The Alaska *Brides* Collection

BARBOUR
PUBLISHING

Golden Dawn © 2007 by Cathy Marie Hake
Golden Days © 2007 by Mary Connealy
Golden Twilight © 2007 by Kathleen Y'Barbo
A Light in the Window © 1999 by Tracie Peterson
Destiny's Road © 1999 by Tracie Peterson

Print ISBN 978-1-62416-739-3

eBook Editions:
Adobe Digital Edition (.epub) 978-1-62836-293-0
Kindle and MobiPocket Edition (.prc) 978-1-62836-294-7

All scripture quotations, unless otherwise noted, are taken from the King James Version of the Bible.

This book is a work of fiction. Names, characters, places, and incidents are either products of the author's imagination or used fictitiously. Any similarity to actual people, organizations, and/or events is purely coincidental.

Cover image: Image Source

Published by Barbour Publishing, Inc., P.O. Box 719, Uhrichsville, Ohio 44683, www.barbourbooks.com

Our mission is to publish and distribute inspirational products offering exceptional value and biblical encouragement to the masses.

Member of the
Evangelical Christian
Publishers Association

Printed in Canada.

Contents

GOLDEN DAWN

by Cathy Marie Hake

Dedication

To Kelly and Tracey, because you're so fun to brainstorm with. To Tracie for her enthusiasm, and to Christian sisters everywhere who make mission fields of their homes and let their lights shine for the Lord.

Chapter 1

April 1897, Oregon

B ess and I are ready to go." Ian Rafferty set down the pail from the morning milking and kissed his mother's cheek.

"Not until you eat a sound breakfast." Though Ma's words sounded cheerful, her forced smile and the way she clung to his sleeve warned Ian she'd still not accepted his decision to go to Alaska. For the past three weeks, she'd split her time between helping him supply himself for this trip and begging him not to go.

Bess brayed outside, a sure sign she resented being hitched to the post. As soon as the mule wore a yoke or a pack, she wanted to work.

"Buckwheat pancakes," Ma coaxed. "You'll not be getting those in a good, long while. Sit yourself down."

"Okay, Ma. Just for breakfast."

Da entered the kitchen and sniffed the air. "Braden, if I'm not mistaken, I smell your wife's sugar-cured ham."

Ian's brother nodded. "You do. There's none better than my Maggie's."

The family gathered around the table. Eggs from their henhouse, ham from their hog, and cream from their cow all testified to God's providence. Da took his place at the head of the table. Instead of folding his calloused hands as he normally did, he reached over and took Ian's and Braden's hands. Braden promptly took Maggie's, and their sister, Fiona, and Mama completed the circle.

"Almighty Father, we give You praise for all You've done on our behalf, for the safety and love and bounty we've enjoyed by Your hand. Now, Father, we ask You to extend those blessings to our Ian as he ventures on in life. Though we'll be parted in body, keep us close in mind and heart we pray, amen."

"Thanks, Da."

Da squeezed Ian's hand. "I have faith God will be with you on your adventure."

Fiona sighed. "I wish I were going."

"You"—Braden waved his fork at their sister—"would gladly go anywhere so long as it was away from here."

"It makes no sense." Ma dabbed at the corners of her eyes with her napkin. "Your da and I risked life and limb coming across the trail so our children would have a better life. There's not a place in the world half as lovely as the farm we've established."

"The Oregon Trail was your adventure," Ian said as he passed the bowl of scrambled eggs. "The Yukon will be mine."

Ma shook her head. "There's no need to go seek your fortune, Ian. Your da and I claimed sufficient land for both of our sons to farm. Fertile land."

"The land's not going anywhere." Ian set down the platter of buckwheat pancakes without taking any. He'd wanted to leave at daybreak just to avoid this unpleasantness. Ever since the day he'd announced his plan to join the Alaska gold rush, Ma had pleaded with him to reconsider. The tears welling in her eyes tore at him.

"I'm a proud man, but I'm not a fool. If I get up there and things are truly as miserable as you believe, I'll come home and admit I chased a rainbow." He softened his voice. "Now that I've given that pledge, let's not waste our last hour together with harsh words."

Ian looked across the table at his older brother. Braden plowed through life with unshakable confidence. He'd loved their farm and grown up looking forward to working the acreage, marrying his childhood sweetheart, and rearing their children here. *He's already done the first two, and a more content man I'll ne'er meet. How can it be that he's so stable and I'm so restless?*

Braden cleared his throat. "Maggie and I—we thought this would be a grand time to lighten your hearts by telling you all that we're going to have a babe."

Maggie patted Ma's hand. "Braden's already decided this will be a son, and he's planned on twelve more babes—a baker's dozen, he calls it. I'll be grateful for your help."

Ma promptly swiped the coffee mug from Maggie and shoved a glass of milk in front of her. "You need to drink plenty of milk. Hedda Libman told me while I carried Braden 'tis an old wives' tale that a woman loses a tooth for each child. All she has to do is drink a quart of milk a day."

Da chuckled. "Aye, 'twas sound advice. Look at your beautiful smile."

Ian rapidly wolfed down his food in hopes that the conversation would last long enough to let him slip away. Bess brayed again, and he shot to his feet. "Ma, those pancakes were the best ever. Maggie, same with your ham. Sis, keep on with your studies. Smart as you are, someday you might be a schoolmarm yourself."

Fiona scowled. "Not me. I'm going to become a doctor."

Da laughed aloud. "A few years back, you planned to become a librarian. Before that, you wanted to be a famous painter."

"Those were childish dreams." Fiona's chin lifted in a stubborn tilt. "I'm of an age to plan my future."

"And 'tis time I set out to meet my future." Ian bent to press a kiss on Ma's pale cheek. "I'll be careful."

He hugged his sister and whispered, "'Tis no shame to dream."

"It's not just a dream, Ian," she whispered back.

He straightened and turned to Maggie. "I remember you bringing your doll to church because you wanted her to learn about Jesus. With all that practicing, you'll be a fine mother."

Maggie blushed and murmured something that got lost in Braden's proud, "I'll watch out for her."

"You do that." Ian unashamedly embraced his older brother.

Braden growled, "Go and enjoy yourself. Don't be sheepish in the least if you decide to come back to us. You're no prodigal, but even if you were, Da would have to race me to the barn to kill the fatted calf."

Ian chuckled. "If you'd seen the supplies I have waiting in town to take, you'd think I'd already killed that calf! Ma thought up more stuff for me to take than you can shake a stick at."

"You'll be glad to have it," Ma predicted.

Da promised to take good care of things.

With a heavily laden mule, a Bible, and high hopes, Ian set out on his adventure.

Goose Chase, Alaska

Wind whipped the air, and chunks of ice cracked and knocked together as the river began to thaw. Meredith Smith turned her face to the weak spring sun and relished the small bit of light and warmth it yielded. After a long, dark winter, even the slightest ribbon of light lifted her spirits.

Tucker straightened from the bank of the river and lifted his net. "Sis! How's this?"

Tilting her head to the side, she studied the fish. "If it were any bigger, he'd be eating us for dinner!" Her twin grinned, and Meredith's heart soared. Tucker seldom smiled. She understood why, but that made these rare moments all the sweeter.

"Bring me a bucket. I'm going to see if I can't catch more."

Meredith lugged a wooden bucket to him. "If the others are anywhere near that big, the only thing that'll hold them is a bathtub."

"It'll be good to have fresh meat." Tucker dumped the trout into the tub and turned back to try to net more. A craggy formation of rocks stuck out into the river from their claim; then the river suddenly widened from that point. The water continued to rush past, but some swirled into the wider space in an eddy in which fish sometimes took refuge. When Tucker spotted that land feature, it cinched this as the land he chose for their claim.

Meredith watched the fish thrash in the confines of the bucket. "You've caught us a tasty lunch."

"Wish we had some cornmeal. Then he'd taste better when you fry him."

"I might be able to find some herbs. I'm starting to see a few sprouts coming up here and there."

"Don't try anything you're not sure of." He leaned forward and squinted at the water.

Meredith didn't reply. She and Tucker saw life from opposite perspectives: he saw the pitfalls, while she looked for the possibilities. Long ago, he hadn't been that way. Ever since the debacle, Tucker's view of life had changed. She'd learned to allow her brother his mutterings and weigh whether they bore consideration or were merely manifestations of the burdens he shouldered.

"Sis?"

Meredith turned around. "Yes?"

Tucker grimaced. "I know we need to buy supplies, but I owe plenty of folks money. Make a list of the absolute essentials, and we'll talk it over later."

"Are we going to town tomorrow?"

"I haven't decided. I don't want to leave you here, but taking you is dangerous."

"Dangerous?" Meredith laughed. "We made it through a winter in Alaska. We're tough enough to survive a trip to town."

"I knew it. I knew you'd grow to hate this isolation. You—"

"Tucker, if you dare say anything about me leaving here and going to Uncle Darian, I'm going to push you in the river. Never once—not a single time—have I regretted coming here with you. We're family, and we belong together. No matter where I live, there'll always be challenges. In Texas, it was the heat and lack of water. Before that, it was the tornadoes in Kansas."

"Last time, you said it was the thunderstorms and flash floods," he grumbled.

"See? That just bolsters my argument. I'm going to make that list of essentials, and at the very top of it, I'm going to write 'handcuffs.'" Her brother gave her a startled look. Meredith shook her finger at him. "God linked us together the day He created us as twins. If locking us together is the only way I can keep you from trying to send me away, I'll do it."

"It's not right—"

"I agree." Meredith knew she'd abandoned her manners by interrupting him, but too much hung in the balance. "It's not right for you to try to send me off to Uncle Darian."

"He's family."

"Not as close as you are." She folded her arms across her chest. "I'm winning this argument. You know I am. You haven't come up with a single valid point, and we've gone round and round about it for more than a year."

"You're stubborn as a mule."

Meredith closed the distance between them. She hugged her brother. "I love you, too."

"You ought to." He tugged her to the side. "I just caught another fish."

They'd survived the winter on smoked fish, beans, and corn mush. To be sure, Tucker also supplemented their diet with snow hare he snared and meat for which he bartered.

"With the river thawing, this is going to be a good fishing day. I'll fill this bucket with water, and we can keep a few alive in the cabin so they'll be fresh the next couple of days."

"Wonderful!" She thought for a moment. They'd made it through the winter only with very careful planning and God's providence. The number of meals she had sufficient supplies left to make could be counted on one hand. "I'll gather wood, and we can smoke some fish, too."

"I don't want you wandering off."

"I'll stay close by." Glancing at the empty claim beside theirs, she added, "I wonder if Percy made it to town."

"Based on pure orneriness, I'd say he did." Tucker jerked up on the net and growled when he saw he'd caught nothing.

"Are you referring to his orneriness or yours?"

Tucker gave Meredith his full attention. "You're full of sass today."

"And you're grumpy. I guess we deserve one another." She laughed as she walked away.

A stand of trees stood a ways back from their tiny cabin. As the snows began to melt, branches that had fallen were revealed. Meredith dragged back a spruce limb. It sledded along the icy ground, making the task manageable. Tucker would take an ax to it later. Gathering fuel was essential both for cooking and for heat. Especially for heat.

Meredith pulled her rust-colored woolen cloak more tightly about herself. Though the calendar indicated spring had arrived, cold was a constant companion.

Percy, their neighbor, came to Alaska on the same ship she and Tucker had traveled on. They'd taken neighboring claims. By midwinter, Percy had declared that if he survived the cold, he'd return home and live out his days in the blessed warmth of California.

After dragging over two more branches, Meredith sat down and started composing a list of essentials. She did so on a slate. Paper was too costly up here. More important, she could erase items and script in some other much-needed item without Tucker being any the wiser. Eager to enjoy the sunlight, she sat on a rock and leaned against the cabin wall.

"Coffee," she wrote. They'd run out of coffee halfway through the winter. As much as her brother loved coffee, that counted as a severe hardship. Had just she and Tucker been drinking it, they would have been sufficiently supplied, but men dropped by a lot. Since most of them arrived in this icy frontier alone, they often came over with mending or laundry or questions about cooking. Hospitality prompted Meredith to offer them coffee, but survival forced her not to feed them.

An odd economy developed. Men who sought her assistance soon brought firewood or meat from game they'd shot. Twice she'd earned enough coffee to make a pot. Just the memory of the taste and aroma of coffee made her mouth water. Oh, and the blessed heat each swallow imparted. Certainly, coffee rated as an essential.

Beans. Rice. Cornmeal. Oatmeal. Salt. Lard. Meredith paused and stared at the list. Flour and sugar would be wonderful, but they'd make do without those luxuries. She didn't want to write down anything for Tucker to eliminate. He'd feel bad if he denied her a single thing.

One item she craved above all else, but she didn't add it to the list. They'd done fairly well with a damaged one this past year. Tucker wanted a decent one just as badly as she did. If she wrote it on the list, it would only cause him needless anguish. Maybe next year they could splurge. Right now she needed to be sure they wouldn't starve.

"Be sure to put down thread and needles and some buttons," Tucker ordered as he walked up.

"Okay." She bowed her head over the slate.

"Your sewing kept us from starving this winter." He set down the bucket.

"My sewing was responsible for us running out of coffee." She leaned sideways and peered at the fish. "That's a feast for fifteen in there!"

"Four at the most." Though her brother muttered the response, Meredith knew Tucker was proud of what he'd caught. "Why don't you fetch the twine? I'll start a fire, and we can string these up and smoke 'em. Whilst they smoke, I'll catch more."

The fish milled in the bucket, and Meredith gave her brother a delighted look. "You caught a Dolly Varden!"

"It took you long enough to notice." His gruff tone didn't begin to hide his pleasure.

"I'm not smoking it; I'm fixing it for dinner."

He grunted and turned back toward the river.

"Don't you dare pretend that you're slaving away. I know good and well how much you love going fishing."

He shouted over his shoulder, "I deserve this. No doubt, tomorrow you'll pester me into hoeing a patch for your garden."

"I always said you were smart." Meredith looked to the side of their tiny cabin and imagined how wonderful it would be to coax something other than gold from the ground.

Mud sucked at Ian's boots. He'd tied them as tight as they'd allow, but the mud still tried its hardest to rob him of his footwear. Bess trudged along, patiently bearing the packs on her back and the seven-and-a-half-foot sled she pulled. Sure-footed as ever, she didn't seem to mind the bone-chilling cold. Good thing, that. When his mule decided she was too thirsty or tired, she exhibited the famed stubbornness of her kind.

Ian readjusted the straps of the pack on his own back. Despite the cold, excitement pulsed through his veins. Every curve he rounded, every step he took, seemed to feed his sense of adventure. After days on the boat to come up here, he'd gotten his fill of being stuck in close quarters with greedy men. Instead of taking the White Trail or traversing the

Chilkoot Pass, he'd determined to go elsewhere. Goose Chase wasn't even on the map, but he'd overheard a few men in Skaguay talking about the tiny town. Taking that as a cue from the Lord, Ian went to Goose Chase.

Everything fell into place. Upon reaching Goose Chase, he met a prospector. Mr. Percy willingly exchanged his claim's deed for ship fare to return to Washington. The ticket cost a pittance—ships emptied of their stampeders gladly booked passage to Seattle at greatly reduced rates just so they'd earn a little rather than none at all.

Then, too, the snowmelt hadn't yet hit the point where the path would turn into an endless mud bog. Bess didn't like mud puddles, and they slowed down her pulling. Enough snow and ice covered the ground to let the sled skim across the surface.

Well, most of the time it did, Ian thought as he struggled to yank his right foot free from a sucking, muddy morass. He straightened up just in time to spy a hawk floating on the currents of the icy north wind.

"Lord, 'tis a majestic place You created here. I can feel it in my bones—'tis where You'd have me be." Ian consulted his map again. "Not far now, Bess. We'll be getting there."

A few minutes later, something struck his shoulder. Ian wheeled around.

"Git offa my land!" A haggard, hairy man stood several feet away. Even from a distance and despite the stranger's unkempt mustache, Ian could see his sneer.

"Just passin' through."

"No, you ain't." The man's eyes narrowed. He bounced his hand up and down, giving Ian a glimpse of the rock he held as a weapon. "Not 'less you brung vittles."

"You're hungry?"

An ugly laugh filled the air. "Boy, you're dumb as a stump. Ain't nobody up here who ain't had his belly growlin' worse'n a grizzly."

From his reading, Ian knew the winters would be horrendous, but he also knew game abounded. He frowned. "Is the hunting hereabouts bad?"

"You gonna gimme grub, or are you gonna turn tail and get offa my claim?"

"A hungry man oughtn't be turned away." Ma's words echoed in his mind. Ma and Da sometimes spoke of how carefully they had to ration food while traversing the Oregon Trail.

Da's advice followed just as swiftly. *"Don't give away more than you can safely afford."*

"I can spare a wee bit."

The man drew closer. "A lot. I wan' a lot."

Christian charity prompted Ian to share; prudence demanded that he make sure he kept enough to supply his own needs for a long while. "Here." He pulled the sandwich he'd bought in town from inside a burlap bag. That sandwich cost the exorbitant price of two dollars.

"That's a start. What else you gonna gimme?"

"This and my thanks. If that's not enough, I'll walk the border of your claim and carry on."

The man grunted, swiped the sandwich, and lumbered off.

By the time Ian made his way around the last bend in the river before nearing his new claim, he'd met two more surly miners. *Whate'er I endure here, Lord, help me stay civil to my fellow man. And, Lord? If You're of a mind, I'd appreciate a good neighbor.*

The next instant, a gunshot tore the air.

Chapter 2

H ey!"
"Next shot won't be a warning." Though no one was visible, the voice came from a stand of trees.

"Mr. Abrams?" an unmistakably feminine voice called from across the river. "Are you all right?"

Ian watched in utter amazement as a woman in a rust-colored cape came into view. What was a woman doing out here in the bitterly cold wilds? He immediately whisked off his hat. "Ma'am."

"Mr. Abrams?" she repeated.

"Got me a claim jumper."

Ian heaved a sigh. "I've a claim of my own. I don't want yours."

"You don't want mine?" Mr. Abrams finally stepped into view. "Well, how do you like that? Meredith, this whippersnapper is insulting my claim!"

"I'm sure it's a grand claim." Ian nodded to emphasize his point.

"Indeed, it is. A very fine claim," the woman tacked on.

"But I'm eager to set to work my own stake." Ian reached into his coat pocket and produced his map. "And I ought to reach it as soon as I cross the river here."

"Did you buy Percy's claim?"

"That I did." Ian squared his shoulders. "Word in Skaguay was that the Chilkoot Pass is nigh unto impassable, but folks are clamoring about the benefits of going that direction anyhow. By now, most of the decent claims have to be gone. I reckoned that heading off in a different direction made sense."

A man joined the woman, and it didn't escape Ian's notice that he held a rifle. She smiled up at her man. Gently pushing the butt of the rifle toward the ground, she said, "This gentleman is our new neighbor."

"Ian Rafferty."

The man studied him, then rasped, "Tucker and Meredith Smith." It didn't escape Ian's notice that Tucker Smith kept a tight grip on his weapon.

"Pleased to make your acquaintance." Cold as it was, Ian longed to slap his hat back on, but that would be rude. He turned a shade to his left. "And I gather you're Mr. Abrams."

Mr. Abrams kicked the muddy sled. "You might make it 'cross, but ain't no way to get your b'longings over."

The woman looked at the chunks of ice bobbing on the rough current. "I'm sure the gentleman must have a plan, Mr. Abrams." She turned her gaze onto Ian.

"Indeed, I do."

"Tucker and I are willing to help."

Tucker's head dipped once in curt agreement.

"Name him a steep price," Abrams advised. "He's got plenty."

"I will not!" Tucker boomed in outrage. He turned his attention on Ian. "We offered our help, and it's yours. What's your plan?"

During his trek, Ian had considered this eventuality and formulated a plan. "I've a ball of twine—"

Abrams hooted with laughter.

Ian pretended the miner hadn't made a sound. "I'll tie one end to an arrow and shoot it into that pine. Once 'tis on your side, if you can pull the twine, I'll tie a sturdy rope to the end. Once we've hitched the line betwixt trees, I can ferry parcels across."

"No use you doing that much work—especially with the river so mean right now." Tucker shook his head. "We can each have a line and stay on opposite sides. It'll be safer and quicker."

"That's a generous offer. I've a pair of pulleys. They'll make things glide more smoothly."

"Now just you hold on a minute." Mr. Abrams scowled. "You're supposing I'll allow you to use one of my trees."

Lord, give me patience. This old coot's quibbling over something that petty?

"Smith might be willing to help you outta Christian charity, but I'm not." Abrams smacked himself in the chest. "Bible-thumpin' folks can do what they please, but charity begins at home, and you're standin' on my property."

Ian set aside his irritation over the man's greed as his heart jumped at how quickly the Lord had answered his prayers to have Christian neighbors.

"Mr. Abrams," the woman called in a sweet voice, "I'm sure you'll be willing to help out while I prepare supper. Then we can all break bread together to welcome Mr. Rafferty properly."

Abrams's eyes lit up. "You got bread? Real flour-built bread?"

Even from across the water, Ian watched as her features pulled, then quickly resumed a strained smile. *She's out of flour.* He blurted out, "The first thing I'll send over is flour. It's only right that I contribute something to the meal."

"Oh, that would be wonderful!" The joy in her voice was unmistakable.

"I hope it's not too much trouble for you to bake it."

"Not at all!" Suddenly, her beaming smile faded. "Oh. Well, I mean, I have soda. I can bake biscuits. We ran out of flour awhile ago, so I've lost my starter."

"I've a small packet of sourdough starter I bought from an old woman in Skaguay. That and a few cakes of Fleischmann's yeast." *For all of her upset o'er me leaving, Ma gave me fine directions on the essentials. I'd have never thought of starter.*

Mrs. Smith pressed a hand to her bosom and said in a shaky voice, "You have starter?"

The last thing he wanted to do was set a woman to tears. Ian scuffed a small pebble with the toe of his boot and wondered what else they'd run out of. Whatever it was, he'd do his best to share. They'd already offered their friendship and help. He could do no less. "I'd take it as a favor if you'd use the starter I brought and freshen it. Left to myself, I'm afraid I'd not bake for another few days and have it go bad."

Tucker said something to her, and she nodded before walking off.

"We ain't got all day." Abrams motioned at Ian. "Get busy." As soon as Ian pulled out his bow, the crusty man gave it a dubious look. "Sure you can hit the broad side of a barn with that?"

"I'll be hitting that spot where the bark's scraped off of the pine," Ian called out to Tucker. A moment later, the arrow cut the air and landed precisely where he'd said it would.

Tucker whistled. "Impressive."

"I'd be more impressed if he'd hit something I could eat." Abrams watched as Ian tied his end of the twine to a rope. Tucker pulled the twine until the rope spanned the river. Once Tucker secured it to the pine, Abrams started dragging the other end toward a fat old red alder. "Got them pulleys, or are they stuck somewhere in that big mess of junk you hauled up here?"

"Here they are." Ian pulled them from the burlap bag he'd tied with string. He felt every bit as eager to get to his claim as Abrams was to eat.

Tucker stood with his feet braced apart and rested his hand on his hips. "Don't give in to the temptation to go fast and heavy on the loads. Make them light and well balanced. Better that you take time and save it all than go quick and drop something in the drink. You can't afford to lose anything up here."

It took just slightly under four hours to set up the rig and transfer his possessions over the tumultuous water. As the last load went across, Abrams kicked the sled. "What're you gonna do with this now?"

"Taking it over." Ian had plans for every part of that sled.

Abrams scowled at him. "You tetched in the head?"

"Not that I know." Ian chuckled. "But if I were, I suppose I'd be the last to know."

"Humph."

Bess balked at crossing the river, but she finally did so. She twitched, shook, and brayed once she hit land. Tucker picked up what looked to be a burlap sack and started to dry her off a bit.

Lord, You exceeded my very thoughts and wishes with the Tuckers for my neighbors. They're God-fearing, helpful, and even show consideration to a beast. Thank You for settling me next to them.

Ian held fast to the rope and swung his feet up. Mud splattered off his boots as he crossed his ankles over the rope. Pulling himself from one side of the river to the other didn't strain him in the least. If anything, each moment managed to invigorate him further. As soon as he hit ground, he went over to assume Bess's care.

"She's fine." Tucker ruffled the mule's coarse mane. She wandered off and cropped at some fresh grass.

"Thanks for seeing to her." Ian took out his bandanna and dipped it in the water. As he started to wash the grime from his hands and face, he called out, "Come on over, Mr. Abrams. The rope's sturdy."

Abrams coughed and spat. "I'm too old for that nonsense."

"Oh, but supper will be ready in a jiffy," Mrs. Smith called to him. "I set a place for you."

"Can't disappoint the lady." Abrams swung up on the rope and shimmied over with more dexterity than Ian had expected. The old man dropped down next to Tucker Smith. "Been so long since I had me some bread, I woulda swum over here to have a taste."

"You can't swim," Tucker said.

"Woulda lernt how." Abrams marched toward the cabin.

Until that moment, Ian hadn't paid much attention to the small building. Percy said he'd erected a shelter on the claim. Though small, it looked sturdy enough. If anything, the nine-by-ten-foot log cabin would be generous for a man on his own. *A bigger place would require more wood to heat. This is perfect for me.*

He and Tucker followed close behind the old man. "Once we eat and Abrams makes it back to his claim, I'll help you use the rope to hang your provender."

Ian gave Tucker a surprised look. "I appreciate the offer, but it hardly seems necessary."

"Bears and raccoons are active. Most of this could be gone in a day."

Ian shrugged. "The cabin looks quite sturdy."

Confusion plowed lines on Smith's forehead. "You want me to store your goods?"

"Dinner's going to get cold," the woman called to them from the door.

At that moment, Ian realized this was her home, not his. "My apologies. I mistook your cabin for mine."

Tucker's brows shot upward. "What cabin?"

"Hooo-ooo-ey!" Abrams wheeled around and laughed so hard, he started coughing. "Percy snookered you!"

Dread filled Ian. "He swore he'd constructed a shelter."

"He did." Abrams pointed to a half-hidden jumble of logs. "He just didn't tell you what kind."

When he stared at the ramshackle lean-to, Ian questioned the sanity of his plan for the first time.

Chapter 3

Tucker caught an abundance of fish today."

"I brung my appetite with me. I could eat the legs off a runnin' skunk." Abrams smacked Ian on the shoulder. "Betcha you're starvin' after walking all this way."

Until he'd seen the lean-to, Ian had felt ravenous. But his appetite had disappeared. Just before he said so, he looked at Mrs. Smith. *Miss Smith*, he thought as he got a closer look at her abundant brown hair and warm hazel eyes. Her features were finer and softer than Tucker's, but there could be no mistaking the truth. They weren't man and wife—they were brother and sister.

"Are you hungry, Mr. Rafferty?" Her glance darted to the lean-to and back.

Ian suddenly remembered his manners and whisked off his hat. He didn't want to lie, so he settled on the only truth he could muster. "Something smells wonderful, ma'am."

"It's your bread." She inhaled deeply. "In the Bible, there's talk of incense burning before the Lord. I don't know about all the sweet-smelling things they used, but I won't be disappointed if heaven smells like fresh, hot bread."

"If that was true, I might could think 'bout mendin' my ways and getting churchified." Mr. Abrams plowed on into the cabin.

Accustomed to stomping the field soil from his shoes and wiping his feet on the veranda mat, Ian noticed the Smiths had no such mat. His next realization was that the cabin had a dirt floor. Nonetheless, he stomped his feet and did his best to knock off the worst of the dried crumbles.

"No need for that," Miss Smith murmured.

"I'd beg to disagree. Your floor is hard packed; the soil on my boots would scatter all over and make a mess." He flashed her a wry smile. "Besides, my ma would wallop me if she ever heard I tracked dirt into anyone's house."

Miss Smith laughed.

A table made of raw-cut timber completely filled the space between a pair of beds. Packing crates formed a crude storage area along the far wall on each side of a stone fireplace. Most of the dishes sat on the table; an appalling lack of food on the shelves stunned Ian. *And still, they invited me to supper.*

"You men can sit on that side." Tucker waved at one of the beds. He sat next to his sister on the other.

"How lovely to have you gentlemen join us." Miss Smith's hazel eyes sparkled with delight.

She's living on the edge of hunger, yet she's glad to share. Ian smiled at her. "Honored to be invited, ma'am. It's generous of you."

"Yeah." Abrams nodded as he swiped the biggest slice of bread and stuffed half of it in his mouth.

"In our home, we ask a blessing before each meal." Tucker folded his hands.

Abrams crammed the rest of the bread in his mouth and bowed his head. The second Tucker's prayer ended, Abrams grabbed for another slice of bread and squinted at Tucker. "Dunno much about all that God stuff, but didn't you forget one of your lines? The one 'bout daily bread?"

"That's the Lord's Prayer." Tucker lifted the platter of fish and started to pass it to Ian.

Ian tilted his head toward Miss Smith. "Ladies first."

Tucker's brow rose, but he held the platter so his sister could serve herself.

Abrams took a gigantic bite of the bread and spoke with his mouth full. "Ain't all the prayers His?"

Miss Smith served her brother first, then herself. "All of our prayers are said to the Lord, but Jesus taught the disciples one as an example of how to pray. We call that the Lord's Prayer."

"Humph. Just as well." The old man took the platter and speared the largest fish with his fork. As he lifted, the fish flaked apart and half flopped back onto the platter. He scraped the fish directly from the platter onto his plate and plunked the platter down without offering it to Ian. "I recollect there's another part of that prayer that don't settle with me. I ain't no trespasser, and I ain't a-gonna forgive nobody else for trespassing on my claim."

"Jesus forgives all of us if we ask Him to. Christians want to be like Him, so we try to forgive others." Miss Smith deftly lifted Abrams's mug and pressed it into his hand as he reached for a third slice of bread.

Tucker pushed the bread toward Ian. Tucker's eyes gave a silent bid for him to hurry and claim his fair share.

Ian took a slice and immediately gave the plate to Tucker. "After you and Miss Smith help yourselves, perhaps you could set this behind you."

"No reason to do that," Abrams roared with outrage.

"Of course there is. I'm clumsy." Ian pointed at the serving platter that lay off center in the middle of the tiny table. "I aim to scoot that closer, or I'm going to drop fish on the table and make a mess." He proceeded to pull the entrée over and serve himself.

"As I said"—Tucker cleared his throat—"bears can be a problem around here."

Ian grimaced. "Then how did Percy live in a lean-to?"

"Stink." Abrams bobbed his head knowingly. "He stunk so bad, bears like to thought he was a skunk."

Miss Smith coughed. *Is she really choking, or is she trying to hide laughter?*

"Tucker, whap her on the back a few times. Something's going down the wrong pipe." Abrams waggled his fork in the air. "Yep. Stink's what kept the bears from Percy."

Miss Smith's cough turned to a splutter. If Mr. Abrams had bathed even once in the past six months, Ian would have been amazed. Out in the open, his smell hadn't been quite so overpowering, but in the close confines of the cabin, Abrams's stench grew stronger by the second. Opening the one tiny window wouldn't begin to help.

"Miss Smith"—Ian looked across the table at her—"do you need some fresh air?"

Tucker grabbed his plate and hers as he shot to his feet. "Good of you to understand, Rafferty. Come, Sis. We'll all go on outside to finish supper. After the long winter, it's best you get as much light and fresh air as you can."

"Since you insist." She rose with alacrity.

"Go on ahead." Abrams sounded downright jolly. "I'll get the bread."

"I'll tend to that." Ian smiled. "Since her brother's hands are full, I'll help the lady with her cape."

Miss Smith nodded. "Then I'll carry the bread."

Abrams made a disgruntled sound and trundled outside.

Ian took Miss Smith's cape from the peg by the door. "I hope you'll leave some of the loaf in here so you can have it tomorrow morning."

"You won't mind?"

"Why would I?" He slid the russet wool over her shoulders. "You baked it."

"But it's your flour." She said that last word almost reverently.

"No, it wasn't." He couldn't help himself. He moved her thick, glossy brown braid. It felt every bit as soft as it looked. "Just as your brother shared the fish he caught and you shared your labor, I shared the flour."

"You bringin' that bread out here?" Abrams hollered.

Ian chuckled. "Now set aside some for yourselves before that ornery old man eats it all."

Meredith sat outside by the fire. Smoke filtered up from it and through the fish Tucker had strung earlier in the day. That bounty alone already caused her to praise God for His provision today. The bread just proved how generous the Lord continued to be toward her and Tucker.

"You gonna eat that bread, or are you just gonna stare at it?"

"Of course she's going to eat it," Tucker half growled.

Mr. Abrams stuck out his lower lip like a pouting toddler. "No need to get touchy. Just didn't want good food to go to waste."

"It was good food." Mr. Rafferty set his plate down on the rock beside him and nodded at her. "Miss Smith, you're a grand cook." After she murmured her thanks, Mr. Rafferty gestured toward the line of fish. "And Tucker, you're quite the fisherman. That's an impressive day's catch. I know for certain I'll never come close to a haul like that."

Though she appreciated the compliment Mr. Rafferty paid to her cooking, Meredith especially appreciated how he praised her brother. Tucker enjoyed fishing and was proud of having provided well for their meal. Having someone recognize his contribution—that mattered.

"I'm a miserable fisherman," Mr. Rafferty continued. "But I do like to hunt. Once I erect a cabin, I'm planning to build a smokehouse."

"You handled that bow well today." Tucker skidded the last bite of his bread over his plate, gathering the last little flakes of fish. "Even so, I'm glad to see you brought a firearm."

"I read a fair bit when I decided to come north. Judging from the landscape and region, I'm hoping to get grouse, pheasant, and rabbit. My bow will serve me well with those wee creatures. As for my rifle—one good-sized mountain sheep or caribou would certainly provide endless meals."

"No caribou here. No deer, either." Abrams burped loudly. "You'd be smart to pan gold and pay for more supplies to see you through the winter. That canvas you brought—just double it over the lean-to, and you'll be snug enough. You don't have time to waste building a cabin, let alone a smokehouse. That plan's pure foolishness."

Mr. Rafferty stared at the fire. Most men would have been insulted, but he didn't react. After a moment's silence, he asked, "Are you folks familiar with a man by the name of Wily?"

"Yes," Meredith said.

"Who isn't?" Abrams scowled. "Worthless waste of a man."

"Wily's a good man," Tucker disagreed. "Salt of the earth."

"Salt?" Abrams spat off to the side. "If that's what you want, he'll bring it. Won't deliver what's important, though."

Tucker shrugged. "A man has the right to run his own business. Wily's reliable. If he agrees to ferry someone or deliver something, his word is his bond."

Relief radiated from their new neighbor. "Percy introduced me to him. After I learned that Percy had hedged regarding the shelter, I wondered if he and Wily were in cahoots. Wily's to bring the remainder of my possessions in his boat."

"You've got more stuff a-comin'?" Abrams leaned forward. "Like what?"

"Necessities."

Abrams slapped his knee. "Now that was downright smart of you. Wily wouldn't pry. You said necessities, and he don't think the way you and me do. He won't guess what you got. I'm your neighbor. When—"

"If you're thinking I have spirits or tobacco coming, you're mistaken. Neither appeals to me, and they're certainly not essential."

While Abrams moaned and groaned, Tucker rose. "Speaking of necessities, we'd better string up the supplies you brought before we lose our light."

"Hold on a second." Abrams looked like a drowning man grasping for even the smallest twig. "Ain't you gonna brew us up some coffee now, Meredith? You always make coffee when you got guests."

"Which is why we ran out." Tucker locked eyes with Mr. Rafferty. "Learn from our mistake. There'll be no coffee tonight."

"Now why'd you hafta go ruin it?" Abrams trundled toward the rope. "No use me stickin' round here any longer. Time's better spent workin' my claim." Once he crabbed his way across the river, the old man untied the rope from his tree. The cold air carried his dark mutterings.

As Mr. Rafferty pulled the rope over to his claim, Meredith gathered the dishes. The men sorted the supplies, and Meredith forced herself to wash the dishes. She oughtn't bustle over and stick her nose in the new neighbor's business. Though he seemed friendly enough, she didn't want him to feel as if they were trying to get on his good side so he'd give them food.

It didn't take them long to suspend the food from a tree. Rafferty accompanied Tucker back to their fire. "Sis, Mr. Rafferty's asked to sleep by the fire here tonight. He'll add logs so the fish'll smoke."

"Will you be warm enough?" As soon as she blurted out the question, Meredith regretted her haste. They didn't have blankets to spare.

" 'Tis kind of you to ask, but I've warm blankets aplenty." He set down the bundle he'd carried in his left arm and carefully propped his rifle so it pointed away from the cabin.

The fire flickered again, and Meredith's breath caught. Atop his dark wool blanket rested a brown leather book. "Is that a Bible?"

"It is." He smiled. "It's a blessing to know I have believers for my new neighbors."

"Could you. . .would you. . ." Tears filled her eyes.

Tucker wrapped an arm around her shoulders and pulled her close. "Our Bible got wet. We tried to dry it, but pages started to mold. I cut the spine and salvaged half of it. I think my sister is asking if you'd mind reading something aloud."

"Not at all." He picked up the Bible and held it out to her. "Why don't you choose what you'd like? Tucker, you can read it to us."

She relished the weight of the whole Bible. How could something that felt so heavy make her heart feel so light?

"What would you like, Sis?"

A psalm? A passage of Exodus where the children of God were in the wilderness? Job, who suffered the unthinkable and turned to praise God? The choice overwhelmed her. "Anything. Anything at all."

Tucker let out a low, long rumble of laughter.

In that moment, Meredith knew she'd never forget this moment or the neighbor God sent to make it happen. Mr. Rafferty hadn't brought bread alone. He'd brought the Word of God, and he'd done the impossible. He'd broken a year and a half's bleakness by making her brother laugh.

Chapter 4

Ian squatted by the fire and moved the speckled enamelware coffeepot. The brew would feel good going down after the cold night. Odd, how yesterday had been so bitterly cold, yet a warm wind replaced the frigid gusts today. All around him, patches of snow melted away, and the river widened as the frozen edges thawed.

Through the night and even now, Ian kept the fire low—just enough to keep a nice, steady stream of blue smoke wending up to the fish.

The cabin door opened. "Good morning!" Miss Smith sounded as cheery as a lark.

"Morning." Her brother sounded downright surly.

"Top o' the mornin' to you both." Ian grinned. He'd grown up with his father saying that phrase, and somehow it seemed right to use it now, himself.

Tucker's eyes widened. "Is that coffee?"

"It is. You declared there'd be no coffee last night. I didn't want to make a liar of you, so I waited 'til this morning to brew a pot. It should be ready any minute now. Go get your mugs."

"You're not obliged to share," Miss Smith murmured.

"I'm happy to."

Tucker cleared his throat. "I'm a proud man. I'm glad you offered, because I might have sunk to begging for a sip if you hadn't."

Ian finally stood. "If my sister were here, you might have to do just that. Fiona's been known to drink an entire pot of coffee all on her own before breakfast ever reached the table."

"Smart gal." Tucker nodded his approval.

"You don't know just how smart she is." Ian stretched out the words with relish. "Whilst I gathered my supplies, she insisted upon me bringing another can of Arbuckle's. Said it would keep me warm in the dead of winter."

"Arbuckle's," Tucker groaned.

"His favorite." Miss Smith laughed. "I'll go fetch the mugs."

"Bowls and spoons, too," Ian called out to her. "I'm not much of a cook, but oatmeal doesn't take much attention."

While she disappeared into the cabin, Tucker shifted his weight and studied the toes of his boots. "We're not in a position to return your—"

"Seasoned. That's what they called it." Ian squatted, stirred the oatmeal, and repeated, "Seasoned. When the colonists first came to the New World, someone who made it a whole year was called 'seasoned.' That's what you are. There's plenty I don't know. If I ply you with coffee, I reckon it won't seem so much like I'm pestering you with my questions."

Miss Smith reappeared. They said grace and breakfasted outside. Scents of smoke, pine, coffee, and fish mingled in the air. Casual conversation flowed. Miss Smith reached out and touched one of the fish that hung over the low fire. "In another hour or so, I'll be able to store those away."

"I'll catch more today."

She shook her finger at her brother. "Not until you start my gardening plot. You promised you'd hoe me one as soon as we got our first chinook."

"A chinook is an unseasonably warm wind," Tucker explained. He turned back to his sister. "The growing season's not long enough to make it worth your while."

Unable to bear the disappointment flickering across her face, Ian spoke up. "I brought seeds, myself."

Miss Smith's jaw dropped. "You did?"

Tucker gave him a wary look. "Most men wouldn't bother. First and only thing they care about is getting gold."

"I'm not like most men." Ian lifted the coffeepot and poured the last of its contents into Tucker's cup. "Getting the gold is only part of my plan. But I came to succeed, not to plunder the land and run off. Having a solid roof over my head and food for my table—that will allow me to remain put and be a success in the long haul."

Tucker took a sip of coffee and said nothing.

"You folks have been more than kind, but I don't want to test your hospitality by making a mistake again about the property line. What landmarks did you and Percy establish?"

"The pile of rocks right there"—Tucker nodded toward the riverbank, then tilted his head in the opposite direction—"to the red alders back there."

"Mr. Clemment holds the land on your opposite side." Miss Smith stared into her mug. "There's a bramble between your properties, and you're best to leave it alone. He means no one any harm. He's rather. . .eccentric."

"I'll keep that in mind." Ian surveyed the area and thought aloud. "There's enough for my mule to forage for a while, but I won't be able to keep her in feed all winter long. For a while, she'll be useful, though. I can hitch her to pull the logs for my cabin. Until I fell the trees, she's got nothing to do. Would you like to use her to start your garden?"

"Nice offer." Tucker sounded like a man doomed to a tedious chore. "But we don't have a plow."

"Neither do I, but I have a plan."

About an hour later, Tucker looked over the odd apparatus they'd put together. "You know, this thing just might work, after all."

They'd taken the skids from the sled Bess had pulled the supplies on and used them along with a spade, a plank, wires, and leather straps to create a plow. "It's a sorry-looking oddity, but it'll work." Ian jostled it. "Pretty sturdy, all things considered. We'll hitch it up to Bess, and you can start that garden for your sister."

"Nope." Tucker rested his hands on his hips. "You plow both gardens, and I'll chop down trees. Believe me, I'm better with an ax than a plow."

Ian wagged his head from side to side. "Your plot is cleared; I need to clear stones. I—"

"Under the best of circumstances with a normal plow, I'd make a fool of myself. In the time it would take me to plow the garden with this contraption, you could have done yours, ours, and more to boot. We're simply trading skills."

"Tell you what: I'll clear stones while you catch more fish. I'm not looking to put in a huge garden—just enough to get by. Then we can start in on that deal."

Tucker chewed the inside of his cheek and looked at their claims. "How much seed did you bring?" A minute later, he cupped his hands and called, "Sis?"

Miss Smith came around the side of their cabin, her arms full of deadwood. "Yes?"

"C'mon over here." He cupped his chin in his hand and tapped his forefinger against his cheek as if he was pondering something perplexing.

Ian threw back his head and laughed. When Tucker looked at him as if he'd lost his senses, he smirked. "You just made a big mistake."

Meredith dropped the wood and walked toward the men. Tucker was giving her the sign. Her brother was going to make some kind of a deal, and he wanted her to hear the bargaining and give her opinion. She respected that about her brother: he included her in decisions and tried hard to be scrupulously fair to whomever he dealt with.

"Sis, I think we need to come to an agreement with Ian. He brought enough seed to sow a good-sized garden, and he has his mule and this plow."

"A plow your brother helped construct."

Meredith looked at the strange creation. "That's, uh. . .quite a plow, Mr. Rafferty."

An impish twinkle lit his blue eyes. "You might say that."

"I proposed that if Ian would plow your garden in addition to his own, I'd spend the morning felling trees for his cabin."

"No, no." Mr. Rafferty started tapping his foot. "That's not right. I'll spend half the day clearing stones from the plot on my side. Yours is already clear."

"But you have the seeds. Sis, he's got seeds for everything from beets to radishes."

"Wonderful!" She brightened at that news. They'd had so little variation in their diet that even the smallest change thrilled her. "I have beans and cabbage."

"What kind of beans might they be?"

She smiled. "Green pod beans and yellow wax beans."

Tucker started pacing. "That's nice, Sis. It's a nice start. But it's not much. He's got everything. Carrots. Turnips. Table beets and lettuce and potatoes—and that's just part of it."

Watching her brother left her feeling slightly dizzy, so Meredith focused back on Mr. Rafferty. "Carrots? Oh, they sound delicious! And beets—it'll be so nice just to have color on our plates instead of white and brown food. I do hope it doesn't sound as if I'm complaining. Well, maybe I am, a little. But God's provided for us. We've had enough to eat."

"We'll plant plenty and store up sufficient for a long winter."

Tucker turned back around and headed toward them. "But your seeds and labor. Whatever is extra—"

"We'll sell or trade with our neighbors."

"That's a wonderful plan, Mr. Rafferty." Meredith started thinking of the things she'd put on the list of necessities. Maybe she could reduce some of the amounts if their garden grew bountifully.

"Your garden. Your plow." Tucker stepped closer to their new neighbor. "Your seeds. You—"

"I," Mr. Rafferty interrupted, "propose that we'll all labor and share equally in the yield."

"But there are two of us," Meredith pointed out. "We'll eat more."

"And unless I miss my guess, Miss Smith, you'll be far more efficient in making sure things are preserved."

Tucker didn't stop pacing. He walked toward the riverbank and back, each time expounding on a concept or challenging Mr. Rafferty's assertions and offers.

Mr. Rafferty continued to interrupt him. Of course, he couldn't stand still. That would have made it far too simple. He'd stoop and heft a rock, then pitch or carry it off a ways. With one man moving up and down while the other paced from side to side, Meredith found herself leaning on the crazy makeshift plow so she wouldn't be so dizzy.

"Well?" Tucker finally stopped.

"Do you agree, Miss Smith?" Both men looked at her.

"Let me get this straight." She shook her head to clear away the confusion. "You'll both build a smokehouse, which is to be spaced evenly between our homes. Since the fish are plentiful right now, you'll use the logs from the lean-to so the smokehouse will be ready tomorrow when Tucker returns from fishing all day. While my brother fishes, Mr. Rafferty will plow a garden—a large garden which is now marked by the four boulders he's laid out."

"Perhaps a wee bit larger," Mr. Rafferty mused.

Before Tucker could charge into further negotiations, Meredith blurted out, "Mr. Rafferty and I will sow the seeds, and we'll mind the garden. Because it's his plow and the lion's portion of the seeds is his, and he's doing half the labor, and there are two Smiths and only one Rafferty, I'll be in charge of preserving as much as possible for the cold months. Whatever excess produce might grow will be bartered or sold, with the proceeds being split evenly."

Just summing it all up exhausted her. Meredith sucked in a deep breath.

"I'm thinking it all sounds good so far." Mr. Rafferty nodded.

"I don't." Tucker started pacing again. "It's lopsided. We're taking advantage of you."

Mr. Rafferty cast an exasperated look at Meredith. "Explain the rest to your hardheaded brother. If anything, the deal's heavily weighted to my advantage. In fact, I think—"

"I think you both need to let me finish stating the agreement." Tucker escalated the speed of his pacing, and if Mr. Rafferty went back to rock clearing, she wouldn't be responsible for her actions. "Tucker, do stop wearing a path in the ground. I'm dizzy from watching you."

"Are you feeling poorly, Miss Smith?" Mr. Rafferty solicitously cupped her elbow as if she were a feeble grandmother.

"I knew it. Uncle Darian's is where you belong. It's too harsh up here for you." Tucker grabbed her other arm.

"Nonsense." Fearing she'd soon be caught in a tug-of-war, she pulled away from both men. "I'm stronger than that mule."

"Maybe not as strong, but every bit as stubborn," Tucker mumbled.

"You're a braver man than I, Tucker. If I ever said something like that about my sister, Fiona, I'd never hear the last of it."

Meredith cocked a brow and glared at the men, who now stood side by side. She cleared her throat.

"Sore throat? I've some medicaments—"

"Nah," Tucker said, stopping Mr. Rafferty. "She likely needs a sip of water. I'll fetch it."

"So help me, if you so much as take one step away from here before we finish this deal and shake on it, I'll push you in that river, Tucker!" She shot Mr. Rafferty a look that dared him to say a single word.

The man had the audacity to grin at her like a simpleton.

"My brother will help you chop down trees and build your cabin—"

"The logs come off my property," Mr. Rafferty inserted.

Tucker nodded agreement, so Meredith continued. "In return for your assistance in putting a floor in our cabin—"

"Which will come from trees felled on our claim," Tucker said.

Meredith didn't bother to look at Mr. Rafferty. She rubbed her temple. "And Mr. Rafferty insists we receive half of whatever meat his hunting yields." She barely sucked in a breath and hurried on so they couldn't interrupt yet again. "During the next week or so while this construction is under way, I will prepare meals for the three of us using Mr. Rafferty's supplies. Thereafter, Tucker may ride Bess to town and use her to pack in our supplies. Furthermore, we are welcome to borrow your Bible unless you're reading it, which is at sunrise each day, but since sunrise is a ridiculous notion in Alaska, we will assume it to be at the outset of the morning. There. That had better be the end of this deal."

The new neighbor shook his head.

"What else, Mr. Rafferty?"

"Since you'll be preparing my meals—"

She lost all composure. "Seward bought Alaska from the Russians with less trouble than this agreement!"

His eyes twinkled, and he nodded somberly. "And they called the purchase Seward's Folly. Well, all I wanted to say was that I'd take it as a favor if you'd call me Ian instead of Mr. Rafferty."

"If she calls you Ian, then you'll call my sister Meredith."

Afraid they'd plunge back into the bargaining they'd embraced with such relish, Meredith shouted, "That's it! We all have a deal."

"It blesses my heart to see you're so happy with it." Ian beamed.

Tucker bobbed his head in satisfaction.

Meredith stalked back toward the cabin muttering, "Alaska isn't going to turn me into a raving lunatic. It's the men who will!"

Chapter 5

Wastin' your time, I tell you!" Mr. Abrams shouted across the river. Water sloshed over the edge of the pan he swirled. "Two grown men playing house—that's what you are."

"He's a crazy old coot." The log slid into the notch with a solid thud. Tucker tacked on, "Nosy, too."

"A smokehouse, and now a cabin?" Abrams tutted loudly. "Next thing, it'll be a privy and a summer kitchen." The old man cackled as if he'd told a hilarious joke. "Yep. A summer kitchen. Because summers here are so long and hot!"

Ian shot Tucker a quick look. "A privy. I didn't think—"

"Chamber pot works fine."

Ian nodded curtly.

Abrams's cackling laugh drifted on the wind. "You'll still be roofin' that place when I move back to Seattle and live off my gold."

"Pay him no heed. He talks just to keep himself company."

Ian chuckled softly. "Had the Lord not blessed me with fine new neighbors, I might well have developed that same habit myself in a few years. As I've both a brother and a sister, I'm accustomed to being teased. As long as he's not holding that rifle of his, Abrams is harmless." He and Tucker lifted the next log and dropped it into place.

"His motto is 'Shoot all trespassers.'"

"I found that out firsthand. Tell me, how good of a shot is he?"

"He's as good a marksman as I am a plowboy."

"Speaking of which—"

"We're making good time on this." Tucker kicked a small chunk of wood out of the way and pretended Ian hadn't interrupted.

"Thanks to your help. But our deal was—"

"Ian, the ground was frozen solid. It would have taken dynamite, not a plow, to turn over the soil. The ground is still hard as rock. Give it another day or so."

Meredith ventured over. "Lunch is ready."

"It smells wonderful. Your brother and I've worked up an appetite."

As they finished eating, Meredith gave Tucker a tentative look. "Did you ask him?"

Tucker's face puckered as he thought for a moment.

"The laundry," Meredith reminded him softly. A fetching blush tinted her cheeks.

"Oh. Forgot about it." He turned to Ian. "Sis is doing laundry this afternoon. You're welcome to toss whatever you have in the wash pot."

Ian opened his mouth to accept, but Meredith's blush changed his mind. "Thank you for the kind offer, but I'll do my own."

"The wash pot will already be boiling," Tucker pointed out.

"Aye, it will." Ian smiled at Meredith. "And I'll thank you not to dump out the suds. Once you're done, I'll see to my own wash."

"Hey! Wily!" Abrams shouted.

"Where is he?" Meredith tilted her head.

"There. Rounding the river bend," Tucker responded.

Meredith's brow puckered. "Of course Wily is coming on the river. But where is Mr. Abrams?"

"Did you come to your senses?" Abrams hollered to Wily, who paddled his odd-looking boat closer. "I ain't choosy—beer, whiskey, vodka—"

Ian didn't bother to hide the astonishment in his voice. "Abrams is up in that red alder. The lowest branch."

Laughter bubbled out of Meredith.

Wily squinted toward Abrams's claim. "You're going to break your neck, you old fool."

"It'll be your fault for not bringin' me likker. I have to hang upside down to straighten out my spine bone."

"Men who drink spirits don't have a backbone," Wily shot back. He nodded his thanks as Ian reached out, took a rope, and tied the boat to shore. A young man jumped from the other end of the boat and tied it as well.

True to his threat, Mr. Abrams dangled by his knees from the branch.

Tucker's voice went wry. "Ian, don't reach for your bow and arrows. That's not a giant possum. That's just a crazy old coot."

"I ain't crazy. My back's painin' me, and since I don't have any medicinal spirits, I gotta resort to this."

"I'll make you a willow-bark tea."

"Won't help, Meredith." Abrams continued to hang there. "Standin' knee-deep in that icy water's gonna cripple me. I need a good belt of Oh-Be-Joyful every hour or so to keep my innards warm enough."

"This is my nephew, Joe." Wily gestured toward the young man. "He's normally on a trawler, but this load was too heavy for me to move alone."

"Thankful for your help." Ian shook Joe's hand, then grabbed the first bundle from Wily.

Tucker and Meredith stood on the bank and stared at him.

"Meredith, how's about you taking the list I have here and checking everything off so Mr. Rafferty knows I brought everything?"

"Why, yes. Of course I will."

"Sis doesn't need to check a list." Tucker stepped forward. "You brought half a mercantile."

"The wrong half!" Abrams shouted. "It wouldn't have hurt to bring along a few bottles."

"One more thing and the boat would have sunk." Tucker tromped toward Ian's claim.

Meredith accepted the list. "The flour and sugar are obvious, but how do you know what's in the crates?"

"I have them numbered."

Wily scratched his nose. "Didn't imagine you'd already have a cabin goin' up. We can just pass everything in so you don't have to move it again."

With four men unloading the supplies, things went smoothly. Joe elbowed Tucker. "Those stampeders walking the Chilkoot Trail are idiots. They have to carry caches, backtrack, and carry in more. Canada won't let 'em in without a ton of supplies."

"He's not exaggerating. Canadians demand a full ton. Nothing less, or the prospectors will starve." Wily thumped down a sack of cornmeal. "Might take you longer to coax as much gold from the ground here, but you'll still be alive."

Ian hefted another sack. "Tucker, since Meredith is cooking for us, it's stupid to keep all of this at my place. Let's take a bag each of flour, cornmeal, sugar, and beans over to your cabin."

Meredith ran her hand over a sack of flour. "Tucker, when you go to Goose Chase, try to buy flour in this sack if you can. It's pretty."

"Rafferty came up here with his supplies." Joe trudged past with a washtub full of sundry items. "Socks doesn't have anything like that."

A look of disappointment flickered across her features, but if Ian hadn't been facing her, he knew he wouldn't have seen it. She shoved a pin back into her bun to keep it anchored. "I suppose I ought to be thankful Socks has flour at all!"

Ian decided he'd give Meredith the sacks—but he'd wait until he could "bargain" with her so she wouldn't feel as if he was treating her like a charity case. He gave her a quizzical look. "Socks?"

"The owner of the mercantile in town." She smiled at him—a warmhearted smile that proved she'd already set aside her disappointment. "Rumor has it that he was so cold his first winter up here, he unraveled a pair of socks and knit them into a hat."

"He knit something himself?" Ian couldn't imagine a man fiddling with yarn and knitting needles.

"It's a fact, not a rumor." Wily shook his head. "Never saw a man more proud of himself. He wouldn't take off that hat. Come summer, Socks finally peeled off the ugly thing. He'd gone bald as an egg. We tease him and say he ought to have washed the socks before he made them into a hat."

"He couldn't afford his own soap to wash 'em. Prices on everything are sky high." Joe shook his head. "The trawler I work—the captain said he'll keep us in coffee, but we have to drink it black now because sugar is twenty-five cents a pound."

Meredith gasped.

Joe nodded. "Yep. And it's fifty cents for one can of condensed milk."

The strained grooves bracketing Tucker's mouth told Ian the Smiths hadn't mined enough gold to buy supplies at those outrageous rates. He'd read about the inflated prices and hedged against that eventuality by paying shipping for his provender.

"Good thing you're such a fisherman." Ian slapped Tucker on the back. "I haven't hunted yet because everything is scrawny in the springtime. Come autumn, I'll see about bagging a mountain sheep or two, some pheasant, and plump hares."

"With all of that and our garden, we'll be well set." Meredith nodded.

"Garden?" Perplexed lines carved Wily's face.

"Aye." Ian gestured toward the area behind the smokehouse. "I'll be plowing that field in the next few days. Meredith and I are planning to sow a bounty of vegetables."

"My ma lives in Skaguay. She roped me into helping her plant every year." Joe shrugged. "Now all I do is take fish heads and guts home to her. She claims it makes everything grow better."

"Aye, and she's right." Ian nodded. "Fish enrich the soil."

Meredith tugged on Tucker's sleeve. "All the more reason to give thanks that you're such a good fisherman."

"Didn't realize the fishing around here is so good." Wily gazed at the river.

"I don't have to be back until Friday, Uncle, but I pull in nets of fish every day. Don't expect me to join you." Joe cast a glance at the partially built cabin. "Don't mean to sound boastful, but the fact is, I'm good with an ax. I've won contests. Trees don't stand a chance around me."

A sick feeling hit the bottom of Ian's stomach. He hated admitting how little money he had left. "I, ah. . .don't know what the going rate—"

Joe reared back. "I'm offering my help. I don't want to be paid. This is Alaska. We help our neighbors!"

"I meant no offense, and I'll gladly accept your help."

Wily cocked his head to the side. "It's past noontime. Dawn's the best time to fish. Those are some nice, straight logs over yonder. I could split them—maybe even get a few planks for you."

Thrilled by that offer, Ian seized it. "We promised Meredith a plank floor for her cabin."

Meredith blinked and then shook her head emphatically. "Getting a roof over your head is far more important."

"Those logs are from your property." Tucker scowled at him.

Ian shrugged. "So you'll trade me for some from yours."

Meredith started to back away. "Oh no! Wily, Joe—run quick! Once Tucker and Ian start bargaining, they don't stop."

"I tell you what." Ian grinned. "We'll just leave that as the only swap as long as you agree to cook for Wily and Joe, too."

"Of course I'll cook for them. What kind of hostess do you think I am?"

Ian didn't hesitate for a single second. "The grandest in all of Alaska."

"That's not saying much." She arched a brow. "There are probably all of ten women in the whole region."

"Other women heard of your gracious talent and stayed away because they couldn't bear the thought of falling short of your example."

"That proves it." She turned to Tucker. "You said he's a Scot, but he's not. Only an Irishman would be so full of blarney."

"You thought I'm a Scot?" Ian growled at Tucker. "That's nearly as bad as the insult your sister just gave me."

"Scots are good men." Tucker sounded downright bored. "What insult?"

"Scots might well be good, but Irishmen are grand. 'Tis no more a boast than Joe's telling us he's capable with an ax." Ian turned his attention back to Meredith. "But I'll not stand here and have you consider my praise as bluster or blarney. With your merry heart and willing hands, you're a rare woman. 'Tisn't the fare or china on the table that makes a body feel welcome. Like the proverb in the Bible, I'd far rather have a humble meal of herbs with pleasant company than a feast where there's strife."

"I agree." Wily clapped his hands and rubbed them together. "But we'll see about adding a plank floor to that cabin. Where are the tools?"

Ian grabbed a couple of axes and headed toward the woods with Joe. Joe tested the weight of one ax and mused, "Meredith Smith is a spirited woman."

"Indeed, she is."

"I've only seen her once before. She's certainly worth a second look."

Ian locked eyes with Joe. "She's adventurous and friendly, but Meredith Smith is every inch a lady."

A lazy smile tilted one corner of Joe's mouth. "I wondered if you were taken with her. Can't blame you." His ax bit into a tree trunk.

Ian paced to the other side of the tree and started swinging the other ax. Until now, he'd focused on the tasks at hand. Suddenly, the truth struck him. He'd come on the journey of his life and found a woman whose sense of adventure matched his own. From times of prayer and Bible reading, he knew she loved the Lord. With each blow of his ax, he listed her qualities—her virtuous ways, her kind heart, her warm smile, the sunny outlook she maintained—

"Hey!"

Ian gave Joe a startled look.

"Step aside. This one's ready to go."

Ian joined Joe on the other side of the trunk. "Timber!" he bellowed. Then they nudged the trunk above where they'd chopped. Branches rustled, air whistled through the limbs, and the last bit of the trunk cracked as the tree plunged down.

"That one fell hard and fast."

Ian nodded as he continued to think of Meredith. *So did I.*

Chapter 6

Meredith waved. "God go with you!"

Wily and Joe's umiak floated around the river's bend and out of sight.

Behind her, Ian nickered to Bess. He'd already plowed two rows since breakfast—a true feat considering the still-frosty ground and the odd "plow" he'd concocted.

Meredith turned and watched as the fabric of his shirt went taut over muscles in his arms and shoulders. He fought the stubborn soil, and Bess strained, but inch by inch, foot by foot, they made progress.

Carrying a washtub filled with sand, Tucker staggered past Meredith.

"Let me help!"

"Open the door. It blew shut."

Meredith dashed ahead and yanked open the door to their cabin. Each evening the men had dragged stones into the cabin and cobbled a section of the floor. As dawn broke today, they'd dragged out what little furniture she and Tucker owned and carried in logs split in half. Those puncheons now formed a real floor, but instead of staying steady like planks would have, the puncheons rocked and tilted.

Grunting, Tucker dumped the sand onto the floor. He cast a look at the door. "Sis, Rafferty's a fine man."

She blushed. "That's my assessment, too."

"But I don't care how nice he is. You made a promise to me, and I expect you to keep it."

"I haven't said a word to him."

Tucker hefted the empty bucket. "Don't. Some things stay in the family. It's no one else's business."

She hitched her shoulder. "It doesn't matter to me, Tucker. It's important to you, so I'll stay quiet."

"Good." He stared at her, looking as though he expected her to say more.

"I'll work the sand into the floor." Meredith dragged her instep across a ribbon of sand and watched it filter through the cracks. "I'm starting to notice a difference. The sand's keeping the logs from rolling and tilting so much."

Tucker heaved a sigh. He knew her well enough to see that she'd changed the subject. But she'd told him she'd stay quiet, so he went on to the new topic. "Even when I get the puncheons stabilized, the floor'll be rough, Sis. You're liable to get splinters in your feet."

"Nonsense. You men used files and rasps to smooth the surface, and the sand will take care of most of the tiny stickers. I'll braid a nice, warm rug to go between our beds, and we'll be snug as can be."

"We don't have cloth for that."

She flashed her twin a smile. "Anything worth having is worth waiting for."

Tucker snorted and tromped back outside to fetch more sand.

After building a fire and setting the huge wash kettle over it, Meredith hung the quilts out to air. The laundry she'd planned to do days ago desperately needed to be done. In the past, she'd hung her unmentionables in the cabin by the fire to dry. Fearing Ian would take a notion to help her brother with the floor, Meredith decided she'd better hang her small clothes on a line between the quilts. With Tucker's shirts on one side and britches on the other, no one would be able to spy her garments.

As Meredith rinsed the whites, Tucker began to whistle softly. *"Rock of Ages, cleft for me. . ."* The hymn's lyrics ran through her mind.

"Let me hide myself in thee," Ian sang. Or at least, that's what Meredith thought he was trying to do. Not even two of those words were sung in the same key.

"Sis, forget the laundry." Tucker hauled more sand. "Hurry up and make lunch so he'll stop singing."

Ian had his back to them and continued to plow as he caterwauled, "Let the water and the blood, from Thy wounded side which flowed. . ."

Tucker winced. "Sounds like blood's flowing, all right. Just not the sacred variety."

"Be of sin the double cure. . ."

"I never would have guessed it, but Abrams is right," Tucker muttered. "Some afflictions deserve a stiff belt of whiskey."

Meredith giggled. "I don't think whiskey can cure that."

"It wouldn't be for him—it would be for everyone who has to listen."

Straightening up, Meredith wrung out a petticoat. "Bess doesn't seem to mind."

"Dumb mule doesn't know any better. I mean it, Sis. Take pity on me and make lunch. It'll stop him from—"

"Singing?" she filled in.

"I refuse to lie and call that singing."

"Are you sick or just dying?" Abrams shouted across the river.

Ian halted midrow. "Someone's sick?"

"You gotta be. Ain't never heard sounds like that come outta someone unless they was sufferin' real bad."

"He's going to say something about spirits," Meredith whispered to her brother.

"Couple of stiff swigs of whiskey would fix your throat. I'm telling you, Wily needs to deliver spirits to us. They're medicinal."

"Nothing's wrong with my throat." Ian stretched his back.

"That's a matter of opinion." Tucker set down the bucket of sand.

"Had a gelding break a leg once." Abrams continued to swish water and silt in his mining pan. "Sounded just like you. I put him outta his misery."

"I guess I should be thankful you're holding a pan instead of your rifle." Ian's voice held an entertained lilt.

Meredith couldn't help wondering, *How can he have such a deep, true speaking voice yet sing so dreadfully?*

Tucker rested his hands on his hips. "Do you whistle or hum any better than you sing?"

"Nope." Ian grinned like the Cheshire cat from *Alice's Adventures in Wonderland.* "I'm so tone deaf, I got out of having to suffer through music lessons. I take heart in the verse that says, 'Make a joyful noise unto the Lord.'"

"It's noise, all right," Tucker said.

"Sounds like someone's slaughtering you." Abrams dumped out the last of his pan. He'd gotten nothing for his efforts. "Take pity on the rest of us. Call it Christian charity."

Ian's grin widened. "In Luke 19, Christ said if men were silenced, even the rocks would cry out His praise. I take it you'd rather hear the rocks?"

"No one means to insult you," Meredith said.

"Speak for yourself." Abrams scooped up another pan full of silt. "Maybe if the rocks cried, they'd be tears of gold."

"For that, I'd keep my silence." Ian nickered to Bess and flicked the reins. As his plow split the stubborn earth, he disappeared behind the smokehouse.

"Do you still want lunch right away?"

Tucker looked at the little droplets of mud her dripping petticoat created on the ground between them. "Nah. Go on ahead and finish whatever you need to."

After lunch, Meredith shoved her hands in her apron pockets. "Ian, the wash pot is empty now."

"Good. I've gotten to the point that I wouldn't have to put pegs on the walls to hang my clothes. They're all about to stand up on their own. Since we're using your wood and soap this time, next time we'll use mine."

"Meredith!" Abrams bellowed from his side of the river. "I gotta little laundry. Some mending, too. What's your asking price?"

Unladylike as shouting was, she walked toward the riverbank and modulated her voice. "How much mending?"

"Some buttons. A few rips, and my socks need darning."

"How many rips and buttons, and do you still have the buttons?"

Mr. Abrams looked like a sulky toddler who'd been caught tugging on the dog's tail. "You can't expect a man to remember where stupid little buttons roll off to."

"I don't have many spare buttons."

"I'll pay you a pinch of gold dust for it all."

Meredith laughed. "You'd pay that much for one splash of whiskey in town."

"It's going to take all my gold to buy vittles for next year."

"Provender is expensive." She nodded. "Tucker was saying the very same thing. It's going to take all we have to supply us for the next year, too."

"You're putting in a garden. That'll cut your costs. Two pinches, and that's as much as I'll offer."

"You have months' worth of grime in those clothes, so it's going to take me half of forever to wash and mend them. Four."

"Four!" Abrams roared.

"Or. . ." She paused.

"Or?"

"You come help put the roof on Ian's cabin and allow us free transit across your claim whenever we go to town."

"Do I look like a carpenter to you?" He spread out his arms, and water sloshed from his gold pan onto his sleeve and back into the river.

"You're a man of many talents, I'm sure." She smiled. "And though I don't wish to be rude, you are a man in sore need of a woman's assistance. Your clothes are in tatters."

Ian wandered over and stood beside her. "You don't have to pay the man to help me, Meredith. 'Tisn't right."

"I'd do his laundry anyway, Ian."

He shot her a sideways glance. "Self-preservation?"

"Precisely."

Ian grinned. "Abrams—let's make this deal better for everyone involved."

Abrams brightened. "You do have some whiskey, after all!"

"No, no." Ian folded his arms across his chest. "What I have in mind is a far better proposition."

"Ain't nothin' better than a coupla long swigs of Who-Hit-John."

Ian ignored Abrams's grumble. "You'll provide the logs to make a pontoon bridge across the river, and—"

"A bridge? I'm a miner, not a carpenter. I need to spend my time prospecting."

"Just listen. The river's about twenty feet from here to there. One of those spruces on your claim will more than do the trick. Just a medium one."

"How do you reckon that?"

"I'll help you cut the lower portion into four pontoons, and we'll split the rest of the trunk in half lengthwise to lie over them."

"Why bother splitting it?"

"For Meredith." He cupped his hand on her shoulder. Big as his hand was, he didn't rest the weight there. Warmth radiated from him, though.

It wasn't just physical warmth. A sense of his kindness washed over her. She'd never once said a word to Tucker about how she was stranded on this side of the river. Ian understood the issue and created a solution.

Speaking in a man-to-man tone, he continued to address Abrams. "We need to make sure Meredith will have secure footing when she crosses. Splitting the log and placing the puncheons side by side ought to make the bridge wide enough. In fact, due to her full skirts, a rail might be smart."

"No. No rail. A rope is good enough." Abrams's face grew dark. "But what do I get out of this?"

"You"—Ian stretched out the word as though he were preparing to crown a king—"may use Bess to go into Goose Chase and back on the day of your choosing next week. With your back paining you as much as it does, I know it would help for a sturdy mule like Bess to haul your supplies."

"That's very generous of you." Meredith smiled at Ian. "Bess is a fine mule."

"Aye, she is. And by next week, I'll have finished plowing and dragging timber."

"Compared to the time it would take you to do your laundry, mend your clothes, and make several trips to Goose Chase to bring back supplies," Tucker said as he scooped up more sand, "one day of roofing and a few hours to make a bridge is nothing."

As Ian withdrew his hand, Meredith fought the urge to lean toward him to prolong the contact. Instead, she concentrated on the old man across the river. "My brother is right. That trade is heavily in your favor, Mr. Abrams."

"I dunno." Abrams combed his fingers through his grungy beard.

"Well, don't worry about it." Ian turned to Meredith. Mirth crinkled the corners of his oh-so-blue eyes. "I'm sure whoever is across the river from my claim will be more than happy—"

"Hang on a minute. A man deserves a minute to think through a deal." Abrams bobbed his head. "Yup. I'll do it. But if Wily gets het up about you blocking the river so he can't take that sorry excuse for a boat any farther, you gotta deal with him."

"Wily won't mind," Tucker said. "He never goes any farther upriver than Clemment's."

Mr. Abrams let out a cackle. "He'll take it as a favor. Nobody wants to deal with that crazy old coot!"

"It's not a problem. With a pontoon bridge, we can let one end float downstream and pull it back in place after Wily's boat goes through," Ian reasoned.

"The real problem will be Abrams." The corners of Tucker's mouth tightened. "The minute that bridge is built, he'll come tromping over every time he smells coffee or food."

"What if we make a deal where we won't cross onto his claim and he won't come over here, unless we've gotten permission?" Meredith shrugged. "It's good manners."

Tucker snorted. "Abrams wouldn't know good manners if they bit him."

"How would the two of you feel about telling him he's invited to Sunday supper each week—provided he worship with us first?" Ian hooked his thumbs in the pockets of his jeans. "The rest of the week, we'll have the bridge float along our side of the river. I'll link it from the midpoint of my claim so you won't feel it's impinging on your panning, and Abrams won't worry about whether it diverts any gold that would flow his way."

"What are you all yammerin' about over there?" Abrams scowled.

"My brother and Ian are making sure everything will work out fairly." Meredith gestured toward the river. "They're concerned that the bridge might block the flow to your bank and affect how much gold you wind up with."

"Then there ain't gonna be no bridge!"

"We worked it all out," Ian declared. "The bridge will normally float parallel to our shore. Whenever we need to cross, we'll pulley it into place."

"Humph."

"But we'll worship every Sunday, and you're invited to join us." Seeing the horror on the old man's face, Meredith hurriedly tacked on, "And of course you'd be welcome to stay for Sunday supper."

"I ain't makin' no promises."

"Take your time. You can decide from week to week." Tucker wrapped his arm around her shoulders. "But you know what a fine cook Sis is."

"Aye, that she is!" Ian turned to her. "Why don't you go ahead and see to our neighbor's laundry? It's silly for me to wash my clothes when I still have plowing to finish."

"I am looking forward to having a garden."

Ian smiled at her. "Good. I'm thinking 'tis a shame, though, that I didn't bring any flower seeds. Ma always likes to plant a patch."

"Soon we'll have flowers all about us. Alaska is harsh, but wildflowers abound."

"I should have known." Ian studied her for a long moment. "The fairest of all are brought about by God's hand."

Meredith felt her face grow warm. Men in the region dropped by and tried to flatter her in hopes of getting a meal or a cheaper rate on mending. In the thirteen months since she'd been in Alaska, never once had a man complimented her without having an ulterior motive. Ian walked away before she could form a response.

Chapter 7

*I**shouldn't have said anything. Not so soon. I've barely met the lass.* Ian tied twine to an arrow and shot it over onto Abrams's property. *I embarrassed her. She's too kind to say so, but her blush made it clear as day.*

"I'll send a rope over now." Tucker attached rope to the twine. "It's best if Abrams ties the rope on his side first. I aim to yank hard when I secure it on this side. That way, if he didn't do a decent job, nothing is lost when it gives way." Tucker paused a second. "I can't help thinking, though, it might be a blessing if his laundry took a dunking before Sis has to wash it."

Ian looked up at the clouds and started whistling. He turned and walked off.

"Ian!" Tucker shouted at him. "You can't whistle any better than you sing!"

"Want me to start humming instead?"

"Spare me the agony."

Ian considered humming just for fun, but he had to harness Bess to the plow. Bess didn't like his music any better than Tucker did, so Ian decided garnering her cooperation was more important than needling Tucker.

Plowing the virgin soil took great effort. Even the best plow would be tested by the plot, and Ian ruefully fought to keep control over the rudimentary one he'd designed. The soil looked rich, though. Each foot would mean another cabbage. Each yard would support a trellis of climbing beans. As the crops grew, he'd be able to spend time with Meredith. Perhaps then, if he were patient, he'd reap more than just vegetables. If God willed it, Ian hoped to cultivate Meredith's affection, too.

"Just how much more do you plan to do?" Tucker leaned against the smokehouse and scanned the garden.

"May as well do a few extra rows. I was thinking that when you go to town, you could see if they have any of the seeds from Sitka."

"What does Sitka have to do with seeds?"

"The Russians settled here first. I read that the czar ordered each settlement had to have a garden. Since America bought the land, the government decided the Russians had a good notion. Sitka sends out seeds for free. I'm thinking Meredith might like some parsley and mustard. Rhubarb, too."

"Rhubarb!" Tucker moaned. "I don't remember the last time I had rhubarb pie. Maybe you ought to plow twice as much."

Ian opened his mouth to reply, but the plow caught on a stone and veered to the side. "Looks like you're out of luck. The soil's shallow and rocky here."

"What about another row farther back?"

"Sure, and why not? We may as well coax as much as we can from the land. How's Meredith's new floor?"

"Done." Tucker looked at his cabin. "Nothing shifts when I walk across it. I'll lead Bess over to the back of the plot. You bring the plow."

A moment later, Ian set down the plow. "We've got a good six feet here. I can get at least three more rows in. Maybe four."

"With the size root cellars we both have, you'd better make it four. I figure we'll finish off your cabin tomorrow; then I'll go to Goose Chase. If there's anything you need, write it down. I'll try to get it for you."

"I'll think on it. Ho there, Bess. All right, girl. Let's go." He clicked his tongue, and his mule started pulling the plow. That row was difficult. The next fought him even more. Halfway across, Bess stopped dead in her tracks.

"Aww, c'mon, Bess." Ian jostled the reins.

Her tail started to spin in a circle—a sure sign she'd made up her mind and wasn't in any mood to listen to his plans. "Bessie, Bessie, Bessie," he crooned.

She turned to the side and gave him a baleful glare. Mules in general, and Bess in particular, would hit a point where they got tired and simply refused to work another minute. Her scraggly tail spun again.

"All right. You've done all you can today." Ian released the plow and walked up to give her an appreciative pat on the withers. "You're a good girl. You've worked hard."

Freed from her obligations, Bess wandered away. Ian hung the harness on the hefty pegs he'd driven into the outside of the smokehouse. He paced back to theplow. Leaving it in place was okay, but he needed to scrape off the worst of the muck so it wouldn't dry and turn into a heavy, jagged crust.

"Done?" Meredith asked.

"Not yet. Bess decided she'd worked enough for the day, so I'll finish the last two rows first thing tomorrow." He scraped off one last glop. "How's the laundry going?"

"My laundry line is full. I wanted to know if you'd mind me pinning clothes to the rope over the river."

"I don't think that's the best idea."

Meredith wrinkled her nose. "I understand. I was afraid something might fall in."

"Not something. Someone." Straightening up, Ian slid his knife back into the belt sheath. "Clothes can be replaced. Fast and cold as that water is, we can't risk you. I'll string up something."

"We don't have any more rope, Ian."

"Ah, but lass, I have wire. It ought to serve." He located the crate containing the wire, and Meredith decided where she wanted him to string it. Cheery as a lark, she chattered and laughed as he wound the wire securely around a branch. When Ian reached to secure the second side, Tucker shouted his name.

"What?" Ian called back.

"Get over here." Tucker stood with his arms akimbo. His voice sounded harsh as a whip. "We've got to have a talk."

Until now, Tucker had been a shade taciturn. Wry, too. But he'd never been overbearing. *He's protective of his sister. He doesn't want me around her.* Ian decided to finish his task. "I'll be over in a minute."

"Now," Tucker ground out.

Chapter 8

S omething's wrong." Meredith scurried toward her brother. Ian hastened alongside her. Tucker stepped back into the shade behind the smokehouse. He yanked her arm and shoved her past himself.

"That's no way to treat a lady!" Ian glowered at Tucker.

Ignoring Ian's protest, Tucker rasped harshly, "Look."

"Ian's done a wonderful job, Tucker." Meredith gave her brother a puzzled glance. "It'll be a fine garden, indeed."

"No, it won't."

"Tucker, you can't say that. We have solid plans."

Ian hunkered down, then shot to his feet. "We'll change our plans."

Meredith gawked at him. "What has gotten into the two of you?"

Ian held out his hand. A small white stone with a tiny thread of color was nestled in his palm. "Gold fever."

Staring at his hand, Meredith tried not to let her hope run amok. That one small glint of yellow wasn't enough to sneeze at.

"Look." Tucker stooped down and brushed away more dirt. "White quartz. Gold is most often found in white quartz."

"The vein is slim as a cobweb, but it's there." Excitement pulsed in Ian's voice. "Glory be to God!"

Tucker rose and wiped his fingers off on his pants. He stuck out his hand. "Congratulations, Rafferty. You've struck gold."

Meredith shot a startled look toward the woods. Tucker was right. The quartz was a solid four feet from the property line—and on Ian's claim.

Ian extended his right hand, clasped Tucker's, and shook. "We've struck gold."

Lord, look at Tucker. He's trying so hard to be honorable. You know how much he needed that gold. But if someone else is to have it, there's no finer man than Ian Rafferty. Meredith swallowed the bitter taste of disappointment. "You're right. The plans will change now. Ian won't need a garden."

"Nonsense!" Ian turned loose of Tucker's hand and faced her. "We'll need good, hearty food to prospect. It's just that instead of coaxing mustard yellow from this spot, we'll mine gold!"

Meredith managed a tipsy smile. "That was clever. We're very happy for you, Ian."

His brows knit. "For me?" His eyes widened. "Oh no. No, no, no. This belongs to all of us."

"It's on your claim." Tucker sounded as if he'd backed into cactus.

"And you discovered it." Ian folded his arms across his chest. "I'm going to be stubborn, so you'd best just agree. This is a fifty/fifty partnership."

"Don't be a fool." Tucker turned and started to walk off.

"Tucker Smith, we struck a bargain. I'm holding you to your word. You are a man of your word, aren't you?"

Meredith gasped.

Tucker wheeled around. "You're questioning my honor?"

A slow smile lifted the corners of Ian's mouth. "You agreed that anything coming from the garden would be split half and half. An honorable man's word is his bond. Either you stick with that bargain or you renege. What's it going to be?"

"It's not that clear-cut."

Ian turned toward her. "It's plain as can be to me. You were there. Did your twin agree to an even split?"

Unsure of how to answer, Meredith tried to recall exactly what they'd said. Part of her wanted to agree with Ian and remove some of the financial burden from Tucker's shoulders. On the other hand, she didn't want to take what wasn't rightfully theirs. "We were discussing the garden. We said we'd all labor and share equally in the yield, but—"

"There's no *but*. We agreed." Ian's smile would be smug if he weren't being so astonishingly generous. He looked from her to Tucker and back again. "I'm holding you to your word."

"All our neighbors combined aren't as demented as you are." Tucker stared at Ian. "We don't expect you to do this. The discussion was about produce, not gold."

"Yield." Ian stared her brother in the eyes. "I distinctly remember the word *yield*, and so does your sister. The matter is settled. We are going to have one problem, though."

Tucker looked wary. "What's that?"

"Abrams. The minute he comes across the bridge and sees this, he'll be a problem. I can just imagine him going to Goose Chase, getting soused at the saloon, and blabbing."

"So he won't know about it." Meredith reached up and tucked an escaping tendril of hair behind her ear. As soon as she finished the mundane task, she realized Ian was watching her intently. *What is he thinking? The other men in the area all want to marry me to ease their lives. Ian hasn't said a thing, and he's even doing his own laundry. He isn't like anyone else. I can't figure him out.*

"Why not?" He still didn't stop gazing at her.

"Why not?" Meredith echoed as she scrambled to recall what they'd been conversing.

"My guess is, Sis figures Abrams will think you're spending all sorts of time gardening."

"Exactly!" Relief flooded her.

"That excuse won't last long."

Tucker shrugged. "No, but it'll at least last through next week. By then, he'll have gone to town and returned. Meredith and I have been panning at the river's edge. A few prospectors in the region are digging shafts. With you being new to the claim, no one will give a whole lot of thought to you going about things your own way."

"Good." Ian smiled. "You asked if there was anything I wanted from town. Another pickax would be smart. A sledgehammer, too."

"I have both." The tiniest bit of pride rang in Tucker's voice.

"Now how do you like that?" Ian's eyes twinkled. "The partnership couldn't be off to any better start than that!"

"One more thing. I'm holding you to your word, too." Tucker jabbed his forefinger at Ian. "You said if the rocks cried out, you wouldn't sing. Well, the rocks cried out. I personally think it's God's way of sparing Meredith and me from having to hear you slaughter tunes."

"Well, now, you do have a point." Ian scuffed his boot in the overturned soil. "I won't sing."

"Fine." Tucker walked off.

Ian winked at Meredith. "You're my witness, lass. I vowed I'd not sing. I said nothing about whistling or humming."

Ian admired his handiwork. Meredith would be so pleased when she saw what he'd made! He'd encouraged her to go to town with Tucker yesterday. They'd be back late this afternoon.

Ian stepped backward. *Squish.* He gritted his teeth at the disgusting sound. Distracted as he was, he'd gone directly into a puddle of mud that now threatened to suck off his boot. *It'll be too hard for Meredith to walk back on paths like this in one day. It might be tomorrow ere they return. All the better. I'll get more done and surprise her.*

Two days ago, while Tucker, Abrams, and he had roofed his new cabin, Meredith had planted her cabbage and beans. Ian fought with himself whether to plant the rest of the seeds and surprise her, or to wait and have an excuse to spend time in the garden with her. In the end, he compromised and planted potatoes and carrots in her absence. The rest they'd do together.

Spending the last two nights under his own roof had felt odd. Lonely. While he'd slept outside by the fire, the arrangement seemed temporary. A whole canopy of stars kept him company. But sleeping indoors—well, it didn't seem right for the house to be so impossibly still.

Back home, Da snored. Ma often mumbled in her sleep. Fiona's bed creaked in protest when she'd flop over to be closer to her lamp so she could read late at night. The only other time he'd felt this way was when Braden married and moved from the room they'd shared and carried Maggie over the threshold of the small cabin next to the farmhouse.

What would it be like to marry Meredith and start a family here? Though larger than the Smiths' cabin, Ian's still wouldn't be big enough to hold the big family he hoped to have. *When the time comes, I'll add on.*

His stomach rumbled. Ian headed back into his house to rustle up something to eat. He'd burned the cornmeal mush for breakfast. That experience made him decide he'd probably do no better cooking in a fireplace than he did over the fire pit he currently used. When Abrams went to town next week, Ian would have him post a letter. He'd already sent one with Meredith—a short one that reassured Ma that he was safe and had good Christian neighbors and a sound roof over his head. The next letter would give Ma a special task: Send a stove!

He'd never given much thought to how hard Ma worked at the stove to cook. Meredith made it look easy as could be to throw together delicious meals at the hearth in her cabin. After a prolonged search, Ian found the recipe book Ma had created just for him to bring along.

Twenty-five minutes later, he peered into the pot and wondered why the rice looked so soupy.

Abrams lumbered across the bridge and sniffed. "I reckoned you'd be gettin' vittles. What're you making?"

"A mess."

The old man sauntered closer. "A mess of what?"

"It's supposed to be rice."

"Looks like a bowl of maggots."

Ian slapped the lid back on the pot.

"Squirrel. That's what we need. Chuck in some squirrel meat, and it'll be a fine stew. Grab that bow and arrows of yours. I don't wanna wait all day. I'm hungry."

Ian's stomach growled. "You know how to make stew?"

"Yep. Any idjit can. Just dump in the right stuff, and there you have it." Abrams pulled the rice from the fire. "Gotta set that aside, else it'll burn."

Abrams proved to be astonishingly adept at cooking. By the time Ian skinned and chopped one squirrel, Abrams had done the other two. "Son, gotta tell you, that squirrel is lucky he died quick from your arrow. Nothing deserves to be hacked up like that. It woulda been called torture if he was still alive."

"It'll still taste good."

"No thanks to you. We need a pinch of salt and a dash of pepper. What other seasonings d'ya have?"

"What else do you want?"

"Sage and thyme. Onion, if you've got one."

Almost an hour later, Ian slapped a glob of mud over the twigs he'd jammed into the spaces between the logs of his cabin. Chinking the cabin was essential—but it didn't take his mind off the delectable aroma wafting from the pot. "Abrams, I'm washing my hands. After that, I'm going to dive headfirst into that stew."

"It'll be ready by then."

As they sat and ate, Ian motioned toward the pot with his spoon. "If I didn't know just how tired Meredith and Tucker will be when they get back, I'd eat every last drop and lick that pot."

"We could make a second pot for them."

Abrams looked dead earnest, but Ian decided to treat his remark like a joke. He chortled. "You've a fine sense of humor."

"Well, you got a lotta food, you know."

"Not really. I brought what the recommendations are for one man for a year."

"I watched when you unloaded all the stuff Wily delivered. You brought more'n two hundred pounds of sugar and least a hundred pounds of cornmeal 'stead of fifty."

"I did." Ian nodded. "But I brought less canned fish and meat. I'm also hoping to grow more vegetables. Tucker and Meredith have advised me to ration my food very carefully, and I figure they know what they're talking about."

"Humph." He scraped the bottom of his bowl. "You can't be sure they'll be back today."

Instead of arguing, Ian changed the topic. "Do you have any empty bottles on your claim?"

"A few. Why?" Abrams squinted. "Don't tell me you're gonna wrap yourself up in a temperance banner and preach all the evils of alcohol. I'm a grown man. I can do whatever I please."

"It's not for me to condemn you. I wouldn't mind having some empty bottles, though."

"Most of 'em don't got a lid anymore. And if you're plannin' to store food in 'em, it won't work. They're nothing but trash."

"I see." Ian stood. "Well, I suppose we can leave the pot off in the ashes and hope the stew tastes half as good at suppertime as it did for lunch."

"Better. The longer it rests, the move flavor you get." Abrams stood up. "I'll bring some bottles when I come for supper."

Ian smothered a smile. It didn't escape his notice that Abrams had invited himself to supper. Anticipating that had prompted him to bag three squirrels at the outset. "You do that."

"We gonna have coffee?"

"Might. Then again, might not. How many bottles do you have? I'm talking quart-sized, not dinky, piddling ones. Round ones."

"Dunno. I'll check." Abrams scuttled back across the bridge.

Ian went back to chinking his cabin.

"Six," Abrams shouted. "I got six so far."

"Is that all?" Ian didn't doubt for a moment that Abrams had plenty more. For the rest of the afternoon, Abrams kept hollering as he scrounged up more bottles, and Ian would simply nod.

"Twenty-nine! Dunno why you want 'em, but that's gotta be all I've got."

"Twenty-nine?"

"You wantin' 'em round's gonna give me fits. I never paid any mind to how many things come in rectangular bottles."

"Bring over everything you've got."

"Shoulda said so in the first place." Glass clinked in the metal washtub as Abrams crossed the bridge. It took him three trips to tote over an eye-popping assortment of bottles that once held everything from beer to whiskey, cod liver oil to hair tonic. The empty containers turned a patch of dirt into a glittering heap. "That's a lot of bottles. You have to admit, it's a fine assortment."

Ian gave Abrams a good-natured shove on the shoulder. "At lunch, you said they were trash."

"I gave up valuable time I coulda spent panning for gold. My time's worth plenty."

"I agree. We'll have coffee after supper tonight."

Abrams's eyes narrowed. "Strong coffee—not that stingy, dishwater-weak brew."

"Strong enough to float a horseshoe. Between now and then, I have work to do."

Abrams shook his head. "Work is prospectin'. I have yet to see you work a lick. If all you wanted was to be a farmer, you shoulda settled somewhere else."

"My family has a grand farm in Oregon. I wanted something more, something different."

"Sure don't look that way," Abrams muttered as he left.

Ian stared down at the bottles. As he'd expected, most of them had once held spirits. Those didn't capture Ian's attention. He stared at the other ones. Braden insisted upon Maggie's taking a daily dose of Dr. Barker's Blood Builder because she'd always been on the delicate side. Fiona used Princess Tonic Hair Restorer. It seemed ludicrous that old Abrams used both of those products, too—but the proof lay there. On occasion, Da used Peptonic Stomach Bitters. Ma insisted that everyone take a teaspoon of Norwegian cod liver oil each morning. Odd, how ordinary glass bottles would bring back so many memories.

Ian surveyed his claim. Much as he hated to admit it, Abrams had a point. Like a good farmer, Ian had come, built a sturdy home, seen to a smokehouse, and plowed a field. *Did I leave home only to recreate the exact same thing here?*

Chapter 9

The last rays of sunlight dimmed as Meredith hit the edge of Abrams's claim. "See? We made it."

Tucker gave her an exasperated look. "If you say, 'I told you so,' I'll push you in the river."

"No, you wouldn't. I'd push you in first because I've listened to an endless string of grumpy mutterings all day."

"You'd have to fight an army of mosquitoes to get close enough to make good on that threat." He batted away a buzzing insect.

"They are thicker this year." Meredith readjusted a strap on the knapsack she wore. "Hello! We're back!"

"It's about time." Old Abrams popped into view. "Rafferty over there's been holdin' off on supper until you took a mind to show up. I'm about to suffer a sinking spell from hunger."

"We can't have that!"

Abrams waited until they came abreast of him. He lowered his voice and leaned closer. "One of you better talk sense into Ian Rafferty. He's whilin' away his time with foolish pursuits. At this rate, come spring of next year, he won't have more'n a pinch of gold dust. He'll have to slink back home with his tail betwixt his legs 'cuz he can't afford grub for the next year."

"He's a grown man," Tucker grumbled. "He can do what he likes."

"Once you see what he's been up to, you'll think nutty old Clemment's downright sane by comparison."

The man on the other side of Ian's claim displayed a wide array of peculiarities. Meredith couldn't imagine what Ian could possibly do to earn such a comparison. Instead of saying anything, she headed for the bridge. Knowing she'd reach the other side of the roiling river without any effort convinced her Ian Rafferty was clever, not crazy.

"Welcome back!" Ian walked over and immediately took the knapsack off her back.

"Careful! I have eggs in the top."

Ian inclined his head to acknowledge her warning. "I'll help Tucker unload everything. Abrams, why don't you dish up supper?"

Weary as she felt, Meredith stepped into her cabin and almost wept with gratitude. Ian had started a fire so the house would be warm—but better still, he'd filled the galvanized tub with water and left it on the hearth. She'd just wash her hands and face now, but as soon as she finished supper, she'd come and spoil herself with a good, long soak.

"Did Bess behave herself?"

"Never thought I'd like a mule," Tucker confessed, "but she was a godsend."

The men dropped off the knapsacks and went back outside to unload the provisions. It would take at least two more trips to carry in everything they'd need for the next winter—but each bag of beans and every pound of flour testified to God's faithfulness.

"Sis,"Tucker said as he plopped down the last parcel, "don't bother arranging everything. I'm starving, and if we don't hurry over, Abrams is going to drink all of the coffee."

Meredith laughed. "Is it hunger or coffee that's driving you?"

"Both."

Moments later, Meredith knocked on Ian's door. He walked up from behind her. "Go on in. My home's always open to you."

She and Tucker went inside. Four crates surrounded a cot. What had once been the base of a sled lay across the cot, turning it into a table.

Abrams thumped the speckled coffeepot in the center. "Chow's on. Grace better be short, 'cuz I've waited to eat longer than a man ought to."

Too hungry and tired to be sociable, Meredith and Tucker sank onto the crates. They listened as Ian thanked the Lord for granting them traveling mercies and providing for the meal, then started eating. Very little conversation flowed. Once the meal ended and the coffeepot was emptied, Ian looked at Abrams. "Ready?"

"Sure." Abrams rose from the table and carried the lamp out the door, leaving them with the light of a single candle.

Ian waited a moment, then urged, "Turn around."

Meredith's skirts tangled and snagged on the rough crate. She carefully disentangled herself and pivoted. Her breath caught in her throat.

"It's beautiful!"

The lamp Abrams held outside filtered through an assortment of bottles.

"That," Tucker's tone echoed with wry disbelief, "is undoubtedly the strangest window I've ever seen."

"Stained glass. You made a stained-glass window." Meredith could scarcely speak in more than a reverent whisper. She walked toward it. Her forefinger hovering a mere inch above the open bottles' mouths, she traced the dark cross that deep brown bottles formed in the center.

"Well?" Abrams hollered. "Do they like it?"

"My sister is captivated."Tucker started talking to Ian about heat loss.

Ian answered back about thick mortar between the bottles and the air trapped inside them.

The precise content of their conversation didn't matter to Meredith. Her cabin had one window just large enough for them to squeeze out of in case of a fire or something blocking the door. All winter long, shutters and a tightly nailed length of leather closed off that window. The notion of having a sliver of light or color enthralled her.

The light behind the window faded. Abrams stomped back in. "It's purdier from the outside. Leastways, it is after dark. Makes me regret not keeping them bottles for myself."

Meredith took in the pattern of color Ian used: green, blue, and brown bottles alternated around the outside, amber ones formed the next row all the way around, then the entire center was clear with the exception of rectangular and square brown bottles that formed the cross. "Just imagine waking to this."

"Had I known how much you'd like it, I would have made mine half that size so you could have one, too." Ian motioned toward a few odd bottles lined up on the floor directly

THE ALASKA BRIDES COLLECTION

beneath the window. "You're welcome to have those as a start."

Meredith stooped down and frowned. "Oh, Mr. Abrams. I recognize this bottle. It's Positive Rheumatic Cure. My mother, bless her soul, used it."

"Folks don't know how bad the rheumatiz gets. 'Specially in the winter. I'm gonna have to load up on the cure. Ran out last month."

"We would have brought back a bottle for you."

The old man patted her cheek. "Darlin', you put me in mind of my daughter. Violet's got that same streak of kindness."

"You have a daughter?" Tucker blurted out.

"Yup. I'm gonna go back home to her soon as I strike it rich." He shuffled uncomfortably. "Well, I'm going on over to my cabin now."

"Tomorrow is Sunday." Ian leaned against the wall right next to the window. "Will you be worshipping with us?"

"And having Sunday supper?" Meredith tacked on.

"Nah. Gotta make up for lost time."

Ian and Tucker didn't say anything, but they each took an oil lamp and stood by the riverbank as Abrams crossed the bridge. They knew he couldn't swim and was too proud to confess he was afraid of falling in. Meredith watched as they stood like sentinels, keeping watch—two strong men who wouldn't have hesitated a heartbeat about jumping into the frigid, fast-moving current to rescue a peculiar, grumpy old man. The sight didn't frighten her in the least. She had every confidence in them and believed that God would let no ill befall them.

Waves of weariness washed over her as the men turned and approached her. Meredith didn't want to confess how exhausted she'd grown from the muddy ten-mile trek from town. Instead, she went back into Ian's cabin and started clearing the table.

"Leave that," he ordered. "I have one last thing to show you ere you go home."

Meredith and Tucker accompanied him around the cabin, past the plowed field, and toward the stand of trees. She kept looking down, trying to avoid tripping over a stone or a rut.

"Well?" Ian sounded jubilant. "What do you think?"

Tucker started laughing.

Delighted, Meredith looked at her twin. Twice now, Ian had gotten him to laugh. Tucker reached over and turned her head to the side so she could see what tickled him.

Ian swept his hand in a gesture that would do a snake-oil charlatan proud. "Only the best for those who want the comforts of home."

Meredith's jaw dropped.

Chapter 10

Meredith slipped from the outhouse early the next morning, unsure whether to be sheepish or delighted. A lady didn't discuss such topics, but she couldn't help wanting to thank Ian again. And again. And again.

Just to keep from flinging her arms around Ian in thanks last night, she'd clung to Tucker's arm and babbled in delight. She'd probably made a complete fool of herself, but Ian was far too polite to say so. She'd finally stammered something and run back home to soak in the bath. She didn't take as long as she wanted to. Tucker had to be tired, too, and she wanted him to enjoy hot water. She'd no more than lain down when she heard him come into the cabin. A mere breath later, she'd fallen fast asleep.

"Ian wants to know if you want to worship here or over at his place."

"Do you mind if it's at his place? The light shining through that window would be perfect."

"Okay. Ian invited Abrams again, but that ornery old man won't come. I'm going to go see if Mr. Clemment is interested."

Tucker coaxed Mr. Clemment to come over and worship with them. Mr. Clemment arrived in overalls that he wore backward. He looked slightly confused and grew wary as Tucker introduced him to Ian.

Ian slowly extended his right hand. "I'm glad to meet the neighbor on the other side of that fine bramble that separates our claims."

"God never made a better bramble!" Suddenly, Mr. Clemment warmed up to Ian and started telling him all of the varieties of birds that would peck the berries.

Ian listened and asked a few questions. Treating the odd man with respect, he managed to steer him into the house and seated him beside Meredith. " 'Tis grand to have neighbors worship together, isn't it?"

Meredith patted Mr. Clemment's hand. "We're glad you came."

Ian reached over and took his Bible from the table. Meredith watched her twin. When they'd gone to the mercantile, she'd seen Tucker longingly running his fingers over the cover of a Bible. He'd not picked it up, though. Since Ian shared his Bible, they could do without buying one for themselves. Even though that was the case, Meredith knew her brother missed having a complete Bible every bit as much as she did.

"Tucker, here." Ian handed his Bible to Tucker. "Why don't you read to us from the Word of God today?"

Tucker accepted the Bible, sat down, and reverently rested his hand atop the leather cover for a long moment before opening the pages.

Meredith looked from her brother's hands to Ian as he sat on a crate. Ian's kindness and generosity and Tucker's reverence stirred her heart.

After Tucker read from the Psalms, each of them took turns speaking of the Lord's goodness. Ian ended with a prayer. Although an altogether simple service, observing the Lord's Day still felt good.

Tired as she'd been from travel, Meredith decided beans would make for an easy and filling meal—especially since she had eggs. One precious egg allowed her to make a pan of corn bread.

After Sunday supper, Mr. Clemment paced around the garden plot. "I like sunflower seeds. Are you planting sunflowers?"

"No, they don't have sufficient season to grow up here." Ian proceeded to explain the crops they planned.

"Oh!" Meredith perked up. "Socks is going to send to Sitka for free seeds for us. They ought to come in a week. The only seeds he had were for parsnips, so I took a packet."

"Been a long, long while since I had parsnip soup." Mr. Clemment scratched his side. "Don't suppose you've got a recipe for it."

"I do. Once we have a nice crop of parsnips, I'll be sure to make soup for Sunday supper especially for you."

"Hold on, Sis." Tucker gave her a warning look. "You can't go counting your chickens before they hatch."

"Chickens are fine birds," Clemment said.

Meredith didn't want to be rude, so she nodded acknowledgment to Mr. Clemment. "Tucker, we live by faith."

"Not by faith alone. You have to face facts, too. Life brings hardships and trials. No matter how hard you and Ian work in that garden, you can't count on anything coming of it."

"Just like prospecting," Clemment agreed. "You can work your fingers to the bone and hardly get a thing for all your efforts."

"Don't be faulting the lass for her bright outlook. Naysayers never get anything started and done. Her cheerful attitude is a wondrous thing." A slow smile tugged at the corner of Ian's mouth. "I'm thinking your mother named you well. A merrier woman I'll never meet."

"Mama called me Merry when I was small."

The smile broke across Ian's face. "And with your leave, I'll call you the same. 'Tis a fitting name indeed for you."

Delight rippled through her. "Please feel free to."

"Good. Merry you are, so 'tis Merry you'll be."

⁂

"Merry?"

She ceased planting lettuce seeds, sat back on her heels, and faced Ian. "Yes?"

"You've mentioned your mother a few times. Tucker said she's passed on. What about your father?"

She looked away and rasped, "He's no longer with us."

"Ahh." He stretched out the sound in such a way that it carried the flavor of sorrow, as well as understanding. "I apologize. I didn't mean to add to your grief."

She bowed her head and covered the infinitesimal seeds with a fine layer of soil. The first batch of lettuce was starting to mature. By staggering the planting, they'd stretch the time they'd be able to enjoy the produce. Merry tried to concentrate on her task, but she worried that the way her hand shook would tell Ian how much he'd rattled her composure.

Why did I ever promise Tucker I wouldn't tell anyone? Keeping the secret is so hard. I feel like

48

I'm lying or dancing around the truth. Ian is such a good man, yet we're repaying his generosity and kindness with deceit. Meredith swallowed to dislodge the thick ball in her throat, but it didn't help.

Silence hung between them. The song of birds didn't begin to cover the awkwardness.

"I won't mention him again, Merry. I can see how much I've upset you, and I'm truly sorry."

Tears blurred her vision as guilt mounted. Unable to speak, Meredith merely nodded.

Ian continued to work. The steady sound of his hoe made it easy for Meredith to know precisely where he was. He'd moved down that row and now came back toward her. Normally, they'd carry on a comfortable conversation while working in the garden. The strain of the silence pulled at her conscience. Bound by her promise to Tucker, she couldn't say anything— but the topic weighed so heavily on her heart, nothing else came to mind.

The sharp sound of a slap made her look up. Ian frowned while looking at his forearm. "I've seen hummingbirds smaller than the mosquitoes around here!"

"Tucker says that Alaskan mosquitoes must not have heard the rule that everything is supposed to be bigger in Texas."

"I'm sure the onions in Texas are larger. The few that did grow certainly weren't worth the effort."

"I'm not so sure about the parsnips, either. Mr. Clemment will be so disappointed if we don't succeed with them."

He leaned on his hoe. "Do you think the parsnips are actually normal in size? I'm thinking that the carrots, potatoes, and parsnips will be ordinary, but the long, long daylight hours are making things above the ground grow huge. Anything by comparison would look meager."

"I hadn't thought about that." She scanned the garden. Calling it a garden seemed ludicrous. Early on, they'd had to thin the vegetables. Instead of tossing aside anything, Ian decided it would be good stewardship to plow a few more rows and transplant anything they thinned. But he'd had to do a few more rows. . .and a few more again.

Miners who'd paid Meredith to do their laundry and mending last year came by again. One look at the garden, and they'd eagerly bartered for vegetables. The funds from those first transactions paid for canning jars and more buttons.

Meredith and Tucker had come to an agreement: any of the money or goods she earned with laundry, sewing, and the garden would go toward their own needs. Tucker didn't want any of that to go toward repaying everyone back in Texas. He alone would do that with whatever gold they mined.

"Aha!"

Ian's sound made Meredith jump. She gave him a startled look.

"You think my question holds a grain of truth. Much as I love potatoes—and what self-respecting Irishman wouldn't?—'tis a crying shame that they don't grow so big here. But I'm thinking we'll have enough to get us through the winter. Don't you?"

She looked at that area of the patch. "I'm not so sure. . . not if I roast those two hares you snared today. Potatoes and carrots and roast. . ."

Ian looked up at the sky then heaved a sigh. "How am I to know when 'tis suppertime? The notion of living with the midnight sun sounded novel when first I came. But now I can't sleep worth a hoot and don't know when 'tis mealtime."

"Time doesn't have much meaning up here. If you're having trouble sleeping, you can hang something dark in front of the windows and by the door. That helps."

"I drove nails into the log directly above my window last night. Knotted the corners of a brown blanket 'round the nails."

"Good."

"Not so good. Just as I was finally falling asleep, one end slid off and pulled the other down with it. I gave up and put the blanket over my head—but then I could scarcely breathe and started roasting."

"Oh dear."

His mouth formed a self-deprecating smile. "I'd call myself a pathetic wretch, but I'd be lying. Just one look around, and I can see how blessed I am. I've a claim, a garden, and godly neighbors. What more could a man ask for?"

For his godly neighbors to be forthright instead of putting up pretenses. The answer shot through her mind. Unable to face him any longer, Meredith rose to her feet and dusted off her hands as she walked to the water bucket. Sipping water from the dipper, she fought to regain her composure.

"Hey!" A pair of men appeared on the edge of the woods. "Didn't think it was possible a woman was round these parts, but Matthews said we'd find one here—and there you are!"

Ian appeared at her side in an instant. "Did you men need something?"

"Heard tell the gal takes in laundry and mending."

"She might." Ian's voice sounded controlled and quiet, but at the same time, those two clipped words made it clear he wouldn't put up with any nonsense.

The men drew closer. "Now that winter's over, we've got clothes that need washing." One raked his fingers through his greasy hair and beard. "A haircut would suit me fine. A shave, too."

Meredith shook her head.

"The lady's not a barber." Ian stayed close and murmured, "If you don't want to do their laundry, put your hand in the pocket of your apron. If you'll do it, slip your hand into mine."

Every bit of money she could earn mattered. Meredith slid her hand into Ian's rough, warm palm. His fingers closed about hers. He squeezed gently, and Meredith struggled to stay composed.

I'm living a lie, and he's protecting me.

"Well, that answers that," one told the other.

"What?" Ian half growled.

"Heard the gal was here with her brother. That feller over yonder looks like her. He's gotta be her kin. Kinda hoped she'd take a shine to one of us and marry up. Guess you beat us to her."

"Crying shame, too. She's pretty."

Ian didn't look at her. He simply stepped forward and tucked her behind himself.

"We ain't meanin' to insult you or scare your missus," the other said to Ian. "Havin' a wife to do the laundry and cookin'—well, you're set real fine. Us? We just need some stuff done."

Ian didn't budge. "Women are worth far more than just being laundresses. This woman, in particular."

"You're right. Betcha she's a fine cook, too."

Meredith could feel the way Ian bristled at their comments. Whenever bachelors happened by, they invariably proposed. They wanted a woman to cook their meals, tend their clothes, and warm their bed. Even Mr. Abrams and Mr. Clemment had suggested marriage. Ian alone bore the distinction of being the only man she'd seen in the past fifteen months who hadn't asked for her hand.

Does he have a wife or sweetheart back home? Or does he think I'm as attractive as last week's fish?

"How much laundry do you have, and what kind of mending?"

He remembered me asking those same questions of Mr. Abrams. She stood on tiptoe and peeped over Ian's shoulder.

"Two pair of britches and two shirts apiece. Most everything's short a button or two."

Elbowing his companion, the other jerked his head toward the garden and moaned. "Matthews was right. They've got fresh truck. Lots of it!"

Tucker sauntered over. His hooded expression wouldn't allow the strangers to know what he was thinking, but Meredith knew full well he noticed Ian's protective stance. "What's going on?"

"We're looking to have some laundry and mending done and to buy up some of those greens you folks are growing."

Ian turned to Tucker. "Meredith's planning to can any of the green beans and wax beans we don't eat fresh."

"You got all season to grow more. Surely you could spare us some now. And some lettuce, too. That's lettuce, isn't it?"

The man had good call to wonder. Ian had never seen lettuce even half that size. "Aye, it's lettuce. And beside it—that's cabbage."

The two men whispered to each other. One finally cleared his throat. "One buck, cash money, and a pinch of gold dust. We get two quarts of fresh beans, two quart jars of beans the gal's put up, two heads of cabbage, and two heads of lettuce, and the lady does our laundry and mending."

Ian snorted.

"Two bucks."

After supper one night a few weeks back, Meredith, Tucker, and Ian had come to an agreement regarding the price of their goods. For the effort they put into the garden, they needed to make a profit. After all, it did take away from the time Ian would prospect. But the money earned would also be a fine way of making it so others wouldn't realize they'd found that sliver of a gold vein. Even so, if any of the three of them felt led to sell at a reduced rate or even give away food to someone in need, that would be fine.

Ian and Tucker exchanged a stern look. Then Tucker looked at her. Ian still didn't budge—he kept her directly behind himself, out of their view. Something in the way the strangers acted didn't put Meredith in a generous frame of mind. She gave her head a slight shake.

"The mercantile in Goose Chase charges a buck and a half for hamburger steak and onion in a can," Tucker said. "One stinking can for a buck fifty. I don't doubt they'd pay that much for a head of cabbage."

"Probably pay us that much and charge a customer more," Ian chimed in.

"The three of you can't eat all that," one of the men wheedled. "It'll just go to waste."

Merry slipped from behind Ian and stood between him and her brother. "I'll just slice up any extra cabbage and whip up batches of sauerkraut. It'll keep in crocks for months on end."

"Other men are eager to buy our excess, and for fair prices." Ian stared at the men. "But those men also understand the value of having a lady do their laundry and mending. Bad enough, you've offered gracious little for the food, but I'll not stand by and let you insult Meredith. It would be best if you went off and struck a deal with someone else."

"We can't do that. There aren't any other women, and no one else planted a garden."

"You should have thought about those things before you made such a paltry offer." Tucker made a shooing motion. "Go on and get off my land."

"Six bucks!"

Ian folded his arms across his chest. "No. You insulted the lady. She'll not be lowering herself to wash your clothes at any price."

"Then five bucks. Forget the laundry or mending. We'll pay you five bucks, cash money, and you give us two heads of lettuce and two heads of cabbage and—"

"No more," Tucker ground out.

"My brother means to say," Meredith blurted out, "we'll agree to five dollars for the items you just specified." She felt sure her brother was going to send the men packing even though they'd offered an exorbitant sum.

"Deal!" One of the men scrambled over.

"But you don't come back. Ever." Tucker stared at them.

After they left, Tucker ignored her. He looked at Ian. "I don't care how much they offer. Sis isn't doing their laundry or mending. Ever."

"I agree. And they'll not buy another morsel of food."

"Are you going to bother to ask me?"

"No," they said in unison.

She huffed. "I have a mind of my own."

"Aye, you do. And a sound mind it is." Ian then tacked on, "But you've also a tender heart. What kind of men would we be to stand by and let anyone abuse your helpfulness or hurt your feelings?"

"My feelings aren't hurt."

Ian shook his head. "Lass, that just proves our point. You've forgiven those louts already. Fact is, they didn't care about your feelings. They had sufficient money to make a fair offer. They had no honor. Never deal with someone who lacks integrity."

For the rest of the day, while the men used pickaxes and the sledgehammer to chip deeper into the stony earth, Ian's words pounded into Meredith's mind over and over again. *"Never deal with someone who lacks integrity."* How would Ian feel when he learned the truth?

Chapter 11

Thanks." Ian accepted the dipper of water from Meredith and took a long, refreshing gulp. Tucker had loaded Bess with garden truck and led her to town. Several more trips would be essential—both to sell the produce and to bring in supplies for the coming year.

Meredith accepted the empty dipper. "Thank you for sending Tucker to town today. He can be so stubborn!"

Ian grimaced. "Aye. But that thumb has to be paining him something awful."

She nodded. "He knows better than to be using a wet sledgehammer on a rainy day. He's lucky lightning didn't strike him."

"I'd be a hypocrite to condemn him for that. We get so much rain, there aren't many days' work we'd get done if we ran inside each time the sky took a mind to spit."

"I wonder how far he'll get before someone stops him and asks to buy something straight off Bess."

"Not far." Ian lifted his pickax. "I knotted everything on with a diamond hitch, so he'll be able to take things off without her losing balance as long as he keeps the sides fairly even."

"That's good."

"Best you know, Merry, that the vein in the stone isn't getting any wider yet. We'd hoped it would grow big and fat."

"It still might. Even if it doesn't, you're getting more than we ever panned."

"I saw you panning yesterday."

"Why not? I was waiting for the laundry pot to boil. I got about a pinch and a half of gold dust. With gold at sixteen dollars per ounce, that's not a bad show for an afternoon's work."

"Pure gold is sixteen dollars per ounce, Merry. Gold dust is impure. When it's all melted and the dross is removed, it weighs far less."

"Oh."

The disappointment on her face tugged at his heart. "Every bit counts."

"Yes, it does." She smiled. "Did Tucker speak to you about removing rock now in as much bulk as possible?"

"He did." Ian found a comfortable grip on the pickax. "I'm in full agreement. We'll be able to crush it down and put it through the shaker box during the worst of the winter."

"So you don't mind?"

"Why would I mind?" He gave her a surprised look. "Long days like this can allow us extreme amounts of outdoor work. When we're locked inside by the most frigid part of the winter, we'll still be able to make progress."

"It'll make a mess of your cabin—all the dust and grit."

"Man came from dust and will return to dust."

53

Merry's laughter filled the air. "Woman came from bone. Where does that leave her?"

"If all goes as God intended, it leaves her right by her man's side and inside his heart." *And that's where I'd like you to be.*

"Well, for now, this woman is going to do a few chores. Tucker said he'll be back tonight, but I'm not so sure."

"I believe he will. The sunlight will allow him to travel safely, and he's got a lot of stamina."

"That's true." Her pretty hazel eyes sparkled. "I think it's more a matter of stubbornness. Once my brother sets his mind to something, he pursues it with a singleness of mind that is nearly unshakable."

"Old Abrams said something to that effect last night." Ian remembered the old man's bluster. "Only he wound up calling your twin a thickheaded bulldog."

The matter neither of them addressed was glaring: Until now, Meredith and Ian hadn't been alone. She'd gone to town with Tucker on the other trip. His leaving her behind and in Ian's safekeeping showed a measure of trust that Ian understood. He planned to be worthy of that trust. Clenching the pickax helped him do just that. Otherwise, he'd cave in to temptation, grab Meredith, and help himself to a sweet, sweet kiss.

"Anything special you'd like for supper?"

He stopped. "You needn't cook for me, Merry. I've put beans to soak. I can boil them later."

"It's no trouble, Ian. I don't mind."

"I do, though. Our bargain ended. You have no call to cook for me."

Resting her hands on her hips, Merry gave him an exasperated look. "That deal? Don't be ridiculous. You've been sharing your food far longer than we agreed to, and you've plowed more than twice what we agreed upon."

"You've helped weed, thin, and transplant." He readjusted his hold on the pickax. "Add to that all the beans you've canned."

"In jars you bought." She stooped down and pleaded, "Ian, let's not haggle. Please let me cook. You have every reason and right to claim the gold here."

"No, lass, I don't. The Lord was present when we made our agreement. He knew where the riches lay—and He had Tucker see them first. The believers in the Bible worked together and shared all they had in common. Tucker and you are working every bit as hard as I am. I couldn't face myself in the mirror or my Maker on Judgment Day if I hoarded this for myself."

"You're being honorable." Tears shimmered in her eyes. "How, then, can you want us to partake in your blessings and refuse to accept what we have to offer? From now on, I'm making the meals."

He shook his head. Every morning of his life, he'd seen Da give Ma a good-morning kiss, and she'd give him another as he left for the fields. Since the day Braden and Maggie married, they'd taken up that same tradition. *If I sit across the breakfast table from this woman, I'll long for that same closeness.* Refusing her offer would hurt her, though. In a voice every bit as rough as the gravel he was creating, Ian said, "Midday and supper. I make my own breakfasts."

The smile on her face made him glad he'd compromised. She rose with grace and went off to see to her chores.

Ian chipped away at the ground. The pickax did a fair job, but sinking a hole into anything took a lot of effort. Even though it was summer and sunlight ruled both day and night, the glacial rock didn't care. As long as Ian worked, he kept warm. After a few minutes of stopping and talking, the insidious cold started making his muscles knot.

Spying a small offshoot of gold, Ian wanted to significantly widen the area they'd begun to dig. He established a rhythm and kept at it.

"Ian!"

Merry's voice brought him to a halt. "Are you ready to eat?"

"I'm always ready to eat." He set down the pickax and hopped out of the hole. A quick backward glance made him say, "It looks like I'm digging a grave."

Merry shivered. "Don't say that!"

"Oh, lass, I'm sorry. I wasn't thinking." Recriminations ran through his mind. Grief still held great sway over her—so much that she couldn't bear to mention her father. *I have to mind my tongue. That was a terrible slip.*

"Never mind." The blithe tone she used didn't take away the sadness in her eyes.

They sat on crates over by the river to eat. "I'll never tire of this view." Ian watched as the water bubbled and whooshed by. "The sight and sound are lovely indeed."

"It's pretty in winter, too. Because we came from Texas, I'd never lived with snow before."

"I'd think the novelty would wear off once the cold sets in."

"Boredom is just as big an enemy as cold. Tucker's suggestion of taking rocks inside to pulverize and extract the gold—it's his way of staying busy. He spent two solid weeks last winter weaving us snowshoes."

"This winter, we can draw a board on wood or cloth and use rocks to make a game of draughts."

"We did that." The corners of Meredith's mouth twitched. "But that game grows tedious. Tucker came up with a different use for those rocks. He nearly drove me to distraction trying to learn to juggle them."

"Did he, now?"

Meredith shook her head. "Not really. He never did manage to keep three in the air. They'd fall somewhere, and he'd scoop up more. He wouldn't give up until he'd used up all the stones and they peppered the beds and floor."

"That's a man acting out of desperation. What did you do to keep busy?"

Laughter bubbled out of her. "I dodged stones."

After his laughter died down, Ian said, "You're a delightful lass, Merry Smith."

"Look at the two of you," Abrams groused loudly.

Ian bristled at the old man's intrusion. Having just paid Merry a compliment, he wanted to follow up and say something more.

"Coulda invited me to lunch," Abrams continued on. "Since Tucker went to town, the bridge is spanning the river."

"But the bread I'm baking won't be ready until supper." Meredith stood. "Wouldn't you rather come tonight?"

"Now that's more like it! What else are you fixin'?"

"Why did you waste your breath to ask?" Ian slapped his hat on his head. "You know whatever Merry makes will be far better than anything you or I would rustle up."

Abrams shouted back, "I'm a better cook than you, Rafferty!"

"That's not saying much. Anyone's a better cook than I am."

"You more than make up for that lack with your farming and hunting." A pale pink suffused Meredith's cheeks. She swiped Ian's plate from his hands and walked away.

Ian fought the urge to dash after her. Instead, he made a quick round of the snares he'd set. Every last one lay empty. *Lord, You know I'm falling in love with Merry. You own the cattle on a thousand hills. I'm not asking for a fatted calf, though. Couldn't You please see fit to fill my snares with a couple of hare or grouse? Don't let her confidence in me dwindle. She's always had Tucker to lean on. He's a fine man, Lord, but if Merry becomes my wife, she needs to see me as the one who can provide for her.*

"Ian?"

"Ian?" Meredith called again as she walked around a stump. Spying him, she changed direction toward him.

He shot to his feet.

She glanced at the empty snare. Methodical as he was, she knew this would be the last one he'd check. Ian always went in a clockwise sweep of the traps and snares. His hands hung empty at his sides. "I know how important it is for you to be prospecting. Just because I said you're a good hunter, please don't feel I wanted you to bring in supper tonight."

"Sad fact is, nothing's caught yet."

"I was afraid of that—oh! Not that there wouldn't be anything. That you'd feel obligated to bring in the meat. We have a fair store of smoked fish, and I made several jars of confit with the squirrels you've gotten. I'll come up with something."

"We've hours to go before suppertime." His voice sounded strained. "I'll check the snares in a few hours."

"All right." She looked down at the dusty hem of her dress and then back at him. "The salad and bread are wonderful additions to our table, and we're thankful for each bite. Please don't think there's anything wrong with a plate of beans."

"Are you reminding me to be thankful for whatever we have?"

"If that's so, it's unintentional. I wanted to let you know that *I'm* thankful. Tucker and I are eating better now than we have since we came up here." As soon as she spoke, Meredith wanted to take back those words. "I didn't mean that the way it sounded. Tucker works hard, and we've done just fine."

"Your brother is a good man." Ian gave a definitive nod. "Hardworking, God-fearing, and he loves you."

Tension draining out of her, Meredith grinned. "Almost as much as I love him."

"I hold no doubt that he'd disagree." Ian dusted off his hands. "You're a rare woman."

Pleasure thrummed through her. "Thank you. That's kind of you to say."

"I'm not just saying it. I'm meaning it." He cast a look around them. "Since I've arrived, I've seen any number of miners tromp over here. You sew and do laundry and write letters for them. Every last one has spoken of marriage to you."

Her jaw dropped.

"Before you think I've eavesdropped, a handful have proposed to you in my presence, and Tucker told me the rest have done likewise. Know this, Meredith Smith: I'm speaking from an earnest heart, not out of flattery in hopes of gaining a wife to wash and mend my clothes."

"Oh." She wasn't sure what more to say.

"I'd best get back to work."

"Me, too." She watched him stride over to the smokehouse, hop down into the hole in the earth he'd been digging, and take up his pickax. *So he's not attracted to me. Ian's the first man I've met in Alaska who appeals to me, and he doesn't even want a wife.*

Chapter 12

I did it. I finally told Merry I'm courting her. The way those strange men dump filthy, stinking clothes at her feet and ask her to be their wife—it shows no respect or caring. A huge chunk of rock yielded to the pickax. Thoroughly pleased with himself, Ian kept working. *Now that she knows I appreciate her for her kind heart and lively spirit, she'll understand I'm different.*

He'd work himself to death if necessary to be sure Merry had whatever she needed. To be sure, the lass never wanted much at all, but Ian was determined. He'd hunt and farm so she'd never have to be satisfied with a meager meal, and he'd coax every last fleck of gold from the claim in order to provide for her.

Twice that afternoon he paused from work only long enough to drink water and check the snares. Empty. They remained empty.

Lord, I'm counting on You. Merry needs to see how I can provide for her.

A gunshot sounded.

Ian leapt from the hole and snatched the shotgun he always kept within reach. "Merry, get in the cabin!"

"Git offa my claim!" Mr. Abrams shouted.

Instead of obeying Ian, Meredith came running toward him. Ian turned toward Abrams's claim and shoved Meredith behind his back.

"Settle down, you old geezer." A man stood in the middle of Abrams's claim. He held two huge salmon. "I'm fixin' to trade. Feller named Smith sent me."

"What do I get? You're on my property."

Meredith popped out from behind Ian. "Why, Mr. Abrams, letting him cross your property is your contribution to our supper tonight."

"Merry, get back behind me." Ian didn't wait for her to comply. He stepped in front of her.

"I'm in no danger." She started to shift.

Ian kept hold of his shotgun and reached back with his other hand. He grabbed her and held her in place. "Abrams has that rifle in his arms. There's no telling what he'll shoot, but it's not going to be you."

"Rafferty, what do you say?" Abrams shouted.

"Put down your rifle and let him come across."

Abrams shook his head. "Dunno. Bears like salmon. Might be one takes a mind to follow this man. Can't let down my guard."

The stranger pushed past Abrams. "A bear would want the salmon, not you, you old goat."

Meredith muffled a giggle.

As the man started across the bridge, Tucker glanced at her. "You like salmon."

"I adore it."

"It's written all over your face. One look, and he'll know he has the advantage on this barter. Go on inside. I promise, you'll have salmon for supper."

To his relief, Meredith walked to her cabin and went inside. He didn't want men ogling her. Once she shut the door, Ian folded his arms across his chest and waited. Whoever spoke first in a bargain always walked away with the shorter end of the deal. Meredith wanted salmon, and Ian determined he would strike a bargain whereby she'd get both of the ones this man carried.

"Coffee," the man said as he stepped off the bridge, onto the shore.

"Coffee," Ian repeated, surprised Tucker would have sent anyone to trade fish for his beloved drink.

The man nodded. "Erik Kauffey. Sounds like the drink but spelled different. I brought these to barter. You've got to admit, they're beauts. Big ones, too."

"I'm Ian Rafferty. Smith's my partner." He motioned toward a stump. "Set those down over there."

"Where'd the little lady go?"

Ian gave him a steely glare. "Did you come here to barter or to banter?"

Kauffey heaved a so-that's-the-way-things-go sigh. "The salmon were fresh caught this morning. One's female, so you'll even be getting roe in the bargain."

"Never could stand the stuff." Clearly, Kauffey accepted that Meredith was off-limits, so he pursued the barter by pointing out the advantages of Ian's obtaining the salmon. Ian knew better than to jump in and agree, so he shrugged. "I've heard roe makes for good fertilizer."

"Roe's good to bait snares for birds. Lots of ptarmigan here."

"Ptarmigan. They're in the grouse family, right?"

"Yeah. White-tailed ones are local. Wings are always white, but come snow season, they're all white. Good eating." Kauffey sauntered over toward the vegetable garden.

"I haven't seen many."

"Funny birds, ptarmigan." Kauffey headed toward the far corner. "They show up and disappear in a wink. You ought to be glad they haven't been around much. They'd eat every last leaf you have here."

"They'd have to fight the hares for the privilege."

Kauffey squatted down and inspected a head of lettuce. "If you take it into consideration, I'm not averse to taking something if a rabbit or bird took the first bite."

"I'm sure we can work something out."

Ten minutes later, Meredith exited her cabin and met Ian over by the stump. "That man practically danced across the bridge to go home."

Ian grinned. "You know those two heads of lettuce and the cabbage that the hares nibbled? He took all three, and I tossed in some rhubarb. The way he dashed off, I think he was afraid I'd change my mind."

"Up close, these salmon are even bigger than I thought. A quarter of one will be a feast for us. I can smoke the rest. Oh! If I put some of it in a pail and tuck it in the cleft of that rock over there, the water will keep it chilled. We can enjoy fresh salmon again tomorrow!"

"That's clever of you." He pulled his knife from his belt sheath. "I'll—"

"You'll let me see to them. With Tucker loving to fish, I'm a dab hand at this. You have more important things to do."

"Like what?"

"Put in a fireplace."

"I've decided to put in a stove."

She reared back. "A stove? How will you ever get a stove?"

"I know Socks has one in his mercantile for thirty-two dollars. 'Tis highway robbery. But shipping one from Oregon to here will be reasonable."

"I—I didn't mean the cost." Hectic color filled her cheeks. "I wondered how you'd transport it. Wily's umiak would sink the minute you loaded the stove aboard."

"Wagon wheels. By affixing axles and wheels to the box, I can have Bess pull it in."

"You're serious!"

"That I am. Sears won't ship to Alaska, but the catalog shows a Southern Sunshine cookstove. It's a dandy thing. My folks will find one and ship it here. I figure the crate it comes in can serve as a wagon of sorts. It'll be easier to haul produce into Goose Chase."

"Are you sure you want to sell Bess when the weather changes?"

"There's insufficient feed for her here. I just wanted to mention about the wagon so if there was anything heavy or bulky that you and Tucker might want, you could take advantage of the opportunity."

"Thank you. We'll keep it in mind."

Something in her tone of voice struck him as odd. Ian cleared his throat. "Forgive me if I'm out of place, but it occurs to me that Tucker is your only family. My family back in Oregon would be more than willing to locate goods and ship them for you. It's far cheaper."

"That's a kind offer. Tucker and I actually have an uncle, but we already have everything we need."

Ian didn't challenge her. To his way of thinking, Meredith didn't have half of what she needed.

Over the next two months, Ian grew increasingly perplexed at why she and Tucker bought only the barest essentials for themselves. It made no sense; the garden flourished and brought cash, gold dust, and a wide variety of items in barter—not enough to make them all rich, but certainly sufficient to provide comfortably for their needs.

Perhaps they're worried next year will be harsh and they're trying to set aside for lean times— like Joseph advised Pharaoh to do. With that in mind, Ian determined to work even harder to reassure Merry that she'd not have to worry.

⁂

Merry stretched as Tucker twisted from side to side. Ian emerged from the smokehouse. "All done?" he asked.

"Yes." She watched as he carefully latched the door shut. "I don't think we could wedge one more thing in there. That mountain sheep was enormous."

"God's provided well."

"You're right." Merry smiled at Ian. He'd gone out hunting and returned with enough meat to get them through much of the winter, yet he didn't boast. "But there's no reason we can't credit that the Lord used you to supply for our needs."

"Hold on a second. Tucker's the one who brought in all the fish."

Tucker shook his head. "Nope. I caught the trout and Dolly Varden, but the salmon— that's your doing. Kauffey must have come here a dozen times to trade for the greens from that garden of yours."

" 'Tis *our* garden." Ian's brows scrunched into a stern line. "Merry's labored in it every bit as much as I have. And though Kauffey caught the salmon, Tucker, you sent him here to barter."

Merry wanted to hug Ian for how he'd turned the conversation. Instead of boasting about his hunting acumen and all of his success, he'd emphasized Tucker's contributions. Tucker already struggled with feeling indebted. The last thing he needed was to face that same burden in his own home.

"With Merry preserving jars and crocks of everything she gets her hands on, we'll be eating like royalty all winter long."

"He's right, Sis. You've gathered at least five times as many berries this year, too."

"We missed strawberry season entirely. Now that we know they can grow up here, I'd love to plant some next year."

Tucker shook his head.

They're probably too expensive. I shouldn't have said anything.

"Without Bess, Ian won't be able to plow the land. This year's garden was great, but you can't count on it again next year."

"Ah, but we will." Ian smiled. "I came to an agreement with Wily. He gets my mule for the cold season; I get her for the warm. If you're of a mind to be farmers with me again next year, I'd be pleased to continue the partnership."

Merry's heart sang at the promise of another season of working side by side in the garden with Ian. They'd had wonderful discussions and lively debates and had shared concerns while in the garden. *Maybe next year he'll feel settled and ready to take a wife.*

"If you don't mind, I'd like to have Bess drag down more wood for the winter."

"I'm happy to help you down a few trees."

"Wait!" Merry backed up. "Don't you dare start haggling and making another deal. At least not in front of me."

The men exchanged a baffled look.

"The way the two of you wrangle, it's a marvel someone's firstborn child isn't already named."

Eyes twinkling, Ian turned to Tucker. "Now there's a fine notion!"

"Something biblical," Tucker mused. "I always liked Amminadab. That, or Ahaseurus."

"Methuselah's got a nice ring to it."

"You can't do that!"

Tucker crooked a brow. "Give me a couple of good reasons why not."

Feeling a tad sassy, she proclaimed, "Since we don't have the Old Testament, you wouldn't spell it right."

"That's not a problem." Ian stood beside Tucker and smiled like a rascal. "We already have an agreement. You're welcome to borrow my Bible anytime. What kind of man would I be if I went back on my word?"

"Sorry, Sis. You need a better reason."

"All right, I'll give you a great one. Because that poor, defenseless child never did anything to deserve such a terrible fate!"

Ian turned to Tucker. "Don't you think naming a child something like Jehoshaphat would help him develop character?"

Meredith burst out laughing. "Any son either of you have will already be a character if he takes after you."

"Sis has a point."

"Fine." Ian shrugged. "Then we'll just leave the boys out of the bargain and go for a daughter's name."

Chapter 13

That's all mine?" Ian stared in disbelief at the packages, crates, and tins.

"Yup." Socks readjusted his cap. "I need it outta here. Came in three days ago, and I'm already tired of chasing folks away from it. You got stuff there I can't get in. It's makin' my mercantile look bad."

The weather had changed. Ian knew Bess belonged with Wily now. Even with careful packing, she wouldn't be able to carry everything—and Ian didn't want to risk taking her back only to have her freeze or starve because be couldn't get her back to Goose Chase.

Wily leaned against the counter. "By the time January or February comes around, Rafferty, you'll be glad to have all that stuff."

"Probably." Ian stared at the goods his family had sent. He knew they'd really stretched the budget and been incredibly generous. Still, gratitude warred with practicality. He didn't know how he'd get everything to his cabin, and even if he did, he didn't have room in the cabin for all of it. Suddenly, Merry and Tucker's careful and lean planning made a lot more sense.

"Don't worry. I'll help you out." Wily hefted a crate. "It's the least I can do."

It took a lot of consideration and careful balancing, but they managed to load everything into Wily's umiak. "I appreciate this." Ian got aboard and took up a paddle.

Wily settled in, and someone pushed them off. "I reckoned this is as good an excuse as any for me to get a morning of fishing. Probably won't catch anything other than the ague, but you won't hear me complain if I do. I've spent every waking moment of the past three weeks making deliveries. I'll just be glad to have folks leave me be."

It took a lot of effort to row the heavily laden vessel upriver. When they finally reached Ian's claim, Tucker met them at the riverbank. He took a rope and secured the umiak.

"Welcome back." Merry pulled a shawl about her shoulders. "Hello, Wily. How nice to see you, too. I have coffee ready."

Ian didn't want to blink. He'd been gone from Meredith for less than a day, and it felt as if it had been forever. He looked into the sparkling depths of her hazel eyes and knew if that was the only gold he ever found, he'd be the richest man on earth.

"Lookit all that." Abrams traipsed across the bridge.

"Don't bother to ask," Wily snapped. "I didn't bring any spirits."

"I wasn't talkin' to you, you old coot. Ian, got anything there for me?"

"Rafferty's an honorable man. He wouldn't transport whiskey or beer on my umiak."

Ian drew an envelope from his shirt pocket so he could stop the quarrel. "Socks gave me a letter for you."

"It must be from Violet." Merry tucked her hand into the crook of Abrams's arm once he claimed the missive. "I'd love to hear how she's doing."

As they walked off, Wily murmured, "He can't read a lick. Marks an *X* for his signature.

Meredith's got such a kind heart, she covers for him."

"Yeah, well, he'll wrangle his way into staying for supper now." Tucker grimaced. "Not only will he drink the entire pot of coffee she has going, he'll bug me until I make another pot after supper."

"If he didn't, I would." Wily shoved a burlap bag into Tucker's hands. "Make yourself useful."

Tucker didn't move. "Rafferty, if there are any bottles in here, I get them. I'm going to put a window in for my sister. Never paid any mind to the color, size, or shape of them 'til now. The blue and the green ones are scarce as hen's teeth. Meredith hasn't said anything, but I know she has her heart set on a pretty window like yours."

"I have absolutely no idea what is in all of this. Once we get inside my cabin, I'll take stock."

Wily barged into Ian's cabin and stopped. "When did you do this?"

"The partition? About a month after the roof went up."

"Doesn't make sense." Wily set down his load. "Why's your bed here with the kitchen stuff instead of in the other room?"

Ian shot Tucker a questioning look. Folks were highly secretive regarding anything about their prospecting.

Tucker hitched his right shoulder in a motion as if to say, *Who cares?*

"We spent valuable time farming, so we've hauled in stuff to process during the cold weather."

"Hope it pays off for you. Socks has a habit of talking too much. Just the other day, he was jawing about whose claim gave up a lot of color this year. I'm not naming names, but only three claims used gold dust to buy their winter provisions."

"Three." Tucker grimaced.

"Could well be that some got more and just didn't use it to pay the storekeeper." Ian set down a crate. "They're smart if they don't. Socks has the biggest hands God ever made. Socks taking a pinch of dust as payment is the same as someone else taking two."

"Yup." Wily slapped Tucker on the back. "Last time you went to town, coupla fellows were just coming back from Sitka. Did you notice that they paid Socks with cash?"

Tucker thought for a moment. "You're right. They did."

"They're crazy as loons. They should have bought supplies in Sitka. Anyplace else has to have cheaper prices than Goose Chase."

As the men carried the last of the goods to Ian's cabin, Merry and Abrams reappeared. Abrams trailed after Ian. "That's far too much stuff for one man. You won't have room to turn around in your cabin with all that in there. You bein' my neighbor and all, I reckon I could buy some of it off you. For a good price, of course."

"No." Ian wanted to shoo off the pesky old man.

"Oh, go on ahead," Wily said. "Abrams is your neighbor. And he's said he'd pay you a good price. Of course, you and I will have to split the delivery charge."

"Hold on there just a minute!" Abrams scowled at Wily. "Mind your own business."

"I am. I deliver goods. Everyone pays for that service. Since you just told Rafferty that you'd be willing to deal fairly, that means you'd pay your share of the shipping fee."

"I would not! He was coming this way anyhow. It didn't cost nothing extra for you to cram a little more in that odd boat of yours."

"I'm keeping all of the shipment, so the matter is settled."

"Tucker?" Meredith rested her hand on his arm. "Coffee's ready back at our place."

"Sounds good, Sis."

"Don't mind if I do have a cup." Abrams scurried after Tucker.

"Unless I miss my guess, that old leech already had a cup." Wily shook his head. "Leaves me in a quandary."

"How is that?" Merry asked.

"Don't know whether to hope he strikes it big so he'll cash in and leave, or to hope he never gets more than enough to live on because civilized society won't know what to do with that old skunk."

"He's a character, but he has a good heart."

Wily brushed a kiss on Merry's cheek. "You'd find something nice to say about the devil himself."

As Wily went to get coffee, Merry stayed in the doorway.

Ian fought the urge to go over and claim a kiss, too. Only he'd never steal a kiss, and though he was sure of his feelings, Merry seemed oblivious to his interest. He looked at the bundles then saw the question in her eyes. "I'm not sure which bundle your gift is in, Merry. I'll be sure to hide it from your twin."

"Thank you. It's nippy. Why don't you come warm up with some coffee?"

"I'll have a cup with dinner. Wily's going to spend the night and fish in the morning. I need to clear some space for him."

Meredith nodded. "Supper will be ready whenever you are. It's nothing special—just rice and beans."

"You're a fine cook, so don't take this the wrong way, but it's not the fare that makes a meal. 'Tis the fellowship. I've yet to eat a meal you've cooked that didn't please me."

Long after she left, Ian basked in the warmth of her smile. He quickly sorted through things and determined where to store each item. Putting the food away was simple and straightforward, with the exception that he hid away the new can of Arbuckle's coffee.

The birthday and Christmas gifts he'd requested for Merry and Tucker fit into a crate. He also slid Merry's Christmas gift for her brother in with them. Two paper-wrapped parcels bore Ma's lovely penmanship: "Do Not Open Until Christmas." Ian carefully slid that full crate beneath his bed.

They'd grown parsley and mustard, and Merry now boasted a good supply of those dried herbs. Ma had sent spices, though. Ian opened the cinnamon and inhaled. The scent evoked myriad memories of family and home.

Ma had sent him a union suit and a handsome blue plaid flannel shirt. Da had tucked in seeds for next year's garden. Braden's contribution—a pair of thick catalogs—came with a teasing note about their being a "housewarming gift" for the outhouse. Ian chuckled with joy when he saw that Fiona had sent him popping corn.

Last of all, Maggie had sent a flowery tin. Her note said, "Everyone else was practical. Sometimes the impractical is more essential." Puzzled, he pried open the lid. An exotic blend of chopped-up dried leaves gave off a faintly spicy aroma. Tea. Maggie knew he didn't like tea. In a flash, Ian understood. His sister-in-law had sent this for him to give to Merry.

One by one, he prayed for each member of his family. Each night he did so, but being surrounded by reminders of their thoughtfulness and love made Ian appreciate all the more how blessed he'd been to have such a family.

Someday, Lord, I'd love to wed Merry and start a family with her. Could You bless me with her as my wife?

⸺

"Something's burning." Tucker gave Merry a wary look.

She pushed him into Ian's cabin. "You're letting out the heat."

"I'm letting out the smoke." Tucker waved his hand in the air. "Ian, are you in here somewhere?"

Ian threw back his head and laughed. "Sure and enough, I am. Merry, did your brother ever do school theatricals? He's got a penchant for acting."

"The only thing I have a penchant for is coffee."

Ian pointed toward the stove. "Over there."

Tucker went over, poured himself a cup of coffee, and let out a long, loud sigh of bliss.

"For complaining about the smoke," Ian's mouth twisted with wry humor, "you're breathing just fine."

"Coffee makes everything better."

Merry dared to peer down into the small pot on the stove. "What is—no, *was*—that?"

"Oatmeal. I added some berries. The middle part tasted okay, even if the edges got. . . crispy."

Ian's mishap couldn't have happened at a better time. Merry and Tucker had just decided to bargain with Ian—she'd use his stove to cook all of their meals there.

"I put a little water in it. Once the water boils, it'll soften the mess, and I'll be able to scrape it out." Looking utterly pleased with himself, Ian added, "I'm going to use it to bait snares for ptarmigan. Birds like grain and berries."

"So you're going to snare some?" Tucker slurped more coffee. The men started to talk about hunting.

Merry continued to stare at the glop in the pot. "Why bother to snare the poor birds?"

"I thought they'd taste good. Don't they?"

"Nothing that eats this would taste good."

Ian slapped his hand to his chest. "I'm wounded!"

Merry laughed. He'd teased Tucker about having a propensity for theatrics, but Ian often waggled his brows or pasted on ridiculous expressions just because he knew it tickled her. She made a show of looking into the pot and shuddered. "You're lucky you're only wounded. I'd think this might be deadly."

"It's supposed to be deadly—for the ptarmigan."

"If it's like anything else you've cooked, it will be." Tucker gulped the last of his coffee.

Ian gave him a smug look. "You're drinking something I made."

"Why do you think I pray over everything I eat or drink?"

Ian approached Merry and clasped her hand in his. "Lass, you're a wondrous fine cook. Aye, and don't let your brother say otherwise. When he eats something I make, there might well be truth in what he said, but when you've done the cooking—well, the prayers are strictly in thanksgiving."

"Thanksgiving! I'm so glad you brought that up." Delighted to have that segue, Meredith rushed ahead. "We ought to invite Mr. Clemment and Mr. Abrams to join us. If we do, we'd need to use the table you made from your sled. It's the only one big enough to hold a meal for all five of us. And if it's okay with you, I'd like to use your stove to bake."

"I told you the day I brought that home, you're always welcome to use my stove."

"You wouldn't be as liable to burn yourself on the stove, Sis."

"You burned yourself? When? Where?" Ian pored over her hands.

Merry withdrew from his touch. Until now, it had never bothered her to have short nails and chapped hands. Pulling her share of the load rated far above vanity. But suddenly, she felt self-conscious of just how rough her hands had become. "It's nothing. Really."

Tucker snorted. "She burns a finger almost every week. It's impossible to control the flames in a fireplace. A stove's much safer."

"It uses less wood, too. From now on, Meredith Smith, you'll cook on my stove. Had I known this before now, I'd have built a fireplace and given you my stove."

"It's too late now. Temperature's dropping." Tucker glanced to the side to make sure Ian wouldn't see; then he winked at her. "From now on, Meredith will have to cook breakfast here, too."

"I could have breakfast started."

"Whatever you start"—Tucker cracked his knuckles—"would undoubtedly finish me off. The only person in the world who cooks worse than you stares back at me in the mirror."

Ian went to his bed and got down on his knees.

Tucker poured himself another mug of coffee. "Ian's praying he'll never have to eat anything I fix."

Pulling a crate from beneath his bed, Ian declared, "Meredith would take pity on me. She'd never subject me to such suffering. Would you, Merry?"

"Of course not. What are you doing, Ian?"

"Getting something." He lifted the lid to the crate in such a manner as to block her view of the contents. It wasn't right for her to snoop, anyway. Meredith turned her back. She heard Ian mutter something. Then the lid slammed shut, and she heard the crate scrape across the floor planks.

"Merry." Ian's voice sounded close.

She turned around and practically bumped into him. "Oh! I'm sor—" She blinked.

"We've established that Tucker and I are no help in the kitchen. I'm trading you this for cooking for Thanksgiving." He held out a stack of folded flour sacks. They were all the same pink floral she'd admired months ago.

"How did you get more?"

"I wrote Ma. She sent these. The top one—Ma slipped in a few whatnots you'll be needing to make a frock for yourself."

"Oh, Ian!"

"Tucker, we've work to do. Finish up your coffee." Ian pressed the gift into her hands, shrugged into his coat, and bolted out the door.

Meredith started to shake. She set the fabric down on the table, and pink thread, ribbon, buttons, and airy white lace tumbled out. Meredith couldn't blink back her tears. Looking at Tucker, she rasped, "I can't go on like this. He deserves to know the truth."

"It's none of his business." Tucker's face darkened. He headed for the door and stopped abruptly. "You gave me your word, Sis. I expect you to keep it."

Chapter 14

"Days are growing shorter." Ian watched the shadows lengthen at an astonishing rate. Tucker picked up the pheasant he'd shot. As he straightened, he gave the twine on Ian's shoulder a meaningful look. "Long enough for you to take care of Thanksgiving."

"Buckshot's bound to bring down more than a rifle shell." Three pheasants dangled from the twine. "And face it: Clemment and Abrams will each eat a whole bird. Nothing much to eat except the legs on these, anyway. We needed that one you got."

"I'm not so sure Clemment will eat pheasant." Tucker headed back toward the cabins.

"I've noticed he likes birds. Talks about them every time I see him." Ian didn't mention how he'd seen Clemment biting berries straight off the bramble or how he'd stuffed fists full of twigs into the pockets of his overalls. It didn't seem right, finding amusement in someone else's oddity.

"He's getting mighty peculiar."

Concern shot through Ian. "So it's not just my imagination. Do you think it's safe to have him around Merry?"

"He's harmless. Up here the long winter's night bends some men's minds. Last year he came visiting a few times. Merry adores him, and he fancies she's like his daughter. Wasn't 'til the very last of winter that he showed signs of cabin fever. Him already getting bizarre, that's not good."

They paused at the tree line and dressed the birds. As he worked around the sharp spur on the back of a pheasant's leg, Ian cleared his throat. "Tucker, if I've done something to upset Merry, you need to tell me."

"She's fine. Why?"

"I knew she liked that pink material, but she's had it for almost two weeks and hasn't done anything with it." Feeling ridiculous for having blurted out his thoughts, he concentrated on dressing the second pheasant.

Tucker grabbed the last one and worked on it. "You haven't done anything. Well, in a way, you did. You went beyond the agreement we made. Merry would cook on your stove, and we'd have Thanksgiving at your place. Giving her the material—"

Ian snorted. "You got it wrong. She's cooking breakfast in exchange for using my stove. Anyway, I saw straight through that whole act. You and Merry already had made up your minds to strike that deal with me before you left your cabin that morning."

"You sound awful sure of yourself."

"And you're evading the issue. I'm not faulting you, Tucker. If anything, I'm trying to convince you that you're bargaining with the wrong party. You and I need to team up. We're already business partners. We need to figure out ways to help our Merry."

"*Our* Merry?" Tucker stared at him.

Ian didn't hesitate. "Aye, our Merry. Like it or not, I have feelings for the lass. Strong feelings."

"Merry has me."

"I expected you'd say as much. I'd not ever question the fact that the two of you are as close as can be. I don't even challenge that bond. But Merry has a bottomless heart. If I have my way, she'll find room in her heart for me."

"Every single man up here wants Sis as his wife."

"I've seen that firsthand. It riles me. Those men don't think past what they want. Merry deserves a husband who cherishes her."

Tucker picked up his rifle. "We're losing our light. We need to go back."

"I aim to court her."

"You might get everything you aim a gun at, but you don't win a woman just because you want her." Tucker dumped a pheasant on the ground and kept walking.

"I agree." Ian refused to waste the bird. A hunter didn't kill just for fun. He scooped it up and lengthened his stride so he walked abreast of Tucker. "What Meredith wants is more important than what you or I want. If she wants nothing more than my friendship, I'll settle for that. If God blesses me by opening her heart to me, then I'll count myself the luckiest man alive."

Tucker shook his head. "This isn't going to work."

"And why not?"

"Just because you and Sis are thrown together for the winter and bored, you'll mistake companionship for romance. Any little thing she does, you'll interpret as a sign of her affection. You're putting her in an untenable position. Just accept her friendship and be satisfied."

"It's her decision to make, Tucker. Merry is easygoing and adjusts with a cheerful heart. That doesn't cancel out the fact that she's a strong woman with hopes and dreams."

Tucker stopped. "No one knows her better than I do. Yes, she's strong—but Meredith is also fragile. I won't let you break her heart."

"That's the last thing I'd ever want. You and I are in full accord over that. But that's as far as what we want matters. I'm not going to pressure her, and I trust that you won't, either. The decision she ought to make is whether I'm the man God wants her to marry. Don't make this a situation where she has to choose between the twin she adores and the man she loves."

"You're taking a lot for granted."

"No, I'm living in hope." Ian shoved a pheasant at Tucker. "You dropped this. Your sister has grand plans for setting an abundant table. We don't want her disappointed."

"Just because you're my partner, I don't have to like you."

Ian threw back his head and belted out a laugh. "Ah, but you do, Tucker. In spite of yourself, you do."

Merry sat down and shook her head at the mess on the table. "I was afraid Mr. Clemment and Mr. Abrams were going to come to blows over the last of the stuffing."

"For once, I'm siding with Abrams." Outrage rang in her brother's voice. "Clemment crammed half of the rice into his pockets."

"Now, now. He did offer to put it back in the bowl." Ian's eyes twinkled. "And his hands were clean, thanks to Merry."

"Probably the first time either of those old men used soap in a month of Sundays."

Tucker headed toward the other room. "Speaking of which, I'll dump the tub."

"I'll do that. Go on over and stoke up the fire in your fireplace."

As the men saw to those tasks, Merry started to stack the plates. She didn't have to scrape them—not a single morsel remained. To her surprise, Tucker came back first.

"Ian's dunking the tub in the river. Don't know if it'll ever come clean."

"The river's starting to freeze over. Go make sure he doesn't fall in."

"I'm going—not because I'll have to fish him out. Because we need more water." He grabbed a pair of buckets and sauntered out.

They returned with the tub half full of water and set the huge thing directly atop the stove.

"You can't do that. I need to dip water out of the reservoir to do dishes."

"River's probably going to freeze over in the next day or two." Ian looked around. He took a large pot and the pitcher to his washbasin. "Tucker and I decided to go ahead and put by a fair supply of water in advance."

"That's smart, but—" The door shut before she finished.

Though she'd need hot water to wash the dishes, cool water would work well enough to rinse them. Meredith dipped the rinse basin into the galvanized tub and pulled it out. Next she dipped the dish basin in and filled just the bottom. When the men returned, she insisted, "I need you to move that tub. Even a little."

"What's the rush?" Tucker motioned for her to sit down. "We want to fill the buckets from our place, too."

"You'll be glad we did. You know how cranky your brother gets if he has to go without his coffee."

Deciding that she'd have to solve the problem herself, Meredith poured water into two loaf pans and put them in the oven. While waiting for them to heat up, she fiddled about the "kitchen" and straightened the food on the shelves, set the spices back in order, and swept the floor.

Ian and Tucker returned. Ian scowled at the tub. "Where's all the water?"

"I dipped some out so I can do dishes."

He dangled his fingers in the water and wiggled them. "Water's warm. How long 'til it's hot?"

"Not long. She drained half of it." Tucker shot her a disgruntled look.

"We can add the water from the reservoir." Ian scanned the room.

Merry asked, "What do you want?"

"A pot. You've used all of them, haven't you?"

"Thanksgiving dinner takes a lot of dishes." She gestured toward the table.

Tucker poured the water from the pitcher into the washbasin. "Here." He shoved the pitcher at Ian.

"Tucker, tell your sister our bargain."

"Okay. Sis, I wash and he dries."

"What kind of deal is that?"

"A smart one." Ian elbowed Tucker in the ribs. "If he puts the dishes away, you'll never find anything again."

"I—"

"You're getting your birthday present from me two days early." Tucker grinned. "Here." He pulled something from his pocket and handed it to her.

She held the item a little closer to the lamp. "Victoria's English cottage rose glycerin soap. Tucker!" She lifted the beautifully wrapped bar and inhaled deeply. "The fragrance is wonderful. How did you get this?"

"When Wily was here, I asked him to tell Socks to order it."

"Thank you." She wound her arms around her brother. "I love it!"

He squeezed her. "While we do the dishes, you're going to shampoo and soak."

Merry laughed for joy. "That's what the water is all about!"

"We thought to mix water from the reservoir with the buckets so you could rinse your hair." Ian motioned for her to move away from the door to the other room. "It'll take time to heat up more dish water, so you're to soak to your heart's content."

"I put water in loaf pans in the oven to use for the dishes."

"That'll work, but it still doesn't mean you have to rush. Tucker, grab a few candles so she'll have some light."

Ian carried the tub, and Tucker grabbed a pair of candles. Meredith followed them into the room. Tucker pulled a towel from beneath his shirt. "Happy birthday."

Meredith emerged a long while later. The men had done the dishes and were drinking coffee. "I feel utterly spoiled."

Tucker sniffed. "You smell girly."

"Thanks to my brother." She smiled at him. "This was the best birthday present you could have dreamed up. Why don't you go use the water?"

Tucker looked horrified. "And smell like roses?"

"You can use my Ivory." Ian motioned him toward the stove. "Fill a pitcher from the reservoir and heat up the tub."

While Tucker bathed, Ian scooted a stool over toward the oven. "Sit here and sip some coffee. I'll rub your hair dry."

Reaching up and touching the towel wrapped around her head, Meredith hesitated. "I'll wait 'til I get home."

"It's too cold out for that. Here." He patted the stool. "I didn't mean to offend you. If you feel it's improper for me to help you, then please still take care of yourself. Would you like to borrow my comb?"

"If you don't mind."

He handed her his comb. "Whatever I have, you need only ask."

"You're too generous."

"Nay, lass. Our heavenly Father has faithfully provided for me. 'Tis His generosity I extend whenever I share. Today's Thanksgiving—a day to count our blessings. I've my family who loves me, and I've you and Tucker as my new friends. 'Tisn't just my belly that's full. My heart overflows."

"Mine does, too." Afraid she'd been too forward, Meredith hastened to tack on, "Tucker's, too. This year we have so much for which to be thankful."

Chapter 15

H appy birthday!" Ian shoved his door shut and helped Meredith remove her cape.
"Thank you."

For a fleeting second, Ian allowed himself to brush a spiraled tendril of her hair from her nape. It felt baby soft, a realization that made him smile, seeing as it was her birthday.

"I'm the older one. Sis, scoot over. I'm dying for a cup of coffee."

Meredith poked her twin in the ribs. "Being five minutes older doesn't give you leave to be bossy."

"I'm not bossy." He eased past her and tacked on, "Just surly."

"You hardly even say a word to Ian except for wanting coffee."

The last thing Ian wanted was for her to be put in the center of a tug-of-war between him and her brother. He shook her cape and hung it on a peg by the door. "I understand. Tucker knows what he likes."

Tucker paused with the coffeepot in midair. "I know what I love."

"So go on and have a cup." Ian gently nudged Merry toward the table. "And have a seat. Breakfast is ready."

"You cooked breakfast?"

"Oh no." Tucker consoled himself with a swig of coffee.

"I'd be insulted if your reactions weren't warranted. In the past, some of the things I made were—"

"Burnt offerings." Tucker's voice rated as funereal.

"There are a few things that"—Ian grabbed a pair of pot holders—"I did learn to make. These are one of my favorites, so I hope you like them, too." He opened the oven and took out a heaping plate of buckwheat pancakes.

"Flapjacks!" Tucker scrambled to the table.

"How did you manage flapjacks?" Merry gave him a disbelieving look. "It takes eggs to make them."

"Yep. Two of 'em." Ian grinned. "I brought them back from Goose Chase packed in cornmeal. It's a trick my ma used while on the Oregon Trail. Once I got home, I oiled them."

"Enough talk." Tucker patted the table. "Let's eat."

Ian set down the platter and sat opposite Merry. He'd rather sit beside her, but her brother made a habit of doing so—a point Ian noted with a twinge of irritation. *Lord, this is all in Your hands. Help me to have the right attitude.*

"Whose turn is it to pray?" Merry wondered aloud.

"Actually, it's your brother's, but I'd like to ask a special birthday blessing for the both of you." Ian bowed his head and folded his hands. "Our dear, praised heavenly Father, we come before You to start another day. 'Tis a special one—and I'd ask You to look down on Your daughter Merry and Your son Tucker. You've brought them through the past year, and I ask You to hold them in the hollow of Your hand this next year. Grant them health, happiness, and a closer walk with You. Thank You for the food before us, and know how glad we are to be Your children. In Jesus' name, amen."

"Thank you for that lovely prayer, Ian. Among the blessings God bestowed upon Tucker and me this year, you are at the top of the list."

"That's high praise, indeed. I'm honored." In years past, Ian gladly would have eaten every last buckwheat pancake himself. This morning he found contentment in eating only two and urging Meredith and Tucker to have more.

Once breakfast ended, he went to his bunk and moved the pillow. "I have a little gift for each of you. Tucker, here."

"No, have Sis go first."

Merry laughed as he swiped the last bite from her plate. "Tucker is older. He should go first."

"Ma taught me not to argue with ladies." Ian handed Tucker his gift.

"A cribbage board? I haven't played cribbage in years." Tucker's joy dimmed. "But we don't have cards."

"Ah, but we do!" Ian pulled a deck from his shirt pocket with a flourish.

Tucker concentrated on the wooden board and ran his thumbnail over the rows of tiny holes. "Thanks."

"What a wonderful gift!" Merry bumped Tucker's shoulder playfully. "Now you won't have to try to learn to juggle. That"—her eyes twinkled with glee—"is actually Ian's gift to me: that I won't have to dodge the rocks you try to juggle."

"Nay, lass. You've a gift, too." Ian could hardly wait to see her reaction. He scooted the pillow completely out of the way, picked up her present, and walked back to the table. "Here you are."

Her hand flew to her mouth, and she stared at his hand. From behind her fingers, her voice sounded breathless. "Hair ribbons."

"Your hair is your crowning glory, Merry." He set the gift on the table before her. As he did, the ribbons shifted, revealing a pair of hair combs and a card of hairpins beneath the lengths of pink, blue, and white.

"Hairpins! Socks doesn't sell ribbons or hairpins." Her warm hazel eyes sparkled with delight.

"Why would he?" Ian chuckled. "The man's bald as a shaved egg. I wrote home and told my family all about the two of you. I asked for the ribbons. My sister, Fiona, never can keep track of her hairpins. Half the time, she's searching for them at midday. I can't say for certain whether 'twas she or Ma who sent them along."

"Please give them my thanks." She turned to Tucker. "You knew about this, didn't you? That's why you arranged for me to wash my hair! The way you work together—it is such a joy to see what great partners and friends you've become."

"Tucker, we could spend the whole day jawing around in here, or we could actually go out to work and put some muscle behind that partnership."

"Go out to work? Why don't you work inside today?"

Tucker shook his head. "I can't stand being cooped up. There'll be plenty of days when we can't go out. I'm glad to have breathing room." He stood.

Once they'd left Merry and were out of earshot, Tucker stopped. "What you did—it was nice. But that doesn't change things. You can't buy Meredith's affections."

"I'd be a fool to believe otherwise."

"Why did you let her think I knew what you'd gotten her?"

"I neither agreed nor disagreed. We both want Merry to be happy. Aye, we do. On that we agree. And I credit you with loving her so much that you'd have decided to make our gifts complement one another for her benefit."

Tucker shook his head. "I don't know what it is up here that addles a man's mind. There's Abrams and Clemment, and now you. You're all crazy."

"Abrams is a rascal. Clemment—well, I thought perhaps we ought to discuss him. He's not right in his mind. I worry that he'll not take proper care of himself and be a winter casualty."

"Merry keeps track of things. You can write a note to his family. If she doesn't have an address, she can wheedle it out of him."

"I'll get word to his family. 'Tis the least we can do for a neighbor."

Tucker started rocking the wood-framed steel mesh rocker cradle as Ian dumped small chunks and gravel into it. He added water, and they winnowed through the stones that were worthless.

"Ian? Does Meredith have your family's address?"

Ian didn't pretend to misunderstand what Tucker meant. "Listen here, Smith. If you think I'll bolt off to my old hometown, you're the one who's showing a bent mind. Like this here, I've sifted through stones and pebbles and gravel. I finally struck gold in the form of the comely hazel eyes of your sister. Aye, and that's enough to make me feel as rich as Midas."

Ian dumped the top two levels of unremarkable chips of stone. He stuck his forefinger into the very bottom of the rocker box and brought it back up with a mere breath of gold dust on the tip. "A thimble full of this is an ounce. A refiner's fire burns off the dross and leaves it pure. You and I—we're standing in the furnace, but the Lord has different works to do within our hearts and souls. You can call me crazy, but 'tis commitment—commitment to His will and to the woman I love."

"A man who plays with fire gets burned."

"To me, Merry is worth whatever fire I must walk through."

Tucker stopped rocking the box. At the very bottom, only a few flakes glinted. "No matter how much you work at it, you don't always get enough of what you want in the end."

Somewhere, sometime ago, a woman hurt him. Compassion replaced Ian's frustration. "Tucker, whenever a man courts a woman, there's always a danger that things won't work out. I've not pursued anyone 'til now, but that's changed for me. To me, Merry is more than worth the risk."

Chapter 16

Merry tilted her head and squinted. Ian's bottle window was beautiful to look at but difficult to see through. For the sake of warmth, he'd tacked a hide up over the window and shut the shutters, but for the scant three hours of daylight they had, he'd roll up the hide and open the shutters.

It's so much nicer than last winter. Even a little light is wonderful, and the colors are pretty. They'd gone through a five-day blizzard recently. Being in the small, dark cabin she and Tucker shared felt suffocating. He'd been restless. He'd also muttered about partnerships and not getting enough in the end.

Lord, You know how he worries about the money. If it's Your will to provide enough to cover the debts, we'll be grateful. If You don't want us to be free, then please grant us grace.

She opened her sewing box and pulled out her knitting needles and yarn. For a few hours, she could work on Christmas gifts. Her mind whirled as the yarn played between the needles. *Tucker was upset when we were in our cabin and Ian was over here. He already feels beholden to Ian. Knowing Ian was working here with the rocker cradle while we weren't helping—that has to bother Tucker. I should have realized it before now.*

After finishing several rows, Meredith put away her knitting. She went to the stove and stirred the stew. Mountain sheep, two sizable potatoes, some carrots, and assorted spices mingled to give off a mouth-watering aroma. After filling a jar, she covered the stew once again and put on her russet cloak. She barely touched the door, and the wind blew it wide open. Snow from the past two days spread before her. Using leather thongs, she strapped on the snowshoes Tucker had made for her. Even with them on, it took effort to walk to where the men were working.

"What are you—"

"Doing out here?" Tucker finished Ian's question. They both looked at her as if she'd taken leave of her senses.

"I'm worried about Mr. Clemment. I'm taking him some stew."

"I'll take it to him." Tucker came toward her with far more ease than Ian did. Merry didn't comment on that fact; Tucker was weaving a pair of snowshoes for Ian as their Christmas gift. They'd be done in time for the worst of the cold months.

"I want to go, too. You can't expect me to stay cooped up all the time."

"Go on ahead." Ian rubbed his gloved hands. "I'll check the snares."

Tucker and she were halfway to Mr. Clemment's claim when Meredith dared to voice what was on her mind. "Ian's cabin has a lot of room. When blizzards hit, if we stayed there, you could work alongside him."

"What's wrong with our cabin?"

"Nothing at all. We made it through last winter just fine. I was thinking more of how he used the rocker cradle and coaxed gold from the silt while you and I did nothing during the last storm."

"I can take a bag of rocks back to our cabin and pan by the firelight."

"Yes, you could. I could, too."

"No, you can't. I'd have to do it over the dishpan so we don't end up with water and ice on the floor."

Meredith said nothing about how Ian had stretched the mountain goat's hide so that it now formed a big, warm rug in his main room. Instead, she said, "We can take turns."

"No," Tucker replied in a harsh tone. "You did all that gardening and earned what we needed for this winter's supplies. I'm doing the prospecting."

"I don't mind, Tucker."

"I do." His voice was colder than the arctic wind.

Mr. Clemment didn't answer their knock. Tucker kicked the door, and it swung inward. The biggest mess Meredith had ever seen stretched before her. Tucker stepped in first, pulled her in, then shut the door. In a low tone, he ordered, "Stay right here. I'll give him the food."

Meredith released the jar and watched her twin shuffle around the mess and toward the table. Mr. Clemment sat cross-legged in the center of the table. He gave Tucker a big smile and gestured grandly. "Home, sweet nest."

"We brought you some chow." Tucker set the jar on the table. When Meredith took a step forward, Tucker motioned her back.

"Food looks good. It'll warm me clean down to my gizzard."

"You enjoy it, old-timer." Tucker came back to her side. "There's not much sun. I need to get Sis back to a warm cabin."

"Off with you, then." Clemment made a shooing motion.

Once he shut the door, Tucker stared at Meredith. "He's not right in the head. Ian and I discussed writing to his family. Do you know if he has any?"

"A brother. I have the address."

"Good. You don't come here alone. Ever."

"You don't want me to get out at all." She sighed. "Honestly, Tucker, I—"

"You're going to listen to me. Clemment was as ordinary as anyone we knew when he first got here. Being here has made him go crazy. You can't trust him for one minute. And like it or not, we're not going to stay with Ian during blizzards. There's no telling if his mind will snap, too."

<hr>

"A Christmas tree?"

Ian nodded. He could tell how important it was to Meredith. She'd popped out of his cabin, eyes wide with anticipation. "Aye, lass, if you're wanting one, we can do that."

Merry's face lit with glee. "Oh, I do want one!"

"Fine, then. Let me set these inside." He opened the door to his cabin and put down a brace of snow hare he'd snared. Leaving them outside would invite predators.

"Do you want pasties with those, or roast?"

Ian shrugged. "Whatever pleases you."

"I'll let you decide while we choose a tree. I've already crocheted little snowflakes, and we can string cranberries."

"I'm far more liable to eat those cranberries than to string them up."

"You may eat popping corn instead. I don't think we need a big tree. Something about. . . this high."

"Come walk with me. You can choose whichever one you fancy." He'd far rather walk with her alone, but Ian knew Tucker wasn't about to put up with that notion. Instead, he called over, "Tucker! Merry wants a Christmas tree. Why don't you come along and help us find one?"

"There's no room."

Merry smiled. "We can share the one Ian puts in his cabin."

"There's a grand notion." Ian slid her hand into the crook of his arm.

Tucker rested his hands on his hips. "We don't need a tree."

"You're grouchy as a bear." Meredith reached up to pull the hood of her cloak up because it had started to slip.

"I'm not grouchy. I'm hungry."

"Then dress the hare. Ian and I won't take long. Then I'll fry the rabbits, just the way you like them."

Ian steered her off to one side. "I need to fetch my hatchet." He claimed it from just inside the smokehouse. "Now what kind of tree did you have in mind?"

"Pretty. And green and fragrant."

"Any particular variety?"

She hitched her shoulder. "I'll know it when I see it."

They tromped through the snow. Merry made a point of having them walk entirely around each tree so she could make sure it was shaped well and full. Just to prolong their time together, Ian started pointing out flaws.

"You think this one's lopsided?" Merry tilted her head to the side.

"Look at the top. See how the sprigs are veering off?"

"Now that you mention it, they do." She headed toward another one. "The top is pretty on this. I know the bottom has a bald spot, but can't we just chop off the top?"

Ian shook his head. "If we take the tree's life, 'tis only fair the whole of it is used."

Finally they found one that didn't quite reach Meredith's waist. "Oh, it's perfect! Look at it—all around, it's full and green."

Ian had to agree. "It's a beauty. Is this the one you want?"

"Oh yes!"

The crisp air rang with the sound of the ax as Ian chopped down the little pine. Much to his regret, he still needed to carry the ax and drag the tree, so he couldn't hold Merry's hand.

Bubbling over with enthusiasm, Merry cupped her hands to her mouth and called, "Tucker, we found it!"

"It's about time," he hollered back. "It's getting dark, and I'm half starved."

As they drew nearer to the cabin, Merry's footsteps dragged. Ian figured out what the issue was. "Merry, I'm going to stop a few minutes so I can level off the bottom of the tree. Do you mind standing back a little ways? I don't want any chips to fly up and hit you."

"Okay."

A minute later, Tucker stomped over. "What have you done with my sister?"

"Shh." Ian jutted his jaw toward the outhouse. He raised his voice. "You have to agree, this is a dandy little tree."

"Then my sister picked it out."

"That she did."

"I knew it. You can't sing worth a plug nickel. You can't cook. It was a safe bet you can't find a tree without help."

Meredith reappeared. "You boys behave yourselves."

"Speaking of behaving, I'm going to go check in on Mr. Clemment tomorrow." Ian hastily tacked on, "Alone. He's getting worse by the day. Mr. Clemment probably isn't dangerous, but we're taking no chances."

"We agree." Tucker's words about knocked Ian out of his boots. "Either of us men can stomp over and make sure he's alive. You're not getting near him."

Lord, are we making progress? Is Tucker finally seeing things in a better light?

Meredith could scarcely stand waiting until Christmas supper was over. She'd made gifts for Ian and Tucker—even going so far as to hide them each in sugar sacks so the men wouldn't know what they were. They'd be so surprised!

"Ladies first this time." Tucker went into Ian's other room and came out with a length of wool.

"Tucker! It's beautiful!" She smoothed her hand over the blue, gold, and beige plaid. "So soft and warm."

"Thought you could make a skirt for yourself."

"And it'll give me something to keep me busy. Oh, thank you!" She smiled. "You even chose colors that match my shirtwaists." Tucker and Ian exchanged a look, and she burst out laughing. "Even if you didn't do it on purpose, it worked out perfectly."

Ian went over and pulled a crate from behind the tree. The strings of popcorn and cranberries danced on the fragrant green needles. "Let's see what we have in here." He lifted the lid.

"Dessert." He lifted out a tin plate.

"Fudge," Merry breathed softly.

Ian chuckled. "Braden's wife and Fiona love Ma's fudge. I'm not certain how Ma managed to sneak any off to us, but here it is."

"The spices and the pink flour sacks and now the fudge—your mother's thoughtfulness..." Merry's voice died out as tears prickled behind her eyes.

"Ma's a grand woman. Proverbs 31 says a godly woman's children will rise up and call her blessed. 'Tis easy indeed for me to sing her praises."

Tucker groaned. "Speak them; don't sing them."

Ian chuckled and drew out a handful of pure white candy canes. He hung them on the tree. "We'll save these for another day."

Next he drew out a tin box. "This is from Ma and the girls, for Merry."

Merry blinked in surprise. "But I—"

" 'Tis in keeping with a Rafferty tradition. Each Christmas, everyone receives something practical and something impractical. You'd not want to ruin my Christmas by objecting, would you?"

Merry accepted the tin. "Thank you." She smiled at the beautifully painted scene on the lid. "This is so charming!"

"Did I tell you what Sis did with the paper wrapper on that soap?" Tucker didn't pause. "She flattened it out and has it pinned to the wall by her bed."

"Did you, now?"

"It's pretty, and so is this." Merry bowed her head and opened the tin and gasped. "Embroidery floss!"

"Doesn't sound all that practical to me," Tucker groused.

"The colors are beautiful." Merry couldn't figure out why Tucker had to be so moody—especially on Christmas.

Bless him, Ian laughed off Tucker's grumpiness. "Lift the paper, lass."

Meredith gently pushed aside the floss and discovered a sheet of paper. A paper of pins, a package of needles, four spools of thread, and dozens of buttons lay below. "I can truly use these. Thank you, Ian." She closed the tin and traced the lid again.

"These are for you, too, Merry." Ian held something out to her.

She looked up. "Skates?" She'd seen pictures of ice skaters, but she'd never actually seen skates.

"With the river frozen, I thought we'd have a lot of fun skating over it." Ian grinned at her. "The surface of the ice is surprisingly smooth."

"It does sound like a lot of fun. Thank you!" She accepted the skates and ran her fingers over the white leather shoe portion. "How did you know what size?"

"He asked me." Tucker's mouth twisted wryly. "It took me three times to check on your old shoes. You kept waking up or turning over."

"I never make things easy on you, do I?"

"Nope."

She beamed at them. "The two of you are incredible. These skates and the material—you've been so thoughtful. I'll remember this Christmas forever!"

Ian returned to the crate and pulled out a brown paper parcel. "Tucker, this is yours."

Tucker tore off the paper. "Netting!" As the netting spilled across Tucker's lap, a thin leather folder fell into view. He opened it. "Hooks and lures. Rafferty, you made a huge mistake. I'm going to ache to fish, not prospect."

"You've brought in many a tasty meal. I'm not complaining about your fishing." Ian reached into the crate yet again. "Tucker, this is for you."

Something jumbled and tumbled inside as Tucker accepted it. "Sounds like a rattler."

"I've never eaten one, but I understand they're edible." Ian tilted his head toward Merry. "I have no doubt that Merry would make it taste fine."

"I wouldn't get near one of those things!"

Tucker lifted the lid.

When he didn't say anything, Merry leaned forward and peeked. "Chess pieces!"

"Do you play?" Ian asked.

"It's been a long time."

Merry dipped her head and ran her forefinger over the metal blade of one of the skates. She didn't want to let out Tucker's secret. He loved to play chess—almost as much as he loved to trick someone into thinking he was a novice. He never wagered on a game. For him, it was a challenge to see how long it took his opponent to realize Tucker knew what he was doing.

Ian said, "We'll have to play a game sometime."

"Sure." Tucker managed to sound offhanded.

To keep from giggling, Merry went to the tree and opened a burlap bag she'd tucked beneath the boughs. She pulled out the smaller sugar sacks and gave each man his. Since

Tucker had just opened a gift, Ian went first. He unfurled the blue hat and scarf she'd made for him. He whistled under his breath. "My ears and nose are about to freeze off. This is great! I like blue, too."

"The color of your eyes." As soon as she spoke the words, Meredith realized they probably sounded coy. Embarrassment washed over her. "And—and that nice wool shirt your mother sent."

"'Tis true." Ian didn't seem the least bit offended. "And the fabric for your skirt that Tucker gave you—the golden stripe in it matches the centers of your eyes." He turned his attention on her twin. "Tucker, what have you there?"

Tucker gave her a funny look. All her life, Merry had been able to read his expressions. Recently, it hadn't always been easy, and on occasion, it was impossible. He opened his sack and drew out a brown hat and scarf. "Real nice, Sis. Thanks."

She smiled and motioned toward the door. Tucker walked over, opened the door a mere crack, and pulled in the gift he'd made for Ian. "These are for you, Rafferty."

"Snowshoes! I've been needing a pair something fierce."

"Yup." Tucker handed them over. "I've gotten cold just watching you wallow in the snow."

"Merry's scarf and hat will keep me warm whilst I learn to walk in these. I've no doubt I'll trip over my own shoes and tumble many a time until I get as good as the both of you are."

"You'll be faster than Sis. She dawdles."

"If you wore skirts"—Merry shook her finger at her brother—"you'd be slower, too."

Ian elbowed Tucker. "You? In a skirt?" He threw back his head and laughed.

"She meant both of us. Didn't you?" Tucker gave her his agree-with-me look.

Merry pretended to sigh. "Actually, either of you would trip on the hems and break your neck if you had to wear all of these layers. Perhaps what I ought to do is use that wool to make myself trousers."

"Over my dead body!" Tucker roared.

"If you were dead, she'd just wear your britches." Ian folded his arms across his chest and surveyed Tucker. "She'd have to hem them up to the knees and take them in a ways, but Merry's a clever lass. She'd wind up with a brand-new skirt and a couple pair of britches to boot!"

"If anything ever happens to me, you're to put Merry on the next ship out. Uncle Darian lives in Seattle. Give me your word on that right now, Rafferty."

"Enough of that talk! You're too ornery for anything to happen to you." Meredith rested her hands on her hips. "And how dare you try to send me to Uncle Darian?"

"He could buy you anything your heart desires."

Scowling at her brother, Meredith demanded, "What kind of woman do you think I am? The things that matter to me can't be bought."

The cabin fell silent.

Chapter 17

Ian clapped his hands and rubbed them together. "Well, most things that matter cannot be bought. Merry?" He gestured toward the crate.

Excitement replaced her irritation. Meredith half ran to the tree, stooped beside the crate, and rose. "We've saved the best for last. Here, Tucker."

His jaw dropped as she pressed a new Bible into his hands. He cleared his throat, then cleared it again. Emotions flashed across his features. "How?" he rasped.

She'd anticipated his worrying about the cost and had a ready answer. "Ian offered to have his mother shop for me. Things are economical in Oregon, and keeping the secret from you has been fun."

Ian slapped Tucker on the back. "A Bible—now you can't get a more essential gift than that."

"And Ian gave you the chess pieces, so he upheld the Rafferty Christmas tradition—though I have to say, I think having you play chess is practical for me. You'll be too busy with the game to try juggling rocks. I'd rather spend time stitching a sampler than dodging stones."

Tucker held fast to the Bible and cracked a smile.

"While he pores over that," Ian said, "why don't you and I go skate?"

"You have skates?"

He smiled. "My dad sent them to me. They're my impractical gift."

Within minutes, Ian had set several lamps on the bridge. The bridge always floated just a few feet off the water. Meredith looked at the sight and smiled. "It's hard to remember the bridge is frozen in place. The way the lanterns glow on it makes it look like a shooting star."

"I'd not thought of it that way, but you're right. I noticed instead how they set everything to sparkling—especially your eyes."

Meredith's heart skipped a beat. *Could he be feeling more for me than just brotherly love?*

He chuckled. "Don't be so surprised, Merry. You're a comely lass." He started lacing on his skates. "Fiona always complains 'tis hard to get her skates on tight enough once she's bundled in layers to skate. Braden or I help her. Would you care for some help?"

"Why, yes. Yes, please. Thank you." Meredith couldn't figure him out. He'd complimented her and then compared her to his sister. What did that mean?

A few minutes later, he took her hand in his and helped her step onto the ice. "Ready?"

"I'm not sure. How do I balance on these?"

He gave her an astonished look. "Haven't you ever skated?"

Meredith shook her head.

"You'll do fine. You're always so graceful; it won't be hard at all. Wait here a second and watch my feet. You don't step. Simply glide one foot a little from the front to the side, then the other."

He slid across the ice. "One foot, then the other."

"You make it look easy."

"It is. Here. Hold on to my arm."

Meredith scooted off the bridge and onto her feet. As Ian threaded her hand through the crook of his arm, her legs started to wobble and her feet started to slide. "Oh no!"

"It's okay. I have you."

She clung to him for dear life.

"See? You're doing fine. You're staying upright."

But for how long? She didn't ask.

"Standing is hardest."

"If I can't stand, how can I move? I—I. . .whoa!"

"Here." He transferred her right hand into his right hand and wrapped his left arm about her waist. "How's this?"

Wonderful. Just as quickly as that reply flashed through her mind, Meredith felt her left foot betray her. "I'm like a newborn foal. All wobbly and awkward."

"Not for long."

"Ian?" She held to him in desperation. "If I fall, you'll fall."

"So what? I've fallen hundreds of times."

She jerked away. "That's hardly reassur—ah! Ah! Ohhh!" Her shriek echoed in the air as she tumbled.

Ian sat beside her on the ice. "Not half as bad as you feared, was it?"

"Twice as bad," she whispered.

"Are you hurt, honey?"

Honey. He called me "honey." Warmth rushed through her.

"Merry." He tilted her face up toward his. "Are you hurt?"

She blinked then ducked her head. "No. Just embarrassed."

His finger tickled her cheek. "It's only me. You don't have a thing to be embarrassed over." He stood and helped her up. "It gets cold down there, doesn't it?"

She nodded and clamped both of her hands around his forearm. "What if the ice isn't thick enough? I could fall and make us crash through."

"A dab of a lass like you?" His laughter rang in the nippy air. "There's no danger of that. Come now."

He made it look so simple. He skated backward and let her hang on to him. Knees and ankles locked, she allowed him to tow her out a ways.

"Merry, you're stiff from the middle clear down to your toes, but the top half of you is bobbing like a washerwoman at the scrub board. Shoulders back. A little more. Yes. Excellent!"

Eventually, she tried to glide her feet the way he did. She plunged down onto the ice and yanked him down along with her. "I'm going to break your neck."

"No, you won't."

Meredith glared at him. "Oh yes, I will. If I live to get off this ice, I'm going to study the Bible and see if there is any situation where murder is condoned."

Ian had the nerve to laugh.

Just about the time Meredith decided to tell him she was an abject failure, she managed eight strokes before stumbling. Amazingly, she didn't fall.

"You're getting a feel for it. You're doing wonderfully."

Just then, Erik Kauffey wandered over. "Well, look at you!"

"Merry Christmas!" Merry and Ian said in unison.

Kauffey motioned toward them. "Same to you. That looks like loads of fun."

"Merry's got natural talent. This is her first time."

Kauffey hooted. "I strapped a pillow to my backside the first few times." He laughed so hard he coughed.

Tucker came out of the cabin. "What's going on?"

"I hoped you'd all be in the Christmas spirit and be willing to trade. I got a plug of tobacco and two peppermint sticks."

"Neither of us uses tobacco." Tucker gave Ian a questioning look.

Ian hitched his shoulder. "Go on ahead and dicker over a cup of coffee, Tucker."

Meredith giggled. "You don't truly think the two of them will have only one cup apiece, do you?"

"It's Christmas. Let them enjoy themselves. I sure am enjoying myself."

"This is sort of fun."

Ian kept praising her. He stayed close and helped her up over and over again. Finally, they managed to skate together halfway around the circle. "We're coming close to the bridge. Do you want to go around one more time?"

Her feet and legs shouted, *No!* But he had his arm around her. Meredith rasped, "Okay. One more time."

"That's my girl!"

Oh, if only I were your girl. That lovely thought kept her going and sustained her almost all the way around. Then a terrible thought struck. *I have no business wanting to be more than a friend to Ian. I'm not really a friend, either. Not a true friend. He has no idea about what happened.*

"Here we go. I'll glide you right next to the bridge. At the last moment, just hold me. I'll spin and slip you right down on the planks."

Moments later, Ian knelt on the ice and unlaced her skates. "How are your feet? Do the skates rub anything?"

"They're comfortable. Truly, they are."

"Good. We'll come skate often." He sat beside her and changed out of his own skates and back into his boots. He tied the laces of the skates together, carried them over his shoulder, and helped her up. "The air is bracing, but as you skate, you stay reasonably warm."

"That's hard to imagine."

"What's hard to imagine is that you've never ice-skated. Now that I think about it, it makes sense. I grew up thinking skating and winter were synonymous. Did you always live in Texas?"

"Most of my life." She didn't want to go into details.

"So tell me more."

She shook her head. "I'm boring, Ian. Nothing about me is worth knowing." *Liar!* Conscience aching, she stammered, "I'm realizing my clothes are damp. I don't want to catch a chill."

"Go change right away. Better still, go on up to my cabin. I'll go fetch you dry clothes."

"No!"

"But your cabin won't be warm enough."

"I'll bundle up and maybe take a nap. I have a feeling you and Tucker will keep me up late tonight when you start playing chess. You certainly did when you played cribbage!"

"All right. I'll walk you—"

"Nonsense. You need to go change, too."

Later that evening, they ate leftover roast. As a special treat, Meredith watered down a can of Borden's milk and added cocoa. They all sipped hot chocolate and had a piece of fudge.

"You're quiet tonight, lass."

Meredith startled.

"You wore her out skating." Tucker turned toward her. "I'll go on over to Clemment's place tomorrow morning and get the dishes."

"I'm still not sure we should have let Mr. Kauffey drop off the food."

"Clemment's odd, but I don't consider him dangerous." Ian took another sip and hummed appreciatively. "Old Abrams, on the other hand—you get a rifle in his hands, and we'd all better be caught up on our prayers!"

Tucker gave Ian a funny look. "Sis meant that she was afraid Kauffey probably ate the food himself."

"No, no. You're both mistaken. I fear Mr. Kauffey might be taking the ague. His voice was rough, and he was coughing. The thought of him walking any extra distance concerns me."

"The ague?" Tucker shook his head. "It's tobacco. He smokes it whenever he can get some, chews it the rest of the time. That causes a gravelly voice and hacking."

"I've seen that before." Ian unrolled the cloth they'd drawn a checkerboard on. "So, Tucker, are we playing draughts or chess tonight?"

"Draughts. Tomorrow we can play chess. I want to be well rested. It's a complicated game."

"Aye. Then again, so is cribbage. Once you memorize all the rules, things come quickly."

Tucker gave Ian an assessing look. "You sound like a man who enjoys the game."

Ian gave him a long look. "I don't back away from a challenge."

Chapter 18

Ian's lantern cast a halo of light into the darkness of the morning. Drops of ice sparkled along the rough, thin fences he'd made of willow branches. Every two yards or so, Ian left a break about the width of his fist in the fence. He grinned in satisfaction that the snare in the next opening held a ptarmigan.

Ptarmigans seemed to prefer the willow branches, and the birds had a habit of dragging their feet in the snow. They'd scurry along the fence and step into one of a series of loops in a length of string. By dragging their feet, they tightened the snare.

Ian set down his lantern and took off his gloves only long enough to take the ptarmigan and reset the snare.

"Well, well." Tucker sounded pleased.

Ian tugged back on his glove, wound the ptarmigan's legs onto the string, and grabbed his lantern. "I'm falling every fifth step," he announced as he lifted one foot. Though he waddled like a drunken sailor on the snowshoes, it beat having to slog through knee- and thigh-deep snow.

Tucker lifted his own lantern higher. "Is that a complaint or a boast?"

"A boast, of course. When first I set out this morning, I fell or stumbled every other step."

"My sister did better than that." Tucker lifted his chin.

Ian didn't take the bait. "I don't doubt that in the least. Merry's a graceful woman. She took to ice skating right off. Aye, she did." Though he'd been facing both of them, Ian focused directly on her. "And I was proud of you for that, lass."

"I have a patient teacher."

"And an impatient brother. I'm hungry, and if Ian didn't start a pot of coffee yet—"

"You needn't bluster. I have a pot on the stove." Ian held out the string of ptarmigan. "We've three of these, Merry. Tucker can dress them whilst I check the rest of the snares. I'm hoping for more."

"I'm drinking my coffee first. I have to wake up. Otherwise, Ian's going to whip me at chess."

"Oh, now." Ian huffed. "The man's going to be making me sorry I brewed that coffee."

Merry laughed. "Listen to the two of you. You sound like boys wanting the first chance on the schoolyard swing."

"Swings are for girls. Tell her, Rafferty. No self-respecting boy wants anything to do with them."

"I'd be lying." Ian paused a second, then added, "Even when I was a mere lad, I always found the lasses fascinating."

Merry didn't bother to muffle her giggle.

Tucker swiped the birds. "You knew what I meant."

"Ian, I can't tell you how thankful I am that you've been so generous about sharing your coffee. Tucker was surly like this once we ran out of coffee last winter."

"You deserve a medal for that." Ian shamelessly took advantage of the opening. "Seeing as I have no medal, I'll take you ice skating this afternoon."

"We're playing chess today." Tucker glowered at him.

"Of course we will. But you promised Merry you'd go pick up the dishes over at Clemment's. I reckoned you'd do that during the light, and she and I can spin around the ice." Ian didn't want to give Tucker a chance to ruin his plan. "I'll be in soon. I just have a few last spots to check."

He walked off. Sound carried exceptionally well on the icy air, so he heard the Smiths go on into his cabin. "Lord, Tucker's starting to wear on my patience. I don't want things to turn ugly. Could You please open his eyes so he understands I'll not shove him out of Merry's heart and life?"

He reached the last part of his trap line then returned to the cabin empty-handed. "Sorry I didn't get anything more."

"But these are nice plump ones. I think I'll save the white meat in a bucket of ice for tomorrow and make chicken and dumplings today. That way, Tucker can take something to Mr. Clemment. I worry about him."

Ian nodded. They'd sent a letter to Mr. Clemment's family, but he wasn't even sure if Merry had a correct address for the man's relatives. No one could rely on what the bizarre man said.

Merry plucked a fistful of feathers and added them to her bucket.

"I'll be done here in a minute. Tucker, please stir the Quaker oats."

Tucker complied. "Rafferty, come spring, I want to send a request to your family. I'm hankering after grits."

"Okay. In the meantime, is there someone who might have some? We could arrange a trade."

Both men turned to Meredith. Her brow puckered. "I'm trying to recall where people are from. I doubt Northerners or Westerners would have grits." She named a few possibilities.

Tucker and Ian alternately ruled out each candidate. Most of them lived too far away. With frigid conditions and barely three hours of light, prudence dictated not going any distance.

"I'm more likely to find gold than grits." Tucker sounded downright morose.

"Come spring, we'll turn some of that gold into grits." Meredith set aside the second bird and started on the last.

"Aye, you're right." Ian turned to Tucker. "I suppose that means you and I had best start working." They went into the adjoining room.

As they'd excavated along the vein of gold, the men had separated out the rocks and gravel that showed promise. Anything that wouldn't bear working, they'd used to make paths between the houses, right by the smokehouse. Come spring, that gravel would keep them all from getting mired down.

The stone they'd chipped out that bore any glimmer of golden hope filled crates and bags in the second room. On the coldest or stormiest days, the men processed the silt in the rocker cradle. On clear days, they'd spread a sheet of canvas outside and use a mallet to pulverize rocks.

"Feels like we're due for more snow."

Tucker nodded. "Guess we'd better bash up some rocks so we can stay busy during the next blizzard."

"We've made faster progress than we anticipated. We're liable to run out of anything to process ere the spring thaw comes."

"It's the rocker cradle." Tucker picked up the canvas and the mallet. "Sure beats standing in icy water with water sloshing over my sleeves."

Ian grimaced. "Wouldn't you know you'd say that? I was thinking that when the thaw comes, gold might wash downriver. I wondered if we'd be smart to devote time to the riverbank, then go back to digging when the ground softens."

"The idea holds merit. If I could do it without having to listen to old Abrams shouting across the water at me, I'd be more inclined to agree."

"He's a character." Ian hefted a sack. They went to the door, set things outside, and then returned only long enough to put on their hats, scarves, and gloves.

"The two of you are going to catch pneumonia," Meredith fretted.

Tucker snorted. "Just yesterday you said I'm too ornery to die."

"We've each a union vest and two wool shirts on. 'Tis sweet of you to worry, but needless."

"It's more dangerous to sweat and ice up than it is to be a little chilly." Tucker threw open the door.

Ian followed him out. Turning to close the door, he gave her a reassuring smile. "We'll not be out long."

They worked steadily, and just as Ian finished pulverizing the last rock, he caught movement out of the corner of his eye. "Abrams is on his way across the bridge."

"Old goat's probably angling for a meal again."

Abrams tottered over. "Reckon dinnertime's here."

"Sundays, after worship, you're always welcome to stay and eat supper with us." Ian stood back as Tucker carefully gathered up the canvas.

"But it's Chrisssmesss."

Tucker stopped fiddling with the canvas and folded his arms across his chest. "I don't let drunks near my sister."

"Awww, Schmith, I only had a few nips. For my rheumatiz."

"That's a few too many."

Abrams pouted like a baby. "Iss your cabin, Ian. Whaddya shay?"

"You don't want Merry to see you like this. It would upset both of you. Go on home."

"But I'm countin' on holiday grub. Mer'dith'll lemme eat. I've been eatin' beans forever."

"You're full of beans, all right," Tucker muttered.

"Thass right. I'm fulla beans. Betcha Merry'll fix me a big ol' roast or ham. Maybe both." Abrams nodded so emphatically he lost his balance.

Ian threw his arm around Abrams. "C'mon. I'll walk you home."

"But I wanna eat. Juss not cat."

"Cat?" Tucker and Ian said in unison.

"Uh-huh. You Bible-thumpers feed folks the fatted cat. Don't want cat. Wanna ham. Thass pig, you know."

"Yes, I know." Ian steered Abrams toward the bridge. "We don't have any ham, but that can't be helped. Next week is New Year's. If you're sober as a judge, we'd be honored to have you over to celebrate."

Abrams squinted up at him. "You're not gonna push me off in that room and make me take a bath in the middle of winter, are you?"

"Let us make a deal about that."

Abrams stopped at his cabin door. "I getta make the deal. If I take a bath, nobody feeds me that fatted cat." He stuck out his hand. "Schake on it."

"We won't feed you cat. Now let me stoke the fire in your fireplace, and you can go to sleep."

From the outside, Abrams's cabin looked small; from the inside, Ian realized he could reach out and touch both sides at the same time. The sight inside would have made Merry's hair stand on end. Items littered the floor, and sacks of staples lay heaped in the corner. A single log burned low in the fireplace. Icicles hung from the ceiling around the edges. To Ian's astonishment, the old man reached up, broke off one of those icicles, and shoved it into a bucket on the hearth.

"Water." Abrams tumbled onto his cot. "I'm schmart. And I don't eat cat."

Ian stoked the fire, added snow to the bucket by the fire, and left the old man to sleep.

Meredith set steaming bowls on the table. "You're right on time for lunch."

"Thanks. It smells great!" Ian peeled off his hat, scarf, and gloves.

She fought the urge to smooth down his riotous hair. The man desperately needed a haircut. Then again, so did her brother. Thanks to the hair combs, pins, and ribbons Ian had given her, she was able to keep her own hair contained into a reasonably ladylike style. *Ian called it my crowning glory. He likes my hair.* That thought made her shiver with delight.

"I invited Abrams over for a New Year's meal, provided he's sober. I hope you don't mind." Ian tacked on, "He agreed to take a bath before the meal."

Laughter tinting her voice, Merry said, "You could have been a politician instead of a prospector!"

"Are the two of you going to yammer the whole day, or can we eat while chow's still warm?"

Meredith sat down next to her twin. "I forgive you for being impatient. It's just that you want to be done here in time to use the light to go to Mr. Clemment's, isn't it?"

Tucker grunted.

After asking the blessing, they ate with very little conversation. Meredith couldn't wait to go ice skating—not because she felt any confidence, but because she wanted to be with Ian again. *He called me "honey" yesterday. And I've caught him looking at me. Can it be that he's developing feelings for me? I hope so. It would be so thrilling to be his wife.*

"Sis? You're not paying any attention. I asked what I'm supposed to take the food to Mr. Clemment in."

"I filled a canning jar. It's over there." She wrinkled her nose. "Please bring back as many dishes of ours as you can find."

"Easier said than done. His place is a mess."

"I know you'll do your best."

Tucker rose. "You haven't been out much. Why don't you strap on your snowshoes and come with me?"

Heat filled her cheeks.

"Nay. The lass and I already planned to skate. She can go on a visit to Clemment next time."

Tucker yanked on his coat and scarf then stood by the door.

"Tucker, you forgot the food for Mr. Clemment!" Though the scarf covered her brother's nose and mouth, Meredith could see the ire flash in his eyes. "And take a lantern!"

"I know the way."

"We don't have a lot of light. If you stay awhile—"

"I'm not tromping over there to keep that crazy loon company."

"I don't care how ornery you get—I'm going to match you with my stubbornness."

Tucker let out an impatient growl as he yanked on his hat.

"Give my best to Mr. Clemment." Meredith handed a jar to Tucker. "Tell him to come for New Year's."

"You already told me to do that twice during lunch."

"You're wasting time." She made a shooing motion.

"You're the ones who are wasting time. You haven't taken a hint. I'm not leaving until the two of you are out on the ice."

Mortified that her brother implied they'd do anything improper, Meredith gaped at him.

"The ice is thick." Ian carried his bowl over to the dish basin. "You needn't hold any concern that we'd fall in."

Tucker stood by the door. Ian gave him an opportunity to confess he was worried about their welfare instead of their morals, but he didn't. His silence embarrassed—no, irritated—her. He'd been impossibly grouchy all morning, but this went beyond reason. In a low tone, she demanded, "Apologize for insulting both of us."

Tucker didn't bother to lower his voice. "I won't apologize. In fact, it would be best if Ian took the food to Clemment."

"Well, he's not. He invited me to go skating, and I accepted. Furthermore, you volunteered to go check on Mr. Clemment. No one's changing the plan. You men are going to play chess tonight." Tucker looked ready to say something, so she cut him off. "I'll just leave the dishes to soak now while we skate."

"I'll help you with your cape." Ian took it from a peg by the door and draped it over her shoulders. As she buttoned it, he shrugged into his own coat.

A minute later, they stood outside. Tucker looked at the skates and lanterns Ian held. "You'd better take those down to the river then come back for Sis."

She knew he was trying to get rid of Ian. Meredith didn't want to listen to another insult or a lecture about keeping the secret. "Nonsense. I can carry a couple of the lanterns." She grabbed two and started toward the river. Over her shoulder she called, "Tucker, come back in a better mood, or I'm going to hide the coffee."

"That would darken his mood more, Merry."

"It couldn't get any uglier than it is already!"

Chapter 19

The men exchanged a few words, but the wind whipped them away from Meredith. *I'm an idiot. I should have stayed there. No telling what Tucker is saying to Ian.* Right as she decided to turn back around, from the corner of her eye, Meredith spotted her brother walking away.

Ian joined her on the bridge a few minutes later. "I'll set out the lanterns first." He did so and then quickly yanked off his boots and laced on his skates. "Let's have you sit on the edge, like last time." He stood on the ice, took her hand, and helped her sit on the edge of the bridge.

Meredith took a deep breath. "About what my brother implied—"

"I've handled it." He looked into her eyes, then knelt to help her with her skates.

Unable to let the matter drop, she asked, "How?"

He started lacing her right skate. "Your brother's having a bad day. We're all bound to have a few. Even so, I told him I'll not stand for him questioning your honor or my integrity."

"I'm sorry, Ian."

"Nay, lass. Don't be. Tucker loves you. His concern was misguided. He needed to be reminded of a few things. There, now. Hand me your other skate."

Meredith decided not to ask further questions. Tonight when she and Tucker were alone, she could. Maybe when he got back from Mr. Clemment's, he'd have reconsidered and repented. That would clear the air.

"You'll be more confident today once you realize you've learned to balance." Ian helped her onto the ice.

"I'm not so sure of that." She stared downward. "Why are there lines on the ice?"

"I swept it this morning."

"You swept the ice?" She gave him a startled look.

"Aye. Last night's wind carried pine needles and such onto the ice. I didn't want anything to cause you to stumble." He smiled. "And look at you—skating so well."

Her focus shifted. "How did I—ohhh! Ohhh!"

"Here." Ian braced her before she fell. His chest vibrated against her as he chuckled. "You were doing fine until you decided to fret. Let's just have some fun, okay?"

"All right."

Ian stabilized her, but he started holding her hand instead of wrapping his arm around her. When she slid or fell—even when she bowled him down—he never lost patience. "Ian?"

He lay still and propped his head in his gloved palm as if he lay on ice every day. "Yes?"

"How long does it take to get good at this?" She pushed against the ice and sat up.

"To my thinking, you're already doing everything right."

"I fell." She crooked a brow and stared at him. "And I knocked you down. This is the fifth time."

"Sixth, but who's counting?" The corners of his eyes crinkled. "Falling isn't what matters. The important things are if you get back up and if you enjoy yourself."

"I'm having a wonderful time!" She tried to plot a graceful way to get up. "It's the other part that's difficult."

With a lithe move, he got up and extended both hands. "Ah, lass, you don't have to do that alone. Sometimes, 'tis fellowship in the struggle that makes overcoming it all the sweeter."

"As long as you don't mind my struggles." She accepted his help.

He held fast to her hands. Even through their gloves, Meredith felt his warmth. "Mind? Not at all."

"Sis! I thought you were supposed to be skating."

Meredith twisted around. Had Ian not compensated somehow, they both would have fallen again. "Tucker!" She couldn't believe he was back already.

"Sitting around on the ice is idiotic—unless you have a purpose."

"You're not one to talk," Ian called back. "You're lying on the bridge."

"And I have good reason." Tucker took a hammer and struck the ice.

"Tucker!" Terror shot through Meredith. "What are you doing?"

"The ice is too thick for that to cause problems," Ian told her.

"I'm going to fish!" Tucker proceeded to take a saw and cut the hole larger.

All her life, Meredith had loved having a twin. Suddenly, she reconsidered. He had to have run over to Clemment's cabin and back. He was making a pest of himself.

Tonight, when we're alone and under our own roof, I'm going to give him a piece of my mind.

Shouting woke Ian. It took a second for him to realize the source. He immediately yanked on clothes and raced out his door. Tucker never raised his voice to Merry, but he was bellowing at her now.

Ian didn't bother to knock. He plowed straight into their small cabin. Meredith stood close to the fireplace, as if it would stop her shivering. But Ian knew she wasn't quivering from cold.

Tucker scared her.

Irate, Ian turned to Tucker. Tucker paced a few steps back and forth across the cabin. His speech was garbled. He turned to Ian, pointed, and shouted, "Don't know. Go 'way."

Ian stepped toward him. Just as he drew closer, Tucker spun back around. He took two steps then crumpled to the floor.

Chapter 20

H e's burning up." Ian flopped Tucker into bed and tried to remember what little
medical knowledge he'd gathered over the years.

"He's never sick. Never."

The panic in Meredith's voice forced Ian to take charge. "Throw everything you need
for a few days onto your bed. I'll carry them to my place and then come back for him. Put on
your cape while I'm gone."

There didn't seem to be any rhyme or reason to what Meredith pitched onto her bed.
More than anything, they'd need the bedding. Ian gathered up the corners and ordered, "Be
quick, Merry. I'll be back in just a minute."

"All right."

He hastened to his cabin, threw another log into the stove, and pulled back the blankets
on his own bed. Until that moment, Ian hadn't realized he was barefoot. After yanking on his
boots, he went back to the Smith cabin.

"Merry?"

"Come in."

He went straight to Tucker. "I'm going to take him over now. I'll have a better hold if he's
not in the blankets. You follow me with them, okay?"

"Okay."

Tucker was limp. Ian told himself that was far better than having to deal with a combatant.
Carrying deadweight on a snowy path taxed him, but Ian made every effort to make it look
easy so Merry wouldn't have anything more to worry about. She slid past him and opened the
door to his cabin. Ian draped Tucker on the bed and turned back to Merry. "I'll put him in a
nightshirt. Your cots fold, don't they?"

"Mine does."

"Go back and get it."

Moments later, Ian informed her, "He's got a roaring fever. No rash. That's a good sign."

"What do we do?"

"I have just a few medicinals."

She moistened her lips. "Willow bark is good for fevers."

"Excellent." He cupped her face. "I'll do everything I can, honey."

She nodded, but tears filled her eyes. "That broth powder—I'll make some."

Ian forced a smile. "Only because he's sick. Tucker would far rather have coffee."

Tucker muttered something unintelligible.

—⁂—

"The willow bark isn't working." Meredith's heart twisted as she tried to sponge the heat
from her twin's iron-hot skin.

"I'll go see if Abrams has anything."

How long Ian was gone, Meredith didn't know. It felt like forever. A gust of frigid air blasted into the cabin as he returned. She turned with every hope that he'd have a curative. The bleak look on Ian's face chilled her far more than the cold air.

"Clemment's no help at all. Abrams managed to get a good supply of spirits. He's celebrated the holidays and isn't in any shape to make a difference."

Meredith sank down onto the stool and swallowed hard. She reached over and curled her hand around Tucker's. The scar on his thumb he'd gotten from building their cabin still puckered. He squeezed—but so weakly, alarm pulsed through her.

"I'm going to town."

It took a minute for Ian's declaration to sink in. Merry gawked at him. "There's no path. You'll get lost. It's impossible. No one even tries in the winter."

"God will help me." He pulled on the hat she'd knitted him. The scarf, too. Ian came and knelt by the bed. He rested his hand atop hers and Tucker's. "Heavenly Father, You know the concerns of our hearts. You know what Tucker needs. Please, Lord, help us to help him. Keep him in Your hands and give Merry strength and wisdom, and speed me back to them with something that will cure him. In Jesus' name, amen."

Meredith shivered.

"Here, honey." Ian slipped a blanket around her shoulders. He tested her forehead with the backs of his fingers. "You're not sick. That's the best news yet. I'm putting another log in the stove."

"I'll keep trying to get him to take the broth."

"Good."

"Ian? I'm afraid for you to go. And I'm afraid for you not to go."

He looked at her, then said quietly, "We'll make a pact. I'll pray for you and Tucker. You'll pray for me and Tucker. I think he needs our prayers most."

"Okay."

"We'll trust the Lord to make a way." Ian reached for his coat. He yanked it on and fastened it. Hanging from the same peg were his skates. He snatched them. "Merry, God's already made the path."

He left, and she tried to watch through the bottle window as he skated away. Both of the men she loved were in danger.

Ian's hand stung from the cold. He pounded on the doctor's door anyway. He'd not yet met Doc Killbone, but that didn't matter. What did matter was that Tucker's best chance of survival lay with the doctor's knowledge and skill.

Thump, thump, thump. Still no answer.

Finally, the door opened a mere crack. "Doc's sicker'n a dawg. Can't help you none."

"He can still give me advice and medicine." Ian pushed his way past a short, squat man. "Where is he?"

"Asleep."

Ian hollered, "Doc? Doc!"

"He's sick, I tell you."

Ian turned and spotted a gaunt old man in a nightshirt. "Are you Doc Killbone?"

"Yuuuusss." The affirmative sounded as weak and drawn out as possible.

"Tucker Smith's sick. High fever. Nothing's making it break. What do we do?"

"Everybody's sick." Doc rubbed his temple. "I'm outta stuff."

"The mercantile—what does Socks have that would work?"

"No telling what he has." Doc shuffled back toward his bed, but he melted to the floor halfway there. Ian and the man who had answered the door lifted the doc into bed.

Doc closed his eyes and whispered wearily, "Sorry, son. Can't help."

Ian knew beyond a shadow of a doubt that under normal circumstances this man would have come. But these were not normal circumstances.

He went to the mercantile. Instead of going to the front door, Ian went to the back room where Socks lived.

Shoving open the door, Socks groused, "Makin' nuff noise to wake the dead."

"Tucker Smith's sick. High fever. What do you have?"

"Not a thing. Everyone else got whatever it is."

Ian refused to accept that answer. "You've got to have something." He brushed past and went into the mercantile. Most of the shelves were empty—but Wily had told Ian that was normal during the winter. Ian lit a candle, whispered a prayer, and scoured the place. Nothing.

"No miracles to be had here. You shoulda had those folks send you medicine instead of all that other junk they shipped."

Heavyhearted, Ian left the mercantile. He walked about ten yards, then jolted. Wily. He was in Skaguay for the winter—but he owned a place here in Goose Chase. He might have something.

Typical of Alaskan practicality, the doors to Wily's home were never locked. Matches and wood sufficient for a fire and food for a meal waited for any desperate wayfarer. Ian bypassed all of that. He rifled through Wily's other possessions.

Please, Lord. Please, Lord. Please. A leather satchel hung from a hook on the back of the door. Tucker grabbed it. The chink and tingle of glass hitting glass made his hopes soar. There, inside the bag, rested four small bottles and half a dozen vials. Each was numbered, and a palm-sized black leather book told what was in each numbered bottle and what its purpose was.

Snow started falling just moments after Ian laced on his skates and started skating up the iced river. With each passing minute, the flurries grew. His muscles tensed and cramped. He wrapped the scarf Merry had made for him over his nose and mouth, but the air was so cold, he felt as if he were inhaling shards of glass. When it became too difficult to see more than a few feet ahead, he kept close to the side of the river. As long as it was on his left, he knew where he was.

Until he fell.

<hr />

Meredith heard a sound. She hopped up and ran to the door. "Ian!"

He staggered in, and she slammed the door shut.

"You made it!"

He nodded and unlooped a leather strap from around his neck. She shoved him onto a stool and put a mug of coffee into his hands, then took the blanket from her own shoulders and wrapped him in it.

"Everyone. Town. Sick."

"Oh no."

He nodded wearily. "Got medicine bag. Wily's house."

"I was worried sick. This is the worst blizzard I've seen."

Ian's mouth tilted upward. "Bridge. Hit it. Got me home. God was with me."

Meredith set the bag on the table and carefully took out each jar and vial. "Quinine." She read. "Quinine! I know that's for fever!" The tiny book gave the proper dosage. Once she spooned it into Tucker, she turned back to Ian. "Your clothes are soaked. You have to change. Now."

He looked up at her. Though weariness painted every feature, his eyes still twinkled for a moment. "And you called your brother bossy."

Merry kept hopping up to give Ian more coffee and broth. He kept nudging her back onto a stool beside Tucker and draping a blanket over her shoulders. They took turns drizzling fluid into her brother.

"Merry, it's not going to do Tucker any good for both of us to be exhausted. We'll take turns. You lie down awhile."

She gave him a puzzled look.

Ian led her over closer to the stove. The heat radiating there felt so good. He'd set up her cot and had blankets waiting. "Lie down. I'll wake you if I need to."

"Are you sure?"

"Absolutely."

She lay down, but rest wouldn't come. Guilt mounted. Finally, Merry threw off the covers.

"It's my fault. Him being sick. It's my fault. We've always had each other. I made a promise to him. I've been begging him for months now, but he wouldn't release me from my word. I told him that I couldn't keep it anymore. It's anger. That's what this is. It's burning him hollow on the inside. He's mad that I was going to choose you over him. I am all he has, and I was going to betray him. He told me to go ahead and tell you. He told me I could, and he meant it, but look what it's doing. It's killing him. Now he's going to die, and you'll never trust me."

"Merry, honey, he's going to get better. I have faith he is. Aye, I think he's feeling a bit cooler. And he's not restless like he was."

"I didn't lie, but I did. Because I didn't tell you stuff I should have. I'm ashamed. I was living a lie because I didn't tell you something."

"But was it something I needed to be told?"

"Women are supposed to know about healing and stuff. I never learned it. Mama had a doctor, and once she went to her eternal rest, we were so healthy we never needed any help. What if he's not getting better? What if—"

"You're exhausted. 'Tis your fears talking, not your faith. Why don't you rest? It does no good for us both to stay up. If there's something you want to tell me later when things are back to normal, you can."

"You're being noble. That makes me feel even worse. The conviction I carry in my heart tells me it's just as wrong to withhold information as it is to give false information. You've asked about my family, and I've evaded telling you the truth."

"You don't have to tell me anything you don't want to."

"But I want to tell you!"

"But Tucker doesn't want me to know it?"

"I've reasoned with him. He didn't do anything wrong. Our father did. Only Tucker feels our family's honor is gone." She leaned closer. "Father swindled a lot of people back home. They'd just recovered from the awful depression, and Father tricked them into trusting him.

We once had a spread with prizewinning livestock. Now the bank owns it."

"I'm sorry. It must have been tough to live through giving up your land and livestock."

"It was, but worse, Tucker was engaged to be married. The girl's father called it off."

Ian looked indignant. "There was no call for that. Tucker is an honorable man."

Meredith couldn't seem to stop wringing her hands. "Worst of all, Father. . . c–committed. . ." The word was too hard to speak aloud. "He took his own life. Tucker feels honor-bound to repay all of those people what Father swindled from them."

Bowing her head, Meredith added in a hushed voice, "And now we're no better than Father was. We've misled you. We've taken your food. We've even been mining gold on your claim. That's not the way to return the Christian charity you've shown."

Ian clasped both of her hands in his. "Merry, none of that matters to me. I wish I had enough money to pay back those people so Tucker and you could be free of that burden. God holds us accountable for our own actions, but I think you and Tucker are extraordinary. You aren't responsible for paying back the investors."

"You're not mad?"

"The two of you trusted your dad. He wasn't worthy of your trust. Discernment is a gift, but it's also a matter of wisely gathering information. I thank you for feeling you could trust me, but I don't fault Tucker for taking longer."

Tears streaked down her cheeks. "Will he have that time? Will he get better?"

"God willing."

Tucker's fever broke. Ian fought the urge to whoop with joy. He wouldn't do that—Meredith needed her rest. She'd no more unburdened her soul than she'd fallen fast asleep. How she'd managed to curl up like a kitten on one of those cots amazed him.

Ian filled a small cup with apple cider and lifted Tucker's head. Tucker took a few sips then stopped. Every few minutes, Ian coaxed him to take more.

Weariness dragged at him. At one point, he decided to hum.

Tucker's left eye opened a mere slit, and he frowned. "Liar."

"Tucker Smith, are you calling me a liar?"

"No singing." His voice sounded as gravelly as the silt they mined.

Ian leaned a mite closer. "I wasn't singing. I was humming. I gave you my word I wouldn't sing, but I never said I wouldn't hum or whistle."

"Ugh. Hum? Thought. . .mosquito."

Ian grinned. "You'd best open your eyes wider. I'm too small to be an Alaskan mosquito."

"No tune. Mosquito."

"You being sick, you just didn't recognize the hymn 'The Solid Rock.'"

The corner of Tucker's mouth twitched. "I'm better. I'd be sick if. . .recognized that tune." Suddenly, Tucker's brow furrowed. "Sis?"

"Sleeping. She's worn out." Ian lifted Tucker's head and tilted a cup to his mouth.

"Cider." Tucker scowled. "Coffee."

"Nay. Water, cider, or stew. Take your pick."

"Picking." Tucker looked over at his sister. "She picked you. Loves you."

"I was hoping so. She's a rare woman. I'm wanting to marry her, you know."

"Maybe not. Our dad—"

"Your father's not here for me to ask, so I'm asking you for her hand."

"But—"

"Tucker, whatever is in the past is done. No one should have to assume the guilt of another's deeds. Christ alone did that. God is the only Judge, and He grants forgiveness freely through His Son. I don't care what your father did. What I care about is you being my friend, and more important, you being my brother-in-law.

"I'll love Merry 'til my dying breath. Now are you going to give me permission to take her as my bride, or am I going to have to force you to drink more water?"

"Coffee, deal."

Meredith woke to the smell of coffee. She sat up on the edge of the cot and cried out, "Tucker!"

"He's too ornery to be sick." Ian stood and stretched.

"He needs hearty food, not coffee. Ian, you come lie down. I'll sit with my brother for a while. Oh, wasn't the Lord good to us?"

Tucker sat on the edge of the bed and groaned. "I feel like someone hit me with a two-by-four."

"That's not possible." Meredith started to ladle up stew.

"There's no milled lumber around here," Ian said.

"But there are the finest cabins in the world," Meredith countered. "Who else has a bottle-glass-stained window?"

"You'll have one soon, Sis."

"How did you get enough bottles?"

He shrugged—but it was a forced action. "I just have a feeling."

The blizzard still howled. "Do you have any feelings about how long we're going to be burrowed in here?"

"What does it matter?" Ian shrugged. "We have chess, draughts, and cribbage."

"Don't forget juggling," Tucker added. "You need to learn how to do that, Ian. I'll teach you."

Meredith burst out laughing.

Tucker turned to Ian. "What's so funny?"

"I heard you still need to perfect your technique."

"I'm up to two stones at the same time."

Ian plastered a solemn look on his face. "Two. I see."

"Yes, and they're matched, so I can't count on the different colors guiding me."

"Why haven't you taught Merry such a valuable skill?"

Tucker shook his head. "No, no. She'd run off with the circus and leave me behind. I can't have that."

"Wait a minute." Meredith approached her brother. "Are you saying you can't allow me to go off with the circus, or are you saying I can't leave you behind?"

"Unh-huh." He slumped back down and closed his eyes.

"You need more sleep." Ian pointed toward her cot.

"I've had more than you have."

He grabbed a few blankets. "I'll make a pallet."

"You can't do that." Meredith tapped her toes on the floor. "This is far too hard."

"Compared to ice, the floor is soft."

In the middle of the night, the blizzard abruptly stopped. Ian sat up and wondered at the odd hush, followed by a strange singing.

Merry lifted her head. "Oh. The northern lights!"

"I've got to see this." Ian yanked on his boots and coat.

Merry hurriedly grabbed her cape. They slipped outside and looked up. Green and red waves and flames danced in the sky.

"What makes the noise?"

Merry shrugged. "I don't know. Sometimes it's much softer. Tonight it's loud."

Ian held out his hand. "Let's go look at them from the bridge."

She slid her hand into his and stood out where they'd have a better view. "Breathtaking."

"Yes," Ian agreed.

Light arced upward and swirled. "I'm so glad I came here."

"So am I. It's been every bit the adventure I wanted, and more." He stared upward. "You know, your brother and I figure that the vein we've found probably isn't going to get much larger. It's worth pursuing, but it won't make us rich."

"I already am rich." She gestured upward. "I have a symphony in the sky and my brother is well. We have a Bible and enough to eat and a good friend and neighbor. What more could I ask for?"

Ian stayed silent.

Finally, Merry got up the nerve to look at him.

He was staring straight at her. "I don't know what more you could ask for, but I know there's still something else I'd want. I long to marry the woman I love."

Merry held her breath so long she got a little dizzy.

"Are you going to ask me who she is?"

She shook her head.

Ian rubbed his warm, calloused fingertips down her cold cheek. " 'Tis you, Merry. You've stolen my heart just as surely as I breathe. If the only gold I ever got from Alaska was the gold in the center of your eyes, I'd die a happy man. Will you be my bride?"

"Oh yes, Ian. I don't know exactly when or how, but you stole my heart, too. My mama once told me love is the greatest adventure of all. You're the man I want to share that adventure with."

As they shared their first kiss, God painted the sky with color and sound.

Epilogue

I get to kiss the bride."

Ian gave Abrams a disgruntled look. "Later. Let me marry her first."

"Can't do that. Once she's your wife, she's a married woman. I wouldn't kiss some other man's wife!"

"I saw the ring," Mr. Clemment said. He wore his overalls the right way around for the special occasion. "It's gold." He nodded. "Gold as the first rays of the Alaska dawn."

"It ought to be. I had the ring made from the gold on our own claim." Ian craned his neck to see out his door. "What's keeping them?"

"They're twins," Abrams opined. "Takes 'em twice as long."

The minister shot a strange look at Ian. "You're only marrying one."

"Don't worry; we'll be sure he picks the right one," Mr. Clemment said in an earnest tone.

The minister tugged on Ian's sleeve. "Can you tell them apart?"

"Yes, Parson, I can. Abrams, go get my bride."

Abrams stepped out the door and hollered, "Hey! This man you wanna get hitched to is gettin' itchy. Best you shake a leg."

The parson tugged at his collar. Ian leaned forward. "Seeing my neighbors reminds me that God has an imagination."

"A big one, indeed."

A few moments later, Tucker stopped just outside the threshold. He set down his sister and brushed a kiss on her cheek.

"See? We kiss her before you swap the 'I do's'!" Abrams and Mr. Clemment both raced over and gave her a kiss on the cheek.

With no church for miles around, Merry wanted to get married in front of Ian's stained-glass window. A golden ribbon of sunlight cast a glow through it.

The parson stood in silence.

Merry finally whispered, "What is he waiting for?"

"I'm sure you want your sister to share this joyous occasion." He bobbed his head.

"What sister?"

Ian fought to keep a straight face. "Parson, Tucker is Meredith's twin."

"Yes, yes. Well, I can see how you're able to tell them apart."

Meredith smoothed the front of her pink dress.

"You look beautiful," Ian told her.

She beamed at him, and the brightness of her smile promised a love that would glow for a lifetime.

GOLDEN DAYS

by Mary Connealy

Dedication

I wouldn't be writing this dedication without Cathy Marie Hake. God put her in my life.
Christy Barritt and Suzan Robertson helped make me the writer I am today.
And the Seekers are the best support group ever. They're a gift from a loving God.

Chapter 1

April 2, 1898
Seattle, Washington

The Alaskan Gold Rush had turned Seattle into a madhouse.

Amy Simons hurried along the noisy, teeming street. She had taken over the job of running errands for the mission because the other teachers dreaded going outside.

Amy staggered as rough, crude men shoved past, trying to move faster. The tread of booted feet and the loud shouts of gruff voices overwhelmed all other noise. Ahead, a busy street rushed with carriages and wagons. People sick with gold fever darted across. The loud lash of a whip broke through the noise. Amy glanced at an oncoming wagon drawn by four horses.

A hard shove sent her stumbling off the wooden sidewalk. Something caught her foot, so she tumbled to her hands and knees into the path of the charging horses. As she fell, she heard the shouts of alarm mingled with raucous laughter.

A roar of warning from the driver barely reached her. With a shriek of terror, she threw herself out of the path of iron-shod hooves. One hoof landed solidly against her side, and her head hit the hard packed ground with a sickening thud.

"*Hintak xóodzi!* Papa, the hintak xóodzi! The white bear is coming!" With a deep-throated growl, a huge white bear reared up on hind legs, its claws slashing in the air.

Her father lay bleeding on the frozen ground in front of the roaring bear. He needed help. He needed her. "I will help you. I am coming, Papa."

"Amy, wake up."

The cold of artic ice bathed her face. The polar bear growled and slashed.

"Papa!" Amy swiped at the ice on her forehead. Her eyes flickered open. The dim light blinded her. Mercifully, she left the nightmare behind. An agonizing pain in her head nearly kept her from recognizing Mrs. McGraw holding a cool cloth to her forehead.

"You're safe, Amy. I'm here." The parson's wife who helped run the Child of God Mission had been mothering her since she'd arrived as a confused, grieving twelve-year-old.

Amy's eyes fell shut against throbbing pain; then she forced them open. Her stomach heaved. Mrs. McGraw became blurry, and there suddenly appeared to be two of her sitting on the bedside.

"There you are, young lady." The scolding voice echoed as if Amy heard it from across a great chasm. "Finally, you've come back to us. Whatever on earth is hintak xóodzi?"

Where had Mrs. McGraw learned the Tlingit term for the great white bear? Amy hadn't spoken a word of her mother's language since she'd come south.

"It is the great white bear, a polar bear." Mother's accented English slipped from Amy's lips. Years of struggling to speak more like others in Washington State were forgotten as Amy remembered the dream of her father in danger.

"Oh, polar bears. I've heard of those. You sounded as if you were being chased by one, dear. Were you in danger from polar bears where you lived?"

"No, although they've been known to rove far from their territory, I've never seen one. But my mother's people were nomadic and often traveled to the far north lands. I heard stories of them." The vicious, beautiful beast seemed to follow her into wakefulness, to roar and slash inside her head, or was the roaring and slashing from the pain?

Nausea twisted her stomach. She rested one hand on her belly as she fought down the urge to vomit. As Amy squinted up at the two Mrs. McGraws, one of them faded away while another remained behind, sitting at her side on the bed. Amy realized that, although the McGraws knew of her heredity, she never spoke of her mother's Tlingit tribe to anyone.

Struggling to sit up, every movement sent pain tearing through her body. Her chest blazed with an ache so deep it seemed to come from her heart. Her head pounded. Agony wracked one arm and her neck.

"Now just you stay put." Mrs. McGraw's strong, gentle hands eased Amy back. "You're going nowhere."

"But dinner. I promised to help. And I. . ." Amy tried to remember what happened. "You needed flour. I am so sorry I did not get that chore done. What happened?"

"Lie back, Amy. You were run down by a freight wagon three days ago."

"Three days?" Amy lurched upright again. The movement sent a shaft of pain through her chest and her right arm. Her left arm lashed her with pain when she moved it to clutch at her chest. Amy encountered heavy bandages wrapped tightly around her ribs. She stifled a groan. "The children and the classes—I have left everything for you."

Mrs. McGraw's chubby, competent hands rested with gentle firmness on Amy's shoulders. "We've managed, child. We missed you, but we got by. Now don't fret."

Amy knew that was more than true. She wasn't needed, but Mrs. McGraw was too kind to say so. It hadn't mattered so much when she'd been paying tuition to go to school and helping out with teaching duties. But this year, her father's tuition money hadn't come. Amy had been trying to earn her keep, but due to Mrs. McGraw's hard work and efficiency, there was little to do.

"You're battered and bruised everywhere, but nothing's broken. You just need rest and lots of it, and you'll be good as new. I'm mighty relieved you're awake, though. You've been as still as death for the most part, then restless at times as if a nightmare gripped you. We've near worn out God's ears with our prayers."

Amy forced herself to lie still, though she felt an urgency to be on her feet, caring for herself.

Mrs. McGraw carefully passed a bowl of steaming chicken soup to Amy. Amy forced her left arm to work as she took the bowl. With an encouraging pat, Mrs. McGraw left to feed the children in residence at the orphanage. Amy quit pretending to be strong. She set the spoon aside and drank the soup using only her right hand.

The dream of her father fighting for his life haunted her. He needed her.

A few minutes later, Parson McGraw stopped by. "Awake at last, young lady? Excellent!" The parson's sparkling blue eyes, half concealed behind a shaggy head of dark hair threaded with gray, reminded Amy of her father.

"Parson, I've got to go home."

His eyebrows snapped together. "What's this? Why, Amy, home is Alaska. You don't want any part of these madmen heading north."

The newspaper called them *stampeders*, and Amy thought that described them very well. "I have to go. There has been no letter from Papa in too long. And I'm taking up space better given to the children."

"Now we've been a spell between your father's letters before. Not this long, but it's too early to worry. And there's always room in our home for you."

"I know, and I thank you for that. But Seattle has never been my home; you know that."

The parson nodded. "I've always known you'd return to the north country, but now isn't right. My heart tells me you should wait."

Wait on the Lord. The words startled her as if someone had spoken them aloud but from within. She refused to be deterred. "I am going. I have to."

Parson McGraw's eyes softened, and his kind expression grew serious. "This morning during my Bible-reading time I found a verse that seems very appropriate to this moment. In fact, I'm wondering if God didn't guide my hand to select those pages and that passage."

"What passage is that?"

"It's from Isaiah. It says, 'They that wait upon the Lord shall renew their strength; they shall mount up with wings as eagles; they shall run, and not be weary; and they shall walk, and not faint.' The verse touched me because we'd been so worried about you, and those words encouraged me greatly. But now I'm wondering if God didn't lead me to them for you as much as for me."

Amy swallowed, fighting to keep her determination strong in the face of the parson's gentle wisdom.

"I have such a powerful desire to go home, Parson. I cannot stay here knowing Papa has tarried so long with his letter. He may be in danger. I have to go see."

He tried to dissuade her. Later his wife took her turn. Amy slept poorly that night, awakening in pain every time she shifted in bed, haunted by nightmares when she did slumber.

And under the pain and the nightmares, both awake and asleep, whispered a voice that said, *Wait.*

Perhaps the Lord Himself urged her to accept the generosity of these kind people. But rest went against her nature, and taking charity hurt her independent spirit nearly as badly as the bruises hurt her body.

She wanted the midnight sun.

She wanted the vast, rugged beauty of her home.

She wanted Alaska.

Chapter 2

A thick-soled boot nearly landed on her drawn-in toes. "Miss?"

Amy jumped at the gravelly voice. Her ribs punished her for the sudden movement. The man crouched beside her, entering her line of vision as she looked up. Worry cut lines between his dark red brows. "I noticed you didn't eat."

She twisted awkwardly to face him and gasped as pain stabbed her.

"Are you all right?" His hair shone red, longish and neglected like her father's. Unruly curls blew in the saltwater breeze.

His skin was fair, his cheeks chapped by the cold spring air. His face bore the stubble of their weeklong passage on the ship. Between the rolling of the ship and the absence of hot water, shaving was impossible. One large freckled hand with clean, blunt fingers, held a plate full of what passed for food on this wretched ship. The bracing wind had banished any aroma of the plate of beans. Just as well. The aroma amounted to a stench.

She didn't answer his question. Admitting how weak she felt put her at a disadvantage. She knew too well the ways of the wild where a wounded member of a herd faced the destiny of being picked out by the wolves. For pure survival, she forced herself to eat once a day, but she preferred hunger to the mob scene in the galley.

Amy looked at the man's shining blue eyes and felt as if she could see the wide Alaskan sky. She was tempted to search their depths until she saw home. As she looked closer, she saw that something dimmed the glow. He seemed to bear some weight that surrounded and smothered him. The missionaries had spoken sternly of proper behavior, but nothing about this man seemed dangerous.

"Thank you. That is very kind." She reached a hand toward the plate and nearly snatched it back when she saw how it trembled. She didn't think of herself as weak, but her hand told a different story. She didn't like her weakness revealed to this stranger.

He handed the plate over along with a fork, then turned and settled on the deck beside her. "This is a nice spot. I hope you don't mind my intruding."

She noticed he shifted around until his body blocked the wind for her—another kindness. "No, of course not. It is so close inside. I needed some fresh air."

"Close, huh? A nice word for people packed like sardines into the belly of a converted freighter with no windows, no baths, and no manners." He turned to look at her as she scooped up the first bite.

She smiled at the Irish lilt in his voice.

"Name's Braden Rafferty. It's a sad day when a little lady like you sets off with a boatful of madmen on the hunt for a pot o' gold."

Amy grinned. "I am Amy Simons." *Amaruq Simonovich.* She was tempted to tell him her real name. Papa had thought she'd be treated better with a more American name, and she'd respected his wishes.

"My father is in Alaska close to the area where they found gold. I am forced to accompany seven hundred madmen north." She flinched and turned, mindful of her ribs. "I am sorry. I did not mean to imply you are a madman."

She glanced sideways. Braden smiled. The smile broke slowly across his face. It seemed at odds with the downward furrows around his mouth as if his natural expression was always sad. And the smile didn't reach his eyes—as if no amount of amusement could touch him. But for all of that, it was a nice smile.

"In my own way I reckon I *am* a madman. I'm joining my brother. He's got a claim north of Skaguay. He didn't go all the way into the Klondike. Some old trapper convinced him he'd find all the gold he wanted far closer to civilization."

Some old trapper made Amy think of her father.

"Not sure if he's found any. He didn't send much money home to buy supplies. But he has found himself a wife, built a cabin, and sounds content." Braden's smile faded. "Now here I am, leaving a prosperous farm and my parents, who need me. That's madness, I reckon."

Amy scooped up more food, only now realizing how hungry she'd become. She did her best not to taste the bland, mushy mess, but she felt steadier as her stomach filled.

"So, you're going with this horde to Dawson's Creek—is that right?" Braden settled against the bulkhead as Amy scraped the last bite of food off her plate.

Shaking her head, she swallowed. "I am taking this ship to Sitka, then on to Skaguay. From there, I will hike up the Skaguay River to my father's cabin. He is deep enough in the wilderness as it is. No need to tramp another five hundred miles." Amy heard her voice taking on the sound of her mother. More and more since the accident two weeks ago, she'd found herself reverting to the heavily accented English she'd learned from her Tlingit mother and Russian father. She liked the sound of the broader vowels and the simplicity of speaking without contractions.

Braden sat up straighter and faced her. "I disembark in Skaguay, too. If you're familiar with the land, maybe you could look at the directions my brother sent." Braden reached inside the patch pocket of his buckskin jacket.

Another man stepped in front of them. His body blocked the few pale rays of sun. Annoyed, Amy looked up.

A stocky, middle-aged man in ill-fitting work clothes dropped to his knees on the deck squarely in front of her. With the constant flow of miners at his back, he crowded too close to Amy. Then he smiled at her in a way that reminded her that her name *Amaruq* meant wolf.

"Mind if I steal a bit o' space out'a the wind, folks?"

Since the deck wasn't hers to give or take, Amy didn't see how she could say no. She did notice that the man wasn't out of the wind. He looked blue-lipped and miserable. No light of fanatic gold fever shone in his eyes. Amy glanced at the man's hands—soft city hands. Lots of city folks had thrown in on the hunt for gold, but you could read the hunger in their eyes. Why would this man be going north if not driven by that same hunger?

"Name's Barnabas Stucky, miss. I see you're travelin' alone. Y'ever need any help, you ask for Barnabas, and I'll come a runnin'."

Barnabas Stucky struck her as more dangerous than most men, and she trusted her instincts.

The fur traders she'd grown up with came in all kinds. Although with her Russian blood,

Amy didn't have coloring or skin as dark as most Tlingits, when she was with her mother, she had faced occasional prejudice. She'd met those who would be kind to a Tlingit child, those who would avoid a child out of awkwardness, and those who were dangerous to anyone, child or adult. Stucky fit with the latter group.

"Thank you, sir. I am fine, but I will remember your offer." She looked away, hoping the man would leave.

Braden took the plate from Amy. Amy glanced at him, then sideways at Mr. Stucky. Stucky's eyes narrowed. He took a hard look at Braden, making obvious motions for him to leave. Stucky's eyes sharpened as if eager to be alone with Amy.

She grabbed Braden's hand.

Chapter 3

W e were going to discuss the way to your brother's cabin, I believe?" Amy's hand dug into Braden's wrist even through the buckskin.

He heard the soft cry for help in her question. Her quiet voice, with the echo of some nearly forgotten accent, stopped him from returning the plate to the galley.

Braden looked from her unexpected touch to her wary eyes. He relaxed back against the steel wall behind him. Of course it had to do with the city slicker. Braden hadn't liked the looks of him, either. She'd chosen him to protect her.

"You're my strength, Braden."

Maggie's voice haunted him every waking minute. He'd been a protector before and done a poor enough job of it. If he had any sense, he'd run and leave this foolish little woman to fend for herself. She appeared ill equipped for the rugged life of Alaska. Frail and withdrawn, too thin, too pale, afraid of her own shadow, she didn't even have the sense to feed herself. Easing his shoulders flat against the wall, Braden admitted her reasons didn't matter. She wanted him to stay—he'd stay.

A heavy, black braid rested over her shoulder and reached down long enough to curl in at her feet in front of her drawn-up knees. Her eyes, black as midnight, were pretty, but her lids looked heavy, as if she were near collapse. She had a faint upward slant to her eyes and a dark complexion, lightened by the pallor of a woman who avoided the outdoors, like his Maggie had. Even with her father there to protect her, any fool could see she wouldn't survive an Alaskan winter.

Braden clenched his jaw to keep from telling her just that. Instead, he settled in close and pulled Ian's letter out of the pocket of his heavy, well-lined buckskin coat. Then he began to pick up the conversation they'd been having before Stucky's interruption.

"My brother and his wife live upstream, east of Skaguay." Braden extended the letter to Amy.

She smoothed back the sheet of white paper. Its crinkle sounded civilized against the huffing of the steam engine and the rough voices and clomping feet of the passing men.

Stucky leaned forward, as if trying to sneak a peek at the letter. Braden couldn't imagine why unless he thought they had a treasure map leading straight to a mountain of pure gold. Well, let the man look. He'd soon see it was no such thing.

Amy jerked her chin up, and her huge, dark eyes lit with interest. "This is very close to where my father lives. I will be going this way out of Skaguay. I can guide you."

Braden stifled a sigh. Aye, and he could do all the work so she didn't get her lily white hands dirty and carry her so she didn't stub her toe. Dandy. "Sure, we can travel together. I'll see you to your da's house; then you can get me headed in the right direction for my brother's claim."

Amy smiled, her straight white teeth shining. She looked little all over, more than half a foot shorter than his six feet one, with fine-boned hands, and a stubborn chin under that pretty smile.

For a second, Braden forgot what a burden she would be. But then he remembered Maggie's smile and knew what lay ahead. With a sigh, he swallowed his irritation. Sure, and he'd deliver the lass to her father because it was his Christian duty. And he'd use the burdensome chore as a reminder, every step of the way, that a man paid too great a price for trying to be someone else's strength.

Someone walked her way on the deck in the dark. Amy'd expected him to come. With a twinge of shame, she thought of how weak she'd been since the accident. But despite her shame, pleasure stole into her heart and raised her spirits. She looked up to see Braden with a plate of those awful beans.

He crouched beside her and handed her the plate, then scooted around to block the wind with his broad shoulders.

"You did not need to do this, Mr. Rafferty." Amy scooped the first bite in her mouth, feeling as if she'd been given a gift.

"It isn't right for you to fight your way though that rabble." Braden pulled his hat low over his eyes. "Although, I 'spect I qualify as rabble myself."

Amy grinned as she chewed the bland meal.

His eyes were shaded by his hat, but he must have seen her smile, because one shoulder hunched.

She swallowed. "The wind is kind tonight. You do not have to shelter me. Go ahead and rest your back against the wall."

Turning her attention back to the plate, she ate quietly for a while before he finally slid down to sit on the deck.

As they sat there in the full dark, a long, thin ray of green light climbed in the sky. Amy sighed.

"Sure, and the sunset is giving us quite a painting to watch tonight," Braden said, easing his shoulders and shifting a bit so there was only an inch between them.

The lilt to his voice was pleasant to Amy's ears. "It is not the sunset. That is past. Rather, it is *gis'óok*."

"What?" Braden lifted his hat with his thumb.

"Uh, I mean it is the northern lights, a miraculous moving night sky." Feeling as though she were a liar, Amy didn't explain the native words she'd learned from her mother's people. She knew Braden wouldn't care that she was of another nationality than he. Or did she? Father had seemed so sure her Tlingit and Russian blood would set her apart. Being set apart from the gold-seeking madmen would be glorious. She clenched her jaw to keep from speaking about the Tlingit legends surrounding the gis'óok.

Braden sat up straight. "I've heard of these lights. This is the first night I've come out on deck after dark. It seems like the night drives a man to bed. But I saw you'd missed the meal again, so I came up here lookin' for you."

Amy turned away from the growing light show and smiled. "Thank you."

He tipped his hat at the sky. "That's the northern lights, heh?"

"It is said that you can see them in Seattle, but where I lived in the city there were streetlights—and many children to put to bed at the time I would normally gaze at the sky."

"Where's that?"

"The Child of God Mission." A streak of red slowly lifted alongside the green. "Ah, God hangs a curtain of crimson beside the green tonight. Far more often it is shades of green and white. The color of flame is a rare gift."

Braden stiffened a bit, and Amy wondered if she'd said something wrong. She chose to be still rather than make it worse.

"So you think God goes to the bother of giving us pretty colors in the night sky, do you?"

Amy nearly flinched at his bitterness. Unsure how to answer, she silently watched the colors climb and fade, new ones following old, each a different color, some bright, some so faint they were barely visible.

The lights soothed her soul. At last, into the glorious, colorful darkness, Amy said, "I think God set the world into motion. He made the dark and the light, the rain and the clear sky. I believe in Jesus to protect my soul, but I think God expects me to use the intelligence He gave me to protect my life. He lets the world work as it would, and He gives us the sense and strength to survive in it."

"Or not survive."

"I cannot argue with what you say. There was no one stronger than my mother. No one more equipped to handle the rugged land and more wise in its ways. And still, she fell on a narrow trail crossing one of her beloved mountains and broke her leg. She, who had never been sick, caught the fever and died. So yes, some don't survive."

"How long ago did she die?"

Amy turned and saw that Braden watched her, not the sky. "I was twelve summers. I wanted to stay and care for my father and stay in my land. But Papa would not hear of it. He needed to be gone for long weeks in the winter, running his trap lines, collecting the furs that supported us. He said the loneliness of our remote cabin would drive me mad—if it did not kill me."

Braden nodded. "Your father sounds like a wise man."

"He said it was the most painful thing he had ever lived through save the death of my mother. At the time, I only saw it as losing the only person alive whom I loved." Amy looked away from Braden to watch the sky and hide tears. "If my grandfather had still lived, he would have come. Together, we might have been able to convince Papa to let me stay. But Grandfather had died by then. When I left, I felt torn away from life as surely as if my heart had been ripped out of my chest."

Silence settled, and Amy decided Braden would say no more to her.

Just as she'd have turned away to watch the sky, he said, "I'm sorry. I'm so sorry that happened to you, Amy."

The mystical lights rained down from above. Their eyes met. An eternity stretched between them.

Braden leaned toward her for one confusing, exciting moment. A feeling Amy didn't understand stirred in her chest. Then he jerked back, his expression suddenly as cold as the icebergs that lined the passage through which they traveled.

Braden turned away, his shoulder hitting the wall behind them with a dull thud. Amy didn't know what to say or do.

Wait on the Lord.

This once, the whisper touched her, and she savored the closeness to God, glad that she wasn't completely alone in the world. Braden by her side, so distant and quiet, reminded her of just how alone she was. She turned back to her plate and finished the beans quickly, ignoring the spectacular night sky, dim compared to the rainbow of pain arcing across her heart.

The moment Amy had cleaned her plate, Braden took it from her and rose. "I'll find you here in the morning, then." He walked away quickly, leaving her so alone that the deck took on a menacing feel.

Sitting in her dark, lonely place, she felt the push of fear telling her to go in where there were people. For once, the echoes of God's guidance weren't urging her to wait.

She heard a muffled footfall in the direction opposite of the one Braden had gone. Instinct drove her to her feet. Her ribs protested the sudden movement, but she didn't tarry. She scurried down to the putrid little cabin full of bunks stacked three high, a room she shared with so many others. For once, instead of smothering her, the close quarters offered protection.

Unable to sleep because of the early hour, Amy was glad the cabin window stood open, offering a bit of fresh air that only partially dispelled the miasma of sickness and filth. She watched out that tiny open circle and enjoyed the curtain of light until she fell into a fitful sleep. Footfalls chased her in her dreams, a pursuit that lasted throughout the night.

Faithfully, Braden brought Amy three meals a day, and they ate together on the cold deck. Amy had never spent time with a young man before, and she found she enjoyed visiting with him. They talked of many things, though she noticed he never spoke of his past.

By the time the *Northward* arrived in Skaguay, Amy's ribs didn't stab her quite as often. Fatigue still plagued her. *Why didn't I stay at the mission and heal for a few more weeks?*

She'd have been welcome. She even knew God wanted her to take time to rest. But that knowledge hadn't seemed important. Home would renew her strength, although getting there might well kill her. She had no strength yet, and a long journey lay ahead of her.

The Skaguay dock, from which she'd departed nearly six years ago, shocked her. The sleepy little village of a dozen houses and more dogs than people had turned into a boomtown. Ships lined the narrow pier. The creak of ropes and pulleys off-loading supplies from various vessels blotted out the serene voice of the wilderness. Skaguay loomed ahead of her like an ugly sore on the pristine land.

Amy leaned on the railing along with as many stampeders as could fight their way forward. Ignoring the unwashed bodies and rough voices that surrounded her, she fought back tears at the destruction of her beautiful Alaska.

She thought of her mother. Harmony had existed between Yéil Simonovich and the wilderness. Alaska, a land of abundant food and fuel, its beauty stretching so high and wide it seemed eternal, looked like an extension of heaven. The territory stretched in all directions so vast Amy had believed everyone could come and there would still be room for more.

She was wrong. It was ruined.

Touching a hand to her trembling lips, Amy watched in silence as the *Northward* inched its way to the dock. The stampeders surged forward, jostling Amy, making her grateful for her nearly healed ribs. A heavy hand seemed to settle on her back, although she felt certain the touch wasn't personal. For an instant, Amy remembered that busy Seattle street and the careless shoving hands accompanied by cruel laughter that had sent her tumbling into the path of a carriage.

Amy grabbed the waist-high railing. A fall over the side would be fatal with the distance to plummet and the heavy drag of the *Northward* pulling water beneath it as it inched along. Amy turned sideways, determined to force her way back from the rail.

She looked up into the eyes of a man she'd caught watching her from a distance several times. That alone didn't surprise her. A lot of men watched her. They watched all the women. But this one's eyes had been sharper than most, with something in them different than that male gleam a woman came to recognize.

Had he been the one pushing on her? A shudder began deep inside as she thought of the long fall to certain death.

"Miss Simons?" The man touched the brim of his slouching brown hat. It might have been a cowboy hat at one time, but it had been battered until it sagged over his ears and only curved in the crown because his head held it in place. He seemed to be shoved forward at the mercy of the pack.

He had a saddlebag over one shoulder with a flat seining pan clattering softly against a pick anytime the ship bobbed or the shifting mass of humanity bumped him.

Keeping a firm grip on the railing, she said, "Yes?" She didn't like him knowing her name, although she imagined few secrets remained about her after all this time aboard ship. Her wariness didn't ease just because he had a few manners.

"My name is Thompson, Miss Simons, Darnell Thompson. I couldn't help overhearing you discuss your journey with Braden Rafferty." The man smiled, but to Amy his expression seemed calculating.

He shrugged under his shearling coat. "I'm headed in much the same direction myself. I wondered if I might travel along with you once we leave the ship."

Amy couldn't bring herself to casually include him. "Whether we travel the same trail or not is surely not my decision."

The man watched her. Looking around for a long moment, his eyes focused over her shoulder as if he saw someone he knew. He gave one firm nod. "Fair enough. More men on a trail makes for safe passage. I'll discuss it with Rafferty."

"You do that." Amy stared into the man's eyes. They were a strange hazel color, brown flecked with gold. The mission teacher had taught her to be wary of men, and though she'd made an exception for Braden, this man didn't inspire such trust.

Mr. Thompson tugged on his much-maligned hat and left her by the railing. Although he'd looked past Amy's shoulder at someone or something, he turned and went in the opposite direction. Seconds later, Stucky appeared at her back.

Amy clenched her jaw, preparing to use all the cool manners she'd learned from the missionaries. Before she had to bear the miner's questions, Braden approached. Amy glanced around, expecting Thompson to come up again and invite himself on the trail. He'd melted into the crowd even though moving through this mob seemed nearly impossible.

She tried to spot Thompson so she could point him out to Braden.

He was gone.

Chapter 4

He was gone!

Braden pushed roughly past the men that separated him from Amy. Complaints and return shoves didn't stop him. Where had that man gone? Their eyes had met for just a second, and Braden hadn't liked what he'd seen.

As Braden reached Amy's side, he breathed more easily. "One of the crew members said we should be able to hop off this crate in an hour. Standing by the railing won't get you off a second faster." Without mentioning the man who'd taken off, Braden caught her arm.

Now past the grumbling men, Braden noticed that worthless Barnabas Stucky standing at Amy's elbow—another overly interested miner.

Amy's eyes widened at his firm grip, but Braden felt an urgent need to get her out of this crush. He nodded at Stucky, then parted the throng of stampeders, dragging Amy away from the edge. Since the men were all trying to get closer to the railing, they let Braden pass with little trouble.

Braden worked his way around the ship. The side not facing port was nearly deserted, and he leaned against the wall. He'd seen that Amy had her meals here every morning, noon, and night since that first time he'd brought her food. The ship served no breakfast this morning because the crew had been occupied since before dawn with navigating the Skaguay port. But they'd dock early so they'd find a meal on shore.

Disgusted with Amy's lack of survival skills, Braden wondered if she'd have even lived through the trip without his help. He leaned against the wooden walls of the wheelhouse and crossed his arms. "We'll just wait here until the captain tells us to disembark."

"Thank you for helping me through that mob." Amy spoke quietly as she always did. Her voice carried a note of calm, a husky sweet sound that soothed his battered heart. She leaned beside him, one arm wrapped around her chest, staring straight forward at the mountains across the bay from Skaguay.

Through the entire voyage she favored her side, although in their long days together on the boat, she'd never mentioned being hurt. Of course, Braden hadn't talked about himself much, either. They'd discussed the trek to Ian's house and the rough voyage and the conditions Braden could expect in Alaska, but he'd never so much as said Maggie's name.

Maggie would have shared every trouble. Amy's lack of complaint told Braden she wasn't hurt, just weak, probably stiff and sore from the rugged voyage. She never should have taken this trip.

"Welcome." Braden nodded and stared at the majesty of Alaska looming high over the ship. When the beauty of the mountains had worked its way into his soul, he produced his letter from Ian one more time and discussed the route with Amy until long after the ship had docked and the deck had cleared.

Amy overflowed with ideas for the journey home, and Braden found it easy to trust her.

"I don't trust him." Braden whispered to Amy.

The gaunt, bearded man to whom Amy had led him limped away.

"Why'd you pick this man to haul my supplies?" Braden watched the man, looking more animal than human, scratch his neck as he hobbled along. His long, snarled hair, black and streaked with gray, straggled below a fur hat with dangling ear covers.

"Wily? He has been carting supplies up the river all my life. He will do fine by us." Amy barely glanced at Braden and then followed after the foul-smelling man.

Braden suspected the man had been avoiding baths all his life.

The man snagged his suspenders with his thumbs from where they drooped around his hips and snapped them over his shoulders. Then he stooped over, grabbed a pair of ropes off the ground that were attached to an oddly shaped boat, and began pulling the strange contraption down the bank toward the vast bay that opened on the south side of the settlement of Goose Chase.

Amy got on the uphill side of the thing. It looked like a flat boat wrapped in animal hide. She dropped to her knees in the sand with a groan Braden heard from ten feet away, and began shoving. Braden looked at his sizable stack of supplies, which he'd transported from the ship to Goose Chase by paying an outrageous sum to rent a rickety handcart.

Amy shoved, and Braden decided that even if it meant letting someone steal everything he'd brought for Ian, even his mother's precious mantel clock, he couldn't let Amy do hard labor she was obviously unsuited for.

He moved to her side. "What is this thing?"

Amy looked up from her position on her knees. "It is an *umiak*."

"What?"

"It is a boat called an umiak. It has a wooden frame, and Wily has his covered with walrus hide. It is suited for shallow water and heavy loads."

Braden thought about it and figured if a walrus wasn't waterproof then nothing was. His supplies—six good-sized boxes—would nearly fill it. Good thing Amy didn't seem to have anything beyond the small satchel she slung over her neck and shoulder. Just more evidence of how ill-equipped she was for this journey.

"Let me do that." He dropped on his knees beside her and gave his head a little sideways jerk to get her out of the way.

With a grateful smile, Amy got to her feet and let him take over. Between him and Wily, they had the boat launched in a couple of minutes. Wily pulled the floating umiak down the bay toward Braden's supplies.

Braden and Wily worked in silence loading. Wily looked up at Amy and asked, "Ride, little Amaruq?"

Braden tried to figure out just what he'd heard. *Amaruq?* The man slurred his words like he almost never used his voice, which Braden could believe considering how little he'd spoken so far.

"Until you hit the current." Amy nodded. "Then I'll walk." She climbed in.

Braden noticed the lack of room for him in the umiak. He didn't get a chance to ask where he was supposed to sit before Wily began leading the boat up the bay, away from Goose Chase and civilization.

Amy and Wily were about twenty feet away from him before Braden realized he was walking, no doubt all the way to Ian's camp, over twenty miles away through some of the roughest territory in the world. The steamship had docked early, and they'd walked the miles to Goose Chase as quickly as possible, towing the cart. The trip could be made in one day easily in the normal course of things. Then Braden looked ahead at the big, blue water of the bay. It narrowed in the distance and cut between two mountains that sprang straight up from the water's edge. How were they supposed to walk through that?

A rustling of bushes behind them reminded Braden of the men who had shown interest in accompanying them. It made no sense. The stampeders headed up the Chilkoot Pass toward Dawson's Creek. Why would a gold-hungry miner want to follow them? Braden had turned down an offer of company from Stucky and that sharp-eyed stranger named Thompson, who'd hovered too close to Amy on the boat. Neither had seemed as interested in the gold as they were in Amy.

Braden had done his best to lose them in the horde at the dock, even though they had to tug along the cart Amy had found. They'd headed out of Skaguay, walking down what looked like a game trail to Goose Chase. He'd thought they'd slipped away unnoticed. Now those rustling bushes made him wonder.

Should he investigate? He studied the undergrowth then looked forward toward the mountain Wily seemed determined to walk over. Braden forgot the bushes and trudged forward, filled with dread.

Filled with wonder, Amy leaned forward, so eager to get through the bay and into the narrow waters of the Skaguay River that she could barely stay seated. Hearing her Tlingit name for the first time in years renewed her spirit. She'd known Wily from her earliest memory.

The beauty was so profound Amy wondered if God had created Alaska as a drink for a thirsty soul. She longed to get out of Wily's slow-moving umiak and march away from this easy water passage and into her wilderness. She stayed put, of course. She was in a hurry to get to Papa. Now wasn't the time to reacquaint herself with her magnificent home. And she knew there'd be no riding when Wily's umiak started scraping along the bottom of the river. They'd need every hand on the ropes. With her ribs still aching, she did the practical thing and saved her energy. Alaska, by dint of trying to kill everyone who came here, taught a person to be practical.

Amy looked at the contents of the umiak behind her and wondered what pile of impractical frippery Braden Rafferty hauled in those crates. It was just more evidence of how ill-equipped he was for this journey.

Amy had a single change of clothes, her knife, a cloth book of needles, and a small cast-iron skillet. The indulgence of the skillet nearly shamed her, and Amy hoped Wily never found out about it. He'd shake his head as he had so many times when, as a child, she'd shown fascination with the things Wily hauled. He didn't talk much, but he'd let her know she'd gone soft.

She could easily enough create a pan out of a soaked slab of bark from a cedar tree. Her mother had raised her right. The cedar even added a nice flavor. But a skillet worked better and took less tending. With her sore ribs and aching muscles, she'd been inclined to spoil herself. When she'd sold off her things to pay for the trip home, she found a few coins to spare for a frying pan in case she ended up camping along the trail. But there'd be no camping. Because of the early docking of the ship, she'd be home in a single day.

Of course, some of Braden's things would be supplies. And Amy wasn't innocent of indulging her papa. She'd sent a bit of sugar and a few pounds of flour to him every spring, even though he only asked for traps or tools.

Amy sighed, wondering where Papa had gotten to. Her stomach twisted. Why hadn't he written? He was an old man by her Tlingit people's standards, nearly forty. He might not be tough enough to tackle Alaskan winters and survive all this territory threw at him. She wished suddenly that she'd had the money to bring her papa a few treats. Perhaps she shouldn't fault Braden for toting foolish things over a mountain.

"Can I help pull?" Braden's voice turned her to face the shore. He held out a hand for one of the two ropes Wily had slung over his shoulder. Wordlessly, Wily handed one over. She watched Braden loop the rope until it was a bit shorter. Braden fell in, following a few steps behind Wily. The going was easy now, but the terrain ahead would be rough.

She couldn't wait to get into the mountains. As she drank in their beauty, she realized that away from these mountains she'd only been half alive.

This mountain wanted him dead.

Braden's foot slipped off a rock, and he sank to his ankle in the icy river. The weather was mild, but the water still held the frigidity of winter within it. Wily had given him a pair of waterproof boots. Amy told him they were made of walrus intestines so his feet stayed dry—bitterly cold, but dry. The spring thaw allowed them to pass, but ice patches still lined the river, and in places, the umiak had to break through a thin sheet of stubborn spring ice. They'd been going at a forced march since they docked at Skaguay this morning, and Amy had assured him he'd sleep at Ian's tonight.

Enjoying the motion that stretched his muscles, long inactive on the boat, wouldn't have been so bad if his feet weren't frozen lumps.

"Papa's cabin is just ahead." Amy eased the rope off her shoulder and straightened.

Braden watched her for signs of collapse. She'd worked hard once the water got shallow and they'd crossed to the other side of the river, throwing her shoulder into the rope. Braden had protested, sure Amy would collapse within a mile, but Wily and Amy overruled him. Wily handed over the rope to Amy then waded behind the umiak, pushing it over the sand when it bottomed out. Braden had insisted on taking the lead rope, pulling for all he was worth to keep Amy's work to a minimum.

They'd started as quickly as they could get off the ship and get to Goose Chase and had been dragging this blasted umiak—or whatever Amy called it—for hours.

Braden's shoulder ached. The fabric of his shirt was tattered. He'd shed his coat long ago.

Amy sighed so loudly Braden stopped. He looked back to see if she was in danger and saw a huge grin on her normally somber face. Her white teeth flashed.

"We are here." She faced the woods.

"Your father's cabin is near here?" Braden looked at the steeply pitched, heavily wooded area. Amy was visibly exhausted. Even smiling, she had dark circles under her eyes, and despite the brisk spring air, her face had an unnatural pallor.

"No, it *is* here." Amy pointed into the forest. Suddenly, it popped out at him. A cabin sat about one hundred feet back into the woods. The place blended completely with the rough-and-tumble woods.

Braden noticed they were out of the wind and no snow lay on the ground around the cabin. A shaft of sunlight shone down through a gap and shared its generous warmth with the house. A man wise in the ways of the wilderness had chosen this spot. With a sigh of relief, Braden knew that despite the odd, tumbled-down look of the cabin, the man inside possessed wood smarts and would keep his daughter safe.

Braden looked at Amy. She glowed.

"Let's go say hello. Then you can point me toward my brother's place."

Amy nodded, but then her eyes narrowed, and the bright smile faded from her face.

"Your brother's on up the stream a piece." Wily's voice sounded farther away than it should be. "I'm gonna keep headin' up."

Braden heard the faint scrape of the bottom of the umiak on the rocky river bottom and turned to see Wily moving along.

"Something is wrong." Amy strode toward the cabin.

As Braden hurried after her, he realized that there was more to this house than he'd first thought. A second room had been built on at an angle. The roof sloped sharply upward, most likely to keep the snow from piling up, but it looked sizable enough for a loft.

Dark furs hung on the front, a long one that must cover the front door and two smaller ones that could only be windows. Patches of cedar bark and branches made it resemble a stack of trees blown into a pile by the wind.

"I can see something's wrong. It's been damaged." Braden decided he'd help with the repairs.

"No, it always looks like this."

"The windows have always been broken out?"

"No, we have always covered the windows with furs." Amy arched an eyebrow at him as if he'd said something ridiculous. "Where would a person get glass?" She hurried on.

Braden stayed at her side. "Then what's wrong with the place?" By the look on her face, he knew whatever bothered her was serious.

"There is smoke coming out of the chimney." Amy's breath sounded labored as she quickened her pace.

That's a silly reason to get so upset. "Maybe your da needed to heat the place up. Maybe he's cooking."

"Papa? Need heat or cook inside? This late in the spring?" Amy began running toward the house.

Chapter 5

The journey up river had almost finished Amy. She'd used every ounce of her strength, tapping deep inside for the courage to go on, knowing she would soon rest in Papa's house.

As she rushed toward her home, a whisper on the wind, one she didn't care to heed, told her to wait on the Lord. She'd heard this ever since she'd awakened after the accident in Seattle, determined to leave the city, but she'd ignored it. Yes, God might be trying to make things easy for her, but she didn't need easy. She could take care of herself.

Her legs wobbled as she forced them forward. Her ribs punished her for running. She clutched them to quiet the pain and held herself erect by sheer will. It shamed her to rely on someone else. She should have been able to take care of herself.

Shaking off her fear, Amy reached for the grizzly pelt that kept the wind out of the cracks in the door.

She hesitated, remembering her manners learned from the McGraws. It was home; she should just go on in. But she'd been gone so long. She stood on the slab of gray rock centered in front of the door and knocked, her fist muffled by the bear skin and the rugged door frame. No one came to the door, and her jaw tightened with impatience as the moment stretched. Why had Papa stopped writing? Why had he worried her like this for so long?

"Amy, maybe we should—"

"Should what, Braden?" She whirled to face him. "I am home. This is the end of my journey. There is nowhere else for me to go."

No one answered her knock on the log framing the door, so she pulled back the pelt and shoved on the door. It was firmly latched. Papa hadn't even had a latch on the door while she lived here!

Her fear was too much to face, so she grabbed hold of a flicker of annoyance and turned it to anger. Pounding on the door, she glanced up at the smoking chimney. Someone was here but not Papa. He wouldn't abide stifling smoke when he could breathe the pure Alaskan air.

If he was here, he must be sick. If Papa couldn't come to the door, then she'd beat the door down and go in uninvited.

"Papa, it is Amy! Open this door!" She hammered with the side of her fist on the saplings that had been lashed together into a tidy door, heavy enough to keep out the winter wind and a pack of hungry wolves.

Suddenly it flew open. Braden caught her before she fell into the arms of a stranger. The man who stood before her was certainly not her father.

"I dunno an Amy. Beat it!"

The door began to swing shut. Amy threw herself forward and blocked it open. Her ribs hurt from the impact. On a gasp of pain, her vision blurred. "What are you doing here? Where is my father?"

The man's eyes narrowed, lost in a full beard and coarse, knotted hair. He sneered at her. Teeth bared green and broken. "No father in this place. Now git!"

Amy spoke quickly. "My papa, Petro. . .Peter Simons, owns this cabin. Tell me where he is."

The man quit sneering. He quit trying to get his door shut. His eyes were suddenly cold, and he studied her intently. A vile smell rolled off the man and out of the cabin. When Amy had lived here, the cabin had a clean, woodsy aroma.

"No need to get riled, mister." Braden shifted slightly so his shoulder blocked the man who had invaded Amy's home.

The man's conniving eyes slid toward Braden, and with a little clutch of her heart, Amy knew only Braden's presence kept her safe. That whispering voice had warned her. God knew of the danger. But Braden *was* here, although it galled her that she needed him.

"Pete Simons din't have no kin. He lived alone long'ez I knew him. And he never made no mention of any daughter. No woman is gonna come in here layin' claim to what's rightfully mine."

"Yours?" Amy's temper built until she was too upset to be afraid. "That is a lie! It belongs to Peter Simons."

"It did 'til he sold it to me."

Amy gasped. "Papa sold the cabin?"

"Sure as shootin' he did. Got me a bill of sale'n ever'thin'." The man looked her up and down in a way that made her skin crawl. "An' I knew Pete for years. Never heard him talk of a daughter. Who put you up to makin' a claim to my place?"

Her father loved this cabin. He wouldn't have sold it, because he didn't see it as belonging to him. Her father had been deeded this place by an old Russian friend. Papa loved his rugged life and carved out a home here. No bill of sale would convince her differently.

Then Amy thought past all her anger. "Where is my father? If he sold you the cabin, then he must have moved on somewhere else. Tell me where he is."

The man crossed his arms. "You expect me to believe you're Pete's daughter 'n you don't know he's dead?"

Amy gasped. "No! No, I do not believe you. I would have heard!"

Amy backed away from the awful words. Braden slipped a strong arm around her waist.

"I don't b'lieve you're his daughter. You're on my property, and I want you off. The next time you hammer on my door, I won't come unarmed." The man glanced again at Braden then turned his cruel gaze on her.

Amy shuddered to think what might have happened if she'd come here alone.

The man gave her one last wild glare and then stepped back and slammed the door in her face.

A cry ripped out of Amy's throat, and she launched herself at the door. Braden caught her around the waist and swung her away.

"Stop. We have to get out of here. You heard what he said about a gun. Let's go. I'm sorry about your da, but you can't stay here."

Amy looked up at Braden and met his sad eyes. She'd known he carried a weight, though he'd carefully avoided talking about anything personal. His sadness came from grief. She recognized it because it echoed everything she felt.

"You have lost someone, too," she whispered.

Braden's eyes darkened as if a cloud had gone over the sun and turned the blue sky gray.

He held her gaze silently; then at last, as if it hurt to move his head, he nodded.

She had no one in the world who cared if she lived or died. Nowhere in the world to call home.

"Papa." Her knees buckled, the world swirled around, and her vision faded to black.

Braden caught Amy as she collapsed, and swung her into his arms. He held her close, saw the utter whiteness of her skin. The frail woman weighed next to nothing, so he lifted her a bit higher in his arms.

"You're my strength, Braden."

His strength hadn't been enough for Maggie. Now, without any wish to provide it, he'd have to be the strength for Amy. He turned back toward the river. Ahead, he saw Wily disappear around a curve in the ever-narrowing water. The days were nearly split twelve hours of dark, twelve hours of light this time of year. It was just past noon, the sun high in the sky. They had miles to go, and darkness would catch them soon enough.

Alaska, the land of the midnight sun. What had he been thinking to come here?

Ian expected him. There'd been time to write, assuming a letter got out this far, but no time to get a response. Braden hadn't left immediately after Maggie died. He couldn't abandon his father that way, even though every day spent in the house where he and Maggie had lived with his parents and little sister was pure torture. Braden had stayed three months, finishing spring work; then he'd walked away before he could fail anyone else. Deep inside, he knew walking away added to his failures.

When he announced his plans to live in Alaska, his mother cried and scolded. Da turned quiet and spent a lot of time in the barn. His sister, Fiona, harangued him with her quick Irish tongue. Still, he'd left. Staying hurt too badly.

When he rounded the river bend, he saw Wily ahead, pulling his umiak as if it were a well-trained dog. The river flowed slightly deeper here. Braden couldn't see any rocks through the crystal clear water. He could ask Wily to let Amy ride, but he wouldn't. As much as he resented the burden she'd added to his life, her grief was too new. Only a monster would expect her to endure it alone.

Just for today, he'd be her strength.

"Your brother's house is up that slope."

Braden's head came up and followed the direction indicated by Wily's gnarled finger.

He'd made it. They'd been walking for nearly twenty hours now, with only the most meager moments to rest. But they were here at last. Wily had taken him nearly to his brother's back door.

In the full moonlight, Braden made out a cabin barely outlined against the trees.

"I'll see to the load. You get the little one out of the night air." Wily had smeared some flat, strong-smelling leaves on his skin and insisted Braden do the same and also use it to protect Amy. Though the swarm of bugs didn't bite, they buzzed around Braden until the air was thick with them.

Amy, her faint changing to a more natural slumber, had slept the afternoon and evening away in Braden's arms.

"Thanks. Come on up to the house for the night."

Wily shook his head. "Downstream's a sight faster'n up. I'll sleep at home tonight." Then the grizzled old man had given Amy a worried look. "Uh, mister, I'm right sorry I didn't warn Amaruq about her pa. I thought she knew. I'm never one to talk out of turn. But I'd a spared her that if'n I'd a known she 'spected to find her father to home."

With a shake of his head, Wily turned and began unloading the umiak.

Amaruq? What did that mean? A native word of affection for Amy, most likely. Braden turned toward Ian's house. He followed a path that climbed and twisted into the forest. Hoping Amy's extended unconsciousness came from simple exhaustion and shock and not something more serious, he reached Ian's door. "Ian, open up!"

A shout of joy sounded from inside the cabin. "Merry! He's here!"

The door flew open. "Braden, it's great to—" Ian, standing there in red flannel long johns, quit yelling. His expression faded from pure happiness to worry as he looked at Amy. Then he slung his arms around Braden awkwardly, trying not to squish Amy, but as if he couldn't contain his need to make contact.

"It's so great to see you. What happened? Who is she?"

Before Braden could speak, a pretty brunette in a hastily donned blue gingham housedress came dashing up from behind Ian. Ian stepped back just inches from Braden as if he couldn't bear to be farther away. A furrow cut through Ian's brow.

"You look done in, Braden. Let me take her." Ian reached for Amy, but Braden shook his head and angled away from Ian.

"Thanks, but I'm fine. I'll take her the rest of the way." Empty arms seemed like an extension of an empty life, and Braden couldn't face letting go right now. Bleakness washed over him.

" 'Tis a long walk from Skaguay." Ian stepped back a bit and laid a hand on Braden's shoulder.

Braden nodded. "I've left some supplies on the shore."

"This is Meredith." Ian tipped his head at his pretty, brown-haired wife. Ian's smile glowed with affection. Jealous pain slashed through Braden's heart.

Meredith nodded with a welcoming smile. "You must be exhausted. Is the woman hurt? Does she need medical care?"

Braden shook his head. "This is Amy Simons. She planned to return to her father's home. Peter Simons owns a cabin a few miles down river."

Ian nodded. "Knew him. He was an old trapper who's been here longer'n most anyone except the Eskimos. Never heard tell he had a daughter, though. Of course, he didn't talk much. Rumor had it he died last winter."

"Amy just found out."

"Let's get her inside. We can talk." Ian stopped and turned toward the river. "Say, is there coffee in those supplies?"

"We got one letter from you this year. Ma got so excited she sent everything you asked for and more. Let me lay Amy down. Then I'll see to it."

"You've got to be hungry." Ian nodded toward the house. "Let's get Amy to bed. Then you can eat while I holler for Tucker to help haul in the goods."

Braden knew of Meredith's twin, who had staked a claim nearby. "I didn't come here to make more work for you, Ian."

"If there's coffee in that pack you brought, I'll carry *you* down to the riverside, dancing all the way."

Braden scoffed. "That I'd like to see, little brother."

Grinning, Ian said, "I hardly qualify as your *little* brother anymore."

Braden noticed how broad Ian stretched across the shoulders these days. That kind of muscle came from long days swinging a pick for gold and an ax for wood. Braden wanted that kind of work. He wanted exhaustion that made him forget the torment of his memories.

Braden followed his brother into a tiny bedroom and lay Amy on the rumpled sheets. Ian and Meredith had obviously been long asleep when he arrived. Meredith pushed past him as he let his burden go with surprising reluctance.

Meredith busied herself fretting over Amy. He saw strength in Meredith's slim shoulders. She'd make a fine partner.

He couldn't stop his mind from turning to Maggie and all her frailties and complaints about the rugged life. The guilt hit him with an edge as keen as an ax. Feeling as if he were betraying her memory, Braden decided that tomorrow he'd start earning his keep. He wouldn't be a burden to his brother. He wouldn't.

Chapter 6

Amy's eyes flickered open. She stared at the ceiling overhead and wondered where she was. A noise made her turn her head, and she saw woodlands through an open window. The cool, crisp air and the sharp, sweet smell of cedar cleared her head. Alaska. Home.

Papa.

The memory hit her hard. A cry of pain nearly erupted from her throat. She choked it back, and it felt as if she swallowed jagged stones.

She'd never see her father again.

Fighting tears, she pushed the thick bearskin cover aside. The room felt sharply cold in the spring morning, but she'd been comfortable beneath the heavy fur. As she moved, her muscles protested.

Before she could sit up, the door opened, and a young woman entered.

"I thought I heard you moving in here." The pretty, dark-haired lady carried a tray. Amy could see a plate piled high with eggs, most likely duck eggs this time of year. Someone who knew the woods could feast in the spring. The plate had a slab of meat on it, too. Amy smelled mutton. If she'd been home, her father would have gone fishing early and brought in fresh salmon for breakfast.

Her eyes spilled over.

The woman set the tray down on a short table and dropped onto the bed beside Amy. "I'm Meredith, Braden's sister-in-law. Braden told us you just found out your father died. I'm so sorry, Amy." The woman wrapped her arms around Amy's shoulders and pulled her close.

Braden had talked about his brother and his new wife. The future had been safe to discuss; it was the past he'd avoided. Amy couldn't resist the warm arms. She held on tight and cried her eyes out.

When the storm had spent itself, Meredith eased Amy away.

Amy saw tears on the kind woman's face.

"I'm so sorry about your father." Meredith drew a square of cloth from her apron pocket. She handed it to Amy, then dried her own eyes on her apron. "I know we can't begin to take the place of your father, but please stay with us. I was so thrilled to see Braden bring a woman yesterday, I nearly cried at the sight of you. I'm so lonely for a woman's company, I told Ian I was about to head out for Seattle to kidnap a woman off the street, bring her here, and force her to talk to me." Meredith smiled. "You've saved me a lot of trouble."

Amy burst out laughing. Somehow the laughter was almost as wrenching as the tears. "You mean I'm a prisoner?"

"Don't even think of trying to escape. I'm a desperate woman."

Amy smiled. "So, you just survived your first Alaskan winter, then?"

Meredith's eyes widened into perfect circles. "It's dark for six months!"

Amy felt the smile hold, which shocked her when her heart hurt so badly. She couldn't remember ever being this fond of someone on so short an acquaintance. "I lived in Alaska until the age of twelve when my mother died. I noticed the long winters."

"You'd better eat your breakfast. You're going to need plenty of strength to sit and listen to me talk for the next six weeks." Meredith reached for the tray and slid it in front of Amy. Arching her eyebrows, she said, "Make it six months."

"I don't need breakfast in bed. I'll come out to the kitchen." Amy tried to set the tray aside.

"No, that'll take too long. You just start eating. I'll tell you about my life. When you're done eating, it will be your turn. It all started when I came up here to live with my twin brother, Tucker."

Amy enjoyed every bite of the breakfast. She'd forgotten the special flavor of duck eggs. The bighorn sheep reminded her that her father had shot and smoked one every year, but the tough, stringy, savory meat was a treat, not something to be eaten every day. They mainly ate salmon, halibut, seal, and even an occasional bit of whale when Amy's Tlingit relatives came past on their way north after a successful sea hunt.

They'd eaten the meat of whatever he trapped for fur, if possible. Mother made muskrat into a tasty stew combined with the greens and roots she'd coax out of the cold Alaskan dirt.

Amy would have had lapses into grief if Meredith hadn't chattered on while Amy ate, talking about her family and pointing out the window she'd had Ian add to the room so that they could get better air movement. Amy knew from Meredith's kind expression that the lady was deliberately putting herself out to be comforting.

When Amy finished her meal, Meredith said, "I've been heating water so you can have a warm bath."

Amy sat forward so eagerly she nearly fell out of bed. "Warm water?"

"Yes, and plenty of it. There's wood to burn and water to heat if nothing else. Especially now that spring is here and we don't need to burn constantly just to keep the bitter cold at bay."

"Thank you. You shouldn't have. I could have bathed in the river." Amy'd done it many times and learned to think of the icy water as invigorating. Still, a warm bath was one of the things she'd liked best about Seattle.

Meredith shuddered. "Many's the time I've bathed in the river. You'll have to do it, too. But not this first time—not when you're so exhausted from the trip and drained from the awful news."

The mention of her father twisted Amy's wounded heart. "Is Braden here?" She saw the curious gleam in Meredith's eyes and wished she'd held her tongue.

"Yes, he's staying with us, of course. He slept nearly as long and hard as you did. But he's already up and going strong. He's like his brother and mine when it comes to work. Our lives will be much easier with three men to do the heavy chores. It kept Tucker and Ian hopping to heat both cabins."

"You'll meet Tucker at dinner." Another gleam came into Meredith's eyes.

Amy could imagine what Meredith was thinking this time. The teachers at the mission had tried to persuade Amy to court. But she'd always planned to return to Alaska. No sense attaching herself to some man who might not want to come.

"I know you'll like my brother. We. . ."

Settling back a bit until Meredith wound down again, Amy enjoyed the talk of Meredith's family. A movement drew her attention, and she saw Braden standing in the open door, holding a steaming bucket in one hand and a large wooden tub in the other.

Amy reached quickly to tug on Meredith's sleeve. Meredith looked at Amy then turned to the door.

Rising from the bed, she said, "Bring it in, Braden. Don't let it cool.

Amy waited until she stood alone in her room then quickly prepared for her bath. She longed to soak her aching muscles, but there was too much to do for her to linger. She'd already wasted a good part of the day in bed. She could see by thesunlight climbing the bedroom wall through the window that she'd slept half the morning away. She finished her tub bath in mere minutes even with taking the time to unbraid her hair and wash it with the bit of soap Meredith had left.

Amy combed and braided her hair while it was still wet. She pulled her other dress out of her satchel and slipped it on, then washed out her clothes and draped them on nails on the wall. Then she stepped out to the main room to see if she could be of use.

The first thing Amy noticed was a lovely window in the opposite wall. Someone had taken time and love to create it. A glass window was hard to come by in Alaska because glass was so fragile. But this window had been made with bottles of different colors. A cross had been fashioned from deep brown bottles in the center of it. Amy had already sensed Meredith had God in the center of her life, and this window just made it all the more certain from whom this family drew its strength.

The front door stood wide open, and Meredith worked outside, leaning over a table.

Amy wanted to go to Braden and thank him for getting her here yesterday. She couldn't remember anything after she left her father's house. Braden had stepped in, as he had the whole trip, and taken care of her. She felt shy to talk to him for some reason, so she took a step toward Meredith and froze.

For the first time, she noticed the crates Braden had brought up the river with him. They were piled high throughout the cabin. Amy's eyes widened at the things that draped out of the boxes and sat here and there on the floor.

Pure garbage.

A white and gold china figurine of a fine lady, her hair piled high on her head, holding out her long skirts as if to curtsy. Bolts of cloth—pretty but lightweight and impractical. A set of glass dishes. Only a few plates and cups survived intact.

A mantel clock, large and ornate. Amy shook her head. The clock ticked away on the roughly built kitchen table that took up half the room. But what did time matter in Alaska? Time was simple: dark and light, winter and not winter. Besides, the Raffertys didn't have a mantel. She remembered the Simonovich cabin did. The beautiful mantel in her father's cabin had been carved by her grandfather. The contents of its hidden drawer might prove that her father hadn't sold the cabin.

She had to go back. She had to open that secret drawer. If her father had sold the cabin, the deed would be signed over to the new owner. If the deed still lay hidden in that drawer, then the man had taken the cabin and perhaps even killed her father.

A wave of grief stopped her from charging outside and heading straight for her father's house. She wasn't even sure how much farther they'd come upstream, although she had no doubt she'd find her way home without trouble. She needed to wait until she'd regained her strength, and she needed to repay the Raffertys for their kindness.

Amy walked outside in the spring warmth and sunlight, savoring the feel of a cool breeze against her damp hair. She noticed Braden splitting logs and approached Meredith. "Why is Braden doing that, Meredith?"

Meredith, standing over a cobbled-together table and slicing sheep steaks, straightened. "Call me Merry, please. He's chopping wood." Meredith smiled. "Who knows why? Ian told him to pick it up off the ground, but Braden seems determined to do it the hard way."

Amy glanced at the tidy stone fireplace on the side of the cabin. "What he's splitting is too fresh. If he picks up windfall branches, they're already cured. The fresh wood smokes."

Meredith, her hands covered in blood from her carving, looked a little pale, but she smiled. "We told him all that. He just said he needed to work off some energy, and it'd be cured by winter. Which is true. Ian told me to leave him to it. I think it has something to do with Maggie. He must need to keep busy."

"Who is Maggie?"

Meredith's eyes widened. "I thought you'd traveled here together. He said he met you on the ship."

"We did."

"He never told you that his wife died three months ago, giving birth to their first child?"

Amy's grief, fresh and deep, swept over her. She remembered that moment when Braden had faced her at Papa's cabin. She'd known he mourned someone. Tears burned her eyes. "No, he never told me."

Meredith shook her head. "I'm sorry to have spoken of it. You're thinking of your father now; I can see."

There was no time to spare for tears. Amy dashed to wipe them away then straightened her spine and turned to the day's chores. "Why are you having sheep again? It's tough, and they're heavy to cart home. The skins are nice, but I prefer bearskin or sealskin." Amy clamped her mouth shut, realizing she sounded rude. She'd always had trouble not speaking her mind.

Meredith calmly turned to a pail of water and washed her hands; then she took off her bloody apron and tossed it over a tree stump that stood next to her makeshift table. Without warning, she whirled around, launched herself the few feet separating her from Amy, and hugged her.

Amy staggered back. Her healing ribs protested, but she caught Meredith and hugged her back. "What is it?"

Amy looked over Meredith's shoulder and saw Braden pause in his chopping to look at them and arch an eyebrow. Amy shrugged.

Whispering, Meredith said, "I'm so sick of mutton I could die!" Her voice broke. Amy felt Meredith's shoulders shudder, and tears dripped onto her neck. Amy controlled the urge to smile.

Braden shook his head and disappeared into the woods, no doubt walking past perfectly cured wood lying at his feet to do things the hard way.

"The reason we're eating it right now is that Ian and Tucker love fresh meat. So do I, as a rule. We need to refill the smokehouse before winter, but in the meantime, my menfolk want fresh steaks!"

"What about salmon? It's time for the salmon runs."

Meredith nodded. "Ian's been watching the river. He'll bring in a good supply of that soon."

"I know a place a few miles downstream that's away from the river. I'm not sure how far we came yesterday, but that stream may be closer to you than it was to my home. I'll find it. My mother and I used to spear enough fish to last all winter with only a couple of days' work."

Tears filled Meredith's eyes. "That sounds good. But for now, I've got to finish cutting the steaks off this beast then cut the rest in strips so I can start smoking it." Her shoulders sagged, and she looked over her shoulder at the raw meat.

"I'll smoke the meat, Merry."

Meredith dashed her wrist across her eyes. "I'm just being silly today. I'm sorry. It seems I cry at the drop of a hat these days. I'll finish this. I'm almost ready to light a fire in the smokehouse. Go tell Braden to stop chopping and start picking up the wood that's lying thick on the ground." Meredith smiled then turned back to her chore, fastening her apron firmly around her slender middle.

Amy turned to hunt up Braden, and for the first time she really saw the cabin.

Tiny.

Amy's face heated up as she realized the cabin had only one little room tacked on, and she'd taken it. The log cabin, little more than twelve-feet square before the extra room half that size was added, had barely enough floor space for three people to lie on the floor.

She'd ousted Meredith and Ian from their bedroom. Well, that couldn't happen again, not for one single night. But she couldn't share a room with Braden. What could she do? She headed around the cabin to tell Braden his long morning's work was a waste of time.

Chapter 7

And then she has the nerve to tell me I'm wasting my time." Braden's irritation with the little woman wouldn't ease as he tromped through the trees. He'd have ignored her if she hadn't told him Meredith agreed.

Braden picked up sticks, Amy's voice taunting him. *Just pick wood up off the ground. It's a fraction of the work, and it's cured and ready to use.*

He filled his arms a dozen times, admitting the pile of wood grew far faster than when he'd split logs. Amy picked up sticks, too, although he'd deliberately gone in a different direction from her for fear of what he'd say in his irritated state.

He should have gone mining with Ian and Tucker, but he'd wanted to stay here and start earning his keep. He emptied his arms and turned to go into the woods again when Meredith came outside carrying a small bundle covered with a large gingham cloth. Braden recognized it as being among the things he'd brought from home. He still winced with embarrassment when he remembered the clock. He'd been in Alaska a day and already learned that time didn't matter.

"Did you notice the cabin up the river, on past Tucker's?" Meredith asked.

"I saw a trail leading off that way, but I haven't followed it. I thought Ian wrote to us about a man who lived across the river from you, quite a character. Abrams, isn't it? Someone else lives around here?"

Meredith sighed. "If you can call it living. You're right about Mr. Abrams. He lives across the river. But Mr. Clemment lives on our side of the river, and I've been feeding him since the first chinook blew. Ian went to see how he'd come through the winter. Not everyone can endure six months of dark. He's not. . .thinking clearly."

"Not thinking clearly?" Braden narrowed his eyes at his sweet new sister. "What does that mean?"

Meredith shrugged and handed Braden what turned out to be a plate, still warm. "Just leave this at Mr. Clemment's cabin and bring back the dishes from yesterday. I don't have any to spare. And Braden?"

"Yes?"

"Uh, if Mr. Clemment should happen to be on his roof when you get there. . ." Meredith lapsed into silence.

"He's repairing the roof?"

"No, he. . .well. . .sometimes he thinks he needs to. . ." Another extended silence. "He's usually down by now."

"Meredith. . ." Braden drew her name out slowly and shifted his weight impatiently.

"He's harmless." Meredith scuffed one foot on the still-frozen ground and clasped her hands behind her back as if afraid Braden would hand the dish back. "In fairness, it helps Tucker get up in the morning."

Braden's eyes fell closed. "Tell me what's going on."

Ian came up the sloping hill, spotted the cloth, and said, "Don't tell Rooster Clemment he's not a chicken. He gets mad."

"Rooster?" Braden looked at the seemingly sane pair.

"He climbs the roof every morning and crows, right at dawn—except in the winter. We suspect he just stayed up there waiting, hoping the sun would rise."

"He stayed on his roof all winter? An Alaskan winter?" Braden felt his eyebrows arch nearly to his hairline.

Ian looked at Meredith. "Probably not. He's alive, after all. We were shut in pretty tight ourselves, so we really didn't check. We just went to see him this spring and found him up there." He shrugged. "When we began having a few minutes of daylight, Rooster'd crow it up then crow it down. Now I think he's afraid to come down. He doesn't make much sense most of the time. But based on a couple of things he said, I believe he thinks the sun will go down if he isn't up there."

Braden shook his head in disbelief.

Ian grinned at him. "Anyway, say hello whether he's on the roof or not. He gets mad if you ignore him. Then go on inside, get the old plates, and leave the new. He's harmless."

"If he's harmless, why do I have to worry about making him mad?"

Ian appeared to be thinking that over. "Maybe I should take the food."

Braden rolled his eyes then set off with the plate, still warm to the touch.

Ian called after him, "If he laid any eggs, go ahead and bring 'em home!"

"Ian," Meredith chided, "be nice."

Braden glanced back to see her cuff Ian on the arm. Ian started laughing, grabbed Meredith around the waist, and swung her in a circle while she giggled.

The stab of jealousy shamed him, and Braden turned away. He didn't begrudge Ian his marriage to such a sweet lady as Meredith. But it reminded him that he'd never touch his Maggie again. Seeing Ian's happiness hurt.

Braden passed Tucker's neat little cabin in a tiny clearing. It was one room built just for a gold miner who spent all his life outdoors, panning in an icy stream or slamming his pickax into a hillside. Tucker didn't spend any time there except for sleeping. He even ate all his meals with the Raffertys, which Ian said was fair because Tucker helped hunt the food and cooking for three was as easy as cooking for two.

Ian and Tucker admitted at breakfast that they hadn't made a big strike. They found enough color to support themselves but not enough to draw their own herd of stampeders. Both men thought it was a good tradeoff.

He walked on. A few steps farther, Amy came out of the woods with an armload of branches. As he reached her side, he saw a barely visible game trail climb up the sheer, heavily wooded land that hugged the narrow path. How had she found that tiny trail so quickly? Her hair dangled loose from her braid, and dirt smudged her face here and there. She had a bag slung over her shoulder, the same one she'd carried all the way from Seattle. The bag bulged, and what looked like a slab of bark stuck out the top. Twigs and leaves had snagged her dress and tangled in her hair as if she'd fought her way through a bramble. But she didn't complain or fuss at her appearance. His Maggie had always been so tidy.

"You should be resting." Braden clamped his mouth shut before he could say anything else. Whether Amy wore herself out wasn't his concern.

Amy smiled. "I intend to help wherever I can. I have no wish to be a burden to Ian and Merry. What are you doing?" She nodded at the dish in his hands.

"Near as I can tell, I'm feedin' the chickens."

A smile quirked her lips. "There are not any chickens in Alaska." She dropped her load of sticks in a neat pile alongside the trail and dusted off her hands. Coming close, she peeked under the cloth. "And if there were, we would not give them mutton for breakfast."

"Want to come along? I might need someone watching my back trail." Braden hadn't meant to invite her along. The words just came out.

"In case you are attacked by a flock of the chicken's friends?" Amy turned and walked beside him on the trail. Braden realized they'd become friends on the trip here. They'd talked a lot on that long, boring journey but not said much about their pasts. Memories of Maggie still rubbed too raw. But they'd talked plenty about their ideas for the future in Alaska. Both of them trying to stay out of the stampeders' way. Neither of them held much interest in gold—the only interest for everyone else.

Hitching her bag higher on her shoulder, Amy stretched out her stride to match his, even though her legs were much shorter. "Braden, I want to go back to my father's cabin. I need to be sure that man has a legal claim. I can do that if I can get inside. Father had the deed hidden, but I know where it is."

"I'm real sorry about your da, Amy. But what good would it do to go back? You can't live there alone."

The trail disappeared ahead, around a curve of rock. Braden saw the stubborn set of Amy's jaw and knew she'd commence to nagging any second. When the cabin appeared right around the bend, he breathed a sigh of relief and changed the subject. "I can't believe how close the cabins are to each other."

"No use for forty acres here." Amy seemed to drink in the beauty around her, looking into the heavily wooded land that barely made room for this narrow path. A stream chuckled through the little clearing, and sunlight cut through the towering pines to bathe the gap in sunlight.

Braden had to admit the scenery looked breathtaking. "True enough. No one's planting a corn crop."

"But about my father. I think. . . ." Amy fell silent.

As the cabin came fully into view, Braden saw a man standing on the roof on one leg, his hands tucked into his armpits. The man stared up at the beams of sunlight as if he were soaking himself in them. Braden—now understanding Ian's amusement—exchanged a look with Amy. Her brow furrowed. Her dark eyes gleamed with compassion.

"Good morning, Mr. Clemment." Braden tried to remember all the ways Ian had said you could make Rooster mad. "I'm Ian Rafferty's brother. I've brought you some dinner."

The man lowered his curled leg to the roof and jammed his hands on his hips. *Uh oh, that looks like mad.* Then the man, with a head of brown hair and a full beard sticking in all directions like a dark sunburst around his face, stuck his arms back where they'd been. He flapped his elbows as if he planned on taking off, looked at the sky, and crowed at the top of his lungs.

"You take the food in, Braden. Let me talk to Mr. Clemment for a while."

"I'd better stay out here instead. You maybe shouldn't be alone with him. There's no telling what he might get up to."

"He looks harmless to me, except maybe to himself." Amy began walking toward the house.

Harmless. Probably true. Ian had said so. Glancing up at the man, he whispered to Amy, "Yell if you need me."

Amy threw him a confused look as if unable to imagine ever possibly needing him.

Braden went into the tiny cabin to set the food on the table. There wasn't one. The cabin was packed to the rafters with wood, bark, furs, and leaves. Braden had walked into a nest.

A trail of trampled down sticks led to the middle of the room. In the center of the chaos, as if Clemment *had* laid an egg, were a few plates like the one Braden carried—no doubt Meredith's. Braden set the food down, picked up the used plates—still dirty, but Braden didn't expect a chicken to wash dishes—and picked his way outside.

When he stepped outside, Amy had vanished. "Amy, where'd you go?" Braden turned in a circle, looking for her. His heart sped up. A cold sweat broke out on his forehead. Before he could holler again or step back far enough to see Rooster, Wily and another man approached the cabin by the trail Braden and Amy had used. Then Braden heard voices. Turning, he saw Amy sitting on the roof, chatting with Rooster Clemment. Rooster had settled down on the peak of the roof beside her, his knees drawn up to his chest, and his arms clamped around them.

The man with Wily approached Braden. "If you're Ian Rafferty, thank you for contacting me and telling me about my brother. I'm here to take him home."

"I'm Braden Rafferty. Ian's my brother."

"Well whoever you are, thank you. We had no idea where Wendell had gone." The man reached a hand out to Braden, who balanced the plates in one hand and shook with the other.

"You've restored my brother to me. God bless you." The man pulled a piece of paper from his pocket. He scribbled on it, lay it face down on the gingham cloth, and turned to the man on the roof.

"Wendell, come down!"

Rooster, busy visiting with Amy, turned at the sound. From the ground, Braden could see the man's eyes widen with recognition. "Carlton?"

Rooster slid down the roof, dismounting as gracefully as if he really could fly, and flung himself at the man. Braden could smell Rooster from twenty feet away.

The newcomer didn't so much as flinch as he pulled Rooster into his arms. "Father and Mother and I want you to come home. We miss you so much. Please say you'll come with me."

Rooster pulled free of his brother's arms and looked back at his cabin.

Amy dropped off the roof and came to rest her hand on Rooster's arm. "The sun shines for long hours all winter back home. You need to go, Wendell."

Wendell looked at the sky and then back at the roof as if he were worried about abandoning his vigil.

"It will be fine, Wendell." Amy patted his shoulder. "I will see to your work here. Your family needs you. Think of the sunlight and warmth. There are no long days of darkness where your brother is going."

"You remember Texas, don't you? Even in winter, we have warm days and lots of sun," Carlton added.

Rooster nodded but seemed hesitant. A man who thought he crowed the sun up wouldn't want to leave his post. Braden admired Rooster's dedication.

Between Amy and Carlton, Rooster allowed himself to be talked into leaving, walking away from the cabin with nothing. What would he pack anyway? Sticks?

Braden stood quietly nearby with Wily.

Carlton and Rooster—one dressed for civilization in a suit adorned with Wily's walrus intestine boots, the other dressed in rags—their arms slung around each other, headed down the trail.

Wily muttered, "Alaska ain't for everybody."

Braden wasn't sure which man Wily was talking about. "How'd you get back up here so fast? You've barely had time to walk home."

Wily shrugged. "I kin catch a current home and ride most of the way. Mr. Clemment stood there a'waitin' for me when I arrived, half crazed with worry 'bout Rooster. He convinced me to turn around and hightail it back."

Braden looked at the gaunt man. His weathered skin barely showed through his beard. "You must be exhausted."

Wily twisted his beard into a long, gray rope. "I been tired a'fore. I reckon I'll be tired agin." He trudged down the trail after the Clemments.

As the men disappeared from sight, Amy came up beside Braden. "I am glad his brother came. He needed to go home."

Which reminded Braden that Amy needed to go home. Not Ian's home but civilization home—Seattle. "While you were talking Rooster down off the roof, Carlton said Ian wrote to him and told him Wendell wasn't well. He thanked me. I didn't do anything."

"I am sure they did not want to take the time to hunt up Ian and thank him. What is that paper he gave you?"

Braden looked at the folded paper on top of the crumpled gingham. Shifting the plates, he unfolded the paper.

"A deed to Rooster's claim." Braden looked after the men and took a step after them. "He wrote Braden Rafferty on it. He meant it for Ian not me."

Amy caught his arm. "Do not worry about it. If you want Ian to have it, just sign it over."

Braden nodded. "Yep, that's okay then. Ian can have it."

※

Ian didn't want it.

"So, Rooster's brother came and got him?" Ian studied the handwritten note Carlton Clemment had scribbled Braden's name on.

Meredith straightened from the table, where she snipped at green wool for Ian's shirt. She folded the cloth with sharp, tidy snaps. "That's good. He needed to go home."

"How'd you get up on that roof so fast?" Braden asked Amy, who set the little bag she'd kept at her side all the way from Seattle in the corner of the kitchen.

"Flew up just like Rooster does?" Ian offered the deed back to Braden.

Amy smiled, shook her head, and said nothing.

"I'm not taking it." Braden tucked his hands in his pockets. "You and Merry've been caring for him. You'll be the ones takin' his claim, and that's that."

Amy crouched on the floor by the wall, her bag beside her. Braden watched her digging around in what looked like twigs and crushed leaves. What had she gathered that for? Kindling?

"Stubborn big brother." Ian narrowed his eyes, then shoved the paper into the breast pocket of Braden's brown broadcloth shirt. "I don't need another claim. This isn't like Oregon where we want to add to our acreage to grow more crops. I'm getting a living out of the rock I'm hacking at now. A few ounces of gold a month trickle out of there. We don't need much cash money. And I'm as busy as I want to be."

"But what if there's a big gold strike on Rooster's land? It should be yours."

Ian looked at Meredith. "He's right. I could be handin' away a fortune."

Meredith's eyes twinkled. "Why do I doubt that?"

Ian laughed, and Meredith joined in. "Keep the claim, Braden. The house is the real gold mine."

Braden thought about the mess inside Rooster's house. *Why do I doubt that?*

"We're too crowded here." Meredith tucked the fabric into one of the wooden boxes Braden had brought that nearly filled the little cabin. "And if God wants Ian to strike it rich, he will. He won't have to go around grabbing up every claim that comes his way."

Ian nodded. "I'd rather hunt than dig any day. We can't eat gold."

Amy smiled. "That sounds very Alaskan of you."

Tucker came in carrying a platter of raw steaks. Braden noticed Meredith turn from her brother and move to the open window. She stood casually looking out and breathing slowly. But her stance struck Braden as deliberate.

Braden pulled the deed out. "I can live in the house without owning it."

Tucker gave his sister a close look that made Braden wonder if the two of them were up to something. "I saw Wily going downriver with Rooster and another man. What's going on?"

"Rooster's brother came to get him." Braden quickly told Tucker what had happened that morning.

"Wasn't Wily just here last night?" Tucker looked away from his sister then began to skewer the steaks with a pointed metal spit and hang them over the gently crackling flames in the fireplace.

"He told me he'd sleep in Skaguay," Braden remembered. "Downstream's faster than up, and he expected to get home before it got too late."

Ian nodded. "True enough. Rooster's brother must have pushed him hard."

Amy rose from digging around in her bag, and Braden noticed her favoring her ribs. His thoughts went back to Rooster's house. "Why'd you go up on the roof anyway? You could have fallen off and gotten yourself killed."

Amy turned and sank into one of Ian's roughhewn chairs. "I've seen people driven half mad by the long winter before. I hoped I could talk some sense into him—talk him into going back down south. He let me pray with him. Then just when we were praying, his brother came as if God Himself had sent help."

Tucker added sticks to the fire.

"Here's how it's gonna be, big brother." Ian laughed and slapped Braden on the shoulder hard enough that Braden nearly staggered. "You're taking the claim."

Braden felt his jaw tighten. "I might be robbing my own brother of a fortune. I won't do it."

"Braden." Ian shook his head, grinning. "There's no great wealth to be chiseled outta those rocks."

Braden didn't want to take the chance of striking it rich and alienating his brother forever. "I'll take the claim, but anything I find, we share."

Ian shrugged. "Sounds fair enough if you'll agree to the same thing on my claim. I don't want you digging on Rooster's claim anyway. I want you digging on mine."

"I'm not taking half your gold!"

Tucker straightened. "We always work together without much mind to which claim we're on. It's safer to stay together, and the isolation of working a claim gets to a man after a while."

"Like it did Rooster." Ian's gaze hardened. "So, I'll take your deal of sharing, Braden. A three-way split between you, me, and Tucker. And offer you the same deal back on my own claim."

"I'll take it." Braden couldn't imagine what he'd need gold for. But if he got any, he'd spend it on his brother and Meredith somehow or send it home to Da and Ma. "I need a house, and you need the space."

"Merry and I will do what straightening we can to your new house today," Amy said quietly. "I looked inside a window as I climbed up. It needs. . .quite a bit of work.

An understatement if Braden had ever heard one. He remembered Rooster's man-sized chicken coop. Braden wondered if he'd be the one on the roof next.

Chapter 8

"Have you been inside Rooster's cabin, Merry?" Amy and Meredith started down the path toward Braden's new cabin as soon as they'd cleaned up after lunch. Amy thought of the work ahead of them to turn a nest into a home.

The men were long gone exploring Rooster's claim.

"Oh my, yes. The contents of Rooster's house will make a year's worth of kindling. All we have to do is carry it outside."

"That's all, huh?" Amy and Meredith exchanged a dry look; then Merry started laughing. The urge to laugh surprised Amy. She'd always been very reserved with people, and she'd spent little time around women her age. There were some in the school, of course, but Amy went home only to the McGraws, who were wonderful to her but were more given to quiet smiles than to giggles.

The two of them set to work. Amy ignored her aching ribs. The pain was no longer sharp and frightening. Amy noticed that Meredith had turned pale and worked more slowly as the hours passed.

"Why don't you go back to the cabin and start supper? I can finish here."

The pale color of Meredith's cheeks took on a faintly greenish tinge, and her shoulders slumped. "There'll be mutton again tonight." She said the words like she was reading a death notice and then walked away.

Exhausted by the time the light faded from the sky, Amy swept the cabin free of the last bits of twigs and leaves and then hurried back to help Meredith. Amy's strength waned far too quickly. To make the meal more interesting, she gathered a few greens on her way. Noting a berry bush, Amy planned the dessert she would make when they were ripe.

She spotted a moss her mother had brewed into a tea that helped reduce fever and another useful in a poultice to prevent wounds from turning septic. She needed to lay in a supply of medicines, so she made a note of the location.

She stepped in the cabin just as Meredith set the steaks on to cook in a large iron kettle full of water. Meredith straightened from hanging the kettle and staggered backward.

Amy rushed forward and caught Meredith before she fell.

"Are you all right?" Amy turned Meredith to face her. Meredith's cheeks were ashen, and her eyes weren't focused.

"A–Amy?" Meredith groped for Amy's arm as if she couldn't see where to hang on.

"Sit down." Amy urged Meredith to the table, settling her on a chair.

Meredith folded her arms on the table and laid her head down. "I must have straightened up too suddenly."

"Are you feeling ill?" Amy ran a hand over Meredith's disheveled hair. Meredith's forehead glowed with sweat.

"No, don't worry about me. I'm fine." Meredith lifted her head then looked toward the fireplace, clamped her mouth shut tight, and laid her head down again.

"Is the smell of the steak making you dizzy?" Amy couldn't imagine why that would be. Influenza had gone through the school in Seattle, but that kind of illness was rare in remote areas of Alaska. Other people had to bring the disease. If Amy had gotten sick on the boat and brought some sickness with her, that would make sense. But neither Amy nor Braden had experienced so much as a sniffle.

Meredith, her voice muffled by her arms and the table, said, "I think I need some fresh air."

Amy watched as Meredith raised her head and shoved herself to her feet. Amy didn't trust her not to fall again, so she took a firm grip on Meredith's arm and steadied her until they got outside.

The stump Braden had used to chop kindling stood only a few feet from the house. Amy helped Meredith reach it then eased her down.

"I think I know what's wrong." Meredith lifted her head and managed a true smile, even though her skin carried the chalky white of a long blizzard.

"What?"

"It's better outside. I hadn't realized how much the smell of cooking meat bothered me."

"What is better? What is wrong?" Amy sorted through the illnesses her mother had taught her and the treatments. Did Meredith have a wound that had festered? Had she fallen and sustained some internal injury? Amy crouched down in front of Meredith to quiz her.

A secret smile on Meredith's lips stopped Amy's questions. A blush crept up Meredith's cheeks, erasing the frightening pallor as Meredith's hand slid to her stomach.

"I think I'm carrying Ian's child." A soft laugh escaped Meredith's lips, and she quickly moved one hand to catch the sound.

Amy dropped the rest of the way to the ground. "Really?" A smile spread across her face as she looked at Meredith's joyful expression.

"I've been wondering for a couple of weeks, but I wasn't sure. That must be it, don't you think?"

Amy knew something about babies and how they were born because her mother had occasionally been called in to do some doctoring for her people. Amy asked questions about Meredith's condition, and they decided together that a baby was definitely on the way.

"Have you told Ian yet?" Amy clutched Meredith's hands, excited about the new baby.

The smiled faded from Meredith's face, and her pallor returned. "I'm afraid to even suggest it."

Amy got on her knees and leaned close to her friend. "But why?"

Meredith's lips curled down, and her eyes filmed over with tears. "Ian worries, and now that he's heard about Maggie's death. . ." Meredith shuddered. "Braden, Ian, and Maggie practically grew up together. I'm afraid to tell Ian I'm expecting. I know it will frighten him. He's already overprotective of me. This will make it worse."

"You are going to have to tell him, Merry. This is not the kind of thing a woman can hide for long."

"Oh, I know. I'll tell him soon. But now that I know I may have trouble cooking, he'll worry all the more. He's already so busy with the mine that he comes home exhausted every night. Now he'll think he needs to cook and do any lifting around the house. He'll take even more on himself. I understand that this stomach upset and the dizziness don't last. If I could just wait to tell him until I'm feeling stronger, I think he'd handle it better."

Amy nodded. "And Braden is going to be even worse than Ian."

Meredith took Amy's hand. "He seems so sad, and he has yet to even speak Maggie's name except when Ian asked him a direct question. Has he talked to you about her?"

"No, the first I knew his wife and child had died was when you told me about it this morning."

Meredith straightened and looked over her shoulder toward the woods. "Tucker will take his cue from Ian and Braden. I'll be lucky if the three of them don't order me to bed for the whole time. And I wouldn't mind them being so protective if it didn't land a burden on all of them."

Amy nodded. "Then here is what we will do. We will wait as long as possible to tell the men. In the meantime, I will help you with the things that upset your stomach—like the cooking. We will get you outside in the fresh air every chance. Since I have newly arrived, maybe they will not realize you are doing a bit less and I am doing more."

"But you're still exhausted from your trip."

"So, we will work together. Surely the two of us together, even in the shape we are in, equal one fully functioning woman."

Meredith's eyes got wide; then she erupted into laughter. The two of them hugged.

"Congratulations." Amy pulled away to arm's length. "This baby is going to be such a precious blessing to this home."

Meredith's eyes filled with tears of joy. "I can't wait." She hugged her stomach again.

Amy hopped to her feet. Despite her long day and lingering injuries, she felt renewed strength. "I am going in to finish the dinner. You rest a bit. If you are able, you can stack the branches Braden and I brought in today. I think the fresh air is all you need. When the meat is done cooking and the room airs out, I will call you in. Can you eat? Sometimes new mothers are nauseated."

Meredith shrugged. "I've had a good appetite so far. I think it's just the smell of it cooking that got to me. I've had several episodes like the one tonight, but no one caught me with my head on the table." Meredith stood and threw her arms around Amy. "Thank God for you, Amy." Meredith burst into tears.

Amy shook her head and patted Meredith on the shoulder until the tears eased. "I remember my mother saying crying at odd times was a symptom of a baby on the way."

Meredith dried her eyes on her apron. "Well, I've definitely got that."

"Sit back down for a while. Make sure your head is clear before you start bending and stacking the branches. And do not let me catch you lifting any heavy ones, or I am telling Ian about the baby tonight."

Meredith nodded, then sat and folded her hands in her lap like a prim and proper schoolgirl. "I'll behave, Mama. I promise."

Meredith dissolved into laughter, and Amy joined in.

Amy finally went to the house and set about preparing dinner for the Rafferty clan.

Swirling the pan, letting the crystal clear water overflow the edges, and watching for bits of gold, Braden hadn't seen a fleck of gold yet. He wished he'd catch gold fever because, unless he did, panning for gold was never going to be any fun. He didn't see much sign of the gold madness resting on Ian or Tucker, either. The only time they got interested as they worked about twenty feet apart on the icy murmuring stream was when they talked about hunting.

"I saw polar bear tracks a stone's throw from my house." Tucker worked the rocker with the steady swish of water against a sieve. Occasionally, he straightened and flicked at the bottom of his pan with a negligent finger and then tossed the contents away.

"Are you sure it wasn't a grizzly?" Ian sat on a rock, swishing away, staring into the pan. "I've never heard of a polar bear this far south."

The two men seemed to prefer working close enough to talk, showing none of the normal miner's ferocious knowledge of his property line. Braden wasn't even sure where the boundary of his claim lay. Of course, only the three of them were mining in the area, so who'd argue about property lines?

"There were tufts of pure white fur. The old boy must be shedding his winter coat, because the fur scraped off as if he were snowing."

Ian looked at Tucker. "It'll be hungry and cranky. We'd better keep Merry close to the cabin."

"Amy, too." Braden tossed the slushy sediment back into the water. He saw a silver fish flash past in the fast-moving stream. He thought their time could be better spent fishing than mining.

"So, have you spoken for the little woman?" Tucker asked.

Braden straightened and looked at Ian's brother-in-law. "Of course not. I didn't come up here hunting for a woman."

"Hmm. . ." Tucker kept rocking.

"What's that supposed to mean?" Braden couldn't hide his irritation. He wrestled his temper under control.

"Doesn't mean a thing." The quiet scratch of rock against metal almost covered Tucker's mild comment.

"Her father just died. She's not interested in any man right now."

"She tell you that?" Tucker, bent at the waist, working his rocker, turned his back to Braden.

Braden's eyes narrowed on Tucker. "Are you saying you're interested in Amy?"

"I'm not saying a thing. Asked a simple question is all. Just makin' conversation."

Braden frowned at Tucker's back. Then he glanced at Ian and saw Ian swirling his pan and watching Braden when he should be looking for gold dust.

Braden decided to change the subject. "So, you've actually found some gold here?"

Tucker laughed.

Ian tossed the contents of his pan away and grinned at Braden. "We get some color out of here once in a while."

Tucker stood and tugged his suspenders. "I keep hoping I'll catch gold fever, but so far, this is just plain boring."

Ian grunted in agreement and then shrugged. "It pays the bills."

"What bills? I thought you lived off the land."

"Good thing, because gold wouldn't pay any. It's almost suppertime." Ian packed his scanty supplies and gathered up his rifle. Braden and Tucker followed suit. "Let's go down the trail in the direction you saw the bear, Tucker. Seein' his tracks'd tell us what we're up against."

Companionably, the three of them began the hike through the heavy woods.

Chapter 9

For the next two weeks, Amy did the lion's share of the work, and Meredith got the credit.

Amy neatly rolled the pallet she slept on in the main room as Meredith talked to her through the window. "I feel like a fraud sitting out here day after day."

"You are working." Amy talked to Meredith through the cabin window as she set the salmon steaks on to roast in the covered skillet. "You have almost finished that shirt for Braden."

The day before, Amy had hiked to the spawning beds and speared enough salmon to last a month. She'd cleaned them at the stream to keep from luring hungry grizzlies to the cabin, then dragged them home with a travois she rigged out of cedar branches. Hanging them high in a tree a good distance from the house so a bear wouldn't get to them, she planned to spend the morning building a separate smokehouse for the salmon to separate the fishy smell from the bighorn sheep and other meat, then go fishing again in the afternoon. The salmon would run for two weeks. By the time they were done, she'd have enough to last the winter.

She'd seen bear sign between the cabin and the stream and was tempted to go hunting. The fur and lard would come in handy, and she loved bear meat. But it would be wiser to wait until the end of summer for that, when the bear's fur grew thick and its belly fat.

"Ian loved his shirt, didn't he?" Meredith got a faraway look in her eyes. Amy remembered Ian's delighted thank-you to his wife when she showed him what she'd sewn. The affection between the two of them had awakened a longing in Amy, but for what she didn't know.

Ian had worn it for the very simple church service the Raffertys held each Sunday morning. Then, because the Raffertys kept the Sabbath and did no hunting or mining on Sunday, he'd worn it the rest of the day.

Braden had attended the service, but he remained solemn and offered nothing when Ian read the Scripture. Amy was nearly brought to silence when Ian read the verse that she'd so studiously ignored when she'd headed north.

Ian read from Isaiah the same verse Parson McGraw had read her when she lay mending in Seattle: "But they that wait upon the Lord shall renew their strength; they shall mount up with wings as eagles; they shall run, and not be weary; and they shall walk, and not faint."

Wait.

How clearly she'd heard God's urging. But what purpose did waiting serve? Her father was dead, and she needed to find out why and make sure justice was done. She turned her thoughts from that part of the morning's message and joined in with the group's discussion of God's blessing. She heard an eagle cry overhead, and her heart pounded more quickly as the encouraging words from Isaiah settled in her soul. Yes, those words called her to wait. But they also promised strength to soar, to run, to walk and not faint. A request from God and a promise in return for obedience.

Meredith needed strength. She needed to not be weary. With a sigh of relief, Amy claimed this verse for Meredith. It was good Amy had come to help out the family so Meredith could rest.

After their day of rest, Meredith chose a length of fabric to make another shirt, this one for Tucker.

Enjoying the feel of a piece of smooth, lightweight calico, Amy said, "I can't believe Mrs. Rafferty sent all those bolts of cloth." It served no purpose to make a dress of the calico. It wouldn't protect against mosquitoes in the summer, and it was too thin to keep a body warm in the winter.

"We could take it to Skaguay and sell it for a fortune." Amy shook her head at the waste.

"Well, we're not. We're keeping it all to ourselves. We'll be the best-dressed people in Alaska. And what doesn't work for clothing, we'll use for curtains and tablecloths." Meredith threaded a needle and knotted one end. She dug her needle into the soft flannel.

Amy saw Meredith finger the red plaid and envied her working with the bright, smooth cloth. Then the smell of the salmon teased her nose—a delicious smell she'd missed—and she decided she had the better of the two jobs.

Once the juniper berries were on to simmer, sprinkled with a bit of the precious sugar Mrs. Rafferty had sent, Amy headed outside and went to work, piling the stones for her smokehouse.

Wanting to build it well away from the cabin so the smoke wouldn't torment Meredith, Amy chose a spot near a tumbled pile of stones at the base of the mountain. The Raffertys' sturdy little log smokehouse stood close to their cabin, nearly depleted of stores after the long winter. Ian's recent luck hunting bighorn sheep had kept them fed, but Amy wanted a change of diet for Meredith. Starting with heavy flat stones for the foundation, she rolled them into a circle, wanting it big enough to get the dozens of salmon steaks all cooking at once.

She worked the morning away, carefully selecting stones that went well together. The tighter she made it, the faster the salmon would cook. Every foot, Amy left good-sized holes in the chimney, and by the holes, she rigged drying racks of fresh saplings.

The work reminded her of her childhood. Her mother had smoked salmon just this way. The pangs of loneliness for her papa still hit her hard at times, but she knew her papa's faith. Picturing him in heaven—surrounded by white-capped mountains and soaring eagles, sparkling, rushing streams, and heavily furred animals that now were his to caress without needing their fur for warmth—made her grief bearable. Then she thought of the man who lived in her father's house, and her anger burned. She needed to go back and find out if the sale was real. If not, that man might have. . .

Amy veered her thoughts away from the awful man and her father's fate. She couldn't go now. She had to care for Meredith. The need to gain justice for her father festered like a sliver embedded under her skin, but it would have to wait.

Sweating from exertion, Amy felt better than since before her accident. Using smaller and smaller stones, she narrowed the smokehouse, five feet across at its circular base, into a chimney. The stones were still heavy, nearly the size of a man's head, but her ribs didn't protest when she lifted them. She felt healthy and happy and at home. Just as the structure reached waist level, the trees rustled behind her.

With a start, she turned.

"What are you doing?" Braden dashed across the opening around Amy's smokehouse. He grabbed the rock she held as if it were preparing to drop on her head.

"I am drying salmon. Is it midday?" Amy wondered if she'd lost track of time. "I am sorry if your meal is late." She glanced at the sun, not quite overhead. If she hurried, she had time to finish the chimney, lay out the fish, and start a smoldering fire.

Dusting her hands, she pointed at the smokehouse. "Just rest the flat side right there."

Amy noticed his stunned expression as Braden laid the stone into place on the half-built wall. She turned and selected another rock.

"You did all this?" Braden shifted the piece of granite he'd taken from Amy.

Impressed with his feel for fitting the stone in place, Amy said, "Of course. We have to preserve the fish for winter."

"What fish?"

Amy reached for one of the cedar branches she'd laid over the salmon and flipped it aside. "These fish."

Braden's mouth gaped at the dozens of filets. "Where did you get all this?"

Amy tilted her head at the silly question. "Uh, the river? You know fish come out of the water, right?"

Braden pivoted to face her, his eyes narrow.

She grinned.

A spark of humor relaxed his features. "Yes, I know where fish come from."

"I went fishing yesterday afternoon. I left after you'd gone back to the gold mine and got home ahead of you. I forgot to mention it. The salmon are running. Meredith says Ian gets them out of the river, but I knew of a little stream nearby that angles off the Skaguay River." Amy arched her brows. "The one we came up to get here."

"I remember the Skaguay River." Braden crossed his arms. "I walked in ice water for half a day. I couldn't forget that river if I tried."

"Good." Mindful of the time, Amy grabbed a rock and set it on the narrowing smokehouse.

Braden took it from her. "Tell me where to set it."

"If you want to help, then get your own rock. I am not going to stand here and point while you do the work."

Braden set the rock in place then stopped to stare at her as if he'd never seen a woman before. "You're going to help me?"

"Braden! I am not going to *help* you. I am going to do it myself. Maybe, if I am really lucky, you are going to help me. I have already finished with the hard part. We are to the little rocks now." She bent for another rock.

Braden grabbed it.

She held on, glared, and asked, "Do you not have some gold to mine?" She had a brief tug-of-war with Braden, her calloused fingers slipping on the rough piece of rubble.

Then, as if the sun came out from under a cloud, a smile broke out across his face. It reached his eyes in a way she'd never seen before. "You'd throw me out and do it yourself?"

Amy jerked the rock free of Braden's hands. "I mean this in the nicest way possible, Braden, but get your own rock, or go away."

A gurgling sound startled Amy into looking at the pesky man. Braden was laughing. His voice tripped over the sound coming out of his throat as if he didn't remember quite how to laugh.

The laughter sang like sweet music in Amy's ears after seeing the weight of sadness Braden carried like a load of stones. The joy of the moment made her laugh, too. He released the rock when he laughed, and Amy set it in place. Then side by side they enjoyed the day and their silly argument and each other.

Ragged corners of Amy's heart, tattered from her father's death, knit together as she laughed with Braden. When the laughter faded, she remembered anew how this beautiful land had been like God's own cathedral when she was growing up, as if Alaska sat on the top of the world closer to heaven. Amy felt more at peace than she had since she'd left her northern home six years ago. Braden's laughter had brought her closer to God.

With a silent prayer of thanks and a quick flutter of her hand at Braden, Amy shook her head. "Enough nonsense. I am in a hurry. I have got to get dinner on." She grabbed another rock.

Braden hesitated for a second as if he seriously considered taking this stone from her, too. She angled her back to him to protect the rock.

Braden bent down and selected his own stone. "There's no hurry. Merry does all the cooking."

Amy froze with the rock resting on her smokehouse wall. In the closeness of the moment, she'd forgotten they'd been hiding the news of the baby from the men. Knowing all Braden had been through, Amy thought it even more important to keep the news from him than Ian.

The silence must have told him something was amiss. "Merry does the cooking, right?"

Shifting the rock around to suit her, as if fitting it just so was a matter of life and death, she bent to get another one. Neither she nor Meredith would lie if they were asked. But they didn't want the men to know yet. Meredith had felt better the last couple of days. A week from now, maybe two, she would be ready to announce her wonderful news.

Calming herself, Amy forged on, hoping Braden would forget her careless words. "I do want to help her, though."

She felt Braden studying her as she kept her back to him and busied herself with the smokehouse. Suddenly, Braden's big hands appeared beside her and picked up a rock.

Sighing with relief, Amy worked quickly, glad she'd fooled him but feeling guilty. They'd had such a nice moment together, and now her dishonesty had placed a barrier between them.

As they worked on the smokehouse, her mind went to her mother, who'd taught Amy the skill of building an *atx'aan hídi* to preserve their food, and from there her thoughts went to Papa.

"Braden, I want to go back to my father's house."

"I'm really sorry about your da." The dry scratch of stone on stone made a hushed backdrop to Braden's solemn voice.

Amy regretted that the laughter was gone.

"I haven't told you how sorry I am for your loss because. . . well, there hasn't been time." Braden's height made the stone structure go up faster. As the smokehouse wall grew higher, Amy began handing him rocks rather than nesting them herself, and the system worked smoothly.

Amy knew there'd been plenty of time for Braden to mention her loss. They'd been here nearly two weeks, and they'd eaten three meals a day together. But they'd avoided each other. The long journey here had forged a friendship between them that confused Amy. Worrying about her father and his home, and now caring for Meredith and three hungry men were all she could handle. An attraction to the kind man who had cared for her but still loved his wife was a complication she didn't need.

For Braden's part, she knew he still mourned his wife. His perfect wife. He'd spoken of her a few times, how ladylike she was, how gracious and soft-spoken. Amy glanced at the calluses on her hands and the tan she'd already gotten from working outside for long hours. Her Tlingit heritage showed far more since her return to Alaska. Relearning the ways her mother had taught her enhanced her resemblance to her native people. With a sad heart, she knew she looked and acted nothing like the woman Braden had loved and lost.

"It takes a lot of hard work to make a go of Alaska," she said quietly. "There is not a lot of time to visit."

"I think you're better off forgetting about the house. It's sold. I know you must miss your home."

A high scream overhead pulled their eyes upward. A golden eagle swooped across the cloudless blue sky, its wings spread wide as it played on the cool spring air currents. The breeze ruffled the cedars surrounding Amy's smokehouse, creating the music of nature with their sway and the eagle cry. The white cap of a mountain peak soared above the treetops.

Amy's throat swelled at the beauty all around her. She had missed her home. But her home was the land, not that cabin. She didn't want the building, only the information it contained. She couldn't rest peacefully until she knew what had happened to her father.

As another scream from the eagle reached her ears, she felt as if God spoke to her. " 'But they that wait upon the Lord shall renew their strength; they shall mount up with wings as eagles.'" Amy quoted. "My mother favored that verse mainly because of the beauty of the eagles that lived all around us. That verse always lifted my heart as surely as the wind lifts an eagle's wings."

Amy glanced at Braden. His shoulders stiffened. "You do not talk much of your faith, Braden. Can you find no comfort in knowing that your wife has gone home to God?"

Braden looked up from where he worked. "My wife is with God. I'm sure she's in a better place. But that doesn't leave any excuse for my making her life harder than it needed to be. I should have been stronger."

Stronger how? Amy held her tongue. *"Wait upon the Lord. . .mount up with wings as eagles."* A beautiful image. The wind seemed to whisper through the trees, *Patience, wait on the Lord.* In this one thing, questioning Braden, perhaps it would be better to wait. He seemed far from being ready to talk of his loss. But waiting for Braden's heart to heal was not the same as waiting to find the truth about her father. Braden needed time, but time was the enemy of the truth. Waiting might mean the man got away with murder.

Amy had cared for herself since the age of twelve and believed God wanted her to. So why did the Lord nudge her to wait? Did she hear God's voice carried on the wind, or was it just her imagination? The Raffertys offered her safety and an easy life. But if she needed to face something hard, she'd just as soon get on with it. She turned back to the rock pile and selected the next stone.

"There is a hidden compartment in the mantel. It held Papa's important papers." Straightening with the next piece of granite, she added, "If he really sold the cabin, then he would have handed over the deed. But if—"

"Your home is gone." Braden laid his hand on her shoulder. "You need to accept that, lass."

Amy's jaw tightened. "Nobody *accepts* their father's unexplained death and the theft of their home. You haven't accepted your wife's death, have you?"

Braden took the load from her hands and rested it on the ever-narrowing chimney that had grown to chest level. "It's not about accepting. I—I just know God took her from me, and I want her back. If I'd taken better care of her, God would have blessed my efforts and let us be together for a long life. I failed. And now you want to risk confronting that man with his gun just to get a house back you don't need and you can't live in. Well, I'm not going to let you go."

"Not *let* me?" Amy clamped her lips tight and turned back to the smokehouse. She worked harder, wanting to keep her sharp words locked inside. Braden didn't deserve to be barked at. In his own overprotective way, he meant to be kind.

The smokehouse was soon done. Amy had left small, arched openings at each level. Now she knelt at the base and loaded the damp moss and green branches and wood chips. She found the match she'd tucked in the pocket of her gingham dress and carefully struck it on the stone. The matches were a wonderful convenience—though she certainly didn't need one to start a fire.

A pile of shredded bark resting on a larger slab of bark blazed to life, and Amy eased it into the base of the atx'aan hídi.

The sweet sound of crackling wood came from inside the smokehouse. The warm smell of cedar smoke tickled her nose. As the fire blazed inside the rounded opening, Amy used each level of the smokehouse, with its neat openings, to lay out her salmon.

Braden caught on quickly and worked at a different level so they wouldn't get in each other's way.

It only took moments for the blazing fire to die down and begin smoldering. Smoke billowed out of the hundreds of cracks of the chimney. They finished putting the salmon into the smoky chamber and stood back to keep from choking.

The sense of accomplishment eased Amy's temper, and she shared a smile with Braden. "This will burn for hours. I need to add wood twice a day. We will keep the fire going overnight. Tomorrow, about noon, this batch will be done, and I will take it out and add the salmon I spear today."

"Today?"

Amy nodded. "I need to get enough for the winter right now. It is easy when they are spawning. There are plenty of salmon in the river, of course. But my stream is better. And it needs to be done now. Later in the summer, I might sit all day and only spear enough food for a single meal. I will do that, of course, so we can eat fresh fish during the summer."

"Earlier, when I mentioned Merry doing all the cooking, you acted like something was wrong. What's going on?"

Amy had hoped he'd forgotten that blunder. But this talk of food had obviously reminded Braden. She toyed with a small rock, fitting it into an opening to keep a bit more of the smoke inside. The chimney wasn't meant to be tight. She fiddled with the rock to give herself time to think.

Braden pulled her hands away from the smokehouse and turned her to face him. "I asked if something was going on."

Amy studied her toes peeking out from beneath her brown calico dress, not a bit sure she could keep an innocent expression on her face. Suddenly, he caught her upper arms in his hands and lifted her until she had to look at him. "What is it, Amy? Is Merry sick?"

Amy shook her head. She couldn't outright lie, and from his worried expression, she knew Braden wouldn't let the subject drop. "The smell of cooking meat makes her sick because. . . because. . ." Amy prayed that Meredith wouldn't be too upset with her. "She is expecting a baby."

"A baby?" A smile bloomed on his face. Then, as if the bloom were slashed off with a knife, his forehead furrowed, and the corners of his mouth turned down. Braden released her hands as if he'd found himself holding a rattlesnake. His jaw formed a taut, straight line; deep furrows showed on his brow, partly covered by his unruly red hair.

He stepped back from her. "No."

Amy felt the pain and fear rolling off Braden in waves. "She will be fine." She rested one hand on his wrist. "I know you lost your wife and you are worried for Merry, but babies are a blessing. She will be fine."

"You can't know that."

"She is a strong woman. There is nothing more natural than having a baby. God will take care of her."

"Like he took care of Maggie?" Braden shook off her touch and shoved both hands into his hair as he turned away.

Amy had lived with the Tlingit ways for too long to fear the birth of a baby. It was a reason for joy. Her mother had assisted whenever a baby came along, and Amy knew the way of bringing a child into the world. But how could she reassure Braden?

Amy knew the truth. If Braden didn't want to hear it, she couldn't force him. Speaking just above a whisper, she said, "Maggie's time to go home to God came. I know you miss her. You loved your wife and wanted that child, but God called them to Himself. To be angry at God for doing it makes no sense."

With a twist of guilt, Amy realized she'd been ignoring God's urging for patience. For a moment, she wondered if that also made no sense. But it wasn't the same thing. She accepted her father's death. She only wanted to see justice done; that bore no resemblance to anger with God.

"I've heard it all before." Braden dropped his hands to his sides, his fists clenched. He looked at Amy, his blue eyes smoldering like the stones behind them. "Why would God send a child only to take it away before it drew a single breath? Why would I hear Maggie's screams only to be useless as she lay and bled to death in my arms?"

"Oh, Braden." She laid one hand on his wrist, hurting for him. "I am so sorry. I did not know you went through all that."

He jerked his hand away as if she'd burned him. "Sorry for me? Maggie's the one who died. I don't deserve your sympathy. And I won't accept that as God's will. How can I? To accept it means God wanted to hurt me. What kind of God is that?"

"We cannot know the ways of God." Amy looked into pain that permeated the depths of Braden's heart. She remembered the bitter loneliness she'd felt when her mother had died. Nothing had come close to easing her pain except when her father held her. Despite the way Braden had rejected her touch, she couldn't stop herself from taking the few steps toward him and throwing her arms around him.

His hands went to her wrists behind his back as if he'd tear her loose. Then, with a sudden groan of pain, he released her wrists and pulled her hard against him.

Burying his face in her shoulder, he wept.

Chapter 10

Tears escaped as if a dam had burst when Braden felt Amy, solid and alive and strong in his arms. Her vitality and calm filled him with the courage to face the pain of Maggie's death. Until this minute, he'd clung to his anger and guilt, afraid of the tears as if once he began to cry he might never stop.

Vaguely, he felt Amy pat his back. He heard murmurs of comfort spoken so quietly he couldn't make them out. He thought she spoke of God, or maybe she spoke to God.

Braden knew a prayer was long overdue. *God, forgive me. I've blamed You. I've been angry at You. I'm so sorry.*

Braden remembered the words Ian had read to them one Sunday morning. *"But they that wait upon the Lord shall renew their strength; they shall mount up with wings as eagles; they shall run, and not be weary; and they shall walk, and not faint."*

"You're my strength, Braden."

But he hadn't been strong enough. Even though Maggie had demanded a lot of Braden, God had promised to renew his strength. *God, why didn't you make me strong enough?*

The awful sight of Maggie bleeding, begging him to save her, dying in his arms faded into the memory of how she'd been before. She had a wonderful smile, though not so bright as Amy's. Amy's white teeth glowed out of her tanned face. Maggie had a gentle laugh, precious to Braden because he hadn't heard it often. Amy had at first appeared to have an overly serious nature. One of her gentle smiles had been rare indeed. Now, on occasion, she shared a husky and generous laugh. He'd even heard her giggle with Meredith while they set the meal on the table. Once, under Tucker's merciless teasing, Amy had laughed so hard she'd held her stomach as if it hurt.

Braden realized he was comparing his wife to Amy. His tears stopped as soon as he realized the disloyalty of his thoughts. He felt compelled to say, "My Maggie was a gracious, gentle lady. Aye, she had the manners and temperament of an angel."

Braden thought of a few times Maggie hadn't been so sweet. She didn't lose her temper, but she did complain and gave way to tears and long, pouting silences. Braden had learned to give her what she wanted to keep peace in his home.

Amy had lost her father; she'd been left homeless with only a stranger to care for her. She'd been exhausted from the trip. But she'd handled it all. She'd fought her way through the loss, the exhaustion, and the fear. She'd squared her shoulders and taken on the household so Meredith could rest. And she'd done it quietly.

Even Meredith, tired out from the baby growing inside her, hadn't whined and demanded Ian stay in the house as Maggie had with Braden. Meredith had accepted Amy's help out of necessity but kept working. She'd sewn three shirts this week out of the fabric Ma had sent, one for each of the men. Braden had seen no new clothing for Meredith or Amy as of yet.

Braden remembered how Maggie needed to be complimented for things. He'd loved to put that glow in her eyes when she'd show him a shirt she'd mended or a cake she'd baked. Even while he did it, Braden thought of his mother baking daily for the large household, gardening, canning, and cleaning all day. Ma sewed or knit in the evening, her hands never idle, her thoughts always on what came next and who needed her help.

Amy reminded Braden of his mother, a hard worker with no need for thanks because she saw herself as part of the family and worked to make the family run smoothly. Ma and Da had trained their young'uns to say please and thank you, but they didn't work for the thanks they earned with it. Not his mother, not Amy, not Meredith, only Maggie.

Braden realized he still held Amy. It had felt so natural he'd kept hanging on. He stepped out of Amy's arms, pulling away so abruptly that she stumbled toward him when she didn't let go quickly enough. He dashed his shirt sleeve across his eyes.

He saw the confusion in her eyes and dropped his gaze to her soft lips. He thought of the northern lights in the sky when they were together on the trip up here. He'd been drawn to her then, and the very idea had shocked him. Now he wanted to pull her close. He wanted her warmth and strength not just for a day but forever. Braden shoved his hands in his pockets to stop himself from reaching for her. The pain of losing Maggie was too fresh; caring for another woman felt like a betrayal. He had to say something to rebuild the wall he needed to protect his heart.

"There's no room in a family for lies and secrets." His tone shocked him. The rough edge of it calling Amy a liar. "If you women don't tell Ian the truth, I will."

He found safety in his anger and looked at the little woman who'd just built a smoke-house and had plans that would feed the family for the winter. Amy had gone fishing yesterday, leaving Meredith home alone all day. Now here she planned to do it again. Maggie never would have done that. Maggie would have stayed at the house where she belonged.

Glaring, his temper came rapidly to a boil to cover his guilt. "If you're going to go off on your own and leave Merry, you'd better tell us so someone can be there in case she needs help."

Amy's jaw dropped. He saw the tracks of tears cutting through her grubby face, tears she'd cried for him. She'd worked up a sweat building the chimney and then apparently scratched her nose and cheeks with dirty hands.

Maggie kept herself neat and clean.

"Braden, what is wrong?" Amy's kindness only made him more furious. He felt like a polar bear, lashing out at her for no reason except his own bad temper. But he couldn't stop.

"Are you going to keep lying to Ian or not?"

"We did not lie. We just—"

"Just didn't tell the truth." Guilt rode him like the gnawing hunger of an empty belly after a long winter's hibernation. "Don't dress it up fancy to make excuses for yourself. That makes you a liar."

Amy's head jerked back as if she'd been slapped.

Braden had to lock his muscles in place to keep from reaching for her and telling her she was wonderful, beautiful, brave, and strong.

Amy met his eyes, as if she accepted his condemnation and believed every word. "I—I will tell Merry. Now that you know, she will need to tell Ian, of course. I think we should let her be the one to tell him."

Braden held her gaze for a moment longer. Then with a single nod of his chin, he said,

"Do it before the end of the noon meal, or I will."

He turned and plunged into the woods, afraid to be near her for another second.

❦

Amy sank onto the nearest rock. What had happened? One second she'd been in Braden's arms, comforting him, feeling closer to him than she ever had to another human being. The next, he'd been calling her a liar and threatening her if she didn't admit everything to Ian.

She never should have hugged him. The mission teachers had told her about a woman's proper demeanor. She'd shocked Braden and once again reminded him of how poorly she compared to the refined wife he'd lost.

A gust of wind carried a thick blanket of fish-flavored smoke over her, setting her to coughing. If it hadn't been for that, she might have sat on that rock forever.

The smoke reminded her of dinner, and fighting back tears of shame for the way she'd flaunted herself at Braden, she hurried toward the house. She needed to give Meredith a few minutes to prepare herself before Ian got home.

She strode toward the cabin, her mind jumping around like a speared salmon fighting its fate. A sudden crackling in the brush drew her attention. She turned to face the noise, resting her hand on the hilt of her knife, tucked in its scabbard and tied around her waist with a thin leather belt. She always carried it in case she needed to cut saplings or dig for roots.

Ian and Tucker had warned her that they'd seen the white fur of a polar bear and its tracks in the woods, but not this near. She knew how hungry the huge animals were in the spring. The smell of smoking salmon would draw them. That's why she'd used the heavy rocks to build the smokehouse, rather than just hang the fish over an open fire. Keeping a watchful eye on the woods, she listened for the heavy breathing of a bear, watched for a flash of white fur against the brown of the trees and the green of the cedar branches.

She heard something more, but it didn't sound like a bear, more like a footstep. Human. A cold chill raced up her spine as she backed away from the thick undergrowth and remembered the menace of those soft footfalls that late night aboard the *Northward* and how she'd never stayed on the deck alone again. She pulled her knife. "Who is there?"

She continued backing away, keeping her eyes open, listening for movement that meant someone circled her. She heard nothing. As soon as she put enough paces between her and that thicket, she pivoted and raced for the cabin.

By the time she got to the house, she had begun to doubt the strange flash of fear. Feeling foolish for racing through the woods, she slowed her steps and tried to steady her breathing. Running a hand through the wisps of black hair that had escaped her braid, she tidied herself. No sense frightening Meredith just because Amy jumped at her own shadow. With a shake of her head, Amy entered the cabin to see Meredith sitting on Ian's lap.

They were both grinning.

Amy forgot all about that strange moment in the woods. "You told him."

Meredith nodded. Ian jumped from the chair with Meredith still in his arms and whooped, twirling her around in the air.

Amy stepped back so she wouldn't get plowed over in the tiny cabin, laughing at Ian's antics.

"Ian, stop. I'm going to throw up." Meredith slapped at his shoulder, but then she went back to holding him tight. She didn't look sick. She looked wonderful. Amy saw none of the greenish hue to her skin. Her eyes glowed with joy, her cheeks were flushed pink from laughter, and her lips were slightly swollen, no doubt from Ian's kisses.

"Well, good," Amy said, "because Braden found out today. He insisted that we tell Ian... *today.*"

Meredith, perched in her husband's arms, arched a brow at Amy. "You talked with Braden this morning?"

"Yes." Amy refused to say more despite Meredith's open curiosity. "Ian, take your wife outside so I can cook some dinner. This cabin is not big enough for me and a dancing couple."

"I'm feeling better." Meredith squeezed Ian's neck until he grunted. "I think I could help cook today."

"Not right now." Amy shook her head. "I think you need to go and spend a few minutes with your husband. You can try cooking tonight."

Ian smiled, whirled Meredith one more time, and then swept toward the door with his wife still in his arms.

Amy jumped out of the way, laughing at Ian's nonsense. She turned to watch them go and saw Braden standing at the edge of the clearing. Ian and Meredith didn't see him; they were too caught up in their own joy. Could it have been Braden she'd heard in the woods? Would he have kept quiet if she'd come upon him, rather than speak to her, even after he'd seen her fear?

With his heart in his eyes, Braden watched his brother and Meredith. The grief cut lines into the corners of his mouth and deepened the lines in his forehead.

The happy couple vanished into the woods, and Braden turned to Amy.

Anger replaced grief, and even from this distance, she could see the accusation, as if she'd betrayed him somehow. The betrayal boiled down to Amy being alive while his beloved Maggie was dead.

I am in love with him.

From out of nowhere, the knowledge swept over her as powerfully as an avalanche. His expression couldn't have hurt as much as it did for any other reason. At that moment, she'd have done anything to take away his pain, even given up her life in exchange for his Maggie's if God granted her the power to make such a trade.

Her eyes held Braden's. Then, as if he couldn't bear the sight of her a moment longer, he turned away and disappeared into the trees in the opposite direction his brother and sister-in-law had gone.

Amy fed the family and, with some argument, settled Meredith in for an afternoon nap. After the excitement of telling Ian her news, she looked exhausted. Meredith protested, but she fell asleep almost before Amy left the room.

Amy tended the fire in her smokehouse, then set off through the woods. She planned to haul home a much larger catch today. Knowing she had the smokehouse to build first, she hadn't taken the time to carry more salmon home yesterday. Settling into the long, silent strides her father had taught her when he took her along to his trap lines, she covered a mile and had two more to go. She moved easily up the rugged mountain, reveling in the beauty of her home.

She might not have come after the uncomfortable moment in the woods earlier if she hadn't convinced herself the noises, assuming they were human, were from Braden sulking. That stopped her from mentioning the incident at the table while they ate, too. Although she should have said something, the meal was a joyful one with Meredith and Ian elated over their news, and it had been easy to keep her vague fears to herself.

A still, small voice whispered to her to wait, to take someone along, to not strike out alone in the woods. The only thing that gave her pause was leaving Meredith alone. But Ian and Tucker had always left Meredith when they went to the mines, so they must believe it to be safe. Amy ignored her doubts in favor of action.

Her mind firmly on Braden and the way he'd held her and then pushed her away, she only distantly noticed the terrain. She'd climbed this path before, after all. She reached the summit of the modest mountain that separated her from the rich salmon run. She paused at the top, drinking in the hundreds of scenic peaks that made this look like a footstool for God's grand throne. The small mountain she stood on wasn't even high enough to be capped with snow. She followed a trail that skirted a cedar stand on her right hand and on her left dropped away in a sheer fall.

Only a few stunted trees clung to the rugged mountainside. A lip of the trail stuck out far enough that the cliff face wasn't visible for nearly a hundred feet. She looked over the edge and saw, far below, the silver waters of the stream she sought.

Beautiful—the rushing waters audible even from this high, the soft hush of the wind flowing over her like the breath of God. Sighing, inhaling the cold crisp air, she turned to head down.

Swift footfalls sounded behind her.

With only seconds to react, Amy whirled to face the direction of the running steps, but hard hands caught her before she could turn fully around. A vicious shove launched her into midair. As she fell, cruel, satisfied laughter rang in her ears. Laughter she now remembered. Laughter she'd heard in Seattle as she'd fallen under the hooves of a charging horse.

Chapter 11

Amy twisted and clawed at the cliff. A stunted tree grew out of the rock. Her chest slammed into it. The tree crackled, and the limbs cut her hands as she scrabbled for a hold. The impact jerked her fingers free, and she fell again.

A protruding rock jabbed her belly. Amy grunted at the blow, fighting to draw a breath. She hung draped over the rock, head and feet hanging down. The world swayed. The narrow rock under her belly gave her no room to balance. She began to slide feet first off the ledge. She grabbed at the jagged wall beside her, shredding her palm.

Her gaze darted around. A little crack in the rock formed a V. Amy's left hand clawed at the fissure. Her other arm swung in a wild arc over the long drop.

Her battered fingers slipped from the niche. She clenched her fist and punched it into the fissure, ripping flesh. Her weight locked her fist in the narrow opening. The protruding rock now pressed against her face.

Her body hung, suspended from one arm, wrenching her shoulder. For a sickening second, only that tremulous fist stood between her and death. Her strength wouldn't have held her. The rock pinched her fist tight, trapping her, saving her.

Amy turned her face away from the scraping rock and looked down. Below her kicking, dangling feet was a sheer drop of a hundred feet. Dizziness swept over her. Nausea twisted her stomach. She wrenched her head sideways to block her vision, choosing to focus on the rough rock scraping her cheek rather than the sickening knowledge of just how far she'd fall if her hand gave way.

With her other hand, she found a lip on the protruding rock and grabbed hold.

She fought her way back onto the tiny ledge. Once steady, she realized the rock she'd hit cut back into the cliff a few inches. Sliding into the indentation, she found a secure spot.

Careful not to lose her balance, she turned her back to the cliff and pressed against the rocks. Once tucked into the little cleft, she worked her hand free of the crack that had saved her. Looking up, she saw the cliff overhang.

Her stomach burned from the blow against the ledge. Blood streamed off her knuckles, and both her palms bled from frantically clinging to the stunted tree. Her blunt nails were torn and bleeding. Pain radiated from her face where it had ground against stone. When she gingerly touched her throbbing cheek, her fingertips came away stained scarlet with blood. Her back, undamaged in the fall, burned with the feel of shoving hands.

Someone had tried to kill her. A wave of dizziness almost upset her balance, and she forced her mind to remain clear. She had to think.

Wait on the Lord.

God chided her for striking out on her own after the meal. Or did He mean that she should wait now? Don't climb to safety. Wait for help.

She decided it meant the first. God had tried to warn her that the woods held danger for her. Well, she knew now, and she'd be careful. *I'm sorry I didn't listen, Lord.*

She turned her eyes upward to see if she could climb out.

Wait on the Lord.

Perhaps she would rest up for a few minutes.

Catching her breath, she listened for any sound from above. Never one to ignore hard facts, she faced the truth. She had no doubt that shove was a deliberate murder attempt. With shocking clarity, she realized someone had tried to kill her in Seattle, also. And maybe on the boat that night she'd been alone on the deck and that day by the railing. And someone had been lurking in the woods near her smokehouse. She wondered if Braden's presence had headed off an attack earlier.

Who?

She thought of the man who'd come to her father's door. Would that man silence the only person on earth who might dispute his claim?

There had been others on the ship who'd made her uncomfortable. Darnell Thompson, with his too-watchful eyes, had been close that day at the railing. Had he hoped for one last chance to kill her?

What about the oily little Barnabas Stucky?

Both men had claimed to be stampeders. Both had offered to accompany her home. No gold miner on his way to the Klondike took a side trip to go sightseeing. Not even a woman in a nearly all-male world could turn those madmen aside.

Amy sat and thought it through as her breathing steadied and the worst of the pain eased from her hands. When she had quit trembling, she began to assess her situation.

Studying the sheer wall below her, she knew going down was impossible. Amy had scampered around mountains many times in her childhood. She tried to pick out footholds and handholds in the rock face and found none.

Above her, Amy could see a way, precarious but possible for about half the distance to the top. After that, the cliff curved out of sight for a few feet before ending at the overhang. Her climb might lead her all the way up or leave her stranded, possibly unable to go back, hanging over thin air.

But if she did get to the top, what awaited her? Someone who even now had noticed that she'd stopped her headlong fall to death? Or had he shoved her and run like a sneaking coward who would attack a woman from behind?

Amy sat quietly, listening. She'd been preoccupied as she'd walked, a foolish mistake that she'd never have made before her years in Washington. But even distracted, she'd have noticed any blatant sounds. That meant whoever had pushed her knew the woods.

And that made him smart enough to wait quietly and make sure he finished his job.

Amy looked at the sun still high in the sky. She knew the patience of the north country. She knew what it meant to out-wait a stalking cougar or a hungry bear. This ledge twenty feet down a cliff felt safe. For now, maybe the safest place between here and the Raffertys. She'd stay.

Wait on the Lord.

For now, she'd wait.

———

"Honey, what are you doing out here?"

At the sound of Ian's worried voice, Braden turned from the rock he chiseled. Meredith stood near their most recent digging, her trim body silhouetted against the sunlight. Her shoulders rose and fell as she panted.

Ian and Tucker had worked their way through solid stone during the last year. Braden had already found a couple of thin streaks of the golden wealth that God had created and sewn into the fabric of the earth. None of the streaks went deep.

He couldn't see his sister-in-law's face, but he could feel her tension. He dropped his pick and heard two other metallic clangs from Tucker and Ian as they advanced on Meredith.

Ian got there first. Braden and Tucker were a step behind.

"Amy's never come back." Meredith flung herself into Ian's arms. "I should have waited, but I've just got this terrible feeling. She promised to be back in time to start dinner. I told her I'd do it, but she insisted, and she's never failed to keep her word."

Ian lifted his wife, her feet dangling above the ground, and carried her out of the mine. He brushed the wisps of brown hair off her flushed cheeks.

"You shouldn't have hiked all the way up here."

Ian, Meredith, and Tucker all turned on Braden when he spoke.

Worry creased Ian's forehead as he turned back to his wife. "Are you all right?"

"I just couldn't wait. I feel fine. I was careful." Meredith turned away from Ian, who kept his hands around her waist. Her eyes blazed at Braden until he could feel the heat.

"I couldn't sit at home *when I'm fine* while Amy might be in danger."

Braden arched a brow at Meredith's fierce strength, so different than anything he'd known with Maggie. Another pang of guilt hit him as he compared Maggie to another woman and found his wife wanting. Not everyone was strong. Not everyone had what it took to tackle an unsettled land. That wasn't Maggie's fault.

Clenching his jaw to keep from defending Maggie when no one here had said a word against her, Braden nodded. "No, of course you couldn't."

"Where did she go?" Tucker stepped past Braden and studied his twin. He pulled a handkerchief out of his hip pocket and mopped Meredith's sweaty, dirt-streaked face. The walk up here was strenuous.

Braden's stomach clenched in fear for Meredith's baby—and for Amy. Meredith spoke the truth about Amy's dependability. Something had happened to her. Why had he let her set off in the wilderness? What if that polar bear had attacked her?

Braden fought down his growing panic. "She said she needed more salmon. She mentioned the spawning bed. Where is that?"

Tucker and Ian exchanged a glance over Meredith's head. Ian looked at Braden. "I don't know. The few salmon we catch come from the Skaguay River. The two of you talked about the smokehouse, but she never said where exactly she'd caught the fish."

Meredith spun around to face Ian. "You can find her. You can track her down and bring her home."

Braden remembered his brother in the woods when they were young. He'd moved with the silence of a cloud of smoke. He'd made a game of sneaking up on wild animals.

"Yes," Braden said, "you can do this, Ian."

Ian looked at Tucker. "I want you to walk down to the cabin slowly with Meredith. Make sure she doesn't overdo it."

"Ian, I'm fine!" Meredith clenched her fists.

Ian rested a hand on her cheek. "I know you are, honey. But let Tucker take care of you, please. Braden and I are going after Amy, and we're going fast. That means I'm leaving you behind, and it'll take a load off my mind if I know you're being easy on yourself."

He lowered his hand from her cheek to her stomach. "You told me you get dizzy sometimes. That's a mighty serious business when you're walking alone with no one to catch you if you fall. Let Tucker get you home safe. Please."

Meredith rested her hand on top of Ian's. To Braden it looked like the two of them were holding their unborn child. The sight warmed his heart, and for once he felt no pain when he thought of a baby.

Meredith nodded. "I'll behave." She reached up and gave Ian a quick kiss on the cheek. "Now get out of here and find Amy. If I lose that woman, I don't know what I'll do." She said it lightly, but there was nothing humorous about a missing woman in the wilderness.

Braden didn't know what he'd do, either.

Ian cut his gaze to Braden. "Let's get moving."

Ian took off down the mountain at a near run with Braden right on his heels.

In the time it took Braden to load both rifles, Ian had found Amy's tracks heading straight up the mountain, away from the river.

"What salmon live up there?" Braden muttered.

"There's a stream that empties into the river. It winds around like crazy, and I've never followed it. I'll bet she's heading for that. Climbing up and down this mountain will be shorter than going around, I'm figuring."

Silently they fell into step, Ian in the lead. He passed through a thick patch of trees and dropped to the ground so suddenly Braden almost tripped over him.

"This is an old game trail. I've never noticed it before. How did she find it so fast?"

Braden could see Amy's footprints heading uphill.

Ian pointed. "You can see she went up and came back down yesterday. But there's no sign of her returning today." Ian looked up through the spruce and cedars grown close together, clinging as if by a miracle to the rocky ground. Shrubs tangled together, mixing with the scent of pine and showing off their summer finery of berries and flowers, sometimes guarded by wicked thorns. Heavy branches drooped across the trail.

Ian set off, pushing through the dense foliage, following her trail easily. She'd moved quickly, her strides long. The rocky soil gave way to solid rock, and a few yards after that the trail split. One side went up, the other down.

Ian crouched to study the ground. He rose and went a few long strides up the slope, then came back to brush his fingers over the lower route. Hunkered down to touch the plants along the trail, he turned at last to Braden. "I can't tell which way she went. There's no sign of a footprint on the stone. This could be the way down to the stream. I'll follow this one." Ian gave the plant one more look as if he could hear it speaking and was listening for Amy's route. Then he pointed at the upward trail. "You see if you can find any tracks that way."

"What if the trail divides again?" It could divide a hundred times, and they could be days exploring all the possibilities.

Ian shook his head. "Let's don't borrow trouble."

Braden nodded then headed up, tension growing in his stomach. Amy was now long overdue. She'd have been on time, toting those blasted fish, and Braden knew it. The stone path stretched ahead relentlessly, as if a thousand years of winter winds had scrubbed every breath of soil from its surface, leaving no chance for a single footprint. He could find no evidence Amy had come this way.

He reached the peak and stopped at the edge of a cliff to look down on the stream far below. He could hear the rushing water. Did that mean she'd taken this path? Or was it the one Ian had followed?

The soaring view, breathtaking in its beauty, made Braden feel closer to God than he had since Maggie died.

"God, where is she?" he prayed aloud.

"Braden, is that you?"

Braden gasped at the voice coming from under his feet and jumped backward. Then he dropped to his knees and leaned out over the edge of the cliff.

"Be careful!" She sounded exasperated. "There isn't room for anyone else down here."

Despite his shock, Braden grinned. "You sound okay." He lay on his stomach and scooted out far enough so that he could look around a scrub cedar and see Amy looking up, her expression disgruntled as if she wondered what took him so long.

Chapter 12

W hat in the world took you so long?" Amy began her cautious ascent, ignoring her shredded hands, dried blood, throbbing skin. She'd been planning to climb up as soon as someone came to find her. After just a couple of months with the Raffertys, she knew to expect them, and she feared facing whoever had pushed her, so she'd waited. Yes, for once she'd waited. She breathed a prayer of thanksgiving for Braden's presence.

She reached the curve in the rock face and got a firm grasp on the stunted tree. Pulling herself up to use it for a foothold, she stopped. With five feet from her outstretched hand to the top, there wasn't a handhold in sight. Her stomach twisted as she thought of being stranded on this sheer rock with her battered hands, trying to back up. The places she'd found to hold were little more than half-inch-wide ledges in the rough stone and then this tree with its rough bark and piercing needles. Now, instead of the mortal danger she would have faced had she refused to wait, she had Braden.

He reached for her. She reached back. Their hands met in the middle and locked together. The pain of his solid grip on her battered hand told her she was alive and safe. She met his gaze and had no fear of letting go of her last anchor. Braden would hang on. He'd pull her to safety.

It struck her again just as it had earlier. Yes, she loved him. And he was a fine man, worthy of her love. It was she who didn't measure up. She could work from sun to sun—and that said a lot in an Alaskan June—but she'd never be the genteel lady who'd won his heart. Amy felt sure that the harder she worked, the more she underlined her unfitness for him.

Braden pulled her up, catching her other arm when it came within reach. Once he had her securely, he slid his arm around her waist and tugged, rearing back on his knees as she came over the ledge. They tumbled onto the trail together. Braden jumped to his feet. He stayed close, as if ready to grab her should she fall back over the cliff.

Amy climbed more slowly upright, every joint in her body aching. Braden kept a steady hand on her arm. They looked over the dead drop; then Amy turned away, shaken to think how close she'd come to dying.

"Thank God, you're all right." Braden's heartfelt words brought her head up. His eyes skimmed over her bruised, bleeding face; then he clamped one hard hand on her waist and pulled her into his arms.

"You could have died." Braden's head lowered. "I could have lost you."

Their lips met.

Braden broke the kiss. Amy's eyes flickered open as Braden stepped away, turning toward the cliff. He rubbed the back of his neck with one hand and stared into space. Where a moment ago, she'd been warm, now the cool, dry Alaskan air chilled her lips.

Amy knew what would come next. Regret. A list of her inadequacies—a list of Maggie's virtues. She spoke before he could.

"Do not touch me again."

Braden's head rose, and his eyebrows arched. "I—I won't. I'm sorry."

Regret. Already. Now here came a list of her inadequacies. She headed him off. "Fine. As long as we are clear."

Amy crossed her arms. "Now what are we going to do about this?"

Braden's eyes dropped to her lips.

"Not that!" Amy snapped.

Braden looked her in the eye, his face flushed.

"What are we going to do about the man who pushed me off that cliff?"

"What?" Braden pushed his battered Stetson back.

"I stayed down there because I feared he might still be here."

"He?"

"The man who pushed me off the cliff." Amy looked around. She'd be on her guard now like she should have been all along. She was lucky she had survived to be more careful.

"A man pushed you off the cliff?" Braden looked around.

"Did you think I fell? Do you believe I am a clumsy city woman who trips over her own feet?"

"Uh, yes, I mean, no, not clumsy," Braden said. "But you're from the city, after all."

"I am from Alaska. This is my home. I am as sure-footed as a bighorn sheep, and I do *not* trip over the side of a cliff by accident." Amy clenched her jaw and fists in the same breath and turned away from him. She forced herself to be practical. Looking for tracks, she saw the solid rock underfoot. There'd be no tracks. Even off the trail, the shrubs grew out of tumbled rock.

"How long ago did this happen?" Braden's sharp, wary voice got her attention.

"I have been on that ledge for at least four hours."

"Four hours?" His brows slammed together as he studied her scraped face. "How did you hold on so long?"

"What choice did I have?"

He frowned then looked into the underbrush, going straight to the most obvious hiding place. "No tracks. Whoever did it picked the perfect spot."

Amy had already learned of Ian's skill in the wilderness. But Braden also looked comfortable studying the trail, searching for signs left behind by the attacker. She watched him run his hand over the ground as if he could feel the presence of someone from hours ago. Father had tracked like that.

Braden turned to Amy. "What did he look like?"

"I did not see him. I just heard someone run up behind me. Then he pushed." *And laughed like in Seattle.* She opened her mouth to tell Braden this wasn't the first attack.

"He? You saw a man?"

"No, I just said I did not see anyone."

Braden crossed his arms. "Then how do you know a man pushed you?"

"Because. . .because. . ." Amy faltered.

Braden's eyes narrowed.

"Because I suspect I was pushed by the man who stole my father's cabin."

Braden shook his head as if her answer disgusted him. "You're obsessed with your father's cabin."

"My obsession did not push me over that cliff."

Braden fell silent. Amy didn't like the look in his eyes.

Braden looked down at her hands and reached for them. "You're hurt."

She saw her palms, scraped raw. He turned them over, revealing several bleeding fingernails broken below the quick. Next his eyes focused on her face. "You're scraped here, too." He touched her cheek with a calloused hand.

The teachers at the mission had warned her to hold herself apart from men, and she always had. Now Braden's gentle touch only brought pain because she knew he had judged her unworthy. She enjoyed the touch even as she knew she should push him away.

"We need to get you home. Can you walk?" Braden slid one arm around her waist as if he planned to pick her up and carry her.

Hurt by his kindness when she knew it carried no affection, Amy stepped out of his reach. "I have been sitting all afternoon. I am as rested as a bear awakened from his winter sleep by the chinook. What about the man who pushed me?" Amy started down the trail.

Braden jogged to catch up with her. "You're sure you were pushed?"

Amy stopped so suddenly Braden plowed into her back. She stumbled from the impact, and Braden caught her arm to steady her. She shook off his hand. "What do you mean, am I sure?"

Braden's fair skin turned pink, and he seemed very interested in the rock he kicked under his toe. "It's just that, well. . .you didn't really see anybody. Maybe you slipped, or maybe a branch fell out of a tree and hit—"

"What branch?" Amy turned back to the site where she'd fallen. "Would it not be lying there if it fell out of a tree and hit me?"

"Not if it fell over the cliff, too."

Speechless, Amy stared at Braden until finally the silence brought his head up. Once he looked at her, she asked rigidly, "Do you think I am a liar? You called me such this morning."

Braden shook his head until the red curls peeking out from under his hat danced. "I didn't say you lied."

"Then you think I am stupid."

"Amy, I. . ." Braden pulled his Stetson off and slid the brim around and around through his fingers.

"Do branches sound like running feet?" She slugged him in the shoulder, and he looked up.

"You never said anything about running feet."

"I did not know I stood in front of a judge, giving testimony. I thought I spoke to a friend who had some. . ." Her voice broke. Shocked at her weakness, she cleared her throat and went on. "Some respect for me."

"Now, you know I respect you. I saw that smokehouse you built."

Amy's eyes narrowed. "And you came running over to help me as if I were some fragile flower about to be crushed under the stones, even though I had obviously already built most of it alone."

"I just thought it looked like. . .like. . ." He went back to playing with his hat.

"Like hard work?" She slapped the hat out of his hands and only through sheer strength of will kept herself from stomping the crown into the stone path when it hit the ground at her feet. "Is that what you were going to say? You did not think I would want to do any hard work? As if I am lazy?"

"No." He looked up from his hat, glaring at her. "That's not what I meant. It's just hard. It's not woman's work. I didn't mean any offense."

"You call me a clumsy—"

"I didn't."

"Stupid—"

"You're not stupid."

"Lazy—"

"You work hard. I never said—"

"Liar."

"Well, you should have told Ian—"

"Is that about it? Perhaps you would toss me back over the cliff before my inferiority destroys your family."

"Now, Amy lass, don't be—"

"Let me tell you something about women's work, you stampeding *g'oon* hunter."

"Stampeding what?

Amy might not have said it if she hadn't been so insulted. "G'oon. It means gold. You're one of the stampeders, are you not? One of the crazy men invading my beautiful Tlingit land for that golden rock."

"Your Clink It land?" He pronounced the word in a clumsy fashion. "What does that mean?"

"It means while you are calling me clumsy and lazy and stupid and a liar—"

"I did *not* say you were—"

"I am born to this land. I have learned how to find the true wealth in it without tearing out its heart with a pickax. My mother was a Tlingit."

"A what?"

Amy jammed her fisted hands on her hips and flinched when her scraped palms protested.

Braden caught one of her hands, and she wrenched it away. "One of the native people who lived for centuries in harmony with the snow and darkness before you came with your big steamer ships and soft ways."

"Soft ways?" Braden scooped up his hat and clapped it on his head. Dust puffed out from the brim.

"And I learned how to live in Alaska from her and my Russian father. Each of them alone is stronger than all you Raffertys put together."

Braden narrowed his eyes. "Y–your mother was an Eskimo?"

Amy remembered as she saw Braden's strange expression that her father had warned her people would treat her oddly if she told them of her native and Russian blood. Amy crossed her arms. Well, now came her chance to see how Braden reacted. This was his test, not hers.

"My mother is half Tlingit, I am one quarter. We're not *Eskimos*. That is a word your people use for all of us because you are too lazy to learn who we are, even while you insist there is a difference between your Irish, your Scots, your English, your Swedes, and your Germans. There are dozens of different groups up here. I am from the Tlingit nation. I know rugged land. I know narrow mountain passages. I know the difference between a falling branch and a running man."

Braden shook his head. "Then why haven't you said anything before? I mean, you said you grew up here, but I had no idea your roots went so deep."

"My name is Amaruq Simonovich. My father is a Russian fur trader, not a man to die easily. Not a man to sell a cabin he does not own. An old friend gave over the lovely spot out of the wind to my father. Papa comes and goes following the fur seasons. He has lived in that cabin for more than twenty years, but it is not his to sell. It is only his to live in."

"Amaruq? I heard Wily call you that, but I thought I'd just misunderstood. Then Amy—"

"My father wished to have me live as an American in Seattle."

"You *are* an American," Braden said indignantly.

"Father feared that I would be treated poorly as both a Tlingit and a Russian. So I abided by his wishes. But I am proud of my heritage, and I know this land. And I never want to speak to you again."

Amy whirled and charged down the trail. She nearly reached the bottom before Braden caught up with her and grabbed her arm.

"Listen, if you really think a man pushed you off that cliff. . ."

Amy jerked her arm loose and jammed her elbow into Braden's gut. It was like hitting iron. He had the nerve to smile as he caught hold of her again.

She defiantly tilted her chin.

Speaking as if he were addressing a two-year-old, he said, "If someone pushed you off a cliff, you'd better not go running away on your own."

"I would rather—"

"If you're tellin' the truth. . ." Braden cut her off, his good humor evaporating. "Then stay with me." His eyes challenged her.

To dash past him back to the cabin would be to admit no danger existed. She thought of those pounding footsteps, and a shiver ran down her spine. She knew Braden felt it, because his grip softened. He rubbed the length of her upper arm as if to warm her.

While she wanted to defy him, it *was* foolish to go off alone. Should she tell Braden her suspicions about what happened in Seattle? He'd just think she imagined that, too. Why not? She'd believed it an accident until just hours ago. That uncomfortable moment on the boat was even vaguer.

It was foolish to go off alone earlier. Especially after I sensed someone watching me. Wait on the Lord.

Amy wanted to scream. She didn't want to wait on anyone. Not Braden, not God, and not the man who had attacked her. She pictured the cruel, bloodshot eyes of the man in her father's home. She wanted action. She wanted to charge straight for her father's cabin and force a confession out of that man.

She turned and stood at Braden's side like a well-trained dog. "You are right. It would be foolish. I will stay beside you as we go back, and then we will plan together how to oust this evil man from my home."

"The cabin again. What about us? What about Merry? We need you here. What good is a cabin goin' to do you all alone in the wilderness? You can't live there."

"Of course I can." She wrenched her arm away from his tender touch.

"But why would you? That's no life, one woman alone. Why not stay here with us?"

"It is not the cabin I care about; it is justice for my father I seek. That man most likely killed him. That is not something I will forget, especially since the same man is trying to kill me."

"If he is."

They stared at each other. Amy saw the stubborn line of Braden's jaw and knew he'd never help her, never see justice done. God wanted her to wait. Now Braden wanted her to wait. She couldn't do it.

"Ian should be meeting us down lower." Braden nodded toward the trail. "He took another path."

"That one leads into a ravine cut by a spring. It empties into this spring a long way to the south. You can get to the salmon beds from there, but my way is quicker."

"Now, tell me again how you know someone pushed you."

Amy retold her story, more carefully this time, including every detail. She even told Braden about the noise she'd heard earlier in the woods. As they walked, Amy's tension eased, and she felt the safety of a strong man at her side. It reminded her of her father and how he'd always cherished her.

Looking sideways at Braden, she said, "My mother's name was Yéil; it means 'raven,' a sacred creature to my people. My mother and her village became Christians, but the old names are still special to them, and they often name a child after animals. My name, Amaruq, means 'wolf.'"

"Now that you say it, I can believe that you're an Eskimo."

Amy arched a brow.

"I mean a Clink It," Braden added with a faint blush. "But brown hair and brown eyes are common."

"Mother was a half-blood Tlingit raised in a Tlingit village and wise in their ways. My father is Petrov Simonovich, a Russian fur trader, born and raised in Alaska. They were both strong people from races suited to the cold, dark land." Amy crossed her arms and looked at Braden. "I have inherited their strength."

"You were barely surviving on that boat."

"That is because of an accident in Seattle." She clenched her jaw to keep from adding her suspicions to her story. "Part of the reason I decided to come home was the frantic pace of the city. Also, I could not support myself after my injuries. And I—" Amy stopped, then gathered her composure. "I missed my father. I had not heard from him in a long time. I needed to make sure he was all right."

Braden, his stride shortened out of concern for her, turned as they walked together. Amy saw him study her in the spring sunlight dappled by the hardy cedars and slender spruce that lined the narrow game trail, barely wide enough for two people. The sun sank lower in the sky, but hours of daylight remained.

"Amaruq, huh?" He grinned at her.

Amy tried to remember why her father thought it important to keep her heritage private.

"Amaruq Simonovich. Well, I guess you being here makes more sense than an Irish farmer."

Amy managed a smile. "A lot more sense."

Braden smiled and then laughed. Ian appeared from a little side trail and gave Amy a startled look.

"I am fine." Her mouth spoke the words, but her heart knew the truth. No one was fine who had someone trying to kill her.

Chapter 13

"S omeone tried to kill you?" Meredith clutched Amy as if she were hanging off a cliff right that very minute.

Tucker jumped from his seat at the table, knocking his chair over. His eyes were wary, his body tense, coiled for action as if the attacker might come into the room at any moment.

Amy decided someone needed to build sturdier furniture for this household, and she was just the one to do it.

She saw Ian's eyes darken with worry as he hurried to Meredith's side and slid his arm around her to calm her. Braden stood beside Amy, the two of them just inside the door. He rubbed the back of his neck and shook his head at Amy as if she were upsetting Meredith deliberately.

"He did not succeed." Patting Meredith's hand, hoping to calm her, Amy added, "From now on I will be on my guard. Do not get all in a dither."

Meredith, always as sweet and cheerful as her name, squared her shoulders and clenched her fists. Despite Meredith's bout of sickness caused by the baby, Amy remembered that Ian's wife had survived the frigid Alaskan winter and cared for two men, all without complaint—and certainly without climbing on a roof and crowing the sun up in the morning.

Meredith's eyes narrowed. "I am not in a dither." She turned on Ian. "What are we going to do about this?"

"Well, I thought—"

"We are going to my father's cabin and have it out with that man." Amy cut him off.

Amy shifted her gaze from Braden to Ian to Tucker. "You know that is who pushed me. Until we prove that, no one is safe. Such a dangerous, ruthless man. He could harm anyone if his twisted mind told him to."

"Ian, you've got to see to this." Meredith wrapped her arm around Amy's shoulders.

"You don't know he did anything wrong." Braden dragged his hat off his head and hung it on the peg beside the door. "You didn't see anyone."

"We'll get to the bottom of it, honey." Ian slung an arm around Meredith.

Amy pulled away from Meredith and whirled to face Braden. "Are you going to accuse me of being a liar again?"

"We can't go off and leave the women at home." Tucker shouldered his way between Meredith and Ian. "You stay, Ian. You're a married man going to be a father. Braden and I will go to Amy's cabin and take care of this."

Braden ran both hands through his hair, his agitated motions making the unruly curls wild. He raised both hands in front of him as if surrendering. "I never said you were a liar."

"You called Amy a liar?" Meredith ducked under Tucker's arm and scowled at Braden. "Why, she's the most honest woman who ever lived."

"That is not the way I remember it, Braden Rafferty." Amy shook a finger under Braden's nose. "You accused me of—"

"Now, honey, don't go getting mad at Braden." Ian circled Tucker's huge frame and rested his hands on Meredith's shoulders.

Amy jammed her fists on her hips. "Why are we wasting time talking when we should be heading for Father's house?"

Wait on the Lord.

Amy shook her head to clear it of the impossible idea. Now was the time for action—past time in her opinion. "You are not going without me. Tucker, Braden, and I will go. Ian and Meredith can stay here."

"I did not say you lied."

Amy glared at Braden.

"We can all go." Meredith wrung her hands as if she were afraid of being left out. "I have been in this cabin nonstop for six months."

Meredith was practically confined indoors thanks to the bear tracks Ian had seen. The only time she went outdoors was when Amy cooked their meals. And then she sat in the yard, within feet of the house. Amy knew anyone living like that would be eager for a change.

"Now, we can't do that." Ian rubbed Meredith's shoulder. "I wish we could, honey. I know you'd like to go to town."

"Are you out of your mind?" Tucker turned on Meredith. "We're not going on a picnic. You can't come. It's dangerous."

Despite the rudeness, Amy saw how dearly Tucker loved his sister.

"We are wasting time." Amy's arms flew wide. "If none of you are going, fine. I'll go myself."

"Are you out of your mind?" Braden leaned until his nose almost touched hers. "You're not going anywhere alone again as long as you live." Braden's orders only made her more impatient. "And I didn't call you a liar. I wondered if you might be mistaken, is all. It's hard enough believing someone is capable of murder, but to accuse a man with no evidence—"

"The evidence"—Amy jabbed the second button on Braden's brown broadcloth shirt—"is his presence in my father's cabin. I am telling you for the last time, my father would not have sold it."

She pulled her hand back for another good jab.

Braden caught her hand. "Stop that."

Amy jerked against his grip, and he let her go.

"When you said 'for the last time,' you didn't even begin to mean it, did you?" Braden sounded exhausted.

Amy clenched her fists.

"Now, Amy, you can't know that about your pa. He might have sold the cabin." Tucker hooked his thumbs into his suspenders.

"He's her father. Who would know better?" Meredith shoved Tucker sideways.

Not budging an inch, Tucker scowled at Meredith.

"And that means it was stolen." Amy ignored Tucker and jabbed Braden again. "So if my father died under unexplained circumstances, then this man is suspect in his murder."

Braden caught Amy's hand. "I told you to stop that."

"Amy's word is good enough for me, Braden. We have to help her. Stop being so stubborn." Meredith crossed her arms, the very picture of stubbornness.

"The law needs more than Amy's suspicions." Ian stuck his head between Tucker and Meredith.

Tucker quit glaring at Meredith and turned to Amy. "Don't even think of going down there by yourself."

Amy pulled against Braden's grasp.

Braden didn't let go. Fire flashed from his blue eyes.

Common sense said to give an angry man some space. She stepped closer and rose on her tiptoes. "Then you had better quit making excuses and come with me. Let us go see if the deed is still in the hidden drawer in Papa's mantel. It is just an old paper given to him by the Russian trapper who lived there before him. Father would have signed it over if he'd sold. And if the man killed my father and stole the cabin, that deed will be tucked in there, all the proof you and the law need."

Braden rolled his eyes. "We can't just go off in these woods and leave everyone behind."

"Why not?"

"It's not safe to leave Ian and Merry alone. You, Tucker, and I would be fine, unless there's really someone after you."

Amy gasped. "You just called me a liar again." Amy whirled to face Meredith. "Did you hear that?"

Meredith stepped up to stand shoulder to shoulder with Amy. "I most certainly did."

"Not a liar, mistaken."

"Then we will go, just the two of us," Amy said to Braden. "We will sneak up to his place, wait until he is away, go in, and have a look in the mantel. If everything is in order, we will leave. Tucker and Ian can stay here. That way, Meredith will be safe."

"You can't sneak into a man's house," Ian pointed out. "It's against the law."

"It is not sneaking in if it is my father's house. I am welcome there."

Braden shook his head. "But you can't know if it's your father's house until after you sneak in. So it's wrong. Finding something that makes it right later still makes it wrong when you first do it."

"What are Ian and Tucker keeping me safe from?" Meredith threw her hand in the air. "Until this man attacked, I have felt as safe as a babe in arms."

"What about those bear tracks Ian saw?" Tucker reminded her.

"That was days ago," Ian said. "The bear must have moved on, because the tracks are old. This isn't his regular territory. I can tell by his size he's an old fellow, and I've seen no sign of him before."

"Bears roam widely. Just because he has never been here before does not mean he is passing through," Amy said.

Ian shook his head. "He's miles from here by now, heading north. And I should be the one to go. Once we're in the wilderness, I'm the one who can find a trail and keep an eye out for trouble. And now that the bear's gone, whoever stays here will be perfectly safe."

A crash shook the cabin and startled Amy into stumbling against Braden. He wrapped his arms around her as they whirled toward the sound. The cabin door hung on one hinge, and the paw of a polar bear poked through the opening. The fierce roar of the hungry bear nearly rattled the timbers that held up the cabin.

Tucker dived for the shotgun hanging over the door. "Perfectly safe, my—"

The bear slashed at Tucker, and he stumbled back. The door tilted open at the upper left corner.

Braden grabbed Amy around the waist. He tucked her behind him. Ian caught Meredith by the shoulders and shoved her at Braden. Snagging Meredith around the waist, Braden put his body between both women and the bear. Ian ran for the door.

The bear roared. A paw slammed. The leather hinge on the bottom broke. Only the rickety wooden latch held the door closed.

Tucker, landing his back with a hard thud against the sturdy row of cedar saplings that formed the door, shoved it into place. His body and the protesting latch stood between the rest of them and a thousand pounds of enraged bear.

Tucker reached over his head, lifted the gun down off its pegs, and tossed it. Ian snagged it in midair. Braden ducked beside the door and lifted the heavy bar they dropped in place every night to secure the cabin.

Amy dashed for the bag of herbs she'd been collecting ever since she'd arrived. Thrusting her hand deep in the bag, she dug until she found the leather pouch she'd so carefully filled.

The beast barreled into the door with a vicious snarl. The door shook, and Tucker staggered forward a step. Bracing his legs, Tucker jammed the door back in place.

"When I say so, let the door go." Ian lifted the gun, keeping the barrel pointed upward over Tucker's head.

"No!" Braden shouted, lifting the massive beam. "Let's get this bar in place. It'll be enough to keep the bear out. He'll go away eventually. If we let him in, you might not get him before he hurts the women."

Amy swung the wooden shutter in the bedroom aside and poked her head out the window, looking toward the bear.

Braden caught Amy's movements out of the corner of his eye. "What are you doing?" He turned toward her.

"Scat, hintak xóodzi! Shoo, bear!" She tugged the slipknot that held the pouch closed. The bear swung its massive head at her. He fixed his beady black eyes on Amy as if he could already taste her tender flesh. The bear reared up on its hind legs. She threw the bane at the bear, pouch and all.

The pouch hit the bear full in the face, and a little puff of the bitter herb dusted its snout. The growling roar cut off and turned to a whine. He retracted his claws and swiped at his face.

Braden grabbed Amy around the waist. "Get away before he—"

The bear's whining grew louder. Braden quit hollering and turned to see the animal drop on all fours and shake his head frantically, sneezing and rubbing his face on his furry foreleg. The bear looked up, and for a second, Amy stared into his eyes.

"I know it hurts, hintak xóodzi, old friend, but you should not have come here. The salmon swim thick just over the hill. Quit being lazy and go find your own food. Leave us in peace."

Meredith shoved herself in beside Amy.

Ian stepped up behind his wife. Amy saw Tucker ease the door open an inch and peek through.

The bear seemed to be crying. Amy grinned. She knew the bitter powder would do no harm, but for a while it would sting something fierce. "Big baby."

The bear shook his head again like a dog shaking off water. Huffing, his nose and eyes streamed. Then, with a wail as if he'd been soundly spanked by his mama, he turned and galloped into the woods. Amy hoped he was going fishing. The water would soothe the sting.

Meredith turned once the bear disappeared. "You have a bear repellant in your case?"

"Of course." Amy laughed. "No one lives in the midst of wolves, bears, and wolverines without a supply of it. I call it water carrot."

Tucker set the door back in place, and when it fell toward him, he dropped the bar across it with a loud clatter. "Water carrot?"

Ian stepped away from the window. "I'm really familiar with these woods. I've never heard of water carrot."

Amy shrugged. "It resembles a carrot and smells of it a bit. That may not be its true name. It is something my people use. We also call it *yán*. Before the missionaries came and told my mother's people about Jesus and the one true God, we used yán as a magic charm to ward off evil spirits."

"And bears?" Meredith asked, shaking her head, still glancing nervously at the woods where the bear had disappeared.

Amy laughed. "Yes, all large dangerous animals. Now we know it is not magic; it just burns."

"And where do you find this water carrot?" Ian's brow furrowed.

Pleased Ian showed this eagerness to learn more about this new homeland of his, Amy said, "I will show you. It is dangerous though. I'm careful to never, never touch it with my bare hands. It is a deadly poison if eaten, and the juice would make you very sick if it touched your skin."

Amy thought of the plant for a second and then added, "Oh, I remember now, one of the missionaries told us yán goes by another name in the English language."

"What name?" Braden asked.

Amy carefully turned away from the group and washed her hands thoroughly as she tried to remember. "It was something about one of your ancient teachers. We studied him a bit in school." She dried her hands and turned back to the four of them, only then noticing the way they were staring at her, as if she'd wrestled the bear single-handedly rather than just tossing the bane at him. And that's when she remembered.

"Socrates." She nodded with satisfaction.

"What about him?" Meredith asked.

Ian slipped his arm around Meredith and rested his big hand on her slender waist.

"He drank the potion from this plant."

Silence stretched long in the room.

At last Meredith asked, "You mean hemlock?"

Amy snapped her fingers. "Yes, some people call it hemlock."

Ian dropped his arm from Meredith and buried his face in both hands. "Bear repellant."

"She's got hemlock in a bag." Tucker's shoulders began to tremble in a way Amy couldn't define, almost as if he were laughing. But what was funny about any of this? He ducked his head then turned his back and went to the door. He must be preparing to mend it.

"Well, he will not be back, and it is time to fix supper. I will get smoked salmon. It will cook up quickly."

Braden rested his hands on her shoulders and turned her back to the dry sink Ian had fashioned out of a three-foot section of a hollowed-out bud gum tree. "First, before you cook our supper, why don't you wash your hands once more?"

Amy reached for the pail of water, but Braden blocked her hands and poured the water for her, then carefully wiped the bucket where she'd grasped it moments earlier. Amy let him help as she washed again, though she couldn't imagine why. Had he seen a smudge on her hands that she'd missed?

As Amy washed, Meredith came up beside her and handed her a bar of soap. "What else do you have in that bag?"

Amy accepted it and kept scrubbing. "Oh well, tundra rose, of course, and mooseberries. A bit of devil's club, although not enough. I got tired of dodging the thorns and will go back later for more. I brought in a bit of spruce tip—hard to run a home without that. And there are crushed leaves that make a wonderful mosquito repellant. We can rub it on our skin and—"

"It's not made out of nightshade, is it?" Amy noticed Meredith wringing her hands together.

"Nightshade? I have never heard of that. Does it grow around here? Does it make a good tonic?" Amy wiped her hands again on the flour-sack towel hanging on a peg near the sink. When she finished, Braden took it between two fingertips, held it far from his body, and tossed it out the window.

"How about foxglove?" Tucker kept his back to her, apparently fascinated by the door, his shoulders shaking harder now.

"Foxglove? My, no. That is not an Alaskan plant. Do you people know nothing about the northern lands?" Amy crossed her arms, wondering why they were all staring at her except Tucker, who ignored her as blatantly as the others stared.

"Wolf bane, maybe?" Ian asked. "That'd keep the mosquitoes away, I'm thinking. After all, it stands to reason that anything that'll scare off a wolf'll scare off a mosquito."

Amy frowned at them.

"Any poisonous mushrooms in that bag, Amy darlin'?" Braden shook his head at her. "Or maybe you've stored up a little rattlesnake venom?"

Suddenly they all burst out laughing.

Just as Amy's feelings began to pinch, Meredith threw her arms wide and hugged Amy until she could barely breathe.

Meredith whispered in her ear. "I'm so glad you're here."

The words and the tight hug were so sweet Amy hugged her back. She thought of Braden's arms around her on the cliff, then later when he tossed her here and there as he stood in the breach between her and a savage bear. It was a completely different kind of feeling from Meredith's hug, but he'd been trying to save her, even if it had slowed her down. It healed a lonely place in her heart to know he'd put her safety above his own.

The laughter quit hurting, and soon she joined in.

Meredith pulled away. "What in the world is a hintak xóodzi?"

"It is my people's word for the great white bear."

"Your people?" Tucker asked.

Braden and Amy exchanged a glance. Braden gave her an encouraging nod.

"Braden, you and Tucker run and fetch me the salmon. Ian, get a fire started in the fireplace. Meredith, you get comfortable at the table. I am hopeful the salmon will not upset your stomach as much as the mutton. When we are together, I will make supper while I tell you all about hintak xóodzi and my people."

Chapter 14

Amy wanted to march straight down to her father's cabin and confront the man who now lived there. It galled her to admit it, but she was too frightened to go alone. She didn't want to further frighten Meredith, so she didn't try to get the whole family to help her. She focused on Braden, but although two weeks had passed since the attack on the cliff, he still refused to help.

She was turning into a nag, and it was all his fault. He also wouldn't let her go anywhere alone. Amy got some satisfaction out of ordering the stubborn man around while he followed her. It neared mid-June. The days were hot, but a cool breeze kept them comfortable as Amy tramped through the woods with Braden ever watchful at her side. The snow had melted away from all but the mountain peaks.

"Pull that limb down so I can cut it." She jabbed an impatient finger at a stunted little tree with bright scarlet branches as thin as a whipcord. Amy simmered like a pot over a hot fire with the lid clamped down tight. She wanted to go to her father's, and she couldn't with Braden watching her every move.

"What are these good for?" He took notice of everything she did and helped any way she asked. This time, she was cutting tender red twigs off a dogwood tree. She respected his wish to know all about this new land. She'd been a teacher in Seattle, and it seemed natural to share her knowledge.

"I will weave a design into baskets with them." Holding up the narrow, supple twigs, she drew strength from their beauty. "The red makes a nice border design."

Satisfied with her stack of colored twigs, she went on to a stand of alder trees. Braden followed along, acting as pack mule. Amy noticed he never fully relaxed or let his attention wander from the woods around them.

"The alder bark treats infections, and I use it to tan hides." She carved slices of bark, careful to leave plenty intact so the tree would heal.

Another day, Amy pulled out the wickedly sharp knife, her only tool, and began carving. "This is a bud gum tree. Ian used a stump from one for his sink. We can also make buckets from the bark, then waterproof them with the gum. Then we will dig into the ground and steal roots. They make excellent rope."

Braden shook his head as if the bounty of nature amazed him. She climbed hills and scrambled over rocks, ignoring the ache of her hands, which still bore scrapes from her fall off the cliff. The scabs on her hands and face were mostly gone, and the skin had toughened. She hacked away at trees and shrubs without giving a thought to asking for help. He insisted on helping, of course, but she'd have let him stand by and keep watch if he hadn't offered.

She moved on to a thicket. Long yellow spines stood guard over the tender inner branches, and fragrant white flowers dotted the bushes.

Amy pulled leather gloves from her pocket and tugged them on. She had tanned the sheepskin and cut out the fine leather to make them. "Do not help with this one. You do not want a thorn in your skin. It will fester, and it is very slow healing."

Braden caught her arm as she reached for it. "Then why don't you leave it alone?"

Amy smiled as she straightened away from the plant. "This plant does not want to share itself, but it is a plant my people prize, and we have learned our way around the stubborn thing."

"Prize for what?" The large stand of shrubs with their fierce thorns formed an impenetrable thicket that reached up the steep incline in front of them.

Amy's smile turned into laughter. "My grandmother would tell you it wards off witches and bad luck."

"Witches, huh?" Braden had set the bulk of his load on the ground, keeping his gun at hand. "Well, we don't need that since I don't believe in witches."

"Neither do I, but it makes a restorative tea, and I want some for Merry." Amy smiled. Then the smile faded. "She is getting much better, I think."

A stubborn expression came over Braden's face. "Yes, much better. This is the third morning in a row she hasn't been sick, and she stayed in the cabin while you cooked breakfast. She's still not ready to be left alone."

They'd talked of going to her father's often. Braden always had excuses why now was not the time. "She would not be alone. Ian would stay with her." Amy's eyes narrowed. "You know I need to go."

"Amy, we just can't—"

"If it were your father," she cut him off, "you would go. Do not tell me otherwise."

"It would be different in Oregon with a sheriff in town and a marshal's office to keep peace in the countryside. In Alaska, with no law closer than Dyea, the sheriff would never tramp hours into the woods after a criminal. Alaska is still a territory, and the law outside of town resembles the law in any wilderness."

Amy turned away from the nasty plant. Jerking her gloves off, she clutched them in one hand and whacked her other hand with the soft leather. "I know, and I have been patient, but it is time, Braden. We could be down there and back in one day."

Braden snorted. "The sun doesn't set. One day lasts six months."

She slapped the gloves into her hand again. "I am tired of waiting." *Slap.* "I am giving Merry a few more days." *Slap!* "Then I am going with or without you."

Braden caught the gloves, an irritated expression darkening his eyes.

"I am not going to fight the man. I am going to wait until he is gone, then slip in and out quickly." She held tight to the other end of the gloves and yanked on them.

Braden refused to let go. "You're staying right here."

"Now that I have been warned, I do not need a bodyguard." She wrenched at the gloves and stumbled forward. "I know how to move through the woods. I know the signs of others in the area. I would be fine."

One hand landed on Braden's chest, the other firmly grasped the gloves. She looked up at Braden.

He dipped his head and kissed her.

Her lips softened. Braden jumped away and turned his back.

"I have enough."

Braden turned. "What?"

"I said, I have enough. Let us go home."

"Listen, Amy." Braden caught her arm. "I'm sorry. That. . . that shouldn't have happened."

Amy turned. "You are right. And it will not happen again. I do not let men. . .close to me like that, Braden. If you would have asked, the answer would have been no."

Temper sparked in his eyes. "That wasn't only me. You kissed me back."

Amy gave his hand clamped around her upper arm a hard look. "Are you finished?"

"Yes. The afternoon is waning." Braden looked at the sky. "The sun is going to set in, oh, about six hours, I'd say."

A tiny laugh escaped Amy's tingling lips, and she shook her head. Braden let go of her. He picked up the load she'd been gathering, and she filled the fur-lined bag she always carried, slung it over her shoulder, and filled her arms besides.

They went back toward the house together. As they neared the clearing, they saw Tucker stacking windfall branches. Meredith sat on the stump they'd used for chopping wood and sewed another shirt for Ian or one of the other men. She was keeping them all supplied with clothes.

"She is almost better, Braden."

"Just be patient, woman."

"I have been patient. More patient than any of you have a right to expect. I need to find out what happened to Papa." Amy turned and blocked the path in front of Braden. He stopped, or he'd have run over her. They faced each other with arms filled with bark and branches, leaves and roots. "Take me to my father's, or I will go alone."

Braden leaned forward until their noses almost touched, despite the load they both carried. "Fetching after your da's house is the way of a greedy woman. You have plenty here. Why do you need more?"

"I am not greedy, Braden Rafferty. This is not about that cabin. This is about justice."

"If it's not about greed, then it's about revenge."

"Justice is not revenge."

"You can't bring your father back. You can't live in that house alone. You can't even be sure someone attacked you."

"Again you call me a liar." The twigs Amy hugged to her chest snapped.

"Mistaken, not a liar. We've seen no one around. Ian, Tucker, and I are fair hands in the woods. But none of us is as good as you, are we, Amaruq Wolf Girl?"

"No, not a one of you is as good as me." She realized how boastful that sounded, and bragging wasn't what she intended. She'd merely spoken the truth.

"So, have you seen him?"

Amy raised up on her toes to shout at him before she truly thought about what he'd said. She dropped, flat-footed. "No. No, I have not seen him, nor any sign of him."

She blinked, trying to focus all her fears and finding doubts taking their place.

"Maybe that's because he doesn't exist." Braden arched one skeptical eyebrow. "Or maybe it's because some winter-crazed man like Rooster was passing through and did something cockeyed for no reason other than 'cause he's a loon."

Amy knew it wasn't true. She remembered the laughter. She'd heard it in Seattle, hadn't she? What about the menace on the *Northward* that night Braden had left her alone? What about her fear as she stood too close to the railing? It couldn't all be her imagination. She had too much respect for her instincts for that. But she was tired of wasting her breath trying to convince Braden.

"Fine, if you want to explain away what happened on that cliff, you do so. But hear this, Braden Rafferty. I am going to my papa's cabin. I am going, and I am going soon. Merry is my friend, and I will care for her as long as she needs it."

"But no longer?" Braden's eyes narrowed and anger tinged color into his freckled cheeks. "You won't turn left nor right from your obsession with your father, even if it means betraying all of us when we took you in."

"Betraying you? You are betraying me with your doubts and insults. So no, I will not be swayed from my course."

"You're not goin' anywhere." Braden's cheeks were so crimson with anger Amy thought if she touched them her fingertips might sizzle.

"Am I a prisoner, then?"

"No, there are no door locks to keep you here. But if you go, you walk away from all of us."

"By whose order? Merry would let me return. I live in her home, not yours."

"You live with the Raffertys. Do you think Ian will keep you here if I tell him I want you to leave? Do you think he'll stand by while your recklessness frightens Merry, maybe enough to make her lose their child? You already made her walk a long distance to find us when you needed help. How many times will you do that before Ian says enough?"

Amy's heart sank. Braden's words reminded her that she was indeed the outsider here. She was alone in the world. And it was for just that reason that she had to find justice for her father. She had to find the truth.

Wait on the Lord.

No! she shouted in her heart. She'd waited long enough. Too long.

"So be it, Braden. When I go, I will go for good." She whirled away and charged across the opening surrounding the cabin. She went inside and shut the cabin door before Meredith or Tucker noticed they'd returned.

Braden stared at the closing door. He wanted to go in and shake her and hold her and kiss her and. . .and. . .

The ideas that came into his head shocked him, ideas of marrying Amy and having her fill up the empty places in his heart. He prayed for self-control.

Self-control. Lord, when did I start needing that?

Braden felt a weight crushing his chest as he realized Amy was in his heart. Amy was the one prompting his prayers for self-control. Amy was the one.

And she wanted to go on a long hike in the woods. Alone with him. Just the two of them. His heart beat faster as he thought of the long hours he'd spent with her this last month and how much he'd learned and how he loved seeing her in the sunlight and twilight and any other time of day.

He took a step toward the cabin and stopped. He couldn't do it.

It would betray Maggie. Wasn't failing one woman enough? The self-control he prayed for surged to life as he realized he was forgetting the wife of his heart. The woman he'd played with as a child, held hands with as a young man, killed as a husband. God wouldn't ask him to risk another woman.

Through the window, Braden saw Amy at work over the fireplace. Amy, caring for them day and night. A true friend to Meredith. So wise in the ways of Alaska that all their lives were better for her presence.

The aroma of mutton wafted out of the cabin. Braden saw Meredith turn her head toward the scent and lose all the color from her cheeks. Clamping her hand over her mouth, Meredith jumped up. She dashed for the underbrush near the cabin and disappeared.

Tucker exchanged glances with Braden to make sure they were both aware. Braden jerked his head toward the house. Tucker nodded, hefted his Winchester over his shoulder with a quick, fluid move, and started after his sister just as the sound of retching came from the bushes.

Braden set Amy's treasures outside the cabin door when he wanted to go inside and beg her to care more for him than for her missing father. Instead, he turned his hand to collecting firewood, staying within sight of the cabin.

Protecting her from afar to protect his own foolish heart.

Chapter 15

*B*ut they that wait upon the L*ord* shall renew their strength; they shall mount up with wings as eagles; they shall run, and not be weary; and they shall walk, and not faint."

Amy lay on her makeshift bed in the main room of Ian's cabin and read the passage of Scripture by full daylight at ten-thirty at night.

Unhappy with the message, she set her Bible down gently, resisting the urge to clap the book shut. It seemed every Bible verse she read called her to wait.

"I have waited," she whispered into the empty room. "I have been here two months now, Lord. I believe You wanted me to stay and take care of Meredith, but the summer fades quickly. I must see what happened to my father. I cannot spend a winter in comfort with the Raffertys while my father's death goes unpunished. Make a way for me to go, Lord."

Amy almost stopped before she uttered the next words of her prayer. But the need to act drove her, and she spoke quietly into the silent room. "Or I will do it on my own. You gave me a life that taught me independence. I take care of myself. I work hard. I have the skills I need, and I believe You want me to act. You are a God of justice. You do not want an evil man to hurt my papa and pay no price."

Amy lifted her Bible again, this time more tenderly, and asked God to forgive her disrespect. The book fell open, and her eyes fell on Psalm 27:14. *"Wait on the L*ord*: be of good courage, and he shall strengthen thine heart: wait, I say, on the L*ord*."*

She recalled another verse, and for the first time applied it to herself. She knew what it meant when Moses had argued with Pharaoh to "let my people go" and the Bible said, "Pharaoh hardened his heart."

She knew because Amy hardened her own heart at that moment. She deliberately chose a path she feared God didn't bless. Meredith was feeling better. The summer was wearing itself down. She was through waiting on the Lord or anyone else, especially Braden Rafferty.

Instead of listening to the still, small voice that whispered on the wind, she made plans. Braden stayed with her nearly every minute. How could she slip away from him for long enough that he wouldn't just come after her and drag her home?

Amy sat up straight. Braden wasn't here right now. Yes, the nighttime, when she was in Ian's care, was the time to go. If someone lingered in the woods, that someone had proved to be a coward and wouldn't attack the house directly. So they'd come to expect Amy to go inside and stay. Anyone lingering in the woods wouldn't be on watch in the night.

If she slipped out as soon as the Raffertys went to bed, she'd reach her father's cabin before that horrible man got up in the morning. She'd find a hiding place, wait for him to leave, and then sneak in. She'd quickly find the deed and be halfway home before the Raffertys knew she was gone.

Why, she'd even leave a note so if she didn't get back before they woke, they'd know her entire plan. And she'd meet them a few miles down the river because they were sure to come after her.

The only flaw in her plan was the worry she might cause Meredith. That was the one thing Braden said that almost swayed her. Thinking of Meredith hiking to the mine twisted Amy's stomach. Meredith could have fallen. The baby could have been lost. Amy knew she'd have to hurry to minimize Meredith's concern. Maybe if she drove herself hard, she could be down and back before the Raffertys climbed out of bed.

Meredith wouldn't even have to cook breakfast. Amy would be home in time.

She looked out the window, considering setting off right now. But she wanted an earlier start. She'd make sure Meredith was feeling okay; then she'd go to see what had happened to her father.

Wait, I say, on the Lord.

Amy only heard the wind as she turned over and fell asleep.

Meredith's unruly stomach had a relapse. Amy, caring for Meredith and the rest of the family, fell into bed exhausted each night for the next week. Braden was as diligent as ever guarding her—so much so that his guarding felt less like protection than like a lookout for an escape attempt. It didn't matter. Amy wasn't about to abandon Meredith. . .yet.

Amy's heart twisted when she thought of the warmth that had passed between her and Braden. It had vanished since their fight over her need to go home. Something had been lost between her and Braden. Or maybe not lost. Maybe for Braden it had never been there.

Early the next week, Meredith took a turn for the better, and Amy knew it was time to go. The first night Amy was able to stay awake long enough to hear Ian's soft snores, she tossed back the covers on her sleeping pallet and stood, fully dressed.

After tucking her knife into the sheath around her ankle, she smeared on a paste made from yarrow leaves to repel the mosquitoes. She eased the door open and closed, knowing Ian slept lightly. She stuck a note—one she'd had written for a week—on the outside of the front door.

Pulling on her walrus-gut boots, Amy strode toward the river, listening for any sound that didn't belong in an Alaskan wilderness. As she hurried along the water's edge, she startled a porcupine and her spring babies drinking from the river. The *slap* of leaping salmon called to her as if she needed to be fishing instead of being about her father's business. When the shore allowed it, she ran, racing against the coming morning and the Raffertys' worry.

In these early days of August, the sun settled into a brief dusk, but Amy's night vision was excellent. With the moon and stars shining off the river, she found her way easily.

The river chuckled over stones. The sound soothed her agitated spirit and made her sleepy, reminding her that she'd worked a long, hard day, caring for her family.

Her family? Were the Raffertys hers? Whatever she proved about her father, she still had no one left to call her own. Meredith was like a sister to her; Ian, a protective big brother. Tucker teased Amy just as he did Meredith. Braden. . .Amy could summon no sisterly feelings for him. She'd declared that when she left, she'd leave for good. But in her heart, Amy hoped desperately that they'd welcome her back. She wanted Papa, but she wanted to belong to the Raffertys, too. Especially Braden.

Amy turned her mind away from Braden and his strong arms and the kisses they'd shared. Picking up her pace, she tuned her senses sharply toward the forest and any danger lurking there. She rushed along, setting sights for home and justice, ignoring the quiet urging in her soul to wait.

Hours later, a mile upstream of her father's cabin, she slipped away from the water and hiked into the rugged woods. The land climbed sharply upward along the riverbank, and staying under cover was hard, slow work. Her mother and father had taught her to ease her way through the woods, like smoke drifting between heaven and earth. She took great care to be silent as she pulled herself along the steep incline, hanging onto shrubs along the side of the mountain.

When her father's cabin came into sight, Amy dropped behind a large stand of cottonwood trees. She rested her head against the tree, the bark rough on her cheek. She ran her hand lovingly over the wood and remembered learning very early how to tap the cottonwood to take just a bit of the sap and then eat it fresh. These trees were the equivalent of a candy store and held precious memories for her. She looked overhead and saw the first tinge of yellow in the fluttering leaves. Already summer was slipping away. To have waited longer to see to the man who had harmed her father would be madness.

Settling in, Amy let the nature that had fed and clothed her wrap itself around her like a cloak. She heard the sharp, high cry of a raven as it swooped and dived overhead. A high, majestic scream lifted her eyes to heaven, and she saw sunlight glint off the bald head of a soaring eagle. A rustle in the bushes nearby revealed a marmot making its way to the water's edge for an early morning drink.

There was no sign of activity in the cabin. But it was too early to believe the occupant had risen for the day. An hour slipped by as she waited, and then another. Amy thought of Meredith, awake now and worrying. Amy forced herself to wait when she couldn't bring herself to before. A sound out of place with nature pulled her eyes toward the cabin. Coughing. Riveting her eyes on the front door, Amy waited, her muscles coiled, her heart thudding.

She pictured the mantel her Tlingit grandfather had carved. It had been a gift to her parents on their wedding day. The mantel carving was an intricate design in perfect harmony with the world outside the door. Grandfather had loved working with wood, and Amy had been allowed to sit by his side and watch as the beautiful creations emerged under his patient, talented hands.

He'd made her a noisy rattle and figures of animals and fish. But the mantel had been her favorite. Many endless winter days, she'd lazed in front of the fire, making up stories about the animals etched into the alder wood. She'd loved the sun and the moon. The river Grandfather carved along the bottom seemed to move when firelight flickered in the fireplace below. And the crackle of the flames passed for babbling water. Salmon were suspended, eternally leaping out of the stream, and some days Amy could almost hear them splash as they hit the water.

But most important right now was a thin drawer, its edges hidden by Grandfather's intricate carving. The drawer held the few family possessions that mattered. The deed had been ignored for the most part. Amy's father had enjoyed telling the story of the old trapper who had, with grand ceremony, presented the deed when he gave the cabin away and headed south to live out his old age with his brother.

Petrov Simonovich had never considered himself the owner of this land, so he wouldn't sell it. But if someone persuaded him to give away the cabin, he'd sign over the deed with the same pomp as the man who had handed it to him. Amy knew how to touch the carved raven and stretch her fingers wide to touch the sun, then press in on the drawer to pop it open. The deed to the property would be there.

Another cough sounded from the cabin, and Amy hunkered down a bit more. Smoke appeared in the chimney, and the smell of salmon cooking teased her nose and reminded her she hadn't eaten for hours. At last the cabin door swung open, and the man who'd driven her away from her home stepped out.

He carried a pickax over his shoulder and a shovel hanging from a pack on his back. Amy saw the man tuck a chunk of jerky into his pocket and close the door. A gust of wind carried his foul smell to Amy where she crouched twenty feet away. The man walked heavily, feet plodding along unevenly. Amy was almost certain that shuffling gait couldn't belong to the man who had pushed her off the cliff. She clenched her jaw, wondering if she'd created this whole threat out of her own fears.

He went around the side of the cabin, ragged clothes swinging their tatters in the wind. Amy remembered a game trail that led from the cabin up toward the mountaintop. He must follow it to some mine he'd found.

With a sigh of relief, Amy knew she'd have the cabin to herself. That didn't mean she'd linger. She'd grab the deed and go home. The man wouldn't even know she'd been there. Then she'd present the deed to that stubborn Braden as proof her father had met with foul play.

As Amy stood, she wondered if Braden, Ian, and Tucker would act when presented with evidence. Why had she come? Why had she ignored the urging to wait?

God, what good will it do to know my father did not sell the cabin?

The only answer she got—*wait on the Lord*—was one she refused to heed.

The miner's lumbering footsteps diminished on the path. She remembered cruel hands on her back. Saw the yawning emptiness in front of her as she hurled over the mountain's edge.

And she felt hands on her back on the *Northward* as she stood by the boat railing. Hands on her back on a busy Seattle street corner. She remembered those stealthy footfalls onboard the ship when she sat alone on the deck. Braden couldn't explain those three things away by attributing it to some person driven mad by the long, black winter. No, someone had come after her, possibly four times. She had no reason to believe he'd stop now. This had to be dealt with.

The man's footsteps faded completely. Amy squared her shoulders and ignored the internal warning that seemed to ring louder than ever. Why would God ask her to wait now? Why, when she was so close and the danger so minimal? She hurried toward the cabin.

Mindful of the way sound carried, she lifted the heavy front door, hinged with worn leather, to keep it from scratching as she swung it open. Leaving it barely wide enough to slip through, Amy headed straight for the mantel. There was no reason to stay a second longer than necessary.

Amy reached her left hand for the precious raven and the sun that glowed in the bright sheen of aged wood.

The wicked laugh she'd heard twice before rumbled behind her.

Hands shoved her into the mantel.

Amy's chest slammed into her grandfather's intricate carving. She staggered sideways, caught her balance, and whirled around.

Braden still battled the long daylight hours. He had adjusted somewhat, but he'd wake up to full light and have no idea whether it was 1:00 a.m. or high noon. As a result, he'd learned to roll out of bed quickly, feeling late.

He pulled on his clothes. His belly told him it was breakfast time even if the sun wouldn't cooperate. Maybe Ma did the right thing, packing that fancy clock. Leaving the cabin, he walked down the path to Tucker's, looking for a clearing overhead that would give him a good look at the sun. He still stung from the ribbing Tucker and Ian had given him the time he'd awakened Tucker just one hour after they'd gone to bed.

Finding a likely spot, Braden studied the sky and decided it was a wee bit early. He'd go on to Ian's, gather wood for a while, and leave Tucker sleeping for another hour. As soon as he stepped into the clearing by Ian's cabin, he saw the white paper fluttering on the front door. Braden rushed forward and pulled the note free.

> *I have gone to get proof of what happened to my father. Do not worry about me. I will be back in time for breakfast.*
>
> *Amy*

Braden stared at the note, fury riding him as he thought of the headstrong, impetuous woman. She might meet up with whoever wished her ill. The ache in his heart at the thought of losing Amy forever nearly drove him to his knees.

"Ian, wake up!" Braden hammered on the front door with the side of his fist, regretting that Amy's reckless behavior was going to put all of them in jeopardy.

Ian opened the door in his bare feet and long underwear.

Braden shoved the note into his hand. "You can't leave Merry. I'm going after Amy."

Meredith appeared in the door, peeking over Ian's broad shoulders.

"Get Tucker first," Ian said. "I don't want you out there alone."

Braden shook his head. "No time." He turned toward the river.

"Braden!" Ian's voice stopped him.

He turned back.

Ian reached over his head and pulled down the Winchester. He thrust it at Braden. "Wear those boots, too. They're waterproof." Ian jerked his chin at the boots that lay on the ground. Braden realized there'd been four pairs lying there last night. Now there were three.

"I don't want to leave Merry home alone. We'll go for Tucker together. He'll be after you as soon as he can get on the trail."

Braden jerked the boots on and ran for all he was worth toward the river. He glanced over his shoulder to see Ian and Meredith walking swiftly toward Tucker's cabin in their nightclothes, Ian's arm protectively wrapped around Meredith's waist.

Braden charged down the rocky beach. When the creek bank grew too steep, he'd weave into the shallow water, his feet splashing, his lungs heaving as he pushed himself. The gun hung heavy in his grip as his arms swung in time to his long-legged pace. The voice of God pushed him as surely as if the wind had hands. And the cry of the raven shouted for him to *hurry, hurry, hurry*.

Chapter 16

Amy looked into the shifty eyes of Barnabas Stucky.

"Well, if it isn't the pretty little lady from the boat." Stucky's clothes, new on the boat, now hung off him like filthy rags. The smell of him nearly made her retch. His hands with broken, dirt-caked nails, reached for her, and she backed away until her shoulders were pressed against the mantel.

"You've been a hard one. But you're not gettin' away this time."

The look of pure cruelty on his face spurred Amy to action. She grabbed for the knife in her ankle sheath. Stucky's hands closed on her wrist before she could reach it. He dragged her forward, shoving her into a chair so hard it knocked the wind out of her. Jerking at his belt, he pulled it free and bound her hands in front with the coarse leather.

"Who are you?" Amy's heart hammered in her chest. Why hadn't she waited?

"My brother sent me to find you when he got this cabin. He knew you were the only one on earth who'd complain."

"Complain? Because Papa sold out?" Amy's stomach sank, knowing the truth without the man speaking another word.

"No, 'cause your pa refused to sell out. Here's your plumb stupid old man sittin' on gold that'll make the Klondike Gold Rush look like a little pile of granite. Your father owned it all and didn't even know it was there. When Owen found the gold, he took the claim. This is a land for the strong, and your father was an old, weak man."

"That is a lie. My father was getting older, but he was still a strong man. The only way your brother could have hurt him is to shoot him in the back or push him off a cliff."

Barnabas was close enough that she could smell his fetid breath. His teeth, yellow and broken, were bared at her in a savage mockery of a smile. "Reckon that's what he done."

"So, your brother is a coward just like you," Amy taunted. "He would never take on a strong man face-to-face when you are too afraid to face a woman half your size." Amy thought of her knife. If she could goad him into releasing her, perhaps to prove his courage, she could win any fight they had.

Barnabas laughed and tightened the belt around her hands. "Once Owen got to the cabin, he found all your letters and the daguerreotype you sent your pa. He wanted to make sure you never found your way home."

"And he knew just the snake that would do his dirty work, didn't he?" Amy strained under the leather binding as she spat the words at her captor.

Barnabas laughed. "Owen knew I was fresh out of Yuma prison and needin' money. I wouldn't have had to come all the way here if that wagon had done you in on the streets of Seattle."

"You almost pushed me off the boat." Amy shuddered at the man's twisted smile. The full beard he'd grown, only stubble on the boat, made him look more animal than man.

Stucky's eyes, as cold and dark as an Alaskan January, narrowed. "I lost you at Skaguay. Figured you'd go all the way to Dyea and weren't payin' attention. That's the only reason it took me as long as it did. Then I came home after you went over the cliff. I never dreamed you came out o' that fall alive."

He bent down until his face was level with hers. "You're a hard one made for a hard land, ain'tcha, missy? Well, I'm a hard one myself. My brother finally let me move in with him onest you was dead. He's gonna pay me cash money to clear his rights to this holding."

Amy lunged for his throat with her bound hands. With a crude, growling laugh, Stucky blocked her, snagging the belt that held her hands. Amy kicked at him, landing a hard blow to his ankle that knocked one of his feet out from under him. He fell forward. Amy jumped from the chair. Stucky lunged at her and sank his fingers into her long braid. He jerked, slamming her back on the chair.

"You want to fight? We'll fight." Stucky grabbed Amy by the throat. His powerful grip tipped the chair backward as he stood and fumbled for a leather strap hanging over the mantel.

Amy clawed at his hand, fighting for breath. Clumsily, he bound one leg to the chair, then the other. Once she was pinned down, he wrapped a longer strap around her waist. Panting from the exertion, he moved away from her.

Completely immobilized, Amy saw the rage in Stucky's eyes and knew she had to talk fast if she wanted to live. So far, Barnabas Stucky had shown interest in only one thing. "How much is he paying you? I could pay you more."

Stucky laughed. "A hundred dollars. And don't think you can trick me. I already checked in Seattle to find out how much money you had. People have bought their way out of trouble with me before. You didn't have enough to beat Owen's offer." He laughed and curled his fingers into claws, then reached for her throat.

"One hundred dollars? While he gets my gold mine?" Amy nearly stumbled over her words. "You saved it for him. You deserve half that mine. If you helped me get it back, I would give you the whole thing."

Stucky stopped short, his hands extended. The calculating look returned to his eyes, this time layered with something other than cruelty. Greed.

"You'd never hand over this claim. I know better than that. But my brother should be payin' me more. If he's gonna be a rich man while I'm doing all the dirty work, then I deserve to be his partner." Stucky's high-pitched laughter filled the room again.

Amy heard the nervous mania that was so evident in all the stampeders. If he would just go, she might be able to get to her knife, then free herself and get away.

Oh God, forgive me. Forgive my impatience. If only I had waited.

"If Owen wants me to clear the title to this land, he's gonna have ta pay." Stucky checked Amy's bonds, then gripped her chin and lifted her face. "I'll be back, li'l Amy. Nothin's gonna change for you, but it is for me. You're gonna make me rich."

Laughing, he turned and raced out of the cabin.

The second Barnabas vanished, Amy struggled to reach her ankle. The tie at her waist kept her from bending. Her leg wouldn't rise. Minutes ticked by as she fought the leathers; they only tightened. She had no idea how far Barnabas would have to walk to find his brother. With a near howl of frustration, she pulled her hands to her mouth and began chewing on the brown, tough leather of Stucky's belt. As the minutes turned to an hour with only a bit of headway on her bonds, she fought down panic, knowing he couldn't be gone much longer.

The door flew open, and Braden charged inside, his leveled Winchester sweeping the room.

"Braden," Amy choked, losing a battle against tears.

"Are you alone?"

"Yes, there are two men, both of them gone. But they will be back. We have got to get out of here!"

"I'll be right back."

Amy wanted to scream at him not to leave. She fought down the impulse. She knew Braden well enough to know he wasn't about to abandon her.

Braden checked the bedroom Amy's father had built for her.

Amy sighed with relief when he came back out.

"No one here." He drew his knife from his belt. With a slash, he freed Amy's hands, then made quick work of the rest of her bonds.

He helped her from the chair. "We've gotta get out of here before they come back. We'll get you home. Then Ian, Tucker, and I will come and settle this." Braden tried to slide his arm around her waist, but she stepped away.

"Let me get my father's deed first. It will only take a second."

"It can wait, Amy. We've got to get clear of this place."

"He admitted that the man who lived here killed my father." A renewed spate of tears shook her body.

Braden's jaw tensed. "Make it quick."

She turned toward the mantel.

"We won't let him get away with it. I'm sorry we didn't come here sooner and find out what happened."

Amy reached for the raven and sun. "No, it is my fault. God has been telling me right along to be patient, to let Him set the time for justice. But I did not listen. And you put yourself in danger because of my stubbornness. I should have waited for help. I am so sorry." Her tears blinded her as she fumbled with the stiff wooden levers.

Braden rested one hand on her trembling shoulder. His strength helped ease her tears.

"This is the first time you've ever admitted you were wrong."

Amy glanced over her shoulder, glad for his teasing tone that steadied her. "That is because this is the first time I have been wrong."

Braden coughed, then laughed out loud. "And it's the first time you've ever said you needed help."

Amy looked up at him and opened her mouth.

Braden laid one finger on her parted lips. "Don't say it. I know. You've never needed help before, either."

Amy shrugged and felt sheepish because that's exactly what she'd been planning to say. "Let me get the deed. Then we will get away from here. He will be gone a while, I expect, but I do not want to take a chance."

Braden jerked his chin in agreement. Amy reached for the carved mantel again just as heavy footsteps sounded on the path behind the house.

"They are coming." Amy started for the front door.

Braden grabbed her by the wrist. "Too late!"

Chapter 17

B raden raced for the back room, dragging Amy along. He swung the door open, lifting so it made almost no sound. Amy held her breath as the two men's voices grew closer. Once in the back room, she ducked behind Braden, who swung the door shut and turned to face it. Amy sensed Braden's rigid attention to every sound outside the door. He lifted his rifle so it pointed toward the ceiling, his thumb on the hammer, his finger on the trigger.

The men were arguing as they strode down the trail.

"You'll pay up or you'll kill her yourself."

Amy heard Stucky's vicious, heartless discussion of her life and death reduced to a matter of dollars and gold dust.

"I ain't gettin' my hands dirty killin' a pretty little woman in a territory where there's only about ten of 'em," Stucky continued. "Not for a measly hundred dollars. An ole trapper disappears—nobody thinks too much of it. A young woman living with a solid family like the Raffertys goes missin', and questions'll be asked sure as certain."

"I'm not givin' you half this claim," Owen raged. A hard fist pounded on the outside door. "I'll up the price to two hundred dollars, but that's highway robbery. We made a deal. And no one knows you're here. No one's gonna blame you for nothing."

Owen's voice sent chills down Amy's spine. This man had killed her father. This man had hired a man to murder her. All for gold. Now he bartered for her life with less emotion than most people would show buying a bolt of cloth.

Braden watched through a crack between the saplings bound together to make the door. He took a second to look away and gave her a nod of encouragement. His eyes, sharp and intelligent, told her he'd protect her with his life. She stood behind him, her left shoulder pressed against the wall like his. The fingers of his right hand steady on his rifle, he reached behind with his left and caught her hand, lacing his fingers together with hers.

Amy had never felt more connected to another human being. Braden offered her protection, using his body to shield her. She tightened her grip on his hand as his strength drove the chill away.

"Thank you," Amy whispered. She pulled her hand free of Braden's so he'd be able to move quickly.

The door to the cabin swung open.

"She's gone!" Stucky's voice mixed with shouting from Owen.

"You said you'd tied her up." Owen's fury cut through the room. "We've got to find her."

Amy froze. The walls weren't that solid, and movement could possibly be seen through cracks. Any creaking wood, even just from shifting weight, might draw the men's attention to this room. She saw Braden's shoulders tense beneath his brown shirt and didn't realize what he meant to do until he'd moved.

Swinging the door open, Braden stepped into the main room. "Put up your hands."

Gun level, his voice bitter cold, he froze the two men in their tracks.

Amy peeked around Braden's broad shoulders. Neither man had a gun. She could see that now. Braden must have noticed this fact and decided to end the nightmare right here.

"Both of you sit down." Braden gestured with the muzzle of his gun toward the two chairs in the room. One of them still had leather straps hanging from where Amy had sat bound.

"What are you doing in my house?" Owen backed away, looking between Braden's eyes and the gun. "This is trespassing. I'll have you arrested."

"This is one of them Raffertys," Stucky said.

Owen cut him off. "He don't have no proof a' nothin'." Owen scowled at his brother and then slumped into a chair.

Amy slipped out of the back room and stood behind Braden.

Both men's eyes widened. Barnabas Stucky's face turned beet red, and Owen bared his teeth until Amy expected him to growl. The two men looked alike now that she saw them together. Middling tall, stout of build, dark hair streaked gray, full shaggy beards—in that they looked like most of the men who came north. But they also shared ruthless blue eyes and cruel lips. Hate etched the same lines into their faces.

Braden held them captive, but now what did they do?

As if she'd asked the question aloud, Braden said, "Stay behind me." He planted himself between the front door and the two snarling men with Amy at his back. "Tucker's on the way. We'll hold 'em here 'til he comes, then go on into Skaguay and leave them with the sheriff."

"We ain't done nothin' wrong," Owen erupted from his chair.

Braden leveled the rifle. Amy couldn't see Braden's expression, but she saw Owen blanch and sit back down.

"Whatever you want here, mister, just take it," Owen sputtered. "I'm a law-abidin' man. I don't know what you're talking about, takin' us to the sheriff. There's no call—"

"You killed my father." Amy stepped up beside Braden, her temper too hot to think of safety. "You have tried to kill me four times."

"He's tried four times?" Braden glanced at her, his brow furrowed. Then he went back to watching his prisoners.

Amy nodded and pointed at Stucky. "He admitted it. On his brother's orders, he tried to kill me in Seattle, then twice again on the boat. He never caught me alone for long enough."

She looked at Owen. "So do not waste your breath with lies. Braden came in and found me tied up, and we heard what you said to your brother when the two of you came back to the cabin. It is not my word against yours. Braden is a witness, too. You cannot explain that away."

"Hey, whatever my brother did ain't no business o' mine." Owen glared at his brother.

Stucky's jaw tightened. Fury burned in the man's eyes until Amy thought he'd attack Owen. She realized that unless they could break Owen's story, Barnabas, who had tried to kill her but never managed it, might be arrested. Owen, the man who had murdered her father, might go free.

Before Barnabas could accuse his brother, a noise caught their attention from behind. Amy whirled around and looked into the eyes of Darnell Thompson, the other man who'd paid so much attention to her on the boat. He held a Colt revolver in his hand, pointed steadily at Braden's midsection.

Braden's finger tightened on the trigger. Amy prayed, knowing her recklessness had brought Braden to this moment. She might be responsible for his death.

"Ease off, Mr. Rafferty. I'm not here for you. I'm here for him." The gun shifted from Braden to Owen. "I've been hunting you for a long, long time. I lost your brother's trail in Dyea, and it's taken me a long while to get here. But this is the end of the line for you and your claim jumpin' ways."

Thompson, dressed like a stampeder with three-months growth of beard and a probing, assessing look in his eyes, reached into the pocket of his brown wool pants and pulled out a badge. "I'm a Pinkerton. If you even remember anymore, you killed a man in Texas nearly four years ago and sold off his homestead. You prey on men who live alone, far from anyone. But this Texan had friends. He was a loner, but his father is a powerful man back East who kept track of him quietly. When his son came up missing, he called in the Pinkertons."

"So you have proof he is a thief and a murderer?" Amy stepped sideways to let Thompson inside.

"I followed Stucky north, hoping he'd lead me to his brother. I saw Stucky gettin' ready to shove you over the railing of the *Northward*."

Amy's eyes widened in shock. "You saw him? Why did you not arrest him?"

"I saw what was in his eyes, miss," Thompson said. "The evil intentions he had toward you. But he didn't do anything because I stepped in with that trumped-up story about wanting to come with you. I was just makin' talk until your watchdog got there."

"Watchdog?" Amy's forehead wrinkled.

"Rafferty. I saw him coming your way, and when he got close enough so Barnabas couldn't hurt you, I eased back. Another reason I didn't accuse him of anything was because I wanted him to lead me to his brother. Now, I'm taking Owen back to Texas to stand trial. And I reckon we'll just throw Barnabas right on in with him."

"But what about my father?" Amy looked between Thompson and Braden. "How does a jail cell in Texas add up to justice for Papa?"

"A noose, when it comes, collects all a man's debts." Thompson tugged the front of his Stetson low on his forehead. "He'll pay for it all, miss. Don't you worry. I'd like you to write a letter explaining all that happened here for me to take back. He's done this a heap of times and left a trail of death across this country. But this is the first time he's ever stayed put long enough for me to catch up with him. He'd kill the landowner, sell the property as his own, and then move on. Not sure why he stayed here."

"I know why." Amy nodded. "This is the first time he has ever found gold."

"It's mine. No one is going to take it from me." Owen lunged out of his chair at Amy.

Braden grabbed his shoulder and sat him down hard.

"We'll just have your word for this theft, because there's no proof your father's dead without a body. Some old trappers keep moving. But your testimony will add weight to the charges."

"I can do better than write a letter. I can prove he stole this land."

Thompson gave her a long, sharp look.

Braden smiled encouragement at her.

She carefully skirted the two outlaws and went to the mantel.

Touching the sun and the raven at the same time with her left hand, she pressed in on the hidden drawer until she felt the catch snap. Sliding the drawer open, she stared down at the old deed, yellow with age. She slid the papers out carefully and gently unfolded the brittle document. This was the last thing connecting her to her father. Tears burned her eyes as she thought of the gruff but loving man who'd brought joy to her childhood and whom she'd missed terribly all her years in Washington. She'd never see him again.

Turning, she took the deed to Thompson. They looked down and saw that the land title was unreadable.

"What is that?" Braden glanced at the papers but went back to watching Owen and Barnabas. Amy noticed Thompson's watchful eyes only looked away from the men a second at a time, too.

"It is in Russian." Amy's voice faded. She swallowed and continued. "I had forgotten. I always knew the drawer was there and what it contained, but we did not get it out often. Probably not since I was too young to read."

"That isn't a deed. It's chicken scratchin's that prove nothin'," Owen raged. "And some man comes in here and says he's a lawman." Owen glared at Thompson. "He don't have any say over me up here in the Alaska Territory."

"You won't be in the Alaska Territory for long." Thompson pulled shackles from the pack he carried on his back. Thompson gave one last grim look at the deed. "Too bad that's in Russian. To have solid evidence in Alaska would strengthen my case in Texas. Don't reckon there'll be anyone between here and there that'll read Russian."

Amy's heart ached when she thought of her father and all she'd lost. "He killed the only man I knew who could read it."

"He's covered his tracks with killing for years."

"This time he picked a man who didn't kill so easy." The deep voice filled the cabin.

They all whirled around.

Petrov Simonovich stepped into the cabin.

"Father!" Amy launched herself at the thin figure who had replaced the robust man who'd raised her. She'd take him however he looked.

Her father caught her to him with a soft grunt. "My Amy." His arms wrapped around her with a strong grip that belied his slender frame. "You've come home."

Amy heard a crash and turned to see Owen running toward the small cabin window. Thompson dove for him and dragged the killer to the ground before he could escape. Barnabas jumped at Braden, who'd lifted his gun off the prisoners when Amy had distracted him.

Amy's father set her aside, reached for the man grappling for the gun, and hurled him against the solid wood mantel with a dull thud.

Braden took one look at Barnabas as he crumpled unconscious to the floor and then turned to Thompson. "Let him up. I've got you covered."

"Yep, 'n' if you don't, I do." Petrov chuckled.

Braden gave Petrov a narrow-eyed look.

Petrov clapped Braden on the back. "Sorry, boy. I know you're doin' fine." He turned back to Amy and pulled her firmly into his arms.

"They told me you were dead, Papa."

Petrov grunted. "Not the first time nor the last they'll prove up to bein' stupid."

Amy smiled and clutched her father tight, afraid to believe her own eyes. "Where have you been all this time? You stopped writing months ago."

"That one there"—Petrov nodded at Owen as Thompson pulled him to his feet—"shoved me over a cliff last winter, clear up north of here. Broke my leg in the fall. He stood over me and laughed about leaving my body for wolves."

Amy turned and pulled back her leg to give Owen a swift kick.

Her father stopped her, laughing, and hugged her again. "Always was a feisty one, my Amy."

Amy saw Braden nod and heard him whisper to Thompson, "That's the honest truth."

Amy's father looked over her shoulder for a long time. Amy pulled back far enough to know he was staring at Braden. A firm jerk of her father's chin seemed to settle something between him and Braden. Then Papa set her on her feet and reached for the deed, which had fallen to the floor.

"I'll do more than translate this for you. I'll go with you back to Texas and make sure he stands trial for all he done to me."

"But Father, what about me? I want you to stay here in this cabin with me."

"I'll be back." Amy's father turned to her. "You're in good hands here with your young man."

"He is not my young man." Amy glanced over her shoulder at Braden.

Braden grinned. "Sure I am."

Braden lowered his rifle now that the Stucky brothers were securely shackled. He came forward, his hand extended. "Petrov Simonovich, I'm Braden Rafferty. And I'd be proud to take care of your daughter, sir."

"I—I cannot live with Ian and Merry any longer," Amy stuttered.

Amy watched Papa shake hands with Braden as if they were sealing a bargain.

"No, you can't." Braden released her father's hand and took hold of hers. "That'd never be fittin' for a married woman."

"A what?" Amy's jaw went slack.

"Her mother was like this, too, son." Petrov chuckled again. His full beard quivered. Amy remembered his broad, deep-chested strength.

"But Father, what happened to you after Owen shoved you?"

"Now's not the time for that. You need to talk to your young man."

"Tell me!"

Papa and Braden exchanged a long look. Her father shook his head and sighed. "I got taken in by your mother's people. They found me before the wolves did, but they were on their way to their winter hunting grounds and didn't have time to bring me back. My leg was mighty slow in healing. Looked for a time like I might lose it. One of your mother's uncles seemed way too willin' to be the one handling the knife when the time came. It was a powerful incentive to keep on healing up."

"But still, why would it take you so long to get back? Summer is nearly over. You could not have been healing all this time."

A high-pitched wail came from outside the cabin.

"Come on in. It's safe."

A woman, dark and quiet with the serene eyes Amy remembered from her mother, came into the cabin, carrying a baby.

"We had to wait until my son was old enough to travel." Petrov smiled.

"Son?" Amy saw two little fists reach up from a blanket woven of fine goat hair. She leaned against Braden without thinking about it. He wrapped his arm around her waist and pulled her close.

"Amy, this is my wife *Guwakaan*."

" 'Deer,' what a beautiful name." Amy left Braden's side and rested a hand on the petite lady, quite a bit older than Amy but still a young woman, svelte and graceful as a deer. She could give her father many sons and daughters yet.

Amy had to smile, thinking about her father with little ones around his knees. He'd been a wonderful father to her, and he'd been alone for a long time. This would make his life rich again.

"And we called the baby *Ch'ak'yéis'.*" Petrov nodded with a look so proud Amy thought the laces on his buckskin shirt would burst.

" 'Young Eagle.' Perfect," Amy said.

"I s'pose." Her father frowned. "I wanted to name him Boris."

Guwakaan looked up. She'd been demurely shining her midnight eyes on her son, but now she smiled at Amy and rolled her eyes. Amy had to fight to hold back a laugh. She knew she and Guwakaan would be good friends.

"Are you interested in a trip to Texas, Guwakaan?" Amy asked.

"I will go where Xóots leads. I would enjoy seeing more of this great land."

"Xóots? You call my father Grizzly Bear?" Amy giggled.

Guwakaan nodded. "But he is a skinny bear these days. He lost too much weight healing, then more growling because the healing was slow. I will fatten him up." Despite her teasing, she turned adoring eyes on Amy's father, and he pulled her into a gentle hug that included the baby.

Amy remembered her mother using the same tone when she talked about her father. This one would make Father very happy.

"Uh, Mr. Simons?" Braden squared his shoulders.

"It's Simonovich, son. Done with all that passin' for anything I ain't. Proud of my Russian blood."

"Good. What I was going to say is, uh. . .you're rich, sir. Aye, you've got yourself a gold mine. And if these two speak the truth, it's a good one."

Guwakaan spoke quietly. "We cannot eat góon. I can see it if it makes a good spear tip or a pot, but why the madness around the góon?"

Petrov said to Braden, "You take it, son. I've found plenty of ways to dig a living out of this frozen world. I don't need a bunch of yellow rock to make me happy."

Braden shook his head. "I'm finding enough of my own. Just traces, nothing big, but that suits me. I hate the thought of another gold rush, this one aiming straight at me. I think I'll just leave it for you. Maybe someday Ch'ak'yéis' will want the gold."

"We will raise him better than that, Xóots. Just wait and see." Guwakaan and Amy's father exchanged a look that spoke of complete agreement.

"So when do we head for Texas?" Petrov looked at Thompson.

Amy's stomach sank when she thought of her father leaving. Then she remembered what Braden had said about getting married.

"Right after the wedding." Braden turned to Thompson. "You're a lawman, closest thing we've got around here to a judge. You can speak some vows."

"True enough," Thompson said. "I'm sworn to do such things by the state of Texas. I'm not sure if it's okay up here, but no one will care."

"Well, I certainly care!" Meredith stepped into the cabin, her hands on her hips, her cheeks flushed. "You'll be married by a proper minister, and that's that."

"What is going on here?" Ian asked.

Tucker stood behind him.

Braden gave them a shortened version. The nearest minister was in Skaguay. Thompson, the Stucky brothers, Petrov, Guwakaan, and Ch'ak'yéis' were all heading that way anyway. So it was decided the Raffertys, Tucker, and Amy would accompany them, have the wedding, and return home together after seeing Amy's father off.

Meredith acted as if she'd been given a priceless gift when they decided she could go.

Amy stood listening to them, her temper growing until she thought her insides would explode. She opened her mouth to tell them all their planning was for nothing because someone had yet to properly propose.

Wait on the Lord.

Amy froze. If she'd waited, her father would have handled these men, then written and sent for her. If she'd waited, she wouldn't have risked her life on that cliff when Barnabas pushed her. If she'd waited, she wouldn't have been at the mercy of Barnabas Stucky. Had she learned nothing?

She calmed down and turned to Braden.

He smiled at her. "I think we've forgotten something mighty important, haven't we, little Amaruq?" He took her arm and led her out of the cabin. With a backward glance, he said, "And you all give us a few moments of peace while I ask this woman to marry me."

Her calm turned to serenity as Braden pulled her to stand beneath a cottonwood turning to blazing yellow. The leaves fluttered overhead like the wings of angels. A raven swooped low and called out. The river rustled and bubbled nearby as it rushed toward Skaguay. She and Braden would soon rush along with the river toward Skaguay, too, because of course she was going to say yes if he ever got around to asking.

Braden wrapped her in his arms.

She waited for the sweet words of love every woman longs to hear.

"When I realized you'd run off this morning, I wanted to wring your neck."

Amy lowered her expectations considerably. So Braden didn't have the Irish gift for sweet blarney. So he didn't possess that poetic Irish soul she'd heard tell of. So he was a lunkhead. So what? It didn't matter. She loved him.

Braden brushed her hair off her forehead and leaned close. "I knew if something happened to you my life would never be the same. And I'd have to live with the knowledge that my unwillingness to help you with something so dear to your heart might have cost your life."

"Oh, Braden, it would not have been your fault. God told me as clear as the call of a raven that I needed to wait. He has been trying to slow me down since I decided to climb on that steamship and come hunting my father. If I had left everything to God, all would have worked out. My father would have handled Owen and Stucky. Thompson would have shown up to take the men back to Texas just as he did today without me in the way causing trouble. Then Papa would have stopped in Seattle to see me, and I would have come home.

"It was all my fault. I want to charge in and do everything, but God wants me to learn to wait. He wants me to learn patience. From now on, I am going to listen to God's voice and wait on His timing. I understand how this land works. I have always waited for spring to come again with no desire to force my own ideas about light and dark, winter and summer. I have learned now that I need to do that in everything."

"Uh. . .can you wait right now?"

Amy tilted her head. "Wait for what?"

"For me to get a word in edgewise. I want you to marry me, Amy. I love you. And if you'd waited, we'd have never met."

"Yes, we would have. I would have come home with Papa on his way home from Texas. You would have been my nearest neighbor. Oh yes, we would have met, because God wants us to be together."

Braden nodded.

Amy had to speak of the one worry that plagued her heart. "And if I had waited, you would have had the time you needed to grieve for your beloved wife. In that, too, I did damage, forcing you to compare me to your graceful, ladylike wife with my crude mountain ways."

"Stop." Braden laid his hand gently on her mouth. "Is that the way it seemed to you?" Braden pulled her tightly into his arms. "Forgive me, Amy. It's true that my grieving hadn't run itself dry. But all I felt was guilt and anger, not sadness. You even got me past that."

"Guilt?" Amy pushed away from him far enough to look in his eyes. "Why would you feel guilt for your wife's death?"

"Maggie was never strong. Having a baby was very hard on her. She was not cut out for life on the frontier, and I knew that. But I couldn't imagine living in the city. If it hadn't been for me, she'd have gone back East. She had a chance, because she had an aunt back there who would have taken her in. But I loved her, and she wanted to stay with me. I wanted to have a family. Every way I looked at it, she seemed to have died because of me, and I couldn't forget her dying in my arms, crying for me to save her. I left home, feeling like a failure."

"But Braden—"

Braden shook his head. "Let me finish."

Amy waited.

"I know now there is no sense in those thoughts. The Lord giveth. The Lord taketh away. God gives no man the strength to save a life if God wants to bring one of His children home. When I compared you to Maggie, my guilt came because I found Maggie so lacking. Maggie never would have stepped in and cared for the family like you did. She'd have complained and handed off every job there was to someone else. I loved her and cherished her, but she wasn't fit for the rugged life we live. You are perfect for it. Perfect for me. She was the love of my youth, and I'll always cherish her. But you are the love of my life."

A smile spread across Braden's face. "You're the one God wants me to spend my life with. I know that as surely as I know the sun will rise in the morning." Braden looked up at the always-light sky. "Okay, I really don't know if the sun will rise in the morning anymore."

Amy patted him on the chest. "You will get onto the ways of Alaska in time."

"I will. I love you and want you to marry me." Braden kissed her lightly on the cheek. "What do you say, lass? Are you going to wait this time? Or is this one time you can plunge right in?"

Amy smiled and then laughed and looked up at the wide, glorious sky, the towering pines, the soaring eagles, and the shining sun. "I do not hear God saying to wait. Not for this."

He kissed her again. She didn't wait an instant before she kissed him back.

Epilogue

They made it to Skaguay in time to lock the Stucky brothers in the town jail to await the next steamer and their ride back to Texas and justice.

Meredith tried to talk Amy into buying a new dress, but the prices horrified Amy.

"I prefer sheepskin anyway, Merry. Why would I spend money like this for a dress made out of thin calico that won't last?"

Meredith fussed at her, but Amy wouldn't be budged.

Braden left the women to shop for other things while he found a preacher.

Parson Henderson had come to bring God to thousands of madmen and admitted he found his work trying. He insisted on spending the day with them.

Braden and Amy were married in front of a tent—Parson Henderson's church. Amy's father and his wife and son were there, along with the Raffertys and Tucker.

Guwakaan had gathered a bouquet of yarrow and daisies for Amy. Amy held them easily, surprised by the strong assurance from God that she and Braden were meant to join their lives.

Pastor Henderson, a gaunt man, tall and gangly but with a serene smile that reflected his devotion to God, spoke the vows.

"Do you, Braden—"

"Pastor Henderson, excuse me, but can I make my own promises to Amy?" Braden interrupted.

Looking surprised, Pastor Henderson said, "Of course, if the vows are made to Amy before God."

"They are." Braden turned to her and took her hands in his. He smiled gently, and Amy's heart became his without a word spoken.

"Your hands are calloused." He held them snugly as if trying to warm them.

"I am sorry." Was this when he remembered his fine, gentle wife?

"I love that about you." Braden cradled her hands against his chest.

Amy's doubts faded away under the shining light in his eyes.

"I love that you are strong. I love that you know this land and respect it and understand it. I think I loved you from that first day I sat beside you on the boat, but I was too afraid to trust my heart and the voice of God telling me He'd led me straight to you. You are going to be a source of strength for me all our lives."

"You do not need my strength, Braden. You saved my life. You were there, helping me on that cliff and at Papa's house because of your strength and wisdom and your caring spirit."

"Although I have my own strength, I need yours as well," Braden said. "Having a real partner to stand beside will make us more than we are alone. I promise before God to always love you, always honor you, and always cherish you."

"And I promise before God to love, honor, and cherish you, too, Braden."

"And obey?" The twinkling light in Braden's eyes made it easy.

"Yes, I'll obey you. Because I know you will not ask anything of me that is not right. And I know you will listen to me."

Braden nodded. "And I know that if you object to something I say, it will be for a good reason. I'll listen to that reason, and we'll decide what's best together."

Amy whispered, "Amen."

"Amen." Braden kissed her.

Pastor Henderson blessed their vows.

Amy kept expecting that warning voice to tell her, *Wait.* It never came.

She and Braden had waited until this golden day, until God's own time. They'd waited long enough.

GOLDEN TWILIGHT

by Kathleen Y'Barbo

Dedication

To Cathy and Kelly Hake, who prayed me through this one, and to Mary Connealy, whose dream of writing about Alaska gave birth to the stories and characters that became the Alaska Brides series. Also, I am deeply indebted to Karl Gurcke, historian of the Klondike Gold Rush National Historical Park in Skagway, Alaska, for his insights into the rich history of the area around which the fictional town of Goose Chase is set.

Chapter 1

As far back as she could remember, Fiona Rafferty wanted to be a doctor. While other girls her age were cutting paper dolls from the Sears Roebuck catalog, she spent her time patching up ornery barn cats and setting bird wings—when she wasn't fishing with Da. By the summer of her tenth year, she'd even saved the life of her father's prized spaniel after the old gray mare kicked him.

Her brothers, Braden and Ian, told her she had a talent for healing. If only that talent hadn't failed her the one time it mattered most. With the proper training, Fiona had no doubt she could have saved Ma.

Fiona shrugged off the memory of her mother's illness and forced the feather duster to continue its path down the spines of the books in Da's library. For a man who made his living from the earth, her father was an educated man. He'd mortgaged his dreams to buy this farm, only to see the love of his life buried beneath the uncompromising Oregon dirt.

From nothing, John Rafferty had made a life for his family. Surely he would understand her need to do the same. To make her own life.

Even as she entertained the thought, she knew better. With Ma gone, the only reaction Da had when Fiona broached the topic of medical school was a frown and a swift change of subject.

She heard the door open and close. Da was home for lunch. Smoothing her hair back from her face, Fiona dropped the feather duster beside the bookcase and scurried to the kitchen to prepare the table.

Today he would have his favorite, a thick beef stew with carrots and potatoes. Fiona had outdone herself with the corn bread she'd whipped up, and she made sure fresh butter sat at the ready. Da did love his corn bread with ample butter.

Along with the meal, Fiona planned to serve up a side dish of careful conversation. She patted the pocket of her apron and smiled. The letter had finally come, and she would soon be going away to study medicine. All that remained was to break the news to Da.

Fiona headed for the dining room but stopped short when she heard a second male voice. The words were soft, a murmur almost, but she distinctly heard her name mentioned in the same sentence with "Alaska."

She drew in a breath and let it out slowly. Surely Da had told the visitor of his sons and daughters-in-law who lived in the North Country, then made mention of his remaining younger daughter. "Yes, that's it," Fiona said.

Touching the letter in her pocket one last time, she fashioned a smile and stepped into the dining room. Soon his remaining daughter would leave, as well, but not for Alaska.

"Ah, there's Fiona now." Da rose, as did the man sitting across from him. A woman of plain countenance and plainer dress remained seated at the stranger's side. "Welcome our guests, daughter. Rev. and Mrs. Minter, may I present my daughter, Fiona?"

"Pleased, I'm sure, Miss Rafferty," the reverend said.

"The Minters are headed to Alaska to start a church among the miners at Skagway," Da continued.

"And from what we've heard, we'll be working with some independent characters," the Reverend Minter added. "Your father said your brothers are up that way. Maybe they've written to you about how many of the locals are protesting the U.S. Post Office changing the name of their town from *Skaguay* to *Skagway*. Can't see as how it makes that much difference, but even the local newspaper refuses to change the spelling of the name. In any event, we hope to contact your brothers and send back word of their welfare."

"And don't you forget to hug my new grandson." Da patted the letter he'd carried with him since its arrival some two weeks ago. "I have it on good authority that Douglas Rafferty is a fine and healthy boy, not that we Raffertys would have anything less."

The men shared a laugh while the pastor's wife unabashedly studied Fiona. When Fiona met the woman's pointed stare, she was greeted with a smirk.

"Fetch extra plates, daughter," her father said. "We men are famished."

Fiona quickly rejected Mrs. Minter's offer of help and bustled off to the kitchen to retrieve the necessary plates and utensils. Because of the unexpected guests, the corn bread would all be eaten with the noon meal, leaving none to mix in a glass of sweet milk for Da's bedtime snack.

The kitchen door opened, and the pastor's wife stepped in. "Are you sure you don't need any help?"

"Oh no," Fiona said. "Da would tan my hide if I put guests to work. My ma raised me better than that."

The woman nodded and stepped back to let the door shut, but not before she gave Fiona a look that said she doubted the statement.

"Humph," Fiona whispered. "I sure hope they don't plan on spending the night."

Fiona returned to the dining room to see that the guests were made welcome then proceeded to serve the meal. Finally, she joined them, sitting at the opposite end of the long table from her father, who offered a genuine smile before returning to his chat with the Reverend and Mrs. Minter.

When the pleasantries had been dispensed with, Da said grace. As Fiona lifted her head, she noticed the reverend's wife staring again. Their gazes met, and Mrs. Minter quickly looked away, but not before Fiona detected something in the woman's gray eyes.

Pity.

Fiona sucked in a deep breath. Why would a mouse of a woman feel sorry for her?

"Your father tells me you're quite a seamstress," the reverend said.

"Actually, I'm not really a—"

"Indeed she is," Da interjected. "Her mother made certain Fiona was adept at all the womanly arts." He paused. "Rest her precious soul," he added in a near whisper.

"She's in a much better place," the reverend said. "One where there is no death or illness."

Mrs. Minter added her sentiments on the topic, while Fiona could barely contain her thoughts. Who were these strangers to comment on Ma? They didn't know her. They'd never listened to her Irish tales or hung on every word of a prayer spoken in her soft brogue.

Da offered Fiona a broad smile that fooled only the lunch guests. Fiona knew better than to miss the warning foretold by his drawn brows and direct stare. "Perhaps after lunch you might show Mrs. Minter the needlepoint you've recently completed."

At the thought of the torture known in polite circles as needlework, Fiona suppressed a groan. Little did Da know that the work she'd done with needle and thread had been to pass the evenings with an excuse not to talk about Da's favorite subject: Fiona's status as a single woman over the age of eighteen.

Pretending to be absorbed in her work had kept Fiona from suffering the embarrassment of discussing which poor fellow Da might feature as a prospective husband. It seemed that since Ma's death two winters ago, Da was more worried than ever about marrying off Fiona and less concerned about allowing her to get the education she must have in order to become a doctor.

Now that the boys had found wives and Da had Douglas, he was beside himself with joy. With each passing year, Fiona knew her brothers' wives would add to the number of grandchildren in the Rafferty family until there would be no end to the Goose Chase, Alaska, branch of the family tree.

While she loved babies and pretty houses as much as the next woman, Fiona believed the Lord had put quite another goal before her. The gift of healing had been entrusted to her, and to ignore that gift seemed to border on blasphemy.

That would be worse than giving up coffee—or fishing.

For that reason, she'd prayed extra hard for just the right opportunity to tell Da of her impending departure. The fact that they had lunch guests must mean the Lord didn't intend her to speak to Da on the issue until dinner.

No matter. She'd been called by the Lord to heal, and nothing would stop her from reaching that goal.

Besides, she'd promised Ma she would follow her dreams wherever they led. And this dream seemed to be leading to a career in medicine.

"Did you hear what the reverend said, Fiona?"

Fiona shifted her attention to the preacher. "I'm sorry, Rev. Minter. What did you say?"

The reverend shook his head. "Understandable. After all, I'm certain if I were about to embark on an adventure of such magnitude, I might be a bit preoccupied, too." He set his fork down and nudged his wife. "Why, I *am*, aren't I?" he said before dissolving into laughter. "I appreciate you allowing us the use of your spare room until the final leg of our journey is upon us."

Da's expression turned somber. "Perhaps we should discuss this after the meal."

Both men looked toward Fiona before concentrating on their plates. Only Mrs. Minter continued to stare.

Fiona cleared her throat and took a bite of corn bread. Still, the woman's gaze bore down on her. "So, Mrs. Minter," Fiona finally said, "what is it that you do, exactly?"

"Do?" The mouse of a woman looked perplexed. "Whatever do you mean, Miss Rafferty?"

Fiona dabbed at the corners of her mouth, then settled her napkin back into her lap. "What I mean is, what sort of talents do you have? What is it you do all day?"

Pink flared on the woman's cheeks, and she cleared her throat. The reverend had stopped chewing to watch the exchange with what looked like interest. Da, however, seemed ready to spring from the chair at any moment.

"Well, I. . ." Mrs. Minter cast a sideways glance at her husband. "During the day, that is, once the reverend is out and about, I. . ." She dropped her gaze to her plate. "I don't suppose I do anything much at all, actually. We'd hoped for children to occupy my hours, but the Lord seems to have had other plans."

The reverend set his fork down and patted his wife's shoulder. "We must thank Him that He's given us a new ministry instead, dear."

Mrs. Minter's smile didn't quite reach her eyes when she said, "Yes, you're right. He has given us that, hasn't He?" A weak hiccup followed the statement, and the pastor's wife began to dab at her eyes.

"Fiona. Apologize at once."

She didn't have to look at Da to know she'd committed a grievous error in judgment. Before she could speak, her father addressed Mrs. Minter.

"You must forgive my daughter. She has delusions of a career." He paused for effect. "In medicine, no less. Can you feature it, Reverend? A medical school wanting to train a girl?"

That did it. Fiona had happily stepped into Ma's role of running the Rafferty home, and she'd even endured the endless hours it took to tie just the right knot and choose just the right colors to make useless needlepoint pillows. To be rewarded by having her choice of career mocked was just too much.

Fiona rose and arranged her napkin on the back of the chair just like Ma used to do. When she cleared her throat and met her father's astonished stare, the room tunneled and contracted until there were only two people present: she and Da.

Shoulders squared, she opened her mouth and let the pent-up words loose. "Perhaps you've missed this fact, Da, but medical schools have been training women for quite some time."

Da's eyes flashed a warning, but he kept a calm expression. "Perhaps you've missed the fact, daughter, that in this family our women are made for a much higher purpose, that of a pursuit in the domestic arts." He looked to the reverend for confirmation. "Have you heard anything so ridiculous as a Christian woman seeking a career?"

While the pastor and his wife shared a quiet chuckle, Da looked completely unamused. Fiona's heart pounded. Slowly, she stepped away from the table, intent on walking away without comment.

Then she spied the look on Mrs. Minter's face. Pity had been replaced by something akin to satisfaction. Fiona's pulse quickened.

"She's been set on this since she was a wee girl. Can you feature it?" Da joined in the laughter.

That, for Fiona, proved to be the last straw.

"I assure you the admissions board at the medical college did not find the issue of my medical training so funny."

She reached into her pocket and withdrew the envelope, depositing it in the middle of Da's plate. He looked down at the paper and knocked the corn bread crumbs off it with his fork. Fiona's breath caught in her throat as her father's gaze scanned the return address.

While Fiona watched in horror, her father tore the letter in half and let it drop to the floor.

"Unlike Mrs. Minter, you have no husband to hold you here, Fiona." The pastor and his wife could not have missed the tremble of anger. "You'll be of much help to Ian and Merry and to Amy and Braden."

Da turned to the Minters and began an explanation of how both his sons were living in the "vast Northland," as he put it. Fiona had heard her father brag of his sons' adventurous streaks and the fine matches they'd made so many times she could practically recite the words right along with Da. This time, however, she could barely hear his voice for the ringing in her ears.

Her father cast a brief glance in Fiona's direction. "The domestic arts are the only career a woman of good character should pursue, don't you think, Rev. Minter?"

"Oh, I do indeed." He turned to his mouse of a wife. "What say you on this, dear?"

Their gazes met. A brief flicker of what may have been sympathy from Mrs. Minter was quickly replaced by a broad smile. "I say that with all those stampeders looking for wives, even a woman not given to cooking and cleaning could do quite well for herself." She punctuated the statement with a smile.

Fiona looked to Da in appeal. Before she could open her mouth, her heart sank. Her father actually looked. . .relieved.

"I had prayed for a solution. After all, she refuses the hand of every suitor who crosses the threshold," he said. "And I feel this permanent arrangement will be beneficial to Fiona."

Well, at least Da thought it a permanent arrangement. Fiona, on the other hand, knew better. The Lord hadn't given her brains so that she might learn to mend a better set of trousers or make a tastier beef stew. And as for those suitors? Contrary to what Da thought, she'd given each one prayerful consideration, then praised the Lord loudly when He deemed them all unsuitable.

She took a breath and let it out slowly. Despite what Da thought, the Lord had made her smart for two reasons: to become a doctor and to figure out how to get out of Alaska. Both objectives, she knew, would take time.

The latter, however, would come soon. All Fiona had to do was keep her outspokenness in check and learn a bit of patience. Surely she could appease her brothers and their wives by fitting into the absurd culture of frozen winters and of summers with no darkness—until she found an escape.

When Fiona dared to look toward the reverend's wife again, she found only pity on the woman's face. But then, Mrs. Minter had no idea Fiona had another envelope upstairs in her room—one that just might save her from a life in the "vast Northland," a life spent in Goose Chase, Alaska.

Taking notice of Fiona's gaze, Mrs. Minter formed her plain features into some semblance of a smile. "Don't worry, Mr. Rafferty," she said sweetly, never removing her attention from Fiona. "We will take good care of your daughter. Have you given any thought to the issue of her transportation? We have acquaintances in Skagway who might be of assistance in seeing that she reaches her destination safely."

As Da warmed to the topic, Fiona returned to her seat and stabbed her knife into the butter, slathering it between layers of corn bread. How she arrived in Alaska was of little concern to her, certainly not worthy of missing a good meal.

Her exit, now, that would be much more interesting.

Chapter 2

A half day's walk from Goose Chase, Alaska

Tucker Smith straightened his back and eased his pick down beside him. A roll of his shoulders loosened muscles hardened from nearly three years of work in this very tunnel.

It didn't start as a tunnel, of course. Way back then, it was just a good idea—a hunch that he and Ian Rafferty had to better themselves and their families by finding gold in the frozen Alaskan land. Who would have known that the discovery of gold in the soil they were digging up for a garden would eventually lead to carving out a tunnel in the face of the mountain?

He cast a glance at the sunlight a few feet away, then turned his back on the day to stare at a wall of midnight-colored earth. Yesterday he had stood in this same spot, and tomorrow he would do it again.

"Hard to believe I used to complain about working all those hours in the sun back in Texas."

Texas.

The reminder of his home, or rather his former home, made him reach for the pick and begin swinging again. Before long, he'd cut a sizable chunk of rock from the wall. Rubble lay around his boots, and specks of dirt littered the shirt his sister had sewn for him last winter. As he brushed the soft wool, Alaskan earth fell like brown snow.

A glint caught Tucker's attention, and he knelt to nudge the mud away. Pocketing the nugget in the pouch at his waist, he went back to work. By the time Tucker heard Ian coming up the path, he'd made a tidy haul.

"Hey, take a look at this. I think we've found a—" The look on his brother-in-law's face stopped him cold. "What's wrong? Has something happened to Merry?"

"Merry?" Ian shook his head. "It's Douglas, actually."

"Douglas?" Tucker let his pick fall. "What's wrong with the baby?"

"You wouldn't believe it."

Tucker's heart thudded in his chest. If anything happened to his nephew. . . well, he just couldn't imagine what he'd do.

"Rest easy, Tucker. My son rolled over today. One minute he was on the blanket just as peaceful as can be, and the next he just flipped right over. Smiled after he did it, too."

Another less jubilant feeling quickly replaced the relief that flooded Tucker. Envy. If not for the way he had turned tail and run from Texas, he, too, might be a papa with a little one he could be proud of.

Tucker took a step back and scrubbed his face with his palms. Where had that come from? Three years had passed since he left home. He knew he still had to work on eliminating the shame he felt over that retreat, but until now he thought he'd done pretty well handling the rest of it.

Ian gripped his shoulder. "You all right?"

Tucker nodded and reached for his pick. "Yeah," he said as he forced his thoughts back to Ian. "Just happy for you and Merry, that's all."

But as he said the words, Tucker followed up with a silent prayer for the Lord to forgive him for his lack of complete honesty. Sure he was happy, but in equal measure, he compared the blessings the Lord had bestowed on them to the same places where God seemed to have forgotten him.

He probably ought to say something. Ian surely would understand. But then, what good could come of admitting to Ian and Meredith—and to Braden and Amy, for that matter—that he envied the life they led?

No, he didn't need anyone to feel sorry for him. The Lord had blessed him with food in his belly and a warm fire in his cabin at night, even if he did sleep alone. That combined with the presence of Meredith and her in-laws left him hard-pressed to complain.

Still. . .

Tucker swung the pick, felt the satisfying *thud* of metal against rock, and knew he'd have to hit a whole lot of rocks before he came close to forgetting.

If he ever did.

"Oh, I almost forgot." Ian reached into his jacket and retrieved what looked like a letter. "From Seattle. I figured it might be important."

The only person he knew in Seattle was Uncle Darian. The address on the front did not belong to his uncle. "That's odd," he said, as he unfolded the letter and began to read.

"Something wrong?"

"There is, actually. It's Uncle Darian." He looked up at Ian. "He died."

"I'm sorry." Ian rested his hands on the handle of his pick. "What happened?"

Tucker folded the letter and stuck it in his coat. "The letter said he'd been ill awhile but wouldn't let anyone write us. Said he didn't want to bother us with his troubles." He shook his head. "That's Uncle Darian for you. Always worrying about everyone else."

"Yes, that fits with how Merry described him." Ian shrugged. "We'd always hoped to show off Douglas to him someday. I wanted to meet him and shake his hand."

"He would have liked that very much." Another thought occurred to Tucker. "Merry will be upset. There was a time when I tried to convince her to move in with him. Times were hard that first year, and I figured Alaska was no place for a lady, you know?"

Ian nodded. "And while Merry would've been wonderful for him, I have to be selfish and say that I'm glad she didn't listen to you. If she'd been there, we wouldn't be together and we wouldn't have Douglas. Did you think about that?"

When Tucker shook his head, Ian continued. "No sense telling Merry now, since there's nothing she can do about it but fret. Best wait until tonight, and I can tell her."

"No," Tucker said. "You're partly right. We'll wait to tell her, but we're going to tell her together."

Ian studied him a minute. "I reckon that's fair enough."

"Reckon so."

Tucker resumed working, as did Ian. He prayed while he worked; then as generally happened, his prayer turned to humming.

Not too long after, the humming became a full-fledged version of "Rock of Ages." His singing voice resounded in the acoustics of the tunnel.

Awhile later, Tucker laid aside his singing. "I'm going to have to go take care of his affairs. That letter was from a lawyer. Said Merry and I've got an inheritance of some sort."

"You'll have to take care of that before winter."

"And Merry can't go." Tucker shrugged. "Not with the baby so small."

Ian landed a blow on the rocks, then reached for what looked like a decent-sized nugget. "Then it's settled. You'll head for Seattle next week to take care of your business. Tonight we can talk about how you'll get there and when you'll go."

"I'll need to speak to Merry, but since you're her husband, you ought to know this, too." Tucker met Ian's gaze with a direct stare. "I'm sure Merry told you that our pa left some debts back in Texas." When Ian nodded, Tucker continued. "Well then, I intend to use whatever Uncle Darian left me to settle those. I know we agreed to share anything between us, but I've got to do this. I wouldn't dream of taking anything off Merry's side, so don't you worry about that."

"I wasn't." Ian laid down his pick. "But he was Merry's father, too, so we'll be shouldering our share. End of discussion."

"No, it's not." In all the time he'd worked and lived side by side with him, Tucker had never wanted to challenge Ian Rafferty to fisticuffs. He was about to change that record when Ian spoke.

"What am I missing here, Tucker? Merry will want to pay for half, and you know it."

"Yes, I know it." Tucker studied the toe of his shoe a moment before lifting his gaze to meet Ian's stare. "I'm telling you that, as the last male in the Smith line, this is my responsibility. I reckon the job of making her understand is going to be your responsibility."

Ian chuckled. "Want to trade with me?"

Tucker went back to his work with a grin. "Not on your life, pal. You chose her for a wife; now you're going to have to live with that."

"That may be," Ian said, "but one of these days you're going to find a wife, and then we'll see."

Skagway, Alaska

Fiona began to plot her return to civilization before the ship left the dock in Seattle. The Minters had stayed a full week while Da went about preparing for his only daughter to be shipped north against her will. Keeping mostly to herself, Fiona left her room only to prepare meals.

When the ship left Seattle, she calmly waited in her stateroom until the vessel had cleared the sound. She'd said her good-byes to Da at the farm, knowing the situation was temporary, but even then she'd cried.

By the time they disembarked at Skagway, Fiona had substituted praying for plotting. She'd crafted two more letters, which she mailed early on the third morning in the city.

The reverend and his wife made her feel welcome in their new parsonage, but she itched to get on with the process of settling in Alaska. The sooner she was settled, the sooner she could make her departure. Bad weather and the lack of a suitable guide kept her from taking the land route to Goose Chase.

While waiting for the weather to clear and the ships to begin plying their routes, she settled into an uneasy peace with the Reverend Minter but never managed the same with his wife. Finally the day came when Mrs. Minter gave her the good news: A suitable mode of transport to Goose Chase by water had been secured. She would leave on the morrow.

"How do you feel about fishing?" Mrs. Minter asked.

"Outside of the good Lord and a hot cup of black coffee, that's about my favorite thing. Why?"

A knowing smile had been the only response. Until Fiona set eyes on her mode of transportation, she'd had no idea what that smile meant.

Upon arriving at the docks, however, Fiona realized she'd been booked on a trawler that reeked of the fish it sought. The reverend escorted her aboard and saw her settled into a storage room that was the closest thing to a stateroom before muttering a brief prayer and making a swift exit.

Much as she loved to fish, she generally declined to inhabit spaces within reach of their scent. This time, she obviously did not have that option.

The trip upriver was uneventful, yet Fiona found sleep elusive at night and an object of desire during the day. Finally, when their destination was within sight, Fiona wandered up to the deck.

"I will never get the stench out of my trunk," she muttered as she watched the crew prepare for docking in Goose Chase.

"Oh, I don't know, miss. I find a decent bath and a scrubbing will reduce the smell a bit."

Fiona whirled around to see the elderly captain, a man she now knew to be Mrs. Minter's uncle, Boris Svenson, also known as Captain Sven, grinning in her direction. She adjusted her traveling hat and clamped her mouth shut. No good could come from making a response.

"It helps if ye rinse the first time in saltwater." He shrugged as he stepped over uneven boards with nimble feet then called out instructions to the crew before turning his attention back to Fiona. "Worked for my wife. She never once complained after I'd scrubbed meself proper," he said as he removed his cap and studied the deck. "May the Lord rest her soul."

"Oh," she said softly. "I'm terribly sorry about your wife."

"Worry not, miss." His downcast look was replaced by a twinkle in his eyes. "The dear woman only wished for my happiness. I've been lookin' for a gal t'keep me warm come winter." He inched closer. "So, you're quite the lovely lass. Are ye meetin' someone special in Goose Chase? If ye are, my niece didn't mention it."

Fiona bit back the caustic words that threatened and forced a smile. "Why, yes, I am," she practically purred. "Two of them, actually."

"Two?"

"Yes, indeed." The smile broadened as she cast a glance toward the little town. "Brothers, actually."

"Brothers?" The captain's busy brows went skyward as he sputtered for a response.

Taking pity on the poor man, Fiona gathered her coat about her. "My, but it's chilly out."

"Chilly? Why, this is practically a heat wave compared to what it's usually like up here. The Lord's been kind in giving us mild temperatures. Just wait until the winter sets in."

Winter? A time when ship traffic ground to a halt due to storms and ice? Oh, no. She'd be long gone before the snow fell.

"Say, would you happen to know when there's another vessel headed back to Seattle?"

"Seattle?" He gave her a questioning look. "Ye haven't even set foot on the shore, and you're already plotting t'leave? I call that downright odd. What say you, Mr. Smith?"

Fiona followed the captain's gaze to a man standing nearby on the shore. Trying to focus through the sun's glare, she made out the silhouette of a shock of dark hair, a pair of broad shoulders, and long legs.

"Well, now. That depends. You didn't propose marriage again, did you, Cap? That's usually why the girls run off." The lanky fellow shifted positions, deepening the shadows covering his face.

An acid reply refused to be restrained. "I'm no girl, sir," she said through clenched jaw. "I'll have you know I'm going to be a doctor."

"A doctor?" The man's voice was deep and decidedly Southern. "I don't believe I've ever met a lady doctor, especially not one wearing such a hat. What sort of odd bird had to be robbed of that feather?"

"And you'll not be meeting this one either, sir." With that, she added a decidedly unladylike frown and turned on her heels. "If you'll excuse me, I believe I've left my other glove in the stateroom."

"Stateroom?" the fellow on the docks called. "Since when does this old tub have staterooms? Cap, did you redo the place when you heard you'd be transporting lady doctors? I sure hope you polish the chandeliers before I board. You know I like things just so."

The sound of the men's laughter sent Fiona skittering below deck. The glove retrieved, she returned to the deck to find both the captain and the arrogant rapscallion gone.

Fiona picked her way across the deck and negotiated the narrow plank that served as an exit, all the while waiting for the irritating man to return so she could educate him on the proper treatment of a lady. Her foot slipped on a patch of ice, and she nearly went sliding toward the dock. Skidding to a stop atop her trunk, Fiona gathered her skirts and her wits.

"It's only temporary," she whispered. "Keep smiling." Then she spied her brothers and the smile broadened.

Braden saw her first and called her name, but Ian outran him to lift her into the air and then envelop her in a bear hug. "Welcome to Goose Chase, Fiona."

Chapter 3

"Oh! Ian! Put—me—down!" Fiona gave her brother a playful swat as her traveling hat tilted and obscured her vision.

Ian complied, but not before he made one last spin. He set her down on the uneven boards, then feigned exhaustion while Braden grasped her shoulders to keep her from landing on her posterior.

"I didn't expect to see both of you," she said as she recovered her balance and straightened her hat.

"Amy's visiting her father for a few days." Braden's buttons nearly burst as he straightened his shoulders. "It seems as though I'm going to be a father."

Fiona's squeal of delight nearly drowned out Ian's peal of laughter. While Ian clamped his hand on his brother's shoulder, Fiona wrapped her arms around his middle to give him a tight hug.

"Thank you both," Braden said. "Amy couldn't wait to tell her da."

Ian took a step back. "You don't seem excited about this. What's wrong?"

Braden shook his head. "It's nothing, really. I mean, I know women have babies every day, but..."

Fiona reached for her brother's hand and met his gaze with an unwavering stare. "Braden, you can either spend every minute of Amy's time waiting for something to go wrong, or you can open your eyes every day and thank the Lord that He has entrusted you with a new life." She paused to let her statement sink in. "Which will it be?"

"You've grown up, Fifi." Braden swiped at his eyes with the backs of his hands then gave her a wry smile. "What happened to the little girl I left behind?"

Ian released his grip on Fiona and reached for her bag. "Braden, you know how she hates to be called Fifi."

The serious moment passed, and her brothers returned to being, well, her brothers. Some things never changed.

Braden chuckled. "I know," he said as he sized up the stack of items she brought. "You still like coffee as much as you did before?"

Fiona gave him a serious look. "More."

"I sure hope you brought some," Ian said. "Tucker's about to drive us mad, worrying you might forget."

"Who's Tucker?"

"That's Merry's twin brother," Ian said. "Remember, I wrote to you about him."

"Ah, yes," she said. "I remember."

"He obviously doesn't know our Fiona." Braden shouldered the bag, grabbed another, and then turned to head down the dock. "She wouldn't think of starting a day without a cup, eh, sis?"

"Hey, Braden, remember the time she walked all the way to town for coffee beans because Da wouldn't let her take the horse and buggy out alone?"

"We were out," she said.

While her brothers chuckled and made short work of moving her things, Fiona studied her surroundings. On first glance, Goose Chase seemed nothing more than a collection of ramshackle huts perched alongside a river so narrow it barely supported a decent vessel. In truth, other than the trawler she arrived in, the favored conveyance seemed to be small canoelike rowboats made of what looked to be some sort of hide.

"Am I going to have to ride in one of those?"

"Actually, your things are," Ian said. "Most of the time you'll be walking."

She crossed her arms over her chest and stared up at Ian in disbelief. "Walking?"

"Yes, but only if you want to get to your new home," Ian responded.

She bit back the bitter response that would let her brothers know exactly how temporary this situation was. "I'm sorry. That was rude of me." She gave each of her brothers another hug. "I'm afraid the trip's made me unconscionably cranky."

"I don't mind a cranky sister. I'm just glad you're here. I've missed you," Braden said, then added a greeting in his wife's native Tlingit. "That's from Amy. She's thrilled to have you living so near us."

"And Merry can't wait to talk your ear off, I'm sure." Ian shrugged. "I'm afraid our wives are starved for female companionship. I promised to fetch you home as soon as our business in town was done."

"And the baby," Fiona said, "how is he?"

"Douglas is, no doubt, the most brilliant of all the Rafferty men. It won't be long until he's calling me Da."

"Ian, he's only four months old." Braden looked past Fiona to frown. "We're going to have to keep a close watch on Fiona. Look at the attention she's drawing."

Ian followed Braden's gaze. "You're right," he said. "But then, when's the last time an unattached beauty arrived in town?"

"Hush now," Fiona said. "The men can't be that interested in me. I'm as plain as they come. Now let's make haste for home. I've got a nephew and two sisters-in-law to meet."

One glance at the streets of tiny Goose Chase, and Fiona had no doubt her brother's statement *was* true. As she followed them down streets muddy with the beginnings of the spring thaw, she saw men everywhere. Old, young, and every age in between.

And obviously, they all saw her.

"You're causing quite a sensation," Braden said as he steered her away from a particularly large mud puddle. "Like as not there will be a line of suitors at Ian's place before dark."

Ian must have noticed her expression, for he reached to grasp her hand. "Braden, you go on to the mercantile. Fiona and I will wait for you in the *umiak*. I think all this attention's a bit much for her."

Fiona shot Ian a look of thanks and then followed him back to the docks in silence.

Somehow her trunk had been transferred to one of the leather-clad canoes. She glanced over at the trawler and then returned the captain's wave.

"Remember the red canoe Da built for us when we were children?" Ian gestured to the leather boat. "This is much like it. It's called an umiak," he explained. "Braden and Amy built it with skins I trapped." He paused. "And we won't be traveling with it all that far." Ian's grin turned tender. "I know all of this is new to you, but I promise you'll love living in Alaska. Just give it a chance."

Once again, Fiona chose not to comment.

As promised, Braden returned quickly, and their trip upriver began. Fiona marveled at her brothers' ability to maneuver the small vessel, given that they used ropes to achieve the task. Many long hours later, they crossed a small bridge and steered the umiak to a stop near a collection of buildings that Fiona prayed were not homes.

Unfortunately, they were.

<hr />

"Did Da really say that?" Eyes twinkling, Ian Rafferty took a healthy sip of coffee and set the mug on the rough wooden table. His lovely wife, Meredith, swiftly refilled the cup from the pot brewing on the small stove.

A little over two weeks had passed since Fiona had landed in this strange community, and she'd almost caught up on her sleep. While she'd quickly learned to love the women her brothers had married, she had yet to find an equal fondness for the land where they settled. Why, even the bridge that linked her brothers' land to the opposite shore was a temporary structure. Except when they used pulleys and ropes to swing it into position, it stood useless, parallel to the river's edge. Her brothers had explained this was necessary to keep the bridge from causing the water—and the flecks of gold it might carry—to flow away from the opposite shore and the miner who held legal claim to it.

As her brothers had predicted, a constant barrage of suitors seemed to appear at random from the vast wilderness surrounding them. Ian and Braden took great delight in her discomfort, while Meredith and Amy encouraged her to ignore the whole lot of them. Fiona kept her thoughts to herself and counted the days until she could make good her escape.

That morning over breakfast, the talk had once again turned to matchmaking. Unlike before, Fiona spoke up when Ian began his teasing.

"I fail to see what's so funny. Did our father mention that my lack of a mate is the main reason he banished me to this place?" Fiona took a healthy sip of coffee then glanced over at Meredith, who gave her a nod. "Da feels I should be a wife and mother and not a doctor. To paraphrase, Alaska may do what Oregon did not."

"Get you married off?" Ian shook his head. "And why not? If you haven't noticed, the population in Goose Chase is decidedly male. Why, I'm surprised Merry gave me the time of day, what with the pickings being so plentiful."

Meredith brushed past Ian, pausing only to kiss the top of his head. Fiona watched her disappear behind the fur curtain separating the eating area from the other parts of the tidy but claustrophobic abode. While Fiona understood the need to protect its inhabitants from the dreaded Alaska winter, the odd dwelling seemed more like a tomb than a home.

And the facilities, well, to say the least, Fiona did not relish her morning ablutions or the occasional nighttime trip outside. Then there was the complete lack of a proper day and night. She rose and slept by the clock, not the sun, having been warned by Braden on her first day that one might lose track of days and nights unless a diary was kept. Amy advised her that by the time summer set in, she would be able to read a book at midnight.

How her brothers and their families stood it all was beyond Fiona. Even baby Douglas seemed to adapt better than she to the odd life his parents lived.

Fiona forced her mind back to the topic at hand. The courage to speak might not return; seeing the conversation through to the end was best done only once. She took another sip of coffee and stared at Ian.

She would have to have this conversation again with Braden when the opportunity presented itself. Perhaps it was better to divide and conquer when it came to the Rafferty men.

"What if I don't want to be married off, Ian? What if I want to be single the rest of my life so I can devote myself to the calling the Lord's placed on me?"

Shock registered on Ian's face, even as heavy footfalls sounded outside.

A gust of icy wind preceded a tall man bundled into a parka that showed only a pair of brown eyes and a lock of ebony-colored hair. "How did I get so fortunate as to meet the one woman on earth who isn't looking for a husband?" As he peeled off the topmost layer of outerwear, the stranger thrust a gloved hand in her direction. "Tucker Smith," he said. "And you must be Ian's sister, Fiona."

His hand enveloped hers, the fingers strong and warmer than she expected. So was his expression when he removed his cap and shook free a mane of hair that needed a good barbering.

Odd, but something seemed quite familiar about the man. And the voice? Fiona was almost certain she'd heard that voice somewhere before.

Ian motioned for the man to take a spot at the table, then reached for the coffeepot and a spare mug. "Fiona, meet Merry's brother. Tucker, this is Fiona. He's a Texan, so don't pay attention to half of what he says and ignore the rest of it."

So this was the mysterious Tucker Smith, the man she had heard Meredith and Ian whispering about when they thought she was not listening. Something about a mission to Seattle. A deceased relative whose will needed tending to, perhaps. She'd not been able to piece out the story from her limited knowledge, but truthfully she'd been too tired to muster more than a passing interest.

Fiona sized up Meredith's brother, being careful not to attract his attention. To her surprise, the man acted not at all like the other men who sought her favor.

If Fiona had not been so relieved, she might have been offended.

Tucker shared a laugh with Ian before turning his attention to Fiona. His gaze swept over her and then settled on her eyes. Was that amusement? Recognition?

Surely not.

Ian had written of his brother-in-law and most likely had also told Mr. Smith about Fiona. *Yes, that's why he's staring at me as if he knows me.*

"Well, now, pleased to meet you, ma'am," Mr. Smith said.

The man spoke in a slow drawl, a voice that shook the timbers of her heart with its depth and richness. She wouldn't be surprised to find Tucker Smith had a talent for music, such was the melody of his speech. So this was the mysterious fellow her sister-in-law so often remembered in her prayers.

Tucker settled onto the chair beside Fiona, then swiveled to face her. Rather than stare into the man's startling, sky blue eyes, she settled her gaze on his red suspenders.

Ian leaned forward and rested his elbows on the table. "You get everything handled?"

His yes came out in a weary sigh.

"Were you able to wire the money to Texas?" Merry asked as she pushed back the fur curtain and returned to the room. "I know that was first on your list of things to do after you signed the papers."

"Enough of that." Ian gave Meredith a look of gentle warning. "Let the man rest, dear. He'll give us the details soon enough."

She turned to Fiona. "Tucker's been taking care of some family business. He's been in Seattle for a spell."

Fiona lifted her gaze from the red suspenders to their owner's face. A tinge of the same scarlet color decorated his cheeks. Tucker caught her staring, and she looked away quickly.

Meredith paused beside her husband, but her gaze landed squarely on Tucker. "Funny how the supplies last twice as long when you're away. I think you only came back for the food."

"And I always appreciate the pleasure of your company and the taste of your stew, Merry, so it's no mystery why I'm here." Tucker smiled, and Fiona's stomach did a flip-flop. "The mystery is why you're here, Fiona. What brings a pretty girl to Goose Chase, Alaska?"

When Fiona didn't respond, Tucker looked around the room as if asking for the answer. Thankfully, neither Ian nor Meredith spoke for a full minute.

Tucker gave Fiona a sideways look. "Well, now, a woman with secrets. I'm intrigued."

"Never mind, Tucker," Meredith finally said. "Now tell me all about Seattle."

Fiona sighed. This was a temporary reprieve at best.

Soon, everyone in town would learn why she was banished to this frozen wasteland, and she'd be humiliated for sure. With the ratio of single men to unclaimed women quite out of balance, she'd soon feel the stares, anyway.

Well, no matter; she'd be gone soon enough.

Tucker leaned conspiratorially in Fiona's direction. "Let's make a pact. You keep your secrets, and I'll keep mine. Together, we'll keep this pair guessing. What say you?" Before she could respond, a look passed over his face. "Is. . .that. . .*fresh* coffee?"

Fiona glanced down at her cup and then back at Tucker. "It is. I brought it from home."

"Tucker, you only just returned." Meredith stopped behind her brother to muss his already unruly locks, then smiled at Fiona. "My brother's appetite for coffee is matched only by his appetite for caribou steaks."

"Are we having caribou steaks tonight?" Tucker looked like a kid in a candy store. "Don't tease me, Merry. Seattle is great, but it's not Alaska."

"And I, for one, am grateful." The words were out before Fiona realized she'd spoken them.

"My sister's been banished to Alaska against her will," Ian said to Tucker.

Fiona cringed as she waited for Tucker's sarcastic comment. It never came. Rather, Tucker seemed sympathetic.

Meredith met her gaze. "Same as my brother and me, actually," Meredith said. "Tucker and I never expected we would leave Texas for Alaska. Sometimes your family makes decisions without thinking of how they will affect you, and there's nothing you can do but live with them."

Ian looked stunned at his wife's statement. Tucker, however, rose and put his hands on his twin sister's shoulders. "Sometimes the Lord lets us slide into sticky situations faster than He lets us climb out of them. What happened back in Texas is better left back in Texas. I reckon I'm not willing to say any more than that on the subject, and I'd be obliged if you'd do the same, Merry."

The baby began to whimper, breaking the silence. Meredith looked as if she might speak and then clamped her lips shut. A quick nod of her head was followed by Meredith turning on her heels to follow the sound of her son's cry.

Chapter 4

Tucker eyed the pretty redhead a split second longer than proper, then forced his attention on his brother-in-law. Something about her tugged at his thoughts. He never forgot a face, and this face he'd seen before. But how was it possible?

He returned to his chair and tried to think of how he might have seen a woman with such fire and promptly forgotten the experience. It seemed impossible.

"You look like you're pondering something important, Tucker," Ian said.

"Do I?" He decided to move his attention elsewhere. Now was as good a time as any to break his idea to them gently. "Did you hear the Harriman Expedition's heading toward Sitka?"

Ian met his gaze. "I did."

"Wonder what you think of that?"

Ian tipped his chair back and ran his hand over his chin hairs. "I reckon somebody's got to do it. We need the maps, and there's no telling what else they'll find." He nodded. "I say, good for them."

That went well enough. Tucker decided to go ahead and spring the whole plan on them. "What would you think if I signed on for the adventure?"

His brother-in-law set his chair down with a *thud* and then shook his head. "Sign on for the adventure? Are you serious?"

Tucker caught the redhead staring at him. "Dead serious, actually," he said. "I met a fellow on the way back from Seattle, a mapmaker. We got to talking, and it turns out they need folks like me who know their way around the tundra." He paused. "So, Ian, what do you think? Can you do without me for a month or so?"

Ian seemed to be taking the news in and chewing on it. Tucker knew his brother-in-law rarely spoke before cogitating a bit. Most times, he liked that about Ian Rafferty. At the moment, however, he was ready to jump out of his seat and shake an opinion out of him. If Meredith hadn't bustled the baby out of the room to feed him, she probably would have spoken her piece by now. He had little doubt, however, what she would say. Ian, on the other hand, just might like the idea.

"I've heard the expedition's going to bring along an artist," Ian's sister said. "How wonderful to see the flora and fauna of the Arctic Circle."

When Tucker looked her way, green eyes stabbed him with something akin to disgust. He made the mistake of chuckling.

"Do you find my statement amusing, Mr. Smith?"

Tucker grimaced. "Forgive me, Miss Rafferty," he said slowly, "but there are more important things in the world than flora and fauna."

"Such as?" Her eyes glinted a challenge stronger than her tone.

"Such as. . ." Dare he hint at the real reason he wanted to be aboard that ship? Probably not. This one seemed to be devoid of the usual cognitive handicaps associated with being born female. Unfortunately, she'd obviously acquired the feminine art of putting a big-mouthed man in his place, most likely a hazard of growing up alongside Ian and Braden. Unless he said something brilliant soon, she'd most likely do just that.

"Such as," he said with false bravado, "making maps so the railroad can go through and towns can be built. You never know when space is going to run out back home in the States. We need to be ready when they start looking for land in our direction." He looked to Ian for support and found only amusement.

Fiona's harrumph let him know exactly what she thought of his answer.

"You have a better idea, do you?" His voice rose. "Perhaps a picture of some tree or fern that will save the world?"

Hands on hips, the redhead pushed away from the table and met his gaze. "Or perhaps some plant with medicinal qualities that will save people." Fiona rose. "If you'll excuse me, I have some things to take care of."

He watched Ian's sister sweep from the room as if she were the queen of England.

"Since when do you want to get on a ship and leave because some fellow down south's living too close to his neighbor?" Ian asked. "Something else is going on here, Tucker Smith, and I want to know what it is."

"I think I know." Meredith's firm reply startled them both.

Tucker whirled around to see his twin sister standing in the doorway, holding Douglas against her shoulder. A look passed between Meredith and her husband, and after a moment, Ian rose. "It's a fine day for a walk down to the creek. I believe I will go see if I can find a bit of gold with the pan."

"That's a fine idea, Ian," Tucker said. "I'll go with you."

Meredith reached him before he stood and pressed her free hand on his shoulder before handing the baby to him. "You're needed here, Tucker," she said. "If Ian needs any help, he can take his sister."

"Take my sister panning? Are you. . ." Ian looked from Meredith to Tucker and then back at Meredith again. "Fishing with Fiona. Ah, yes, of course. Why didn't I think of that?"

"You did," Meredith said. "Just now."

"See what a man needs a wife for?" Ian smiled and then kissed both his wife and his son. A moment later, he was crossing the yard toward the red-haired spitfire.

"See what a man needs a wife for?" Tucker felt the stab of guilt down to his gut. A wife. A son. Maybe a daughter someday. . .

"Tucker."

His twin's gentle voice drew his attention. He looked up at her and smiled. "Are you going to lecture or listen?"

She settled into the chair next to him and dabbed at the baby's smiling mouth with her handkerchief. Tucker reached for Douglas and held him close against his chest. One hand on the baby's back, Tucker felt the soft fuzz of his nephew's hair tickling his nose. He was, for a moment, lost in the sweet baby smell.

"You won't enjoy him so much when his dinner's digested."

Tucker adjusted his nephew to the crook of his arm and held him slightly away from his body. Meredith giggled and retrieved her son.

"You men never cease to amaze me. You can gut a fish or skin a caribou, but you go weak at the thought of a baby doing what babies do best." She arranged Douglas in her lap then lifted her gaze to Tucker. "I do believe I know what's wrong, Tucker, but I wonder if you'll say it before I have to."

He shrugged and rose then reached for the coffeepot. While pouring the last dregs of his favorite beverage into his mug, Tucker watched Ian and Fiona disappear over the rise in the distance.

Alaska was beautiful, especially this time of year. Only Texas held this kind of sway over him, and as the years flew by, the hold of his native land lessened.

The sound of Meredith cooing to her son drew his attention. He turned and took a deep breath and then hauled himself and his coffee back to the table.

"Save me the time and say it, Merry," he said before taking a sip of the hot, strong brew. "No matter what words I might have to defend myself, I am sure you will have more to add to them."

"That's not fair." Meredith's expression softened. "Or maybe it is." She seemed to be searching his face. "I don't pretend to know why the Lord blessed me with Ian and Douglas here in Alaska when you had to leave all your dreams behind in Texas. I don't deserve all this happiness." Her eyes welled with tears. "And you don't deserve to be alone."

As he expected, his sister knew him too well. Tucker could deny it, but any statement other than the truth wouldn't be worth the breath he wasted on it. Diversion seemed his only option.

"I'm not alone. Between your family and Braden's, I never have to worry about too much peace and quiet." He paused to take a sip of the cooling coffee. "Especially now that Amy and Braden will be giving you a new niece or nephew. Before long, Goose Chase will be overflowing with Rafferty children."

"But that's just it." Meredith shook her head. "Don't bother to deny it. I've seen how you are with Douglas. Oh, Tucker, you should be having babies of your own."

He faked a laugh in another attempt to sidetrack the discussion. "Now wouldn't that be something to see? Last time I checked, it was the wife's job to have the babies."

She tossed her handkerchief at him and rose to walk the baby the length of the room. "Have you written her since we left?"

"Her?" He feigned ignorance. "Since when do I write letters to anyone?"

Meredith halted her pacing. "Stop it, Tucker. You know who I mean."

"Yes, I do know who you mean, and no, I haven't written her." He took a deep breath and let it out slowly. "I told her before I left that I'd never ask her to be tied to a man whose family couldn't hold their heads up in town."

"So that's why you broke it off with her. Because of our father."

His temples throbbed as he tossed back the last of his coffee and set the mug on the table. "No, Merry, I told Elizabeth's daddy that I released her from the promise to me because the situation had changed. She was standing right there when I told him, and she seemed to be fine with it."

"Seemed to be fine with it or struck dumb with shock?" she asked as she patted the sleeping baby's back. "You know, Tucker, you are stubborn as a mule." Meredith paused to shake her head. "No, that's not right. I don't want to insult the mule."

"You, Merry Rafferty, always were the dramatic one."

From the look on her face, Tucker could tell he'd done it this time. He and his twin rarely shared harsh words. Their closeness generally prevented any conflict, but at times like these, it was that closeness that gave him the knowledge of just what words would hit the mark.

The last time they had argued, it had been over a play toy. He couldn't remember who won that argument, but he never forgot how much he hated seeing his sister cry.

Like now.

"And you, Tucker Smith," she said as the first tear wove a path down her cheek, "were always the dense one. You mope around here wishing you had a wife and baby like Ian, yet you went and messed up the one chance you had. No wonder you want to run off and hide on some expedition to the North Pole."

"They're not going to the North Pole. They're—"

"Who cares what the destination is? The only reason you want to be on that boat is to get away from the consequences of your choice. You could have brought Elizabeth with us as your wife, you know."

"Now why would I want to do that? The woman can't brew a pot of coffee to save her life, and she surely doesn't know which end of a fishing pole goes in the water. Why would I want to burden myself with such a woman?"

She refused to be put off track by humor—that much he knew from looking at her. Tucker tried another tack.

"Maybe she didn't want to go, Merry. Have you thought of that? Maybe she didn't want anything to do with a man whose father had no better morals than to defraud half the county."

"It wasn't half the county, and you know it."

"What I know is that I had no choice in what my father did, but I do have a choice about whether to stay here and listen to you telling me what I ought to do."

Tucker rose and headed for the door. If Meredith wanted to question him further on his love life or anything else, she'd have to follow him.

And he intended to walk fast.

———

Fiona was so mad she could have walked all the way back to Oregon. Instead, she settled for storming away from a conversation where her brother refused to admit that she belonged in medical school rather than Alaska. Ian held the archaic view that his baby sister should be seeking a husband instead of following a dream.

"You're wrong, Ian," she called over her shoulder as she stormed away. "It's not something

I want to do; it's something I have to do. There's a difference."

"Oh, Fiona, be serious."

His teasing laughter chased her along the path by the river, and then it brushed past her to echo against the snow-covered hills up ahead. She counted her steps, picking her way around patches of mud and jutting rocks.

How had a lovely stroll with her brother turned into an argument—something she and her brother never had? Ian didn't intend to be mean, and she knew it. He was just a man and, as such, held to a whole bunch of ideas that didn't fit anymore. To listen to Ian Rafferty, one would never know there was a brand-new century dawning in less than seven months.

Fiona would have loved nothing better than to shout back to Ian, reminding him of that fact, but to do that, she'd have to backtrack and catch him where he could hear her. Instead, she allowed herself to think about where she might be when the clock struck midnight on January 1 of the year 1900. She'd be at the medical college, of course.

"What better time to write a letter of acceptance to the university?"

The question, spoken aloud to no one in particular, brought a smile, and she wore that smile until she reached the open door of her temporary home. Once inside, she stopped short when she saw Meredith bent over a sheet of paper, writing furiously. Her sister-in-law seemed so involved in whatever she was working on that she had no idea Fiona stood watching.

"Merry?"

She jumped, grasping her chest. The pen clattered to the floor, where Fiona quickly retrieved it.

"I'm so sorry." Fiona handed Meredith the pen. "I didn't mean to frighten you."

Meredith folded the letter in thirds then set it aside. "No, it's fine," she said as she smoothed back her hair. "I was just writing a letter to someone back home."

"Would you have extra writing materials I might use? I think I'd like to do the same thing." She gestured behind her. "I think I'll enjoy the outdoors. It's nice out."

"Of course," Meredith said, her voice still a bit shaky. "There's a lovely spot just over the hill beside the river."

When Fiona arrived at the spot, she found it already occupied, so she turned, intent on retracing her steps. Tucker Smith sat so close to the water that he could reach over and stick his hand in if he wanted to. He gave no notice he saw her, and it was only when he called her name that she realized he was aware of her presence.

"Fiona, wait. You don't have to go."

She stopped. "No, I'll find another place to write."

"Suit yourself," he responded without looking in her direction.

Fiona wandered around until she found a secluded spot a few hundred yards upstream. Spotting a rock large enough to sit on, she perched atop it and hauled out her writing kit. Writing the letter of acceptance took almost no time. It was the letter to her father that she agonized over.

Despite her father's old-fashioned ways, Fiona loved him with all she had. Unlike her brothers, she'd been her father's shadow. Tagging along beside him, baiting his hook, and cooking his meals had cemented a bond between them that nothing could shake.

She might not like his choice to send her to live with her brothers, but she understood it. A man of his generation would never think of letting a woman choose her career, at least not where her father came from.

As much as she did not want to write him of her plans, Fiona knew she must. So with dread and prayers, she began a letter to her father.

She'd used and discarded three sheets of paper when Tucker Smith strolled into sight around the bend in the river. Fiona frowned. Just when she'd finally decided how to break the news to Da. What did the irritating man want now?

He walked tall and swift, making his way over the rocky ground without so much as a glance toward his feet. Unlike her, Tucker had made peace with this place.

"I surrender." He paused. "And I apologize."

Well now, she hadn't expected that. "For what?" came out before she had time to think.

Even an irritating man can look handsome when he grins, and Tucker did. "I won't tell you what Merry called me, but I will tell you she was right."

"I see." Fiona set aside her writing and studied the ink stains on her fingers as she blew out a long breath. "Tucker. . ." She spoke as slowly as she moved, lifting her head as the words fell softly between them. "I owe you an apology, as well. I shouldn't have spoken to you in the manner I did. It was rude."

He reached for a stone to throw toward the river. It hit the middle of the stream with a plop then disappeared below the rippling surface. "We're a fine pair. How about we start over?"

He rose and bowed low, as if he were greeting the queen of England. "Name's Tucker Smith of the Texas Smiths. The pleasure's all mine." He took two steps back and affected surprise. "Say, aren't you Ian and Braden Rafferty's sister?"

The slightest smile threatened to escape, so she looked away. My, but this one could be charming when he wanted. The last thing a woman on her way out needed was to find an interest in a man who wasn't going with her.

A movement on the other side of the river caught her attention. From where she sat, she watched a silver-haired man slide from behind a rock to crouch beside a stand of trees. "Tucker," she said slowly, "someone is watching us."

Chapter 5

Tucker followed Fiona's gaze to the other side of the river. He chuckled when the fellow had the gall to wave.

"Do you know him?"

"I'm afraid so." He returned his attention to Ian's sister. "That's Mr. Abrams. He owns the land on that side nigh on up past the creek."

"Does he always spy on the goings-on over here?"

"Well, I can't be sure." Tucker shrugged. "But I believe he busies himself with working his claim most days. Leastwise, Merry's never complained about him."

She clutched her paper and ink. "Wonderful."

"Looks like you've caught his attention. Maybe he can't help staring because he thinks you're the prettiest thing he's seen in some time."

The expression on Fiona's face told him how little she liked that idea. Tucker hoped his own expression didn't give away how much of that statement described his feelings, as well.

"So he's not dangerous?" Fiona swung her gaze in his direction before taking another look at the fellow across the river. "Are you sure? He seems a bit. . .well. . . odd. Look, he's climbing that tree."

"Miss Rafferty," he said slowly, "I assure you, old Mr. Abrams isn't any more dangerous than I am."

She cut him a sideways glance. "And that's supposed to make me feel better?"

For a minute he couldn't tell whether or not she was serious. Then her lip twitched, and he knew she was hiding a smile.

A cry for help prevented Tucker from answering. Fiona jumped to her feet and raced toward the sound.

"It's your neighbor," she called, as she jumped off the rock and searched for a spot to cross the river. "I think he fell out of the tree. Look!"

She pointed to Abrams, who lay on the ground. Tucker stood watching for a moment, until he realized the panicked female was about to try and swim across.

"What are you doing?" Tucker called. "The water's freezing. You can't go in there." He caught up to her. "Go back and fetch Merry. She will know what to do."

"There's no time," she said. "Get me across the river." When he didn't react immediately, she took off walking again.

"Miss Rafferty, what are you doing? If you get in the water, you'll—"

"Help me across, then, or I'm swimming. That man needs medical attention, and I have the training." As if to prove her point, she made a move toward the first rock nearest the banks. "I can walk across the rocks and—"

"Not on my watch. Ian would have my hide. The bridge is only a quarter mile downstream."

Fiona shook her head. "No time to go that far. He could be seriously injured. There has to be a faster way."

Making up his mind as he sprinted after her, Tucker swept the obstinate woman into his arms, then swung her over his shoulder. "Be still, or we'll both get a good dunking. I'm crossing up ahead where that fallen log is. If you understand that you need to be completely still, say yes now. Otherwise, I'm dumping you right here."

"Yes" came like a squeak from somewhere behind his right ear.

Tucker hauled her closer against him and tested his balance on the log. Before putting his next foot forward, he paused.

"What are you doing?" the Rafferty woman croaked. "Time's wasting."

"Hush, woman," Tucker said, "I'm praying; then I'm crossing. You got any complaints about that, you take it up with the good Lord."

She held silent and still while he finished his prayer and set across. Midway across the stream, Tucker stopped to readjust the slight weight he carried over his shoulder. To his surprise, she neither moved nor spoke.

Three steps later, however, she squealed and grasped handfuls of his shirt when his foot slipped. Tucker righted himself and made the rest of the trip across in short order. As soon as he set her feet on the ground, Fiona began running.

When she reached the fallen man, she dropped to her knees and began to examine him. A half hour later, she had Mr. Abrams trussed up and ready to transport. While Fiona waited with the patient, Tucker raced back to the cabin. Ian and Meredith were in the middle of an animated discussion.

"It's Abrams," he called as he reached the clearing. "Fiona's got him situated, but he's not waking up. She says he needs to see the doc over in Goose Chase."

As quickly as possible, the men used the pulleys and ropes to swing the bridge out across the river until it came to rest on the opposite bank. Ian followed Tucker back over to where Fiona waited.

"Any luck in reviving him?" Ian asked.

Fiona shook her head. "His pulse is slow but regular, and his pupils are even, but he's completely nonreactive. I'm afraid there might be swelling on the brain that can only be relieved in an operating room."

Neither Tucker nor Ian moved. Other than the nasty bump rising on Mr. Abrams's head, he looked as if he might be taking a nap rather than fighting for his life.

Fiona jumped to her feet. "What are you waiting for? This man could die if we don't get him help!"

Ian spoke first. "Fiona, honey, I don't think you realize what it would take to get him to town. You're not in Oregon anymore. It's a half-day's walk, not a ride on a train or a buggy."

Tucker watched while the redhead's expression changed from worried to determined.

"Then we walk. Which of you will go with me?"

Before he realized what he'd said, Tucker agreed to the trip. Ian slapped him on the back and wished them well, then helped Tucker get Mr. Abrams situated in the umiak. Meredith insisted on packing a meal for the trip.

Fiona, however, was only concerned for her patient. She did, however, agree to take a letter from Meredith to the post office in Goose Chase. After all, she had a pair of letters to mail, too.

Fiona set her bag and Meredith's pail of food into the vessel beside the patient, straightened her traveling hat, then reached for the rope. The sooner they left, the faster they would get there.

"What are you doing?" Tucker gestured to the umiak. "Get in and ride. This is no place for a lady to be walking."

Her jaw set in a determined line, she ignored him and tugged on the boat's line. It barely moved. Tucker let her work at it a moment longer; then he reached past her to take the rope away.

"If you want to get him to town in time, you're going to need to cooperate with me. Which one of us has been here longer?"

She looked up, and for the first time, he noticed the up-turned tilt to her nose. He could tell from her expression that she didn't like the answer to his question.

"You," she finally said.

"Then would you let me lead?" He took her hand and met her gaze. "Please," he added in deference to her pride.

"If it will get Mr. Abrams to the doctor sooner, I will do as you ask." She slipped her hand from his and stepped into the umiak. Tucker pretended not to notice how the boat rocked as its newest passenger landed unceremoniously on her posterior. There would be plenty of time for teasing once they reached Goose Chase.

In the meantime, he would keep his peace, and she hoped she would, as well. If only she knew how badly he wanted to start by asking her just what fit of insanity she'd been in when she purchased that ridiculous hat.

Fiona sat stock-still while the vessel slid over the sparkling water. They confronted the crisp wind head-on, and waves lapped up the sides. On occasion, the breeze tried to lift her hat off her head, but the hat pin held it tight and close.

At regular intervals, Fiona dipped her handkerchief in the water and bathed Mr. Abrams's face. Once she thought she saw him blink, but other than that, the old man remained unresponsive.

By the time they reached Goose Chase, Fiona had begun to wonder if the injured man would ever regain consciousness. Tucker pulled the boat ashore and helped Fiona stand.

Fiona's legs complained as she tried to coax them to cooperate. Tucker refused to let her slip from his grasp as they made their way to solid ground. "You wait here, and I'll go fetch Mr. Abrams."

"Wait," she called. "Don't move him yet. How far is the doctor's office from here?"

"Just over there. It's the one with the white porch rail out front," he said, pointing to a wood-frame building several blocks away. "Best I can tell, the only way to get him there is to carry him."

Fiona considered the statement a minute and then nodded slowly. "It's not so far that he'd be injured any further, but, please, be careful."

Tucker went back to the boat and gently lifted the unconscious passenger. Fiona marveled as the miner made carrying the older man look easy.

Racing to keep up with Tucker's long strides, she was nearly out of breath by the time they reached the building with the white porch railing. The sign above the door said R. KILLBONE, PHYSICIAN. Directly beneath that, a hand-lettered note urged prospective patients to knock and come straight in. Bill collectors, the sign went on to state, should knock twice, and then wait for the doctor to answer.

Fiona knocked and then tugged the door open and held it wide until Tucker disappeared inside. She followed the path Tucker took. A neat living area gave way to a room that looked as if it had once served as a bedroom. A worktable stood in the center of the room and a small bed in the corner.

"Doc, you here?" Tucker called.

"That you, Tucker Smith?"

"Yes, sir. I've got a patient for you. It's Mr. Abrams. He fell out of a tree."

A spry man with a shock of dark hair and a pair of wire spectacles came around the corner. "What do we have here?" He noticed Fiona and nodded. "Who're you?"

"She's a Rafferty, Doc. Ian and Braden's sister."

Fiona offered her hand, and he shook it. "Fiona Rafferty, Doctor. Pleased to meet you."

"Likewise, I'm sure." The doctor studied her a moment before turning his attention to Tucker's nosy neighbor. Fiona watched him begin his examination of the older man.

"His pupils are reactive to light," she offered. "There's been no change since this morning."

Doc Killbone looked at Fiona over his spectacles. "You got formal doctor training, miss?"

"No, sir, not yet, but I'm hoping to remedy that soon." She avoided Tucker's gaze. "I did what I could to stabilize the gentleman, but he's not come out of this since he fell. I'm a little concerned about the contusion on his forehead."

"Hmm, yes." The doctor turned his back on Fiona and completed his examination.

While the doctor worked, Fiona snuck a glance over at Tucker only to find him already staring at her. She looked away quickly and then chastised herself for acting like a schoolgirl.

"Is there anything I can do to help, Dr. Killbone?" she asked.

"You say you know your way around an operating room?" When she nodded, he started barking instructions. Before she knew it, Fiona was assisting the doctor in treating the older man.

"If you two don't need me, I'm going to go see if the things I ordered came in at the mercantile. I'll meet you back here in a while."

"All right by me, Tucker," the doctor said.

Fiona watched Tucker disappear down the hall before turning her attention back to the patient.

At one point, the doctor paused to nod his approval. "You're a natural, miss," he said.

"You ought to go ahead with that training as soon as you can. I won't be doctoring around here forever, so I'll need someone to take over my practice."

Rather than explain to him that she'd never return to Alaska once she made good on her escape, Fiona concentrated on the compliments about her doctoring skills that he paid her. When the doctor completed his work, he stepped away to wash his hands in the corner basin. As he toweled dry, he turned to appraise Fiona.

"I don't think I've ever said this to anyone, so you listen close to me, you hear?"

"Yes, sir."

"I've seen a lot of doctoring in my life, but what you did for that man most likely saved his life." He let the towel drop into the basin. "Where are you set to study at?"

Fiona patted the letter in her pocket. "Oregon, sir. I've been accepted into the medical college there."

The doctor rocked back on his heels and studied her again. "That's a fine school, young lady. You ought to do well there. When do you start?"

Emboldened by his praise, she pulled the letter from her pocket. "If this letter reaches the school in time, I plan to start with the new term."

"I'm going to do something to help that along," the doctor said. "My nephew's headed back to Washington State two days from now. What if I were to have him take the letter as far as Seattle? From there, he can see it gets put in the mail. That way, the letter will reach its destination a whole lot faster and a mite safer."

Her heart and her hopes soared. "Would you? That would be. . .wonderful."

The doctor's eyes narrowed. "Now, I'm going to ask a favor of my own." He paused. "I was serious when I said I wanted to know I'd have someone to take over for me if ever I couldn't do my job. You willing to do that, Miss Rafferty?"

Would she? Leaving Alaska for good had always been her plan. Still, what were the odds that the doctor would actually want her to return? And if he did, the Lord would handle the details.

Fiona took a deep breath and let it out slowly. "Oh yes, sir."

"All right. One more question. Do you have your passage set for Oregon?" When she didn't immediately respond, he gave her a knowing look. "You were going to decide on that when the time came?"

She nodded. "I suppose so."

"You leave that to me. I want you back here one week before the term starts. I'll have your ticket ready." He adjusted his glasses. "And lessen you think I've got designs on you, plan to travel alone."

Fiona released the breath she'd been holding and smiled. "Thank you."

Dr. Killbone shook his head. "You just hold off on those thanks. You may want to wring my neck when I call in this favor and ask you to come up here and take over for me."

Chapter 6

Tucker walked into the mercantile like a man on a mission. Bypassing the usual departments, he stepped cautiously into the women's section.

"Merry needing something?"

Tucker turned to see the proprietor of Benson's Mercantile heading his way. "Well, not exactly." He filled the older gentleman in on what he wanted.

"You'll be needing to speak with Mrs. Benson," he said. "Oh, and before you leave, don't forget to pick up those things you ordered last time you were here."

A half hour later, Tucker returned from his errand to find Doc and Miss Rafferty still in the room with Mr. Abrams. He excused himself, retraced his steps, and waited outside the doctor's office as long as he could before he started pacing.

While he walked, he let his thoughts churn. The woman in the office right now was not the one he thought he'd met at the Rafferty cabin. This person was cool and confident, a woman at home in a place where medicine was practiced.

The silly sister of Ian and Braden did not exist there. Rather, she looked to be in her perfect environment.

Why, then, was Tucker so disappointed to figure this out? He'd only just met the girl.

The door opened, and the object of his thoughts appeared, closely followed by Doc Killbone.

Tucker stopped his pacing to shake the doctor's hand. "How's my neighbor?"

"The next few hours are crucial. Like as not he'll wake up tomorrow with a nasty headache and a strong regret that he climbed the tree in the first place."

"I'll sit with him tonight so Doc can get some sleep." Fiona reached into her handbag and pulled out three letters, then handed one to the doctor. "I'm going to go mail these; then I'll serve up whatever Merry sent. How's that?"

"I'd say that sounds like a good plan."

She nodded and took two steps away, then turned on her fashionable heels. "You do have coffee, don't you, Doc?" When he nodded, she looked relieved. "Good. I can put up with just about anything. . . ." She looked at Tucker and then back at the doctor. "But I'm not fit to be around if I miss my coffee."

The men shared a chuckle as Fiona resumed her walk across Main Street.

Tucker turned to the doctor. "I'd best get down to the boardinghouse and make my arrangements before Widow Callen runs out of beds."

"No, need, son," the doctor said. "I've got plenty of space upstairs." He gave Tucker a sideways look. "My boy and me will be here to chaperone, and Miss Rafferty will likely not leave the exam room all night, so I don't see anything improper in the arrangement, do you?"

Tucker studied the subject of their conversation a moment. "No, sir," he finally said. "I can't see anything wrong with the arrangement. Besides, Miss Rafferty's practically family."

"Be that as it may, she's still a fine woman," the doctor said after Fiona disappeared into the postal office. "And one of these days, she'll be a fine doctor." He clapped his hand onto Tucker's shoulder. "You got designs on her, Tucker?"

"Designs? On that one?" He tried to look casual. "Do I look crazy?"

"No," the doctor said. "That's why I'm asking."

The next morning, Tucker was still thinking about the doctor's question. Finally, he had an answer. While he did admit she was a pretty little thing, even with the silly hat, and she'd stood up to the challenge of keeping nosy Mr. Abrams alive, she wasn't the type to settle down and have a family.

So, much as he hated it, the answer to the doctor's question was no.

He knew this for sure as he watched Fiona climb into the umiak. He questioned it only for a moment when they stopped to let her climb out and walk a spell. She hadn't asked about the package he had deposited at her feet, which earned her high marks.

Last thing he could abide was a nosy female.

She'd also stayed awake despite the fact that he doubted she'd had much sleep. Much as he hated to slow down their trip home, he probably ought not walk her so fast. When he adjusted his pace, Fiona looked relieved but held her tongue.

They walked along in silence until Fiona spoke in a wistful voice. "Do you ever get used to how beautiful it is here? Look at the mountains over there."

Tucker nearly stumbled when he followed her directive, so for the next hour he ignored her completely. Finally, the growling in his stomach could no longer be ignored, so he hauled the umiak onto shore and retrieved the food Doc had insisted on sending.

They ate in silence, more due to Tucker previously ignoring Fiona's chatter than anything else. The girl was smart. It didn't take her long to figure out he wasn't going to be much of a talker on this trip.

The sun felt warm on his shoulders as Tucker eased back against the rock, his stomach full and his eyes heavy. When he opened them again, he was alone.

He didn't panic until he heard the scream. Women often overreacted in his estimation. Like as not, the source of her upset was a harmless bug or some other such thing.

He waited a moment. "Fiona?" he finally called.

No answer. Then came, "Mr. Smith!" in the form of a second scream.

Tucker scrambled to his feet and bolted off the rock. The sound came from the south, the opposite direction from the river. What in the world was Fiona doing heading off in that direction?

"Fiona, are you all right?"

No answer.

She screamed his name a third time. A second of silence followed.

Tucker found her teetering on the edge of a rock just beyond his reach. She seemed, on first glance, to be completely fine.

"Fiona, that's not funny. Come down right now before I come to my senses and get mad."

She neither moved nor spoke. Rather, she edged a bit to the left then froze. "I—I can't," she finally said.

He moved a few steps closer. "You can't what? Come down? That's ridiculous."

"No," came out more like a squeak than a word. "I'm stuck."

"You're what?"

She tried to look over her shoulder but teetered and lost her balance. Tucker was there in an instant, catching her just in time.

She landed with a *thud* against his chest, and he held tight to her. The only calamity was her hat, which fell into the dirt at his feet. Tucker took a step to balance himself, and unfortunately, one boot landed on the thing.

At least he'd saved Fiona. She could buy another hat.

As he looked down at the woman in his arms, two emotions hit him hard. First, he felt like laughing. Then, much to his surprise, he felt like shaking her for the fright she'd given him. He set her on her feet and moved off the silly hat, then took two steps back.

"Thank you," she said, assuming her regal bearing once more.

Stifling a smile, Tucker asked the obvious question. "Miss Rafferty, how did you come to be standing on that ledge?"

"I thought to reach that secluded spot."

Tucker looked up in the direction where she pointed and saw the stand of trees. "Why did you want to get up there?"

To Tucker's surprise, the redhead's cheeks flamed to match her hair. "That's rather private, and I'd prefer not to say."

Fiona spied her hat and retrieved it, then studied the bent feather. Knocking the dirt off it made the thing wearable, but the feather would never be the same. Still, the contrary woman set the atrocity atop her head and turned on her heels.

"In the future," he said to her retreating back, "you might want to think twice about wandering off. This time the only danger was falling, but there could be any number of hungry wild animals out there."

"I doubt that, Mr. Smith. If such a danger existed, I'm sure a competent guide such as yourself would have warned me before we set off."

She had him there. He decided to try another tack. "Miss Rafferty, I have to ask. Why didn't you just climb down? Was it those prissy shoes you're wearing?"

"Prissy shoes?" Her shoulders shrugged, but she did not slow down. "I'll have you know these shoes were chosen specifically because they are not only serviceable but also quite attractive and fashionable."

"Well, now, they might be all that, but they are also a menace. Still, if you say they didn't keep you from climbing down, I'll have to believe you."

She picked up her pace. The bent feather bobbed faster. "Yes, I suppose you will," she said. "Now can we change the subject?"

"I'm agreeable to that," Tucker said, "except that my original question still hasn't been answered. Why didn't you just climb down instead of hollering your fool head off and then nearly falling to your death?"

"To my death? My, how you do exaggerate, Mr. Smith."

She sounded a bit out of breath, most likely from the speed she'd chosen to walk. It seemed like the madder he made her, the faster she walked. At this rate, they'd be back to the cabin in record time. He watched the crooked feather on her hat bob up and down and gave thanks for that.

Far be it from him to slow her down, so Tucker decided to give her more reason to race ahead. "So, one more time I'll ask. Why didn't you climb down, Miss Rafferty? And this time, no nonsense. Just give me the plain truth. I promise not to laugh."

Fiona stopped abruptly and whirled around. Tucker nearly slammed into her. "You want the plain truth?"

Tucker looked down into eyes that sparked with anger, and all he could think of was how the freckles on her nose matched the color of her hair just right. He'd have kept staring indefinitely if she hadn't stabbed his shoulder with her forefinger.

"The truth is—" She paused to look away. Without warning, she swung her gaze back to collide with his. "Because I didn't know I was afraid of heights until I got up there. Are you happy now?"

He wanted to laugh, but the look on Fiona's face warned him against it. Instead, he decided to keep his mouth shut. He'd learned in his dealings with Meredith that some questions were best left unasked, especially in regard to the peculiarities of women.

"Yes, I suppose I'm happy as can be, considering the circumstances and the company."

Fiona made a sound of disgust and picked up her skirts, heading toward level ground at a fast clip. As he watched her pick her way across the rocky terrain, Tucker thought of the contents of the package in the umiak.

Perhaps now was the time to get her situated in something sensible, something she wouldn't break her neck wearing.

The moment the thought occurred, Tucker saw Fiona's expensive footwear catch between two stones. She pitched forward and began to stumble, then caught a branch just in time.

With an I-told-you-I-could-take-care-of-myself look, Fiona stared up at him. "I'm fine."

The branch broke. Fiona Rafferty tumbled into the water.

———

When Fiona hit the water, all the air went out of her lungs. She sputtered and clutched at the icy liquid until she felt something solid.

As her head came above water, she saw the thing she'd grasped on to was the broken tree branch. At the other end of it crouched Tucker Smith.

"This branch is old and nearly dried out, so I'm going to have to be real careful pulling you in with it. If we get to going too fast, it'll break. Do you understand?"

"Yes, I understand." The feather from her hat clung to her face, and she swiped at it, sending the hat flying.

"Don't you dare try and fetch that thing, Miss Rafferty. It's not worth drowning for."

"Under the circumstances," she said as she watched her prized traveling hat float downstream with the current, "perhaps you should call me Fiona."

"Fiona, it is, and I'm Tucker," he said. "Now listen carefully. The longer you're in that water, the less likely you are to think straight. That water's still cold. Now, tell me if you can still hang on while I finish pulling you in."

All she could do was nod and wrap her fingers tighter around the rough bark. She looked toward the umiak sitting on the bank. "What about the boat? Can't you get in it and come after me?"

"To do that, I'd have to let go of the stick. You want me to do that?"

She thought a minute. "I guess not, but do you have a better idea?"

"While I pull, I'd be much obliged if you'd start to praying. The Good Book says the Lord pays particular attention when two or more are praying the same thing." He gave the branch a gentle tug. "Oh, and if you were of a mind to, you might pray I don't fall in after you. Between us, we've only got one set of dry clothes."

Fiona did her best to pray and hold tight to the branch, but the harder she tried at both, the more difficult they became. Finally, she closed her eyes and let the waves lap against her as she rested her chin on the branch. The current swirled, causing Fiona's skirts to tangle around her ankles and making it nearly impossible to kick her legs.

Now her only lifeline was the broken tree limb. Without warning, it snapped.

Fiona's feet slammed against the river bottom, and she jerked to attention. Pushing off, she lunged toward the bank. Tucker hauled her onto dry land. Immediately, her teeth began to chatter.

"Fashionable and attractive indeed," Tucker said as he pulled the offending shoe off her foot and tossed it toward the middle of the stream. A second later, the other shoe suffered a similar fate.

Before Fiona could protest, Tucker hauled her onto her feet and handed her a wrapped package. She wanted to ask what it was, but her mouth refused to form the words.

Tucker turned her away from him and pointed to a stand of trees. "Go on, now, and get dry. You have my word as a gentleman that I won't turn around or open my eyes until you tell me to."

While she watched, he turned his back to her and climbed into the umiak to sit. Fiona clutched the package to her chest and tried to decide what to do. It didn't take long to realize that although it was summertime, wearing wet clothing in Alaska was foolhardy at best.

Fiona slipped deep into the stand of trees and, as quickly as she could, exchanged her dress for a blue wool shirt that dipped past her knees and a pair of denim pants with legs much too long for her. The only item in the package that came close to fitting was a pair of fur-covered boots.

She walked out of the foliage with one hand on the overlarge trousers and the other clutching her dripping clothes. Tucker still sat inside the umiak with his back to her.

"Is that you, Fiona?"

"Don't you say one word, Tucker Smith. Not one."

True to his word, Tucker didn't move, even when Fiona tossed the bundle of wet clothing into the boat. As Fiona came around to face him, she saw his eyes were closed. He did, however, seem to be having difficulty keeping a straight face.

With what little pride she could muster, Fiona stepped into the boat and sat next to Tucker. "Can we go home now?"

"I'll need to open my eyes."

"Not one word." Fiona released a long breath. "And no laughing."

Tucker opened his eyes then shut them again. When he didn't move, Fiona poked his arm. "What are you doing?"

He cut her a sideways glance. "Trying to remember if I made a promise about not laughing."

The trip back to the cabin consisted of Fiona riding and Tucker holding the rope. Neither said a word.

When Fiona walked into the cabin, all conversation stopped. Meredith sat beside Amy, who held baby Douglas in her lap. Fiona left her wet clothing on the doorstep and brushed past them to step into the other room.

"Are those new boots?" Meredith asked.

"They're very nice," Amy added. "Aren't they, Douglas?"

The baby grinned and made a cooing sound.

"It's the rest of the outfit I'm a bit confused about." Meredith leaned forward. "Did Tucker help you pick it out, by any chance? I could have warned you the man has no concept of fashion."

Fiona stuck her head out of the door. "Hush, both of you," she said before dissolving into a fit of laughter.

Chapter 7

Three days later, when Tucker hadn't come around the cabin, Fiona went to him. She heard him rather than saw him, the sound of the pickax keeping time with a remarkably good version of "Rock of Ages."

She'd tucked the clothes she borrowed under her arm, along with the odd, fur-covered boots. As an added thanks, she'd wrapped one of Meredith's oatmeal cookies and placed it along with Tucker's lunch in the pail.

Rather than interrupt him, Fiona waited until he got to the chorus and began to sing along. Soon the baritone stopped, and she was left to sing soprano alone.

"I brought your clothes back. Oh, and since you've been avoiding Merry's cabin, she sent lunch," she said when he emerged from the tunnel.

She waited for a response and was rewarded with a combination of silence and an irritated glare. Evidently, the man had forgotten his manners somewhere between Goose Chase and the mine.

"And I wanted to thank you for saving my life."

Tucker let the pick drop and massaged the back of his neck. "Which time?"

He wore a blue shirt nearly identical to the one she'd washed, and he'd left it unbuttoned to reveal a pristine undershirt over dirt-covered trousers. A streak of black mud decorated his right cheek, and it was all Fiona could do to keep from walking over and wiping it off with the corner of her apron.

Fiona set the clothing on a tree stump then situated the boots on top. "Fair enough." She took a step back and studied her ragged nails. "I was wondering something."

Tucker exhaled loud enough to be heard across the distance between them. His stance told her she'd interrupted something important; the facts stated the opposite. After all, it was near to lunchtime, and the gold he hunted sure wasn't going anywhere.

She almost said just that, but she needed his cooperation. "You're leaving to go with the Harriman Expedition, right?"

He leaned against the handle of his pick and shook his head. "You came all the way out here to ask me that? Merry could have answered you and saved you a walk. Besides, I'm not going to take you with me, much fun as that proposes to me."

So his mood hadn't improved.

"I know I'm not your favorite person." At this, Tucker's head jerked up, and he looked as if he wanted to speak. When he said nothing, she continued. "But I don't belong here. I believe the Lord's got other plans for me than to stay here in Alaska and become some stampeder's wife."

When Meredith's brother did not react, she decided to say out loud the thing she'd been holding in her heart since she left Goose Chase. To say anything to Tucker would be dangerous, especially given his mood. If Meredith got wind of her plan, she would tell Ian, and then the jig would be up. Like as not, they'd bundle her off to the far reaches of Alaska before any of them would send her off with their blessings.

Fiona drew in a deep breath of crisp air then let the words escape. "I've been accepted to medical college. All I need is a way to get to Oregon before the term starts."

Tucker yanked his pick up and slung it over his shoulder. In long strides, he reached the tunnel. "I know," echoed over his shoulder as he disappeared.

"You know?" She stared incredulously at the empty opening of the man-made cave. "You know?"

How dare Tucker dismiss her like that? Didn't he realize the risk she'd taken by welcoming him into her confidence?

Hands on her hips, Fiona called to the obstinate miner. His only response was a rhythmic *ping. . .ping. . .ping* from deep in the tunnel.

So that's how he was going to be. "Well, Mr. Smith," she muttered, "I think you've forgotten I grew up with two brothers. I learned early on that if the bear won't come out of the cave, you go to the bear."

The tunnel was dark and narrow, barely large enough for a man of Tucker's size to stand upright. The smell of dank earth was nearly overpowering. So was the presence of Tucker Smith.

She watched his shoulders bunch and the muscles in his arms flex as he slammed the pick against the rocks. "Tucker Smith, we're going to finish this conversation whether you like it or not."

"No, Fiona, we're not." Tucker didn't spare her a glance as he went back to the task at hand. "And I'm prepared to work until sundown with you standing there pouting. I think you've forgotten I grew up with a sister."

Ping. . .ping. . .ping.

"Is that so?" Fiona willed her anger to abate, clearing her mind for a better use of her thinking skills—outwitting Tucker Smith. "Well," she said slowly, "perhaps you're right."

*Ping. . .ping. . .*pause. "What did you say?"

She didn't dare look at him. Rather, she turned to study the dirt wall. "I said, perhaps you're right." *Time to look him in the eyes.* "I can't fool you. You're too smart for me."

"I hope you don't think you can fool me into making a decision." He inhaled and closed his eyes. "Because it won't work," he said as he exhaled.

"But Tucker, I—"

"Out." His voice was low, even, and held more than a little irritation. Yet that sentiment didn't quite reach his eyes, which were twinkling with what she hoped was amusement. "Whatever you're up to, it won't work. Go home."

"That's just the thing, Tucker. I'm trying to go home." Fiona shuffled her feet in the hard-packed dirt. "Well, to be exact, I'm trying to go to my new home."

He shook his head. "Have you ever considered you might already be home?"

"Not even for a minute."

Tucker pushed a lock of hair out of his eyes. "You don't think maybe God's got a purpose for you right here in Alaska?"

Fiona straightened her shoulders and looked Tucker Smith in the eye. Unfortunately, the snippy answer she wanted to give refused to come out. Instead, words that couldn't possibly have originated with her popped out of a mouth too surprised to stop them.

"As much as there's a need for wives in Alaska, there's a greater need for doctors, don't you think?"

Tucker hated to admit too quickly that the girl had a point, so he pretended to cogitate on her statement. As much trouble as she'd caused him just traveling to and from town, he truly couldn't imagine her taking on the life Meredith and Amy lived.

Before the first year was out, the poor man she married would head for the hills or, more likely, drown in the river trying to fish her out. Still, Tucker knew that if he helped Fiona, he'd have her brothers to answer to.

And worse, he'd most likely have to give an explanation to Meredith.

"Well?" she urged. "Will you help me?"

He thought of Ian and how slow the man was to respond. Maybe that approach would buy him some time. "Let me think about it," he said.

Fiona's smile set his teeth on edge. Worse, she looked like she might be getting ready to thank him. Considering he hadn't promised to help her, he surely couldn't accept any appreciation.

Then there was the problem of their close proximity. Compared to the dirt around them, she sure smelled nice.

Tucker cleared his throat. "Don't you need to go help my sister?"

"No," she said. "Not until later. She went over to Mr. Abrams's place to help his niece get settled in. It was my job to pull the weeds in the garden, and I finished that already."

"Wait. Abrams has a niece?"

The redhead nodded. "Evidently so. At least she claims to be."

"Really? Did she bring her uncle home?"

"No," Fiona said. "Mr. Abrams won't be well enough to travel for another week. Violet was fortunate to find her way here with that fellow who delivers the mail."

"I see." Tucker turned his back on the woman and said a quick prayer for strength. As much as he liked to look at the pretty girl, he'd much prefer to do so from a distance.

"Merry said you'd like Violet." She paused and seemed to be thinking over something. "She said Violet was an answer to prayer."

"Is that so?" Tucker reached for his pick and hoped he was wrong about his sister's motives for befriending the Abrams woman. "Well, now that you've caught me up on all the news, you can go on to wherever you were headed next."

"I told you I've got nowhere else to be right now. Besides, that's not all." She leaned toward him. "I felt I should warn you."

"About what?"

"About Violet Abrams." She paused. "And your sister." She shook her head. "You probably aren't interested. Although. . ."

Tucker hated to ask, yet he couldn't help himself. "Although what?"

Fiona shrugged. "Although I felt like a man would want to know when he was about to be set upon by a pretty girl. She's looking for a husband, you know."

He studied the intruder. "She shouldn't have to look far in Alaska. How is any of this my business?"

"I'm not exactly sure except that. . ." Fiona clamped her mouth shut for a second. She seemed to be thinking again. "Except that when she started telling Merry about how she'd only recently arrived in Skagway in the hopes of finding a husband and starting a family, well. . ."

Tucker had just about lost interest. "Well, what?"

"Well, Merry said that she'd come to the right place."

Now he was interested. "Did my sister say anything else?"

"Just that she ought to come for supper tonight."

Tonight? No, that wouldn't do. He had to figure a way out of this mess before it went any further.

He set down his pick and pressed past Fiona to emerge into the sunshine. As much as he loved his twin sister, he couldn't have her pawning him off to the first marriageable female just because he admitted he felt a little lonely on occasion.

There had to be a way to get out of this without hurting Meredith. He'd never do that.

Blinking to adjust his vision, Tucker started walking toward nowhere in particular. He didn't get far before he realized the Rafferty woman was trailing him.

Whirling around to warn Fiona off, she ran smack into him. He pitched forward, and Fiona scrambled backward. As Tucker regained his footing, Fiona lost hers. Only his quick thinking saved her from hitting the ground. Tucker wrapped his arm around her waist and yanked her against him, so that she now stood upright on solid footing. She also stood in his arms. The two women approaching saw it all.

Tucker looked down into Fiona's eyes, and a plan was born.

He took a step back and smiled. "Fiona Rafferty, what if I told you I had a solution to both our problems?"

"I'd say I'm interested." Fiona gave him a sideways look. "But I didn't know you had a problem."

He leaned forward and spoke softly into her left ear. "I don't yet, and if you'll follow my lead, maybe I can keep it that way."

"So if I help you, then you'll help me. Is that what you're saying?"

The pair approached, and he could tell from their posture that they had stopped all pretense of having a jolly stroll in the woods. Unless he missed his guess, Meredith and Violet Abrams were on a mission.

"Tucker?" Fiona tugged at his sleeve. "I need to know if you'll help me get to college."

He looked down at Fiona. "I'll do what I can, but I've never lied to my sister or her husband, and I don't intend to start now."

Fiona chewed on the idea a second then nodded. "Fair enough. The Lord won't bless a venture that's based on lies. So what is it that I need to do?"

"Simple," he said as he leaned closer. "Forgive me when I kiss you."

Chapter 8

Fiona opened her mouth to object then closed it quickly when Tucker aimed his lips toward her cheek. It lasted only a second, but the brush of his lips touched more than her skin. It etched a memory of a dark-haired man and a chaste moment on her heart.

Oh, it was for show, she knew. But somewhere between that moment and the moment their gazes locked, Tucker Smith had become more than just her brother's brother-in-law. Always and forever, he would be the source of her first kiss. Well, almost a kiss, anyway.

And that thought made her madder than a wet hen. She'd dreamed of this moment since girlhood, wondering about the who, when, and why of it over endless hours in the still of the night. Now, with barely any notice, the long-dreamed-of moment had come and gone.

She looked up at Tucker and tried to speak. Her lips, burned by the near miss of a real romantic kiss, refused to move. Funny, but he seemed to be having similar trouble.

He suddenly looked past her and smiled. "Good afternoon, Merry," he said. "Who've you brought with you today?"

Fiona turned to see her brother's wife escorting the neighbor's niece, a pleasant-looking woman with a ready smile, up the hill. As they neared, Meredith's grin split wide.

"Well, hello yourself, Tucker, Fiona."

Flames leaped into Fiona's cheeks as she realized the ladies had seen it all. They had witnessed the whispered conversation and, to her horror, the kiss, as well.

She turned her attention to Tucker, who refused to meet her gaze. "You knew they would see us," she whispered. "You did that on purpose."

"Smile," he said without looking her way. "Or at least pretend to. You do want out of Alaska, don't you?"

Fiona nodded.

"Then go along for the time being. I promise I'll not disparage your reputation. I'm a gentleman," he said softly. "If I weren't, I'd have stolen a real kiss." He paused to let that sink in. "Trust me."

"You're no gentleman," she whispered. "You threw my perfectly stylish footwear into the river. And you caused my traveling hat to get dunked."

Tucker gave her his complete attention. "Your stylish footwear nearly killed you when it caused you to tumble off the rocks and then fall into the river. As for that hat, well, it needed a good dunking."

She was about to protest, but he placed his forefinger atop her lips. "Fiona, it's not like I left you shoeless. I did buy you a pair of the best sealskin boots the mercantile had to offer. And what you don't know is that I placed a mail order at the Sears Roebuck for a few suitable things you will need for winter. That, I admit, was Merry's idea, but I did think of the boots myself."

"You bought the boots for me? I thought they were yours." She glanced over at the ladies, who seemed deep in conversation. "No wonder they came close to fitting."

Tucker looked pleased. "You needed something appropriate. Is that a thank you?"

She pretended an irritation she no longer felt. "Considering you sent a fine pair of kid leather boots downriver, I'm not sure a thank you is in order." She paused to see the ladies draw near. "But under the circumstances, I'm touched that you would be concerned about me."

"Of course I'm concerned." He lifted his gaze toward his sister and Miss Abrams. "To what do we owe the pleasure?"

Meredith gathered her wits. "I came to introduce Tucker to Miss Abrams." She paused and seemed to be at a loss for words. "But perhaps we've come at an inopportune moment."

Tucker made the first move, reaching for the stranger's hand. "Pleased to meet you, Miss Abrams. Do tell how your uncle is faring."

"Thanks to you," she said without noting Fiona's presence, "my uncle will make a complete recovery." She paused. "I've heard our family owes you a huge debt of gratitude."

Tucker placed his hand on Fiona's shoulder and shook his head. "I believe you heard wrong, ma'am. You see, your uncle's alive thanks to this young lady's cool head and excellent doctoring skills. Without her, he'd never have made it as far as town."

"Yes," Meredith added. "God seems to have gifted our Fiona with the art of healing. I saw your uncle, and forgive me for saying this, but I suspected he might be done for."

The conversation spun off from there, moving from the ailing neighbor to the niece's trip from Skagway. Somewhere along the way, the threesome completely forgot Fiona was present.

Or at least it seemed that way. Until she tried to slip off toward the cabin.

"Leaving so soon, Fiona?" Meredith called. "Won't you wait and accompany Violet and me over to the Abrams place? I'm sure there's plenty to be done before Mr. Abrams returns."

Tucker nodded. "What say I tag along? I bet I can find a thing or two that needs my attention."

Meredith looked up at her brother with a broad smile. "Oh, Tucker, I think you already have."

Thankfully, Tucker did not respond. In fact, he didn't say a word until they threw open the door of the old miner's shack and stepped inside. "I'm going back to fetch the toolbox. Looks like this place was falling down around his ears."

Truthfully, Fiona only noticed the disarray. She immediately set to work making the tiny makeshift kitchen shine, while the other two ladies tackled the room where Mr. Abrams had both lived and slept. Tucker returned and began hammering, sawing, and generally making noise in the clearing, which drew Ian's attention.

"Need some help?" Ian called.

Tucker set down his hammer and walked toward Ian, but then Fiona felt another set of eyes on her. Turning, she noticed Meredith studying her intently.

Fiona took a deep breath and exhaled slowly, steadying her hands as well as her nerves.

"If you don't need any help, I'm going to gather the washing and go over to the river."

Meredith gave her a knowing smile. "Of course," she said.

The urge to set Meredith straight bore hard on her as Fiona trudged toward the door. Once outside, she managed to slip past Tucker unnoticed. Ian, however, stopped hammering to watch her disappear around the side of the cabin. By the time she reached the river, her brother's hammer was back in use.

Fiona endured the rest of the afternoon by forcing her thoughts in one direction. As long as she kept her mind focused on where she would someday be rather than where she was, things went well. The distance from the house helped, as did the frigid waters of the river.

At one point, Fiona noticed Ian and Meredith standing a few yards from the house deep in conversation. Perhaps she was mistaken, but it seemed as though the two of them were talking about her. As quickly as she could, Fiona finished her task and slipped past Tucker once again.

She found Meredith cleaning the room's lone window while Violet Abrams bounced a fussy Douglas on her knee. "The washing's done," she said as she walked over to smile at the baby. "Would you like me to take this little one back home and see if he will sleep better in his own bed?"

Violet gave the baby willingly to Fiona and rose. "Most days I think I want a houseful," she said. "But they are tiring, aren't they?"

Meredith chuckled. "I only wish I'd been prepared for the lack of sleep. Now that he's trying to cut a tooth, it seems as though he never sleeps more than a few hours at a time." She gave Fiona a sheepish look. "Ask Fiona. I'm sure the little prince keeps her awake with his howling."

Fiona giggled. "Only the first night. After that, I learned that a feather pillow and a fur blanket placed over the ears make an effective sound barrier."

As if on cue, Douglas began to cry. "Perhaps you should see if he's hungry, Merry."

A moment later while the baby nursed, Fiona listened to Violet and Meredith chatter on about everything from the unseasonably mild weather to the best way to can vegetables. Outside, she could hear the sound of men working, punctuated occasionally by the call of a bird or the murmur of deep voices.

Not soon enough, the baby had been fed and burped. "He ought to sleep well now," Meredith said as she handed the bundled child over to Fiona. "If he proves to be too much trouble, fetch him back here."

"He'll be fine. If he complains too much, I'll put him to work helping me make supper."

Fiona looked down into the drowsy face of her nephew. She could see the image of his father in the tiny face. A cap of red fuzz completed the picture of a little fellow destined to grow into the substantial shoes of his father. The only signs of his mother on Douglas's face were the perpetual smile—except for during the recent teething episode—and the shape of his chin.

"Let's go for a walk, young Mr. Rafferty, shall we?" She settled the baby into the crook of her arm and tossed his burping cloth over her shoulder. "Tell your mommy good-bye for now."

As Violet waved, Meredith kissed the top of her son's head and then looked up at Fiona. "I'd like to talk to you later, Fiona," she said. "I think it likely you can guess why."

Fiona's heart thumped against her chest, and her gaze fell to the cabin floor. What a can of worms she'd opened by agreeing to Tucker's ludicrous plan. It occurred to her that she didn't even know what that plan was. Further, he'd made no definite promise to help her. *What was I thinking?*

"I assure you there's nothing to talk about, Merry. What you saw. . ." She looked up and forced herself to stare at her sister-in-law directly. "Rather, what you think you saw, well, it wasn't what it seemed."

"How do you think it seemed?" Her sister-in-law gave no indication of her feelings on the matter.

"Seemed like you found yourself a husband, Miss Rafferty." Violet grinned. "I don't suppose he has a brother?"

The woman's comment broke the tension between Fiona and Meredith. "Believe me," Meredith said, "as wonderful as my brother is, you wouldn't wish for more like him. One Tucker Smith is plenty."

Fiona glanced out the door and spied the subject of their discussion leaning over the water bucket, dipping himself a drink. Ian stood nearby, obviously waiting his turn at the dipper.

"Yes," Fiona said, "I have to agree with Merry. I think one is definitely more than enough of Tucker Smith. Now, shall we take that walk, Douglas?"

The baby greeted her with a yawn as they slipped out the door and past the conversing men. She'd almost escaped the premises when Ian caught up with her. He spoke to Douglas in the silly manner parents address infants and then fell silent.

For a good quarter mile, the pair walked in silence. Fiona refused to be the first to speak; the emotions churning inside her wouldn't allow it. Occasionally, Douglas would snuggle against her, but most of the time he varied between sleeping and watching his father intently.

"You've got a way with Douglas," Ian finally said. "You'll be a wonderful mother someday."

She allowed the words to settle deep within her heart. With no illusions of ever being gifted of the Lord with children, she had to be satisfied that someone believed she might be good at it.

They reached the bridge, and Ian sent Fiona ahead of him. The baby stayed still as Fiona balanced his weight while crossing the reused logs. Just before they reached the Rafferty cabin, Ian reached for Fiona's arm.

"Lay the baby down so we can chat, Fiona."

"If it's about Tucker, there's no need." She shifted the sleeping infant to her shoulder and rubbed his back to settle him into sleep again. "What Merry thinks she saw is not what was actually happening."

Ian stood his ground and said not a word as Fiona waited for a response. Finally, he pointed toward the door. "Lay the baby down. There's no need to wake him should the conversation become heated."

Fiona complied, taking her time while she made sure Douglas would not awaken. When she returned, Ian was waiting beside the garden.

"I thought I'd pick peas for dinner. What do you think?"

He looked up, and she realized he must not have noticed her. "I'm sorry, what did you say?"

"Peas. For dinner." Fiona knelt beside the cabbage plants and began to pluck at the weeds growing between them. "Never mind. Go ahead and speak your piece, big brother. I'll not be able to persuade you of anything until you've said it all."

Ian heaved a long sigh. "Fiona, for the life of me, I'll never understand why you think you've been exiled."

She looked up quickly. "Because I have."

"Perhaps it may seem that way, but did you ever think our father might have had good reason to pack your things and move you here? Maybe reasons you will never know."

Giving up the pretense of weeding, Fiona settled back and faced her brother. "I know *this*, Ian Rafferty. If you or Braden wished to go to medical college, Da would rush up here and dance an Irish jig all the way back to Oregon with your suitcases on his back. Because I'm a woman, he refuses to consider that I, too, might make a decent doctor."

"Oh, Fiona, don't you see? There's no doubt you'd make much more than a decent doctor. We've all known since you were a wee babe that you had the gift." He paused. "That's not the trouble."

She blinked back the tears that threatened. *I will not cry.* "Then what, in your estimation, is the trouble?"

"Don't you see, lassie? Da, he wants you to be happy."

"But the only way I'll be happy is if I'm doing the work the Lord has for me. How could I possibly be happy doing anything else?"

Ian took a minute to ponder her question. At least that's what he seemed to be doing. When he dipped his head and pinched the bridge of his nose, Fiona knew for sure.

Finally, he lifted his gaze to meet hers. "Fiona, I don't pretend to know what the Lord's got for you. I do know what our father entrusted me to do, and that was to see to your welfare until such time as a proper husband can be found to take over the job." He paused. "I'm sorry, but that's what Da says, and I have to abide by it."

Fiona's Irish blood began to boil, and she scrambled to her feet. Twice she tried to respond. On the third attempt, she found her voice.

"Ian, who do you listen to, our earthly father or our heavenly Father?"

"That's not fair." Ian rose, fists clenched. "You know the answer to that."

She stomped her foot, not caring that she behaved more like a petulant child than a woman with a legitimate complaint. "Then why aren't you listening to the Lord on this?"

Ian squared his shoulders and peered down at Fiona. His cheeks were as red as his hair, and his eyes blazed with anger. "Because, little sister," he ground out, "it seems as though you're the only one the Lord is telling these things to. He certainly hasn't let me know, and I doubt He's spoken to Da on the matter, either."

With that, Ian turned his back to her and headed toward the river. She had to run to catch him. When she reached his side, she grasped his wrist and held on until he stopped.

"Please hear my side of things, Ian." She didn't care if the tears fell. Her brother could think no less of her for crying. "I never said I didn't want all those things. I would love to have a home and family like you. What I said is that I know this is not what God wants for me, at least not now."

"All right." Ian pulled his wrist away. "Fair enough. But if you truly mean what you're saying, why were you cavorting around with Merry's brother today?"

"Cavorting around?" Her pulse jumped. "Is that what Merry told you?"

"Never mind what my wife and I discuss." Ian's voice went menacingly low. "Is it true he kissed you?"

"Much as I wish it were, that's not exactly true," came a voice from behind them.

Fiona whirled around. Tucker strode toward them. "Great. Just what I need. Tucker, go home. I can handle my brother."

"Her brother doesn't need to be handled." Ian pointed to Tucker. "What her brother needs is an explanation. Your sister tells me she saw you and Fiona in an intimate embrace earlier."

"Could I speak to you about that alone, Ian? Man to man?"

"No." Fiona said the word just as Ian gave his permission. "I want to be a part of this conversation," she added.

"No," both men said together.

"Go check on Douglas," Ian said. "It's not good to leave him alone when he's been so fussy."

Fiona wanted to argue, but it would do no good. Instead, she gave her brother and Tucker an I-haven't-said-my-last-word-on-this look and headed for the cabin. Once inside, she checked on the sleeping baby and then watched through the window as the men strolled out of sight over the hill.

"Lord," she whispered, "if I'm wrong about this mission You've given me, would You make it clear to me that I got it wrong? You know I'm hardheaded sometimes, but I really thought You wanted me to be a doctor. I have to admit, though, I sure did feel something when Tucker kissed me. And holding Douglas, well, I could have a half dozen just like him and be happy as can be." She took a deep breath and let it out slowly. "I've never asked You before, Lord, but would You give me some sort of sign as to whether or not I should pursue my dream of being a doctor?"

She leaned against the windowsill and rested her chin in her hands. "One more thing, God. If you want me to stay here, could You perhaps work on Tucker Smith a bit? I can't find too many things wrong with sharing another kiss with him unless You're not agreeable to it."

"I'm going to give you a chance to come clean, Tucker. I've got the highest respect for you, but I want a straight answer about you and my sister."

Tucker swallowed hard. When he had crafted the plan to be left alone by his matchmaking sister, he'd had no idea what sort of trouble he'd be making for both Fiona and himself.

"I have nothing but the most honorable intentions regarding your sister, Ian."

"Then tell me why my wife saw you kissing her. Are you trying to tell me that Merry lied to me?"

"No, never." Tucker held up his hands. "It's just that what she saw wasn't what it looked like."

Ian looked doubtful. "I'm listening."

"When I heard Merry was up to matchmaking, I didn't want any part of it."

"And you figured a woman looking for a man wouldn't be interested in one who was kissing someone else."

"Exactly."

"If I didn't know you better, I'd think you were saying that you took advantage of my sister for your own benefit." He poked Tucker in the chest with his forefinger. "Is that what I'm hearing? Did you take advantage of my sister?"

"No," he said as he stepped back. "I wanted it to look like something was going on so Merry wouldn't force the Abrams woman on me. You see, we recently had a conversation about how I might be feeling a little lonely now that you two are. . . well. . .never mind."

Ian's expression softened. "So my wife took it upon herself to fix your problem with the first female who wandered up?" When Tucker nodded, Ian burst into a fit of laughter.

"What's so funny?"

"I was about to punch you for taking advantage of my sister and courting her without my permission, and it turns out to be a game you and Fiona played to throw Merry off the chase."

Tucker joined in the laughter, but a tiny part of his heart refused to go along with the joke. That little sliver of warmth nestled against the cold loneliness he'd felt since his sister married off kept him from declaring victory.

Rather, he had a sinking feeling he hadn't shared his last kiss with Fiona Rafferty. And that feeling scared him more than anything.

Chapter 9

Ian must have been satisfied with whatever Tucker said, because nothing further was mentioned of the great kiss-by-the-tree debacle. Over the next week, Tucker returned to his pattern of working long hours at the stake and spending what little free time he had at the Rafferty cabin. Eventually, Fiona got used to ignoring the fact that the man sitting on the other side of the table was the same man whose lips had brushed her cheek.

Then she found herself with Tucker after dinner, taking a meal to Mr. Abrams and his niece. By the time they reached the Abramses' cabin, Fiona still hadn't figured out how she had ended up alone on this mission with Tucker. If he had anything to say about it, he kept his peace, speaking only when Violet answered the door.

"We brought supper for the two of you," Tucker said. "It's good to see you back home, Mr. Abrams."

The older man nodded and expressed his thanks while Violet dished the food out and began to feed her uncle. After spending another half hour visiting, Fiona and Tucker made their getaway.

Strolling back under a cloudless sky, Fiona couldn't help but smile. At least she couldn't complain about the Alaskan summer. The long days had been a burden to bear for a while, but now that she'd grown accustomed to sleeping by the clock rather than the light, things went much smoother.

Then there was the friendship that had developed between her and Tucker. It all started when she took to wearing the boots he'd bought her. She found them surprisingly comfortable, and being warm and waterproof made them even better.

The first time Tucker saw her in them, he smiled. He'd been doing so ever since. Oddly, being around Tucker had begun to make her smile, too.

"Penny for your thoughts."

She looked up at the object of her thoughts. "Not on your life, Tucker. I'm never telling."

"Oh? Is that right? Well, I have my ways and. . ."

Fiona stopped midway across the bridge and looked down into the clear river. Several decent-sized frying fish teased her from their watery home. How long had it been since she'd gone fishing? Too long.

"Fiona, are you listening to me?"

"Hmm? I'm sorry. What did you say? I was thinking about fishing."

Tucker gave her an incredulous look.

She held her hands up in a defensive pose. "I'm sorry. I know it was rude. It's just that all my life I've been my father's fishing buddy. Neither of my brothers cared for it, and Da said I was a quick study. As long as I can remember I've had a fishing pole in my hand." She paused. "At least I did until I came here. I didn't realize until just now how very much I miss it."

Silence.

"Tucker?" Fiona said. "Do you realize you're staring at me?"

He nodded.

"Well, stop it." She turned her back and headed toward the cabin, stopping only when she realized Tucker hadn't kept up. "Tucker Smith, get off the bridge and go home. I don't know what's gotten into you, but you are acting silly."

He caught up with her a moment later. "You're serious, aren't you?"

"About what, Tucker?" Fiona stopped to peer up at him. "Is something wrong with you? I don't think I've ever seen you acting so odd. Well, other than on the trip back from town."

"I'm sorry." He scrubbed his face with the palms of his hands. "Did you just say you like to fish?"

"Yes," she said slowly. "Is there something wrong with that?"

⁂

"Wrong?" Tucker's laugh echoed against the nearby hills. "No," he said as he grabbed her by the waist and began to swing her around. "That's wonderful." He set her down then had to steady her when she wobbled a bit.

"Tucker Smith, what's gotten into you?" She primped her hair until she'd smoothed it back into place.

He had to tame his smile to get a word out. "Fiona, I've been living here for nigh on three years, and not once during that time did I ever have anyone to go fishing with. Your brothers are good men, but neither of them has the patience it takes to wait out a decent-sized fish."

She nodded. "That's true."

"Now, mind you, a man likes to fish alone most of the time, but on occasion, it's a fine thing to have someone else to compare your catch with. Outside of the good Lord and a hot cup of black coffee, that's about my favorite thing." He paused to give her a sideways look. "Now *you're* looking at *me* funny. Did I say something wrong?"

Fiona took a deep breath and let it out slowly. "Nothing, really. It's just that, well, I feel the same way."

Tucker eyed the redhead and waited for her to say the punch line. Surely someone as pretty and smart as this one had other things to do than fish.

Then came the absurd question of whether she wore that silly hat and those impractical shoes to fish in. Well, it couldn't be possible.

Maybe he ought to call her bluff. Yes, that idea definitely had appeal.

He affected a casual pose. "So, Fiona," he said as he studied the distance, "what say you and I go fishing after Sunday dinner?" Tucker paused for effect. "Of course, if you're busy, I'll understand."

"Too busy to fish?" She shook her head. "Anyone too busy to fish is just plain too busy. You bring the bait, and I'll fix the coffee."

⁂

On the appointed day, Tucker had the bait packed and ready in the bucket when he arrived at the Rafferty place for their weekly Sunday services. Fiona looked as pretty as ever. Evidently, she had more than one pair of those ridiculous shoes, because the ones she wore with her flowered dress looked just like the ones he'd sent downriver.

He felt a little bad about doing that, but only a little. Still, he shouldn't have tossed the shoes.

"I'll just be a minute," she said as she headed for the kitchen once the services were over. "Do you have a spot in mind?"

Ian looked up from his reading while Meredith watched Tucker from the corner where she held the sleeping baby. Neither spoke, but then they didn't need words to show their curiosity.

"Fishing," Tucker felt compelled to say. "Fiona loves to fish. I just found this out."

"I see," Ian responded curtly, although Tucker thought he might have detected the slightest hint of a grin.

Never had Tucker felt so out of place in his sister's home. "I'll just wait outside," he said as he backed out, running into the door frame in the process.

Sitting on a tree stump and waiting for Fiona, Tucker frowned. "What's wrong with me? It's just fishing. Why, those two act like I've come courting."

"What did you say?"

He looked up. Fiona headed his way with a basket. She wore a pretty flowered dress, a fairly sensible hat with a straw brim encircled by a black ribbon, and the sealskin boots he'd bought for her. To his surprise, she carried her own pole along with the basket.

"Did you bring worms, too?" He gestured to the basket. "I thought I told you I would take care of that."

Her laughter made him smile. "No, it's not worms. Fishing's not fishing without coffee and snacks," she said. "I don't know if I mentioned it, but when I start fishing, I generally stay all day." She stopped short and gave him an appraising look.

"What?" he asked. "Did I do something wrong?"

"Not yet," she said, "but I wonder if you're one of those fellows who likes to talk while he fishes. If you are, I should warn you that we won't be sitting near one another. I like to do my fishing in silence. It's the best time to talk to the Lord, you know. And besides," she said with a wink, "talking scares the fish away." Her expression turned serious. "Unless you like to talk while you fish. I surely don't mean to suggest that—"

"No, it's quite all right. I believe I can abide by the no-talking rule. One question, though."

She set the basket down to adjust her hat. "What's that?"

"Does the no-talking rule apply to snack times? I mean, a fellow might find himself in trouble if he asks someone to pass the salt, so I feel we should spell out the rules beforehand."

Fiona pretended to think hard. "No, I believe talking is allowed during snack times."

Tucker reached for the basket's handle. "All right, then. Let's go fishing."

"Yes, let's. Where are the big ones biting?"

He answered by pointing south. As she walked ahead in that direction, Tucker suppressed a groan, and he turned to a prayer of his own to save him.

Over the course of the afternoon, his fears grew. Not only did Fiona Rafferty know her way around a fishing pole, but she also caught more fish than he had and even offered to bait his hook. It was a side of the redhead that both intrigued and terrified him.

And Tucker Smith didn't scare easily.

For the first time since he had left Texas, he was enjoying himself with a woman who was not his relative. Tucker set his pole into the soft dirt and leaned back on his elbows. Some twenty yards downriver, Fiona was reeling in a good-sized Dolly Varden.

He watched her drop the fish into a bucket that was nearly brimming already. Without missing a beat, she reached over and jabbed the hook into an unsuspecting worm, then cast the freshly baited hook out in a perfect arc toward midstream.

Lord, I'm in trouble. I think I could actually fall in love with this one.

Two hours into their fishing trip, Tucker called a time-out for coffee. To his surprise, Fiona willingly obliged, and soon they were sitting side by side, swapping fish tales about the ones that got away.

When the conversation slowed, Tucker sipped at his coffee and watched his companion as she lay back to look up at the clouds.

"Look, it's a rabbit." She pointed straight up, and when Tucker tried to follow her gaze, he nearly fell over.

"Looks more like a dog to me," he said. "See the tail?"

"That's not the tail, Tucker." She giggled. "That's the ears."

They lapsed into companionable silence, only speaking when the look of a particular cloud needed to be debated. When the silence went on too long, Tucker closed his eyes and let the sun warm his face while his breathing slowed.

"I could get used to this." Tucker opened his eyes and looked over at Fiona, who was no longer at his side. To his surprise, she'd just cast her hook into the river near the bank. "I said that out loud, didn't I?"

To her credit, Fiona shrugged. "I'm fishing. There's no talking in fishing, remember?"

With a chuckle, Tucker closed his eyes and resumed his contemplation of the backs of his eyelids until he reached a state where he could still hear the sounds of the river but he no longer noticed anything else. His sleep was light, barely below wakefulness lest Fiona should need him.

Fiona. He thought of her as he lay there, of his own reasons for escaping this corner of Alaska, and then let his thoughts drift to why he was there in the first place. He'd been running when he got here, and if he headed out with the Harriman folks, he'd still be running.

He'd already lost his past and a good woman to his running. Did he really want to keep it up?

Somewhere during that nap, Tucker gave up all pretense of wanting to leave Alaska, even for a brief time. The Harriman Expedition would do just fine without him. Experienced guides were a dime a dozen in this part of the country.

Women like Fiona Rafferty, however, were not. That realization almost caused him to sit up and smile.

Almost, but not quite. He did feel quite comfortable lying here.

"What did you want to be when you grew up, Tucker?"

The sound of her voice startled him, and he had to gather his wits. He also had to force his eyes to open, but what he saw was worth the effort.

Fiona sat beside him again, a cup of coffee in her hand and the bucket full of wriggling fish. She'd set aside her proper straw hat and captured that fiery hair of hers into a knot.

She scooted closer to lean her back against the tree, ankles crossed, then sat in silence, never pushing him for an answer. She seemed confident she would have one eventually.

Tucker rolled over on his side and supported himself on one elbow. "I don't think I've ever told anyone this, not even Merry." He paused. "You have to promise two things before I will tell you."

"Sounds serious."

"It's very serious. I'm not a man who shares his secrets with just anyone."

Fiona gave him a look of mock horror as she pressed her palms to her cheeks. "Oh, I don't know, Tucker. I'm not sure I'm fit to take on this responsibility."

"Very funny. How old are you?"

"Nineteen." She tucked a loose tendril behind her ear and reached for the hat, setting it on just so. "Why?"

He shrugged. "No reason, I suppose. I just wondered."

"I could ask how old you are, but I'm more interested in this deep, dark secret of yours."

"Twenty-three," he said. "And as for the deep, dark secret, well, I always wanted to follow in my father's footsteps. He was a railroad man. I've dreamed of it since childhood. Do you find that odd?"

Tucker waited for Fiona to laugh. When she didn't, his estimation of her soared.

She seemed to be cogitating on his statement, so he left her to it. Picking up his pole, he urged the line back onto shore and stabbed another worm onto the hook.

"Some fisherman you are," she said with a grin. "You slept through a good-sized trout."

He pretended disgust. "Some fisherman you are. You allowed a good-sized trout to help itself to a feast without getting caught."

"I am a fisher*woman*, thank you very much." Fiona stuck her nose in the air, and her hat tumbled back off her head. She ignored it to give the line her attention.

"Fisherwoman it is." He cast his line out into midstream and watched the hook sink with a satisfying *plop*. "But what excuse do you offer for letting a perfectly decent fish get away?"

Fiona yanked at the line then glanced over at Tucker. "I assumed that since you had no intention of catching him, the least I could do was let the fish eat something so he could get a little bigger before I landed him."

And so they bantered, he about her inconsiderate nature and she about his casual attitude toward fishing. By the time hunger pangs hit, the second bucket was full, and their catch was enough for twice the number of diners at the supper table.

"I suppose we should take these back and clean them," Fiona said. "It'll be supper soon enough."

"Grab the poles and the basket, and I'll take these." Tucker reached for both buckets and turned toward the cabin. "Oh. I should have told you before we left that the rule around here is whoever catches them cleans them."

Fiona looked him in the eye and nodded before hoisting the poles onto her shoulder. "Of course."

They were almost in sight of the cabin when Tucker stopped short. "Fiona," he said, "I had a great time."

For the first time that afternoon, the redhead looked shy. "So did I."

"We should do this again next Sunday."

She agreed quickly. Then her cheeks blazed. "That is," she added as she looked away, "if Merry doesn't have need of me."

Setting the buckets down, Tucker stared down into eyes he only now realized were the deep green of fresh clover. "Of course," he somehow managed to say.

"And if the weather's nice."

He moved an inch closer. Close enough to count every freckle on her nose. "Definitely," he said.

"Next Sunday, it is," she said as she pressed past him to snag the buckets and march toward the cabin.

Tucker couldn't decide whether he'd just missed out on something wonderful or had just missed landing in a boatload of trouble. As he watched the redhead sharpening the knife that would clean the fish, he decided the answer was a little of both.

Chapter 10

For the next three Sundays, Meredith had no need for Fiona, and Tucker managed to join the Raffertys for every meal, breaking his usual habit of showing up only for supper. Never did he seem to mind Ian's ribbing or Meredith's gentle questioning, although he remained steadfastly silent on his renewed interest in family gatherings.

Fiona would have had to be blind to miss the fact that Tucker seemed to be paying more than the usual amount of attention to her. For her part, Fiona feared she might be falling in love—something she dared not do, considering the short amount of time she had left in Goose Chase.

Each time she left the cabin and headed toward the river with Tucker, Fiona couldn't help but smile. Unlike other times, however, today Tucker seemed preoccupied.

At first Fiona ignored him, calculating that whatever ailed the man would soon be set aside in favor of an afternoon of good fishing and even better coffee. Then he had the audacity to complain about the coffee.

"That does it." Fiona stood. "If you can't be decent company, then why don't you try being quiet? Remember, there's no talking when you're fishing."

Tucker's look quickly faded. "All right," he said. "You want company? I'll give you company and talking. I was just wondering if your letter was from the medical college."

Stunned, she asked, "How did you know I got a letter?"

"Because I was with Ian when Braden brought the mail from town." He crossed his arms over his chest. "The one on top of the stack had your name on it."

Her brothers had noticed, too, but they were obviously waiting for her to bring it up. It would have been hard to miss the look Ian gave her when he handed her the envelope. Surely he and Braden had discussed what it might contain.

Fiona hadn't decided exactly what she would say if asked, but she knew she couldn't lie. She also knew she had to be in Oregon when the term began, and according to the letter, that only gave her two more Sundays to fish before she had to leave Goose Chase.

Two more Sundays with the man she'd somehow fallen in love with.

Thinking about it just made things worse, so she decided to lighten the mood. "So you're brooding over the fact I got a letter?" She feigned a playful smile. "Why, Tucker Smith, are you jealous?"

The joke did not have its intended effect. Rather, Tucker stood and dusted off his trousers. Without saying a word, he grabbed the half-filled buckets and stalked away.

Fiona opened her mouth to comment then thought better of it and went back to fishing. If she caught anything, she'd just carry the fish home wrapped in her apron.

She felt a tug on the line and watched as the granddaddy of all trout nibbled at the bait on her hook.

"Fisherwoman, what excuse do you offer for letting a perfectly decent fish get away?"

She didn't have to turn around to know Tucker was walking toward her. "I assumed that since you had no intentions of catching him, the least I could do was let the fish eat something so he could get a little bigger before I landed him."

He came around to stand between her and the river. Somewhere along the way, he'd set aside the buckets, for now his hands were empty.

"I'm going to speak my piece, Fiona, and I don't want you to say a thing. Nod if you understand." When she complied, he continued. "All right, I'm just going to come right out and say it. These last few weeks have, well, they've given me a lot to think about."

Fiona wanted to speak, wanted to say she, too, had found plenty to consider. Instead, she settled for another nod.

"It all comes down to this. Fiona Rafferty, somewhere between the coffee and the fishing, I've fallen in love with you." He began to pace, and Fiona tried her best to keep her focus on him. "Yes, that's right, I have fallen in love. I know it may surprise you, but—"

"No, it doesn't." Fiona smiled. "I've fallen in love with you, too, Tucker."

He stopped his pacing and whirled around. "I'm serious, Fiona. Don't joke with me."

Tears stung her eyes, and she blinked them away. "I'm serious, too. I can't account for it, but I'm ready to admit I'm in love with you." She shook her head. "There's just one problem."

Tucker looked stricken. "What's that?"

"You haven't asked me to stay yet."

"I can remedy that problem right now." He crossed the distance between them to encircle her wrist with his fingers. Lifting her hand to his lips, he softly kissed her knuckles as he met her gaze. "I want to do this right and proper, so I'm going to speak to your brothers since your father isn't here. I just want to be completely sure of one thing first."

Fiona's tears fell as she contemplated the importance of this conversation. She knew what he was going to ask, but rather than answer, she let him speak the words first. "What's that?"

"I've known since we met at that fishing vessel in Goose Chase that you never meant to make this place your home. Can you give up medicine to be a wife to me?"

She took only a moment to consider what Tucker asked. Her heart soared as she whispered, "Yes."

Tucker's yelp of happiness was probably heard all the way back at the cabin. He lifted Fiona by the waist and swung her around, then held her against him and kissed the top of her head. "You've made me the happiest man in Alaska, Fiona Rafferty. If you have no objections, I'd like to go back to the cabin and let Merry and Ian know."

Fiona looked up into the eyes of the man she loved and tried to nod. Tears blurred his handsome face and rendered her useless until Tucker wiped them away with his handkerchief.

"Would it be too forward of me to steal a kiss?"

Fiona smiled. "Why, is Violet Abrams headed this way?"

"If she is, then she'd best close her eyes else she's going to see the best kiss ever given on

Alaskan soil." With that, he made good on his promise.

"Tucker," Fiona whispered some moments later. "Do you suppose you can top that kiss?"

Tucker leaned down and cradled her cheek with the palm of his hand. "I might, darlin', but not until we're married. I'm sure it will be worth the wait, though."

The walk back to the cabin took forever. Of course, it didn't help that every few feet she had to stop and look at Tucker to see if she'd dreamed the whole thing. They got all the way to the clearing before Tucker realized he had left the fish back at the river.

"You go on inside, but don't you dare say a word. I want to speak to Ian before you go blabbing, you hear?"

"I might be convinced, but it will take another kiss."

Tucker complied then sent her toward the door. "Not a word, now," he said as he hurried back toward the river.

Fiona took a moment to compose herself, first by breathing deeply, then by making sure her hair was fixed just so and the tears she'd shed were no longer evident. Just when she thought her nerves had calmed, a male voice called her name, and she nearly jumped out of her skin.

"Mr. Wily," she said as the man rounded the corner of the cabin. "Did you bring mail?"

He nodded. "That and company."

"We have company?" She accepted the packet of letters from Wily, then strained to see inside the cabin. "Who is he?"

Wily scratched his head and shrugged. "Don't rightly know, except that he's a she."

Fiona held the letters to her chest and strolled toward the cabin door. The sound of voices drifted toward her, two female and the other decidedly male. Ian and Meredith had company, but who?

She took a deep breath and said a prayer that she could get through visiting with strangers without giving away her secret. The precious secret she shared with Tucker Smith.

"Fiona, I didn't expect you back so soon."

As her eyes adjusted to the dimness of the room, she found Meredith and offered her a smile. Ian sat some distance away, and if she didn't know better, Fiona would think her brother was royally irritated.

"Dear," Ian said, "why don't you introduce Fiona to our guest?"

Meredith looked flustered. A woman—the one she thought was Violet—dressed in a traveling suit of fine navy wool and matching hat sat across the table from her. The woman's face beamed, and her smile revealed perfect teeth framed by full, red lips.

"I'm Elizabeth," the elegant woman said. "Elizabeth Bentley."

"This is my sister, Fiona," Ian supplied.

Elizabeth reached out to place a gloved hand atop Meredith's. "I want to thank you for your letter. I must say I never expected to hear from you." She paused. "From either of you, actually."

"Yes, well, about that letter." Meredith swallowed hard and cast a furtive glance at Fiona. "You see, that letter was written months ago. Ages, really. I thought that Tucker—"

"Thought Tucker what?"

Fiona turned to see her soon-to-be husband standing in the door. She offered him a smile, but he looked right past her. "Tucker?"

No response. She tried again as he stepped into a shaft of daylight. Still he did not respond.

What Fiona saw on his face, however, frightened her. In the span of half a second, the man she loved had completely forgotten she was in the room.

"Elizabeth?" His voice trembled as he said the woman's name. "What are you doing here?"

"Merry sent her a letter." Ian rose. "She thought you might be. . ." Ian looked over at Fiona with an unreadable expression. "Never mind, I'm going to take our son out for some fresh air. I'll be outside with Wily if anyone needs me." With that, he gathered a sleeping Douglas from his resting spot and pressed past Fiona to head out the door. "Let me rephrase that," he said. "Fiona, I will be outside with Wily when you need me."

An uncomfortable silence descended, and Fiona got the impression she was the only one in the room without the full story. "Someone tell me what's going on here," she said.

"Tucker," Elizabeth said, "you look as handsome as ever."

Tucker remained frozen and mute. The color had drained from his face, and he looked as though he'd seen a ghost. Meredith didn't look much better.

Elizabeth rose and removed her gloves, setting them on the table and arranging them just so. Then she made her way across the room and came to stand close to Tucker. Far too close, in Fiona's estimation, although Tucker did nothing to move away.

Or maybe he didn't notice. His eyes seemed glazed over, and he looked as if anything other than breathing could be accomplished only with great effort.

"Tucker," Fiona said, "what's going on here?"

For a moment, Tucker's vision seemed to clear. He looked at Fiona. "I'm sorry," came out in a strangled reply. "I'm so very sorry."

"Don't be silly." Elizabeth tapped Tucker on the shoulder then let her hand linger there a bit too long for Fiona's comfort. "You're acting as if you're not glad to see me. I know better than that, Tucker Smith. What I don't know is why you didn't write me to tell me that yourself."

"Where you want these, miss?" Wily stood in the doorway with a set of matched valises balanced on one shoulder.

Elizabeth turned to Meredith. "Where am I staying?" She aimed a broad smile at Tucker. "Just for two nights, of course. My father's expecting us in Goose Chase day after tomorrow."

"*Us?*"

Something was wrong. If only Fiona could put her finger on it. Tucker and Meredith were still staring at Elizabeth, and the houseguest was making eyes at Fiona's fiancé while saying her father was waiting to see Tucker and his sister back in town.

Fiona turned to him. "Tucker, maybe this would be a good time to speak to Ian." When he gave her a blank look, she continued. "You know, about that thing you and I discussed at the river?"

His eyes blinked, but otherwise Tucker continued to stand stock-still as a deep red flushed his cheeks. His fists, she noticed, were clenched, as was his jaw. When she touched Tucker's sleeve, he jerked away and then looked down and met her gaze.

"I'm sorry, Fiona." He turned his attention to the visitor. "I thought my obligations had been released."

Fiona heard the words, but their meaning refused to sink in. She reached for the nearest thing—Tucker's arm—to steady herself.

"*Obligations?* Well, Tucker, I don't know what's gotten into you." The stranger turned to Meredith. "I declare, I don't remember him acting this way back in Texas. Do you, Merry? I don't believe he ever referred to me as an *obligation*. Are you really doing that now, Tucker, or was that just an unfortunate choice of words?"

"Elizabeth," Meredith said slowly, "I'm not sure how to tell you this, but certain situations may have changed since I wrote you."

"You. . .wrote. . .to. . .her?" Tucker paused to shake his head. "That explains why she's here, but why did you do it, Merry?"

"You were lonely, Tucker." Meredith took a step toward her brother then seemed to think better of it. "Remember when we talked about how God had blessed me with Ian and Douglas? I wanted you to be happy again. It seems so long ago now. I thought maybe. . ."

"You thought maybe what?" Elizabeth turned to Tucker. "You and I are affianced, Tucker. You and my father may have agreed that due to your father's unfortunate reverses, my reputation would best be saved by ending our association until your fortunes changed, but I don't recall you saying that to me. Do you?"

"Affianced?" Fiona clutched Tucker's arm tight enough to leave a mark while she waited for him to tell the awful woman to leave. Instead, he slid from her grasp.

The room began to spin. Tucker's face went out of focus, but his voice was clear.

"No," Tucker said, "I was afraid to see you alone. Afraid I couldn't leave you like I promised."

"Well, now, you never need fear losing me again." She cast a glance around the cabin. "It certainly looks as though your fortunes have improved, and I know you've made good on your father's unfortunate setbacks." Elizabeth smiled at Meredith. "It's the talk of the town that the Smith family name has been cleared. We all assumed the gold in Alaska had been found in great abundance on the Smith properties."

"Tucker." Fiona sighed weakly as she battled to keep her last meal from making a reappearance on Meredith's clean floor. "Tell her." She looked up into his eyes and saw only sadness. "Please," she managed.

"My father is waiting in Goose Chase for us, Tucker." Elizabeth's voice wavered. "I didn't come here on my own. I was invited." She paused to meet Fiona's stare before turning back to Tucker. "You promised yourself to me, and I to you. True, our plans were interrupted due to financial reversals, but that situation has been remedied." Her voice inched an octave lower. "I thought you were an honorable man."

"An honorable woman would keep her promises, Elizabeth."

Fiona swayed, and Tucker steadied her. Meredith stepped toward her, but Fiona waved her away.

Elizabeth's face flushed bright red. "Whatever are you insinuating, Tucker?"

"I am insinuating nothing, Elizabeth." He cleared his throat and seemed to find his voice. "I received a letter from our mutual friend John Worthington a few weeks ago, thanking me for paying my father's debts. In it, our friend mentioned keeping company with my former fiancée. I passed the statement off as a taunt not worth answering." He paused. "Perhaps it was a warning."

The woman seemed unable to speak. A bright flush crept up her neck and settled in crimson stains atop her prominent cheekbones. "Why, the nerve of. . . the unmitigated. . ."

"Elizabeth," he interrupted, "I am a man of my word." He paused to square his shoulders. "If we are truly still affianced, you would not be keeping company with the town banker."

"Dear Elizabeth, let me help you decide where to put your things." Meredith reached for Elizabeth's elbow and led her out the door. "Mr. Wily, join us outside, please. I believe my brother has a bit of business to take care of, and I would love to show Miss Elizabeth more of our lovely place."

As she passed, her eyes pleaded with her brother; then her gaze landed on Fiona. "I didn't know," she whispered.

Elizabeth ignored the scene unfolding around her and offered Tucker a smile before disappearing outside. "What a lovely place you have here, Merry," echoed through the open door as their footsteps receded. "I had no idea Alaska could be so beautiful."

"Tucker, say something. Didn't you just make the same promise to me?"

He let out a long breath and dropped into the nearest chair, scrubbing his face with his palms as he studied the floor. An eternity later, he looked into her eyes. "Yes," he said slowly, "but I promised her first."

"You promised her *first*?" The words emerged, but her feelings remained numb, stuck somewhere between disbelief and disgust. "First?"

Fiona's nails dug into her palms, and she tightened her fingers into fists. If only she were a man. Then she could slug Tucker and be done with it.

No, she decided as she forced herself to breathe again. She would never be done with this.

Ever.

"Fiona, please say something."

Tucker's pleading look left Fiona cold. If her feet weren't rooted to the floor, she might have run. Instead, she stood still and watched the room spin.

"I love you, Fiona, but I have to honor the promise I made." He rose and took a step toward her. "I thought she didn't want me anymore. I thought—no, I was certain I had been released from my obligation to marry her."

Fiona found her voice and her anger. "But now you've decided you haven't been?"

"It's obvious I am not free to choose you." His anguished whisper did not move her.

"Then you and I have nothing further to discuss."

Without sparing Tucker Smith so much as a glance, Fiona calmly packed what she could carry and walked out into the Alaskan sunshine. Three steps from the cabin door, she went numb altogether, a merciful respite from the feelings formerly battling for release.

A quick glance back revealed Tucker standing in the doorway. "Fiona, please," he said.

She stopped short and whirled around. "Please what? Please stay?"

A stricken look crossed his face. "I can't ask that of you."

"No," she said as she tightened her grip on her bag, "you can't, can you?" Another moment and she might have run back to him, so Fiona turned away.

Just over the rise, she spied Mr. Wily and called to him. He nodded and loped over to relieve her of some of her luggage.

"You'll be fine, miss," he said, and Fiona noted his face showed neither surprise nor sympathy.

"I will, won't I?" she said to his retreating back.

"What's going on here?" Ian called. "It looks as if you're leaving."

Fiona met Ian on the way to the river and kissed her brother and nephew good-bye. "It's time for me to go."

He seemed to be at a loss for words. Fiona decided to help him with an explanation.

"It seems as though there's one too many women here, big brother," she said. "You really ought to go up and get to know Tucker's fiancée. She's quite lovely."

"Tucker's what?" He shook his head. "I thought you and he, well. . .surely you misunderstood. That was in the past."

"Perhaps Tucker misunderstood, because it seems as though he is still affianced to Elizabeth."

Mr. Wily approached, and Fiona handed him the rest of her bags. She waited until he disappeared before continuing her conversation with Ian.

"Now, I hate to keep Mr. Wily waiting, Ian, but I do want to talk about one more thing. Da will not be happy about my leaving so soon."

He shook his head. "Fiona, I'm more worried about what *you're* unhappy about. Please just come back to the house, and let's talk about this. There must be an explanation for whatever you think you've seen."

"I know what I saw." She looked past him to the sky, now a brilliant blue. "You're not going to try and stop me, are you, Ian?"

Ian entwined his fingers with hers, and she glanced back at him balancing the sleeping baby on his opposite shoulder. "Let one of us go with you, Fiona. It's not safe for a woman to travel alone."

"Thank you, but Mr. Wily will see me to Goose Chase. Doc Killbone told me he'd be sure I got to Oregon in time for school if that was what I wanted to do." Fiona looked her brother in the eyes and tried to hold her tears at bay. "I'll help the doctor at the clinic until he can secure passage for me."

Ian looked worried. "Braden and I will come into Goose Chase to see you off. Would that be all right?"

Fiona kissed the top of the baby's head and then did the same on her brother's cheek. "That would be fine, Ian, but it's not necessary."

"I didn't ask if it was necessary." Douglas raised his head and then cuddled against Ian's neck, eyes half closed. "Besides," Ian said softly, "you'll need the rest of your things. If the weather's nice, we'll bring Douglas and the wives and make it a real family send-off."

"All right. I'll take a room at the boardinghouse next door to the doctor's office. It's safe and clean, and the rooms aren't expensive."

"Yes, I know the place." He seemed to be studying her or perhaps trying to think of something to say.

Unable to remain under her brother's scrutiny, Fiona stepped away and glanced over at the river where Wily stood waiting. "Tell Merry I love her. I don't hold this against her," she said. "And tell her I would like it very much if she supported her brother in his upcoming marriage but never mentioned anything to me of the details."

Ian considered the request before saying, "I think you ought to tell her yourself."

"I will," she said slowly, "but not today. I just can't."

"Fair enough," Ian said. "What should I tell Tucker?"

"Tucker who?"

Chapter 11

The trip downriver to Goose Chase seemed to happen in a fog. As was his habit, Mr. Wily said only a few words. He did occasionally nod or shake his head, leaving Fiona to wonder whether he was offering an opinion on the day's events or thinking of something else altogether.

When they reached Goose Chase, she watched Mr. Wily scurry past with her bags. "Where are you going?" she called.

"Boardinghouse," was his curt response.

"Of course."

She followed in a numb state and allowed herself to be led to a small suite on the front corner of the rooming house by the elderly proprietor. As soon as the woman left, Fiona crossed the compact parlor to the bedroom and shut the door behind her. Exhaustion sifted through her like heavy sand, and she lay back on the narrow bed.

"What happened, Lord? I was so happy. Was that just this afternoon?" Tears welled, but she closed her eyes against them. "Or was it a lifetime ago?"

Fiona gave herself over to sleep so deep that she had difficulty awakening. Was it a nap or a night's worth of slumber? The sun shining high in the sky gave no clue, nor did the tiredness in her bones.

This time of year, the sun dipped below the horizon for minutes, not hours, and even then darkness never quite came. To think she might have considered living the rest of her life under such conditions.

Sighing, Fiona let her eyes droop once more. She tried to pray, but much as she wanted to, she could not get beyond the question of why God allowed her happiness to be so short lived. Da would remind her that happiness is never guaranteed, but for the moment, she didn't care to hear it.

"To be truthful, I never *did* care to hear it," she said with a chuckle. "Oh, Da, what will I be telling you about this escapade of mine?"

A knock at the door startled her, and she sat bolt upright, her head swimming. "Yes?" she managed as she smoothed her hair.

"You've got a visitor, miss," the proprietor said.

Fiona's heart leaped. Tucker had come for her. She climbed to her feet. "Tell Mr. Smith I'll be right down."

"No, miss," she said. "It's the doctor to see you down in the parlor. Doc Killbone, that is."

Fiona swallowed her disappointment then walked to the bowl and pitcher. "Tell him I'll be down directly, please."

The image that met Fiona across the basin was a stranger. She quickly averted her gaze and poured water into the basin. Her face washed and hair combed and neatly tucked into a braid, she descended the stairs to meet the town doctor.

"Forgive me for making you wait, Dr. Killbone," she said as she shook his hand.

"Nonsense, dear." The doctor studied her much the same as Ian had only yesterday. Or was it the day before? "When Mr. Wily delivered your brother's note, I must say I was surprised. I had to come and see for myself that you'd actually decided to take me up on my offer to see to your safe passage to medical school. That is why you're here, isn't it?"

She nodded her head. "Yes, absolutely. Did you say my brother sent you a note?"

"Yes, indeed." The doctor patted his front pocket. "Short and sweet it was. Asked me to see to your safety and to send word if he didn't make it to town before you left."

"But how?" She shook her head. "How did Ian send a note?"

"Oh, it weren't Ian. Braden's the one who sent the note." He smiled. "I can see you're confused. It seems as though Mr. Wily ran into Braden on the way out with the woman from Texas. I guess your brother figured you'd be heading for the hills when he found out who Wily was carrying upstream."

"So Braden knew?" Her eyes narrowed. "And you know. Who else knows about my humiliation?"

"There, there, now," the doctor said. "Goose Chase is a small town, I'll give you that, but we're private people. We don't cotton to disparaging words being said about our own."

"Our own," she repeated. "Funny how I didn't feel like I belonged until I had to make the choice to stay or go. I certainly don't pretend to understand what the Lord's planning now."

Doc Killbone crossed his arms over his chest. "Oh, I don't know, Miss Rafferty. Perhaps the Lord is merely guiding you away in order to prepare you for your return." He paused. "Now tell me, Fiona Rafferty, are you certain you want to take those folks at the college up on their offer to educate you in medicine?"

Was she? "Sure as I can be right now," she answered honestly.

Again he studied her. Then he slowly began to nod. "Fair enough. In that case, I believe I can recommend a suitable escort and a ship heading south."

"Escort?" Fiona shook her head. "I came here alone, and I can certainly go home the same way."

"Dear, if I recall, the reverend and his wife sent you forth from Skagway under the supervision of Mrs. Minter's brother, the ship's captain." His brows shot up. "I rarely forget these things."

"Yes, that's true," she said. "It seems so long ago I nearly forgot."

"Time passes quickly, I've found, when we are most happy. I warrant you will blink and find medical college has ended." He smiled. "Rarely do I find someone so well suited to the trade. Now don't forget your promise to come back here and help me someday."

"I won't forget," she said, "but I wonder if I might ask one favor from you."

He gave her a sideways glance. "What's that, dear?"

"Might you write my da? He's going to be awful upset when he finds out what I've done. I wonder if you might tell him what you've told me about my aptitude for the healing arts."

Dr. Killbone considered her words. At last, he nodded. "Of course, I'd be happy to do that. Why, if I had a daughter, I would be proud if she turned out like you."

She almost cried. Instead, she focused her attention on listening to the doctor as he told her about the trip she would be making. "It'll be another ten days before she sails, but—"

"Ten days?" Fiona rose and began to pace. "Forgive me, Dr. Killbone, but I expected I would be leaving much sooner."

"I'm sorry," he said, "but that's the best I could do."

At the kind doctor's distraught expression, Fiona forced a smile. "Yes, well, then I will just have to make the best of it, won't I?"

"Are you sure?"

Ten days spent in the same town with Tucker Smith and his fiancée? No, she'd never make the best of that. Never. "Of course," she said.

"Then let me tell you about the trip. It's a mite confusing, but I'll write it all down if you think that'll help."

"Yes, please," she said.

The doctor removed a slip of paper from his pocket and began to draw on it. By the time he finished, Fiona had more questions than tears.

The biggest question of all, the one she dared not ask anyone but the Lord, was about Tucker. She uttered it later that night as she once again lay on the narrow bed, waiting for sleep to overtake her.

"Lord, why did You let me fall in love with him?"

"Lord, why didn't you stop me from loving her?" Tucker scrubbed his face with his hands, then sat back to lean against the hard rocks where he had once toiled happily. "Why didn't you just stop me? Why?"

The words echoed in the small chamber and wrapped around his broken heart. Never would he forget Fiona Rafferty.

Yet his honor forbade him from allowing these feelings free rein. He must keep his word. To do any less would put him in the same category as his father.

That would never happen.

Then there was the situation with Meredith. The poor girl blamed herself for Tucker's mess, and nothing he could say would assuage her guilt.

Never had anything come between them, but the situation with Elizabeth could if not handled properly. He must convince Meredith that she had done nothing wrong, that he bore her no ill will.

But how?

It was a fine mess. Fiona's absence called to his heart while Elizabeth's claims challenged his honor. In a perfect world, the Lord would answer his prayers by telling him to fetch back the one he loved and send the other packing.

God would never instruct anyone to do wrong. Tucker knew better than to consider it.

Still, he tried to cogitate a way around the conundrum. How long Tucker sat in the cave, he had no idea, but when he rose, the cold had stiffened his joints and numbed his legs. Stomping the feeling back into them felt good on more than one level, so he continued it even after it was no longer necessary.

"What in the world are you doing?" Braden called to him from the ridge. "You look like you're doing some kind of crazy dance."

"Come down and try it," Tucker responded. "It's quite therapeutic, actually."

"Is it, now?" He crossed the distance between them to shake Tucker's hand. "I'm a plain-spoken man, Tucker," he said, "so I'm going to ask you straight out what's going on here."

"Just stomping around, Braden," he responded.

"No, I mean what's going on with my sister and that city woman over at Ian's place?" He paused. "Amy and I met up with her and Wily a few miles downriver yesterday. I found it odd that a woman would travel all the way from Texas with her pa and not even announce herself with a letter before she arrived."

"Now that you mention it," Tucker said, "that does seem a bit peculiar, doesn't it?"

Tucker's hopes soared. Could he have found a loophole?

"Course Amy saw it different. She figured it was just a woman's way of surprising her beau. I'm here to ask if you're that woman's beau."

"Her beau?" He thought on it a minute. "I was once. I asked her pa for her hand in marriage."

"And?"

"And he said yes. So did she."

Braden cocked his head to the side. "Are you saying you were dallying with my sister while you had a woman waiting for you back in Texas?"

Before Tucker could respond, Braden hauled off and hit him. Tucker saw stars and then felt the earth spin. Ian stood over him, demanding he stand up again.

"Stop it right now, you two." Ian pushed Braden out of the way and hauled Tucker to his feet. "Fighting is not going to help the situation."

Tucker swiped at his nose, and his hand came away bloody. "I'd stand here and take punches from now until forever if it would bring back Fiona and fix the mess I've made."

"You leave my sister out of this," Braden said.

"I love your sister," Tucker responded. "But Elizabeth is pressing her suit, and I'm not going to break my word."

Ian looked like he wanted to throw his own punch. "I want to hear how this happened, Tucker. How did you lead my sister into believing you were free when you knew you weren't?"

"I didn't know," he said. "I thought we'd agreed that Elizabeth no longer wanted any part of me. Her pa told me she would never bear the Smith name. Said it belonged to a family with no honor."

He practically spat the words then gave the brothers a look that dared them to comment. When neither responded, he continued.

"I never spoke to Elizabeth directly. I dealt only with her pa, although she stood there and heard every word and never spoke. Under the circumstances, it was the right thing to do, what with Elizabeth being a woman and the flighty sort."

Ian nodded, but Braden barely blinked.

"When Merry and I left Texas, I understood that we did so with no encumbrances except for the ones our father bore. As you both know, I took those on. The Smith name is now clear and free of any hint of dishonor. My intent is to keep it that way."

"So what you're saying," Braden said, "is that you and this woman's da agreed there would be no wedding; only now she's come up here to present herself as your bride?"

"That's the way I see it," Tucker said. "I'm not rightly sure there's another explanation, although it does seem a bit odd that her pa's in Goose Chase, waiting for us."

Ian nodded and rubbed his chin the way he did when he was thinking hard on something. "I reckon we can take the woman at her word. Or. . ."

"Or?" Braden asked.

"Or we can do ourselves a bit of investigating." He gave Tucker a direct look. "What say we all make a trip to Goose Chase together?"

"What do you have in mind?" Tucker asked.

"Just a friendly meeting with your future father-in-law." Ian shrugged. "I have to wonder if he's figuring you've hit it big up here. If so, he might be wanting to change his mind about the value of the Smith name."

Tucker looked at Braden then back at Ian. "I did use my uncle's money to pay off Pa's debts. I reckon Elizabeth's pa might have heard tell I'd done that and figured I'd sent gold money instead of an inheritance."

"Well, did you tell anyone it was an inheritance?" Braden asked.

"I don't remember," Tucker said. "Probably not. I didn't make much of an explanation to anyone." He squared his shoulders. "Much as I appreciate your offer of help, I'm going to handle this myself."

The Rafferty brothers seemed to be sizing him up. Ian nodded first; then Braden slapped him on the back. "You're a good man, Tucker," he said. "I know you'll do the right thing."

There it was again. *The right thing.* How sick he was of doing *the right thing.*

And he hadn't even come to the hardest part yet.

That came the next day when Tucker reached Goose Chase and walked past the boardinghouse and Doc Killbone's office to step into the lobby of the hotel. He saw Elizabeth's pa from across the room and, for one long minute, tried to decide whether to announce himself or run.

But running was for cowards, and Tucker Smith was no coward. Walking like his boots were making their way through quicksand, Tucker pushed across the Deever House Hotel lobby to stand in front of his father's former business partner.

"Well, now," Cal Bentley said as he rose with difficulty, "I'd know Tucker Smith anywhere." His rheumy gaze studied Tucker a moment. He smiled. "You're doing well up here in the frozen North, I've heard. Quite well, indeed."

"Is that why you're here?" he countered.

The older man looked stunned. Then the mask returned. "I'm here because my daughter has decided she can't live without you, Tucker Smith. I'm here to press her case and insist you live up to your promise to marry her."

"Insist?" It was Tucker's turn to do the studying. "Did you anticipate I might reconsider the promise I made?" He took a half step toward the older man. "Were you concerned I might not do the honorable thing, Mr. Bentley?"

"Eh. . .no. . .of course not, son." He fingered the tip of his mustache. "It's just that sending the girl up here without an escort would not have been proper, you see. As her father, it is my duty to see to her welfare until she is safely handed off to her husband." He leaned away from Tucker. "I hope you don't mind, but I found myself with a bit of free time yesterday and wandered up toward the church. I've arranged for the reverend to speak the vows tomorrow morning."

"Tomorrow morning?" As soon as the words were out, Tucker knew he'd shouted them. "Tomorrow morning?" he repeated in a softer voice. "Why so soon?"

Mr. Bentley looked away. "Time is of the essence in these matters. A man can't run his business from all these thousands of miles away, can he?"

"How is the business, Mr. Bentley? Prosperous as ever?"

"Never mind," Elizabeth's father said. "I do just fine. Now what say you and I celebrate the impending nuptials with a juicy caribou steak?"

Food of any kind would have turned his gut, but especially so when Tucker contemplated how he'd be sitting across the table from his father's former business partner, the man who had called in his father's loans and laughed when the elder Smith defaulted and ran.

"Thank you," Tucker said, "but I must decline. Until tomorrow morning," he said as he made his exit. He reached the back of the hotel before he doubled up and lost what little he still had in his stomach.

Chapter 12

P lease stop crying," Fiona said, "or I will never be able to quit."
She looked away from the view of the river out her parlor window to peer at her sisters-in-law through the fog of her tears. Meredith sat on the sofa with her knees beneath her and a feather pillow cradled around her midsection while Amy perched on the edge of a chair.

"Honestly, it's not like I'm falling off the end of the earth. It's just the medical college."

Meredith began to wail again. "But if I'd just kept my matchmaking to myself, you would be here with Tucker and—"

"And Tucker," Amy interjected, "would be marrying for love instead of obligation."

Fiona watched Amy dab at the corners of her eyes with her handkerchief. "Do you really think that's what he's doing, Amy?"

Amy nodded. "Braden thinks so, too."

"Ian's certain of it." Meredith blew her nose most indelicately, then rose to walk to the window. "I'm just so furious at myself, Fiona." She rested her hand on Fiona's shoulder. "Will you ever forgive me? I only meant to. . ." She dissolved into tears.

Fiona gathered Meredith into her arms and patted her back. "Please, dear, don't do this."

A knock at the door silenced Meredith's tears. Amy walked over to open it then stepped back to reveal Tucker.

"Might I have a moment of Fiona's time?"

Meredith whirled about and blew her nose again. "What do you want to say to her, Tucker?"

"Now, now," he replied. "There are things she must hear from me before she goes away." He looked beyond Meredith to Fiona. When their gazes met, she felt the collision down to her toes. "You don't have to leave, Fiona. Please reconsider."

Amy squared her shoulders. "Remember, honor is for the Lord to bestow and not for man to decide upon." With that, she took Meredith by the elbow and ushered her out.

Tucker watched the ladies go, seemingly confused at Amy's statement. When he looked at Fiona, she forced herself to avert her gaze.

"Leave the door open, Tucker," Meredith called. "It wouldn't do to compromise Fiona's reputation when she won't be here to defend herself come next month."

"We are just downstairs," Amy added. "And I wager her brothers are nearby. Remember what I said about honor."

All was quiet. Fiona could hear her own breathing. Tucker's, too, she imagined. Then he cleared his throat, and his feet made a shuffling sound on the wooden floor.

"Fiona, look at me." He paused. "Please."

When she complied, her heart sank. Rather than a man whose heart seemed broken, Tucker looked like a fellow about to be wed. He'd had a haircut and a fresh shave, and he wore the dress shirt Meredith had just finished sewing for him last week.

He'd gone to this trouble for Elizabeth, no doubt. Fiona sighed. Oh, how the ugly monster of jealousy was hard to tame.

No matter, for she'd be too busy at the medical college to think about it.

Or him.

"Fiona, you'll never know how hard it was for me to come here today." He caught a ragged breath. "This was supposed to be my wedding day."

"*Was?*" She wrapped her voice around the single word and breathed easier when she'd spoken it aloud.

Tucker inched closer then seemed to think better of it and returned to his post by the door frame. "I've been given some time. An answer to prayer, actually."

Her stomach did a flip-flop, and she dabbed at the corners of her eyes. "Oh?"

"The reverend was called away unexpectedly."

"I see." She turned her back on him and steadied herself with a death grip on the windowsill. Outside, the usual activity of the wharf carried on as if it were a normal day in Goose Chase.

"No, Fiona. You don't see."

From the sound of his voice, she could tell he was closer. Her fingers gripped their wooden lifeline that much harder.

"I've. . .that is, we've been given a chance."

She turned toward the sound of his voice and found him nearer than she expected. Backing up as far as she could, Fiona pressed her spine against the sharp angle of the windowsill.

"Yes, I suppose so," she managed to say. "A chance to do the right thing."

Tucker winced at her words, a certain sign he'd come to tell her all the reasons why the two of them were meant to part company.

Fiona searched her mind for something to say that would make him leave. A statement that would cause Tucker Smith to turn and run.

Or maybe to dig in his heels and stay.

She wanted neither. And both.

Then he did the last thing she expected. He didn't run. He didn't dig in his heels.

He kissed her.

Tucker waited for Fiona's outrage but hoped for a smile. What he got was stone-cold silence and a face that held no emotion.

Except for her eyes. He thought he glimpsed a spark of hope, perhaps a longing for things to be different.

Then it passed, and she looked away. "Go, Tucker." Her voice was flat as if all the life had gone out of her. "Please, just go."

Tucker threw all caution to the wind and reached for her once more. She sidestepped him, arms crossed around her midsection.

"But, Fiona, it's no use to pretend," he pleaded. "I love you. I always will."

A tear dropped from the fringes of her lashes and traced a path down her cheek to mingle with the strand of hair his embrace had loosened. Tucker knew he would gladly give up all he had to spend his life with Fiona Rafferty.

"Say the word, and I will send Elizabeth packing."

Then came the jab to his conscience. Was this God's plan? Would He suddenly point Tucker away from keeping his word? From doing the right thing and keeping his word to Elizabeth?

Sadly, Tucker knew the answer. Those three words again. *The right thing.*

If only doing the right thing meant having Fiona, as well.

"Tucker?" His name sounded soft as a whisper. Fiona met his stare. "What is God telling you? He wants you to do the right thing, doesn't He?"

He blinked hard. "How did you know?"

"I didn't." Fiona shook her head. "I just know what He's telling me."

Tucker sighed. "And that is?"

She moved toward him, and for a moment, he thought she might fall into his embrace. Instead, she stood up on tiptoe and kissed his cheek.

"Forget me, Tucker," she said as she brushed back the errant strand again. "And I shall attempt to forget you."

"But we're family," he called as she swept past. "How can I forget you? You will always be there at every Rafferty family gathering."

Fiona stopped short and whirled around. "No, Tucker, I won't. But you and Elizabeth will. In time my brothers and their families will come and visit Da. When they do, I'll be there. I ask, however, that you remain absent."

Torment raged inside, and flashes of anger over his predicament made his fists clench. "I won't let you give up your family, Fiona. It's not fair to ask of you."

She shook her head. "You didn't."

"Tucker?" Meredith stood at the end of the hall. "I'm sorry, but Elizabeth is asking for you." She gave Fiona a look that broke Tucker's heart. "I've kept her occupied, but she's threatening to come upstairs. She said you're late for an appointment with her father. Something about him adding you and Elizabeth's children to his will."

Tucker's heart sank at the thought that, as a husband, he would be expected to give Elizabeth children. The reminder, spoken in front of Fiona, seemed too much to consider.

"Thank you, Merry. Tucker and I were just saying good-bye."

Fiona waited until Meredith disappeared back down the stairs before walking purposefully toward Tucker. She stopped close, dangerously close, and Tucker could smell the soft scent of flowers.

Stupid as it was, he inhaled. He was no judge of flowers, but whatever these were, he would always associate them with Fiona. With good-bye.

His heart sank. To his surprise, she reached for his hand and laced her fingers with his.

"I'm letting you go, Tucker, not because I want to, but because I have to."

He was about to protest, about to tell her all the reasons why together they could convince God that their love was good and right. Then she brushed his hand across her cheek, and he felt the dampness of her tears.

She opened her mouth to speak then seemed to think better of it. Instead, she released her grasp and paused. Once again their gazes met.

Without caring about the consequences, Tucker enveloped Fiona in an embrace. Slowly, he felt her arms wrap around his shoulders. Then, as his eyes closed, her fists gripped handfuls of his shirt.

Tucker could have gladly stopped time and stood forever with Fiona's curls tickling his chin and her arms holding him tight. Then he felt her sway.

With a sob, she slid from his grasp and disappeared. The slamming of her door felt like a door closing on his heart.

He knew he would never open that part of his heart again, at least not as long as Elizabeth remained his wife. Lifting his damp fingers to his mouth, he tasted the salt of Fiona's tears. It was all he could do not to add his own to them.

Tucker stood in the window of his room and watched the harbor until Captain Sven's trawler disappeared from sight. He took a step back and let the lace curtain fall.

He'd chosen this place to stay over the more dignified Deever House Hotel for two reasons. First, he knew his bride-to-be and future father-in-law were staying at the hotel in a corner suite—one he would be expected to share with Elizabeth tonight. More important, Fiona was staying in the room down the hall.

It bordered on pathetic, this need to be close to her despite their conversation to the contrary. Yet Tucker hadn't found the gall to go knock on her door.

She wouldn't answer, he'd reasoned, so ignoring the urge to see her saved him from certain rejection. Besides, Elizabeth adored him; he'd be a fool to chase a dream down the hall when he had reality waiting down the block.

And it was the right thing to do.

Tucker waited until he figured his sister and her family and Braden and Amy had returned to their rooms at the Deever House, then changed into his new, store-bought church clothes and reached for his hat. He grabbed his Bible instead. Out of habit, he turned to Lamentations and ran his finger down the page until he reached the verse he sought: *"It is of the Lord's mercies that we are not consumed, because his compassions fail not. They are new every morning: great is thy faithfulness. The Lord is my portion, saith my soul; therefore will I hope in him."*

He closed the Bible and said the words again from memory. Now he was ready.

The hotel was two blocks away, and the church stood across the street. The pastor on duty, a fellow by the name of Minter, did the honors while his wife played the wedding march on an old upright piano. Their vows were spoken quickly and sealed with a kiss that fell just shy of the mark.

An hour after the ceremony, Tucker and his new bride saw Elizabeth's father off at the dock. With nothing further to delay the inevitable, Tucker led Elizabeth up the wide stair-case to the second-floor corner suite his father-in-law had reserved for them.

The room was as elegant as it was expensive, and the same could be said for his bride. Sensitive to his bride's wedding-night jitters, he excused himself to take a long walk while she made her evening preparations.

Standing at the dock, he stared across the waves to the horizon where the northern lights danced in shades of brilliant green. His first thought: *I wish Fiona could see this.*

His second thought: guilt.

Tucker carried that guilt deep in his heart, and no matter how hard he tried, he couldn't cast it off, even when his bride answered the door of their suite with a smile. He knew the source of the smile, and because it was expected of him, he played husband to his wife.

Chapter 13

The next morning, Tucker awoke to the sound of his new wife depositing last night's dinner into the basin. He held her head until she had nothing left then brought a wet cloth to wipe her brow.

He repeated the same process three mornings in a row. On the last day of their honeymoon, when Tucker threatened to haul her off to Dr. Killbone, Elizabeth admitted the hotel cooking was not the source of her troubles. Rather, she was three months along with the child of a cowboy who had been run out of town on a rail by her father. Tucker had been good and truly suckered.

He walked out and stayed gone for two days. When he returned, he half hoped the fellow behind the desk at the hotel would tell him Mrs. Smith had hightailed it out of town in his absence.

Unfortunately, the man handed him the spare key, and when Tucker opened the door, Elizabeth struck up a conversation about the weather as if he'd only gone out for a brief stroll.

Walking past his wife, Tucker stood at the corner window and looked out over the bustling town of Goose Chase. The view of the harbor wasn't as good as the one at the boardinghouse, but he could watch the trains roll in and out of the brand-new station down the road.

While Elizabeth reclined on the settee, a wet towel covering the top half of her face, Tucker watched the noon train pull out. He waited until the whistle stopped before turning around and facing his bride.

"I could end this marriage, and no one would blame me." He clenched his fists. "I've certainly got the law on my side."

Elizabeth peeled off the cloth and gave him a tired look. "You won't do that, Tucker. You're too honorable."

He took a deep breath and let it out slowly. "Why do you think that, Elizabeth?"

His bride struggled to sit upright, allowing the cloth to fall forgotten to the floor. "Because, Tucker Smith, you've enjoyed the marriage bed with me. You'll not leave now. The same moral code that caused you to marry me will keep you from leaving. You're just that kind. You always do the right thing."

She was right, of course.

Tucker brought her home to the little cabin, then quickly agreed the place would never accommodate the two of them. His heart heavier with each passing day, Tucker woke up every morning and put on a smile, even after he acquiesced to his wife's demand that they move into Goose Chase and take up residence in "a proper house."

The house cost as much in gold as the marriage cost in pride, but he endured both with the unfailing hope that the Lord could redeem the situation through the grace He renewed each morning.

Sometime around the fourth week in town, Tucker landed a job with the railroad.

Life became almost good again. Not sweet as it had been in the days with Fiona or before then, when he and Meredith had been making their way as new residents of the frozen state.

Days were no longer filled with empty hours and a wife who paid him no more mind than the barn cats back home or the fellow who delivered the milk. Now Tucker left before daybreak and returned long after Elizabeth had retired for the night. The hours in between were spent chasing the one dream he had left: working on the railroad.

As Elizabeth's belly grew, Tucker played the part of concerned husband. When the day came for her pains to begin, he walked over to Doc's office to inform him, then found Wily and sent word of the impending birth to Meredith.

Meredith needn't have hurried, as Elizabeth labored the rest of that day and through the night. By noon the following day, she'd given up trying and started begging Doc to put her out of her misery.

"There's nothing I can do," Doc explained to Tucker. "I can't hurry something that the Lord's in control of. Besides, the babe's not supposed to come for another month, maybe two, considering you two only married up seven months ago, right?"

Meredith blushed and turned away, but Tucker stood his ground. "That's right, Doc. What are you suggesting?"

Doc Killbone slapped Tucker on the shoulder and shook his head. "You're a good man, Tucker Smith, and I'm not suggesting anything different. What I'm saying is if there's a way to stop this baby from coming, I would have liked to do it."

"There's really nothing you can do?" Meredith asked.

The doctor studied the floor. "There's times when medicine doesn't work. That's when I have to remember that I can still pray." He swung his gaze to meet Meredith's wide-eyed stare. "I suggest you two do the same. That girl in there's not strong like you, Merry Rafferty. I don't know how much longer she can go on. She's lost a lot of blood, and. . .well, frankly, I don't know that she's got much more fight left in her."

A scream sent the doctor running, and a few minutes later, Elizabeth Grace Meredith Smith made her entrance into the world. Meredith fussed over the baby while Doc Killbone saw to Elizabeth.

"Would you like to see the baby?" Meredith hurried over to offer Elizabeth a look at the squalling dark-haired girl.

Elizabeth turned to face the wall. "I can't look at her."

"She's exhausted," Meredith said quickly. "She'll come around when she's stronger."

But she didn't. Three weeks later, when Tucker came home from work, he found a note telling him his daughter was at Doc Killbone's place.

In a panic, Tucker fairly flew down Broadway to the office. The doctor was holding the baby in the crook of his arm and stirring a pot of stew with the other.

"I only stepped out of the examining room for a moment," Doc said as he handed the baby over to Tucker. "When I returned, your wife had disappeared."

"She'll be back." Tucker took the baby home and waited. His daughter's cries brought him back to the doctor's office some hours later. Doc Killbone diagnosed her as being hungry. A substitute was found, and the baby went to live three houses away with the family of a woman who'd only recently lost a child.

Tucker told himself he could get by this way. That he could allow his daughter to grow fat and healthy with a woman who fed her but could not be her mother.

Two days later, he could stand the arrangement no more. Tucker rented out the house on Broadway and went back to his little cabin beside the river. There Meredith helped to feed, diaper, and generally raise the tiny, dark-haired girl she nicknamed Lizzie Grace.

Lizzie Grace's size and sickly condition made mention of the early birth unnecessary, and her dark curls and blue eyes made questions of her parentage unwarranted, for she was the spitting image of her mother. Tucker suspected Meredith hadn't been fooled, but he also knew the question would never be asked. He learned that Elizabeth had left Alaska by ship, and letters asking after her sent to his father-in-law went unanswered. Lizzie Grace assumed that her mother had died in childbirth, and no one told her otherwise.

Tucker existed happily for years in the secluded spot, and Lizzie Grace grew into a young girl with coltish long legs and a mane of dark hair that her father had learned to braid with surprising skill. She could run faster than any of her cousins, male or female, and to Tucker's delight took to fishing as if she'd been born to it.

She and Douglas, the closest to her in age and temperament, practically grew up at the river's bank with poles in their hands. When Lizzie Grace wasn't fishing with Douglas, she was following the poor boy around, imitating his every move.

With his sister and her family nearby and his daughter strong and healthy, Tucker would have been content to live out his days watching his daughter grow in the little cabin. One day, however, Meredith came to him with a plea for Lizzie Grace.

"She's a smart girl, Tucker," Meredith said. "She needs to be in a proper school that will prepare her for whatever God's got for her life, and she needs to be going to a real church. Ian and I have been talking about moving to town, and we want you to go with us."

Just like that, Tucker returned to Goose Chase and the house on Broadway that he'd rented out for years. He also went back to the railroad and found that the man who had originally hired him now ran the show. He landed a job and went to work the same day.

Ian and Meredith and their three little ones moved in with Tucker and Lizzie Grace, and the house burst at the seams until Ian's house next door was complete. Even though walls and a small stretch of yard separated the families, it was just as common to see a Rafferty child—usually Douglas—in the Smith household as to see Lizzie Grace spending time next door with the Rafferty clan.

Amy and Braden visited often. The pair were happily adding on to the cabin Amy's father had given them and making a life with their children. Their occasional visits to town were met with celebration, and each time, Meredith begged Amy to consider staying for good.

Amy and Braden wouldn't, and Tucker knew it. But he also understood Meredith's need to have female members of the family around her. Occasionally he thought of Elizabeth and wondered where she was; more often his musings landed on the subject of Fiona.

She'd completed her schooling at the medical college with honors and gone to work at a hospital in Seattle. Last time the Rafferty clan got together, Meredith had taken a photograph that Tucker still hadn't found the courage to look at.

Not as long as he was still married to Elizabeth. He couldn't. Instead, he concentrated on doing the right thing and pushing away any hope of a life with Fiona Rafferty.

Seemingly while he watched, his daughter grew and thrived. Meredith proved correct in her estimation that Lizzie Grace needed a proper education and a real church to attend. Under the tutelage of the teachers at Goose Chase School, she proved to possess an intelligence far superior to that of her old dad. And in Sunday school classes, she grew in her love for the Lord, often asking questions Tucker had to go deep into the Bible to answer.

Life was good. Then, three days after Lizzie's thirteenth birthday, a letter arrived. The official document told him that his daughter, Elizabeth Smith, was the sole heir of the Bentley estate, which consisted of three hundred acres that ironically had once been Smith land. The rest, the attorney's letter went on to state, had been spent for back taxes and funeral expenses. Attached to the document were the papers Tucker had signed the week before his wedding.

"Surely he meant this to go to your wife," Ian said after reading the documents.

Tucker sent a letter to the attorney, letting him know that there was another Elizabeth Smith out there somewhere, and some months later, another letter arrived. It included a death certificate and a yellowed clipping from a newspaper in San Antonio that told the sordid tale of the murder of a Texas belle named Elizabeth Bentley Smith at the hands of a cowboy.

Tucker lit a match and tossed the paper into the fire. The death certificate he placed alongside his marriage documents in the trunk up in the attic.

A weight fell off Tucker's shoulders even as he grieved for the woman Elizabeth had become. He wondered far too often if he could have done something different, if he might have prevented the tragedy and saved Lizzie's mother.

A year went by, then another, and eventually peace returned. Still, something nagged at Tucker. Some not-so-small piece of the puzzle eluded him, and his prayers failed to reveal what that something was.

One day while riding a long stretch of rail, Tucker had a revelation. The missing piece was a red-haired woman who, by now, had surely forgotten the feelings she had for him so long ago.

Right there in the caboose, with snow-covered mountains slipping past and Skagway behind him, Tucker wrote Fiona Rafferty a note on the only paper he could find: a train schedule. Surely true love cared not for the stationery the sentiment was expressed on.

While Tucker did not know Fiona's address, he felt sure Ian or Meredith did. He practiced the words he would say to them, but when he stopped by Ian's home, the words flew away. He handed the letter to his brother-in-law in silence.

Ian looked Tucker in the eye and nodded, and then slipped the letter into his pocket.

Months went by and no response came from Fiona, so he wrote again and delivered the letter to Ian to send south. Eventually, Tucker concluded that Fiona wanted no part of him.

Not that he could blame her. That's when he tucked his memories away and promised himself he'd live just fine without them. More important, he wouldn't subject Lizzie Grace to the pain, either.

Some things—and certain people—were better left alone.

So he worked hard at the job he loved, and he made it his life's work to finish raising his beloved daughter and to enjoy his old age with any grandchildren she might one day bring him. The years flew by, and the little girl grew into a quite lively young woman who was as much his daughter as if she were made from the same genes.

Lizzie Grace made him laugh and caused him to shed more than a few tears with her childlike faith in him and in the Lord. From the moment he became her sole parent, Tucker had vowed before God that he would be the kind of papa his own father had not been. It made him proud over the years that, while he hadn't done a perfect job, he'd certainly come close more times than not.

The pain in his heart, however, never completely went away. Whenever a thought of Fiona Rafferty intruded into the present, Tucker stopped what he was doing and said a prayer that the woman God never intended him to be with was safe and happy.

That generally worked to channel his thoughts elsewhere. Once he started praying for exasperating females, he naturally went from Fiona to his daughter.

Lizzie Grace had celebrated her seventeenth birthday by doing two things: declaring that from that day forward she would only answer to the more adult name of Grace and begging her father for permission to take a part-time job with, of all people, old Doc Killbone.

Tucker agreed to the first and completely refused to allow the second. The last thing he needed was to lose another woman he loved to the medical profession.

Chapter 14

May 1917, Goose Chase, Alaska

Iit's only six months. After all, the Israelites wandered around on a detour that lasted forty years before the Lord let them settle down. With all the trouble I've been to Him, I should be glad He didn't decide to give me twice the sentence He gave His chosen people."

Dr. Fiona Rafferty continued to mutter under her breath as she guided her motorcar off the boat's wooden ramp and gently around the confusion of stevedores, passengers, and crates, then stopped to consult her notes. Her last glimpse of Goose Chase had been from the deck of a southbound trawler some eighteen years ago, so she'd been careful to include Ian's last letter among her important papers.

The home that she had leased for six months on Ian's recommendation—the one shown on a detailed map she'd tucked into her notebook—was indeed on Third Street, three blocks from the office where she was to report one week from today.

Despite her many misgivings, how wonderful it would be to live near family once again. Some years back, Ian and Meredith had inexplicably moved their growing family to Goose Chase, where Ian went to work for the White Pass and Yukon Railroad. Meredith wrote a long letter attributing their move to better schools and the benefits of being a part of a church community for the first time since she left Texas. Fiona was left to guess whether or not Tucker made the move along with his twin.

"No matter," she whispered. "I'm a grown woman. If I see him—or his wife—it will be fine. We will probably smile, give one another a how-do-you-do, and go our separate ways."

But her words failed to ring true. Knowledge of what she would do would have to wait until the actual moment. In the meantime, she had far too much to consider.

A chill wind ruffled her newly shortened hair and slid inside her collar, making her shiver. While Da had eventually adjusted to his only daughter's decision to become a doctor, her late father probably would have been appalled that she'd lopped off two-thirds of the length of her unruly locks the day after Easter.

Funny how the things she saw as foolish had been so important to Da. Still, the dear man had loved her and the Lord to the very end, only registering the mildest of complaints when she pressed the point of her independence too close to home.

Fiona ran her hand through the abbreviated curls, then set her driving hat atop her head. No matter what Da might have thought, a hairstyle that neither impeded her work nor called undue attention to her womanhood held great merit. At the advanced age of thirty-seven, she'd long since given up the foolishness and frippery of girlhood for a more conservative mode of dress and deportment.

To that end, she would soon have to adjust her wardrobe to Alaska's climate, and fortunately, according to Meredith, a ladies' dress shop stood just around the corner from the office. While Fiona's blue, lightweight wool ensemble was the height of fashion in Seattle, it would soon prove to be the height of foolishness in Goose Chase.

That much about Alaska she did remember—not from experience but from Ian and Braden's tales and from Meredith's letters. When the winter winds blew across the icy terrain, she would be wishing for warmer days—and warmer clothes.

Of all the places she thought God would send her to practice medicine, Alaska was not among them. It was the last place she had expected. Yet God clearly had sent her here, what with the way all the minute details of her move seemed to be orchestrated by what could only be termed a divine hand.

"It's only six months," she reminded herself.

Even with the long-ago promise made to Doc Killbone, she fully believed another doctor would join the old man's practice well before he needed her to move in. Ian's theory was that Doc felt personally responsible for bringing Fiona back to Alaska. Braden, on the other hand, joked that the old man was biding his time until Fiona honed her skills on the unfortunate folks of Seattle.

She smiled at the Lord's unique way of nudging her back to the one place she hadn't quite made her peace with leaving. Fiona shrugged off the thought. "Let it go, old girl."

It was hard to think of either her brothers or Tucker without remembering the idyllic spot where he and the Rafferty men had mined the earth for gold and grown produce twice the size of Oregon's best. But then, it was also hard to think of the man she'd almost given up her dreams for married to another.

Many years had passed, and no doubt Tucker Smith was a happily married fellow who gave no thought to the foolish girl whose heart he'd broken so many years ago. She'd had plenty of opportunities to ask of his welfare or to hear details of his life, but thankfully Meredith had respected her request not to speak of Tucker except in generalities.

Then there were the letters, each destroyed unopened. She hadn't needed to read his apology or suffer his pity. More important, she certainly did not need to be told that their separation was for the best or that his new life was ever so wonderful.

No, best to just let it go. Or rather, to let Tucker Smith go.

And to think she'd actually thought of ignoring her calling and instead live in the tiny wilderness cabin where Tucker probably still resided. What a fool she'd been. She shook her head as if to dislodge the memory.

Fiona stuffed her notepad back into her bag and squared her shoulders. "It's all for the best, isn't it, Lord? If I'd been fool enough to marry the man, I'd never have gone to medical school."

That settled, Fiona adjusted her hat and placed her gloved fingers on the steering wheel. Despite all her confusion and misgivings over her hasty exit from Alaska some eighteen years ago, she was back, and she'd come to stay—at least for six months.

To celebrate her newfound resolve, Fiona picked up her speed. The sooner she found her home on Third Street, the sooner her new life, albeit a temporary one, would begin.

In keeping with safe driving procedures, Fiona drove right down the center of Broadway, veering only slightly to the right or left to dodge the plentiful and disgusting road apples that were a natural hazard of last century's horse-drawn carriages.

Although she avoided those hazards as she motored along, she couldn't miss their scent. "All the more reason to replace such an outdated conveyance with an automobile," she said as she wrinkled her nose. "For transportation there is no finer—"

An impediment of the human variety came charging into her path, and she turned hard to the right just in time to nearly graze him. She might have stopped and given the oaf a lecture in proper pedestrian deportment had the fellow not raised his fist and, in a loud voice, called into question her driving skills.

Rather than waste words on the ruffian, she pushed the Ford to its limit and left him standing in her wake. Like as not, this would be the last she'd see of him anyway. Men of that ilk generally did not frequent places where decent folk were seen.

Tucker chewed on the dust in his mouth and pondered his near miss with eternity. While he loved Jesus with everything in him, he'd never thought when he sipped his first cup of coffee this morning that he might be headed for heaven this afternoon. Besides, he'd always expected the Lord would call him home during one of his fits of apoplexy over Lizzie Grace's latest stunt.

Or as she preferred to be called: Grace.

He set his hands on his hips and stared down the back end of the offending automobile. *Of all the nerve.*

The woman at the wheel hadn't even stopped. And why in the world was she driving down the middle of the road? Even a tried-and-true horseman like himself knew to veer to the right or the left depending on which direction he traveled.

He gave the contraption one last look, then swiped at the road dust with his hat and set it back atop his head. In all his born days, he'd never seen a horseless carriage with a driver that dangerous. Back in Texas, he'd ridden bulls that followed a straighter path.

"Goes to show you the horse can never be replaced, especially not by one of those death traps." Tucker watched the motorcar head left onto Third Street then disappear. "Her husband ought to be shot for allowing such a menace out of the house."

"Well now, that's a fine way for a man to talk."

Tucker turned at the sound of Meredith's voice. "Did you see what she did? Why, the woman practically aimed at me."

"Aimed at you?" Meredith affected that I-don't-believe-you look he knew so well. "From what I saw, you were standing in the middle of the street."

"I wasn't standing; I was walking. And for your information, that contraption was driving in the middle of the street. What person in his—or should I say *her*—right mind would drive down the middle of the road?"

Meredith turned up her pretty nose and shook her head. "The sort of person," she said in a voice that held far too much amusement to be taken seriously, "who is looking to avoid a collision with animals or persons who might be too near the edge of the sidewalk."

"That's exactly the type of answer I would expect from someone with no driving skills." Tucker stepped aside to let a horse and buggy pass and then regarded his sister through narrowed eyes. "I can see now why Ian refuses to allow you to learn."

To Tucker's horror, his twin's eyes welled with quick tears, and she hurried away. He stood transfixed. "I've done it well and good this time."

Mrs. Simpson, wife of the mayor, gave him a look that confirmed his statement as she swept past. "Seems to me a man ought to stay to the sidewalk and hold his tongue unless he's got something nice to say."

"What? Well, for the love of—"Tucker opened his mouth but couldn't get it to cooperate. Finally, he shrugged and ducked his head.

He caught up with his sister on the sidewalk outside Doc Killbone's office. "Come on, Merry. You know I didn't mean it."

"I know a man often says things he means only to discover he shouldn't have."

She shrugged, and Tucker's heart sank. The only thing worse than arguing with Meredith was to watch her give in so easily.

"No, here's the truth. I'm a first-class fool." Tucker gathered his sister into his arms and kissed the top of her head. "Forgive me, please."

Meredith stepped out of his embrace, her eyes glistening. "No, you're right. I'm not fit to drive an automobile."

Tucker crossed his arms over his chest. "Who in the world would want to? One of these days, somebody's going to pass a law against them. I just know it." He caught the beginnings of a smile on his sister's face. "Now that's better. So, tell me. What brings you to town today?"

A strange look came over her, quickly followed by a shrug. "I'm meeting an old friend," she said.

For the first time, Tucker noticed the basket she carried. "What's this?" he asked as he lifted the cloth to spy its contents. "Preserves and fresh-baked bread? And is that a pie? Maybe I'll come along with you to meet that old friend." He took a step back. "Say, what old friend are you talking about? Surely not someone from Texas."

She shook her head. The slightest smile touched her lips then quickly disappeared.

"Merry, you're not going to tell me, are you?"

His twin gave Tucker a direct look then giggled. "If you want to know, you'll just have to follow me."

"Maybe I will," he said as he fell into step beside her. "Say, what's this friend's name?" When Meredith ignored the question, Tucker tried again. "At least tell me whether this is a he or a she."

Meredith stopped in the middle of the sidewalk and set the basket beside her. Hands on her hips, she stood up on tiptoe to come slightly closer to looking him in the eye.

"Tucker Smith, do you honestly think I would be taking a welcome basket to a *he*? What kind of woman do you think I am? Why, I've never even looked at another man since Ian Rafferty came along."

Tucker hung his head. This was not a discussion he would ever win. Time for him to make a good retreat.

As she watched her brother head back up the street, Meredith knew her irritation at him was due more to her conversation with her husband that morning than with anything Tucker might have said. Still, she couldn't tell him that, nor could she tell him of Fiona's return to Goose Chase.

She'd tried many times over the past month, to no avail. The promise Fiona held her to way back in 1899 still tied Meredith to a time that she hated to be a part of. In her haste to see her brother happy, she'd done the one thing that assured he never would find what he sought.

Now, with her prayers answered and Fiona back in Goose Chase, she had no idea how to tell the two of them they were meant to be together. It was silly, this need to make up for the horrible wrong she'd done to them by her letter to Elizabeth all those years ago.

Some days she thought she'd been used of the devil by sending that letter. Then she watched Tucker's daughter, Lizzie Grace, and knew the girl was meant to be in Tucker's world.

Of course, the why and how of that was also a discussion she and Tucker had never had. There was no need. Elizabeth Grace Meredith Smith was as much a part of Meredith's family as were her own children.

The thought of her children brought Meredith to her eldest, Douglas, and the tiff his newest cause had brought on between her and Ian. In nearly twenty years of marriage, she'd only fought with her husband on a handful of occasions, none of which held enough significance for her to be able to remember the details the next day.

This time, however, was different. The son she loved wanted to go to war to make the world safe. What parent would not be proud of a young man willing to give up his life for a cause greater than his own?

Meredith dabbed at her eyes with her handkerchief and hurried up the block to where the motorcar sat. What parent would willingly give up a son? As soon as the thought occurred, she sighed. If her heavenly Father could willingly send His Son, she had no excuse.

Still, did Douglas have to leave Alaska to serve his country? The registration for the draft next month only involved men twenty-one years old and older. Douglas was just eighteen. Why couldn't he wait until he was older? Perhaps there was another way.

Without Ian to support her, she had considered going to Tucker for help—until he proved just how exasperating he could be on occasion. Then there was the situation with Fiona's return.

"Is this person a man or a woman, indeed?"

Then, right there on the sidewalk in front of 233 Third Street, the Lord delivered the most brilliant plan to her. At least she hoped it was the Lord, because she would definitely need His help to pull it off.

Meredith smiled. She'd also need Lizzie Grace, but the dear girl would never have to know.

Chapter 15

Fiona heard the muttering before she heard the knock. She'd been halfway between the kitchen and the small room where she planned to set up her bed when Meredith's voice floated in through the open window.

"Of all the nerve. Thinking I was paying a visit to a he. Why in the world would he even think something like that? As long as I live, I'll never understand why the Lord saw fit to make me twin to a man who—"

Fiona opened the door, ending Meredith's monologue. The basket nearly pitched forward as Meredith enveloped Fiona in an embrace.

"I've missed you terribly." Meredith set the basket down and held Fiona at arm's length. "I know Ian and I saw you three years ago last summer, but it seems like forever." Her eyes went wide. "Fiona Rafferty, you've cut off all your hair."

"Well, not all of it." She patted her shoulder-length bob. "Just the part that got in the way."

Meredith made a complete circle around Fiona, then shook her head. "What's it like? Do you miss it?"

"Miss the mess? Of course not." Fiona reached for the handle of the basket and ushered her sister-in-law inside. "Come get out of this wind. It's going to blow you away."

"Oh, Fiona, that's the hazard of living in Goose Chase. I'm used to it."

Fiona shut the door and carried the basket into the kitchen. As Meredith swept in and began to unload the contents of the basket, Fiona settled at the table and watched her work.

"I'm wondering something, Merry," she said after a moment.

She paused to turn and face Fiona. "What's that?"

"Why did my brother bring you here?" Fiona paused. "The real reason."

Meredith paused before saying, "Fiona, you know I've always respected your request not to speak of Tucker in my letters or on those rare times when we've been together." She lifted her gaze to meet Fiona's. "So, if I were to answer that question, it might tell you more than you want to know."

Fiona opened her mouth to speak then thought better of it. Perhaps Meredith was right. Details of Tucker Smith's life were best left to his wife.

"All right, then," Fiona said. "Why don't I make some coffee? You can catch me up on all the wonderful things my brilliant niece and nephews are doing."

"Brilliant?" Meredith chuckled. "Brilliant at driving their poor mother to distraction." She sobered a moment. "Seriously, they are wonderful children. A mother couldn't be prouder."

Fiona reached for the pail of water she'd drawn only moments before Meredith's arrival and poured just enough in the pot for four cups of coffee. After lighting the stove, she set the pot atop the burner and returned to her place at the table. In her absence, Meredith's face had taken on a worried look.

"Something's wrong. What is it, Merry?"

Her sister-in-law reached for Fiona's hands and held them tight. "It's Douglas." She paused to study the pattern on the tablecloth before looking up. "He wants to join the war effort."

"Why, that's wonderful, Merry," Fiona said. Behind her, the water began to gurgle in the pot. "We all need to do our part for the boys serving our country. What is it he wants to do?"

Tears welled in Meredith's eyes. "He wants to join the army, Fiona. My boy wants to fight for his country."

"Fight?" The word caught in Fiona's throat. To her mind, Douglas would always be the red-haired infant she'd cuddled eighteen years ago. He would be grown now, a man to most of the world.

Back in Seattle, she'd lost a neighbor to the campaign against the Kaiser, and in her practice, she'd seen far too many of the walking wounded who'd been sent home.

"Yes," Meredith said softly.

Fiona squeezed Meredith's hands. "Well, surely Ian will talk sense into the boy."

The first fat tear landed on the oilcloth, followed in quick succession by several more. Meredith's lip trembled as she cleared her throat.

"That's the worst part. Ian's supporting him in this."

"Surely not," Fiona said. "Why, Douglas is still a lad. Why in heaven's name would anyone suggest he'd be fit for fighting?" ˙

Meredith shook her head. "He's nearly nineteen. By the time I was his age, I had already..."

She didn't have to complete the thought. Fiona knew of Meredith's trek from Texas to Alaska, although she'd only been privy to the vaguest details as to why. Something about a bit of trouble Meredith's pa had encountered—trouble Tucker had remedied with an inheritance from their uncle Darian.

Fiona forced her mind back to the issue at hand. "What's the cause of this, Merry? Has my brother encouraged Douglas's patriotism?"

"Yes," a male voice sounded from outside.

Her attention shot to the open window where Ian Rafferty stood. "A little birdie told me there was pie and fresh coffee to be had here."

Bolting to the door, Fiona met her brother halfway. He greeted her with a hug, then twirled her around and set her back down. Reeling, she smoothed her hair back into place.

"Mercy, girl, where's the rest of you?" Ian towered over her, a mock scowl decorating his features. "You've gone and cut off your curls."

"Oh, bother, Ian, get on inside and let's talk about something more important than the length of my hair."

"I like it, actually," Meredith said. "It's much prettier than a plain old braid."

"Never mind, Merry." Ian stomped his boots until satisfied he'd removed most of the mud and then strode inside. "I find your braid to be anything but plain. And I have similar feelings about the rest of you, darling wife."

Fiona watched him kiss the top of his wife's head and then felt an unfamiliar wistful tug. As soon as the feeling came, she pressed it away. Years of training her mind had caused her to perform the action almost without thought.

What good did wishing and hoping do?

"So, do you like the little place we picked out, Fiona, dear?" Ian removed the coffeepot from the stove. "Merry would have preferred something nearer our place, but I told her you'd like being close to your office."

While Meredith engaged Ian in a discussion of the merits of living on the east side of town as opposed to the west, Fiona found three mugs in the second cabinet she opened. Filling two, she slid them before her brother and sister-in-law then reached back to pour hers.

The banter continued for another few minutes before Ian cleared his throat and regarded Fiona with a sideways look. "So, that your Tin Lizzie at the curb?"

"Tin Lizzie?" Fiona chuckled. "Well, if you're referring to my 1916 Ford, then yes, that's mine. Do you like it?"

Ian pretended to think for a moment. "I reckon it's fine for a city girl, but let's see how it fares through an Alaskan winter."

"I'm more worried about how *I'll* fare through an Alaskan winter," Fiona said. "I've heard here on the peninsula the weather's comparable to Seattle. Is that true?"

"Actually, last winter when you all were posting record snowfalls, we fared pretty well," Ian said. "But then, I'm sure my wife will be glad to help you shop for anything you might need to keep warm."

Meredith nudged her husband. "Very funny." She turned her attention to Fiona, placing her hands atop Fiona's. "I'm so glad you're here."

"Thank you." She winked at Ian. "I'm glad I'm here, too. It's not what I thought I'd be doing, but I'm sure it didn't take the Lord by surprise."

"Speaking of surprise," Meredith said, "the whole town is wondering why Doc Killbone suddenly decided to retire. He's not saying a word, but I wondered if maybe you knew."

"Now, Merry," Ian warned. "It's really none of our business." He paused. "Unless the doctor's in ill health. In that case, I would want to bring his situation before the church elders since he's got no family up here."

"No," Fiona said. "He only mentioned that he was ready to pass on his patients to someone younger and that he'd like me to stay on while a proper search is conducted." She shrugged. "I assumed he was ready to retire. Speaking of the doctor, he said he would leave a key with you, Merry."

She shook her head. "Plans changed. He's still in Goose Chase. I guess he figured even a week without a doctor was too long for our bustling city."

Fiona laughed. "Now that's the Doc Killbone I remember. I suppose I should find my way down there this week and visit with him before he goes."

Meredith nodded. "Yes, but wait until tomorrow. I have the most wonderful idea. Why don't you join us tonight for dinner? It's not caribou, I promise."

A positive response lay on the tip of her tongue, but then Fiona thought better of it. She'd most likely see Tucker Smith eventually. It was highly unlikely he would go long periods of time without seeing his twin. Still, she'd traveled a long way to return to a place where bad memories abounded. Perhaps a good night's sleep would better prepare her for whatever situations entering Ian and Meredith's home would bring.

Thankfully, Ian saved her from having to decide. "Not tonight, dear. I've got a meeting of the church elders, and I'm sure Fiona is exhausted."

"Indeed, I am a bit tired." She glanced out the window to see a tall, red-haired fellow driving a wagon, a dark-haired girl at his side. As he halted to swing off the seat, Fiona knew the fellow was Douglas.

She met him at the curb and wrapped her arms around him. "When did you grow to twice my height, Douglas?" She leaned past him to smile at the young lady in the wagon. "I'm Fiona, Douglas's aunt."

The girl held tight to the reins with one hand and shook Fiona's hand with the other. "Pleased to meet you, Miss Rafferty. I'm Grace."

"That's *Dr.* Rafferty, know-it-all," Douglas said. "Now make yourself useful and fetch something out of the box."

"Stay right where you are, Lizzie Grace." Ian strode toward them, and for a moment, Fiona was struck by the similarity of father and son. She might as well have been looking at the same person in two generations. Funny, but had it really been so many years since Ian was Douglas's age? Some days it felt like yesterday.

"Something wrong, Aunt Fiona?" Douglas asked.

"No, darling," she said. "I was just thinking back to when your father was young and strong like you."

"Hey now," Ian called from the back of the wagon, "don't call me an old man yet. I may be the older of the two, but I guarantee I'm the stronger. Let's just see who gets more of these trunks inside than the other."

At Ian's challenge, Douglas picked up his pace. Grace chuckled. "It's always like this. You should see them when it comes to chopping wood. Between those two and my father, the whole town of Goose Chase could stay warm from what they chop."

Fiona drew near the wagon. Something about the young woman seemed so familiar. The eyes—she'd seen them somewhere before. But where?

"Stand back, Dr. Rafferty. Here they come again," Grace called as the door opened and two burly redheads poured out.

While the men and their cargo went in the front door, Meredith came strolling out the back. "Hello, Liz—" She paused to shake her head. "Sorry, it's going to take some time for me to get used to this. Let me start over. Hello, Grace. I see you've met Dr. Rafferty."

When the girl nodded, Meredith continued. "Fiona, Grace reminds me of you when you were her age. We're trying to get her father to understand that perhaps God has plans for Grace that include using her gifts as a healer."

"He's so old-fashioned," Grace said as she rolled her eyes. "He was furious when I told him I was thinking about becoming a nurse so I could join the war effort. Can you believe it?"

"Now, dear," Meredith said, "this is the first I've heard of your interest in such a thing."

The girl edged closer to the side of the wagon. "My friend Helen from church just left to study at Grace Hospital in Toronto. She's got her heart set on joining the Canadian Expeditionary Forces. They go all over the world, you know?"

Fiona noticed Meredith's face had gone white, so she carefully steered the girl away from such dangerous waters. "Why nursing, Grace? Have you ever thought of becoming a doctor? It takes a bit longer, and you'd most likely miss active-duty status in this war, but you'd be helping a whole lot of people back here." She paused. "A great many of our fighting men have returned and are in need of follow-up care by trained doctors. Perhaps you'd like to know what medical school entails."

"Oh yes, do tell."

The girl hung on each word, and by the time Fiona offered to continue the discussion at the office sometime in the near future, Douglas was climbing back onto the buckboard, and Ian looked as if he might be in need of a nap. Meredith mouthed a discreet "Thank you" as Ian came to stand at her side.

"Thank you for bringing the rest of my things," Fiona said. "I could never have managed to get them all inside without you Rafferty men." She turned to Grace. "And it was lovely meeting you, dear. Do come and see me down at the office soon."

"I will," Grace said. "I promise." She offered Fiona a troubled look. "But do we have to tell my papa? He's awful cantankerous when it comes to this subject."

"I think you shouldn't be dishonest with your father," Ian said. "He's a good man and only wants the best for you. If he forbids you to do something, you mustn't do it."

"And while you're contemplating my father's wise words," Douglas interjected, "hand over the reins. I don't ride in a wagon with a woman driving."

Grace objected to the statement and the demand, and soon the pair were embroiled in a war of words. Meanwhile, Ian gave Fiona a kiss on the cheek and headed for the back of the empty wagon.

"Climb in, wife," an exhausted Ian said to Meredith. "I don't believe I'll be walking home today."

"Dear, this happens every time you try to keep pace with Douglas." She allowed her husband to hand her up into the wagon. "Perhaps you should take on our younger son and let the elder one be."

Ian chuckled and gestured to the front of the wagon where Douglas had reluctantly given up on seizing the reins from Grace. "I think our elder son has met his match."

Meredith settled her skirts demurely around her and then smiled at her husband. "Happens every time a Rafferty takes on a—"

"Off with you now," Ian quickly called to Grace. "I'm hankering for a soft chair and a bowl of stew before my meeting at church."

The dark-haired girl set the horses moving and then looked over her shoulder at Ian. "Will Papa be at that meeting?"

Ian's answer was lost in the clatter of horses' hooves, and soon Fiona stood alone in the silence. "Well, Lord," she said as she trudged toward the door and the mountain of boxes that begged to be unpacked, "I don't know for sure what Your plan is, but then, when did that ever stop me from following anyway?"

Chapter 16

Fiona's penchant for neatness kept her up half the night; thus she'd slept well past dawn. Or at least past the time dawn would have broken in Seattle.

Her breakfast, therefore, had become a midmorning snack, and her early morning visit with Doc Killbone had been postponed until after lunch. She found plenty to busy herself with, however, starting with putting away the last of her personal effects.

Only one trunk had remained unpacked last night, and she opened it now. She quickly hung the clothing it contained in the armoire and then removed the paper separating the clothing from her weakness: an extensive collection of shoes. There atop the matched rows of footwear purchased at the likes of Nordstrom's and the Bon Marche sat a hideous pair of eighteen-year-old sealskin boots.

She lifted one out and gingerly examined it. Considering its age and the heavy use it had taken during that one memorable Alaskan summer, the boot had held together remarkably well.

"How many times have I tried to give these away?" Fiona sighed. "More times than I could count. Come winter, I might be glad I saved them."

Fiona removed its mate and set the pair together in the back of the armoire, then began arranging the other shoes around them until the trunk was empty. With the last trunk set on the back porch for Douglas to retrieve that evening, Fiona ran out of busywork. Only her visit to the clinic remained undone.

Forgoing a lunch that likely wouldn't settle well on her nervous stomach, Fiona decided to drive, then at the last minute chose to walk the short distance. She bypassed Doc Killbone's office to browse through the offerings at the Goose Chase Mercantile. While it would in no way be mistaken for Nordstrom's, the mercantile did give the local Sears and Roebuck some serious competition.

She'd walked through departments containing outerwear, underwear, and footwear, when she came to the section reserved for the extreme cold of the Alaskan winter. Not surprisingly, it was the largest department.

A bald-headed fellow in clothing that looked as if it came off the racks from that very department called to her as he emerged from the back of the store. "Need anything, you let me know, miss."

"Thank you," she responded. "I'll do that."

But she wasn't shopping, just looking. It was something to do to pass the time until she collected her wits and retraced the steps of her past to the front door of the medical clinic.

Fiona had almost decided she was ready when she stumbled upon a shelf containing sealskin boots. Front and center were a pair of boots identical to the ones hiding in the back of her closet.

She ran her hand over the soft fur and closed her eyes. The smell of fresh air and freshly cleaned fish assaulted her nose and made her smile. Sunday afternoons at the river rolled past in quick succession.

When the action stopped on the day she first saw Elizabeth's face, she opened her eyes. To her shock, there stood Elizabeth herself. Her heart jumped into her throat, and Fiona gasped.

"I'm sorry, Dr. Rafferty. I didn't mean to frighten you."

The young woman from yesterday leaned against a pile of blankets, not some ghost from eighteen years past. Fiona shook her head and let out a long breath.

"How are you, Grace?" Fiona glanced up at the Regulator clock situated over the handguns and ammunition counter. "Shouldn't you be at school?"

"I am furthering my education," she said a bit too defensively. "I came to see if you're willing to take me on as a student."

Fiona took the girl's elbow and led her away from the memories. "Whatever are you talking about?" she asked when they stepped out into the sunshine.

"Douglas said he heard tell your papa wanted to marry you off, too." Blue eyes stared down from a superior height and begged honesty of Fiona.

"That's true," she said, "and I assume my nephew heard this from his father." When Grace shrugged, Fiona continued. "My father thought I would have a much easier life should I choose to find a husband and bring babies into the world." Strangers were beginning to take notice of Fiona, so she linked arms with Grace and set out walking.

"That's funny," Grace said. "You do bring babies into the world. Many more than if you'd had them yourself."

"Yes, I do." Fiona chose her words carefully. "But if I was to be completely honest, my father was right. To have chosen marriage and a family, well, that would definitely have been the easier life." She paused to let the girl think about her words then pressed on. "How old are you, Grace?"

"Seventeen," she said.

"When will you be eighteen?"

Grace smiled. "Eleven months and two days."

They walked along in silence until Grace stopped short. "I don't know which I want, to tell you the truth. I wonder if you might help me decide."

Fiona shook her head. "Whatever do you mean?"

"Simple." She offered Fiona a broad smile, and the absurd feeling of familiarity returned. "I'm not asking for a job, because that would be defying my papa, which would be wrong."

"Yes, it would."

"But if you were to let me come over to the clinic sometimes, just to watch you and see what you do. . ." She paused. "Well, I mean if I'm not working and you're not paying me, then it can't be a job, right?"

Thankfully, Doc Killbone saved Fiona from having to respond. He stepped out onto his porch and called to her. "I wondered when you two would stop circling."

Fiona embraced the doctor, older now but no less spry. He peered at Grace over the tops of his spectacles. "Well, now, isn't this interesting? Shouldn't you be in school, Lizzie Grace?"

"I got out early today," she said. "Finished up at lunch."

"Does your teacher know that?"

Grace squared her shoulders and affected a serious look. "I'm almost done with school, Dr. Killbone. If I didn't feel so bad that Douglas is still working on his studies, I would've already completed mine."

"She's a good girl," the doctor said. "Always looking out for her—"

"Fiona Rafferty, is that you?"

Fiona whirled around to see an older woman crossing the street toward her. "Yes, I'm Fiona Rafferty. Do I know you?"

"Afternoon, Miz Minter," Doc Killbone said. "Pleasure to see you this afternoon. How's the reverend?"

"Strong, fit, and ready to dance a jig, thanks to your good care," she said.

"Now, now. No dancing for another month or so. Seriously, though, is he staying off that leg?"

Mrs. Minter nodded. "The elders met last night to divide up his duties so that he can follow your orders."

She touched a blue-veined hand to the old doctor's sleeve. "He and I are in your debt."

"You pay that debt every time you say a prayer for me. I am willing to guess it's me who owes you and the reverend by now."

She smiled. "Whatever will we do when you leave?"

Doc Killbone smiled. "Well, now, I'm glad you asked. Meet my temporary replacement, Fiona Rafferty."

"*Dr.* Fiona Rafferty," Grace said.

"Dr. Rafferty," the woman echoed. "Oh, my, then it's true." Her eyes misted. "I thought I'd never see you again to tell you how sorry I am. And now it's twice as sweet because I can congratulate you on making your dream come true."

"Sorry?" She looked from Doc Killbone back to Mrs. Minter. "Do we know one another?"

"Seattle to Skagway, 1899," she said. "Although I actually met you over corn bread at your daddy's table in Oregon."

"The preacher's wife." Fiona shook her head. "Oh, my, I was awful to you. Just awful." She reached for the older woman's hand. "Will you ever forgive me?"

"No, dear, it's I who must ask for your forgiveness. Yes, you were young." She chuckled. "And you were quite brash, if I might be so bold to say."

Fiona flushed and ducked her head. Her cheeks burned with shame at the remembrance of things she'd said to this poor woman.

"No, don't be ashamed, dear," the pastor's wife said. "In truth, your words have chased me for some years. At first I was mad. Really mad."

"For good reason," Fiona said. "I should never have—"

"Oh, no, dear, don't you see? You asked an important question, one that I had to search long and hard to answer." She smiled at the doctor, then squeezed Fiona's hand. "Do you remember asking that question?"

Fiona nodded and met Grace's questioning gaze. "I'm ashamed to say that I asked this dear lady what she did. I treated her horribly. If I remember correctly, I made you cry."

"Oh, no, Fiona. No." Mrs. Minter shook her head. "I'd say we were even. How did you like the accommodations I arranged for your first trip to Goose Chase?" She looked over at the doctor. "I sent her here on my uncle Boris's trawler, and I made sure she didn't sail out until he had a boatload of the nasty stuff."

Fiona giggled. "I still remember the smell of that fish."

The quartet shared a laugh. Then Mrs. Minter reached for Grace's hand. "You're the future, Lizzie Grace. Be bold like Fiona here. Don't be afraid to ask, 'What do I do?' To think she's a doctor now."

"Yes, well, that's a pretty speech, Miz Minter, but if you will excuse us, I'm going to steal Fiona away so we can go over some details before I turn this clinic over to her."

"Come, Lizzie Grace," Mrs. Minter said, "I'll walk you back to school."

"Oh, that's not necessary."

Mrs. Minter released her grasp on Fiona and latched on to Grace. "Oh, I think it is. Of course, I could just walk you home. Is your father there, dear?"

Doc Killbone chuckled as he watched the pair walk away. "Did you really ask her that?"

Fiona ducked her head. "I'm afraid so."

The doctor looked as if he were about to comment, then thought better of it. "Shall we go inside? I'm anxious to talk to you about all those years we've been apart."

"Now, now," she said as she stepped inside, "I did write."

He chuckled as the door closed behind them. "Yes, you did, and this old man saved every letter. Now, what say I put on a pot of fresh coffee while we go over clinic procedures?"

"Coffee?" Fiona smiled. "Doc, you read my mind."

"No, I didn't. Your brother told me that the way to your heart was through your coffee cup. I know we said you would start next week, but I'm itching to leave, so I was hoping you'd take one sip of my coffee and agree to start tomorrow." He paused. "I'm hoping I can get you to agree to a year of work here instead of six months."

"Doc," Fiona said slowly as she caught the first wonderful whiff of coffee brewing, "that had better be some exceptional coffee, because my present obligation is to return to teaching at the university at the end of my six months here."

The doctor smiled. "Well, let's just see, shall we?"

Chapter 17

Tucker paced the parlor, a note from Rev. Minter's wife crumpled in his hand. So Lizzie Grace had skipped out on school again. He'd received a similar note just last week when the preacher's wife had notified him of a conversation she'd had with Lizzie Grace outside the Goose Chase clinic.

Was she just passing by, or was Lizzie Grace at the clinic to beg Doc Killbone for a job as his nurse again? Either way, she'd disobeyed. It wouldn't do to let her get away with such behavior, but short of packing her off to boarding school, what could he do?

She was as strong willed as... He paused to think the statement through and realized he could blame her temperament on no one but himself.

Meredith assured him on a regular basis that his daughter was perfectly normal and well behaved for everyone but her father. At church, she was the model of propriety and an example to the younger ones, while at school, she excelled despite the fact that, because she had entered school late, she was a full year older than any of the other students except Douglas.

No, the problem of her discipline lay in the fact that his daughter knew she had him twisted around her pretty pinky finger. Hard as he tried, he had not yet figured out how to wriggle out of her grasp.

The back door opened and closed, and Tucker squared his shoulders. "Elizabeth Grace, come here, please."

To his surprise, Meredith was the one who stepped into the parlor. "I'm sorry," she said. "I know it's late, but I'm afraid we sat too long over cake and coffee. Grace is helping with the dishes. She'll be along shortly." Meredith touched his arm. "Change of subject. You should have been there tonight. You can't keep avoiding Fiona forever."

"I'm not avoiding her." He crushed the paper in his fist. "Neither am I seeking her. I haven't yet seen her because my job keeps me away for long periods, and you know I've been working that new stretch of track up north." He waved away anything she might have said to the contrary. "Currently my issue is with my daughter. She's missing school again."

"Oh, pshaw, Tucker. That girl could teach at that school. Don't think I don't realize the only reason she still puts up with going is because she wants to see Douglas finish. Another month, and they'll be issuing diplomas anyway. Once she gets that, you'll have a whole other set of worries, but right now, the girl is fine. A little bored, maybe, but fine."

Tucker tried to argue but could find no cause. Rather, he sank into the nearest chair and massaged the bridge of his nose to stave away the dull throbbing that once again threatened.

"Are you having another headache?" Meredith knelt beside the chair. "That's the third one this week."

Truthfully, he'd had one almost without fail every day for the last three weeks, maybe longer. The headaches plagued him mostly in the evening, but on occasion they hit him in the late afternoon, which interfered with his ability to work. Oddly, he never woke up with one.

"I insist you see the doctor about this," Meredith said.

He looked down at his twin and smiled. The effort made him wince.

Meredith climbed to her feet and planted her hands on her hips. "That's it, Tucker Smith. I'm making an appointment for you at the clinic. And before you argue with me, I will remind you that I happen to know that because you've been gone the better part of the last month, you have four days off starting tomorrow." She paused, eyes narrowed. "And if you don't go, I may be forced to use blackmail."

"Blackmail?"

"Yes." Her smile broadened. "I am your twin sister, Tucker Smith, which means I have been party to almost every misdeed you've performed since leaving the cradle. Would you really like any of those stories told to your daughter?"

Tucker furrowed his brow. "I don't know what you're talking about. I was the model of propriety as a lad. Why, the whole town knew what a good fellow I was. I guess you're forgetting about the annual citizenship awards I received."

Meredith shook her head. "I guess you're forgetting about the lye soap-and-honey incident at the church quilting bee. Then there was the suspicious fire at Mr. Jenson's outhouse." She snapped her fingers. "Oh, and there was the time that you and Buzz Landry took the clothes off Widow Cooper's clothesline and strung them up all over—"

He rose and held his hands up then blinked hard to push back the jab between his brows. "All right. You've made your point. I'll go see Doc Killbone tomorrow."

She gave him a suspicious look. "What time?"

"Never mind, Merry."

His sister stood staring, arms crossed over her chest. "I'm reminded of the time the reverend found the pages of his Bible glued together. Then there was the shaved cat incident over at—"

"First thing." He met her gaze. "I mean it."

———

Fiona's first day of work started out with a disaster. The dress she'd carefully chosen and ironed lost a button as she was slipping it on. Choosing a summer frock sprigged in roses, Fiona made it all the way through her morning routine only to spill half a bowl of oatmeal down the front of it while trying to juggle her bowl and her coffee cup. While she took solace in the fact it wasn't coffee she wore on her trek back upstairs to change, she had lost valuable time.

Thankfully, she arrived to find no line formed outside the clinic doors. Stepping inside, she instantly smelled fresh coffee brewing.

"Doc," she called as she removed her hat and set her handbag aside. "I'm sorry I'm late. You wouldn't believe the trouble I had just getting out the door. Say," she said as she followed the luscious scent to the kitchen in the back of the building. "I thought you were leaving yesterday."

She pushed back the curtain separating the kitchen from the adjacent hallway and stepped into a room that held the combined scents of fresh coffee and baked bread. At the cookstove stood Grace.

"What are you doing here?" Fiona suppressed a smile. Obviously the girl's papa hadn't been consulted, nor had her schooling been considered.

To her credit, Grace looked reasonably contrite. "I wanted to make sure your first day went well."

Several different versions of the same scolding came to mind. Instead, Fiona set them aside for possible use later. "Thank you, Grace," she said. "I appreciate the effort you've gone to here."

"I hope you like my coffee. My papa says it's the best coffee in Goose Chase, and believe me, he's particular." She set the pot on a folded napkin then retrieved two cups from the cupboard and filled them. "Be honest. What do you think?"

Fiona blew across the steaming surface of the dark liquid and then gingerly took a sip. It was surely what the coffee in heaven must taste like. To be certain, however, she took a second sip. Then a third.

The dark-haired girl sat wide-eyed. "What do you think?"

"I think. . ." Fiona took another taste. "I think this is possibly the best coffee I've had in a long time."

Grace beamed. "You're not just saying that, are you?"

"Well, I don't know," Fiona said. "I'd better take another taste just to be sure. See, there was this coffeehouse in Seattle. . . ." She drained the cup and held it out for more. "Grace, I have to say that you've bested anything I've ever tried. How did you do it?"

"I've had plenty of practice," she said. "See, it's just my papa and me at home, although we do live next to my aunt and uncle and cousins, so I've never felt like I missed much in the way of brothers and sisters. Anyway, my papa works hard, and sometimes he's gone working for the White Pass and Yukon for a week or two at a stretch."

"That must be difficult."

"Oh, I don't like it much, but my aunt's like another mama to me." Grace paused. "She's the only mama I've ever had, actually. Mine only lived long enough to see me born."

Fiona reached across the table to cover Grace's hand with hers. "I'm so sorry," she said softly. "I lost my mama, too."

A fat tear landed on the polished mahogany. "I'm being silly," Grace said. "I got all off track trying to answer your question about coffee. See, one of the times my papa was gone, I asked my aunt if she would teach me to make coffee. Well, when he came back, I figured I was going to make him real happy with what I brewed up."

"How old were you, Grace?"

"Seven going on eight," she said, her grin returning as she swiped at her eyes with a tea napkin.

"And how did he like it?"

"Oh, he praised and praised my coffee. Then he asked me if maybe I would like him to share his secret recipe." She tapped the tabletop with her forefinger. "Wouldn't you know I was thrilled? The next morning we went downstairs together, and he showed me exactly how to make coffee his way."

"Well, he's definitely got a knack for making good coffee. I won't ask your secret, but I sure would like to find out what he does to make it so. . ." She finished off the contents of the second cup and set it back in the saucer. "So very good."

"I'm glad you like it," came a deep and somewhat familiar voice behind her.

Fiona whirled around in her seat, sending the cup and saucer clattering to the floor. Framed by the curtains he held back stood Tucker Smith.

She'd have known him anywhere. Age had touched his face, but in a kind way, and the creases at his temples she hoped to be laugh lines. Somehow knowing Tucker had smiled in the intervening years made her heart soften. The threads of silver in his hair—now that was a surprise.

Fiona rose on shaky legs and gripped the back of the chair. "Tucker?"

"Papa, what are you doing here?"

He looked past Fiona to Grace. "I could ask you the same question, Elizabeth Grace."

"Papa?" *Elizabeth Grace.* Fiona's knees tried to buckle. The girl she'd taken under her wing was the daughter of the woman who. . .

She couldn't complete the thought.

"Sit down, Fiona," he said. "You're swaying, and I have no desire to catch you."

"No," she said as she stiffened her spine and stilled her wobbling knees, "you never really did desire to catch me, did you?"

"Do you two know one another?" Fiona heard the chair legs scrape against the floor and then saw Grace come around to stand beside Tucker. As she wrapped one arm around his waist, she slapped her forehead with the other palm. "Of course. You're the one my daddy's been in love with all these years."

Silence.

Grace clamped her hands over her mouth, flames jumping into her cheeks. "I said that out loud, didn't I? Oh, no." She buried her head in her hands. "Douglas is going to kill me. Neither of us was supposed to know, but we overheard a conversation between his parents. I swear we didn't tell anyone else."

The room was so quiet Fiona could hear her heart pounding in her chest.

"Go home." Tucker ground the words out through clenched jaws. "I will speak to you about this later."

"Yes, Papa. I'm sorry, Dr. Rafferty. I never meant to. . ." Grace looked up at her father and then burst into tears and ran from the room.

A moment later, the front door opened and then slammed shut. For the first time in almost twenty years, Fiona found herself alone with Tucker Smith.

"I'm sorry you had to hear that, Fiona." Tucker stood arrow straight in the doorway. "Where's the doctor?"

"No apology is necessary, Tucker. Your daughter's obviously misunderstood the situation." She paused to give him a chance to dispute the statement then, to her surprise, felt a bit of disappointment at his silence. "Dr. Killbone is gone," she added. "He left me in charge."

Tucker pinched the bridge of his nose. "For today?"

"No," she said slowly as she avoided Tucker's direct stare, "for six months."

Eighteen years fell away, and Tucker stood at a riverbank with the best fisherwoman and the most beautiful—or was it the most exasperating—girl in Alaska. Tucker shook off the memory and concentrated on where he actually was.

He certainly couldn't do anything about his headache now. In the past, Fiona was the cause of headaches, not the cure.

The past.

Like it or not, the past sat right in front of him. There was no more wondering what he'd do when he saw her. What he did was turn around and walk right out the door he came in without saying another word.

He got as far as the sidewalk.

Chapter 18

The front door slammed shut, and Fiona rose. She took a deep breath and let it out slowly while holding on to the back of the chair for support.

"Six months," she said as she tested her voice. "I can endure anything for six months."

The door opened again, and this time it shut quietly. *Time to go to work.* "Take a seat, please. I'll be right there."

Fiona picked up her cup and saucer and set them in the sink. Then she washed her hands, drying them on the tea towel. *Thank You, Lord, for giving me the chance to help Dr. Killbone.* She turned around. Tucker Smith stood in the doorway.

"I owe you an apology, Fiona," he said, "and it's eighteen years overdue."

She thought to respond, but Tucker held up his hand to silence her.

"Just let me say this. Once I've said what I have to say, you can tell me to leave you alone, and I will."

A piece of her heart cracked, and she leaned against the counter to remain upright. She had dreamed of this moment, this measure of satisfaction over the wrong Tucker had done, for the better part of eighteen years.

When she nodded, he continued. "Good. I assume you'll be keeping the same hours as Doc Killbone."

Another nod.

His expression was unreadable. "Then I'll be here to walk you home when the clinic closes. We can talk then."

The day passed far too quickly, and as the clock edged past four, she found unexpected butterflies in her stomach. She'd just finished giving a new mother advice on a croupy baby when the door flew open. Grace tumbled in with Douglas right behind her.

"Help him," Grace said. "I'm so stupid."

"What in the world are you—"

Grace scooted out of the way to reveal her strapping cousin's pale face. Blood covered the front of his shirt, and his hand seemed to be wrapped in a cloth. Fiona could see stains where the blood tried to seep through.

"What happened?"

"Broken jar. I applied pressure to stop the bleeding and then wrapped it tight and kept it elevated."

Douglas swayed, and Grace slid under his arm to hold him up. Without being told, Grace walked Douglas into the exam room and helped him onto the table. Fiona tagged behind, marveling that the girl knew enough about first aid to assess his ability to move.

"Nerves weren't cut," Grace said. "Looks like you can stitch it."

Fiona cradled her nephew's hand in hers and decided Grace had judged correctly. "Douglas, does it hurt much?"

"No, ma'am," he said. "It stings a bit. It's just that. . ." His face reddened.

Grace leaned toward Fiona. "Blood makes my cousin woozy."

"Does not," Douglas replied.

"Then look at it," Grace said.

"Enough, you two." Fiona placed her hand on Douglas's shoulder. "It's not bad. No glass in the wound. Your cousin took good care of you, and now I'm going to let her help me finish the job."

Douglas looked a bit doubtful. So did Grace.

"Finish the job? What do you mean?"

"Yeah, Aunt Fiona, what do you mean?" Her nephew jerked his hand against his chest then grimaced. "You're not going to let her sew me up, are you?"

"Grace, would you please tell me how many stitches you think it will take to close the wound?"

Fiona watched the dark-haired girl reach for her cousin's hand and study the wound. "It's only a small cut, but it's deep." She paused. "No more than four, I'd say."

"Well, let's see. Go wash up." She squeezed Douglas's uninjured hand. "Would you like something to take the edge off the pain?"

The young man squared his shoulders. "I'm not a baby, Aunt Fiona. If I'm going to fight in the war, I've got to learn to manage things like this."

Fiona bit back her response while she washed up and gathered supplies. Grace returned and stood by Fiona's side, holding Douglas's elbow while the stitches were sewn. True to Grace's assessment, a fourth would be required to completely close the wound.

Fiona looked at Grace and then addressed Douglas. "You're going to need one more stitch. With your permission, I'm going to let Grace do it."

Douglas didn't even blink. "Sure," he said. "Why not?"

"Grace?" Fiona asked.

The girl met Douglas's gaze before nodding slowly. "I won't hurt you any more than I have to," she told her cousin.

Fiona handed her the tools and exchanged places. "Douglas, speak up if you want me to take over for her."

"That won't be necessary. Go ahead, Grace. Just remember: If you mess up, you'll be taking my shift washing dishes."

"Someone's going to have to take it anyway, goofy," Grace said. "These stitches have to stay dry."

"All right, then." Fiona winked at Grace. "Go right ahead, Dr. Smith. I believe the patient is ready. And I know you are. You're a natural."

With deliberate precision, Grace put the last stitch in place. Fiona showed her how to tie off the thread. The girl bound the wound like a pro then dropped the instruments into the pan.

"Would you like me to clean these?"

"Grace?"

"Papa?"

Fiona whirled around. Tucker stood behind her. She suppressed a groan. Surely he was furious with her for letting his daughter perform minor surgery.

On closer inspection, however, Fiona could see no anger on his face. Rather, a slow smile dawned.

"Papa, Douglas cut his hand on a broken jar. If I hadn't been next door. . ."

Tucker pressed past Fiona to embrace his daughter. "I'm so proud of you, Lizzie Grace. I watched you sew up Douglas." His voice caught as he met Fiona's stare over his daughter's head. "Fiona's right. You're a natural, sweetheart."

Grace nuzzled against her father's chest. "Do you think so?"

He lifted her chin with his forefinger and planted a kiss on Grace's nose. "I know so." He turned her around to face Fiona. "I wonder, Dr. Rafferty, do you think my daughter might benefit from medical school training?"

Fiona fought to control her smile. "Why, yes, Mr. Smith. I think your daughter shows great potential. May I have your permission to speak to my former professor at the medical college in Oregon on her behalf?"

"Oh yes, please do," Tucker said.

Grace danced a jig and then regained her composure. "Thank you, Papa," she said. "I promise to make you proud."

Tucker embraced his daughter once more. "I'm already proud, Lizzie Grace."

"I'm so happy, I'm going to ignore the fact that you just called me Lizzie Grace." She addressed Douglas. "You seem awfully happy." Grace nudged his shoulder. "Are you trying to get rid of me?"

"No." Douglas studied his bandaged hand before meeting his cousin's gaze. "But you and I have looked after one another ever since I can remember. If you're not going to war, I don't have to go, either."

Tucker shook his head. "You mean you were only joining up because Grace was?"

Douglas nodded. "Yes, sir. I knew she wanted to join those Canadian nurses, so I figured I could put in for a duty in the same place they sent her and keep an eye on things."

"That's very noble of you, Douglas." Fiona smiled. "Your parents have done a wonderful job of raising you."

The young man shrugged. "I don't know about all that, Aunt Fiona. Most of the time, she's just a little tagalong, but I figure we're family, and we ought to look out for one another."

"Douglas, I'm going to ignore that first comment," Grace said. "I'm sure you're delirious from the pain." She jabbed his shoulder with her elbow, and he gave a playful yelp. "Dr. Rafferty, I believe the patient needs to go home now. Would you like me to wash those instruments before I walk the big oaf home?"

"No, darling, I think I can handle it."

"Fiona," Tucker said, "I believe you and I have plans. Perhaps my daughter should clean up while you and I go for a walk. Should she lock up when she's done?"

Flustered, Fiona could only nod and scurry after her hat and handbag. A moment later, she found herself walking down Third Street beside Tucker Smith.

She took a deep breath of clean, crisp evening air. "It's a good thing you're doing for your daughter, Tucker."

He blew out a long breath. "An hour ago, I would have said something completely different." He paused. "But watching her in there with you, well, I could see it was something the Lord meant her to do."

Fiona stepped around a patch of mud. "I agree."

"Something else." Tucker sighed. "Much as I hate to admit it, I was wrong about you, Fiona."

She gave him a sideways look. "Oh?"

"All those years," he said slowly, "I consoled myself by thinking that you were probably as unhappy as I was. Before you judge me, you ought to know that I believed you were made to be a wife and not a doctor."

Pausing at the corner, they let a motorcar and two horses pass before crossing the street. "And?" she finally said.

"And now I know you couldn't be unhappy, not when you are so obviously suited to this line of work."

Fiona stopped on the sidewalk in front of her house. "Work isn't everything, Tucker."

Her statement seemed to surprise him. She leaned against the Ford and studied him while she tried to decide how much of the truth to tell him.

"Should you be doing that?" Tucker gestured toward the car. "I mean, the owner might not cotton to having you lean on it."

"I assure you the owner is perfectly fine with me touching it." Laughing, Fiona opened the car door. "Would you like to go for a ride?"

Tucker took two steps back. "You own this motorcar?"

She patted the door. "I do."

"I'm assuming it's no small coincidence that I was nearly killed by a woman driving a vehicle that looked very much like this one." He walked in a circle completely around the car. "Ma'am, do you own a black hat with a large feather?" He slapped his knee. "Of course, you do. If I remember correctly, you always did like odd hats." He glanced down at her shoes. "And you had a weakness for fancy footwear, too."

They shared a laugh; then Tucker grew solemn. "Close the door, Fiona. I need to say what I came to say, and I can't do it in that contraption."

"All right." She closed the door. "Merry sent me home with leftovers, and there's always coffee at my house."

Tucker looked up and nodded. "Coffee will do."

Tucker sipped at his coffee and tried to decide where to start. The beginning sounded about right, so he took a deep breath and let it out slowly while Fiona settled across the kitchen table from him.

"Once I get to talking," he said, "I'd appreciate it if you'd let me finish. Then you can send me packing, if that's what you want." When she nodded, he continued. "It all started when Mama died. Papa never was the same. He left Meredith and me to ourselves most of the time, and one day he just didn't come home. The sheriff came to tell us he'd been shot by a man he owed money to."

His throat felt like cotton, so he gulped the coffee and continued before he lost his nerve. "Turns out he owed just about everyone in the county. Only way I knew to take care of things was to bring Merry to Uncle Darian's place and then head for Alaska to make enough to pay everyone back. Turns out my sister had other plans. Merry refused to be left behind, and that's how both of us ended up in Alaska."

Fiona smiled. "That sounds like Merry."

"Yes, well, when I left Texas, I knew I couldn't go back." He lifted his gaze to meet Fiona's. "I was engaged at the time. To Elizabeth." He paused to take another sip of liquid courage. "I spoke to her father, and he agreed it was best that we call off the wedding. Elizabeth was grateful for being spared the humiliation of marrying into my family."

"I'm sorry, Tucker. That must have been very difficult."

He nodded. "Honestly, I didn't blame her, but I found after a while I didn't miss her, either. Then came Ian and the baby, and Braden married Amy. Well, I started feeling like I was the odd man out. Merry knew this and took it upon herself to write Elizabeth. By that time, I had used my share of the inheritance from Uncle Darian's estate to pay the debts. That's where I was going when I ran into you aboard that trawler."

"Oh?"

"I always knew you weren't intending to stay in Goose Chase. You said so that day at the docks." He wrapped his hand around the delicate cup and let the warmth seep into his palm. "I didn't like you much at first," he said with a laugh. "I thought you were a little. . .how should I say this? Prissy."

"Me? Prissy?"

"Obviously you've forgotten the fancy hat and shoes you wore on that first trip back to town."

"Guilty," she said with a grin.

"Anyway, let's just say you grew on me until those fishing trips got to be the highlight of my week. No one was as surprised as me when I figured out I'd fallen in love with you. The day I asked you to marry me, I thought I was free and clear to do so."

His heart ripped in half when he saw that Fiona had begun to cry. "Do you want me to stop?" She shook her head, so he continued. "I know Merry thought she was doing the right thing in contacting Elizabeth. Do you understand why I married her, Fiona?"

"I'm not sure," she said softly. "I figured you still loved her."

Tucker reached across the table to grasp Fiona's wrist. "No, I loved you. I don't think I ever stopped loving you." He released her and continued. "It became apparent the night I married Elizabeth why she was so quick to head to Alaska when she got Merry's letter."

Fiona studied the tabletop. "I don't think I need to hear this."

"Look at me, Fiona." When she complied, he continued. "She was with child. Three months gone with a baby that belonged to some cowboy. When the rogue refused to marry her, she came after me." Tucker paused. "After she had Grace, Elizabeth ran off to meet him. Years later, her death certificate arrived."

The color drained from Fiona's face. "Then Grace is not—"

"Not my natural daughter?" He shook his head. "No, but you're the only one I've ever admitted that to. I'm sure Merry realizes it, but she would never say anything. She was still nursing Douglas when Grace came along, so those two were raised together like twins."

"Like you and Merry."

"I never thought of that, but you're right." He ran his hands through his hair and shored up his courage with more coffee. "I know now that I tried to take back up with you too soon, and I'm sorry if I made things difficult for you by writing those letters. I just wonder now if the Lord has given us another chance. . .if maybe now that we're in our twilight years, it's finally our time."

"Hey, speak for yourself, Tucker. I'm still young." She worried with the coffee cup. "But maybe you're right."

Tucker felt like a weight had been removed from his shoulders—and his heart. "I've been waiting eighteen years to tell you that."

Fiona smiled. "And I've been waiting eighteen years to hear it."

"Sitting here and looking at you now, well, it's like all those years never happened. I'm almost afraid to ruin things by telling you this, but I'm still as much in love with you today as I was the day you left."

She rose and walked to the coffeepot, and for a minute Tucker felt he'd said too much. He was about to backpedal when Fiona turned around and smiled.

Chapter 19

All I know is, he and Ian were locked away in the front parlor for nearly half an hour last night," Meredith said. "You and I both know those two don't have that much to talk about." She paused. "Unless he's asking for your hand in marriage."

Fiona fussed with the ribbons on her hat and tried not to let Meredith's enthusiasm get her hopes up. "True, we have been getting along famously," Fiona admitted, "but marriage? He hasn't given so much as a hint."

Meredith looked undaunted. "I know my brother, and he's up to something. You two have been inseparable for the past month. I don't think he's going to hold off much longer."

"Yes, he is, actually." She leaned conspiratorially toward Meredith. "He's asked me to teach him to drive."

"No!"

"Yes. I'm taking him for a driving lesson today." Fiona touched her sister-in-law's arm. "Please don't say a word. I'm sure it's not easy for a man with Tucker's ego to have to learn anything from a woman."

"Then why bother?" Meredith snapped her fingers. "Of course. You own an automobile, and if he's going to be your husband, he's not going to sit still for his wife driving him around. See, I told you he's about to pop the question."

"Hush, here he comes." Fiona waved at Tucker, then gave her sister-in-law a kiss on the cheek.

"I want all the details," Meredith whispered.

"You've got to be joking." Tucker stared down the length of Broadway, both hands on the steering wheel. "You expect me to learn how to drive by going down the middle of the street?"

"There's nothing on this end of Broadway but empty land. By the time you get way down there, you'll be a natural at driving."

"You make it sound simple."

Fiona nodded. "You're a smart man, and we've been over this a dozen times. It's only a motorcar, Tucker. Surely a man who's worked on the railroad all these years can handle a simple Ford."

His pride trampled, Tucker decided he must do this. The engine purred and rumbled, and the steering wheel vibrated under his fingers. He reached for the stick and followed Fiona's directions. The car lurched forward and promptly died.

To her credit, Fiona didn't laugh. Rather, she gently pointed him in the right direction, and eventually, he managed to get the car rolling forward at a consistent speed.

"Hey, look," he said when he could manage to remain calm, "I'm driving." Tucker began to think about the real reason for this drive, and he pressed a bit harder on the pedal that made the car go. "This isn't hard at all."

"Tucker, slow down."

He looked over at Fiona. "Worried?"

"Tucker!"

Turning his attention to the road, he managed to miss a pair of wagons looming in his path. "How do I turn this thing?"

When she showed him, he tried it at the next opportunity. The vehicle promptly died.

"How about we go somewhere safer?" she offered. "Somewhere with fewer people."

Tucker smiled. "I know exactly the road." He saw it up ahead and turned right without having to start the Ford again. The vehicle sputtered and lurched but smoothed out as it headed over the hill.

Then came the part he wasn't prepared for: downhill.

The Ford picked up speed. "How do I stop this thing?"

"The brake, Tucker!" Fiona shouted as trees whizzed by. "Hit the brake!"

But instead of the brake, Tucker hit the curb and managed a quick left-hand turn that caused the Ford to slide sideways. They rode like that for a full block before Tucker regained control. He straightened the automobile just in time to run up into the yard of the parsonage.

"Get back on the road, Tucker!" she called. "The church is up ahead!"

"I know," he said as he found the brake and brought the Ford to a screeching halt inches from the back wall of the church. He jumped out and ran around to help a shaking Fiona out of the Ford.

"I was going to do this in a much grander manner, but considering we're in the right place for it, will you marry me, Fiona?"

"Marry you?" She leaned against the Ford, and Tucker hoped the flush in her cheeks was excitement at his proposal rather than something to do with their wild ride.

"Say yes, Fiona. We'd like to come out and congratulate the bride and groom." Braden called from around the corner of the church. "Is it safe to come out now, or is Tucker still driving?"

The rest of the Rafferty clan came pouring out of the church, surrounding them. Grace pressed forward to wrap her arms around Fiona before addressing her father.

"I hope you said it like we practiced last night." She turned to Fiona. "How did he do?"

Fiona smiled. "I can honestly say his was the most memorable proposal I've ever had."

"So," Amy said, "he asked, but you didn't tell us what the answer was."

Tucker wrapped his arms around the most beautiful woman in Alaska—or was she the most exasperating? "That's right, Fiona. You haven't given me your answer. If you don't want to go into the church and marry me, I can always drive you home."

⁓

The wedding took place in the little chapel beside the tall trees with Grace as Fiona's attendant and both brothers walking her down the aisle. Meredith, Amy, and Grace had managed to find Fiona a lovely dress and had even acquired an exquisite hat and the most lovely pair of bridal shoes a girl could wear.

Fiona floated through the ceremony, half expecting to wake up from the lovely dream. While Braden drove the car back to Fiona's place, Tucker and Fiona were escorted by wagon to a lovely cabin on the other side of the hills from Goose Chase for a long-delayed honeymoon.

All winter the women planned Grace's trip to medical school in Oregon. The night before Grace was to leave, Fiona slipped into her room with a long list of names of friends and colleagues for the girl to contact once she got settled at the school.

"And no matter what," Fiona said, "you're to return home for Christmas."

"Maybe you and Papa should come to Oregon for Christmas," she said. "You know I don't plan to be there any longer than it takes for me to become a doctor."

"Yes, dear, and I'd like to talk to you about that."

Later that night, Fiona climbed under the thick stack of quilts to snuggle against her husband. "Are you asleep?" she whispered.

Tucker turned to gather Fiona in his arms. "No, I'm just lying here wondering how we're going to fill all the empty hours we'll have once Grace leaves."

Fiona smiled and leaned up on one elbow. "Oh, I don't think that will be a problem, Tucker. A little bird tells me that we're going to be plenty busy come spring."

"Spring?" Even in the dim light, Fiona could see Tucker's broad grin. "Fiona? You're not. Are you?"

"Yes," she whispered. "Isn't God good?"

"Oh yes," he said as he kissed her soundly. To her surprise, Tucker pulled away. "But if you're indisposed, who will be the doctor around here?"

It was Fiona's turn to smile. "Doc Killbone said he'd be sending a replacement in six months. I'm sure he will be willing to stay until Grace returns."

"Grace?" He shook his head. "I don't understand."

"She told me tonight that she intends to return to Goose Chase and practice medicine. That means your daughter will be home in a few years." Fiona stole a kiss from her surprised husband. "Are you happy, Tucker Smith?"

He answered, but not with words.

A Light in the Window

Window

by Tracie Peterson

Chapter 1

Julie Eriksson hastily donned her fur-trimmed cloak and made her way to the viewing deck of the SS *Victoria*. She strained to see the hazy blue outline of land. Nome, Alaska! After five long years, she was finally coming home. For the rest of her life, she would celebrate the seventh of October.

Squinting against the brilliance of the sun as it hit the ice floes in the Nome roadstead, Julie thrilled at the crisp, cold wind on her face. Where other passengers—visitors to her far north—shuddered at the zero-degree weather and went quickly below, Julie felt like casting off her cloak. This was her home, and never again would she leave it. She longed to soak it all up.

The deep blast of the steamer's whistle startled Julie. She remembered back to 1919, when she'd left Nome for Seattle in order to study nursing. Then, the ship's whistle had been a lonely reminder that Julie was leaving home. Now an experienced public health nurse, Julie was returning to her people to offer what skills she'd learned in order to better their lives.

Her only regret was that her mother, Agneta, had passed away while Julie was in school. Having been a sickly woman, Agneta was Julie's biggest reason for becoming a nurse. What little health care existed in Alaska was inadequate to deal with the ailments of Agneta Eriksson. Julie had always desired to bring her mother relief from her torturous bouts with asthma. Julie had learned all she could about the illness, but she hadn't returned in time to help.

Her mother's memory would live on in Julie's heart, but the empty place Agneta's death left would never be filled. With this thought in mind, Julie wondered if her father and brother would be meeting her. Their homestead was some twelve miles northeast of Nome—a short, easy trip by dogsled.

She smiled as she thought of the dogs. It had been so long since she'd driven her own team. City people in Seattle had laughed at her talk of driving dogs, unable to imagine Julie handling the demand.

Of course, some of the rural students had known only too well the love of mushing dogs, and when several had invited Julie to join them at a local winter race, she'd readily accepted. Those simple kindnesses had helped ease her homesick heart that first year.

Glancing at her watch, Julie noted that it was ten minutes till twelve. They'd made excellent time, with perfect weather for their six-day journey from Seattle. During her bleakest moments in the States, it had been hard to believe that Nome was only six days away. Most of the time the distance had seemed an eternity, and had Julie not been resolved to become a nurse, she would have gladly taken the short trip home and forgotten the loneliness that haunted her in the state of Washington.

Julie felt the ship slow as the ice floes grew larger and threatened to halt the *Victoria's* progress. Nicknamed the Grand Old Lady, the SS *Victoria* was one of the only ships to brave the harbor of Nome this late in the year. Julie knew that even the *Victoria* wouldn't challenge the icy waters past the first of November. Insurance premiums would soar due to the risk of icebergs. In fact, after the *Victoria* pulled out of the harbor for Seattle, there wouldn't be another ship into Nome until April.

"All for Nome! All for Nome!" a man called out through a megaphone.

Julie moved toward the man. "Are we going to take the ferry across the roadstead?" she asked as the man moved past her.

"No, ma'am," the man said with a tip of his cap. "The ice is too thick. We're going to walk you across."

Julie nodded. It wasn't unusual for Nome-bound ships to anchor in the ice-laden harbor while passengers walked ashore across the thick ice. Leaning against the icy railing, Julie smiled to herself. Another hour and she'd be on the sandy banks of Nome.

"Oh, thank You, Father," she whispered in prayer. "I'm so happy to be home and so happy to be doing Your work." Julie glanced around to make certain no one was watching her before she continued. No sense in folks thinking she was daft.

"Dear God, make me an ambassador of Your love and good will. Let me help the people in this territory both with my nursing skills and my knowledge of You. And Lord, thank You so very much for allowing the years away to pass quickly and for the good friends You sent my way—friends who helped to ease my burden of loneliness and separation. Amen."

The ship came to a full stop, resting gracefully against the solid platform of ice. Julie raced back to her cabin and gathered her things. It was going to be a glorious day!

The walk across the icy harbor made Julie glad she'd bought a sturdy pair of boots in Seattle before leaving for home. Of course, they weren't as warm as native wolfskin boots with moosehide bottoms, but they got her across the ice without any mishaps.

Some of the "cheechakos," the Alaskan name for greenhorns, were trying to snowshoe or skate in city boots across the ice. If she hadn't worried about hurting their pride, Julie might have laughed out loud in amusement. The only other women on the trip were a pair of frail-looking things who insisted on being pushed across the ice in sled baskets.

Julie wondered about the handful of passengers. Always there were those who came to find their fortunes in gold, but they usually arrived in April or May and departed before the temperatures dropped below zero. There weren't many from the lower forty-eight who, upon hearing of days, even weeks, spent at fifty degrees below zero, would brave the Alaskan winter. Those hearty souls who did usually came for reasons other than acquiring gold.

Of course, some people were running from the law. Alaska provided a good place for criminals to escape from those who might put them behind bars. Others might have family or friends who'd beckoned them north.

Julie surmised the two women in the sled baskets might be mail-order brides. They weren't familiar faces, nor did they appear to be saloon girls. She felt sorry for them as she watched them shivering against the cold. She wondered if they'd ever bear up and become sourdoughs, as those who made it through at least one Alaskan winter were called.

Nearly losing her footing, Julie decided to forget about the other passengers. She was nearly a visitor herself, and she hastened to remember the little things she'd forgotten while enjoying the conveniences in Seattle. She kept her eyes to the ice, determined to keep her suitcases balanced and firmly gripped in her ladylike, gloved hands. *Useless things, city gloves,* Julie thought. She'd be only too happy to trade them in for a warm pair of fur gloves or mittens.

Not that it hasn't been fun to play the part of the grand lady. Given that Nome streets in winter were always in some state of mud, ice, or snow, Julie knew it would be wise to forget about dressing up. *No,* she reasoned, *sealskin pants, mukluks, heavy fur parkas, and wool scarves will be of more comfort to me here.*

The wind whipped across her face and pulled at her carefully pinned black hair. Having spent most of her time indoors in Seattle, Julie's pale skin made an impressive contrast to her ebony hair and eyes.

Julie had her Eskimo grandmother to thank for the rich, dark color of her eyes and shining hair. Having left her Inupiat Eskimo village, Julie's grandmother had married a Swedish fur trapper and moved to Nome. Their only child, Lavern Eriksson, had been born in 1865, some thirty-six years before the famed ninety-seven-ounce gold nugget was taken out of Anvil Creek near Nome.

It was the rumor of gold as early as 1899 that had brought Agneta's family north. While others were eager to make their fortunes, Julie's parents had found a fortune in love. Agneta and Vern had married after a brief courtship and soon Julie's brother, August, had been born. In 1902, Julie's birth had completed the family.

Julie scanned the banks again for a familiar face. She was about to give up hope when her brother's face came into view. His hand shielded his eyes, but Julie easily recognized his easygoing looks.

"August!" she shouted across the ice as she picked up her pace. Her brother pushed through the crowd and rushed across the frozen harbor to greet Julie.

"I can't believe you're finally here," August said as he pulled Julie into his muscular arms.

"Me, either," Julie said as she enjoyed the first hug she'd had in five years. She'd nearly forgotten the feel of supportive arms.

"Here," August said as he took hold of her bags. "Let me carry those. I suppose the rest will be brought ashore some time later?"

"Actually the *Victoria* is unloading immediately. The ice is much worse than they expected, and they want to get on their way."

"Great," August said as they came onto firm land. He put the bags down and asked, "Did you bring much back from the States?"

"Well, there are quite a few supplies for Dr. Welch, and of course the things you and Father requested. Not to mention the dozen or more things that friends wired me to bring back from Seattle. I'd say maybe eight or nine crates," Julie said with a grin.

"That many?" August questioned as his eyes grew wide. "It's a good thing I brought a twelve-dog team."

"You needn't worry," Julie said as she linked her arm through August's. "At least half the crates are for Dr. Welch. They're marked with bright red crosses, so we won't have to spend time figuring out which is which."

"What a relief," August said with a laugh. "Look, you wait here, and I'll go get the dogs." Julie nodded and watched as August walked through the bustling crowd of people. It was good to be home.

An hour later, Julie was helping August load the last of Dr. Welch's supplies into the sled.

"I'll come back for our things after we drop these off at the Doc's. Do you want to drive the sled?" August asked.

"No, you go ahead. I'm just going to walk and enjoy being back," Julie replied.

"Whatever you want," August said and took to the sled. "Let's go. Hike!" he called, and the dogs set out as if the sled basket were empty. They were a hearty, powerful breed of animal, well suited to the work and cold.

Julie trekked behind August, familiarizing herself with the few shops. The post office bustled with activity as the postmaster unloaded the incoming mail. Nome hadn't changed that much during her five-year absence. The Northwestern Commercial Company remained with a number of buildings that lined the main street of town, and folks could still get a meal at the Union Restaurant for four bits.

Up ahead, August had brought the dogs to a halt outside the twenty-five-bed hospital. Julie joined him just as Dr. Welch popped his head out the door.

"You're certainly a welcome sight," Dr. Welch said as he opened the door wide to receive August and Julie. "Let me grab my coat and I'll give you a hand."

August waved him off. "That's all right, Doc. I can handle it."

"In that case," Dr. Welch said with a shiver, "I'll speak with your sister while you unload the sled. You can bring everything around back. I'll have Nurse Seville show you where to put things."

August nodded and drove the dogs to the back of the hospital.

Julie followed the middle-aged man up the stairs and into his office. "I was able to obtain almost all the things you needed from the hospital in Seattle."

"That's a relief," Dr. Welch replied as he offered Julie a chair. "How was your trip?"

"Perfect," Julie answered and took a seat. "Of course, the destination alone made it that. I wouldn't have noticed if they'd stuck me in the galley washing dishes. I was coming home, and that made everything else unimportant."

Dr. Welch smiled and nodded. "I can well understand. Would you like something hot to drink?"

"No, I'm fine," Julie replied as she pulled off her gloves. "As soon as August finishes unloading the sled, we'll need to be on our way home."

"I'm afraid I must insist that you stay at least a day. Preferably two. As this area's public health nurse, you will report directly to me. Our combined reports will then go via mail to the proper officials. There's a great deal we'll need to cover before you can actually begin your work."

"I understand," Julie said thoughtfully, "but I have been working without much time to call my own. I need to go home and see my father, and I need time to rest."

"I confess, I haven't given much thought to your needs. Usually people go to Seattle for a vacation. It's odd to think of someone coming to Alaska for a break. I'm just so relieved to have an extra helping hand with the outlying population," Dr. Welch said as he took a seat across from Julie. "You will actually do many jobs that are often reserved for doctors in more populated regions. Especially as you venture out among the villages."

Julie nodded. "If August agrees," she stated as her brother walked into the room bringing a package, "we'll stay in Nome for one night. Then I really must take a short rest." Both Julie and Dr. Welch looked at August.

"There's no way I can stay. I'm needed to help with the dogs," August replied, reminding Julie of her father's sled dog kennel. "But I can leave part of the team for Julie to mush home tomorrow. I'll need to borrow another sled, however."

"There's one here standing ready for Nurse Eriksson's use," Dr. Welch offered. Julie smiled to herself. It was the first time anyone in Nome had called her that.

"Well, Julie?" August looked at his sister and waited for her approval.

Julie nodded. "I think I can remember the way home," she said with a laugh.

"If you don't," August said, grinning, "the dogs sure will. Especially if it's close to dinner time."

"It's agreed then," Dr. Welch said. "Julie, you are welcome to sleep in the back room. There's a stove and plenty of coal. It's well protected from the wind and shouldn't get too cold."

"Once you get past twenty degrees below zero, it's just about the same. Cold is cold," Julie said like a true Alaskan.

Turning to August, Dr. Welch gave him instructions on where he could leave Julie's dogs and sled gear. "Oh, here. I almost forgot," August said as he handed Julie the package he'd been holding. "These are the things you asked me to bring. I was going to have you change before the trip home."

"You remembered!" Julie said with a note of excitement in her voice. "My sealskin pants and parka!"

August smiled as he secured his parka hood. "I'll tell Pa you'll be home tomorrow. Now if you'll both excuse me, I'll finish unloading the sled and be on my way."

Julie put the package aside and threw herself into August's arms. "Thank you, August. Please tell Pa I love him and I can't wait to see him again." August gave Julie a tight squeeze and was gone.

Loneliness seeped into her heart, reminding Julie once again of the isolation she'd known in Seattle. She tried to shake the feeling, convincing herself that because she was home, she'd no longer be lonely.

As she turned from the door, she could hear the dogs yipping outside, anxious to be on the trail. She understood their cries. She, too, longed to be making the trip home.

Chapter 2

The next morning at breakfast, Julie couldn't contain her excitement. "I can't believe I'm finally home. I can hardly wait to see my father."

"I would've gotten about as much accomplished if I'd sent you on home with your brother. I suppose I should have realized the importance of your spending time with your family," Dr. Welch said as he and Julie accepted a stack of hotcakes from the Union Restaurant's waitress.

Julie laughed in animated excitement. "I feel just like a little girl at Christmas," she said as she poured warmed corn syrup on her cakes.

"We still need to pick up a few things for your trip home," Dr. Welch reminded her.

"Umm," Julie said, nodding with her mouth full. Taking a drink of hot coffee, she added, "I appreciate the supplies you've already loaned me. I'll only need to pick up food for the dogs. It's always wise to keep your transportation well cared for, just in case we get stuck on the trail."

"I heard tell a blizzard is due in," Dr. Welch said between bites. "I'm afraid you'll have to really move those dogs to get home before the storm catches up with you."

Julie glanced out the window. The skies were still dark, making it impossible to get any bearing on the incoming storm. "I'd nearly forgotten about the darkness. How many hours of daylight can I count on this time of year?"

"I wouldn't expect more than seven—especially if that storm moves in as planned. The sun won't be up for another hour or so," Dr. Welch said, glancing at his pocket watch.

"I don't dare wait that long," Julie said thoughtfully. "I'll mush out in the dark. The dogs know the trail in their sleep, and I won't need more than two or three hours at the most, if the trail is clear."

"Are you sure you're up to it?" Dr. Welch questioned. "I don't intend to lose my first public health nurse. I've waited too long for help."

Julie smiled. "Don't worry about me," she reassured. "I've never been one to take unnecessary risks. I'll be fine if I can move out right away."

"Then I'll pay for this meal, and we'll go secure some food for your dogs," Dr. Welch said as he rose from the table.

Julie hurriedly forked the last of the hotcakes into her mouth and pulled on her parka. The warmth of the coat made her feel confident that she could face the trail without danger.

Julie affixed the dog harness to the sled, remembering to anchor the sled securely before attaching any of the dogs. Reaching for her lead dog, Dusty, Julie gave the strong, broad-chested malamute a hearty hug. "Good dog, Dusty. You remember me, don't you, boy?" she questioned as she led him to the harness.

Dusty yipped, and soon the rest of the dogs perked up and began dancing around as Julie talked to and petted each one. Within minutes, they were once again good friends.

After harnessing Dusty in the lead, Julie secured her swing dogs, Nugget and Bear. Two team dogs, Teddy and Tuffy, came next, with two wheel dogs, Cookie and Sandy, rounding out the sled team.

Julie checked the lines and then rechecked them. It had been at least five years since she'd had to be responsible for such a job, and she was self-conscious about doing it right. The wind picked up, reminding her of the expected snow.

"Well, boys," Julie said as she checked the ropes that held her sled load. "I think we'd best be on our way." She left the dogs long enough to go inside and bid Dr. Welch good-bye, promising to return in two weeks.

Taking her place at the sled, Julie paused for a moment of prayer. "Dear Lord, please watch over us and deliver me safely to my father and brother. Amen." She pulled up the snow hook and tossed it into the sled basket.

"All right, team. Hike!" she called, grabbing the bar tightly. She ran behind the sled for a few feet before taking her place on the runners. Soon she'd be home!

Once the dogs made their way out of Nome, they followed a trail that paralleled Norton Sound. Julie was relieved that, because the wind had been surprisingly calm through the night, the trail hadn't drifted much.

Julie barely felt the cold, even though the temperature had dropped to fifteen below. She was so well bundled beneath the layers of wool and fur that when snow started to fall, she barely noticed.

An hour later, however, the snow had worked into a blizzard with fierce winds blowing off the sea. Julie knew the dogs would stay to the trail unless something barred their way, so she moved on without concern.

The wind and ice pelted down ruthlessly, causing Julie to nearly lose control of the sled once or twice. The snow drifted and blew, almost obliterating the trail. Julie reassured herself by remembering that the dogs would be able to find their way through. Nonetheless, she found herself whispering a prayer. It wasn't until Dusty abruptly brought the team to a stop that Julie began to worry.

She couldn't call to the dogs above the blizzard's roar, and the blowing snow made it impossible to see up ahead. Julie wondered why Dusty felt it necessary to stop. She grabbed the snow hook and, after securely anchoring it in the ice-covered snowbank, made her way along the sled.

Taking hold of the harness, Julie made her way down the line past each dog. Finally coming to Dusty, she took hold of the tugline. "What is it, boy?" she questioned as she strained to see down the obscured trail.

Dusty whined and yipped but refused to move forward. Julie turned to move back down the line of dogs when someone grabbed her arm from behind. Her scream of surprise was lost in the muffling of scarves and blowing wind. She turned. A pair of ice-encrusted eyes stared at her.

For a moment Julie did nothing. Her pounding heart obscured all other sounds. She was surprised that the dogs remained relatively calm, and because even Dusty seemed at ease with this person, she began to relax.

The man let go of Julie's arm and motioned her to the sled. Julie nodded while the man took hold of Dusty's harness. Julie pulled the snow hook and grabbed onto the sled bar. The team barely moved as the stranger helped them down a steep embankment and across a solid sheet of ice.

The dogs couldn't get good footing against the slick surface, but the man moved them across with little difficulty. The snow let up just a bit, and Julie could see the stranger urging Dusty up the opposite bank. Whoever he was, Julie was grateful.

The dogs were struggling to get up the bank. Julie knew she should get off the sled and help push. She gingerly took one foot off and then the other. The ice offered no traction, and when Julie pushed forward, her feet went out from beneath her.

Smacking hard onto the ice, Julie lay still, struggling to draw a good breath. Tucking her legs up under her, Julie managed to get to her hands and knees. Just then she felt the firm grip of the man as his hands encircled her waist. Within moments, Julie was up on her feet and, thanks to the stranger, soon up the embankment.

Standing at the top to catch her breath, Julie thanked God for answering her prayers for safety by providing help from a stranger. She quickly resumed her place on the runner of her sled, ready to set out again.

The stranger moved forward. Julie could barely see the outline of another dogsled team. They would now progress together, Julie realized as the man waved her ahead. She felt much better traveling through the storm with a companion.

They progressed slowly, but evenly. Snow fell heavily at times, and the wind threatened to freeze Julie's eyes closed. Just as quickly, the wind would let up and visibility would improve. In spite of the questionable weather, Julie felt confident that nothing would hamper her trip home. She'd put the entire matter in God's hands, and she refused to take it back.

No sooner had this thought crossed her mind than the teams approached a river. Julie waited patiently while the stranger moved his dogs onto the ice. She watched silently as the man expertly maneuvered his animals across the river. It would only be a few more minutes before he'd signal her to start down the embankment.

Then the unthinkable happened. The stranger's lead dog disappeared into the river. Julie watched in horror as the stranger moved ahead of the team to pull his dog from the water. A sudden stillness in the wind carried the sound of cracking ice just before the stranger joined his dog in the water.

Julie had to act fast. She worked her dogs down the riverbank and onto a ledge of even ground. Fearful that the ice would give way and cause more harm, Julie tied a line around her waist and secured it to her anchored sled.

Cautiously, she worked her way across the slippery ice to the place where the stranger's dog team waited for their leader. The stranger was holding on to the edge of the ice, but it was impossible for him to get out. He'd cut the lead dog from the harness and was trying to boost him out of the water.

Julie reached down, took hold of the dog's thick, rough fur, and pulled him forward. The dog seemed fine as he found his footing and shook out his heavy coat. Untying the line from around her waist, Julie motioned the stranger to secure it under his arms.

Following the rope back to her own dogs, Julie took hold of Dusty's harness and pulled him forward down the bank of the river. "Forward!" Julie called against the wind. The dogs worked perfectly, pulling against the added weight of the stranger. Julie kept looking over her shoulder as she encouraged the dogs to pull. When she saw the man roll up onto the ice, she stopped the dogs and quickly crossed the ice to help the man to his feet.

Julie reached out her hand and helped the man stand. He seemed unharmed, yet Julie knew the possibility of hypothermia was great. She motioned to the man to take off his parka, but he shook his head and pointed up the embankment.

She reluctantly agreed to follow the man as he loaded his lead dog into the sled basket and led his dogs away from the broken ice. Julie retrieved her team and feeling more confident of her abilities, urged them up the riverbank. At the top of the embankment, she could see why the man had motioned her on. A light flickered brightly in a cabin window.

With so much of the Alaskan winter months spent in darkness, all travelers looked for that welcoming beacon: a light in the window. Relief poured through Julie as she realized that shelter was so near. She moved her dogs forward and then realized that the cabin she was nearing was her own home. The dogs began to yip and howl as Julie mushed them on. They were home at last!

As Julie stopped in front of the cabin, two bundled forms made their way from one of the outbuildings. Vern and August Eriksson both motioned Julie to the house while they worked together to care for her dogs.

August left Julie's dogs to his father's care and went to the stranger. He motioned him to follow Julie. The stranger pulled August to the sled basket and revealed his water-soaked dog. August nodded and pulled the dog into his arms. He moved quickly to the outbuilding where Julie knew her father kept the sick or weak dogs.

The stranger reached into the sled basket, pulled a canvas pack out, and made his way toward the house. Julie went ahead of him and opened the door. A warm wave of air hit her eyes as she walked into the cabin. Quickly, she made her way to the fireplace.

With no thought of the man behind her, Julie pulled off her heavy fur gloves and scarves. She pulled the parka over her head and tossed it to the floor. Thick black hair tumbled around her shoulders as Julie worked to loosen the laces of her mukluks. Kicking the heavy boots aside, she unfastened the catch on her sealskin pants and let them drop to the floor.

Beneath her sealskin pants, Julie wore heavy denim jeans. She felt them to see if they were wet. Finding her pants in good shape, she straightened up, brushing back the hair from her face. Staring at her from across the room was the stranger.

The shocked expression on the man's face nearly caused Julie to laugh out loud. Her black eyes danced with amusement, and a grin formed at the corner of her lips.

"I'm Julie Eriksson, and this is my home," she offered, extending her hand. She immediately liked his rugged looks.

The man broke into laughter as he took Julie's hand. "I'll be," he said, and his shocked expression changed to admiration. "I must say that's the first time a woman saved my life. I figured you were a man. I mean, well. . ."

He fell silent as he dropped Julie's hand. "Of course," he murmured as he stepped back and allowed his eyes to travel the length of Julie's slim frame, "that's obviously not the case."

"I believe I owe you thanks as well," Julie said, growing uncomfortable under the stranger's scrutiny.

"I think we're more than even. By the way, I'm Sam Curtiss."

"Lucky Sam?" Julie questioned, remembering the nickname from things her brother had told her of his best friend.

"The very same," Sam said with a grin. "Although I think I owe my survival today to more than luck."

Julie nodded. "No doubt."

Sam shook his head. "So you're August's little sister," he said as he took a seat and kicked off his boots.

"I'm also a nurse," Julie said, taking a step forward. "And as such, I know that you're in danger of hypothermia. You should get out of those wet clothes and into something warm and dry."

Sam raised his eyebrows and crossed his arms against his chest. "Yes, ma'am," he said as he leaned back against the chair, "I'd say I owe this encounter to a great deal more than luck."

Chapter 3

Sam refused to take his eyes off Julie while they waited for Vern and August to return from caring for the dogs. He was captivated by this woman as he'd never been by any other. She was so graceful and fluid in her motions, yet the knowledge that she had saved him out on the ice gave Sam a heartfelt respect for her.

As Julie moved about the room and tried to avoid his gaze, Sam couldn't help but smile. She was uncomfortable in his presence—that much was obvious—and Sam wondered why.

Julie ignored Sam as she went about the cabin, reacquainting herself with the home she'd left so long ago. Vern and August, true to their Swedish ancestry, hadn't changed things except to add a portrait of Julie that she'd mailed them while at school in Seattle.

Julie circled the room, touching the things her mother had loved, cherishing the memory of days spent in her company. The house seemed empty without her. She grimaced as she remembered the day months earlier when the telegram had arrived. Because it was February, passage to Nome had been impossible.

Julie blamed herself for not being at her mother's side. Her schooling had been complete in time to return to Nome before ice isolated it from the rest of the world. But because Julie had decided to become a public health nurse, there were certain additional requirements she had to meet.

When word reached her of her mother's death, Julie had had no other choice but to stay on at least until April, when the ports reopened. By then, her mother's body would have long since been cared for, so Julie decided to finish her government training and return in the fall as a fully certified public health nurse.

Julie glanced up to find Sam's eyes fixed on her. His presence made her feel awkward. For the last few years, Julie had spent most of her time with women. Outside of the men she'd helped care for, Julie hadn't allowed herself the luxury of gentlemanly companionship.

The silence grew unbearable, but just as Julie began to fear she'd have to start talking with Sam, the front door burst open in a flurry of snow and fur.

"Father!" Julie ran across the room to embrace the elder Eriksson.

"Julie, it's so good to have you home. Let me look you over," Vern said as he put his daughter at arm's length. "You look more like your mother every day, God rest her soul. Of course, I see a bit of your grandmother Eriksson as well."

"Oh, Father," Julie said with a smile, "come get warm by the fire. Here, let me help you with your parka."

"You're just like your mother. She was always fussing and worrying about me, even when she was. . ." Her father's words trailed into silence.

Julie took the parka as her father pulled it over his head. "Even when she was dying?" Julie finished her father's words.

"Yes." Vern Eriksson seemed to age with the statement. "It hasn't been a year, and it seems forever. Wish it didn't have to be so for your homecoming."

"I thought I'd die for want of home," Julie stated evenly. Her voice strained slightly. "I'd rather it not be this way, but I've still got you and August." The young woman threw herself into her father's open arms. Her eyes grew misty.

"I see you brought Sam home with you," August said as he threw his coat aside.

"I think it was more the other way around," Julie said. "That blizzard hit hard, and I was still at least an hour from home. Sam appeared out of nowhere and, well, here we are."

Julie studied Sam for a moment. His brown eyes were so intense in their evaluation, however, that she quickly looked away.

"Don't you dare believe her," Sam's deep voice boomed out. "She saved my life. Pulled me out of the Nome River when the ice gave way."

"Are you all right, Sam?" Vern questioned with the voice of a concerned father.

"I'm just fine, Vern. Julie's quick thinking and my sealskin pants kept me from getting too wet. That daughter of yours is quite a dog driver. You ought to be proud of her."

"We are, to be sure," Vern said as he squeezed Julie's shoulders. "I'll bet you two could use something hot. Why don't you kick back, and August and I will get something on the stove."

"I'd like to unpack first," Julie said as she picked up her mukluks.

"Your things are already in your room," August offered. "I could pretty well figure out which crates were yours and which weren't."

"Thanks, August," Julie said as she walked over and kissed him on the cheek. "I could get used to being cared for," she said with a smile.

"Somebody as pretty as you ought to be cared for," Sam offered seriously. There was only the slightest hint of a smile on his lips. Julie blushed crimson, uncertain what she should say.

"Don't let her looks deceive you, Sam. She's wild enough to handle when she's got her steam up. I remember the time we were going to have to shoot one of the pups and—"

"I don't think Sam needs to hear about that," Julie interrupted as she shifted uncomfortably. She looked almost pleadingly at Sam, melting his heart and any protest he might have voiced.

"All right, all right," Vern said with a chuckle. "I guess anyone who's worked as hard as you have today deserves extra consideration. Go ahead and do what you need to. August and I will get lunch."

"Sam, you might as well put your things in my room. From the looks of the weather, you're going to be here tonight," August added.

Julie's head snapped up and turned to face Sam. *He's staying the night,* she thought as she met his laughing eyes.

A smile played at the corner of Sam's lips, and Julie was shocked to realize she was paying attention to them. It was even more shocking to wonder what it would be like to kiss those lips.

Julie lifted her gaze to Sam's eyes and found they had sobered considerably under her scrutiny. *What is he thinking? Does he know what I'm thinking?* Julie felt her cheeks grow hot and dropped her gaze.

"I think I'd better get busy," she muttered and left the room. Why did he make her feel so strange? Julie chided herself for even caring. She was a nurse now, and her mother's dream for her was finally realized. There was no way Julie was going to jeopardize that dream by getting involved with a man. Even if the man was the handsome Lucky Sam Curtiss.

Julie marveled that her room hadn't changed in her absence. Her bed was still made up with the crazy quilt her mother had given her for her fourteenth birthday. Julie reached out and stroked the quilt as if it somehow allowed her to touch her mother.

"Remember, Julie," she could hear her mother say, "God only lends us to this world for a short time. What we do with that time, what we leave behind, is our representation of our love for Him. It doesn't matter that we make the most money or have the finest homes. What matters is that we can stand confidently before our Lord and King, knowing that we lived as He would have us live and gave Him our best."

This quilt was only a small part of what Agneta Eriksson had left behind, Julie realized. She'd lived her life for God and had brought both her children to an understanding of salvation. Surely God had welcomed her as a faithful servant.

Julie sat down on the edge of the bed and sighed. She loved the simplicity of her room. A picture of Jesus praying, a small mirror, and a cross-stitched sampler were the only ornaments decorating the walls, while delicate, flower-print curtains framed her window. A small desk and chair completed the room.

Julie stretched out on her bed and listened to the wind howling outside her boarded window. The pulsating rhythm soon put her to sleep, leaving her to dream of penetrating brown eyes and a man she feared would change her destiny forever.

"Julie," Vern called softly as he gently shook his daughter. "Wake up. Dinner's on."

Julie wiped her eyes and sat up. "It's sure been a long time since I've had a wake-up call like this."

Vern smiled and Julie noticed the wrinkles that lined his face and the gray in his beard. *When had he grown old?* she wondered.

"Come on. The food will be cold by the time you make it to the table."

"I'll be right there," Julie said as she got up. "Just let me brush out my hair and change my shirt."

"All right, but it won't be easy to hold back August and Sam. They look mighty hungry," Vern said with a laugh.

"I'll hurry," Julie promised and went to her closet.

The clothes that hung there were those she'd left behind when she'd gone to Seattle. They seemed foreign to her. Finally settling on a navy print with long sleeves and a softly rounded, feminine collar, Julie dressed hastily and dug her hairbrush from her unpacked baggage.

Studying her reflection in the mirror, Julie thought she'd aged a great deal since leaving home. Maybe it was the trials of nursing duty or the loss of her mother, but she looked older than her twenty-two years.

She brushed back her dark hair and decided to let it fall just below her shoulders. There'd be plenty of time to pin it up when she was back at work. For now, Julie was determined to enjoy being a civilian without any obligation to a uniform or dress code.

She finished buttoning the cuffs on her sleeves as she made her way to the table. "Sorry to have kept you waiting," she said, taking her place.

"It was well worth it," Sam said with admiration in his eyes.

"Shall we say grace?" Vern asked and waited for everyone to bow their heads. "Father, we thank You for Julie's safe return, and we praise You for bringing Sam and her through the storm. Thank You for the bounty You've placed before us. Bless this house and all who pass here. Amen."

Julie whispered, "Amen," and lifted her head.

Across the table, Sam lifted a plate of bread and handed it to Julie. When their eyes met, she swallowed uncomfortably and accepted the plate. Sam offered a broad grin before turning his attention to the reindeer steaks that Vern passed his way.

"So," Sam began the conversation while Vern and August occupied their mouths with food, "your brother tells me that you're about to embark on a new career. How soon will you have to report to work?"

"I, uh," Julie stammered, trying to think of what to say. "I told Dr. Welch that I needed a rest. I've been working almost nonstop since I left Nome in order to study nursing."

"That's true, Sam," August said as he paused to take a drink. "My sister never does anything halfway. She completed her courses at the top of her class. She was suggested by none other than the hospital administrator for her position as a public health worker."

"I'm impressed," Sam replied with growing admiration.

It was exactly what Julie didn't want. She tried desperately to steer the conversation in another direction. "I know the need of the people in the villages. My mother was a good example. A doctor can only do so much. As a nurse, I can travel from village to village, and as a native, I'm already known to many and related to a great many more."

"Your mother would be proud," Julie's father said with a smile.

"I only wish I could have finished soon enough to help her." Regret darkened Julie's voice.

"Regret will only grow bitterness, Jewels," Vern said using his daughter's nickname.

Julie nodded. "I know. I'm not going to let it tarnish Mother's dream for me. I want to share more than medicine with the natives."

"Just what did you have in mind?" Sam questioned.

"Well," Julie began slowly as she put her fork down, "I would like to share the Gospel with them. Mother and I talked many times about caring for more than wounded bodies. We felt that there was a need to care for their wounded spirits, as well."

"Do you think folks in the villages will accept your ideas? They might not think too highly of a woman showing up to offer a cure for what ails them."

Sam's voice was lighthearted, but Julie resented his interference in her dreams. Instead of answering, she turned her attention back to the meal.

Vern realized Julie's silence was her way of dealing with things that hurt her. "I believe if the Lord lays a ministry upon your heart, He'll also open the necessary doors," he stated quietly. "Julie's felt this call for a long time. I have to believe that because she's gotten this far, God has been in it from the start. She'll do just fine."

Julie flashed a grateful look in her father's direction before allowing herself to look at Sam's face. She expected to find sarcastic laughing eyes staring back at her, but instead Sam's face seemed sober, almost apologetic.

The conversation took many turns after that, but Julie sensed that Sam wanted to say something more. When dinner was over, Julie insisted the men allow her to clean up the mess. She waited until all three had moved to the front room before she got up from the table.

The wind was still howling outside, and Julie knew without the benefit of an open window that the blizzard was raging. Part of her hated the long, dark winters when windows were boarded up to insulate against the cold, but another part of her loved the raw wildness of it. Days, even weeks, would pass when the only people she would see were those who shared a roof with her. This isolation was part of the region's attraction, and Julie knew she could never leave it for good.

"Still mad at me?"

Julie looked up from the dishes and met Sam's dark brown eyes. "I wasn't mad at you."

"Good," Sam replied, sounding relieved. "I'd hate for you to think lowly of me, especially when I think so highly of you." Julie's puzzled expression amused Sam. "You don't think a guy like me could think highly of a woman like you?"

"I don't know," Julie whispered. "I guess I never thought about it."

"Too busy with your studies and all?"

"I suppose," Julie answered.

"Well then, it's about time you heard it from someone who cares enough to be honest with you," Sam said as he put his hand on Julie's shoulder.

Julie grew painfully aware of Sam's closeness. She had no experience with this. What should she do? Before she could do or say anything, however, Sam leaned down.

"I think I've looked for someone like you all of my life."

His breath was warm against Julie's ear, causing her to shudder. She needed to move away from him, but in order to do so, she'd have to turn and face him. Making her decision, Julie turned quickly and found herself in Sam's arms.

"Don't. I mean, I . . . ," Julie stammered. Why couldn't she say what she wanted to say? Then again, what was it she wanted to say?

"Don't be afraid of me," Sam whispered as he lifted Julie's face to meet his. "I'd never hurt you, Julie."

Julie felt her breath quicken at the sound of her name on Sam's lips. She could feel her heart in her throat. "I know," Julie managed to whisper just before Sam lowered his lips to hers.

The kiss lasted only a moment, but when Sam pulled away, Julie realized she'd wrapped her arms around his neck. Frozen in the shock of what she'd done, Julie met Sam's surprised stare.

"Sam," August's voice called out from the front room, "we've got the chess board set up. If you're going to play, you'd best get in here."

The tension was broken by the sound of her brother's voice, and Julie quickly dropped her arms and moved around Sam. "I'd better get back to work," she said as she left the kitchen with Sam staring silently after her.

Chapter 4

The raging wind and snow left Sam little doubt he'd be staying with the Erikssons through another day. He smiled to himself as he dressed for breakfast. Julie would be there! He could hear her now as she moved around in the room next to his.

Maybe he'd been away from women too long, or maybe he'd been too selfish as a young man to notice, but the existence of a woman like Julie Eriksson was a welcome surprise to him.

Julie beat Sam to the kitchen, where Vern had already stoked the fire in the stove. August had another fire burning brightly in the front room, and several oil lamps had been strategically placed to offer the maximum light.

Julie knew better than to open the door, although a look outside was exactly what she desired most. She could hear the wind and knew the storm hadn't let up. How much snow would this blizzard leave behind? Two, maybe three feet? Julie thought of her upcoming job and wondered how much difficulty she'd have maneuvering the snow-packed trails. Maybe she'd grown too soft for the demands of her duties.

"Good morning," Vern said as he came in from one of the back rooms. "How did you sleep?"

"I was nearly asleep before I finished undressing," Julie said with a laugh. "I was just thinking that maybe I'm not cut out for life in the wilds after five years of civilization."

"Nonsense!" Vern exclaimed. "You have Eskimo and Swedish blood in your veins. That combination will overcome any obstacle in your way. You can do it, Jewels. I have confidence in you."

"So do I," Sam said as he stood leaning against the frame of the door. "I think you're more than able to meet any challenge. Of course, you'll find one or two unexpected surprises along the way, but you're one tough gal. I pity the obstacle that stands in your way."

"That's for sure," Vern chuckled as he motioned Julie and Sam to the front room. "Breakfast will be ready in a little while. You two relax in front of the fire, and I'll call you when it's time."

"I wouldn't dream of it," Julie protested.

Her father wouldn't have any part of it. "I'm still in charge here," Vern said in mock sternness. "Now scoot."

Julie shrugged her shoulders and made her way to the front room. Plopping down on the sofa, she stretched her feet out to absorb the warmth of the fire. Flames snapped and crackled as the logs shifted in the grate.

"You make quite the perfect picture sitting there," Sam said as he took a seat at the opposite end of the couch.

Julie felt the full impact of Sam's stare, and without looking at him she replied, "I wish you wouldn't talk like that."

"Why?"

"Because I'm already humiliated enough. You aren't helping matters one bit," she answered simply.

"Humiliated? Why are you humiliated?" Sam asked as he leaned toward Julie.

She grimaced. "I don't know how you can ask that. I'm totally ashamed of the way I acted last night."

"You mean when August beat you at chess?" Sam teased. Julie couldn't hold back her smile. "That's better," Sam added.

"What is?" Julie asked innocently.

"The smile. I love it when you smile," Sam said softly.

Julie shook her head. "I don't understand you, and I don't know how to deal with you," she said honestly.

"Go on," Sam urged.

"Go on?" Julie questioned as she finally looked Sam in the eye. "What do you expect me to say?"

"I expect you to face up to your feelings. You don't have any reason to feel embarrassment. Especially not on account of our kiss."

Julie put her face in her hands and moaned. "I can't believe I'm sitting here talking to you about it. I get kissed for the first time. . ."

"The first time, eh?" Sam questioned with a teasing grin. "So I was the first man to kiss you. I think I like that."

Julie groaned. "Let's just forget it. Please!"

"I don't intend to forget it," Sam said firmly.

"Don't intend to forget what?" August asked as he bounded into the room.

Julie fell back against the couch and rolled her eyes. Sam only laughed. "I don't intend to forget that your sister saved my life. I'd like to do something nice for her. Something special."

"You've already done plenty," Julie said as she got to her feet.

Knowing that August couldn't see him, Sam made a face, nearly causing Julie to laugh. "I think I'll see if Pa needs any help," she said, struggling to keep a straight face.

Breakfast passed quickly with the men sharing all the news they could think of. Julie remained silent until the subject of the dogs came up.

"I'll need all the help I can get with the dogs this morning," Vern said as he finished a huge bowl of oatmeal. "That storm's wreaking havoc with everything, and I've got to get treatment to the sick dogs and food to all of them."

"I'll be happy to help," Sam said, pushing his chair back from the table.

"Me, too," Julie agreed. "In fact, why don't I take care of the sick ones? That's my field of interest."

"That sounds great," Vern said and smacked his hands down on the table. He'd made that gesture often throughout Julie's childhood, and it always signaled that he was ready for action.

Julie hastily finished her oatmeal and got to her feet. "I'll be ready as soon as I get my coat and mukluks."

"Then the rest of us better get with it, or Julie will have everything done before we get out there," August added.

"Sounds good," Sam said and reached over for his own mukluks.

By the time Julie came back into the kitchen, the men were ready to go. Securing her parka, Julie followed her father and brother, with Sam bringing up the rear. When Vern opened the back door, a gusty wind sent them all back a step, putting Julie squarely into Sam's arms. Despite Julie's push to break away, Sam's grip remained firm. Deciding not to take the action personally, Julie continued to follow her brother into the snow.

"You come with me, Julie. I'll show you what I need done," Vern yelled above the wind. Julie nodded and felt Sam release her as she moved away to go with her father. She watched as Sam went with August to where the dogs were kept behind the house.

Vern ushered Julie into the outbuilding. While it wasn't warm, the building provided welcome relief from the blowing snow.

"Here," Vern said as he pulled Julie to the medicine cabinet. "I still keep all my concoctions and tonics in here. We're blessed to have only five dogs with any health problems. One is Sam's lead dog, Kodiak. He's getting a little extra care after the soaking he got in the Nome River. Other than that, he'll be fine and doesn't really need anything."

"Do you want me to feed him?" Julie asked.

"Yes," her father replied. "I've got a drum of dried fish over in the corner and a barrel of my own special blend for the sick dogs."

"What's wrong with the others?" Julie questioned as she pushed back her parka hood.

"Buster tangled with a trap. He's in the pen along the south wall. I had to put twenty-two stitches in his hind leg. That ought to be easy for you to take care of. The rest have a bowel infection. I have a list on the table of what I've been giving them and how much food they're getting."

"Sounds simple enough. I'll start with Buster."

"If you're all right with all of this, I'll go help the guys with the regular feeding and watering," Vern replied and opened the door. "It's mighty bad out there. If you come looking for us or want to help, be sure to tie a rope to the post outside and then to yourself."

"I will," Julie promised and turned to examine Buster as her father closed the door behind him.

Julie worked for nearly an hour with the sick dogs. She offered each one a tender hand and a soft, soothing voice. The dogs whined and licked at Julie's hands as she stroked their fur.

"You're a good bunch of dogs," Julie said as she dished out their food into individual tins. The dogs cocked their heads first to one side and then the other, as if trying to understand what she was saying.

After giving each dog his ration of food and water, Julie pulled her hood up and dug her mittens out of her pocket. Kodiak yipped and whined for extra attention, and Julie couldn't resist the look on his black and white face.

Putting her mittens on the hard dirt floor, she knelt beside the happy dog. "You're just like your master," she said as she rubbed the dog rigorously. "What is it with you two?" Kodiak licked her hand and then, without warning, gave Julie a hearty lick across the lips.

"You *are* just like him!" Julie exclaimed and got to her feet. She wiped her face with the back of her parka sleeve, picked up her mittens, and went in search of her father.

The wind refused to subside. Standing beside the sick dog building, Julie couldn't see the house, which stood less than twenty feet away. The snow mixed with pelting ice, and Julie winced as it stung her unprotected face.

Forgetting her father's warning about tying herself down, Julie felt her way along the building, knowing that the dogs were just to the north. She strained to listen for any sound of conversation or noise as the men worked with the dogs, but the howling wind blended every sound into one massive roar.

Julie felt her eyelids grow heavy with ice as she moved past the edge of the building and, with outstretched hands, walked in the direction of the dogs.

Taking ten gingerly placed steps, Julie again squinted her eyes against the ice and snow in order to get her bearings. She couldn't see anything but snow. She called out to her father and brother, but the wind drowned out her voice. Fear gripped her heart, and Julie scolded herself for being so helpless. Bolstering her courage, Julie pressed forward. The dogs had to be just within reach.

After struggling against the storm's pressing power for more than twenty minutes, Julie admitted to herself that she was lost. Angry with herself for not heeding her father's instructions, Julie began to pray.

"Lord, I know I've done the wrong thing in not listening to my father. Please forgive me and help me find my way out of this storm." Just then Julie thought she heard the yip of a dog and moved rapidly in the direction of the sound.

She pushed back her parka in order to better hear and instantly regretted the action. Pulling the hood back into place, Julie wandered aimlessly, searching for any kind of landmark that would distinguish her whereabouts.

Cold seeped into her bones, bringing excruciating pain to her legs. Julie regretted having not dressed more appropriately for the outdoors. She'd remembered her mukluks and parka, of course, but she hadn't thought to bring along her scarves or to wear sealskin pants. Now she was paying the price.

Desperation caused an aching lump to form in her throat, but Julie knew crying would only ensure worse problems. A heavy gust of wind took her by surprise, knocking her into a snowbank. Sitting in the snow, Julie suddenly realized how tired she was. Her mind felt muddled from the strain.

"If I rest for a minute," Julie said, rubbing her mittens against her frozen face, "then I'll feel clearer-headed and be able to go on." Something inside her warned Julie that this wasn't wise, but she couldn't fight the need to rest.

Looking up, Julie realized she was snow-blind. There was nothing to indicate that civilization was anywhere nearby. When she moved to shift her weight, Julie heard a crunching sound come from within her parka. Ice had formed on her back and chest from the sweat of her search.

An alarm went off in her mind. That crunching sound meant that she was freezing to death. "Yes," she thought aloud as she got to her feet. "This is the way you freeze. You have to keep moving, Julie. You can't rest, or you won't wake up! Oh, God, send someone to find me. Please God, rescue me before I die."

Stumbling in her blindness and pain, Julie fell against the trunk of a tree. She leaned against it for a moment, licked her lips, and forced her mind to focus on moving. "I don't want to die," she whispered over and over. "I want to live."

Julie wrapped her arms around the trunk and sank into the wet snow. *It isn't at all unpleasant,* she thought. *If a body has to die, freezing to death is at least a simple way to go.* She felt sleep come upon her; they called it "the white death." *Funny,* she thought, *they also call tuberculosis white death because of the thick, white substance that patients cough up from their lungs.* Why had she thought of that? It was strange that something so insignificant to her life as TB should come to her mind now. She'd never need to worry about such diseases again. Not now that she was nearly dead.

"Good boy, Kodiak. You found her. Julie! Julie, wake up." Sam's face floated only inches above hers. "Julie, stand up. Walk with me." Sam was pulling her to her feet.

Julie tried to concentrate on his words as Kodiak whined at her knee. She even attempted to give him a smile. "I'm glad you found me," Julie whispered. She tried to walk, but stumbled and fell against Sam.

Sam easily lifted Julie into his arms and pulled his way back to safety on the rope he'd secured around his waist. Was he too late? There was no way to tell how long she'd been sitting in the snow. Sam gritted his teeth and prayed that she would live. *She has to live,* Sam thought as he moved quickly to the house.

Chapter 5

Julie heard the men rushing around her. She felt her father pulling off her parka, while Sam and August worked to unlace her mukluks. She was dazed and groggy from the cold, and only the pain in her feet reminded her that she'd come terribly close to freezing.

"We've got to get her warmed up," Sam said as he rubbed Julie's feet.

"I'll build up the fire and heat some rocks to put in bed with her," August offered. "We can pack them around her blankets."

"Let's get her to her room," Vern suggested.

"Lead the way," Sam replied as he got to his feet and lifted Julie before August or Vern could move.

Vern nodded and August went to the fireplace. Sam followed Julie's father, ever mindful of Julie's near-lifeless body.

"Put her on the bed," Vern said as he pulled back the covers.

"We'd better get her out of these clothes," Sam said, without any concern for the propriety of the situation. "They're still frozen, but when they thaw, she'll be soaked."

"You're right, of course," Vern answered with a worried look on his face.

Sam was already unfastening Julie's belt as Vern prepared to pull the icy denim jeans from his daughter's half-frozen frame.

Pulling off the pants, Vern leaned over and felt the heavy woolen long johns that Julie had wisely thought to wear.

"These are dry," he said with a sound of relief.

"That's good," Sam said and added, "but this shirt was sweat-soaked. It was frozen solid, but it's already starting to melt. I'd suggest you get her a dry one. I'll leave the room so you can change her privately."

Vern nodded. "I'll take care of it now. You might want to help August."

Sam reluctantly left Julie's side. His brown eyes betrayed the concern in his heart. *Dear God*, he prayed silently, *You must save her!* Pausing at the door, Sam shook his head and took a deep breath before adding, *Thy will be done.*

August was lining stones in the fireplace when Sam entered the front room.

"How is she?" August questioned anxiously. He glanced up and met Sam's worried expression. "Is she going to make it?"

"I don't know yet," Sam said as he handed rocks to August. "She's pretty cold and her pulse is real slow. I wish I had my duck down comforter. It's of little use to anyone back at my cabin."

"We've got a goose down mattress on Pa's bed," August said hopefully. "Could we make use of it?"

"We might be able to cut it open at one end and slide Julie inside," Sam replied in an eager tone. "Would your father mind?"

"Not if it's going to save Julie's life," August said, dusting his hands off as he got to his feet. "It belonged to my mother. It was her most beloved possession. She always said it was like sleeping on a cloud. She wouldn't even use it for everyday. Come on," he motioned. "Let's go get it."

Sam helped August remove all the bedding, and together they pulled the mattress off the bed.

"I can manage this," Sam said as he hoisted the mattress on his back. "You get some of those rocks. Get the flattest ones and we'll put them under Julie. The rest we can put over and around her."

"That ought to warm her up," August said and went to retrieve the rocks from the fire.

Julie moaned, speaking in her delirium. "Tried to find the way," she whispered. "Papa!"

"I'm here, darling," Vern said as he finished buttoning the dry flannel shirt he'd just clothed his daughter in. He patted Julie's arm and talked loudly to her.

"You can't sleep now, my Jewels. It's time to wake up. Come on, we're all waiting for you."

"Too tired," Julie whispered. "Let me sleep."

Just then Sam entered the room, bringing in the feather mattress.

"If you don't object, I'd like to cut this open and put Julie inside. I think the goose down will warm her faster than the wool blankets."

"That's brilliant, Sam," Vern said as he pulled a knife from its sheath on his belt and handed it to him. "Be my guest."

Sam sliced the end of the mattress open just as August came in with a tray of warmed rocks.

"This is going to be a real team effort," Sam said as goose feathers puffed out of the open end of the mattress. "Vern, if you can hold this, I'll lift Julie while August arranges the rocks on her bed. After he's finished, we'll put the mattress on the rocks and put Julie inside it."

The father and son nodded. Sam went to Julie's bedside. She looked so pale and help-less. Her dark hair spread out around her, making her face seem unnaturally white.

Sam thought she looked beautiful, more beautiful than any other woman he'd known. He'd lost his heart to her and prayed that she'd live long enough for him to share a place in her heart.

Cradling Julie as though she were a child, Sam stepped back and let August and Vern work. It was only a matter of seconds before they were ready to put Julie inside the mattress. Together, they eased her down into the goose feathers.

"Now, August, how about some more of those rocks? We can pack them all around the sides and put some on top as well," Sam said as he pulled the mattress up to meet just under Julie's chin.

Julie murmured incoherent words as the men worked around her.

"I'll get some coffee on the stove and warm some cider. That way we can start getting her insides warmed up as well," Vern suggested. "Sam, would you mind staying with her?"

"You know I wouldn't. Go on. I'll be here, friend," Sam replied, and Vern hurried from the room.

When Vern returned, he took turns with Sam and August forcing warm fluids into Julie's mouth. The passing hours filled the men with apprehension. Were they doing enough or had they forgotten something?

As warmth entered Julie's body, she felt as though the blood were thawing in her veins. Pain roused her to consciousness. When she opened her eyes, Sam's face stared back at her.

"Hello," Julie said nonchalantly.

Sam smiled broadly. "Hello, yourself. How do you feel?"

"Buried alive," Julie said as she tried to sit up.

"You stay put, Jewels," her father spoke authoritatively. "You nearly froze to death."

"I remember," Julie said as she fell back against the pillow.

"You gave us a bad scare, little sister," August said, leaning over the foot of Julie's bed. "I think you aged me ten years, and I'm positive you did the same to Sam."

"That's for sure," Sam laughed.

Julie shook her head at the three men.

"How long did it take for you to find me?" she asked.

"That depends on how long you were with the dogs," Sam answered.

"It couldn't have been much more than an hour. Maybe half again as much."

"Well, let's see." Vern figured in his head. "We started around nine. That would've made it ten or ten-thirty when you left the building. We didn't find out that you were missing until noon. After that we took turns looking for you. Sam and Kodiak found you just after two."

"Kodiak?"

"That's right. When we weren't having any success finding you, we decided to get help from the dogs. Since you'd been working with Kodiak, we put him onto your scent, and he helped Sam locate you."

"Is he all right?" Julie questioned weakly.

"Who? Sam?" Vern teased.

"No, no. Kodiak. He didn't get too cold, did he?"

"You stop worrying about that dog. He's doing fine," Vern chided. "We need to know how you feel."

"I hurt," Julie answered honestly. "I suppose that's a good sign. I feel like I ought to be issuing a lot of thank you's." She looked at the three men who watched her so intently and added, "I thank God for all of you."

Vern's eyes grew misty. "Come on, August. Let's get some more rocks heated. Sam, you make sure she drinks more of this hot cider."

"I will," Sam promised as Vern and August disappeared out the door.

Julie looked at Sam. He hadn't shaved, and the shadow of stubble on his face only made him more handsome. "Thank you for saving me," she whispered.

"You've already thanked me," Sam stated as he helped her to drink the cider. "Several times."

"I did? When?"

"When I found you. When you were lying here muttering in your sleep. In fact," Sam said with a self-assured grin, "you said quite a few interesting things."

Julie swallowed hard to steady her nerves. "I did? Well, I imagine the cold affected my mind."

"Oh, I don't know about that," Sam said in a thoughtful way that made Julie wonder what she'd said.

"Just who are you, anyway?" she questioned, causing Sam to burst out laughing.

"What a question! You know full well who I am. Your brother and I have known each other for seven years."

"I know all that," Julie said as she stared at the ceiling to avoid losing herself in Sam's eyes. "I want to know, well, I want to know more."

Sam laughed. "All right. Where would you like me to begin?"

Julie's forehead furrowed slightly as she considered what she wanted to ask. "I suppose at the beginning," she finally answered. "Where were you born?"

"Sacramento, California, in 1889—although we weren't there long enough for the ink to dry on the Bible entry. My father was bent on finding gold. He was always late to everything, including the gold rush."

Julie laughed. "Unlike his son, who seems to make a habit of arriving right on time."

"My father had big dreams. He was one of the reasons I came on up to Nome after my mother died," Sam answered.

"Is your father dead as well?"

Sam nodded. "He got into a fight over a claim. The man took a knife out and killed him then and there. They strung the killer up not twenty feet from where my father lay dead and hanged him. My mother was never the same after that. She was left with three children and had no idea how to support them. The miners were good to her, however. They took up a collection and gave her three hundred dollars."

"What happened after that?" Julie asked, fascinated with Sam's story.

"She moved us around. Sometimes she did laundry for other miners. Other times she'd cook and run a boardinghouse. When my sister married and moved off, I was thirteen and my younger sister was nine. Ma moved us to Seattle, where talk of the gold rush to Nome and the Klondike was all I ever heard tell about. It got in my blood, and I promised myself that I'd one day make the trip to Nome and find the gold that had eluded my father."

"Sounds interesting," Julie said, "but why did it take you so long before you came to Nome?"

"I couldn't leave my mother and sister, and they didn't want any part of it. My mother was getting old, so I went to work. I did a little bit of everything but finally stayed with shipyard work. My sister married at sixteen and offered to take my mother back East with her, but Ma wanted to stay close to where my father was buried. She made me promise to bury her in California, so I stayed on."

"You never married?" Julie asked boldly.

"No," Sam said with a smile. "I never found the right woman. My mother died not long before my twenty-eighth birthday, and right after I got her buried alongside my father, I boarded a ship for Nome and never looked back."

"It must have been lonely for you," Julie said thoughtfully. She knew how the loss of her own mother had left an unfillable hole in her heart.

"Yeah, I guess it was in some ways. Of course, I had the comfort of knowing she was saved. I'd see her again, and that made it a lot easier to deal with."

Julie's eyes opened wide. "So you're a Christian?"

Sam grinned. "Yes, I am."

"Tell me how you came to know God," Julie said as she shifted her weight.

August and Vern came in with a tray full of rocks. "Sam, you take the rocks from the bed, while we put these hot ones in their place," Vern said, using tongs to place hot rocks around Julie's covered feet.

August held the tray, while Vern positioned each rock. Sam put the cooled rocks in a pile on the floor, and when he reached beneath Julie to retrieve the rocks August had placed underneath her, the girl began to laugh.

"I thought this mattress was a little lumpy. Now I see that it was just that I was sleeping on rocks."

Sam bent over her and reached across to get the last of the stones. He gave Julie a wink and quickly handed the rocks to Vern.

"We'll warm up another batch, Sam. How are you doing, Jewels?" Vern asked as he put a hand to his daughter's forehead. "You feel much warmer. That's a good sign. Let's just hope you don't suffer from frostbite."

"Please don't worry, Papa," Julie said and pulled her arm out from the mattress to touch her father's hand. Feathers flew everywhere, causing Julie to sneeze. It was only then that she realized they'd stuffed her inside the goose down mattress. "What a wonderful idea! Who thought to put me here?" she asked.

"It was Sam's idea," August replied. "Sam was determined to save your life, and he usually gets what he wants. They don't call him Lucky Sam for nothing."

"Lucky Sam," Julie echoed as she looked up and met Sam's eyes.

"That's right, and so's the part about getting what I want," Sam declared.

Vern and August laughed as they left the room, but Julie bit her lower lip and stared thoughtfully at the man who remained at her bedside.

Sam returned the look and then spoke. "Now, where was I? Oh, yeah, you were asking me how I came to know Christ. Well, my mother was saved; my sister, too. I always tagged along with them to church on Sunday, at least whenever I could. When I was seventeen, I took a job on a fishing boat. We were pretty far into the Pacific one day when a storm blew up and destroyed the ship. I was left clinging to a piece of the craft, while the storm tossed me back and forth.

"I began to pray like I'd never prayed before. I asked God to save me, and I didn't mean just my worthless hide. I prayed for redemption, and I prayed for deliverance. Some people come to God in a quiet way, but I came to Him in a flash of lightning on the stormy Pacific.

Right after I asked Jesus into my heart, a wave came crashing down over my head, and I kind of figured I'd been forgiven, redeemed, and baptized all at once."

Julie laughed. "What happened next?" she questioned as she caught her breath.

"He saved me. The storm calmed just like the time in the Bible when Jesus stilled the waves. I was found by another fishing vessel about an hour later."

"How fascinating," Julie said with true admiration in her voice.

"Yeah, I guess you could say that," Sam said thoughtfully. "I'm just mighty glad God never gave up on me. He's been a powerfully good friend to have alongside all these years."

Julie liked the open way in which Sam talked about God. It was exactly the way she felt about Him. He was so much more than a figurehead, sitting out there somewhere in heaven. God was a good friend and a constant comfort. Julie felt her thoughts blending to include her admiration of Sam. Had God sent Sam into her life for more than friendship? Already he'd saved her life twice, and whenever she was with him, the aching loneliness she'd known for so many years was absent.

Julie grew suddenly distant, and Sam put his hand out to touch her face.

"Don't," Julie whispered. Instead of getting mad, as Julie had anticipated he would, Sam just shrugged his shoulders and got to his feet.

"I think I'll go find us something to eat," he said and left Julie to contemplate her conflicting emotions.

Chapter 6

Julie recovered quickly from her brush with death. She hadn't suffered any permanent damage, although her pride was sorely bruised. The day after her ordeal, she felt good enough to be up and joined the men in the front room for games of chess and checkers.

"Sometimes," Vern began as he lit one of the oil lamps, "I think I'll be glad when they string electricity this far. Other times, I'm just as glad not to have it to mess with. When the wind picks up past twenty knots, the lines blow down anyway, and then you have to dig the lamps back out."

"Yeah," August agreed as he moved his bishop to threaten Sam's queen, "but staying at the hotel in Nome sure spoils a fellow."

"When did you stay at the hotel in Nome?" Julie asked curiously. "I can't imagine either one of you leaving the dogs long enough."

"It was something your mother wanted to do," Vern answered.

Julie looked up from the table. "Mother? She always seemed to enjoy it here. I never heard her mention a preference for life in Nome."

"Oh, she wasn't partial to Nome. It was just that she knew we'd never lived in a place with electricity or telephone."

"Well, I'll be," Julie said as she shook her head. "I never would have thought it."

"I never would've thought an old sourdough like you would have forgotten how to take care of herself in the snow, either," Vern said as his eyes narrowed ever so slightly. "Julie, you can't be out there on the trail without paying attention to your surroundings."

"Nor to the survival skills that you've no doubt known all of your life," Sam added.

Julie felt as though she were a small child being taken to task. "I know I was foolish. I've readily admitted it, and I've even taken to reading some of Grandfather's books about surviving in the North," Julie said, alluding to books that her mother's father had brought with his family during the gold rush.

"Books can't teach you everything. Besides, you've lived it almost all your life. You need to sit back and pay attention for your own good," Vern said seriously, adding, "August and I will work on your memory."

Julie smiled and jumped three of her father's checkers. "Crown me."

The day passed pleasantly, and as long as they sat in her father and brother's company, Julie didn't feel uncomfortable around Sam. She even enjoyed hearing about his exploits. Sometimes his stories involved August, and Julie shook her head in disbelief.

"I'm amazed that August never brought you home before I left for the outside," Julie stated, calling the lower forty-eight by the term used by most people in the northern territories.

She remembered the five years she'd listened to people in Seattle call Alaska "the frozen North" or "Seward's icebox." Julie just called it "home" and longed for it with all her heart.

"And I suppose that's as much a reason as any," August was saying as Julie stared blankly into space.

"Uh, sorry," Julie said as she cleared her thoughts. "What were you saying?"

"You asked why Sam had never come home with me," August replied.

"And?" Julie questioned over Vern and Sam's chuckles.

"And, I told you. Sam was working a claim that took all of his energy. He didn't dare leave it unoccupied."

"Yeah," Sam agreed. "I was fortunate to have August's help. I don't think I left the claim for the first three years."

"Do you still work it?" Julie asked, suddenly realizing that she knew very little about Sam's current life.

"No," Sam replied as he put August in check. "I sold the claim to the Hammon Consolidated Gold Fields. Mr. Summers, the superintendent, came out to offer me an impressive amount of money for the claim. I'd already made plenty off the mine and was thinking of selling anyway. By the time we'd finished settling, I had more money in the bank than I'd ever need to use."

"You could've sent it to your sisters," Julie said innocently.

Sam's brow wrinkled and behind his beard stubble, Julie could see him grit his teeth. "They're dead."

"Both of them?" she questioned.

"Yes," Sam replied sadly. "My youngest sister was killed in an accident, and my older sister died during the influenza epidemic."

"How awful," Julie replied.

"We lost an awful lot of folks up here as well," August said as he conceded defeat to Sam. "Especially the Eskimos and Indians. They can't stand up to some of the diseases that accompanied the white man north."

Sam nodded and began to reset the chess board. "I know. I remember reading in the *Nome Nugget* that the influenza epidemic left more than ninety-one flu orphans."

"That's true," Julie replied, remembering the awful time. "Poor things. Some of them are still quite young."

"It's always amazing who lives and who dies in a situation like that," Sam said, sitting back. "I always wonder what God's overall plan is when I see a family of youngsters left without their folks."

"Me, too," Julie agreed. "And I have a real hard time when children are the victims of sickness. I've had to nurse dying children," she added, remembering her days in the Seattle hospital. "I don't think I'll ever get used to it." Her words sobered the atmosphere considerably.

"Yet," Vern finally spoke, "we have to trust God's wisdom. He always knows best. I know when your mother was dying, she kept reminding me of Job and how much he endured. 'Curse God and die,' Job's wife told him. Agneta used that example whenever I grumbled too much about the injustice of her condition. She loved to remember Job's patience and strength whenever her own gave way to the sickness. Her favorite verse was Job 13:15: 'Though he slay me, yet will I trust in him.' I admired her loyalty. It strengthened my faith."

"I can well imagine," Sam said with a thoughtful look toward Julie. "A woman of strong faith is one to be cherished. I don't think God intended for any man to live alone."

"You know," Vern said as Julie won the checkers game, "I believe the Bible says that two are better than one."

Sam nodded. "It sure does. It's in Ecclesiastes. Two are better than one; because they have a good reward for their labour."

" 'For if they fall, the one will lift up his fellow: but woe to him that is alone when he falleth; for he hath not another to help him up.' " Julie recited the verse from somewhere in her memory.

Vern reached for his Bible and flipped through its pages to Ecclesiastes four. He continued reading from verse eleven. " 'Again, if two lie together, then they have heat: but how can one be warm alone?' " Julie glanced up at Sam and found his eyes on her.

"That's true," August added. "I remember times when the weather was like this, and Ma would put us all together in bed with you and her."

"I remember that, too," Julie said, forgetting about Sam's fixed stare. "I loved it. I always felt safe and warm. It was so hard to leave and go to Seattle. It was like you were all here together in one safe haven, and suddenly I was left out."

"You were never left out," August said with a smile. "Ma always remembered you in prayers, and Pa talked about you constantly."

Vern nodded and reached across to affectionately squeeze Julie's shoulder. "That's true. Even in Seattle, you were an important part of our family. Almost as if you were never separated from us."

"That's sure not how it felt in Washington," Julie responded. Forgetting about Sam and how he might perceive her, Julie continued. "I remember watching Nome disappear as we steamed to the south. I wanted to jump overboard and come home. I was so lonely. School left so little time for any kind of social life, and I didn't get to attend church regularly because of my hospital duties." Julie needed to say more, but it was difficult to continue, so she fell silent.

"Didn't you have any friends among the other students?" Vern asked.

Julie thought for a moment. "I suppose there were one or two whom I felt comfortable with. We studied together and often worked together, but it wasn't like having a real friend. I suppose that's my own fault, though. I didn't want to be close to anyone."

"Why was that?" Sam asked.

"I guess I was worried about having ties in Seattle. I didn't want anything to hamper my homecoming. I suppose I created my own prison."

"Oftentimes we do," Vern said as he closed his Bible. "Everyone is different, and how they handle their fears varies. I wish I could have saved you the loneliness."

"Truth is," Julie said without thinking, "I still feel empty at times. I have my faith in

God and my family, but, well. . ." She paused for a moment. "I don't know. I guess I'm just anxious to be at my job." Getting to her feet, Julie was just as anxious to drop the subject. "Now, if you'll all excuse me, tomorrow is October twelfth and that means it's August's birthday. I'm going to see what I can whip up in the kitchen."

August grinned. "I figured everybody would forget."

"Just why do you think I braved the weather to come this way?" Sam said and laughed. "Besides, why do you think I let you win at chess yesterday?"

"Well, if it was a birthday present, you should have let me win today as well. I'm a bit humbled by the entire experience," August said as he got up, stretched, and looked at his watch. "I guess I'd better go check on the dogs."

"That'd be a good idea," Vern said. "Let's go."

"I'll lend you a hand," Sam offered.

"No." Vern waved him off. "Somebody has to keep an eye on *her*," he said, pointing at Julie.

"Me?" Julie questioned as she pointed to herself. "I don't need a keeper. I'll be just fine. I promise to behave myself and stay in the kitchen."

Vern smiled at his daughter. "I'd feel better if Sam kept an eye on you."

Julie rolled her eyes and shrugged her shoulders before she let the men go. *Who is going to keep an eye on Sam?* she wondered.

By the time the sun began to set, the weather had calmed, and the temperature had risen significantly. The silence left in the wake of the roaring wind was unsettling.

Julie bundled up against the cold and waved off her father's protests. "I'm just going outside to look things over. There's no wind, no snow, and I'd best get used to the elements. I have a job to report to in little over a week," she said, more harshly than she'd intended.

Vern nodded. "I can't help worrying. I love you, Jewels."

Julie's expression softened as she reached out to put a reassuring hand on Vern's arm. "I love you, too, Papa. Please don't worry. I was very foolish the other day. I realize my mistake, and I won't make it again."

Vern embraced his daughter momentarily and then opened the back door for her. "Have fun," he said. Julie knew it was his way of giving her his blessing and confidence.

Julie walked out into the darkness. She turned back and saw the cheery glow of light shining from the house. Out on the nursing trail, there would only be the lighted windows of strangers to look forward to. Was she doing the right thing? Was she really cut out for the solitary existence her job required?

"You're mighty deep in thought," Sam said as he came from somewhere out of the blackness.

"I was just thinking about my work."

"Apprehensive?" Sam questioned.

Julie looked rather quizzically at Sam. "How did you know?"

"Just something I felt."

"Well," Julie continued before Sam could get personal, "I'm sure everyone has second thoughts. I'm just settling mine, that's all. How about you? What brings you out tonight?"

"I just bought two new dogs from your father. We staked them out with my team this afternoon, and I was checking up on them. They fit right in," Sam said as he moved closer to Julie. "I figure we'll leave sometime in the morning."

"Oh, so soon?" Julie questioned.

"Disappointed?" Sam asked with a grin.

Julie moved away from Sam and noticed the sky. "Look!"

Overhead, the sky filled with pulsating light. Green, pink, and white lights streaked the night blackness, and the heavens exploded with northern lights.

"The aurora," Sam said as he came to stand directly behind Julie.

"I'd nearly forgotten," Julie said. She felt a trembling in her body at the nearness of Sam.

For a long time neither Julie nor Sam said a word. They watched the dancing lights as the colors faded, then radiated and grew brilliant again. The stillness of the windless night made the cold easily tolerated, but Sam moved closer to block the chill from Julie's back.

Julie decided she had to deal with Sam. He wasn't going to go away, and even though he planned to leave the next morning, it was necessary to tell him exactly where she stood.

"Sam," Julie said as she turned to face him. She hadn't realized just how close he was. Sam reached out and quickly pulled Julie into his arms. "Wait just a minute," Julie protested. "You can't keep doing this."

"Oh, yes, I can, and I intend to do it often after we're married," Sam said, refusing to let Julie loose.

"Married? I'm not going to—" Her words fell into silence as Sam lowered his mouth to hers. Julie expected the same brief type of kiss Sam had given her in the kitchen, but instead his mouth was firmly fixed on hers in a deeply passionate kiss. Julie had set out to concentrate on not responding, but easily lost that thought as Sam aroused feelings inside her that Julie had never known existed. Giving in, Julie allowed Sam to pull her tightly to his chest as her arms went around his neck.

When Sam pulled back, Julie felt herself gasp for air. "You'll never stop feeling lonely until you give in to your heart and marry me. Remember, two are better than one," Sam whispered.

"But I prayed about working as a nurse. I know it's my destiny." Julie forced the words from her muddled mind.

"And you are mine," Sam said before silencing Julie's protests with his mouth.

Chapter 7

On the first day of November, Julie reported to Dr. Welch at the two-story Maynard-Columbus Hospital. The whitewashed clapboard building offered the most thorough medical help in northwestern Alaska and had seen more than its share of action.

After meeting with Dr. Welch for a few days, Julie's confidence returned. Dr. Welch was habitually happy. He was at his best when he was working in and around his patients, and his nurses enjoyed his vibrant love of life. Emily Morgan, training to take over as head nurse at the hospital, told Julie that it was Dr. Welch's devoted wife, Lula, who'd made the gray-haired doctor so content.

"You know," Emily said as she showed Julie to a small office, "she married him right after his internship in Los Angeles. She's worked alongside him for many years."

"Yes, I know," Julie said as she slipped out of her parka. "I'm quite familiar with both the doctor and his wife. I was born in Nome."

"I didn't know you were native to Alaska," Emily said. "Oh, by the way, this is Nurse Seville," she added as a rather plain-looking woman came into the office.

"Glad to meet you," the woman said, extending her hand. "I'm Bertha."

"It's nice to meet you as well," Julie said and shook the woman's hand. "I'm Julie Eriksson."

"Well, it's quite a challenge you've carved out for yourself. I've made calls with Dr. Welch to the nearest Eskimo settlements, and I've never really enjoyed the sled travel. Although I must say, Doc enjoys every bit of it. But you'll be out there on your own, driving your own team and facing the elements. I admire your spirit," Bertha said honestly.

"Thank you," Julie answered just as Dr. Welch entered the room.

"Are you ready to go?" he questioned as he took a seat behind a paper-laden desk.

"I sure am," Julie responded. "I came to say good-bye and see if there were any last-minute instructions."

"Take good care of your dogs," Welch answered firmly. "Of course, take good care of yourself as well. Keep detailed records, and let me know if there's anything that needs my attention."

"I will," Julie promised and picked up her parka. "I'd best be on my way. My first stop is nearly two hours away."

"At least the weather's been good. Unseasonably so, if you ask me," the veteran doctor replied. After nearly twenty years in Alaska, he spoke with authority.

"Well, remember me in your prayers," Julie said as she pulled on her coat.

"That we will," Nurse Emily replied.

Moving out on the open trail, Julie had plenty of time to think. Too much time. She'd been working for nearly six weeks, and during that time, she'd seen just about everything.

She'd delivered babies, set broken bones, stitched up wounds, and dealt with a multitude of other ailments. Overall, her experience had been a good one, but always there were the hours alone on the trail when the only thing she could think about was Sam.

How could one man affect a woman so much that she questioned her purpose in life? Ever since Sam had kissed her and told her he intended to marry her, Julie had been confused.

When Julie was younger and there had been only her mother's driving desire to see her daughter become a nurse, she'd felt certain of her destiny. But Sam was just as strong in maintaining that Julie was his destiny.

Julie stopped the dogs for a brief rest. There were only three to four hours of light a day as Christmas grew near. Usually she woke up in the darkness and moved out, only to spend the daylight hours inside a sod igloo, delivering a baby or tending to some other medical need. She was enjoying this rare opportunity to travel during the daylight hours.

Julie checked her compass and pulled out a small map from inside her parka. If everything went according to plan, she'd be in the next village within two hours. Carefully replacing the compass and map, Julie checked her dogs and took her place at the back of the sled.

"Let's go," she called out, and the dogs immediately picked up a nice trotting pace.

Julie alternated running behind the sled and riding the runners. She'd gradually regained her muscular arms and running legs. Physically, she'd never felt better, but emotionally, she was drained.

"God, please help me," she prayed. The winter sky's pale turquoise color was already giving way to the coming darkness. In the distance, Julie saw the telltale signs of a snowstorm. She called to the dogs to pick up the pace before turning her mind and soul back to God in prayer. "Lord, I don't understand why You sent Sam into my life at this time. I thought I knew what You wanted me to do, but how can I do that and care for a husband? And if You don't want Sam to be my husband, then why did You allow him to complicate things for me?" Julie realized how selfish her prayer sounded and fell silent.

She watched the frozen wasteland pass by her moving sled. The horizon stretched out forever, and yet, just ahead Julie would thrill to the light in the window of some thoughtful villager, and once again she'd be safe.

The dogs seemed to sense the end of the journey and hastened to the place where they would receive fresh tom cod and tallow. *They are smarter than human beings,* Julie thought. *They never press on in a storm when they know it's dangerous, and they're content to do their work and take their rest. If only I could be the same.*

Blackness fell long before Julie reached the small Eskimo village. She kept watch through the darkness as the dogs, confident of their trail, pressed on.

Visions of Sam filled her mind, and for a moment Julie allowed herself to wonder what it would be like to marry Lucky Sam Curtiss.

"Surely I'd have to give up my nursing," Julie mused. "He would expect me to give him my undivided attention. And there would be the possibility of children. A man like Sam would probably want a dozen or more," she added sarcastically. "But then, I hope to one day have a big family, too.

"Why did he have to come?" Julie yelled into the darkness. She hadn't noticed that they were nearly upon the village, and only when Dusty brought the team to a stop did Julie realize why.

"Good boy, Dusty. I was daydreaming again," Julie said as she planted the snow hook.

A middle-aged Eskimo man appeared with his two sons. She recognized the man as George Nakoota. She had tended his youngest child during a bad bout of tonsillitis during her first visit to the village.

"There's warm food inside for you," George said as he helped Julie unload her sled. "The boys and I will take care of the dogs." Julie nodded and went inside. As long as the dogs were fed and bedded down, she could rest.

George's wife, Tanana, helped Julie out of her parka and mukluks. "George heard you coming from far off," Tanana said as she placed the parka over a chair by the oilcan stove.

"I don't see how George can hear these things from so far away," Julie said. "He's always saying that he can hear any storm or animal coming for fifty miles. Those are mighty perceptive ears."

"George does not listen with his ears. He listens with his soul. George and the land are close, like old friends."

"The soul can tell a person a great deal, if we choose to listen to it," Julie agreed. "Have you thought about what I told you when I was here before?"

"I remember when your father used to visit with George and tell him about white man's God in heaven. George said it made nights pass faster with stories from your Bible."

"But they're more than stories, Tanana." Julie hoped her old friend wouldn't be offended by her boldness. "I know you're skeptical of the things that white folks bring to your people—the sickness and disease, the mining operations and such—but honestly, Tanana, God has a great deal of love for you and your people."

"I know that," Tanana agreed, "but He loves me in the Eskimo way."

George came in, bringing the rest of Julie's gear. "Your dogs are looking good, Julie. You've been taking good care of them."

"The people have all been so good to me," Julie said as she sat down at the small, crude table where Tanana was dishing up hot food. "They feed the dogs and me and always give us a warm place to sleep. I have no complaints."

"Any trouble with animals?" George asked as he joined Julie at the table. "I noticed that Dusty looked a bit chewed-on."

"He was," Julie said with a nod. "You've got eyes that are every bit as good as your ears, George. He got into a fight with a village dog. The other dog looks worse, so we count it a victory for him. I'd appreciate it if you didn't tell him otherwise."

George laughed. "You spoil him. He'll grow fat and lazy and never run fast, but I won't tell him."

Julie stayed on in George's village for two days. She treated several bad colds and looked in on George's mother, who'd suffered from an infected wound on her hand. Julie was preparing to leave when George's oldest son came running.

"My father's been hurt," he said breathlessly as he pulled at Julie's arm.

"What happened?" Julie asked, pulling her medical bag from the sled.

"The dogs were fighting, and he tried to pull them apart. His arm is pretty bad."

Julie followed the boy on a dead run to the opposite side of the village where George had been carried to his house. When Julie walked into the house, George had already been placed on the small kitchen table. His arm was a bloody, mangled mess, and Julie wasn't sure that she could save it.

She motioned George's son to hold a cloth to his father's arm. "Put pressure here while I prepare my instruments. Tanana, I'll need some hot water. George, George, can you hear me?" Julie questioned as she leaned down.

"I hear you," George said between gritted teeth.

"I'm going to clean your arm and see what's what. I'm going to do a lot of stitching, and I'd just as soon you not have to be awake for it. I've got some chloroform, and I'm going to put you to sleep," Julie said as she prepared a place for her instruments.

"Julie," George whispered weakly.

He was losing a great deal of blood, and Julie knew she'd have to hurry. "What is it, George?"

"You gonna pray for me?"

"Of course," Julie said with a smile.

"Your pa has talked to me before," George paused and drew a deep breath before continuing, "about eternal life. I think I need to have that about now."

George was always good-natured, even when he was bleeding to death, Julie decided. Nevertheless, she continued as if George had nothing more complicated than a splinter. "John 3:16 says, 'For God so loved the world, that he gave his only begotten Son, that whosoever believeth in him should not perish, but have everlasting life.' You must believe that God sent His Son to save your life. Do you believe that, George?" Julie asked as she washed her hands in carbolic acid before pouring a great amount into a bowl for her instruments.

"I believe," George whispered.

"Then pray with me, George," Julie said as she took fresh water from Tanana. "Dear Father, George knows he's a sinner, and he wants your forgiveness," Julie paused to wave George's son away and poured water over his father's arm.

George bit his lip but refused to cry out. "I'm a sinner, God. Forgive me," he said and looked up at Julie.

Julie nodded and continued, "George wants to accept Your Son, Jesus, so that he might have eternal life."

"I want eternal life," George murmured. "I want Your Son, Jesus."

"And Lord," Julie said as she poured disinfectant over the mangled limb, "help me to mend George's arm. Amen."

George nodded, too weak to speak. Julie poured a liberal amount of chloroform on a clean cloth. "I'm going to put you to sleep now, George." She placed the cloth over

George's nose and mouth.

Instantly, George was rendered unconscious, and Julie flew into action. She picked her way through the strips of flesh, cleaning each one thoroughly and moving on to the deep gashes.

Tanana held a lantern to one side. Periodically, Julie felt for George's pulse and respiration. He was doing well, and Julie felt confident that his relative good health and God's direction would see her through the situation.

After two hours, Julie stood back and assessed her work. Barring infection, George would retain full use of his arm. She decided to stay on in the village until she felt confident the wounds were free from contamination.

Dragging her weary body to bed, Julie thanked God for His direction. She fell asleep listening to George's rhythmic breathing.

With George well on the way to recovering and Christmas only three days away, Julie readied once again to return to Nome. She was determined to be home for Christmas, but she hadn't managed to do any Christmas shopping yet.

She was rechecking the dogs' harness when Tanana approached her. "You have my gratitude for saving George's life. I thanked your white God, too."

"He can be your God as well, Tanana," Julie said as she turned from the dogs.

Tanana nodded and held out several packages. "I'll think about your words, Nurse Julie. These are for you. They are payment for George. I know your Christmas is coming soon, and maybe you will need things for your father and brother. I have made two pairs of sealskin mukluks. They have fox fur inside to make them extra warm."

"Thank you, Tanana. I'll give them to my father and brother for Christmas and tell them that you made them."

The woman smiled broadly and backed up a step. "You are welcome here anytime. We'll look forward to seeing you after your celebration."

Julie nodded and rallied her team. "Hike!" she called out and held onto the sled handle as the dogs, eager to be on the trail, moved out.

Nome looked the same as when Julie had left. She knew she ought to go directly to Dr. Welch's office at the Merchants and Miners Bank of Alaska, but keeping in mind that it was Christmas Eve, she took time, instead, to do a bit of shopping.

She searched through several shops, looking for just the right gifts for Vern and August. She finally settled on some tools for her father and a guitar for August. She smiled as she brought the items out to her sled. August had always wanted to learn to play the guitar, and now Julie would hound him until he could play her a tune.

Julie wrapped the gifts safely inside a large fur pelt and loaded them onto the sled. She started to walk down the street to the hospital when something in the store window caught her attention. A handsome, ivory-handled knife was prominently displayed.

Julie went inside and asked to see it in order to better study the detail of the carving. A talented craftsman had skillfully transformed the ivory into an intricate piece of art. The outline of a dog driver with his sled team was highlighted on the handle of the knife.

Impulsively, Julie purchased the knife for Sam. She hadn't seen him in seven weeks, but the urge to buy him a Christmas gift overruled her better judgment.

Adding the knife to the other gifts on the sled, Julie went in search of Dr. Welch.

Chapter 8

Julie found Dr. Welch, and after quickly exchanging her paperwork and personal assessments of the villages she'd visited, she bid him a Merry Christmas and received permission to go home for the holidays.

"You know," Dr. Welch said as he followed Julie outside, "we're having a bit of a Christmas Eve party, and I know Lula would love for you to join us."

"I've never been one for parties," Julie answered honestly. "I'm just a home girl. I want to be with my family."

"I understand," Dr. Welch said with a smile. "You have a well-deserved rest, and I'll see you the day after New Year's."

"I'll be here," Julie replied with a wave.

Making her way to the dogs, Julie started thinking of Sam. Would he make an appearance on Christmas, and if he did, would she be happy to see him? She tried to forget about him and concentrate on getting home, but nothing could get him out of her thoughts.

Julie looked over each of her dogs, checking their paws and bellies for signs of freezing. They were tired and deserved a good rest, but Julie had no alternative but to drive them home.

"Your team looks a bit spent."

Julie smiled before straightening up to meet Sam's bearded face. "I'll give you that much," she said, pushing her parka hood back. Her black hair had been neatly braided when she'd started out that morning, but now wisps of it blew around her face.

"Is that all?" Sam said with a grin. "I haven't seen you in nearly two months. I was beginning to think I'd scared you off. Thought I might have to come find you."

Julie put her hands on her hips. "Same old Sam."

Sam laughed and watched Julie as she finished with her dogs. "I've been thinking about you," he said. "Now that I know what it is to have you in my arms, I couldn't stop thinking about it."

Julie stiffened slightly. She was unprepared for Sam's boldness. How should she react? Nervously, she shifted from one foot to the other. "I certainly hope you don't plan to repeat the scene here in the middle of Nome's Front Street."

"Why not?" Sam said as he took a step toward Julie.

"Oh, no," Julie said, backing up. "You can't mean it. I have a reputation to preserve, if not for myself, for my career."

Sam stopped and shook his head. "I'm never going to do anything but honor and love you. I would throttle any man, or woman, for that matter, who might blemish your reputation.

However, I think your dogs have earned a rest. Let's take them over to my cabin. I'll hitch my dogs, and we'll give yours a break. There's a snow building up, and I don't want you out here alone. I'll take you home."

"No," Julie protested. "My dogs will be fine. It's only another twelve miles. I couldn't ask you to—"

"You didn't ask, and I am telling you," Sam said as he pointed to the sled. "I expect you to get in the basket while I drive these dogs to my house. If you don't get in on your own, I'll put you there myself. Then we'll just see how your reputation withstands the talk."

"I will not," Julie said as she moved to the back of her sled. She thought to jump on the runners and order Dusty into action, but Sam outmaneuvered her and took hold of Dusty's tugline.

Sam raised a questioning eyebrow and waited for Julie to respond. Julie matched his stare. Her breathing quickened as a smile played at the corner of Sam's lips. He waved his hand in front of him and motioned Julie to the sled.

"All right," Julie said and carefully climbed into the sled basket, narrowly avoiding the gifts she'd purchased. "I give up. You win. Take me home."

Sam laughed and dropped the tugline. He walked down the side of the dog team and leaned over Julie. "That's a good girl," he said and dropped a kiss on her forehead.

Julie squirmed away, blushed, and pulled her hood back in place so that Sam couldn't see her face. She wondered who all in Nome had seen Sam's actions, but before she could glance around, Sam moved the dogs out.

While Julie enjoyed the ride to Sam's house on the outskirts of Nome, she was also nervous. Just knowing that Sam stood on the runners behind her made Julie apprehensive. She tried to concentrate on the excitement of seeing her father and brother and celebrating Christmas.

When Sam stopped in front of the two-story clapboard house, Julie was impressed. It wasn't the type of place she'd pictured Sam in.

"We're home," Sam said in a jovial way. "One day I'll say that, and it'll be true."

Julie tried to appear unaffected by Sam's words, but when he reached down to help her from the basket, she nearly jumped out the opposite side of the sled.

"I wish you'd stop," she said and pushed back her parka hood to better see Sam. "I don't know why you insist on doing this, but I want to go home, and if you aren't going to behave, then I'll drive myself." She was determined to stand her ground.

"You're tired, Julie," Sam said, ignoring her protest. "Why don't you go inside and make yourself comfortable?"

"I can wait out here," Julie said anxiously.

"I know you can wait out here. I know you can drive dogs through bitter cold and horrible blizzards. I know, too, that you have a mind of your own, but I'm every bit as stubborn, and I'm telling you to go in the house and warm up." Sam's words were stern, yet Julie knew they were given out of concern for her welfare.

"I'm touched that you care, Sam, but—"

In three long strides, Sam was at Julie's side. He hoisted her over his shoulder as if he were carrying a sack of grain.

"Put me down," Julie yelled and pounded against Sam's back.

"I'll put you down when we're in the house. We're wasting what few daylight hours we have because you can't cooperate," Sam said as he carried Julie into his house.

Once they were inside, Sam put Julie down. She expected him to try to kiss her again, so she moved quickly away. "All right, you've had your way," she said with a trembling voice.

"Not hardly," Sam said with a grin. "I haven't married you yet." He turned with a laugh and walked out the front door.

Once he was outside, Sam stopped laughing. He'd come very close to pulling Julie into his arms and was still trembling himself when he went to unharness the dogs.

He thought about what he'd done as he fed and watered Julie's team. Sam had never imagined that he'd see Julie in Nome. It had been his plan to question Dr. Welch about her schedule and surprise her for Christmas. But the surprise had been his when he found her standing on Front Street preparing to leave town.

Sam rubbed his beard and sighed. She was a beautiful woman, but more than that, she was intelligent and self-confident, although a bit too stubborn. She was exactly everything that he'd prayed for, everything and more.

"Thank You, God, for sending Julie into my life. I feel sure she's the one You would have me marry. I've prayed so long for a Christian wife, and if Julie is the right one, Lord, then I pray You will help her to see me as the man You have chosen for her. Above all else, Lord, protect her from harm. In Jesus' name, Amen."

Sam glanced back at the house. The woman he planned to marry was sitting inside the home he hoped to one day share with her. He would have loved nothing more than to go inside and share her company in the comfort of his home, but he knew it would only make Julie more uncomfortable, so he put the thought aside.

Sam finished harnessing his eager dogs to Julie's sled. He gave his lead dog, Kodiak, a brief pat on the head before going inside to retrieve Julie.

"You're anxious to be on the road, aren't you, boy?" Kodiak whined as though answering, and Sam laughed. "I'm going. I'm going. I just have to go get our girl, and we'll be off."

Sam bounded up the front steps and peered cautiously through the doorway in case Julie planned to throw anything at him. The sight that caught his eye caused Sam to stop in his tracks. Julie lay innocently sleeping on the couch.

Sam called her name, but Julie slept too deeply to hear him. He approached her sleeping form and gently stroked her cheek. It was rosy from the wind, but soft—just as he remembered from the time he'd last kissed her.

Avoiding the memory, Sam went outside and made a place in the basket for Julie. Once he'd placed several blankets in the basket, Sam went back inside. He threw several of his own things into a pack and loaded it onto the sled. Finally, Sam trudged through the snow to the house of his neighbor, Joe Morely, a bachelor who often traded favors with Sam.

Sam let Joe know he'd be gone for several days and asked if he'd mind tending the dogs. After receiving Joe's promise to watch over the house and animals, Sam went back to his house.

Julie slept soundly as Sam lifted her into his arms and carried her to the sled. The cold air caused her to stir and nestle her face against his chest, but she slept on, dreaming of warm arms and a man named Sam.

Chapter 9

Julie woke up just as Sam led the dog team down the embankment of the Nome River. She couldn't believe that he had packed her into the sled to sleep away the miles between Nome and the Eriksson homestead. Wiping sleep from her eyes, Julie worked her way out of the covers and sat up.

The sky was gray and heavy with snow. Julie knew it would only be a matter of time before those clouds would open up and dump another white blanketing on the Alaskan coastline.

"We're nearly there," Sam said as he moved out on the river ice.

"I hope we're not about to repeat scenes from our last shared trip across the Nome," Julie called up from the basket.

Sam laughed good-naturedly. "You'd better mind your manners, or I'll make you get out and walk, and we both know your ability on ice is questionable."

Julie laughed. "I can manage."

"No doubt," Sam said as he reached the opposite bank. He jumped off the runners and pushed as his ten-dog team pulled. Within seconds they were over the top.

In the fading light, Julie could see the welcoming sight of her home. She would be home with her family for Christmas. In the distance the dogs yipped and howled as Sam's team drew near, alerting Vern and August to their arriving visitors.

Sam halted the sled at the back door and helped Julie from the sled. "You go on in, and I'll unload the basket and take care of the dogs."

Julie started into the house but remembered her gifts. "I need to unpack some of it myself," she said as she turned back to the sled.

"I can take care of it," Sam insisted.

"Look, I'm not just being stubborn this time," an exasperated Julie tried to reason. "I have to take care of some of it myself. It is Christmas Eve, after all."

"I see," Sam said with a grin. "Anything for me?"

"That's a rather presumptuous question," Julie replied. "You'll just have to wait and see." She took a step back and crossed her arms against her body.

"I'm not good at waiting," Sam teased. "Especially when I want something and set my mind to get it."

Julie pretended not to understand his meaning. "You must have caused your family a great deal of trouble on Christmas morning."

"I was a perfect child," Sam said, grinning.

"I'm sure."

"Sure of what?" August asked as he came out the back door.

"Oh, never mind," Julie said with a sigh. "Would you mind helping Sam with the dogs while I get some of my gear?"

"You can just leave it all, and we'll bring it in," August said.

Sam laughed as Julie rolled her eyes. "Don't even start, August. She's got Christmas presents and doesn't want any of us to see them."

"Oh," August replied and went to unharness Kodiak.

Julie turned to Sam. "Now, why can't you be more like him?" Sam shrugged his shoulders and went to help August.

Julie managed to get her gifts inside without running into her father. She was coming out of her room when Vern came in search of her.

"Jewels!" he said as he embraced her. "Good to have you home."

"Good to be home. I wanted to let you know about George Nakoota. He tangled with his dogs and had his arm ripped up pretty bad. I stitched him up, and it looks good for a full recovery."

"He was blessed to have you there," Vern said as he walked with Julie to the kitchen. "He probably would have died if you hadn't been. That village is nearly fifty miles from Nome, and he would have bled to death before he got proper care."

"Well, he's doing fine now, and I know he'll follow my instructions on how to care for the wounds. My biggest frustration with many of the Eskimos is their curiosity. I'll stitch something closed and bandage it up, and before I can recheck it, they've unbandaged it so they can see my handiwork."

Vern chuckled just as Sam and August came in through the back door. "You know where curiosity will get you," Vern added.

"Yeah," Sam answered with a grin. "No Christmas present."

Julie had brought extra sugar and eggs with her from Nome. She was determined to bake something nice for Christmas so she cleared the men from the kitchen.

Darkness fell by two o'clock, but Julie refused to let it dampen her spirits. It was Christmas Eve! She baked a cake and rolled out sugar cookies, a tradition started by her mother to pass the anxious hours.

As Julie used each of her mother's cookie cutters, she remembered with fondness the stories her mother would tell about them. The star was for the Bethlehem star that announced the birth of Christ. The Christmas tree, an outline of an evergreen, reminded them of everlasting life in Christ, and the shape of a bell was to bring to mind the joyous music in heaven whenever a sinner accepted Christ.

Taking a final batch of cookies from the oven, Julie put them aside to cool and turned her attention to the finishing touches on a chocolate cake. Setting out a stack of plates and forks, Julie went to the front room to retrieve the men.

"Who'd like some cake?" Julie asked as she entered the room.

"Cake? We should have Julie home more often," August said, deserting his chess game with Sam in order to take his sister's arm. "I'd love some, Julie. Lead the way."

"Yes," Sam said as he rushed to take Julie's other arm. "Lead the way."

Vern laughed and got to his feet. "I guess I'll just bring up the rear," he said and followed the trio into the kitchen.

They gathered around the table, praising the towering chocolate confectionery. Julie cut the cake and heaped huge slices on each plate.

"Let's have the blessing," Vern suggested as Julie placed a pot of coffee on the table and went for cups.

Julie took a seat at the table. The men joined her, and Vern led them in a short prayer.

"Father, we thank You for the birth of Your Son, Jesus, and the free gift of salvation You gave to us through Him. Thank You for this gathering of loved ones as we celebrate that birth. Amen."

"What say we share our gifts now?" Vern suggested after a bite of cake. "Umm, Jewels, this is excellent."

"It sure is," August agreed. "And I agree with Pa. I'd like to exchange gifts."

Julie shrugged her shoulders. "I guess that's fine by me."

"Then I suggest everyone get their Christmas gifts, and we'll move to the front room," Vern said, adding, "Oh, and Julie, please bring the cake and coffee."

"I'll help her," Sam said as he got to his feet. "I'm trying to stay in Julie's good graces." He picked up the cake and coffee pot and moved to the front room.

Julie followed Sam with the coffee cups and then excused herself to retrieve her gifts. She unwrapped the fur bundle that she'd placed on her bed and revealed the guitar. The knife and tools were in separate boxes, so Julie rewrapped the guitar, tucked it under one arm, and grabbed the other gifts with her hands.

She joined the men in the living room and was surprised to find someone had decorated a small Christmas tree and placed it on a table in the center of the room. Beneath it were several wrapped packages of different sizes.

"How wonderful," Julie said as she placed her own gifts on the table. "I remember the last time we did this."

"It was the year before you left for Seattle," August said, taking a package from beneath the tree.

"Yes," Vern remembered, "and your mother was still here. I remember she made the most wonderful meal. I wish she could be here to enjoy this evening, but in a way, I guess she is."

"She sure is, Pa," Julie said as she took a seat on one of the overstuffed chairs opposite the couch.

"Here," August said, handing his package to Julie. "I got this for you. Merry Christmas."

Julie opened the package to reveal a black lacquer jewelry box with beautiful red ornamentation. "Thank you, August. It's incredible." She opened the box to reveal a red velvet interior and added, "I've never seen anything like it."

"It's Japanese," August said proudly. "The guy I bought it from was trying to raise money to get home. He said it was one of a kind."

"Well, I haven't much in the way of jewelry, but I'll cherish it always," Julie said appreciatively. "That large bundle of fur over there is yours. But I need the wrapping back." She laughed.

August unwrapped the fur to reveal his gift. "A guitar! What a great idea, Jewels. Thanks," he said as he took the guitar out and began tightening the strings. "You didn't know I'd been taking lessons, did you?"

"Then you already have a guitar?" Julie asked disappointedly.

"No. I've been using Sam's."

"Sam's?" Julie said, turning questioning eyes to Sam. "You truly are a man of surprises, Mr. Curtiss."

"You don't know the half of it, Miss Eriksson," Sam said with a laugh.

"Well, with both guitars here it would be a nice touch to our celebration if you'd both play us some Christmas songs," Vern proposed.

"Oh, yes, please!" Julie begged.

"Maybe after all the gifts are opened," Sam said and went to the table. "I have a gift for August as well."

He handed August a small package, which, when opened, revealed a dog harness. Vern and August exchanged curious glances, and Julie laughed as Sam cleared up the mystery.

"Kodiak sired a litter of pups last fall, some of the best quality dogs I've seen in a long time. I'm giving August his pick of the litter," Sam announced. "You've been a good friend, August." The men exchanged a heartfelt hug.

"A very generous gift indeed, friend," August stated, knowing Sam could sell any one of his dogs for better than a thousand dollars. "Thank you, Sam."

"You deserve it," Sam replied and took a seat by the fireplace.

"Well, I have a gift for my daughter," Vern said. He pulled several packages from beneath the tree and brought them to Julie.

"I feel like a little girl again," Julie said as she hurried to open each one. She immediately recognized the gifts as pieces of her mother's prized jewelry collection.

"Jewels for my jewel," Vern said and planted a kiss on Julie's forehead. "These were your mother's favorites."

"Yes, I know," Julie said with tears in her eyes. She held up a necklace against her white blouse. The gold of the chain and brilliance of the ruby settings looked good against Julie's dark hair.

"This was always my favorite one," Julie added as she replaced the ruby necklace, "because you gave it to her for Christmas not long after I turned sixteen. I thought it was the most romantic gift in all the world." She wiped at her eyes before looking into the other packages.

"Those pieces were some I thought you would enjoy. I thought I'd save the rest until you marry," Vern stated, wiping tears from his own eyes as well.

"Thank you, Papa," Julie said as she got up to retrieve her father's gift. "I'm afraid my present pales in comparison." She handed her father the package.

"I've already got the best gift in all the world. You've come home to Alaska, and that's enough for me."

As Julie watched her father unwrap the tools, she wondered if she should give Sam his gift. If she did and he hadn't gotten her anything for Christmas, he might feel bad. He might also take her gift the wrong way and think it was a promise of something more than friendship.

"Well, would you look at this," Vern said as he held up a new hammer. "I can't believe it, but they're exactly what I need. I was planning on buying all of these." Julie watched as he tested the blade of the saw and examined the chisel set. "Perfect!" Vern declared, and Julie leaned back, feeling quite satisfied.

"Oh, I nearly forgot," Julie said as she got up and rushed to her room. She came back with the bundle that Tanana had given her. "These are from George's wife, Tanana. She thought I might not get a chance to do any Christmas shopping, and so she made these mukluks for me in pay for sewing up George."

"Anything that woman makes is a prize to be sure," Vern said as he undid the rawhide strip that tied the package shut. He examined the mukluks before passing one pair to August. "It also helps that she knows our sizes."

"Well, this has been a fine Christmas," Vern said as he stretched out his feet.

"Wait," August said as he went to the tree. "There's another gift here. Who's this one for?"

Julie swallowed hard. It was now or never, she decided, and quickly answered. "That one is for Sam."

Three pairs of eyes turned in surprise at her, and Julie wished she could crawl beneath the chair. "I never had a chance to properly thank him for all he did for me. Merry Christmas, Sam," she said quickly to break the tension.

"Well, I must say this is a surprise," Sam said as he accepted the package from August. He unwrapped the brown paper to reveal the knife and sheath. "It's exquisite," he murmured as he examined the craftsmanship. "I've never had one as fine. Thank you, Julie."

She blushed under the intensity of Sam's eyes. The silence was unbearable, and Julie searched her mind for something to say. "How about those songs, now?" she finally questioned.

"Yes," Vern agreed, "now would be the perfect time." He leaned his head back and closed his eyes.

"I'll get your guitar, Sam," August offered and went to his room.

Sam studied the knife before sheathing it and looping it onto his belt. He was more than touched at Julie's extravagant gift. It signaled a change in their relationship. Had Julie come to approve of the idea of marriage? He couldn't wait until a time revealed itself when he could be alone and offer his own Christmas gift.

After several hours of listening to Sam and August, as well as joining in on all the songs they could think to sing, Vern suggested they read the nativity story. Everyone readily agreed, and while Sam continued to strum the haunting melody of "Silent Night," Vern, August, and Julie took turns reading the second chapter of Luke.

When they'd finished, Vern offered a prayer and got up to stretch. "I think I'm going to retire, but before I do, I'd like to say something. I wasn't looking forward to this holiday. It was always Agneta's favorite, and I knew that it wouldn't be the same without her. But I was wrong. The celebration of Christ's birth isn't a matter of the house you live in or the people who share your table. It's a matter of the heart. If the Lord lives here," Vern said as he patted his chest with his hand, "then Christmas is a matter of everyday life. Agneta would want it that way, too. Good night."

Julie watched her father walk from the room. She admired his strength and, in it, found more courage for herself.

"Unless you need help cleaning up, I'm going to bed, too," August said as he ran a gentle hand over the guitar. "This is a swell gift, Jewels. I'm going to enjoy it for a long, long time."

"I'm glad you like it," Julie said, getting up to embrace her brother. "You go ahead to bed. I can manage all of this just fine. Besides, I want to see if the aurora makes an appearance tonight." August nodded, gave Sam a single-fingered salute, and took his leave.

Julie knew that Sam's eyes were on her even before she turned around. What would she say to him? How could she deal with the feelings her heart would no longer let her deny? She cared for Sam, that much was true. But how would it fit in with her nursing? Was it really love she felt or merely infatuation? Taking a deep breath, she turned to meet his eyes.

"Do you have to clear these things away just yet?" Sam asked as he came across the room.

"No," Julie whispered. "I suppose they can wait."

"Good, because I can't," Sam said and took Julie in his arms. His kiss was as gentle as the first he'd ever given her, but the feelings he evoked in Julie's heart were so much greater.

After what seemed an eternity, Julie pushed away. "I can't breathe," she said with a laugh, trying hard to push aside the passion she was feeling.

Sam allowed her the space and led her to the couch. "I want to talk to you," he said as he sat down beside her. "I have a Christmas gift for you."

"You shouldn't have," Julie said in a barely audible voice. Having Sam so close completely muddled her thoughts.

Sam reached into his pocket and pulled out a small box. He opened it for Julie and revealed a ring of gold, with a small diamond. "Julie," he whispered, "will you marry me?"

Julie stared dumbfoundedly at the box. He'd actually proposed. None of his presumptuous attitudes or the self-assured cockiness that he'd delivered before, just the plain and simple heart of the matter. A marriage proposal!

"I don't know what to say."

"Say yes," Sam said as he took the ring from the box and slipped it on Julie's finger.

Julie stared at the ring for several minutes. It was a bit big, but it was exactly what Julie would have hoped for in a wedding ring.

"We've only known each other a couple of months," Julie said, searching for a way she could avoid dealing with the issue.

"We both know it's right," Sam said as he pulled Julie against him. "I love you, Julie, and whether or not you'll admit it, I know you love me."

Julie trembled in Sam's arms. Her breath caught in her throat and made it impossible to deny his statement. Did she love him?

"I don't know what I'm feeling," Julie finally answered honestly. "I won't deny the chemistry between us, but Sam, you weren't in my plans."

"What about God's plans?"

"But I thought I knew what God's plans for me were," Julie said, daring to look into Sam's piercing brown eyes. "I thought I knew exactly what I was supposed to do."

"And now?" Sam questioned.

"Now," Julie said as she took off the ring. "I feel confused. I can't marry you, Sam, unless I know for sure it's what I'm supposed to do." She handed him the ring, expecting an angry retort. Instead, Sam surprised her.

Closing his hand around Julie's fingers and the ring, he spoke. "Keep the ring. I feel confident that God has sent you to be my wife. One day, you'll know it, too, and you'll come to me wearing it, and I'll know your answer." With that, Sam placed a light kiss on Julie's forehead and got up. "Good night, love," he said and left Julie to contemplate her feelings.

Julie held the ring tightly and prayed. "Oh, God, what am I to do? I thought the way was so clear. You had shone a light of understanding on the path that I was to take, and I felt confident that I was making the right choice. Now," she paused and looked at the ring. "Now, I just don't know. I'm so afraid, and I need to understand what I'm to do. I want to serve You, Father. I want to bring glory to You. Can I do this as Sam's wife?"

Several minutes passed. With the ring still in her hand, Julie retrieved her father's Bible and opened it to Joshua 1:9: "Have I not commanded thee? Be strong and of a good courage; be not afraid, neither be thou dismayed: for the Lord thy God is with thee whithersoever thou goest."

"I won't be afraid," Julie said as she reread the verse. "You have commanded me to be strong and with Your help, Father, I will be." Peace filled Julie's heart. "I don't know what the answer is regarding Sam, Lord. But You do, and I am Your servant, seeking to know Your will. Open my heart to Your direction, so that my own plans won't thwart the divine ones You have ordained for me. Amen."

Chapter 10

January 1925 started out cold, with the mercury dipping to thirty below zero. Julie took extra precautions to maintain warmth and safety on the trail by carrying more blankets, additional food, and dry fuel for fires.

She had read several articles in the *Nome Nugget* of the army's findings while experimenting with temperature in the far North. Apparently, it wasn't enough to calculate the outside temperature when determining how dangerous conditions were. The speed of the wind had to be considered as well. The army had concluded that, while a fifteen-degree temperature seemed warm to the natives of Nome, if the wind were blowing at ten to twelve miles an hour, it would feel more like forty below zero. Something called windchill, Julie remembered, and it could create problems for a person on the trail.

The snow had been sporadic that winter, and Nome's streets weren't buried as deeply as they usually were at the first of the year. Julie knew that however good conditions were in Nome, she had no way to tell what would greet her as she moved out across the less-traveled trails.

"We haven't had any traffic from the west or north," she said as she finished her coffee one morning with Dr. Welch and his wife. "So I have no way of knowing what the trails are like."

"I wish I could go with you," Dr. Welch replied honestly. He loved to drive his dogs and found city life a bit stifling at times.

"Actually, I wish you could, too," Julie said with a smile for Dr. Welch's wife. "I love to watch your husband at work, Mrs. Welch."

"Now, Julie, I think we've been friends far too long to continue with the Mrs. Welch title. Just call me Lula; all my friends do."

"I like to call her Lu," Dr. Welch said with a fond smile for his wife, "among other things."

"You're being quite impossible today, Dr. Welch," Lula said with a teasing note to her voice. "You're probably better off with him staying in Nome, Julie. I have a feeling he'd want to wander off and do some ice fishing or visit, if he went on the trail."

Julie laughed and glanced at her watch. It wouldn't be light for another three hours, but the trail beckoned. "I'm going to have to be on my way. Thanks again for the coffee, Lula," she said, trying the name for the first time. "I should be back in a few weeks."

Just then a loud knock at the door caught their attention. "A doctor's house is an open arena," Lula said with a smile. "I'll just see who that might be."

Lula Welch opened the door to reveal an Eskimo man. "I have sick children," he said in

350

a worried way that caused Dr. Welch to jump to his feet.

"What seems to be wrong?" he questioned the man, as Lula brought his fur parka.

"They're burning with fever, and their throats are sore," the man answered.

"How old are they?" Dr. Welch questioned. Lula brought his medical bag and set it on the table.

"One's three, and my baby is only one year old. Can you help them, Doctor? I don't have much money, but I can work hard for you."

Dr. Welch waved the man's concerns away. "Nonsense. We'll discuss such matters later. First, let's see if we can figure out how to help the little ones." He planted a kiss on Lula's temple and turned to Julie. "You can always send me a radio message through the army signal corps, should you need anything or have a problem."

"I'll keep that in mind," Julie said. She pulled on her parka and secured the hood. "Would you like me to drive you to the settlement?"

"No," Dr. Welch said, shaking his head. "There's not so much snow as to impede a good walk, and I need the exercise. Thanks anyway." With that, Dr. Welch hastened into the darkness with the fearful father.

"I guess I'd better be on my way as well," Julie remarked. "I'll be in touch. Thanks again for the coffee."

"We'll look forward to seeing you when you get back," Lula said as she followed Julie to the door. "Be careful."

"I will be," Julie promised and took herself out into the darkness.

The town was quiet, even though there was plenty of activity. Julie felt an emptiness as she watched couples making their way into nearby shops. Maybe she wasn't cut out for public health nursing after all. While she loved nursing and working with the Eskimos, the long, lonely hours on the trail were difficult.

Images of Sam filled Julie's mind. She thought of the ring that lay securely at the bottom of her knapsack. It was a symbol of Sam's devotion. Would she ever be able to put the ring on and give Sam the answer he longed to hear?

In the back of her mind, Julie remembered the verses from Ecclesiastes that her father had read. "Two are better than one. . . . For if they fall, the one will lift up his fellow: but woe to him that is alone when he falleth; for he hath not another to help him up." Loneliness penetrated her heart.

Julie consoled herself with the idea of stopping at home before pushing west. Maybe she could talk to her father about Sam's proposal and her loneliness. He could offer her some idea of what she should do.

Julie checked the tarp covering her supplies and, when she was certain that everything was secure, she took to the back of her sled.

"Were you planning on leaving without saying good-bye?" Sam questioned as he placed his hands on Julie's shoulders.

Julie turned. Dim light illuminated Sam's bearded face. His hair had been neatly cut and his beard trimmed. He was quite handsome, Julie decided. She could do much worse.

"I can't always be looking over my shoulder for you, every time I'm about to go on my route," Julie said, trying to distance herself from the emotions Sam stirred within her.

"I thought you were avoiding me," Sam countered. "I don't suppose you've given much thought to my proposal."

"I've, uh, well," Julie stammered, "I've been busy with my nursing. Since the first part of the month, I've been working with Dr. Welch and haven't even managed to get home. I also have several villages to the northwest to attend to, so you can see I've been very busy."

"That doesn't answer my question," Sam remarked.

"I think it should," Julie said nervously. "I've been too busy to see my family. Doesn't it seem reasonable that I've been too busy to consider your marriage proposal?"

"No," Sam said firmly. "It doesn't."

Julie's mouth opened in surprise. She had banked on Sam's good nature making him drop the issue. Instead he remained a determined force to be reckoned with.

"Do you have any idea what my nursing means to me?" Julie asked seriously. *Perhaps*, she thought, *if Sam knew what my responsibilities mean to me, he'd understand my hesitation.*

"Do you have any idea what you mean to me?" Sam said as he moved closer. His warm breath formed frosty white steam in the morning cold.

"That's not fair, Sam. I asked you first."

"If I answer you, will you give me an answer?" Sam questioned. "I think it's only fair."

"I imagine I mean something quite special to you. After all, you did ask me to marry you," Julie stated evenly. "Now, I've answered your question. Will you answer mine?"

Sam chuckled. "Your father was right. You are something else when you have a full head of steam. Sometime, you'll have to tell me what happened when your father wanted to shoot that pup. No doubt you didn't cut him any more maneuvering room than you are me."

Julie smiled ruefully. "My father told me that pup was good for nothing but taking up space and eating. He said he couldn't be expected to pull his own weight, much less that of a sled. I told him I wasn't all that different. I was too young to bring in any wealth to the family, and certainly I wasn't capable of pulling my own weight. I put myself between the pup and my father's leveled gun and told him he might as well do away with both of us, because the weak were worthless when it came to surviving in the North."

Sam smiled at her determination. "I guess I don't have to ask what happened."

"My father relented. Told me I was spoiled and," Julie added with amusement, "he made me take care of the pup."

"How'd it work out?"

"My father knew best," Julie said sadly. "The pup got in a fight with some of the other dogs. They killed him."

"I'm sorry," Sam replied honestly.

"I learned a good lesson," Julie said as she shook the image from her mind. "Never once did my father tell me, 'I told you so.' He put his arms around me and let me cry. Then he shared the words of Proverbs 1:8: 'My son, hear the instruction of thy father, and forsake not the law of thy mother.' He told me it counted for daughters as well."

"Your father is a wise man," Sam said softly.

"Yes, he is," Julie agreed, "and that's exactly why I need to talk to him before I can give you any kind of an answer."

"I see," Sam answered thoughtfully. "I suppose it wouldn't help if I told you that I've already talked to him about it."

"What?" Julie's head snapped up.

"I talked to your father before I ever asked you to marry me," Sam replied. "I wouldn't have dreamed of approaching you with a proposal unless I was certain your father approved."

"And did he?"

Sam smiled and reached out a hand to push back Julie's hood. "He told me it was up to you."

"That's it?" Julie questioned as she took a step back to avoid Sam's touch. "He didn't say anything else?"

"Should he have?"

"I don't know. I guess I just wondered if he—"

"If he had an answer for you?" Sam interrupted. "I didn't ask your father to marry me. I only sought his blessing. It's you I want an answer from."

Julie turned away from Sam and rechecked her sled harness. Part of her wanted to tell Sam no, but no matter how she tried, Julie couldn't form the word. Why couldn't she simply refuse to marry him and let him slip from her life? "I don't have an answer for you, Sam," she finally said.

"Do you know when you might?"

Julie straightened up slowly, avoiding his eyes.

"Look at me, Julie," Sam said as he reached out and turned her to face him. "This should be a happy experience for both of us. It should be a wonderful and joyful event for two people who love each other. You do love me, don't you?" It was more a statement than a question.

Julie took a deep breath to steady herself. That was the important question. Did she love Sam?

"I—"

"Say, aren't you Julie Eriksson?" a voice called out from behind Sam. Julie recognized the bulky form of her father's longtime friend, Jonah Emery.

"Hello, Jonah," Julie said sweetly, grateful for the reprieve.

"I heard you were back in these parts as a nurse. Say, I'll bet your papa is mighty proud."

"I'll say he is," Sam joined in.

"Why, Sam Curtiss, I should have known that towering frame belonged to you. Well, I'll let you two get back to your discussion," Jonah said with a wave. "You be sure and tell your pa hello from me."

"I will," Julie promised and watched as Jonah moved down the street to one of the small cafés.

"I'm still waiting for my answer," Sam said as Julie turned back to face him.

"I can't give you an answer."

"Then when, Julie?"

She thought for a moment. "I'm going to be gone for a month, maybe more. I'll have an answer for you when I return."

Sam grinned and pulled Julie into his arms. "Then let me give you a reminder to take on the trail," he whispered and lowered his lips to kiss her.

Julie stepped back breathlessly, even though the kiss was brief. She looked apprehensively up and down the street to see if anyone had seen Sam kiss her. When she turned back to reprimand Sam for his behavior, he was gone.

Balancing between relief and disappointment, Julie quickly wrapped several scarves around her face and secured her hood. She could only pray that God would provide her an answer to Sam's question.

"Let's go, boys!" she called out and held on tightly as the dogs fairly burst from the start.

From the dark haven of the entryway to a store, Sam watched Julie move down the street and out of sight. It was hard to let her go without demanding that she accept his love and affection, but Sam had made God a promise. "Thy will be done," Sam whispered in the darkness. "Thy will be done."

Chapter 11

Troubled by her promise to Sam, Julie forgot about going home. She mushed out of Nome on trails that took her west along the ice-packed Bering Sea. The coastline trails were easy to follow, and they often moved off the banks onto the frozen sea itself. This helped drivers avoid heavily drifted snow and hidden obstacles.

Out on the ice, Julie had new concerns to keep her mind on. The wind and pressure often caused the ice to form what the natives called "spears." These ice needles jutted upward from the frozen trail and could pierce the padding of a dog's feet. Whenever spears were evident, Julie took time out to put coverings on the paws of each of her dogs. So far, they'd avoided injury.

As the dimly lit skies gave way to sunlight, Julie pushed back her parka hood. She could tell by the dogs' breath that the temperature had risen. A good driver always paid attention to the degree of whiteness that showed in a team's exhaled breath. Little things like that often saved a driver's life, and Julie, ever mindful of her near-death from the blizzard, paid special attention to such details.

The ice and snow stretched for miles, and the glare of reflecting sunlight caused Julie to shelter her eyes by replacing her hood.

The team moved at a nice trot, and Julie felt exhilarated as she made her way down the coastline. The hills and mountains in the distance, however, reminded her of the dangers that came with isolation. One mistake could be her last.

Thinking about mistakes, Julie considered Sam's marriage proposal. "Lord," she prayed, "I don't know what to do about Sam. He says he loves me, but I don't know if I love him. I suppose I shouldn't be so worried about it—after all, Sam is a Christian."

The miles passed in a blur as Julie continued, "I don't know what to do! My job as a public health nurse takes me out on the trail for weeks, even months at a time. How can I be a good wife to a man while I'm hundreds of miles away inoculating children and teaching mothers about hygiene? Sam deserves more than a pittance of attention every few weeks. I'm sure a man with his zest for living would expect a great deal more, Father. I know he would, and I'd feel obligated to give it to him and leave my job. Since I can't do that, it must be wrong for me to accept his proposal."

That conclusion didn't last long. Unsettled feelings in Julie's mind told her that the issue was far from being resolved.

Sam's never suggested I leave my work as a nurse, she reasoned. *Even when he bids me good-bye, he never causes a scene about my work or says that I ought to be safe at home. Maybe Sam is more sympathetic to the needs of the people up here. Maybe Sam would want me to continue working as a public health nurse, even after we were married.*

"So the answer must be yes," Julie said aloud, but again the feeling that the issue wasn't settled came to haunt her.

"Do I love him?" she asked.

She thought of the way he smiled and the laughter in his brown eyes. The vision of Sam's muscular shoulders and towering frame came to mind. Julie admitted to herself that she was attracted to Sam as she'd never been to another man. *Attraction isn't love,* she reminded herself. *But is it part of love?*

Julie's mittened hands twisted at the sled bar. She couldn't settle on any answers to her many questions.

Please, Lord, I promised him an answer. Please show me whether or not I love him. I must know that before I can answer his proposal because I simply cannot marry a man I do not love.

The daylight hours passed much too quickly. In the distance, Julie saw the flickering light of a lantern hanging on a pole outside a sod igloo. She sighed in relief, eager to rest after only two short stops on the trail.

The village wouldn't recognize their new public health nurse, but Julie knew she'd be warmly welcomed. She halted the dogs as several Eskimos appeared.

"I'm Nurse Eriksson from Nome," Julie offered by way of introduction.

"We're glad to have you," an older man said as he extended his hand. "We have sickness in our village. It is good you have come."

"If you will lend me a warm place to work," Julie said as she reached for her gear, "I'll be glad to examine your sick."

The man nodded and pointed to the sod igloo. "You use my house. I have no wife. I will stay with my brother and his family while you work. Come."

"Thank you," Julie said as she followed the man. "What should I call you?"

The man turned and smiled, revealing several missing teeth. "Call me Charlie," he said and showed Julie inside the shack.

Julie was appalled by what greeted her. The igloo was filthy and very small, leaving her to wonder if these conditions were common in the rest of the village. She noticed the small oilcan stove and turned to Charlie.

"Is there fuel for the stove?"

"Sure," Charlie replied. "I get you nice fire. Plenty warm in here with big fire."

"I'll need water, too," Julie said as she pulled her parka off. It was chilly, but not unbearable, and once she began to clean the room, her body would warm considerably.

"I get you plenty snow, and we melt on big fire. You can have much hot water."

Charlie seemed so pleased to offer Julie his home that she didn't want to hurt his feelings by rearranging everything. "Would it be all right," she began, "if I clean this table so that I can examine the patients?"

"Sure, sure," Charlie said with his broad, toothless smile. "You have plenty fire, plenty water, and plenty clean. Sure."

Charlie disappeared out the door, and Julie could hear him talking excitedly to the villagers. He reappeared and within minutes had a nice fire going in the stove as well as several pans of snow melting on top of it.

Julie rolled up the sleeves of her heavy flannel shirt. While nurses in Nome's hospital wore a recognizable uniform, Julie wore what best suited the climate and elements she would have to combat; warm flannels and wools along with furs and skin pants were of much more benefit to her near the Bering Sea than starched aprons and freshly pressed dresses. She was just pinning up her hair when a young woman burst through the door with her infant child in hand.

"My baby is sick," she cried as she held the infant up to Julie.

Julie reached for the child. His burning skin told her that he had a dangerously high fever.

"How long has he been sick?" Julie questioned the mother while examining the baby.

"He's had a bad cold for two days. He breathes so hard I can't rest for fear he'll stop breathing," the little Eskimo woman said as she twisted her hands.

Julie could hear the labored, shallow breathing of the infant. He was perilously close to death. But why? Julie couldn't find any obvious reason for the baby to be so ill. "I must look in his mouth," Julie told his mother as she pulled a tongue depressor from her bag. "I won't hurt him, but he won't like it." Julie doubted that the lethargic baby would fight her, but she felt better warning the mother about her actions.

The light was so poor that Julie could scarcely see past the child's tongue and gums. "I need more light," she called to Charlie and waited until he brought her a lantern.

"Plenty light for the nurse," Charlie said and went back to his self-assigned task of melting snow at the stove.

Julie positioned the light to give her a good view into the child's mouth. She pried the tiny mouth open and gasped. The back of the child's swollen throat was covered with gray-white patches of dead mucous membrane, the unmistakable calling card of diphtheria. Julie looked up sympathetically at the frantically worried young mother. How could she explain to the woman that her baby would probably die that night?

"Are there any others in the village with this sickness?" Julie asked.

"Yes, there are two other children with sore throats and high fevers," the woman answered. "Can you make my baby well?"

Julie felt the pain displayed in the woman's eyes. "No, I'm sorry. Your baby is very sick, and I can't help him. We've waited too long, and I don't have the medicine I need to help you."

The woman's anxious face fell into complete dejection. She grabbed up her baby and began to wail. Charlie came from the stove and asked Julie what was wrong with the baby.

"It's a white man's disease called diphtheria," Julie said as the crying mother rocked back and forth, cradling her dying child. "I need medicine from Nome in order to save the people from getting the disease. The ones who are already sick may not have enough time left for me to get back and help them. Charlie, I'm going to need your help. Do you have a village council?"

"Sure, sure," Charlie said, repeating what appeared to be his favorite word. "We got plenty people on council."

"I need you to call them together. This disease is very contagious. That means it spreads quickly. Charlie, we mustn't let anyone come into the village or leave it. Do you understand?

I have to go back to Nome and get the antitoxin."

"Sure, Charlie understand plenty good," the old man said with a grave nod. "I keep people here, and nobody else come in."

"Good," Julie replied. "Charlie, I need to have the dogs ready to leave in ten minutes. Can you have them ready for me?"

"Sure, but you plenty tired. You need rest to travel," Charlie answered in a way that reminded Julie of her father.

"Yes, Charlie, I know. But if I don't get the medicine and get right back to the village, many of your people will die. I have to try."

"You try then," Charlie said and patted Julie on the back. "But you don't take the ice. Big wind blowing off the water is making it soft. It might be gone in the night."

"Thank you, Charlie. I'll stick to the land trail," Julie promised.

After speaking with the council about quarantining the homes of the sick and leaving instructions on how to ease the sufferings of those with the disease, Julie repacked her supplies and readied her sled.

Starting with Dusty, Julie lovingly patted her dogs and checked them for any signs of stiffness or injury. Eager to be back on the trail, the dogs seemed to understand the importance of their mission.

Julie moved her team out and ran alongside the sled for quite a distance. She wanted to ensure that she stayed warm, so she only rode the runners when fatigue threatened her with exhaustion. In record time, she saw the lights of Nome and breathed a prayer of thanksgiving.

Julie pushed the dogs to Dr. Welch's house. Mindless of the hour, she pounded on the door. Surprisingly, Dr. Welch himself appeared at the door, fully dressed.

"Julie, come inside. What is it?" Dr. Welch questioned as he ushered the girl to a seat by the stove.

"Diphtheria! The Sinuak village has several cases. One will certainly not make it through the night, and the others I doubt I can help either. I came back for antitoxin."

Dr. Welch looked old beyond his years. Julie worried for his health as he ran a hand through his graying hair and sat down at the kitchen table. "I haven't got any. At least not enough."

"How much do you have?" Julie questioned in a worried tone that matched the doctor's.

"We only have seventy-five thousand units, and I already have cases of diphtheria appearing here in Nome. The two children I was called to care for are dead. I didn't know then that it was diphtheria, as I couldn't get a look inside their mouths. However, little Richard Stanley is also sick, and I saw quite well the patches on his throat. It's diphtheria, all right."

"What are we to do?" Julie asked as she joined the doctor at the table.

"I don't know," the doctor answered bluntly. "It takes thirty thousand units of antitoxin to treat one sick person. I've already got at least four who are sick with the disease and hundreds of others who are exposed."

"To make matters worse," Lula Welch said as she appeared in her nightgown and robe, "the serum we have on hand is over five years old. We'd hoped that the Public Health Department had sent some with you when you returned from Seattle, but they must have been short on it themselves. We didn't receive a single unit."

Julie sat back and took a deep breath. "So we don't know if the serum on hand is effective?"

"That's about the whole of it," Dr. Welch said and put his head in his hands. "We must be prepared to deal with a full-scale epidemic. Diphtheria will only take a matter of days to spread like a flame on dried kindling. The entire peninsula is in danger of epidemic. God help us."

"Yes, He's our only hope now," Julie agreed. "He's our only hope!"

Chapter 12

Julie stayed at the Welch home, and that morning word came that little Richard Stanley had passed away in the night. There was nothing left to do, Dr. Welch decided, but to call upon the mayor and announce an epidemic.

Sitting in the office of the *Nome Nugget*, all eyes of the city council turned to the publisher, George Maynard. As well as operating and publishing Nome's only newspaper, George Maynard was also the town's mayor.

"Diphtheria? Are you sure, Curt?" George questioned Dr. Welch. "We haven't had diphtheria in these parts for over twenty years, and with the ports all frozen up, how would we get the serum now?"

"I can't tell you the how and why, but facts are facts. I wish it weren't so, but the truth of the matter is I've already got three dead children to prove my diagnosis. I'm getting more reports of people taken with fever and sore throat. Frankly, George, it's going to get a whole lot worse before it gets better."

"But don't we have an injection for that kind of thing?" the mayor asked with a hopeful expression.

"We do, and we don't," Dr. Welch explained as he rubbed his eyes with the backs of his hands. "There is an antitoxin, but Nome doesn't have it."

"What are you saying?" M. L. Summers, superintendent of the Hammon Consolidated Gold Fields, questioned.

"I'm saying we have an epidemic, and people are dying. Furthermore, there is a cure, but we don't have it within reach. I have a small amount of antitoxin, but it's over five years old and probably ineffective. There's certainly not enough to stave off an epidemic."

"What do you suggest we do, Doc?" Sam asked as he moved forward from the back of the room.

"We have to quarantine the sick and keep people from spreading the disease. The first order of business is to close the schools and the movie theater," Dr. Welch said as he leaned back in his chair. "As this region's director of public health, I would also like to have a board of health formed to enforce the quarantine. We can't have anybody coming in or going out of Nome."

"Summers, you could take that job on, couldn't you?" Mayor Maynard asked.

"Certainly," Summers answered, feeling honored to be put in the position.

"I'll run a quarantine notice on the front page," Maynard said as he jotted down notes on a pad of paper.

"Thank you," Dr. Welch replied.

"What else can we do?" Sam questioned.

"The biggest problem we have on hand is how to get the antitoxin. I haven't any idea where there might be a supply large enough to help us. It might be in Fairbanks or Anchorage. Then again, it might be as far away as Juneau or Seattle. Regardless, when we locate the serum we'll have another problem on our hands: how do we get it here?"

"If we can locate serum in either Anchorage or Fairbanks," Mayor Maynard began, "there might be a pilot daring enough to fly it to us." Everyone looked skeptical at the suggestion. Flying was new enough to the States, but in Alaska, it was almost unheard of, especially in the winter.

"That might work if it were summer, but I don't think we can afford to risk it in the middle of winter. There's no way of knowing if those engines can handle thirty or forty below zero," one of the other council members said. Murmurs filled the room as the men concurred that flight might be a bad notion.

"Look," Sam said, suddenly getting an idea, "what if we used dog teams? We know they can make it through on the mail routes from Fairbanks. If Fairbanks has the serum, we could start it west and send someone out to meet it. Maybe even relay it across the territory."

"But that will take nearly a month," the mayor argued.

"Not if we send Leonhard Seppala," Summers said, getting to his feet. "You all know he's the best musher in Alaska. His Siberian huskies are faster than any other team around these parts." The council members nodded as Summers continued. "Seppala works for me, and I would gladly allow him the time to perform this courageous act."

"Yeah, those little plume-tailed rats might just pull it off. So we start someone out from Fairbanks with the serum and—"

"So far there is no serum," Sam interrupted the mayor. "We have to send out a radio message and find the serum before we can move it to Nome."

"Sam's right," Dr. Welch said with a nod of his head. "We have to locate the serum first and then worry about how to get it here."

"Whatever it takes," Maynard said as he pounded his fist on the table. "No matter the cost. We all remember the influenza epidemic of 1919."

"Yes, and it didn't help much that the outside had already had its death tolls from it the year before," Welch added. "We were no better prepared for that epidemic than we are for this one."

"Dr. Welch, you give a message to the U.S. Army Signal Corps' radiotelegraph station. We're behind you one hundred percent. Just let us know what we need to do," the mayor replied.

"I'll take you there, Doc. My team's right outside the door," Sam said as he got up to retrieve his parka.

"Very well, gentlemen. I will rely upon you to work with our new board of health director and the mayor as we strive to take control of this nightmare." Dr. Welch got to his feet and followed Sam to where the coats had been haphazardly thrown to one side.

"I'll keep all of you informed," Welch promised and followed Sam out the door.

"This must go priority to Juneau, Fairbanks, Anchorage, and Seward," Dr. Welch instructed as he handed a piece of paper to the sergeant who manned the radiotelegraph station.

Sergeant James Anderson took the paper and read it, paling slightly as he finished its contents. "Looks like we're in for it, huh, Doc?"

"That it does," Dr. Welch said as he cast a side glance at Sam.

Sam was deep in thought over concern for the town of Nome, but especially for Julie. He wished it were possible to make the serum appear on the next mail delivery, but wishing wouldn't make it so.

"I'll notify my superiors, and we'll have a man stationed here twenty-four hours a day until we receive an answer," the sergeant said as he prepared to telegraph the message.

Sam watched the man put on his headset. Turning the dial to adjust the frequency, the man began the message.

"-./—/—/. -.-./.-/.-../.-../.-./—." The radio key clicked out the words, "Nome, calling."

The room seemed shrouded in silence against the rhythmic tapping of the telegraph key. Sam and Dr. Welch stood to one side as the sergeant tapped out the call again. He paused and waited to see if anyone would pick up his signal.

Within seconds the answer tapped back. "Fairbanks, calling. Go ahead, Nome."

The sergeant turned and nodded to Dr. Welch. "It's Fairbanks. I'll relay the message."

The sergeant's finger tapped out the message with expert ease. "Nome, calling. We have an outbreak of diphtheria. No serum. Urgently need help."

Sam and Dr. Welch breathed a sigh of relief. Just knowing that the rest of the world would learn of their need gave them hope.

The sergeant continued to radio the message to Anchorage, Juneau, and Seward. "I'll let you know when I get anything in," Sergeant Anderson said as he took off his headset.

"Thanks, Sergeant," Sam said and offered his dog team to Dr. Welch.

For days, time stood still in Nome. The only thing that didn't slow was the diphtheria. Three children were dead, ten new active cases were revealed, and more than fifty people reported they'd been exposed. Dr. Welch could only use what little serum he had on hand. Soon not a single unit remained.

Finally, on January 25, a message was received in Nome. Anchorage had three hundred thousand units of serum at the Alaska Railroad Hospital. It could be packaged and loaded on the number sixty-six Anchorage-to-Fairbanks Passenger Special and received at the Nenana railhead within two days. The Star Route of the interior mail delivery operated by dogsled from Nenana and could carry the serum as part of its load.

Dr. Welch gave the go-ahead, and Sergeant Anderson wired the message to Dr. Beeson in Anchorage to proceed with the shipment.

"I suggest we call a city council meeting," Dr. Welch said as the sergeant finished his message. "This presents a whole new problem."

Within an hour, everyone had gathered for the meeting. Julie stood to one side of the meeting hall, while Sam kept a determined gaze on her from the opposite side of the room. It was the first time he'd seen her since she'd left for her routes. She'd done nothing to let him know of her hurried return to Nome.

It was also the first time Sam had seen Julie in a dress. Self-consciously, Julie smoothed the white uniform, mindful of the way it displayed her more feminine qualities. She was wearing her uniform because she'd been helping at the hospital with the non-diphtheria patients. Dr. Welch had wisely kept the hospital quarantined for those patients whose ills did not involve diphtheria and required surgery or detailed medical help. Nurse Seville had been dispatched to the Sinuak village to work with the natives while Julie stayed on in Nome.

"I know you've all been waiting for good news," Dr. Welch began, "and finally I have some to report. Anchorage has three hundred thousand units of serum, and they've started it north to Nenana on the train." A cry of excited voices went up. Dr. Welch waited until the crowd had quieted before continuing. "We must decide how we are to get the serum from Nenana to Nome. Anchorage advises me that it will arrive in Nenana tomorrow."

"Leonhard Seppala has agreed to go after the serum," M. L. Summers announced.

"The arrangements have already been made to start the serum west after Nenana," Dr. Welch declared. "Several relay teams will work it down the Tanana and Yukon Rivers. Perhaps we could have Seppala meet the serum, say, at Nulato?"

"That's over six hundred miles round trip," Sam advised. "It would be a hardship for one man and one team of dogs."

"Seppala suggests he take a team of thirty or so dogs," Summers expounded. "He would drop dogs off at the various roadhouses and cabins along the route and pick them up fresh on the way back. That way he could mush night and day. He believes it would only take a return trip of three, maybe four days."

"Three or four days?" one of the other men questioned. "That would average nearly one hundred miles a day! Seppala's huskies are good, but they're not indestructible."

"Have him stand by," Dr. Welch said as he contemplated the matter. "I'm still awaiting word from the governor. I'm not authorized to make the decision on my own."

The men nodded and settled down. Julie took the opportunity to slip quietly from the room in order to avoid Sam, but he was prepared for her action and followed her out. Julie was halfway down the hall and heading for her parka when Sam caught hold of her arm and whirled her into his arms.

"You look incredible," he whispered against her ear.

Julie thrilled to his touch, melting at once against his lean, muscular form. How often had she dreamed of this during those lonely nights spent out on the trail.

"You know," Sam said with a teasing smile, "I never purchase a sled dog sight unseen. I always go over them with a well-trained eye, just in case there are any hidden defects. But you, I was ready to take sight unseen, buried under pounds of furs and leather. Boy, was that a good call!"

"I beg your pardon," Julie said indignantly and pushed away. "Are you comparing your marriage proposal to purchasing a dog?" She clamped her hand automatically over her mouth, grimacing because the very subject she'd hoped to avoid was now open for conversation.

"You know I didn't mean it that way. I just can't believe how beautiful you look in that dress. Now come here, and give me a kiss."

Julie shook her head and backed away. "Remember the quarantine," she said firmly.

"I do," Sam said as he moved forward.

"No close physical contact," Julie reminded.

"Uh huh," Sam agreed, all the while moving forward at a steady pace.

"You aren't going to break the rules," Julie asked as she came to a stop against the wall, "are you?"

"Yup," Sam said and pulled her against him tightly. "If love could kill a man, I'd already be dead," he said as he lowered his mouth to Julie's and kissed her soundly.

Julie's mind went blank as her senses came alive. What was the cologne Sam was wearing, and why hadn't she noticed before how soft his beard was?

Voices down the hall brought Julie back to her senses. She pushed at Sam with both hands and gasped for air. "I've got to get back to work," she said and maneuvered under his sinewy arms.

"We can, uh, talk later," she said, pulling on her parka and acknowledging Dr. Welch as he approached.

Sam grinned at her embarrassment, but let it go at that. He'd have plenty of time later.

Chapter 13

By the morning of January 30, Leonhard Seppala had been given the go-ahead and had moved his huskies out across the trail to press ever closer to the serum.

The people of Nome were frantic. There had been five deaths, twenty-two active cases, and thirty-some suspected cases of diphtheria. All they could do was wait and make those who were ill as comfortable as possible.

Julie was working with Dr. Welch when Sergeant Anderson arrived with a message from Territorial Governor Scott Bone. He was requesting that more relays be set up between Nulato and Nome, as the army reported a severe change in the weather.

"This isn't good," Dr. Welch said as he motioned Julie to follow him. "Sergeant, round up as many of the council members as you can. Julie, you go along with him and get whoever will come with you to join us at the bank. We need more drivers!"

Julie nodded and raced down the hall behind the sergeant, pulling her coat along with her as she stepped into the street. They took opposite sides of the street and worked their way down the storefronts, calling out to those inside as they went.

By one o'clock, a nice crowd had gathered at the bank. Outside the skies had turned overcast, and the wind had picked up. A storm was moving in from the northwest, and Julie was thankful that she wouldn't be required to drive her team out in the blizzard.

"If I may have your attention," Dr. Welch announced. "I have received word from the governor. He has requested we arrange for more relay points along the mail route. The weather forecast has the interior of Alaska turning into a dangerous situation. The suggestion is that more men can travel fewer miles and the risk to life would be reduced significantly."

"But Seppala's already on his way," M. L. Summers declared.

"Yes, I know. He'll no doubt catch up to the serum at one point or another, but instead of having to turn right around and travel all the way back to Nome, he'll only have to make a portion of the journey. I need volunteers to go out along the lines of the mail route and position themselves at the roadhouses."

Several hands went up, including Sam's. Julie caught her breath. What if the storm grew so bad that Sam's life was threatened? Could she stand to see him go, risking his life and the possibility of never returning, without declaring her love?

Her love? Julie tested the thought again. *Yes,* she thought excitedly. *I do love him. I really do, and to lose him now would be devastating.* She didn't hear the rest of Dr. Welch's speech. Her mind was intent on how she could share her heart with Sam. She couldn't throw herself into his arms and tell him, or could she?

The meeting broke up, and Julie recognized Gunnar Kaasen and Ed Rohn, as they had both agreed, with Sam, to participate on the serum run. She waited nervously for Dr. Welch to finish instructing the three men so that she could talk to Sam.

After several minutes, Julie thought better of talking to Sam in public and made her way down the hall. There hadn't been all that much snow, she reasoned, so she'd walk to Sam's house on the edge of Nome and wait for him there.

Julie was concerned to see that the storm was skirting to the east of Nome. It was headed directly toward the path the serum would have to take, so she prayed that it would pass quickly and blow itself out into Norton Sound before it could cause harm to the dog teams. She hurried to Sam's house and went inside to wait for him.

Minutes later, Sam arrived. He was busy with the dogs outside the back door, but Julie knew he'd have to come inside to get provisions before leaving. Nervously, she twisted her hands, wondering what to say when he finally appeared.

Outside, the wind howled, and while it hadn't yet begun to snow, Sam recognized the dangerous look of the storm. He quickly harnessed his best dogs to the sled, deciding to take eight strong malamutes, then made his way into the house.

Julie almost laughed at the shocked expression on Sam's face as he came rushing through the back door, nearly knocking her to the floor.

"Oh, Sam," Julie said as her voice cracked. She was quite frightened for him and threw herself into his arms, just as she'd thought she couldn't do.

"What's all this about?" Sam questioned as he pulled away just enough to see Julie's face.

"I'm so frightened for you, and I just couldn't let you go out there without telling you. . ." Julie's words faded as she lowered her head.

Sam lifted her face to meet his gaze. "Telling me what?"

"That I love you," Julie said and broke into tears. "Oh, Sam, I love you so much it hurts."

Sam laughed out loud and whirled Julie in a circle. Julie sobbed all the harder as she thought of how she'd come to love Sam's boisterous laugh and wondered if, after today, she'd ever hear it again.

"Now stop that," Sam said as he held Julie's trembling body against his own. Her tears pained him in a way he'd never known. "Don't cry, Julie. Everything is going to be all right. You'll see."

"But the storm is coming up too fast, and you have to go so far to get to your point on the relay. I couldn't bear it if I lost you now," she cried.

"Nothing's going to happen to me, silly. I've got too much to live for now that I have you. Did you really mean it? Do you honestly love me?"

Julie rolled her still-damp eyes. "How can you ask that? I thought you knew I loved you before I knew."

"Then everything is going to work out. God sent you to me, and He won't separate us now," Sam said confidently.

"Can we pray?" Julie asked as she wiped at her tears with the back of her hand. "I mean, together?"

"Oh, Julie," Sam's face sobered as he spoke, "I'd love to pray with you. Come on." He led the way to the front room where Julie had previously fallen asleep. He stopped and knelt in front of the small table that held his Bible. "Come here," he motioned, and Julie felt a sudden peace.

Kneeling beside him, Julie felt Sam take hold of her hand in his. With his free hand, Sam began to turn the pages of the Bible. Julie reached up and stopped him.

"May I?" she asked with huge, saucer eyes.

"Of course," Sam replied and let Julie turn to Psalm 121.

" 'I will lift up mine eyes unto the hills,' " Julie read, " 'from whence cometh my help. My help cometh from the Lord, which made heaven and earth. He will not suffer thy foot to be moved: he that keepeth thee will not slumber. Behold, he that keepeth Israel shall neither slumber nor sleep.' "

She paused for a moment, then lifted her gaze from the Bible and recited the words while looking into Sam's dark eyes. " 'The Lord is thy keeper: the Lord is thy shade upon thy right hand. The sun shall not smite thee by day, nor the moon by night. The Lord shall preserve thee from all evil: he shall preserve thy soul. The Lord shall preserve thy going out and thy coming in from this time forth, and even for evermore.' "

"Amen," Sam replied when Julie had finished.

"Amen," Julie echoed. "I feel much better giving you over to the Lord than just worrying about you and struggling through it alone."

Sam helped Julie to her feet and kissed her gently on the lips. "I love you, Julie. You've made me a very happy man today, and when I get back and this epidemic is behind us, I'll expect an answer to my proposal."

Julie nodded and, after one last hug, she rushed from the room and hurried back to work.

By five-thirty, Dr. Welch was sending an exhausted Julie back to the hospital to rest. She had taken to sleeping in the same room she'd occupied her first night in Nome, and after being up and working for over twelve hours, Julie was ready to relax.

Julie made her way through the deserted streets, wondering about the serum that would save the lives of many and whether Sam was safely to his destination. She paid little attention to anything else, until a whining sound at her feet brought Julie's full attention to the source.

"Kodiak!" she exclaimed as she reached down to the dog's obviously cut harness. She felt her heart skip a beat as she recognized blood on Kodiak's fur. Pulling him into better light, Julie could see that he'd been injured.

Scooping the dog into her arms, Julie made her way to the hospital. Mindless of Nurse Emily's protests, Julie took Kodiak to her room and flipped on the lights.

"What happened to you, boy?" Julie asked as she examined the dog. He was suffering from cuts on his face and neck, but otherwise looked to be in decent shape. But if Kodiak had been cut loose from the harness, Sam was in trouble.

Bedding the dog down in her room, Julie pulled the pins from her nurse's cap and tossed it to the table. She slipped out of her uniform and donned heavy wool long johns and denim jeans before pulling on reliable sealskin pants.

She tucked a heavy flannel shirt into her pants and pulled on thick wool socks and her mukluks. Throwing together a bag of supplies, including her medical bag, Julie gave Kodiak her promise to find Sam, locked the door behind her, and went to harness her dog team.

Julie searched unsuccessfully for someone who might help her. She caught up with Dr. Welch at one of the quarantined homes and begged for his help.

"I can't leave Nome, Julie. You know these people are dying," Dr. Welch said firmly. "Try to find someone else to help you. If Sam is hurt, bring him to the hospital, and then I can better serve him."

"I understand," Julie said in a resigned tone. She went in search of anyone who might accompany her, and when no one offered to help, Julie made the decision to go alone.

She packed extra ropes and blankets on her sled, uncertain of what she might need or how far she'd have to go to find Sam. Against her better judgment, Julie retrieved Kodiak from her room.

"I'm sorry, boy," she said as she brought the dog out into the subzero darkness. "I need you to help me find Sam." Kodiak yipped as if he understood and paced back and forth until Julie finished hanging two lighted lanterns from her sled.

She had planned on harnessing Kodiak to her own team, but realized he would be of more help if she allowed him to run free. "All right, boy," she called out to Kodiak. "Find Sam."

She moved the team out behind Kodiak and was surprised to find that the wounded dog responded as though he were in perfect condition. "Dear God," Julie breathed as the wind assaulted her face, "please help me find Sam, and please let him be alive and safe."

Cold numbed Julie's face as she struggled to fix her parka hood. How far would she have to go in order to find Sam? Should she take the time to get her brother and father's help? As Kodiak picked up the pace, Julie decided against any detours. A delay could mean death.

The trail was overblown with snow. Steep, icy embankments lined the Bering side, and darkness made it impossible to see. But Julie was sure of her dogs and pressed on.

After an hour, Kodiak began to yip and slow his pace. Suddenly, the dog howled and danced around. Julie stopped the team and buried the snow hook.

"Sam! Sam!" she called out and listened in the silence for a reply.

Kodiak sat at the side of the embankment and whined. Julie grabbed one of the sled's lanterns and peered over the edge. At the bottom of the embankment rested Sam's overturned sled.

"Sam!"

Julie returned to her sled and pulled out two lengths of rope. She secured them to the sled and threw them down the embankment. She also retrieved several blankets from the sled and tossed them after the ropes. Then, taking her medical bag and lantern, she gripped the rope and worked her way down the embankment.

When she reached the bottom of the icy slope, Julie was stunned by what she saw. Several of Sam's dogs were dead. Her heart beat faster as she righted the sled, praying that it wouldn't reveal Sam's dead body. The sled turned over with a thud and exposed nothing more than an indentation in the snow.

"Sam, where are you?" Julie called into the night. The yips of several dogs sent her in search of their source. A few yards away, Julie found the rest of the team faithfully surrounding

Sam's lifeless form. He'd been able to cut the dogs loose from the tangled harness before he passed out in the snow.

Julie positioned the lantern to offer the best light and spread a blanket beside Sam. The dogs seemed to know that their job was done, and they allowed Julie to work without interference. She gently rolled Sam onto the blanket.

"Oh, Sam," she whispered as she saw the matted blood in his hair. Examining more closely, Julie found a nasty cut along Sam's hairline. She felt quickly for a pulse to assure herself that he was still alive.

Finding a steady pulse and realizing that the bleeding was minimal, Julie wasted no time tending the wound except to wrap it with a length of bandage. She examined Sam's sled basket to see if it was in good enough shape to use. The runners and the basket's side were broken, but the damaged sled would work well enough to get Sam up the embankment.

Working the ropes around the sled, Julie prayed for strength. She had to take off her mittens for several minutes at a time in order to tie the ropes securely. Fearing frostbite, she worked quickly to finish with the ropes.

When she felt confident that the sled was secured, Julie positioned the basket beside Sam's still form. Wrapping the blanket around Sam, Julie rolled his body into the basket and tied him securely in place. The dogs who'd survived the accident scurried up the embankment behind Julie as she prepared to pull Sam up.

Realizing Sam's dogs could help, Julie pulled out an extra harness and added them to her team. Then she pulled the snow hook and took hold of the harness.

"Come on, boys. Let's go," she called as she pulled them forward. The dogs strained against the basket but pulled eagerly as if they sensed the life-and-death issue at hand.

As the basket with Sam's battered body appeared over the top of the embankment, Julie quickly secured the snow hook and went to him. He was still unconscious.

"Please, God," she prayed as she packed Sam in blankets. "Please help me to get him home."

Julie knew the basket containing Sam's body was useless for the trail. Using all her strength, she lifted first one end of the broken basket and then the other until she'd managed to place it solidly atop her own sled. Convinced that Sam was as safe as she could make him, Julie moved the dogs out and headed for Nome.

Chapter 14

Julie paced anxiously while Dr. Welch inspected Sam's wounds. She tried to remain objective, reminding herself that she could only help if she kept her fears under control.

"There's quite a bit of swelling," Dr. Welch said as he finished his examination of Sam, "especially his left eye. We'll watch him closely. Hand me some gauze, please."

Automatically, Julie performed her duties as she would for anyone else, but her heart kept reminding her that this wasn't just anyone else. This was the man she loved. What would she do if he didn't make it? Julie watched Dr. Welch stitch up Sam's head wound.

"Why doesn't he wake up? He should be awake by now." She knew she sounded frantic.

"Julie, you're a nurse. Get ahold of yourself or leave the room. You know these things, especially when they involve concussions, are very unpredictable."

"I know," Julie replied. "I just wish it didn't have to happen to Sam."

"We've done all we can," Dr. Welch said as he taped a bandage in place. "Now, we'll have to wait and see what happens. Come along."

Julie nodded and went to the sanctuary of her own room. As soon as she closed the door, she fell to her knees and threw herself against the bed. "Dear God, I love Sam so very much. Please help him." Julie stayed on her knees praying for over an hour. When the clock chimed eleven, she rose and went down the hall to where Sam lay motionless.

Sitting beside his bed, Julie held Sam's hand and felt for a pulse. Finding it steady and strong, she exhaled deeply. She patted Sam's hand gently and spoke to him as if he were wide awake.

"Sam, I wanted you to know that your dogs have been cared for. I treated them as if they were my own. Kodiak had some nasty cuts, but I washed them out and put salve on them. He'll be just fine. I knew you'd be worried about the dogs, so I wanted to tell you." She grimaced as she leaned closer. Sam's left eye looked painfully swollen, and Julie offered up a prayer for his healing.

"I love you, Sam. Please wake up. Please be all right," she whispered as she held his hand against her face.

Julie sat in the soft light and watched Sam's chest rise and fall in even, rhythmic breathing. She lost track of time, needing to know that Sam was alive, even if he wasn't conscious.

"Julie?"

Julie roused herself, startled to find that she'd fallen asleep.

"Julie?" The strained, husky voice belonged to Sam.

"Oh, Sam!" Julie said, with tears streaming down her face. "You're awake. Oh, thank God."

"Where am I?" he asked weakly.

"The Nome hospital," Julie answered and rinsed out a cloth in cool water. She placed it against Sam's forehead.

"I hurt," Sam said with a sheepish grin. "I guess I took a bit of a fall."

"Just a bit." Julie returned the smile.

"Who brought me in?"

"I did," Julie answered, and nearly laughed at the surprised look that crossed Sam's face. "I tried to get someone to help me, but with the epidemic and the serum run, well, people were just preoccupied."

"How did you find me?" Sam asked as he tried painfully to sit up.

"Stay put," Julie said, with firm hands upon Sam's shoulders. "You took a nasty hit on the head, and you need to rest."

Sam fell weakly back against the pillows. "All right."

"Kodiak found me," Julie said abruptly.

"Kodiak? Is he okay?"

"He's fine. He's cut up a bit, but he led me to you and helped to pull us back to Nome."

"What about the others?"

"There were four dead when I got there," Julie said softly. "I'm sorry, Sam. I know how you love your dogs."

"I remember cutting them loose from the harness, but after that—nothing."

"The dogs saved your life," Julie added. "They were keeping you from freezing to death when I found you."

"They're a good bunch," Sam said, sounding tired.

"You'd better rest now. I'll check in on you from time to time, and Dr. Welch will be back in the morning," Julie said and got to her feet to leave.

Sam took hold of her hand and pulled her down. "Kiss me," he said, refusing to let go of her.

"Same old Sam," Julie said, and pressed her lips gently against his.

Sam smiled up at Julie. "You wouldn't have me any other way," he murmured.

"No," Julie said, "I suppose I wouldn't." She gently let go of Sam's hand. "Now, sleep."

Julie divided her time between Sam and the diphtheria patients. She was glad to see Sam's body healing so quickly, but worried as he became more moody and distant.

"I've brought you a special lunch," Julie said as she brought Sam a tray she'd prepared for him.

"I don't want it," Sam said and continued reading the newspaper that she'd brought him that morning.

"Sam," Julie said as she put the tray on the table beside his bed, "why are you doing this to me?"

"What do you mean?"

"Do you still love me?" Julie asked directly.

Sam's grim expression softened a bit. "This has nothing to do with you. Of course I still love you."

"Then what is this all about? Why are you so angry?" Julie demanded. "It's more than enough that I deal with dying children day by day. It's almost too much to bear that, with all the schooling and training I've received, I still can't help them. Now you're acting strange, and I haven't a clue what it's all about."

"This," Sam said as he threw the paper down, "is what it's all about."

Julie noticed the headlines. They were bold reminders that the life-saving serum was ever closer to Nome. "I don't understand. You're upset because the serum run is nearly complete?"

"I don't expect you to understand," Sam said and folded his arms across his chest. "It's just that I wanted to be part of it. I wanted to help bring the serum to Nome. Instead I'm here in this hospital like a useless lump of coal."

"Sam Curtiss, I don't believe you. You were nearly killed, and now you're feeling sorry for yourself?"

"I told you I didn't expect you to understand. Now just let me alone. I'll deal with it myself."

"I will not," Julie said firmly. "Would you walk away from me if I were behaving this way?"

Sam grinned sheepishly. "You have acted this way and, no, I didn't leave you alone."

"Well, then," Julie said and pulled a chair up to Sam's bedside, "I'm just as stubborn as you are and," she paused and smiled lovingly, "I care just as much."

Sam shook his head. "I've always been lucky, fortunate, blessed, whatever people want to call it. I usually get what I set my mind on, and it's hard not to go on getting my way."

"I'm certain that, for a man like you, missing out on something important is very difficult, but God has all of this in His perfect plan. Sam, it doesn't matter that you won't be the one to bring the serum into Nome. What matters is that the serum gets here safely without any more loss of life."

"I know all that. Believe me, I've reasoned it out in my head, but I wanted to do this. Not just for me, mind you." Sam paused and seemed to struggle to put his feelings into words. "But for God. He's done so much for me, and I wanted to offer Him a small token of thanks."

"You do many things that offer God thanks, Sam. You are a positive asset to God's family, and you simply need to keep in mind that whatever you do, you are doing the work of God."

"Colossians 3:23, huh?" Sam said reluctantly.

" 'And whatsoever ye do, do it heartily, as to the Lord, and not unto men,' " Julie quoted. "My mother was fond of that verse. She told me that anything a person did was a mission for God so long as they committed their ways to Him."

"Kind of humbles a guy," Sam said with a grin.

"It doesn't matter that you didn't run the serum, Sam. It doesn't matter what you do, so long as you do it for God and do it for His glory. I'd love you whether you raised dogs or panned gold. It doesn't matter to me what you do with your life so long as it's committed to God's will and I'm part of it," Julie said with all her heart.

Sam wrapped his arms around Julie. "You will always be a part of my life," he whispered against her ear. "Just as God will always be at the center of it. I'm glad you had the strength of faith to speak directly with me. We're going to be good for each other, because when one of us falls, the other will lift him up."

"Two are better than one," Julie murmured.

"Yes," Sam said. "Reminds me of Genesis 2:18: 'And the Lord God said, "It is not good that the man should be alone; I will make him an help meet for him." ' Will you be that for me, Julie? Will you marry me?"

Julie held up her left hand. "You told me one day I'd come to you wearing this ring and you would have your answer. Well, here I am, and the answer is yes."

Chapter 15

S am was released from the hospital the next day. The first thing he did was to find
a minister who could leave the sick and dying long enough to perform a wedding
ceremony.

Julie was heading from the hospital to the doctor's office when Sam caught up with her.
Protesting all the way, Julie allowed Sam to lead her to the church.

"But Sam," she said as they neared the church building, "I'm still wearing my nurse's
uniform."

"It doesn't matter," Sam said with a grin. "You could be wearing long johns and it
wouldn't matter to me. Besides, it's white."

Julie sighed and realized the weariness that threatened to overtake her. "I suppose
you're right. It's just that, well," she paused as they approached the church steps, "a girl
kind of has in mind all of her life the type of wedding she wants. This just doesn't fit my
dream."

Sam stopped and pulled Julie into his arms. "Look," he said softly, "if you don't want
to get married today, I understand. I won't force this on you."

Julie looked up at Sam, noticing the bandage on his forehead and the discoloration
around his eye. He was still handsome to her and with all of her heart she wanted to be his
wife. "No one's forcing anything on me," Julie answered as she reached up and pushed a
wave of brown hair back off Sam's face. "I want to marry you today."

"Maybe we could have a big church wedding after the epidemic is resolved. I heard that
the serum is due in within twenty-four hours—that is, if the weather holds."

"That would be wonderful," Julie said to both thoughts.

"Well then, let's not keep the minister waiting," Sam said and pulled Julie with him up
the steps.

It wasn't an ideal wedding, but it was more than enough to serve the purpose for which
it was intended. Two people pledged to God and one another that they would love each other
forever and never allow anything or anyone to come between them.

Looking down at the ring on her finger later that day, Julie remembered the hasty ceremony.
She tried to imagine how surprised her father and brother would be when they received the
short letter she'd sent. With the quarantine in place and no telephone at the Eriksson household, it was difficult to get information to them.

Her father would be pleased; August, too. Of that, Julie was certain. How she wished
they could have given her away to Sam. For a fleeting moment, Julie thought of her mother.

Agneta would have approved of the hurried wedding.

Julie's reflections were pushed aside, however, in the face of Nome's crisis. Once again she'd been called to the house of yet another victim of diphtheria, and as she felt the forehead of a small Eskimo girl, Julie's happy memories blurred. The child was burning with fever and most likely would die sometime soon. It seemed strange that something as wonderful as her wedding day would also be the day this child's parents would bury their only daughter.

Julie moved from one house to another. Always, she found various stages of diphtheria. Many were frightened at the news that they were showing the early signs of the disease. Julie worked to calm their nerves, reminding each one that the serum was due into Nome any day. Others were too sick to worry, and Julie prayed aloud for them as she nursed their weakened bodies.

As Julie stood beside the cradle of an eight-month-old baby, she thought how unjust it all was. There was help for this disease. She had training and skills that should save lives, but it still wasn't enough.

"God," she whispered, "why must it be this way?" She thought of the verses in Job and of her mother's dying. Surely her father had voiced that question enough times while sitting beside his dying wife. Hadn't Julie herself asked it of God? She remembered how her mother had correlated verses in Job with everyday life.

"Julie, we don't always know why God allows certain things to happen. We can't have all the answers just yet, because God knows they would be too much for our human minds to comprehend," her mother had told her. "God, in His sovereign wisdom, made all things for a purpose, and how each of those things comes into this world or goes out is entirely up to Him."

" 'Whence then cometh wisdom? and where is the place of understanding?' " Julie's mother had shared from Job 28:20. Julie remembered the moment with fondness. Her mother's greatest desire had been for her family to understand that her illness was neither just nor unjust. It was part of God's overall picture for their lives. That same chapter had answered its questions: "And unto man he said, Behold, the fear of the Lord, that is wisdom; and to depart from evil is understanding."

Julie lifted the dying infant into her arms. The baby's lifeless eyes stared up at her as his tiny lungs drew a final breath. She felt the child's body shudder and knew that he was gone. Gone from this earth but at peace in heaven with his Creator. Julie noted the time, returned the infant to his cradle, and recorded facts about the death before breaking the news to the parents.

Several hours later, Dr. Welch found Julie in a near stupor as she sat beside a child while its mother napped.

"You need to get some rest," Dr. Welch said as he checked the child over. "You've been on duty for over twelve hours by my calculations, and that's too much. Go home, Julie. Go home and get some rest."

"I'm fine," Julie said as she stood on the opposite side of the child's bed. "This is Joey. He's only been showing signs of diphtheria for the last eight hours. Temperature is one hundred and one degrees, and his throat is sore but not overwhelmingly so."

"Good," Dr. Welch said as he finished listening to the boy's chest. "The serum should arrive in time to fix you right up, son." The boy smiled weakly but didn't say anything. He'd already told Julie it hurt to talk, and she had encouraged him to remain silent.

Dr. Welch packed his bag and headed for the open bedroom door. "Don't tarry any longer than you have to, Julie. Go home and sleep."

Julie nodded, even though she had no intention of obeying.

When Dr. Welch returned to his office, he picked up the telephone and put a call through to Sam.

"Sam?" he said as a voice sounded through the line.

"Yes, this is Sam Curtiss."

"Sam, this is Dr. Welch. Look, I need you to come get your wife."

"Is she sick?" Panic filled Sam's heart.

"No, but she will be if she doesn't get some rest. She's ready to collapse, and I've tried to send her home to sleep, but she won't go. I was hoping you could come force the issue."

"No problem. I'll be right there," Sam answered. "By the way, where should I look for her?"

"I left her at the Davises' house. I imagine she'll be there for a while."

"I'm on my way," Sam said and hung up the phone. *Stubborn woman,* he thought as he pulled on his coat and hiked out into the darkened streets.

At the Davises' house, Sam knocked, then opened the door and walked in. Mrs. Davis appeared in the hallway just as Sam stepped inside. "Sam Curtiss," she said in a surprised tone. "What are you doing here?"

"I've come to get my wife," Sam said firmly. "I'm sorry to bother you, but Doc says she needs to rest and won't go home."

The woman nodded and led Sam to her son's bedroom. "She's in there," Mrs. Davis said as she opened the door. "I tried to get her to take a break, but she wouldn't hear of it."

Sam looked in to find Julie's dozing form as she sat beside the sleeping boy. Gently, Sam helped her to her feet and led her from the room.

"Sam," Julie protested. "What are you doing here?"

"Doc sent me," Sam said as he took Julie's parka from Mrs. Davis. "He said you were to go home and sleep and that he didn't want to see you back until you were rested."

"But—"

"No but," Sam said, helping her into her coat. "You're going home if I have to carry you—and you know that's no idle threat—so just be cooperative and we won't cause a scene."

"These people need me," Julie said as the parka fell into place. "I can't leave them."

"You aren't any good to them if you're dead on your feet."

"You don't understand the importance of what I do," Julie said as Sam led her out into the street.

"You're in our prayers, Mrs. Davis," Sam said as he pulled Julie along. The woman waved from her door. "Now listen to me," he continued with Julie, "no job is worth killing yourself over. You have an important duty to these people, but it's certainly not one that anyone expects you to die doing."

Julie tried to jerk away from Sam's grip. Maybe marrying Sam had been a mistake. Maybe he was going to expect her to give up her nursing career. Her mind reeled as Sam forced her along. They hadn't consummated their marriage, Julie reasoned. Perhaps she could dissolve it. But that wasn't what she wanted, either. Besides, she loved Sam, and she had made a promise to God to continue loving and obeying him. If Sam told her to quit nursing, she would have to go along.

Just then, George Maynard came rushing down the street.

"It's the serum," he yelled. "The governor's relayed for us to halt the run because of the weather. Gunnar Kaasen will have to lay over in Solomon until the storm clears."

"He can't," Julie said as she felt her strength give way. "He can't!"

"Hush, Julie," Sam said as he pulled her close. "George, are you sure there's no way to get the drivers through?"

"The wind is blowing up to forty knots, and that coupled with the snow is making it impossible for anyone to get through."

"But people are dying," Julie said, nearing hysteria. "They have to get the serum through. They have to."

Sam steadied Julie's trembling body. "Look, keep us posted. I need to get my wife home for some rest."

"Your wife?" George questioned in surprise.

Sam grinned. "Yeah, we were married in between jobs."

"Well, congratulations! It's nice that something decent can take place in the middle of this tragedy." George went hurrying off, and Sam helped Julie make it to their house.

By the time they'd reached the house, Julie was sobbing. She'd tried so hard to hold everything inside, but with the fear that the serum wouldn't arrive in time, Julie could no longer control her emotions.

Sam guided her into the house and helped her out of the parka. He could hardly bear the sounds of her sobs, and after pulling his own coat off, he took her into his arms and held her.

"They're going to die without the serum," Julie cried. "I can't bear to watch any more of them die."

"I know. I know," Sam said as he reached up and pulled the pins out of Julie's hair. The ebony mane fell soft across her shoulders, and Sam relished the feel of it.

"I can't help them, Sam," she said looking up with dark, wet eyes. "I'm useless to them."

"Nonsense," Sam said. "Come on. I'm going to take you upstairs and put you to bed. You're tired and distraught with what you've had to deal with today. I wish I could have given you a better wedding day."

Julie allowed Sam to lead her to what was to become their bedroom. Neither she nor Sam were thinking about the romance of their wedding night, however. His only concern was to calm her down and see to it that she got some much-needed sleep.

Julie steadied her nerves and dried her eyes. She was too tired to expend more energy on useless tears. Sam helped her to the edge of the bed, where he knelt down and unlaced her mukluks.

"Now," Sam said as he threw the boots to one side. "You rest, and I'll go get a wet cloth for you to wipe your face with."

"No!" Julie exclaimed. "Please don't leave me, Sam. I can't be alone right now."

Sam smiled and unlaced his own boots. "I'll hold you until you're asleep, and even after that, if you like."

"I like," Julie said and moved over to make room for her husband.

Sam eased his weight onto the bed and pulled Julie into his arms. Neither one of them had ever experienced a closeness like this. It was so intimate, so pure.

"Sam," Julie murmured as she put her head upon his chest. "The serum has to get through. We should pray for a miracle."

"You're right, of course. Why didn't we think of that earlier?"

"I don't know. I guess we were just too busy trying to take care of everything ourselves. At least I know I was. I hate myself for always resorting to prayer as a final option," Julie replied.

"Don't hate yourself," Sam stated firmly. "You are a creation of God, and He loves you. I forget the importance of prayer, myself. We'll just pray for a miracle and ask God to deliver the serum into Dr. Welch's hands in record time."

"But if the governor has ordered the race stopped," Julie began, "it would be against the law to continue. Wouldn't it?"

"I suppose it might be perceived that way," Sam said with a nod. "However, a guy has to get the message in order to heed it, right? Maybe Gunnar won't get the message."

"I suppose that's always possible," Julie said with renewed hope. "Thank you for being such an encouragement, Sam."

They prayed together, and Julie fell asleep to the comfort of Sam's powerful, heartfelt words. For the first time in many days, she slept soundly with the assurance that God and Sam were at her side to protect her from the pain of the world.

Sam awoke with a start and, forgetting his wife was nestled in his arms, he woke Julie without meaning to.

"What is it, Sam?" Julie asked as she registered the sound of barking dogs.

"I don't know, but the dogs are going crazy. What time is it, anyway?"

Julie glanced at her watch. "Five-thirty," she replied and got to her feet. "Maybe Dr. Welch has come to find me. Maybe things are worse, and he needs my help."

"You aren't going anywhere," Sam said firmly. "You've only had a little over five hours of sleep, and that simply isn't enough. Get back into bed."

Julie felt as though she'd had a week's worth of sleep and stood with her hands planted firmly on her hips. "I will not be treated like a child, Sam Curtiss. I'm your wife, not one of your dogs."

Sam broke into a hearty laugh. "Well, Julie Curtiss," he said trying the name on for size, "my dogs have better sense than you when it comes to taking care of themselves. However, you are right. I'm used to telling, not asking. I'm sorry. Now, would you please get back into bed?"

The dogs had worked themselves into a feverish pitch, and Julie could stand it no longer. "Sam, please find out what's going on. Please."

Sam lost his resolve as he stared into the pleading eyes of his wife. "Oh, all right. But afterward, you must get some rest."

"Whatever you say, husband."

Sam was gone only a few minutes. When he returned, he tossed Julie her mukluks. "You'd better get these on."

"What is it, Sam?" Julie asked as she hastened to tie her laces.

"Just come with me," Sam said and hurried down the stairs with Julie close behind him. He brought her parka and waited while Julie pulled it over her head.

"Something's very wrong, isn't it?" Julie asked fearfully.

"On the contrary, Julie. On the contrary," Sam said as he opened the front door. "Hurry."

Sam and Julie raced through the darkened streets and Julie knew instinctively that Sam was leading her to the hospital. They rounded the corner. A dog team stood at the front stairs. Julie's heart skipped a beat as she recognized Balto, a big black-and-white husky who was a favorite of Gunnar's.

"Oh, Sam," she breathed against the subzero air. "It's Gunnar's sled! The serum is here!"

"Looks like we got that miracle," Sam said with a grin that spread from ear to ear. "Come on. Let's go see if we can help." Julie nodded and followed her husband up the steps. God was so good!

Chapter 16

G unnar's arrival had attracted very little attention. It was too early in the morning for most people, and no one thought the serum would come through because of the governor's mandate.

Julie stood by crying tears of joy as Dr. Welch received the cylindrical package and hurried inside to reveal its contents. Sam and Julie joined the party, but their hearts stopped when Dr. Welch announced that the serum was frozen. Everyone waited in pained anticipation, wondering if the trip had been for nothing. Finally word came from Seattle that the serum would be unharmed from the freezing and simply required a slow warming to bring it back to its original state.

Gunnar Kaasen and his huskies had covered the last fifty-three miles in less than seven-and-a-half hours. The entire serum run had covered more than 674 miles in a record 127.5 hours, bringing with it the renewed hope of life.

By February 21, Nome's quarantine was lifted. It had been exactly one month since the outbreak of the epidemic.

With every passing day, life seemed to take on a more normal routine. Schools reopened, much to the disappointment of the children and the relief of the parents. Store owners were happy to have full shops again, and everywhere people were glad to have lived through the crisis. George Nakoota even showed up to reveal a perfectly healed arm to Dr. Welch.

It was no different at the Curtiss house. Julie and Sam had settled into a comfortable life at the edge of town, and although Julie had been extremely busy nursing the sick and helping Dr. Welch, Sam had been patient with her absences. Julie wondered, however, how long it would be before Sam's patience wore thin and he would demand that she stay home more.

Several days after the quarantine had been lifted, Julie contemplated the situation as she prepared breakfast. Her heart belonged to Sam, yet part of her belonged to nursing as well.

"You're mighty deep in thought," Sam said as he came into the room and took a seat at the table. He threw the *Nome Nugget* on the chair beside him and smiled. "I suppose you're thinking about the serum run again."

"Well, as a matter of fact, I heard something quite fascinating yesterday," Julie said as she offered Sam a plate of fried eggs and bacon. She returned to the counter, where she retrieved a stack of freshly baked biscuits. Their tantalizing aroma filled the air, and as soon as Julie placed them on the table, Sam reached for one.

"No doubt another miracle," Sam teased. Julie had been enthralled by the stories of miraculous blessings that enabled the drivers to deliver the diphtheria antitoxin to Nome in only five and a half days.

Julie put her own plate of food on the table and joined Sam. "You know how I love the way God moved in this crisis," she said, smiling. "I just can't help being fascinated with it."

"I know, Julie, and I feel the same way. Let's have a prayer." Sam took her hands. "Father, we thank You for the bounty of our table and for the healing of our community. We praise You that the deaths were few and that the medicine was provided in a much quicker time than any of us dreamed possible. Amen."

Sam started eating as Julie began to tell what she'd heard. "Leonhard Seppala cut out a lot of distance by taking a shortcut across Norton Sound. The water was frozen solid, but it was difficult for him to see his way so he had to rely upon the dogs."

"I'd heard that," Sam answered. "It takes a brave man to venture out across an open bay like that. Even if it is frozen solid at the shores, you can't know how it will be once you get out in the middle of the inlet."

"Well, as wondrous as that was, what happened after Leonhard crossed the sound gives even more cause for praise," Julie said, leaning forward. "Not more than three-and-a-half hours after Leonhard crossed Norton Sound, the entire thing broke up, and the ice moved out into the Bering Sea. The crossing would have taken Leonhard's life, no doubt, had he attempted it at a later time. Talk about the hand of God!"

"Incredible," Sam said as he paused between bites. "Our God is truly a God of miracles."

"Leonhard's shortcut saved hours and probably many lives, Sam. I'm amazed that he was able to stay on the sled. After all, he'd driven those dogs for more than one hundred and sixty-nine miles just to get to the serum at Shaktolik. Then to turn around and travel another ninety-one miles to get the serum closer to Nome, well. . ." Julie shook her head. "It staggers my imagination."

"That lead dog of his is something else," Sam said, sipping his coffee. "His name is Togo, and Leonhard never thought he'd amount to much—that is, until he jumped the fence one day and followed Leonhard across part of the interior. Leonhard finally harnessed him up to keep him out of trouble. Lo and behold, the dog's a born leader!"

"Thanks to Togo and the other dogs, Nome is safe, and the epidemic has been defeated," Julie said. "I simply can't imagine the way God planned this all out. Who can know the mind of God?"

"I know how much you've enjoyed learning about the hazards that the men met on the trail. I have one that I think you will find quite rewarding," Sam said with a smile.

"Oh, tell me, Sam! What did you hear?" Julie asked as she leaned forward, her eyes wide in anticipation.

"You remember we heard that the run was to be halted because of the weather?"

"Sure, I do," Julie said with a nod. "How could I forget? I've never lost control like that in my life."

"Well," Sam continued, "it was just about the time we decided to pray that Gunnar Kaasen made the decision to drive on past Solomon and keep the serum moving. He felt compelled to go on and not waste time with a stop. No one had the opportunity to tell him about the mandate from the governor because he never stopped."

"It's just like you said," Julie remembered. "A man can't be faulted for not doing what he knows nothing about. Good for Gunnar!"

"Well, there's more," Sam said as he finished his breakfast. "The wind came up something fierce, and Gunnar couldn't see a thing in front of him. All of a sudden his lead dog, Balto, stopped dead in his tracks. Gunnar couldn't understand why, but Balto wouldn't budge."

"What happened?" Julie asked, captivated by Sam's story.

"Balto had led the team out across the Topkok River, and it wasn't solidly frozen. Balto was standing in running water when he came to a stop."

"Poor thing," Julie sympathized. "His feet could have frozen to the ice. What did Gunnar do? Balto looked just fine when they got into Nome."

"Gunnar's a good man. He thought fast and unharnessed Balto. There was plenty of powdered snow on the banks, so Gunnar rubbed Balto's feet in it until they were fairly dry."

"How ingenious! I've got to remember that one when I'm out on my route," Julie said, braving a reference to her job. Even though the epidemic was over, Julie hadn't found the nerve to talk with Sam about her nursing career. She started to clear the table to avoid Sam's reaction.

"It never hurts to be prepared, and the more you know about surviving accidents, the better off you are. That's what made me so mad about my own accident," Sam reflected. "I knew better than to take the risks I was taking. I should have slowed down a bit and paid more attention. However," he added with a grin, "there was a certain black-haired nurse on my mind. It seems she had just told me that she loved me." Sam pushed his chair back and pulled Julie onto his lap.

"Oh, Sam," Julie whispered against his hair. How she wished she could clear things up and explain how she felt about her work. She was so afraid that if she insisted on continuing her nursing career, Sam would stop loving her.

Sam nuzzled his lips against Julie's neck and began kissing her. Julie found the contact electrifying, yet she knew she needed to finish getting ready for work. As gently as she could, she pushed Sam away.

"I've got to finish up here and get down to the hospital," she said and jumped up abruptly. Sam's surprised face told it all. "I'm sorry," Julie whispered and hurried to wash the breakfast dishes.

Sam's silence worried Julie. She wiped the soap suds from her hands and went back to the table where he was still sitting.

"We should talk," she said and waited for Sam to put down the newspaper.

"What about?" Sam asked hesitantly. Julie hadn't been her normal self the last few days, and he wasn't sure that he was up to dealing with whatever was troubling her.

"Sam, do you know how long I dreamed of becoming a nurse?"

"I know it was a longtime dream. I know, too, that it was a dream you shared with your mother."

"Yes, that's right," Julie said, searching her mind for the right words. "Being a nurse is very important to me, not just because it's a job I do every day, but because of the need. These people are without many of the comforts available in the States, and I want to be a part of seeing to it that they have what they need in the way of health care."

"It's an admirable position," Sam said as he reached out for Julie. "I've always admired your determination and dedication."

Julie stepped back to avoid Sam's touch. He frowned but said nothing.

"It's my determination and dedication to what I believe God wants me to do," Julie said, stressing the reference to God. She paused to see what Sam's reaction might be. His face was unreadable.

"Go on," he said unemotionally. He was troubled by the way Julie had distanced herself from his touch. She hadn't seemed herself since the critical part of the epidemic had passed. Sam was determined to get to the bottom of whatever was bothering her.

"I love what I do, Sam. I love to help people, and I enjoy my work with the natives."

"I don't see what you're getting at, Julie," Sam said more impatiently than he'd intended. "I know that you love your job. I know you love the people and the land. What I don't know is what this has to do with us and why you're acting so strangely."

Sam got up and took two long strides to where Julie stood. He reached out to hold her, but Julie turned away.

"Please don't touch me. I'm trying to explain this to you, and you aren't making matters any easier," Julie said, close to tears.

"Julie, are you sorry that you married me?"

Julie turned back quickly and shook her head. "No, Sam. I love you, and I hope that you still love me."

"Of course I love you." Sam could no longer stand Julie's coolness. He took her into his arms and crushed her to his chest. "I will always love you," he whispered as his lips pressed a long, passionate kiss upon hers.

Julie melted against Sam. She could never imagine life without him. Maybe giving up her career was the only way she could save her marriage. Tears streamed from her eyes. A sob escaped her throat, causing Sam to pull back.

"What in the world?" he muttered and dropped his hands. "I don't understand what this is all about, but I've had just about enough." He stormed out of the room, barely remembering his parka as he went out into the cold.

Julie jumped at the sound of the front door slamming. Knowing it would be impossible to work, Julie retreated upstairs, locked herself in their bedroom, and had a good long cry.

Chapter 17

Julie lost track of time as she contemplated her misery. How could she explain her heart to Sam without hurting him? She loved him so much, yet she felt torn.

She looked around the room that had been hers for a little over a month. Everything here spoke of Sam; the large walnut dresser, the huge four-poster bed, and even the lamps on the nightstands looked masculine and powerful. The room smelled like the heady cologne Sam liked to wear.

"Father," Julie prayed, "I wanted to serve You." Before she could continue, it came to Julie's mind that if she truly wanted to serve God, she'd open her heart and skills to whatever job He gave her. Perhaps the job God wanted Julie to do now involved being a good wife and homemaker. Maybe she was trained as a nurse simply to help during the epidemic.

"I need to understand, Lord. Please teach me what it is I'm to do," Julie begged. "I can't bear to hurt Sam, and I can't bear the way I'm feeling."

Julie reached to the nightstand and picked up her Bible. She flipped aimlessly through the pages, wondering what God might show her there. When she reached Ephesians, Julie began to read through the verses. "Teach me, Lord," she prayed. "I came home to serve You, and now I have a husband to serve and work with as well."

Just then, Julie's eyes fell upon Ephesians 5:22: "Wives, submit yourselves unto your own husbands, as unto the Lord. For the husband is the head of the wife, even as Christ is the head of the church: and he is the saviour of the body. Therefore as the church is subject unto Christ, so let the wives be to their own husbands in every thing." It seemed a clear answer.

"All right, Father," Julie said in earnest, "I trust You to guide me. Sam loves You and seeks Your guidance, and because of this, I believe, without fear, that You will control this situation."

Julie got up and dried her eyes. What should she do? Sam was out there somewhere, and no doubt he was feeling just as confused and troubled as she was. Julie debated trying to find him but chose to wait until he returned. She was determined to make her concerns clear. If Sam insisted she give up nursing, then she'd trust God to give her the grace to do just that.

Julie didn't have long to wait. Within the hour, she heard Sam stomping around through the rooms downstairs. Julie brushed her hair and made her way to the top of the stairs just as Sam was starting up.

"We should talk," Julie said softly.

Sam nodded. The anger was gone and in his eyes shone the love that Julie had come to count on.

Julie made her way down the stairs and took Sam's extended hand. "I'm sorry for the way

I've been acting. I know you deserve a lot better, and I feel bad about it."

"If I've done something wrong, you should tell me," Sam said as he led Julie to the couch.

"You haven't done anything wrong, Sam. That's what makes this so frustrating to me. I've always been able to speak my mind, but something about you makes me forget myself. I suppose it has a great deal to do with my love for you," Julie said softly. She looked down at her hands, avoiding Sam's face.

"You make your love for me sound like something oppressive," he replied.

"Not oppressive," Julie answered. "Maybe restrictive."

"Restrictive?" Sam questioned. "How so?"

"I'm not sure that restrictive is even the right word. I never expected you to come into my life. I don't know why, but I never considered marrying and having a family. At least not until much later in my life."

"And?"

"And," Julie said with deliberation, "I doubt I would have become a public health nurse if I'd known I would be married so soon into my career."

"I still don't understand," Sam said softly.

Julie looked up at him. "I love my job, but I'm ready to give it up if that's what you tell me to do." There! She'd finally managed to get the words out.

"What in the world are you talking about?" Sam asked, confusion spreading across his face. "Why would I ever ask you to quit nursing?"

"Because it takes me away from you. I have to be on the village routes for most of the year, and those absences would keep us separated for long, long spells. I'm not sure I could bear it myself."

"What makes you think that you'll be separated from me?" Sam asked with a grin. "I know what's required of you on your job. I knew it before I ever married you. I even talked with Dr. Welch at length about it."

"You did?" Julie's surprised voice amused Sam.

"I certainly did. You didn't think I'd walk into something like marriage without knowing exactly what I was doing, did you?"

"I guess I never thought about it," Julie replied. "I was too caught up in the epidemic. What did Dr. Welch tell you?"

"He explained your duties and the schedule you'd be keeping as a public health nurse. He told me you'd go by dogsled in the winter months and horseback in the summer. He also told me that the idea of a woman alone on the trails bothered him. I asked him why someone couldn't accompany you."

"And what did he say?"

"He told me there wasn't funding to support two people on the route. It had been hard enough to get support for one. I told him my idea was to accompany you on the trails without being paid."

"What?" Julie's mouth dropped open. "You'd be willing to go with me?"

"I'd insist. I can't imagine anything more enjoyable than long hours in the wilderness with a beautiful woman who just happens to be my wife. I've had it planned from the beginning."

"I never considered such a thing," Julie said in disbelief. "You'd actually go with me? What a wonderful idea! We wouldn't have to be separated, and you wouldn't want me to quit my job." Julie squealed with delight as she threw herself into Sam's arms.

"Is that what your moodiness has been all about?" Sam asked, holding Julie at arm's length. "Did you think I was going to force you to give up your dream?"

Julie nodded. "I wanted to talk to you about my job before we got married. But then, the epidemic came up, and you nearly got yourself killed, and I just let it go. I was afraid to bring it up after that."

"Never be afraid of me, Julie," Sam said softly. "And please don't ever turn away from me again."

"I'm sorry, Sam, it's just that you being the kind of guy you are, I thought—"

Sam couldn't resist chuckling as he interrupted. "You mean to tell me you honestly thought I'd expect you to give up something as important as your nursing? I can't believe you'd think so little of me. I mean, I know I can be a little demanding and—"

"A little?" Julie interrupted. "A little?"

Sam shook his head and pulled Julie into his arms. "Okay, so I can be very demanding, but I certainly wouldn't make a decision like that for you. I married you knowing you had a job to do. I admired you for it. I think helping the villages is an important task, and I believe strongly in spreading the Word of God to those who have never heard it before. I kind of figured I might help you."

"Honestly?"

"Honestly," Sam said firmly.

"I'm so sorry for misjudging you," Julie said as she reached a hand up to Sam's bearded face. "I love you so much, and I love my nursing. I didn't want to have to choose between the two."

"I would never have asked you to," Sam said as he kissed Julie tenderly.

Julie felt a burden was lifted from her shoulders. She thought of her willingness to accept whatever Sam had instructed her to do and knew that her peace came in being willing to be obedient to God.

As Sam pulled away from her, she nestled her face against his chest and thanked God for the husband He'd given her. Almost as an afterthought, Julie raised one last question.

"Sam, there are bound to be times when you'll be needed here or when you can't go with me. How will you feel about that?"

"Nothing will keep me from your side," Sam declared.

"But what if something happens and it does? I can't stay home and forget the people in the villages. We should be in agreement about what we'll do if that happens," Julie said earnestly.

"If that happens, and I don't believe it will," Sam replied, "then I'll simply wait here with a light in the window until you come home safely to me. Good enough?" Sam's eyes were filled with love.

Julie nodded. She no longer had any doubts about being married to Sam. "I love you, Sam, and I love God for giving me the wisdom to marry you. It will be the light of your love that leads me home and keeps me strong."

"Oh, my beautiful Jewel," Sam said as he leaned back and pulled Julie against him. "That's a light that will never burn out. For as long as I live, it will burn only for you."

Acknowledgments

T he 1925 diphtheria epidemic in Nome, Alaska, would have taken more lives and spread farther had it not been for the heroic hearts of the men who shared the serum run. Their names are listed here in honor of their sacrifice and spirit.

"Wild Bill" Shannon—Nenana to Tolovana (52 miles)
Dan Green—Tolovana to Manley Hot Springs (31 miles)
Johnny Folger—Manley Hot Springs to Fish Lake (28 miles)
Sam Joseph—Fish Lake to Tanana (26 miles)
Titus Nikoli—Tanana to Kallands (34 miles)
Dave Corning—Kallands to Nine Mile mail cabin (24 miles)
Edgar Kalland—Nine Mile to Kokrines (30 miles)
Harry Pitka—Kokrines to Ruby (30 miles)
Bill McCarty—Ruby to Whiskey Creek (28 miles)
Edgar Nollner—Whiskey Creek to Galena (24 miles)
George Nollner—Galena to Bishop Mountain (18 miles)
Charlie Evans—Bishop Mountain to Nulato (30 miles)
Tommy Patsy—Nulato to Kaltag (36 miles)
Jackscrew—Kaltag to Old Woman shelter house (40 miles)
Victor Anagick—Old Woman to Unalakleet (34 miles)
Myles Gonangnan—Unalakleet to Shaktolik (40 miles)
Henry Ivanoff—starts from Shaktolik but meets Seppala
Leonhard Seppala—Shaktolik to Golovin (91 miles)
Charlie Olson—Golovin to Bluff (25 miles)
Gunnar Kaasen—Bluff to Nome (53 miles)
And, of course, the dogs!

My special thanks to the Anchorage Museum of History and Art; Anchorage Municipal Libraries; the University of Alaska, Fairbanks; and my husband Jim for their assistance with the historical research surrounding this event.

DESTINY'S ROAD

by Tracie Peterson

Chapter 1

The Royal Canadian Air Force regrets to inform you. . ." Bethany Hogan refused to read any further as the telegram fell from her hand and blew across the yard.

Chubby four-year-old legs ran across the promise of new spring grass to catch up with the papers but were too slow for the job.

Beth watched as two-year-old Phillip followed after his older brother, Gerald. How could she explain to them that their father had been killed? How could she hope that they could understand that a madman named Hitler had made it necessary for their father to give his life in service to his country?

American-born and native to Alaska, Bethany had met her Canadian husband only six years earlier in Fairbanks. He was flying with barnstormers who, for the outrageous price of two dollars, would take individuals up into the air to forget the problems and concerns of the Depression.

John Brian Hogan, "JB" to his friends, wasn't exactly what Beth had been looking for. He was a bit too wild and carefree, with a love of life that oozed over into his conversations and chosen profession. Beth thought him reckless but entertaining.

She remembered standing along the sidelines watching as her girlfriends took turns flying with some of the other barnstormers. JB worked for over an hour, missing several paying customers, in order to coax Beth into the air for free.

It all came rushing back to her as the breeze picked up and blew strong across the open field. The roar of the DH-4's twelve-cylinder engine, the seeming frailty of dope and fabric wings, and the rush of the wind as JB eased back on the stick and the biplane became airborne.

Now he was gone. In his passing, two children were left without a father. Bethany squinted against the morning sun and watched as her children came running back across the field. They were laughing, enjoying the moment, the sun, and the excitement of a new day.

"Momma!" Gerald squealed as he wrapped himself around her legs. Phillip mimicked his brother as soon as his little legs could take him to his mother's side.

Beth hugged her children close, refusing to show them her sorrow. *Oh, JB,* she cried silently. *Why? Why did you have to leave them now? Why did you have to leave me?*

"Momma, was that a letter from Daddy?" Gerald asked in his boisterous voice.

Beth steadied her nerves, lifted Phillip into her arms, and led Gerald with her to sit beneath their favorite towering pine. Gerald, always the more sensitive of the two, sobered at his mother's expression. He waited quietly while Beth settled herself with Phillip.

"The letter wasn't from Daddy, but it was about Daddy," Beth said and took a deep

391

breath. She breathed a prayer, asking God for just the right words. "Daddy has to go away for a long, long time."

"Did he go to heaven?" Gerald asked, surprising Beth with his bluntness.

"Yes," Beth said softly, uncertain that Gerald could really understand. "What made you ask that?"

"Daddy told me he might have to go to heaven instead of coming home after his job was done."

Good old JB, Beth thought. She should have known he would prepare his child for the possibility of his death. "Do you understand about heaven, Gerald?"

"Daddy said it was a really beautiful place. A place where you got to live if you loved God," the boy answered quite seriously.

"That's right," Beth said as she tried to think of what she might say next.

"Will we see him again?"

"Yes," Beth assured. "We'll see him again in heaven."

Phillip seemed oblivious to the news, but Gerald's little forehead furrowed as he concentrated on his mother's answer. Beth wondered if he would cry or if he'd truly be able to grasp the meaning of his father's death. JB had already been gone from Gerald's daily life for several months.

Gerald began to nod his head and Phillip, ever faithful, did likewise. "Then it's okay," he said as he put his hand on his mother's arm. "If Daddy's in heaven, then it's okay."

Beth looked at her brown-eyed son and smiled. "Yes, it's okay, Gerry. Daddy's in heaven and it's really okay."

Phillip squirmed out of Beth's arms and ran after some birds, while Gerald sat beside his mother and held her hand. He seemed to sense that, while his mother's words were filled with hope and eternity, her heart was empty and hurting.

Later that night, after Bethany had tucked the boys into the double bed they shared, she made her way to the sitting room. The rolltop desk gave slight resistance as she pushed it open and took a seat.

There was a great deal to be done in order to get everything arranged. Being American, Bethany was determined to return to Alaska and raise her children as Americans, but where should she take them, and how would she support them? There was the small nest egg that she and JB had saved, but that wouldn't last long with two growing boys.

JB had always teased her about being so meticulous and organized. Beth would make lists every fall and again in the spring of all the things that needed to be done. JB thought it foolish, but inevitably he relied upon them every bit as much as his wife. So Bethany made another list—in fact, several.

Across the top of the paper she wrote: *Things to sell. Things to take. Things to do first.* Under the final heading, she listed the thing that seemed most important: *Bury JB.*

Beth worked long into the night, going over the contents of the house and JB's shop. She thought of choice items to save as mementos for the boys, things that would give them fond memories of their father. Glancing up, she noticed the framed picture of JB in his uniform.

She put the pencil down and reached for the picture. For the first time, Beth allowed her tears to fall. It was impossible to imagine that the big-hearted man she'd fallen in love with was gone.

"JB," she said aloud, "you told me this might happen, but I never believed you. You were always able to get out of any scrape, no matter how bad." She looked at the photo, tracing JB's outline. He'd obviously been told to look serious for the photograph, but his eyes crinkled with laughter.

"I never, ever thought you'd leave me. I trusted God to keep you in His care, which of course He did. I just didn't know He'd choose to care for you in heaven."

Beth got up from the desk and, with the picture still in hand, stretched out across the couch. She intended only to have a good long cry and then go to bed, but instead she fell asleep clutching the picture to her heart.

"Momma," Phillip patted at Beth's face. "Momma, me eat."

Beth roused herself from a dreamless sleep, grateful for a reason to get up. The picture clattered to the floor, momentarily forgotten as Phillip climbed on top of his mother.

"Come here, you sweet boy," Beth said, pulling the two-year-old into her arms. "You don't look like you need food," she teased as she looked underneath Phillip's nightshirt. "But, you look like you could use a good tickling." Phillip's giggles filled the air as Beth ran her fingers lightly across her son's abdomen.

"Tickle me," Gerald called as he climbed on his mother's legs. "I need tickles, too."

The three of them rolled around the couch, laughing and giggling until Beth felt her sorrow melt away. JB wasn't really gone. As long as Gerald and Phillip were here, she would have reminders of JB's love for her.

"Come along, you ragamuffins," Beth said as she set the boys aside and got to her feet. "I'll get you some breakfast and then we have some errands to do."

The boys padded after their mother to the kitchen and waited impatiently for her to prepare steaming bowls of oatmeal. After placing the food on the table, Beth went to the refrigerator and brought cream for their cereal.

"Berries, too, Momma?" Gerald questioned.

"No, I'm sorry. It's still too early for them. I have a little bit of brown sugar, though. I've been saving it just for you two," Beth said as she went to the cupboard and pulled out a small china bowl.

Phillip clapped his hands as Beth spooned the sweetener onto the oatmeal. "Choogar, choogar," he chanted, trying to pick up pieces of the lumpy brown sugar before Beth could blend it in with the cereal.

When breakfast was served, Beth took a seat at the table and she and the boys bowed their heads.

"Father, thank You for the food You've given us," Beth prayed. "We ask for it to nourish our bodies, that we might have the strength and energy to do Your work. Amen."

Gerald and Phillip went to work on their cereal, while Beth pulled a small, worn Bible from the pocket of her apron. Such was their morning routine: breakfast and devotions.

Beth opened to 1 John 2:28 and read to the boys: "And now, little children, abide in him; that, when he shall appear, we may have confidence, and not be ashamed before him at his coming."

She placed the book on the table and turned to Gerald. "Do you understand what that means?"

Gerald got a serious look on his face as his mind struggled to grasp the ancient words. "I know we're little children," he said pointing to himself and then to Phillip.

"That's right," Beth said with a nod. "And abide in him means to live in God and God in you. Do you understand that?" Gerald nodded his head yes and Phillip mimicked the action before Beth continued.

"We are all God's little children and this verse tells us that we are to remain close to Him. It also tells us why. It says we need to do this so that we won't be ashamed when God comes back for us."

"Like He came back for Daddy?" Gerald asked, surprising Bethany.

"That's right. Daddy loved God very much, and because Daddy lived close to God, he wasn't ashamed when God told him it was time to come to heaven."

"Daddy in heh, hehbeen," Phillip joined in.

Beth held back her tears. "Yes, Daddy is in heaven and he's smiling right now because his two big boys are learning about God and how much God loves them. It makes your daddy happy and it makes God happy when you spend time learning about the Bible."

"Will Daddy forget us while he's in heaven?" Gerald asked with a look of concern. "What if we don't get there very soon? Will Daddy know us when he sees us?"

Beth couldn't hold back the hot tears that filled her eyes. "Daddy will always remember us. He won't forget us, and we won't forget him. You wait here for just a minute," Beth said using the opportunity to wipe her eyes as she went back to the living room for JB's picture.

When she returned to the kitchen, the boys were nearly done with their breakfast. She put the picture in the middle of the table and took her seat. "This picture was taken last year when your daddy went away to fight in the big war."

"He went to fly the airplanes, right, Momma?" Gerald queried.

"Yes," Beth answered. "Your daddy flew the airplanes."

"Did he fly his airplane up to heaven?"

"I'm sure that Daddy was in his airplane when he went to heaven. We never know when God will come to take us home to heaven, so we must always be ready. We must always be good and kind to one another, and we should always live close to God and His Word."

Phillip reached out to the picture. "Daddy?"

Beth grieved that her boys would never remember their father for the person he was. He would only be a character in stories they heard and a friendly face that sat upon their breakfast table.

"Yes, Phillip," she said as she allowed him to hold the picture in his chubby hands, "this is your daddy, and he loved us all very much. Whenever we miss him, we can look at this picture and remember that he doesn't want us to be sad. Can you do that, boys?"

Both boys nodded their heads solemnly. They seemed to sense that the moment was quite important. "How long will it be, Momma? How long before we see Daddy in heaven?" Gerald finally asked.

"I don't know, Gerry. But one day we will see him. Of that you can be sure." It seemed to satisfy his boyish curiosity and Beth dismissed them both to play outside.

After cleaning up the breakfast dishes, Beth went once again to the living room, where she looked over the lists she had made the previous evening. Taking three thumbtacks, Beth posted her lists to the wall, determined to mark each item off as she accomplished the tasks. She was reaching for the telephone to call Pastor McCarthy when a knock sounded at the front door.

Beth opened it to reveal her closest neighbor and friend, Karen Sawin. Karen was always bubbly and happy-go-lucky, but the look on her face told Bethany that she'd already guessed or heard about the newest telegram.

"I thought you might be able to use a friend," Karen said as she extended a freshly baked loaf of bread.

Beth accepted the still-warm bread and ushered Karen into the house. "Thanks. You always seem to know the right thing to do."

"So," Karen started uncomfortably, "I guess you heard something official."

"Yes, JB was killed in action," Beth said matter-of-factly as she put the bread on the coffee table and offered Karen a seat on the couch. "You'll have to forgive the way I look. I fell asleep out here last night and haven't changed clothes."

"Why don't you go ahead and take a nice hot bath and let me keep an eye on the boys?" Karen suggested.

Beth smiled and reached out to take hold of Karen's hand. "You are such a dear friend. I'd really like that, if you don't mind. Afterward, we can have a long talk."

"Of course," Karen said. "Whatever you need."

An hour later, Beth emerged looking refreshed. She'd washed and dried her pale blond hair and gathered it back at the sides with mother-of-pearl combs.

"I feel like a new woman," Beth said as she joined Karen in the living room. She wore a freshly pressed cotton dress whose bright peach color was trimmed with a white eyelet collar and armbands. The matching belt showed off Beth's tiny waistline.

"You look so skinny, Beth. I'll bet you haven't eaten a decent meal since JB. . ." Karen fell silent.

"It's all right, Karen," Beth said as she leaned over to pat her friend's hand. "What's happened has happened. JB is dead. We can't change it by not talking about it."

"You're taking it awfully well. I doubt I would be as capable as you," Karen said honestly.

"I'm not handling it that well, Karen. I'm just numb and reliant upon the Lord."

Karen nodded at Beth's words.

"No doubt in a week or two, I'll be beside myself," Beth continued, "but then again, maybe not. I do have to be strong for the boys—after all, they can't be expected to lose both of their parents."

"That's true," Karen said as she pushed back her dark hair, "and we both know JB wouldn't want you to be sad. I don't think I ever saw JB with a frown on his face."

"Nor I," Beth agreed. "JB was a terminally happy man. He always joked that St. Peter would meet him at the pearly gates and ask him what was so funny. JB did love to laugh."

"I'll never forget the night before he left," Karen remembered. "He was laughing and dancing with everyone, including old Mr. Thompson." Karen stopped short and looked away. "Here I meant to come over and get your mind off JB, and I'm doing just the opposite."

"I know what you mean. I tell myself I don't have to deal with everything at once. I mean, it's been nearly a year since JB joined the service. Aside from his few brief letters, the void has been something I've dealt with in an ongoing manner. Yet now that I know he isn't coming back, it seems important to put all our affairs in order and to move on." Beth stared intently into Karen's hazel eyes. "Does that make any sense?"

"I think each person must deal with grief in their own manner. I know I'd be inclined to run away from all of it. Please don't think me unfeeling, Bethany, but I pray to God I never have to know. If something happened to my Miles, I just know I'd crumble."

Beth leaned over and hugged Karen tightly. "I don't think badly of you at all. I pray you never have to know, either. I pray daily that this war will end and Miles will come home safely to you."

"You are such a dear friend, Beth. Is there anything I can do to help you?"

Beth pulled away and got to her feet. "As a matter of fact, there is. I've made several lists." She paused with a grin. "You know me and my lists."

Karen nodded and returned her friend's smile.

"Anyway," Beth continued, "I plan to leave as soon as I can. I want to return to Alaska with the boys and raise them as Americans. After all, they were born in America, and just because their father is—was—Canadian, that doesn't mean they can't share in my heritage as well."

"But where will you go? You haven't any family still living there. Who will take care of you?" Karen questioned in a concerned tone.

"God will take care of me, Karen. Remember Isaiah 54:4–5: 'Fear not; for thou shalt not be ashamed; neither be thou confounded; for thou shalt forget the shame of thy youth, and shalt not remember the reproach of thy widowhood any more. For thy Maker is thine husband; the Lord of hosts is his name; and thy Redeemer the Holy One of Israel; The God of the whole earth shall he be called.' "

"You have a strong faith, Bethany. I'll do whatever I can to help you, but I'll miss you sorely," Karen said as she got to her feet. "Just tell me what I can do."

As spring warmed into summer and the nights grew shorter, Bethany finalized her plans for moving her family to Alaska. She left many of her things with Karen, promising to send for them as soon as she and the boys were settled.

Then, despite the fact that an airplane had claimed the life of her husband, Bethany loaded her boys into the plane of JB's best friend and mentor, Pete Calhoon. With a last look at the place she and JB had called home, Beth turned, resolving to put the past behind her and start a new life in Alaska.

Chapter 2

Crash! Bang! Julie Curtiss cringed at the sound of the slamming doors. The clamor could only mean one thing: her brother was home, and he wasn't at all happy.

August Eriksson came stomping into the room. Mindless that his heavy boots were covered in mud, August marched across Julie's clean kitchen floor and threw his body against the back of a chair.

"Bad news?" Julie braved the words. Her dark eyes were sympathetic as she reached out to touch her brother's sleeve.

"They said I was too old," August grumbled the words. "I'm not even forty-two, and they think I'm too old to join the military."

Julie bit back a remark about being glad that August couldn't go off to the war in the Pacific. Ever since Pearl Harbor had been bombed the previous winter, August had been bent on participating in the defense of his country.

"A lot of other people are going off and serving," August said, dejected. Although he was two years Julie's senior, he seemed like a little boy to his sister.

"Maybe God has another plan for you, August," Julie suggested as she went to the huge cast-iron stove and poured two steaming mugs of coffee.

"I don't think He has any plans for me. I mean, just look at me, Jewels," he said, using his sister's nickname. "Pa died a year ago, and you and Sam took over the house."

"But August, you asked us to move in here in order to help with the dog kennel," Julie said defensively. "Sam and I can certainly move back to town if you like."

"No. No. No," August said as he ran his fingers through his dark hair. "I didn't mean for you to think that. I would have gone mad if you and Sam hadn't moved in here. It's just, oh, I don't know."

Julie patted August's hand. "I know you want to help fight the war, but August, maybe there's something special for you here in Nome."

"I used to think that, too, but after all these years of being alone except for you, Sam, and Pa, I just want to get out."

"Look, August, it's the middle of the darkest days," Julie said with a glance at the calendar. "It's only the end of March, and with all the darkness we have in the winter, a body is bound to get discouraged."

"It's more than that, Julie. I wanted to have a family. I want to get married and be a father. I want a home of my own, something I can build up with my own hands. I want to have a purpose and be needed by others and to need them in return. I just don't belong here with you and your husband."

"But Sam's your best friend," Julie protested.

"I know, I know, and you're my only living relative. That's my point. I don't want to die without leaving something behind," August answered.

"But if you go off to war and get yourself killed, you won't have a chance to marry and have a family. I can't lie and say I'm not relieved," Julie finally admitted. "When the *Nome Nugget* started reporting the facts of the war, I cringed. I wasn't sure what Sam's response would be, or yours for that matter.

"I cried tears of joy when Sam told me he was too old to go. I'm just as happy to have you stay here, but my heart is broken for your anguish. Please don't hate me for wanting you to stay safe."

"I don't hate you, Julie. I couldn't hate you or anyone else, but right now I'm pretty confused and plenty unhappy," August said and got to his feet. "I'm going for a walk."

"It's awfully cold out there," Julie said and bit her tongue. *No sense in mothering August; he'll only resent it.*

"I know," August said, pulling his parka on. "I shouldn't be too long. Maybe I'll run some of the dogs."

"If you see Sam out there," Julie said, trying to sound disinterested in August's plans, "would you mind sending him my way?"

"Not at all," August replied and started to leave. "Oh, I'm sorry about the mud, Jewels. I can clean it up for you."

"Never mind," Julie said and waved him on. "You just get to feeling better. I'll have some lunch in about an hour."

Julie watched her brother leave in silence. She ached for him and went to the living room determined to pray.

August kicked at the snow as he walked. He'd never known a time in his life when he'd felt so completely useless. Nothing in his life seemed right, and he'd lost all faith in the trust he'd once placed in God.

Forty-one didn't seem all that old to August. He felt vital and young. He could run thirty or more miles a day with his dogs, and he was never sick. How could the army tell him he was too old?

Without realizing what he was doing, August hitched a team of dogs to a sled. He hardly gave the process a second thought as he attached his lead dog first, then swing dogs, team dogs, and finally wheel dogs.

Each dog had his own special talent, and those who were weak were quickly weeded out and put to death. The harsh elements of the North didn't allow for anyone, be they man or beast, to exist without purpose. Perhaps that's why August felt so misplaced and out of sorts. He didn't have any real purpose.

August moved the dogs out without any particular destination in mind. He enjoyed watching the muscular frames of the dogs as they ran with a hearty eagerness.

Many Alaskans had traded in their dogs and sleds for gas-powered snow machines, but August found the dogs more dependable. The machines were always breaking down, and often they were incapable of withstanding the subzero temperatures. August reasoned it was impossible to gain warmth from steel and wood if you were stranded in the wilds, but a dog was good to curl up with when the north wind pounded blades of ice into your skin. He'd take his dogs over machines any day.

The dogs worked their way down the roadway to Nome, and when August realized he was nearly at the edge of town, he couldn't decide what to do with himself.

He spoke to no one and didn't offer so much as a wave when people greeted him. He simply anchored his dogs and walked into a nearby café. The look on his face as he pushed back his parka hood was enough to keep people at a distance. Everyone, that is, except his brother-in-law, who entered the restaurant from out of nowhere, on August's heels.

Sam Curtiss ignored August's scowl and motioned the waitress to bring coffee.

"Do you think it will help?" Sam asked, taking a seat opposite August.

"What are you talking about?" August growled.

"Feeling sorry for yourself," Sam said with a grin. "Do you think it will help?"

"If you're here to preach at me, Sam, you can just forget it," August said, refusing to look Sam in the eye.

Sam waited while an older woman poured two cups of thick, black coffee. When she was out of earshot, Sam leaned forward.

"I hadn't planned to preach," he replied. "I just wondered if you were feeling any better."

"No," August answered flatly. "I don't feel any better, and I don't expect talking to you to make any difference."

"Maybe you should give it a try," Sam said, taking a drink. He eyed a questioning look at August.

"Maybe I'd rather be alone," August said firmly. "I don't need you here, Sam. I don't need anybody. The army doesn't want me, women don't seek out my company, and God has apparently deserted me."

"You don't believe that any more than I do."

"I don't know what I believe anymore, Sam." August stared at the steaming cup for a moment before pushing it away. "I trusted God for a full life, and instead I'm left with an emptiness and void that won't be filled. Why should I go on trusting Him when He's left me to stand alone?"

"Think about your words, August. When you accepted Christ as your Savior, was somebody standing there with a list of prizes? Did you think you'd won the All-Alaska Sweepstakes?"

"Don't be snide with me, Sam. I know God didn't offer me a prize package. He did say, however, that I could ask for anything in the name of His Son. He promised to give me the desires of my heart if I put Him first in my life. So where's the fulfillment of that promise?"

"Your life certainly isn't over, August. Why not be patient and let God guide your steps? It isn't a game of, 'I'll give you this, Lord, and You give me that.'"

"I never said it was," August protested as he sank back against his chair.

"Besides, you've had a very good life," Sam reasoned. "Be patient, because God will work a miracle when you least expect it. Just look at your sister and me. I wasn't much younger than you are now when she came into my life.

"I'd been praying most all of my adult life for a Christian wife and, although I knew the chances of one coming to me in the wilds of Alaska were slim, God moved. God hasn't left you alone, August. You must have the faith to get beyond this disappointment."

"It's more than the disappointment, Sam. I just don't know that I can trust God with my heart anymore. Things that once seemed clear and inspiring are just rhetoric now."

"Then remember Psalm 37:23-24: 'The steps of a good man are ordered by the Lord: and he delighteth in his way. Though he fall, he shall not be utterly cast down: for the Lord upholdeth him with his hand.' God hasn't deserted you," Sam stressed. "Have faith that He can get you through this dark time, and you'll soon be walking in light again."

August shook his head. "I don't think I care anymore."

Sam finished his coffee and stood with a smile on his face. "Oh, you care, August. That's what's grieving you so much. You care because you know the truth of the Word. Once you've tasted the truth, Satan's lies can't guide you into any kind of peace. I'm glad you're troubled and in turmoil right now. I'd be more concerned if you weren't."

"I don't get it," August said as he cast a doubtful look at his older friend. "You're glad I feel this way?"

"I'm not glad that you're hurting, but I'm glad that you're struggling against the feelings that are threatening to bury you. You aren't fighting God, August. You're fighting yourself and what you thought God had planned out for your life. Why not go back to Him and seek the answers you're looking for?"

"What if He doesn't listen?" August questioned softly.

Sam nodded knowingly. "What man hasn't asked himself that question? You've got to believe, August. You've just got to step forward and trust God to be there. Now, I'm going home for an overdue lunch. You coming?"

"I guess so," August said as he got to his feet. "There's no reason to sit here."

As August walked out the door of the café, a copy of the local newspaper caught his eyes. "Military Highway to Require Civilian Help," the headline read. August paid the waitress for a copy of the paper and followed Sam into the street.

"Look at this," August said as he scanned the article. "The army is building a road through Canada, the Yukon, and on up to Fairbanks. It says here because of the threat of the Japanese attacking Alaska, the U.S. government feels it's imperative to have access to the territory."

"There's always water routes and air travel. I can't imagine why they're willing to go to the cost of building a road through the wilderness," Sam said, rubbing his chin thoughtfully.

"Well, the paper says that military sources fear the Japanese might have the capability to deny ships passage through the waterways and that their aircraft would be able to shoot down our military planes. It also says they need civilian forces to help the military units with clearing areas for the road and new airstrips."

Sam noticed excitement in August's voice. "I'd imagine an experienced hand at road building would be a tremendous asset," he suggested quietly.

August looked up from the paper with a grin. "I was just thinking that myself. This road will change Alaska's destiny forever. They're bound to make us a state after this."

"It's an awful long ways off," Sam said, wondering if August was seriously considering the job.

"Maybe it's just the right distance to start a new life," August said as he refolded the paper. "I'm going to do it, Sam. I'm going to go build me a road and change my own destiny."

Chapter 3

Beth Hogan worked the dough that would soon be delicious loaves of wheat bread. The kitchen already boasted the aroma of wild berry jelly cooking down, and Beth was grateful for the extra warmth of the stove. The day had turned chilly as a mountain thunderstorm hovered in the distance.

Taking a moment from her task, Beth looked out the window to check on her sons. They were playing happily in the backyard, mindless of the threatening storm. At three and five, the boys were growing up almost faster than Beth liked to see.

Glancing past the boys to the mountains that lined the southern horizon, Beth smiled. There had been so much uncertainty when she'd left Canada the previous year, but when she'd stepped from the plane and viewed the panoramic glory, she had declared this piece of Alaska heaven on earth and arranged for a home for herself and her children.

The land hadn't disappointed her, nor had the people. She had been eagerly welcomed into the caring arms of neighbors and new friends, including an elderly woman who most called Granny Gantry.

Granny had a run-down roadhouse, catering mostly to those who traveled the worn path that residents called a road. While spending the winter of 1941 under Granny's protective wing, Beth had learned a great deal.

Day after day, Beth helped to transform the roadhouse into a prosperous business by adding homey touches. She made rag rugs for the floor and sewed new curtains for the windows. It wasn't long before Beth was even a fair hand at chopping wood and patching walls.

Granny had been pleased with the additional help and company. She seemed to thrive on spoiling the boys by making them special treats. Granny was also a source of Christian fellowship, and Beth relished their times of devotions when the older woman would share her views and knowledge of God.

When Granny passed away suddenly in the spring of '42, Beth again felt the pain of separation. She quickly purchased the property and continued to run the roadhouse, but it wasn't the same without Granny's smiling face.

Shaking off the past, Beth took a deep breath and returned her gaze to the children. They were so little and innocent, but she knew it would only be a heartbeat and they'd be grown. She wondered if they'd be called to war as had so many other mothers' sons. She'd already lost a husband to war; would she lose her children, too?

A cold, ominous cloud had settled over the country since the attack on Pearl Harbor, and there wasn't a citizen from Nome to Tok who hadn't felt fear. The entire world was at war, but Alaskans felt the distance between their homeland and the Japanese empire narrow considerably as rumors of impending attacks ran rampant.

Deaths mounted on both sides, each fighting for what they believed to be right. How long would they battle? How many would have to die? No doubt many more would give their lives before the evil that surged throughout Europe and Asia was taken captive and defeated.

Wiping her hands on her apron and seeking to put thoughts of death and war from her, Beth returned to kitchen chores. Business was booming with the arrival of the U.S. Army. They'd come to build a road, a road that everyone said would protect Alaska from the Japanese and one day link the territory to the rest of the world.

Newspapers throughout the nation boasted stories of the undertaking. They likened it to pioneer trailblazing and merited the army with the civilizing of the Alaskan territory. Surveyors were already placing their marks upon the land at Beth's front door.

Now that the national eye was turned upon the rugged wilderness of Alaska, Beth Hogan had little trouble keeping her children fed and clothed. Instead of a roadhouse where people stopped only on their way to somewhere else, Beth found her home becoming a boardinghouse where customers stayed on a more permanent basis.

The onslaught of new business also helped Beth keep her mind occupied. She still thought of JB and the empty place that his absence had created in her life, but the memories didn't cause her as much pain as they had at first. Sometimes she could laugh or smile at a pleasant memory of her husband.

She kept the picture of JB in a prominent place in the living room, and whenever the boys asked her questions about their father, Beth would try to share bits and pieces of his life.

Just then, Gerald came bursting through the door. "Momma! Momma! Guess what!"

"Calm down, Gerald, and lower your voice," Beth said sternly. She kneaded the bread dough into loaves and placed them in greased pans. "Now, take a deep breath and tell me what you're so excited about."

"I saw boats way down the river. Can Phillip and I go to town and see them up close?" Gerald was still panting from the excitement and his run up to the house.

"Absolutely not," Bethany answered. She turned and put the bread in the oven, unaware of the look of disappointment that crossed Gerald's face. "Haven't I told you boys how dangerous the river is? You mustn't go there alone."

"But it looks like fun, Momma. Please let us go see the boats," Gerald begged.

"No, Son. You have to obey me on this because it's very important," Beth said as she knelt beside her five-year-old. "Do you understand?"

"Uh-huh," Gerald replied as he nodded his head. "It's important."

"Yes," Beth said as she tousled the child's brown hair. "It's very important. I know you're a big boy and you by yourself might do all right down by the water, but Phillip is too little and he might fall in. As his big brother, it's your job to see to it that he's safe—especially since your father isn't here to watch over him."

"Will Daddy see me watching my brother?"

"I imagine so," Beth said as she straightened up and lifted Gerald into her arms. "I love you both very much. Now, why don't you go outside and keep an eye on Phillip for me?"

"Okay," Gerald said and placed a big kiss on his mother's cheek. "I'll be a big help."

"I'm sure you will be." Beth kissed her son and put him down. As he bounded out the door, her mind filled with worry. Had she said enough to prevent Gerald and Phillip's wanderings? She loved them so much, but then she'd loved JB even more and it hadn't kept him from adversity.

She went back to work with her mind only half on her tasks. She nearly burned the bread and scorched the jam, all the while thinking of how vulnerable her children were. Finally, Beth took herself to her writing desk and pulled out a Bible.

"Lord," she prayed, "I know that worry won't save them, but You can. Father, I can't imagine how You ever sent Your Son, Jesus, to a world You knew would hurt Him. I fear letting my sons from my sight for even a minute. I can't bear the thought that they might get hurt or killed. Please watch over them and care for them. I know JB is in heaven, Lord, and that gives me comfort, but please let me keep my children here with me and let them be safe in my care. Let me be a wise mother, God."

She opened the Bible and scanned Psalm 127:3–5: "Lo, children are an heritage of the Lord: and the fruit of the womb is his reward. As arrows are in the hand of a mighty man; so are children of the youth. Happy is the man that hath his quiver full of them. . . ."

Beth smiled, remembering that these verses had been some of JB's favorites. He'd always planned to have a big family, or a "full quiver," as he'd often teased.

"These children are gifts from You, Lord," Beth said with confidence. "I place them in Your hands, Father, and I ask for Your protection of them. Amen."

Glancing at her watch, Beth realized that she was falling behind schedule. Leaving her worries at the feet of her Lord, she returned to her list of duties.

Late that May, August arrived in eastern Alaska. He was more than a little anxious about applying for work on the highway. Even though he'd heard they'd take anyone who could work, August still felt the sting of the army's earlier rejection and wondered if the rumors were true.

August gazed across the valley where rows of tents had been erected to house the army. Beyond these were olive-drab vehicles and heavy construction equipment. The entire landing buzzed with activity while soldiers and civilians rushed to accomplish the business of the day.

After questioning one of the passing soldiers, August made his way to the tent of the commanding officer.

"You need to speak with the area supervisor of the U.S. Public Roads Administration," the officer told August. "I'm certain, however, that you won't be idle for long. We can use every man we can get."

"Glad to hear it," August said and got up to leave. "I'm anxious to get to work."

"Then you're in the right place," the man said from behind his makeshift desk. "You can find the supervisor at the airfield. While we're clearing this path, we're also laying out new landing strips. Just follow the river to the crossroads and turn right. It's just a half mile or so from there. Like I said, you shouldn't have any trouble getting a job."

"Thanks again for your help," August said and left in search of the airfield.

As August walked the short distance down the river to the crossroads, he noticed how different the land was from his native Nome. The fertile valley made Nome seem barren. Tall spruce, fir, and pine weaved a rich green pattern across the land. Wildflowers and carefully tended gardens were visible reminders of the sun's power in a land that enjoyed over eighteen hours of light each day.

August had already been told of cabbages weighing nearly forty pounds and of cucumbers that were longer than a man's arm and nearly as wide around. It was a land of many wonders, and August was only beginning to learn of its richness.

The hike to the airfield did him good, and August breathed deeply of the storm-chilled air. All morning, thunder had rumbled in the distance, but the storm seemed to hang in suspended indifference over the snowcapped mountains.

As August approached the airfield, he discovered that it was hardly more than a cleared path. At one end a windsock had been erected on a pole, and at the other end several tents and wooden buildings stood in sorry contrast to the grandeur of the landscape.

"Excuse me," August said as he approached a mechanic. The man was working on a large tractor, cursing and throwing tools as he did so.

"Whadyawant?" the man asked, garbling the words together.

"I wondered where I might find the supervisor for the Public Roads Administration," August replied.

"Over there," the man said, motioning to the nearest tent.

August thanked the man and walked toward the tent. Suddenly, an older man charged out, nearly colliding with August.

"Sorry, I wasn't paying attention. What can I do for you?"

"I'm looking for work on the road," August explained.

"We can use you," the man said enthusiastically. "Come on inside and we'll talk. Have you any particular job experience that might help us decide where to place you?"

"I can operate most of the machinery," August admitted. "I helped to build roads in Nome."

"So you know the problems we're facing with the permafrost." The man continued without waiting for August to reply. "We have approximately eighty days between frosts and little more. Even at that, a foot beneath the surface the ground is always frozen solid."

"I know the dilemma well," August said.

"The army is in charge of the road, although the Roads Administration has some control because we work in cooperation with one another. Right now, a big part of our civilian effort is aimed at meeting the need for a bigger airfield.

"Our problem is the complications with ground thaw and boggy surface water. Do you think you can render any new thoughts on the matter? With you being an experienced road builder in these conditions, I think you might have a suggestion or two that we haven't considered."

"I'd be happy to offer whatever knowledge and experience I have. I'm too old for the army, or I'd be off defending our country in the war, so I'm open to whatever you have for me," August answered.

"Great. You can start tomorrow. Be here at six and I'll show you around."

"I'll be here," August said as he followed the man outside. "Where can I find sleeping accommodations?"

"That's a good question," the man said as he thoughtfully considered the matter. "I take it you didn't bring a tent with you."

"Nope," August said with a sheepish grin. "I figured you folks were more civilized over here."

"Don't include me in the folks from these parts. I'm from Oklahoma, and this country's a whole sight different from what I'm comfortable with. Your best bet is to ask around town. Some of the folks are bound to have an idea."

"I guess that'll have to do," August said with a nod.

"Wish I could offer you more help, but I've only been here a week, myself."

"No problem. By the way, I'm August. August Eriksson."

"Good to meet you," the man said and extended his hand. "I guess we're a little lax on formalities around here. I'm Ralph Greening, the area supervisor for the U.S. Public Roads Administration."

August shook the man's hand, and after renewing his promise to return at six the next morning, he made his way back to town.

At the crossroads, August noticed that the storm had dissipated and moved to the east. The clouds cleared out to make the vibrant colors of the landscape come alive.

August enjoyed the breeze through his dark hair and the scent of pine as it penetrated his senses. He marveled at the blackness of the glacier silt dirt and wondered at the stories he'd heard of a glacier's ability to physically move its location as much as ten feet a day.

Before he turned to head back to town, August paused long enough to glance down the picturesque winding road. *It might be a good place to call home,* he thought.

A child's shrill scream filled the air and caught August's attention. He listened again, thinking it came from the direction of town, but soon realized it came from down the road in the opposite direction. The intensity of the child's cry for help sent August in a full run down the riverbank.

Gerald Hogan stood on the small wooden bridge that crossed the river nearly a quarter of a mile from his home. "Help! Help!" he screamed. "My brother can't swim."

August arrived in time to see a small, brown-haired child slip beneath the churning water. Without thought for his own safety, August rushed into the river and swam with the current to catch up to the flailing form.

The icy water bit into August's skin as he maneuvered himself better to take hold of the little boy. He stretched out his hand as the child came within reach, only to hit a boulder. The impact sent him careening away.

August knew he'd have to fight with all his strength to once again reach the drowning boy. He lunged forward in the water and grabbed hold of the boy's collar, pulling the child back against his chest.

Fighting the current, August moved toward shore, where the water was more shallow. He pulled the sputtering, crying child with him. Once he reached the riverbank, August fell back against it, breathing hard. Every muscle in his body ached from the stress and cold, but the child was crying and that meant he was alive.

"Are you my daddy?" Gerald asked from overhead.

"What?" August asked in surprise. Drenched and freezing, he was certain he'd misunderstood the boy's question.

"You are my daddy!" Gerald yelled with exuberance. "Mommy! Mommy!" He ran off in the direction of home before August could stop him and set him straight.

Getting to his feet and cradling the cold, crying boy to his chest, August followed in the direction Gerald had disappeared.

"Mommy, come quick. It's Daddy!" Gerald yelled as he ran through the roadhouse's front door.

Beth came rushing from the back room. "What are you saying, Gerald?"

"Phillip fell in the river, and Daddy jumped in after him." The excitement in Gerald's voice left Beth little doubt about the truth of his statement.

"Take me to where Phillip is," Beth said without thought of reprimanding the disobedience of her sons. "Hurry, Gerry. Take me to your brother."

"He's all right, Momma," Gerald said as he led the way. "Daddy came back. Daddy saved Phillip!"

Beth shook her head, unable to understand. "Daddy is in heaven," she said as she took hold of Gerald's eager hand.

"I know, but you said this was heaven," Gerald stated. "Remember? You said this was heaven when we moved here. I knew my daddy would come home."

Beth's heart ached. How could she explain the misunderstanding to her excited five-year-old? She was torn. She had to assure herself that Phillip was safe and alive, but she was also concerned that Gerald accept the truth of his father's death.

Taking her eyes from her son, Beth lifted her gaze to see a dark-haired man approaching down the road. Her breath caught in her throat and her heart beat faster. From a distance, she could almost believe that JB was walking toward her.

Beth stopped in her tracks, while Gerald pulled at her arm. "Come on, Mommy. It's Daddy and Phillip," he insisted.

Beth let go of Gerald and held her hand to her throat. She paled at the ghostly image of her husband. The same dark hair and medium build. The same self-confident stride. Pushing aside such thoughts, Beth rushed forward to take Phillip.

"Daddy saved Phillip from the river," Gerald announced.

Phillip had wrapped his arms around August's neck and, as Beth reached out to take him, Phillip resisted.

"No. Want Daddy," he said firmly.

Beth looked into the dark eyes of the man who'd saved her child. She wanted to explain, to say something that would answer the question in the man's eyes, but words wouldn't come.

"You're freezing," Beth finally managed. "Come with me, and I'll get you something dry to wear."

August nodded and followed Beth back to the roadhouse. She paused to open the door with trembling hands, allowing August to pass through with Phillip. "Thank you," she whispered as August moved only inches from her.

He turned his face to meet her pale blue eyes. He saw the concern for her child and something else. August began to realize that he represented an image from her past.

"You're welcome," he whispered.

Chapter 4

Phillip refused to be fussed over, and Beth watched in silent concern for signs of complications. The boy seemed fine, however, and the only real dilemma was how to explain to him that the man to whom he clung so affectionately wasn't his father.

Beth moved uncomfortably around the room as she built up the fire in the stove and retrieved warm towels for August and Phillip. It was hard to allow the stranger such an intimate role in her son's life, but at the moment she didn't know what else she could do.

"I must apologize for my sons' behavior," Beth finally said, noting the confused expression on August's face. "Their father was killed last year in the war. They have a misconception about his coming back, or, well, that's not really where the misunderstanding occurred, but it's a long story."

She reached out and pried Phillip from August's lap. "I can offer you a robe while your clothes dry," Beth said, turning to leave the room. "I'll have Gerald show you where you can change."

August nodded and watched as the petite woman placed a kiss on her son's forehead. He noted the relief in her eyes and the gratitude. He admired the way she handled herself in the midst of the crisis and the tender way she mothered her children. He was so absorbed in watching her as she left the room that he barely heard Gerald's little voice as he instructed August to follow him.

The boy offered August the robe and turned to leave. "I'm glad you came home, Daddy. I missed you."

"Son, I'm not your daddy, but if I were, I'd love having a big strong boy like you," August said with a smile.

"You're not my daddy?" Gerald questioned.

"No," August said, offering the boy his hand, "but I'd like to be your friend. I just moved here and I don't have any friends. Would you be my friend?"

Gerald wrinkled his forehead as he often did when considering something important. "I wanted you to be my daddy. You look like my daddy." He paused in thoughtful contemplation before adding, "I guess I can be your friend."

"I'd sure like it," August said as he pulled the wet shirt from his body. "Now why don't you go see if you can give your mommy some help while I change out of these clothes." Gerald nodded and left August to contemplate the situation.

"Momma," Gerald said as he came into his bedroom.

Beth looked up from where she was putting dry clothes on Phillip. She'd already checked his body for injuries that had been missed before, but other than a few scrapes and bruises, Phillip had fared rather well. God had certainly been watching over him, even sending the stranger who so closely resembled JB.

"What is it, honey?"

"That man says he's not my daddy. I thought he was my daddy, but he isn't."

Beth lifted Gerald into her arms and hugged him close. "No, he's not your daddy. Honey, Daddy is never coming back. Not here. Not on earth. Heaven is where he lives now, and he's going to stay there forever.

"Someday, we'll all leave this earth and go to heaven, but when that happens, Gerald, we can't come back here. We won't even want to. Daddy is happy in heaven, and he won't ever come back here, but someday we'll see him again. Do you understand that?"

"I understand," Gerald said with surprising acceptance. "I told that man I'd be his friend. Is that all right?"

"Of course you can. Now, you two play in here while I fix some lunch for everyone. I'm counting on you to behave," Beth said, kissing each of them.

"We be good," Phillip said, causing Beth to smile.

"I'll call you when lunch is ready," she said and turned to go.

"Can my new friend have lunch with us?" Gerald asked innocently.

Beth nodded. "I'll ask him right now."

Beth was already busy with lunch preparations when August came into the kitchen with his wet clothes.

"Here," Beth said as she put down the potato she was washing. "Let me take those and hang them out back."

"I hate to be a bother," August said with a grin. There was something about the small woman that captivated him. She seemed so alive and energetic, and August found it hard to believe that she'd never remarried.

Beth glanced up as she took the clothes, and her heart nearly stopped. August's grin was so like JB's. "I suppose," she murmured, forgetting the lunch invitation, "I should introduce myself. I'm Bethany Hogan."

"I'm August Eriksson. May I call you Bethany?"

"Please, or Beth if you prefer."

"I like the name Beth. I hope you will call me August."

Beth nodded and shifted the dripping clothes. "I'm grateful for what you did. Saving my son's life must have taken an incredible act of bravery. I thank God you were there when he needed you." Before August could reply, Beth quickly moved through the kitchen and out the back door.

She pinned the clothes to the line, cherishing the once-familiar weight of a man's clothing. She ran her hand across the collar of August's shirt.

August stood just inside the doorway, hoping that Beth wouldn't see him. He watched as she seemed lost in the moment and wondered if she would ever put her dead husband to rest.

When she turned back toward the peeled log house, August ducked back and quickly took a seat at the kitchen table. He pretended to be preoccupied with his own thoughts when Beth returned to finish fixing lunch.

"I hope you like fried potatoes and ham," Beth said as she continued with her work. "I've also got canned peaches and fresh bread."

"Sounds wonderful, but I hadn't intended on staying for lunch. I never meant to intrude," August said softly.

"Intrude? You saved my son's life. Your presence here is anything but an intrusion. Lunch is an inadequate payment for such a deed."

"Maybe you could tell me where I might find a place to stay," August requested. "I've just arrived from Nome, and I have a job lined up with the Public Roads Administration. I'm not at all familiar with the area, however, so I need some suggestions."

Beth smiled and allowed a bit of a laugh to escape. "It would seem God threw us together for more than one purpose," she mused. "Northway doesn't offer much in the way of accommodations. I run this as a roadhouse, and I just happen to have lost a boarder this morning. I have a small room with a bed, washstand, and dresser. I don't offer regular meals, what with the rationing and all, but the room rates are reasonable."

"Sounds great," August said enthusiastically. Here was the perfect opportunity to stay close by and learn more about this young widowed mother. He cocked his head toward the stove with a chuckle. "What about lunch?"

"What about it?"

"You said no meals."

Beth laughed in spite of herself. "Well, occasionally I offer a meal or two for especially deserving souls."

"If it's half as good as it's starting to smell, I'll try extra hard to be deserving. Besides, where else am I going to find such pleasant company?"

Beth shook her head with a smile. What kind of man was this August Eriksson? He stormed into their lives, saving her child from certain death, and now he sat as relaxed and easygoing as if they were lifelong friends sharing a passing moment.

"What are you smiling about?" August asked as he leaned forward.

"What?" Beth realized she'd betrayed her amusement with the situation and wasn't quite sure how to explain.

"I saw that smile," August answered. "It's a very nice smile, if I might add."

Beth turned back to her work and changed the subject. "What prompted you to move here from Nome?"

August shrugged his shoulders and leaned back. "I heard about the road project, and I wanted to be part of it. I was too old for the army, and I wanted to do something worthwhile with my life—something that would show after I was gone."

Beth nodded. "That sounds reasonable. Did you leave your family in Nome?"

"I don't have any family," August said, and then corrected himself. "Except for my sister and her husband. My father passed away last year, and I've never married."

"I see," Beth said, stirring the cut potatoes into the hot lard on top of the stove. She turned thick ham steaks in the cast-iron skillet, satisfied with the way they were browning.

"What about you? Any family other than the boys?" August questioned curiously.

"No, there's no one else," Beth answered. She retrieved canned peaches from the cupboard before continuing. "My husband, JB, was a pilot with the Royal Canadian Air Force. He was killed shortly after the Battle of Britain."

"I'm sorry," August whispered. "What happened?"

"His best friend wrote me about it," Beth said and realized it was the first time she'd ever shared the details of JB's death. "JB was one of the best pilots in the service. He always managed to get himself and his plane out of any risky situation, except the last time. JB always had a bad feeling about using anybody else's plane. Sure enough, when he died, he was flying another man's Spitfire in a routine maintenance check."

"Was he shot down?" August asked, intent on the young woman's answer.

"No," Beth said, remembering the words of the letter she'd received. "He took off but didn't have enough power to make the Spitfire climb. He reached the end of the runway with a forest of trees directly in front of him and not enough lift to clear them. He crashed into them and was killed instantly in an explosion."

"How awful," August said, considering the fiery death.

"My comfort is that JB was a devout Christian. He loved the Lord more than anything in this world, and I have confidence that he's in heaven."

August grimaced slightly at Beth's reference to JB's devotion to God. He'd once felt that way about God himself. Now there was only bitter resentment for what he'd lost out on.

"What's wrong?" Beth questioned, noticing August's frown.

"Nothing," August replied as he tried to change the subject. "Your boys must have been very young. No wonder they thought I was their father."

Beth realized she'd hit a nerve with August. "They were very young when JB joined the service and went away. I've tried to keep his memory alive by telling them stories of their father and keeping his picture in the living room, but it isn't the same. I worry about them sometimes, but when I get too concerned, I pray about it and turn them over to their heavenly Father." Beth wondered how August would react to another reference to God.

August didn't have a chance to respond, however, as Gerald called from the other room, "Is it time to eat yet?"

Beth watched August's expression change to one of amusement. "Sounds like I'm not the only one who's hungry," he said, chuckling.

"I'll be right back," Beth said after giving the potatoes a quick stirring. She disappeared for a moment and returned with the boys right behind her. "You boys take a seat with Mr. Eriksson at the table, and we'll eat."

"Would it be all right if they called me August?"

Beth nodded. "I suppose, if that's your wish."

"It is," August said with a smile. "Would you boys like that?"

"August is a month," Gerald offered as if it were news to the stranger.

"That's right, and you are every bit as smart as you are brave. I imagine your mother is very proud of you."

Gerald beamed from ear to ear, while Phillip leaned over and reached for August's hand. "Daddy," he stated clearly, refusing to have any part of August's first name.

Gerald reached over and pulled his brother back. "No, Phillip, he's not our daddy, but maybe he will be." Gerald looked up at his mother and asked, "Do you think since our real daddy isn't coming back that August could be our new daddy?"

Beth turned crimson at the question, and August fought to keep from revealing his own consideration of such an idea. He was already more than just a little fond of the young mother and her boys. Still, they'd only met, and August knew there was much more to be considered than physical attraction.

"Why don't you just pray about it, Gerry?" Beth finally suggested. "God will listen to your prayers, and if He feels that it's important for you to have a new daddy, then He will send one to us."

"I did pray for a daddy," Gerald insisted. "I prayed that God would send Daddy home, but you told me he has to stay in heaven. So maybe God sent this one instead." He pointed at August and smiled. "I think you'd make a good daddy."

"I think you're right," August said with genuine fondness for the boy. "Maybe I could be a pretend daddy," he offered with a glance toward Beth. "If your momma doesn't mind, maybe I could take you boys fishing and teach you how to chop wood and hunt for food. Of course, I have to work at my job with the new highway, but when I'm not working, maybe we could do some things together."

Gerald clapped his hands and bobbed up and down in his seat. At his brother's excitement, Phillip squealed with delight and Beth had no idea how to react. She thought it totally inappropriate for August to even suggest such a thing, while the boys thought it perfectly natural.

Unable to hold back her tears, Beth turned quickly to the food on the stove to avoid worrying the children or causing August to question her reaction. Regaining her composure, she wiped the tears with her apron and joined her family at the table with the steaming food. She started to sit and then remembered the peaches and bread.

"So is that okay, Momma?" Gerald questioned. "Can August be our pretend daddy?"

Beth turned to meet August's dark eyes. He seemed to understand her pain and offered a warm smile that reassured her that his intentions were only those that would benefit her sons.

"It's okay, Gerry. You and Phillip can probably learn a lot from August, but just remember to tell me your plans first." She said the latter for August's sake more than the boys. He nodded a promise, and Beth felt calmness wash over her.

She opened the can of peaches and poured them into a bowl, then cut thick slices of her slightly over-browned bread. Bringing these to the table along with the jelly dish, Beth took her seat.

"Would you like to offer grace, August?" Beth questioned, wondering what his response would be.

August shook his head. "I'd like to hear Gerald give grace, if you don't mind."

Beth nodded, thinking how smoothly August had avoided having to pray.

"Dear God," the boy began, "this is Gerald Hogan. You have my daddy in heaven with You, and I want You to tell him that August is going to be our pretend daddy. Tell him we still love him, but we need a daddy on earth."

Gerald's words cut deeply into Beth's heart. She'd tried so hard to be mother and father to her sons and never once thought of the void in their lives.

"And God," Gerald continued as an afterthought, "thanks for the food. Amen."

Beth opened her eyes to find August's gaze fixed upon her. She returned the stare while the boys, mindless of the exchange, helped themselves to bread and jelly.

Beth's expression was almost one of pleading, August decided, but for what? Was she fearful that he'd hurt her young boys, or was she more frightened of how his "pretend fatherhood" might affect her? She looked so young and scared. August wished he could ease her worries.

Without thought, he reached out and placed his hand over hers and gave a squeeze. Then just as quickly, August turned his attention to the food and found himself in an intense conversation with Gerald about the new highway.

A strange sensation crept over Beth. Her heart pounded at the thought of August touching her, yet her mind screamed betrayal. She mindlessly pushed her food around the plate, all the while considering the implication of August's role playing. It seemed such a reasonable arrangement, yet for all she was worth, Bethany couldn't comprehend why.

Chapter 5

A ugust's work with the Alaskan/Canadian Military Highway project took him away from Beth and the boys for long hours each day. Often when he arrived home it was all he could do to clean up before dropping into bed. Gerald and Phillip grew impatient for his company, but Beth faithfully explained why it was necessary for August to spend so much time away from them.

The combined efforts of the United States and Canada resulted in the scheduled creation of a highway that would cover more than 1,486 miles, from Dawson Creek, British Columbia, to Fairbanks, Alaska. Calling it a highway was an optimistic overstatement. The road was clearly nothing more than a bulldozed path through an unyielding wilderness.

Never intended to do more than provide emergency access to the north should the Japanese cut off the water and air routes, this road of mud and ice quickly became a problem of outrageous proportions.

Frozen subsoil, permafrost, muskeg, and long hours of sunlight created problems that made engineers throw up their hands in frustration. Coupled with the fact that there were inadequate supplies and living accommodations for the eleven thousand troops, most of whom were from the southern United States and completely unacquainted with the cold temperatures that seemed to come at will, the highway quickly became a matter of man against nature.

Canada provided access to the lands through British Columbia and the Yukon Territory, as well as much of the needed building materials. All of this was given in exchange for unlimited use of the road following the war.

As engineers and administrators brought their plans together and fine-tuned the design of the project, it was determined that over 130 log and pontoon bridges would be needed to accommodate the hundreds of rivers and lakes that the highway would have to cross.

Added to this were some eight thousand culverts to be dug and reinforced to combat the constant drainage problems created by the swampy soil.

Behind the frustrations of a seemingly endless number of new problems was the threat of Japanese invasion of Alaska. Though few knew of the plan, military experts had found a way to decode Japan's messages in time to learn of Alaska's vulnerability to attack.

Even as far north as the rural villages of Alaska, and perhaps because such vulnerability seemed evident, the mood was one of hushed and guarded silence.

Beth's ten-room boardinghouse was rapidly becoming a common meeting place for the army leadership and the Public Roads Administration. If the weather was cooperative, the group usually assembled outside, where August had placed a number of crudely built tables and chairs. Other times, however, the weather was rainy or cold, and Beth allowed the men to take over her living room while she and the boys holed up in her bedroom.

Glancing outside, Beth could see that the day's weather would allow for an outdoor gathering, and she breathed a sigh of relief. The meetings always made her rather uncomfortable. She never could figure out what disturbed her most: the presence of uniformed men or the worry that military secrets might fall upon the ears of her children, only to be carelessly babbled later.

She finished pulling the last of five wild raspberry pies from the oven as August came striding into the room.

"Ummm, smells wonderful, Beth. Don't suppose you're going to let me buy them for our meeting?"

"What else would I do with five pies?" Beth asked, chuckling. "Are you certain the men will reimburse you? I can't charge you two dollars a pie in good faith if I have to worry that you'll be out the entire amount."

"They stand in line to pay me," August said with a grin and added, "and at thirty cents a slice, they're going out in good shape, and so am I. Helps me pay the rent," he teased.

"I keep meaning to talk to you about that," Beth said as she smoothed back her blond hair and reinserted one of the combs that held it back at the sides.

"Great," August said in a mocking tone of dissatisfaction, "I suppose my rent is about to go up."

"No, not at all," Beth said, mortified that August would tease about such a thing.

"Relax, it was a joke, Beth," August said as he eyed the young woman seriously. "What did you want to talk about?"

"I can't see you having to pay as much as everyone else when you help out so much around here. I mean, you cut most all my wood, you mended the fence and the roof, not to mention that you worked up the dirt for my garden. It's only fair that I offer you some type of compensation."

August smiled and wondered if Beth could begin to imagine the type of compensation he'd like to redeem from her. The fact was, he was growing more attracted to the young widow and her sons each day.

"I'm sure we can work something out," August finally said. "But if you're doing it for my sake, then stop worrying. I'm grateful for the time you allow us to meet and disrupt your home in order to coordinate plans for the road."

"I don't feel it's adequate compensation," Beth interjected. "I'd like to at least reduce your rent. If you have something else in mind, I'm open to suggestions."

August grinned and pushed back his black hair. "Well, an occasional hot meal might do the trick," he said, knowing that he couldn't very well come out and say that he'd like to spend more time getting to know her.

"That seems a simple request," Beth said, realizing how pleasant it would be to have August at her table. "But not an occasional meal. I think it's only right that you share all our meals, if you want to. I'll even pack you a lunch if you'd like."

"You'll spoil me," August said, laughing, "but I'll enjoy it while you do. I'd be quite happy to accept your offer, Bethany."

Beth smiled nervously and made a show of rechecking the oven as if a pie had been inadvertently overlooked. She knew that August was attracted to her, yet she hadn't decided if she liked the idea or not.

It had been over a year since JB had died and longer than that since she'd seen him, but the ghostly image of her husband was never so haunting as when Beth felt the cold, gold band that still adorned her finger. Perhaps when she was ready to put away that last reminder of her marriage, she would be able to deal with the interest of another man.

"Well, I'd best make sure everything is ready for our meeting. The army's bringing the coffee this time, so we shouldn't have any trouble staying awake long enough to resolve any new differences. I'll be back for those pies in about an hour, if that's all right with you."

"They should be cooled by then," Beth said and offered August a smile.

August nodded and left Beth to the task of cleaning up. Beth watched through the window as several army vehicles pulled into her yard, unleashing a throng of uniformed men and a large coffee pot.

A knock on her front door sent Beth to answer it. She opened the door to find two young soldiers looking rather sheepishly at her.

"May I help you?" she questioned softly.

"Ma'am, we're here helping with the road," one of the men began as if Beth wouldn't already be privy to the information.

Beth nodded and the man continued.

"Well, me and Ronnie here, we've been coming to these meetings, and well, ma'am," he stammered for just the right words.

"Go on," Beth encouraged sweetly.

"Well, it's like this. We've been eating your cakes and pies whenever Mr. Eriksson offers them for sale, and we surely do miss our mom's cooking. Army grub just ain't anywhere near as good."

"I'm sure that's true," Beth said, suppressing a laugh.

"We was wondering, hoping really, that we could pay you to make some of our favorite sweet potato pie. We've managed to get our hands on some canned sweet potatoes, and while they won't be near as good as fresh, we'd be mighty happy to pay you to bake us however much it would make. In the way of pies, that is."

Beth felt sorry for the boys. "I'm not sure I have a recipe for sweet potato pie," she said honestly.

"It's pert' near the same as pumpkin," the other boy offered. "But I reckon I can get you a copy of the recipe from somebody."

"Well then, you get me the recipe, and I'll be happy to make your pies. One thing, though, I use mostly honey, due to the shortage of sugar. If you don't think the results will be as good, we'd probably best call off the whole arrangement right now."

"No, ma'am," the first soldier offered. "Whatever way you make it will be just fine. We'll be back when we can bring you the recipe and the sweet potatoes. How much you gonna charge us for the pie?"

Beth thought for a moment. "I think a dollar would be a fair amount," she answered. While she charged August two dollars for most of her pies and cakes, she knew he easily made his money back. These boys, however, were not going to be making much profit because Beth was certain they'd be eating most of the pie themselves.

"Sounds just fine by us," the one called Ronnie said as he looked at his friend. "They charge us nearly that much for a single piece at the café in town, and the army could never make anything as good as what you serve, ma'am."

"Well, I appreciate your compliments, boys. Now you'd best get around back, because I've a feeling the meeting will be starting shortly, and tonight we're having raspberry pie."

"Yes, ma'am!" they answered in unison and hurried to the backyard.

"So our biggest problem at this point," Ralph Greening was explaining, "is the need for a much larger airfield in order to bring in the bigger planes and more supplies."

"It's not just a problem," an army colonel offered. "It's imperative that we have this runway."

"I understand the need, gentlemen. However, the land around us is most uncooperative. We have a tremendous problem with the permafrost. I've asked August Eriksson to address this problem and to let you know about the progress we've made. August, go ahead."

"As we've cleared land for the runway and grated the sphagnum moss from the topsoil, we've run into the constant problem of ground thaw. The moss has always acted as an insulator that keeps the subsoil frozen and firm. When the moss is removed, we get a swamp."

"But we have to have that runway," the colonel insisted.

"I realize that, Colonel, and if you'll hear me out, I'll explain how we're combatting this situation. By experimenting we've come up with a plan that seems to be working. First, we skim off the topsoil and moss, allowing the ground to thaw. When this next layer of ground has completely warmed up, we grate off another portion and allow this section to thaw as well. We do this over and over until what we have is an excavation several feet deep.

"Next, we fill this area with sand from the river bottom. This sand allows the subsoil waters to rise to the level of the surrounding ground's water table. Then, due to the freezing temperatures of the soil, this water freezes and becomes a rock solid surface, while the sand acts as an insulator. This should then allow us to put the regular asphalt apron on top and leave the surface fixed and sturdy year-round."

"Ingenious," the colonel said, offering his first positive word. "Has it been tested?"

"Yes," August replied, feeling rather proud of himself. "It has, and with the exact results we'd hoped for. Our only holdup is waiting for each process of ground thaw. Other than that, we would have the main runway completed in a very short time."

"Might the usage of steam from a portable boiler speed up this process?" the colonel questioned.

"That is a possibility," August said with a nod toward Ralph Greening. "I'm sure my supervisor would be happy to discuss the matter with you."

"Most assuredly," Ralph answered.

"I believe," the colonel said with thoughtful consideration, "we could offer the use of such army equipment when it's not being used for other purposes. Will you have enough manpower for the job?"

"We've hired many of the locals for additional help," Ralph Greening replied. "We're paying a dollar an hour, so pass the word among the civilians as you're out among them. The more hands we have, the quicker the project will be completed, and we'll be able to get those big transport planes in here."

"The Northwest Transport Command will be grateful for that," the colonel said as he sat back in the chair for the first time.

"I'm sure many of the Tanana people will be happy to help," one of the local men who'd been working with August spoke up. "I know these Indians, and they are good people."

"We'll take them all," Ralph said. "Anybody and everybody. If we're to have this road in place by fall, we can't be picky about who works and who doesn't."

"Well, I'd say the situation is well under control," the colonel remarked. "Now, how about one of those delicious desserts that Mrs. Hogan makes for us?"

August smiled and got to his feet. "It's raspberry pie tonight, and you all know the price. Just take up the collection, and I'll borrow a couple of your men to help me bring out the goods."

Instantly the men began reaching into their pockets. As a hat was passed, the money was eagerly handed over. August grabbed the nearest two men and quickly returned with the five pies. The hat was passed to August, as the men gathered around waiting patiently for their pie. Shortly after the food was gone and the coffee drained, the meeting ended and the satisfied men returned to their tents for some much-needed sleep.

August counted out ten dollars for Beth and pocketed the other two. He was tired, but grateful that it was Saturday. He'd managed to wrangle the following day off and hoped that somehow he'd talk Beth into a picnic with the boys. He was considering just how he might ask her, when Beth appeared to reclaim her pie tins.

"Looks like the meeting was successful," Beth said as she stacked the pans.

"Yes, very," August agreed and added, "Do you have to rush right back?"

The light was fading, and in the twilight that filtered through the tall birch and spruce trees, Beth's face seemed shrouded in the shadows. Still, August could see that she liked the idea of remaining.

"I can stay for a little while, although I hate to keep you up," Beth said, putting the pans down and taking the seat across from August.

"That's one of the reasons I asked you to stay," August replied. "I have tomorrow off and hoped that maybe you would agree to picnicking with the boys and me."

"That sounds like a lot of fun," Beth admitted. "Perhaps you would accompany us to church first." She knew August avoided any reference to such things, but she wanted to find out why he was hesitant when it came to God.

To August's own surprise, he agreed to go. "I suppose that would fall into line."

"Church is at eleven, so you should be able to sleep late. I'll try to keep the boys quiet."

"No, don't," August answered. "I want to get up early and play with them."

"I appreciate the way you look after them. I've never seen them so happy. They care quite deeply for you," Beth said softly. "I hope you realize how much they adore you."

"I do," August said and leaned forward. "Does that worry you?"

"I suppose it does," Beth replied. "They suffered the loss of their father, and then I uprooted them and moved them here. They need to feel secure about their home and the people they care about."

"Do you think I'm incapable of offering them stability in our friendship?" August questioned seriously.

"Not really," Beth said thoughtfully. "I suppose my real concern is that soon the road will be completed and you'll be on your way. I know that would be devastating to them."

"Who says I'll be on my way? If I have something to stick around for, I can't see giving that up," August whispered in a low, husky voice. He wondered if Beth would understand his meaning.

"I think as long as you want a reason to stay, you'll have one. The boys are devoted to you, and I want. . ." Beth grew uncomfortable and got to her feet. "I'd better clean up this mess."

August got up and moved behind Beth. "I'd rather hear you finish that thought."

Beth could feel his warm breath against her neck as August spoke. She wanted very much to get away from the loneliness that threatened to strangle her, but she was also afraid of the feelings that were building in her heart.

"I'm not sure it would be wise," Beth finally whispered.

August very gently turned her to face him. He gazed deep into her eyes just before he lowered his lips to press a gentle kiss upon Beth's mouth. When she didn't protest, he pulled her close and held her for several minutes.

"Now, you were saying?" August asked as he pulled slightly away and lifted Beth's face to meet his stare.

"I don't know what to say," Beth answered.

"Just speak what's on your heart," August urged. He wanted so much to hear Beth say something that would indicate her interest in him.

"That's not always an easy thing to do, August."

"No, maybe not," August said, gently stroking Beth's cheek with his thumb. "But it's always the best."

"I'm afraid." Beth's words were barely audible.

"Of me?" August questioned, hurt showing on his face.

"No," Beth replied. "I'm afraid of myself. Afraid of trusting too much, caring too much, needing too much."

"Don't be," August said, kissing Beth's hand and holding it close to his heart. "Just tell me what you started to say. Tell me what you want."

"Stay," Beth murmured. "I want you to stay."

Chapter 6

Days later, Beth sat considering her situation. There was, of course, the constant threat of war hanging over like an ever-present storm cloud. Added to this was the continual demands of the roadhouse and the responsibility of raising two boys without a father.

Her sons concerned her most, along with the fact that Beth was finally admitting how much she missed the companionship of a husband.

She hadn't realized how lonely she was until the night August had held her and kissed her. It was hard to admit to loneliness with hundreds of uniformed men and civilians milling up and down the path that ran in front of her roadhouse, but Beth was lonely. August only made that fact more evident.

True to his promise, August had accompanied her and the boys to Sunday school and church. He had appeared aloof and uncomfortable during the worship service, but he said nothing and acted as though he were simply preoccupied. Afterward, they'd enjoyed a wonderful summer afternoon, picnicking, fishing, and simply enjoying each other's company.

It was hard not to think about those moments with August, as well as their first kiss. Beth had made it very clear to August that she wanted him to stay. What she hadn't said was that she needed him to stay; she needed his company and his friendship in a way she couldn't begin to explain.

August had wanted Beth to talk about her feelings, but how could she when she scarcely understood them herself? And what about the issue of why August was avoiding God? There was a great deal about August Eriksson that Beth didn't understand, and those issues were important enough to her so that she wanted to go slow.

Beth pulled out her ledger books and tried to concentrate on the numbers. She made it through one or two lines before her thoughts drifted off. Suddenly, she was a million miles away from balancing the roadhouse books.

August's appearance in her life had brought so many benefits. The relationship he shared with her sons was a precious friendship that filled some of the void their father's death had created.

Phillip and Gerald accepted August as if he'd been JB returning from the war. It didn't matter to them, even after countless explanations, that August wasn't their daddy. Phillip refused to call him anything else, and often Gerald slipped up and referred to him that way. Beth found it increasingly acceptable for her boys to use the title, and when Gerald put JB's picture in the china cupboard, she realized he was symbolizing an end to his need for JB's memory.

Beth couldn't explain why she didn't fight the action or why it seemed perfectly natural to share her meals and spare time with a man she barely knew. But for the first time in months, her boys were happy, and neither one had bad dreams or moped around looking for a man who would never come home.

Looking down at her hand, Beth suddenly realized that she'd nearly twisted her wedding ring off her finger. She stared at the band for a moment, then pulled it off quickly and put it in the desk drawer. JB was gone, and August was here. Perhaps it was time to deal with the matter head on.

Giving up on the ledgers, Beth made her way through the house picking up toys and misplaced items. What a difference one year made! Where once baby rattles and teething rings had dotted the counters, now blocks and trucks sprouted up. Her babies had grown up so fast that it left Beth aching for the feel of holding them close. Perhaps she'd have more children one day.

The thought stunned her. She hadn't considered remarrying until August came into her life, and now she was contemplating a larger family. Maybe August wouldn't want more children.

"Stop it!" Beth said aloud. "I can't think this way. I've got myself married off and having more children, and all to a man I scarcely know!" The empty house absorbed her words, perfectly content to keep her secrets.

Outside, a summer storm was brewing. Beth could hear thunder rumble in the distance. She fought the urge to cry. Things weren't going badly at all, so why did she feel so blue?

The boys were spending the day in town with the woman who led their Sunday school class at the small interdenominational church. Mrs. Miller was a pleasant woman with graying hair and a grandmotherly shape. Being a widow of several years as well as childless, Mrs. Miller had aligned herself with Beth.

She was particularly fond of Phillip and Gerald, and when the older widow had invited the boys for lunch at her house, Beth had agreed, understanding Mrs. Miller's need. Now, however, Beth reconsidered. The house seemed empty and far too quiet.

Beth sighed. What was wrong with her? She had but to look out her front window and see more activity than most small towns could boast.

The path was being widened to meet road specifications, and Beth could count on no less than twenty different men pounding on her front door daily, seeking everything from water to food to permission to use the privy. She caught on, only after August informed her, that most of the men were doing it to have a chance to talk to the handsome widow of Gantry Roadhouse.

Beth blushed crimson as she remembered August's laughing eyes and boyish grin. He was amused that she had been too naïve to figure it out for herself.

"You're a beautiful woman, Beth Hogan," he had said, "and most of these men haven't had the opportunity to see, much less visit with, a woman of any kind since leaving the States and being assigned to this wilderness. Women are mighty scarce up here, so you might as well get used to being popular."

Beth had feared August would think she'd done something to encourage the attention, but he never spoke of it and never seemed to mind when the boys told stories of visiting strangers.

The highway had been excellent for business, and because of this and the workers' avid interest, Beth could boast a lengthy list of men who were waiting their turn to take residence in her boarding-house. Many of these made the excuse of checking on the availability of rooms and stayed on talking of the weather, the highway, or anything else that would delay their return to work.

Yet Beth was still lonely, and she couldn't understand why.

The clock in the hall chimed two, and Beth realized that her cakes were ready to come out of the oven. She had doubled up on baking, knowing that the next day would be devoted to washing clothes and linens, a job that always took an entire day. Often she was still hanging laundry after August arrived home.

Hurrying to the kitchen, Beth pulled out two cake pans along with an experimental recipe she was trying. The sourdough coffeecake, complete with berries and honey, looked every bit as good as it smelled, and Beth was hopeful that its flavor would match its appearance.

Silently, Beth thanked God for the endless supply of honey that one of her bachelor neighbors provided in exchange for mending and sewing. The older man seemed more than happy to give Beth all the honey she could use and even happier to spend time visiting and telling the boys tales of the old days when he'd lived off the land and searched for gold.

Beth realized that, because of such generosity and bartering for goods, she and the boys scarcely felt the effects of rationing that the war had made necessary. God had been truly good to them.

When her baking was completed, Beth was amazed to realize she still had almost two hours to pass before the boys and August would be home. August had agreed to pick the boys up at Mrs. Miller's house in order to spare either of the ladies from making the trip. At the time, Beth couldn't find any reason not to accept his offer. Now she wished she had a reason to take the long stroll into town.

Heaving a sigh, Beth decided to stop feeling sorry for herself. Instead, she would cook a special meal for her family's return. Putting her hands to work usually occupied her mind as well. Hopefully working on dinner would make the afternoon pass more quickly.

She thoughtfully chose foods that she knew everyone was fond of. Smoked salmon would be their meat, and for a side dish, Beth blended new potatoes, fresh green beans, and pieces of side meat. For dessert, they'd try her new berry coffeecake, a sure way, Beth decided, to know whether or not it was acceptable.

She was just finishing the table setting, using her finest tablecloth and wedding china, when she heard the boys' nonstop chatter as they drew near home. *What a beautiful sound*, Beth thought. She was so used to the constant noise of the road construction that when the men had stopped for supper, Beth hadn't noticed.

She was grateful that the army was taking time away from the project to have their own evening meal. No doubt with the added hours of light there'd soon be another shift at work, but for now Beth was going to thoroughly enjoy the noise that her sons raised and the words that August Eriksson would share at her dinner table.

"Mommy!" Gerald hollered as he came through the door. August followed with Phillip on his shoulders.

Beth smiled and welcomed Gerald into her arms. "Did you have a good time at Mrs. Miller's house?"

"Uh-huh," Gerald said and held up a small sack. "We made cookies, and Mrs. Miller said we could bring them home."

"How nice of her," Beth said, and turned her attention from Gerald to Phillip. "And how about you, buster? Did you have a good time?"

"Had fun," Phillip answered. "Got to ride on Daddy."

"And I believe this child is eating too much," August said as he lifted Phillip over his head and placed him on the ground. "Well, well. What's all this?" he said as he noticed the table.

"I just thought something special might be nice," Beth answered. "I had so much time on my hands with the boys gone. I never knew a body could get so lonely."

August offered a tender smile, and Beth quickly turned her face away to avoid feeling the impact of his clear eyes. "You boys, go wash your hands and we'll sit down to dinner."

Handing his mother the cookies, Gerald scurried off to the washroom with Phillip close behind. Both boys were giggling and chattering all the way, leaving Beth with a much lighter heart.

"I'm sorry if I made you uncomfortable," August said as he paused before following the boys. "I just don't like to think of you lonely. Seems like such a waste, especially when so many enjoy your company."

Beth wondered if it was her imagination or August's feelings that caused her to read more into his statement.

When August and the boys returned from washing up, Beth allowed August to seat her while the boys scampered into their assigned places.

"Who wants to say grace?" Beth questioned.

"I will!" Gerald said enthusiastically.

"All right, Gerald," Beth said, nodding in agreement. "You go right ahead."

"God, this is Gerald again," the boy began. "I sure do like living in Alaska 'cause You sent us a lot of great people and we're having fun here. God, Mommy told me to pray about a daddy for Phillip and me, so I'm praying about it. I like August, God, and I really want him to be my daddy. So if it's okay with You, me and Phillip will take him. Amen."

"What about the food, son?" August questioned softly, noticing that Beth's head was still bowed.

"Oh, yeah," Gerald said and quickly bowed his head again. "Thanks for the food, God. I really like fish. Amen."

August was grinning when Beth raised her gaze to meet his. She grew more beautiful with each passing day, and August heartily agreed with Gerald's prayers that they become a family.

Beth handed Phillip's plate to August. "If you would serve the salmon," she motioned,

"I would appreciate it."

August nodded and filled the plates as they were passed to him. He liked acting as the head of the family, and he enjoyed the warmth and comfort of the company he kept.

Supper passed much too quickly. "I suppose I should be going," August said, getting up. Beth's roadhouse was set up so that the ten boarding rooms all faced north or west and had individual entrances facing the outside.

"Can't he read us a story?" Gerald asked with pleading eyes.

"Please?" Phillip questioned.

"That's up to August," Beth said as she began to gather the dishes. "It's all right with me, August, if you want to read to them."

"I'd be happy to," August said, grateful for the excuse to remain close at hand. He followed the boys down the hall to their bedroom, giving Beth a quick smile over his shoulder.

Beth felt her pulse quicken. What would it be like to have August join her for the evening every night after putting their children to bed? It had been so long since she'd known the warmth and comfort of a man's company. Was it wrong for her to think of such things?

"Well, that didn't take long," August said as he came into the kitchen. "They're nearly asleep."

"Thank you for everything," Beth said, and tried to think of how she could express her gratitude for August's indulgence of their fatherly references. "I appreciate your patience with them. I've asked them not to call you Daddy," she paused, embarrassed as she remembered Gerald's prayer. "But they love you so much."

"I'm sure that they loved their father a great deal. They're just showing me what they can't show him."

"It's more than that. JB was a soldier first. He was so bent on serving his country and being a hero," Beth said as she finished drying the dishes. She didn't see August bite his lip at her words.

"Don't get me wrong," she said, turning to face him. "JB was a good man and a fine father. He loved children and we were planning to have a half a dozen or more, but his need to serve someone else or something else took him away from us. I don't blame him or resent him for his decision, but I don't think I'll ever understand the feelings that drive a man to leave his family and die a world away from those who love him."

"It's a powerful drive indeed," August said softly. "I'm sure JB felt proud, and in his heart he knew that he was offering his children the best he had. He gave his life that others might live free."

"Much like Christ gave His life for us," Beth said, startling August.

"I suppose that's true," he agreed. "If Christ felt it necessary to come on our behalf and give His life, then maybe you can understand JB's desire to offer what he could for those he loved."

"Maybe you're right," Beth said as she considered August's words. "Jesus certainly loves us more than we can comprehend."

August looked uncomfortable, so Beth decided to say no more. "I'd better go," August finally said. "I'll have to be up pretty early, so don't worry about breakfast. I'll get something in town."

"All right," Beth said and watched as August walked quietly from the house. She whispered a prayer that August would find a way through whatever problem was causing him to feel alienated from God's peace.

August made his way to his room. Even though it was still light outside and would be for many hours, August closed the heavy shutters and prepared for bed. It was warm enough that he wouldn't need to light the stove.

He lay awake for a long time, thinking about the things Beth had said and how she constantly tried to steer him back to God. His conscience bothered him as he thought of the truth that he continued to deny.

God clearly wanted his attention, but August wasn't inclined to let go of his bitterness. God still hadn't listened to the desires of August's heart, and because of that, August questioned what purpose faith served.

As he drifted into a fitful sleep, August remembered how his inability to get into the army brought him to both his important job with the highway and Beth Hogan. One door had closed while another had opened and shown him a new way of life. But where did God fit in?

Chapter 7

With the boys busy playing in the backyard tree house, Beth took a moment out of her morning chores to enjoy a hot cup of coffee and a letter from her friend, Karen Sawin.

Karen shared bits of information, including the news that her husband had suffered an injury and was being sent home. Beth wished she could be there to help her friend, but travel was nearly impossible because of the war.

Reading on, Beth was glad to learn that the family who'd purchased her home was being blessed with yet another child and had plans to build onto the house in order to accommodate the addition.

Finishing the letter, Beth noted the fear and apprehension that Karen expressed as she awaited her husband's return. Beth whispered a prayer for her friend as she refolded the paper.

Setting the letter aside, Beth picked up a pad and pencil and scratched out a reminder to write to Karen at the first possible moment. She knew Karen would need all the encouragement she could get.

Beth glanced out the window to make certain the boys hadn't fallen out of the tree. She had faced the tree house with fear, but August had convinced her that boys needed such things. Who was she to argue with his wisdom? Giggles filtered down, assuring Beth that nothing was amiss.

Back at the table, Beth sipped weak coffee and tried to plan out the rest of the day. She jotted notes about lunch and supper, but inevitably her mind returned to thoughts of August. She could picture him standing in the yard playing with her children or chopping wood. He was an appealing man with a handsome face and a gentleness that she'd rarely seen in others. Her feelings for him were growing, but she knew he was troubled about God.

What was it that had hurt August so much that he couldn't deal with God? Beth contemplated that question as she continued to enjoy the quiet.

"Beth?" August called from the front room.

Beth glanced at her watch and then at the clock on the wall. It was only nine o'clock. What was August doing back at this hour?

"In here," Beth called and got to her feet. August came through the kitchen door with a worried look on his face. "What is it?" Beth questioned, knowing that August had something to tell her.

"You'd better sit down," August said and pulled the chair out for Beth.

"What is it?" Beth repeated the question.

"What I'm going to tell you has to be kept secret, at least until you read about it in the newspapers."

"I don't understand," Beth said, and felt her stomach knot.

"You know why the highway was planned, don't you?"

"Sure," Beth replied. "The government felt it was important to have an emergency road in order to get supplies through."

"That's right," August said. "Well, now we may very well need the road."

"Why?" Beth questioned. "What's happened?"

"This is the part you mustn't tell anyone. The army took us into their confidence this morning. The Japanese have attacked the Aleutian Islands," August announced.

"The Aleutians? But that's less than six hundred miles away," Beth said as the color drained from her face. "Dear Lord, preserve us."

"Look, Beth, the Aleutians are a long ways off. We're safe here, but the road project has been stepped up. We've got work to do and not much time to do it in. The troops are holding the Japanese back, but it's critical we get this road through."

Tears filled Beth's eyes. "Are we really safe? I mean, are you sure?"

August saw the tears and heard Beth's voice tremble. He got up and put his hands on her shoulders just as she broke down.

"I can't bear it, August. I can't stand the fear, the worry. I have children whose safety depends on me. I just can't bear the thought of the enemy storming in here and, and. . ." Beth's sobs filled the air.

"Don't torture yourself, Beth. We really are safe. After all, there are more than ten thousand soldiers in Alaska and Canada. There's more than enough manpower here to keep us safe."

Beth pushed away from August and got to her feet. "We probably had thousands of men in the Pacific as well. If men are so capable, why are we at war?"

"We're at war because we have to fight to keep free of dictators like Hitler and Mussolini, as well as military monsters like Tojo. Beth, please don't cry. Everything will work out. You'll see. Just have a little faith."

Beth managed to compose herself. "Yes, of course you're right, August. Faith is the key. Faith in God, though, not in the American military. God will give them strength and wisdom. Prayer is going to be the key to this victory, and I'm sorry that I let go of that wisdom."

August stepped forward and put his hand on Beth's arm. "I just wanted you to know what was going on before you heard about it from someone else. No doubt the newspaper will have enough about it in the days to come, but I never wanted to upset you. I know news like this can be frightening."

"I'm all right now," Beth said as she lifted her apron and dried her eyes. She wanted so much to prove her faith to August. Perhaps he'd once had faith, too, a faith that he'd lost because of tragedy. Maybe this was the reason God had sent August Eriksson into her life—not for love or marriage, but for him to see the truth of God's love.

August studied her for a moment. He wanted to hold her, to make her believe that everything would be all right, but in spite of the feelings that continued to grow, August held himself back.

There was something in Beth's eyes that signaled aloofness. She was content to put the entire matter in God's hands, and it seemed to August that she didn't need or desire his comfort. Shrugging his shoulders, he left the roadhouse with an ache in his heart for something he couldn't explain.

The hot June sun caused sweat to pour down August's back as he maneuvered the caterpillar into position. He was frustrated by Beth's attitude and wondered how he could combat it. She never came out and talked with him about her true feelings. She always managed to hide behind God or biblical principles, almost as if she knew it would distance August from her.

Wiping his forehead with the back of his hand, August acknowledged that his biggest problem wasn't Beth. God was pricking his conscience.

It was the little things that got to him. Things like the way Beth would ask him to say grace or the way Gerald would talk about something from Sunday school. Sometimes it was the simple, quiet moments when August was alone in his room and the silence came over him as if roaring out God's name.

He'd not known a single moment's peace since turning away from his heavenly Father, and the turmoil within his heart only grew. August wanted to shout out for God to leave him alone, but the pressure continued, mounting day by day.

The road work took August away from Beth and the boys for longer periods of time. Sometimes he never made it home because the midnight sun allowed them to work nearly around the clock. Often, August would drop exhausted into a sleeping bag inside one of the administration's tents. The cots weren't nearly as comfortable as the bed back at the roadhouse, but as tired as he was, it wouldn't have mattered if he'd been sleeping on the ground.

Day after day the work continued. They called it "bulldozer surveying," and it was little more than plowing a path through a place where a road had never been intended. Trees, brush, and rocks ended up in messy piles along the road, constant reminders of the haste in which the design was completed.

August would often stare for a long time at the tall spruce and birch trees, trees so thick and full that they were impossible to penetrate with the human eye. It seemed a pity to destroy them.

Dense forests were relieved by brilliant, crystal lakes so blue and inviting that August could almost forget his purpose. Glacier-fed rivers flowed in milky wonder, leaving reminders of the ice mountains that had carved the valleys.

In the distant south, snowcapped peaks rose majestically above green and blue valleys, and everywhere wildflowers carpeted the earth in colors so dazzling and radiant that words could not describe them.

"Eriksson!" a voice called above the roar of the cat's engine. August shut the motor off and climbed down.

"What's up, Bill?" August questioned, recognizing the man beneath layers of dirt and sweat.

"I'm supposed to take over your shift. Supervisor wants to see you."

"Oh?" He wondered about the request as he went in search of Ralph Greening.

Ralph was waiting for August in his tent. "Come on in," Ralph waved him in as he finished up a radio call. "Sorry for the interruption, but I have some good news for you."

"Well, I'm always in the mood for good news interruptions," August said with a smile.

"You've done a tremendous job for us, August, and I'd like to offer you a permanent position with the Public Roads Administration. You'd actually be left in charge of the Northway area after we pull out. They are going to want to establish a permanent road next year, and I can't think of a better man to leave behind."

"I'm flattered," August said.

"Well, you've certainly earned it," Ralph replied as he shuffled through a stack of papers. "I'll be happy to return to the States and get away from these monstrous bugs and all this light. A body needs regular nights and days. I can't figure out how you folks put up with constant light and then endless darkness."

"I guess when you're born here you don't give it a lot of thought. We do suffer in the winter, though. It's hard to wake up in the dark, spend the day in the dark, and then go to sleep in the dark. Coupled with the cold—and I mean bitter, subzero cold—it is a problem," August replied. "But there are winter compensations."

"I don't intend to be here long enough to find out. We plan to have the road completed before then, and after that you can put up with it."

Hours later, August contemplated his promotion and the full responsibility that would be his when Ralph returned to the States. Did he want to head up such a task?

As he settled down for bed, August wondered at the turn of events. Not long ago he'd thought God had deserted him. How did he feel now? Hadn't he proved to himself that he could live life without God?

He missed Beth and the boys. It had been over a week since he'd seen them. They were so important to him, and thoughts of them were never far from his mind. Did they ever think of him? Did they miss him like he missed them?

August closed his eyes, envisioning Bethany as she moved around her roadhouse. She was so gentle and pure, and her heart was devoted to God.

His heart had once belonged to God, too. August shifted uncomfortably as he thought of his efforts to put God away from him. *But whosoever shall deny me before men, him will I also deny before my Father which is in heaven.* August remembered the words of Matthew 10:33 almost against his will.

"But you took away all my dreams, God," August argued, realizing that, for the first time in months, he was speaking to God. "You took it all: my dreams, my hopes, my family. Am I to be forsaken because I dared to think for myself, dared to make goals and dream dreams? I thought you wanted Your children to be happy. Am I to give up my dreams, even my very life, in order to be at peace with You?"

He that findeth his life shall lose it: and he that loseth his life for my sake shall find it. August pulled the pillow over his head as if he could block out the haunting words of Matthew 10:39. The words, however, would not be put aside. God's Word had made its home in August's heart for many years, and it would not leave just because August wished to escape its power.

Chapter 8

After spending two weeks without August in their home, Beth, Gerald, and Phillip were excited to see his weary frame coming up the path late one afternoon.

"Daddy!" Phillip announced when he spotted August. "Momma, Daddy's here!"

Beth glanced out the window, and her hands automatically smoothed back her blond hair. August was home!

Gerald went dancing out the door, rushing into August's arms. "I missed you," he said as August whirled him around.

"And I missed you! Have you been a good boy?"

"I've been very helpful, just like you told me to be," Gerald said as August put him down.

Phillip hurried to be next in August's arms, while Beth stood to the side of the door, wishing she had the freedom her children enjoyed.

August's eyes met hers over Phillip's back. He noticed the softness and grinned at her, causing Beth's heart to pound harder.

"And what about you?" Beth heard August ask Phillip. "Have you been a good boy?"

"Uh-huh. I been helping in the garden," Phillip said, holding up his dirty hands. "See!"

His enthusiasm was contagious. "Yes, I see," August said, inspecting Phillip's hands. "Since you've both been so good, I'll take you fishing tomorrow. That is, if your mother doesn't mind."

"Can we go, Momma?" Phillip and Gerald asked in unison.

"I suppose so," Beth replied softly. "Now, why don't you go inside and get cleaned up? It's almost suppertime."

The boys hesitated as they looked from August to their mother and back again. "You go ahead, boys. I'll be here for a day or two." At August's reassurance, the boys disappeared into the house.

"I've missed you," August said warmly. "I never knew how good I had it until I had to live out on the road. I've missed everything about this place."

"Even the bugs?" Beth asked with a smile.

"The bugs are even bigger down the road. Out there we have to shoot them down rather than swat them." August laughed and Beth joined him. When the amusement passed, silence bound them together.

"You look beautiful." August braved the words and allowed his eyes to travel Beth's form. The dusty rose dress she wore brought out the flush in her cheeks.

Beth didn't know what to say. She was excited by August's appreciation of her appearance, yet she was troubled by the warning her mind kept flashing.

"Are you hungry?" she finally questioned, growing uncomfortable in the silence.

"Yes," August replied. "I suppose I'm keeping you from something."

"Only dinner," Beth answered and opened the screen door. "Come on inside. I'll work while you tell me about the road's progress."

"It's a deal," August said, following Beth into the house and on to the kitchen.

"I took a moose roast out of the freezer several days ago, and we've been eating it ever since," Beth said as she opened the oven door. "We're having moose pie tonight."

"Moose pie?"

Beth smiled as she took the casserole from the oven. "That's right. It's moose roast cut up with eggplant, onions, egg, cheese, and seasoning. It's baked with a pie-crust topping, and that's why we call it moose pie."

"Sounds good," August said, sitting down.

"I can fix up a mess of goose tongue greens, if you've a mind for a salad, and I have fresh sourdough bread."

"Don't go to any more trouble than you already have," August said.

Before Beth could answer, a knock sounded at the front door. "I'll be right back," Beth said as she excused herself.

"What a surprise," Beth said as she opened the door to Mrs. Miller. Ushering the woman inside, she asked, "What brings you here?"

"I know it's last-minute and totally out of line, but I was wondering if I could borrow the boys to help me gather blackberries. I've promised the army a great deal of jam, and there's a huge field of berries ready to pick."

"Well, I'm not sure," Beth said as she led the way back to the kitchen. "Mr. Eriksson is back, and the boys are very fond of him. I don't know if we could separate them just now."

"I understand, but I could sure use the help. I'd be happy to pay the boys," the older woman added as she struggled to keep up with Beth.

"Oh no, you needn't pay them," Beth said as they entered the kitchen. In her absence, the boys had been taking turns playing with August and asking him questions.

"Boys, Mrs. Miller wants to know if you can help her pick blackberries."

"But August just got here," Gerald protested from August's lap.

"And I'll be here for a while," August said and gave Gerald a reassuring pat. "Don't worry about it. You go ahead and help Mrs. Miller. We can certainly catch up on our talking tomorrow while we're fishing."

"Well, I guess we can help," Gerald said once he felt certain of August's presence.

"I'm afraid the boys haven't eaten yet, Mrs. Miller. Would you like to join us for supper?" Beth asked, proud that Gerald had put his own wants aside to help someone else.

"No thanks, and if you don't mind, I'd like to treat the boys to a picnic. I have sandwiches and cold drinks, as well as some special cookies that they are very fond of," Mrs. Miller answered.

"Well, what do you say, boys? You want to have a picnic with Mrs. Miller?" August questioned before Beth could ask. "I'll bet it'll be a load of fun."

"Really, Daddy?" Phillip asked with wide eyes.

"Why, sure. It's a beautiful evening, and Mrs. Miller makes mighty good cookies. I know 'cause she brought us some while we were working on the airstrip."

"Okay," Gerald said as he hopped down from August's lap. "We'll go."

"I'm really grateful, boys," Mrs. Miller said, motioning toward the door. "Let's hurry so we can eat before we pick the berries."

The boys went along with Mrs. Miller, and Beth was left to face August alone.

"I guess we'll have more than enough supper," Beth said as she finished putting the food on the table. She took a seat across from August and realized it was the first time they'd shared dinner alone. Always before they'd had the comfort of the boys to dispel any tension, but now they sat face-to-face, both seeming to know they were going to deal with more than supper.

"I'll say grace," Beth said, avoiding August's eyes. She bowed her head without waiting to see if August would and began, "Dear Father, we thank You for this meal and the fellowship we share. Bless us now and guard us in our steps. Amen."

August held out his hand for Beth's plate, dished out a generous portion of the steaming casserole, and handed it back to her.

"Thank you," Beth said. She wanted to say so much more, yet she felt a sense of quiet come over her, as if it were more important that August begin the conversation.

"This is real good," August said with a nod of approval. "I've had moose steak, moose roast, moose stew, but I don't think I've ever had moose pie. I'll have to send my sister the recipe."

"I'm glad you like it," Beth replied between bites. Food stuck in her throat, and she remembered she hadn't set out any beverage. "I'll get us something to drink. What would you like?"

"It doesn't much matter to me. Whatever you had planned is fine," August answered.

"I have some powdered lemonade that one of the soldiers traded me for pies. I fixed a batch this morning, and it ought to be good and cold by now."

"That sounds good."

Beth smiled and went to fix the glasses and juice. Once this was accomplished, she sat back down to face the unnerving silence.

"I think the boys have grown a foot taller," August said as he ate.

"Yes," Beth replied. "I'm going to have to get them new mukluks this fall."

"Say, I saw some dandy native-made ones just down the road. There's a small village not far from where the highway is going through, and a bunch of us went over to check out the situation and found a wealth of handmade goods."

"It would certainly be great to buy something without worrying about ration stamps. Is it too far to walk?" Beth questioned.

"I wouldn't think so," August said, trying to remember the exact distance. "But maybe you could get someone to run you over, just to be on the safe side. I'll talk to Ralph and see if I can borrow one of the vehicles and drive you there myself."

"Oh, I wouldn't want to take you away from your work," Beth replied.

"It wouldn't take me away from anything," August insisted. "I've been given a couple days off due to the long hours I've been putting in. I'll see what I can do and let you know."

"All right," she reluctantly agreed.

The silence returned to hang between them like an impenetrable veil. Even August shifted uncomfortably and nervously picked at his food. Finally, he put his fork down, folded his hands, and eased back against his chair.

"I have something to say," he began.

"I thought you might," Beth answered and put her own fork down.

August gazed across the table, allowing himself several moments to take in the vision of Beth's beauty. Beth's pale blond hair was pulled back from her face, revealing high cheekbones and soft white skin. Her blue eyes seemed to grow larger under August's stare.

"I don't know all the sweet words or wily ways that men work with women, but what I have to say comes from the heart. While I've been gone I've done a lot of thinking."

"I see," Beth murmured.

"No, I don't think you do," August said softly. "I mostly thought of you. And, of course, the boys." August waited for Beth to make some reply, but she only lowered her eyes.

"I guess I came to realize how important you were to me. I found myself thinking of you and how wonderful you felt in my arms. I thought of the boys and how they always treat me like their father—how Phillip even calls me 'Daddy.' And I had to explain to you."

"Explain what?" Beth asked.

"I love you, Beth. I think I've loved you for a long time, but since I've never been in love, I just didn't recognize it. I knew you were special to me and the boys were always great, but it wasn't until I had to spend a long time away from you, from all of you, that I realized how important you were to me."

"What exactly do you mean?"

"I want to marry you, Beth. I know you're still mourning JB's passing, but I can wait for you. I want to help you make a new life, and I want to be a father to your children and to have more children, together."

Beth wasn't surprised at August's declaration, but neither was she prepared for the proposal. Shadows fell across the room as the sun continued its journey west, and Beth got up to turn on the lights.

August waited impatiently for her to say something, anything that might let him know how she felt. He watched Beth come back to the table and stand behind her chair.

"When I learned that JB was joining the air force, something inside me came undone. Phillip was just a baby, and Gerald wasn't much out of diapers. I cried when JB told me that he would have to go away and that once his training was completed, he'd be sent to Europe immediately. He told me it might be years before we saw each other again, and a part of me died." Beth drew a deep breath before continuing.

"JB had such a love of life and of God, and I knew that I couldn't make him stay. Truly, I didn't want to impose my will upon him, but in my heart I knew he'd never come home again. Of course, I never told JB that. I prayed about it, pouring out my heart before God, and I sought the Scriptures, hoping and praying to find something sensible to ease my worries.

" 'Trust in the Lord with all thine heart; and lean not unto thine own understanding.' That's Proverbs 3:5," Beth said.

"Yes, I know," August replied with a nod. "Go on."

"Well, that was the verse God led me to. I kept wanting to trust my own understanding about things. I reasoned that I had it all figured out. After all, God had sent me a wonderful Christian husband and two beautiful sons. I didn't have any reason to believe that all wouldn't be well, but in my heart I had a gnawing fear that wouldn't pass. When I received notice that JB was dead and knew that my fears were fulfilled, I almost felt relieved. Does that sound strange?"

"Not really," August said and added, "everyone deals with things the best way they can. You were anticipating the worst and the waiting is always the hardest part. When the worst that could happen finally happened, you were able to relax, knowing that things were as bad as they were going to get."

"I suppose that's true," Beth said as she gripped the chair back. "I turned my heart and soul to God for comfort. There was nothing else to do and no one else to pull me through. Do you understand?" August nodded. "I hold my relationship with Him quite dear. He pulled me through losing JB and kept me sane so that my children didn't suffer from the loss."

"Why are you telling me all this? I already know that you still mourn JB. I wouldn't intrude on that. I only ask to remain close at hand until those feelings pass."

"That's what I'm trying to say," Beth said softly. "I've already buried the past and JB. He was an important part of my life, but he's in heaven now. I don't have to worry about JB anymore. I miss him occasionally, but those times come rarely now. I've been able to get on with my life, and JB's death is no longer an issue with me. But my love of God and His Word are."

"I don't understand."

"You have an obvious problem when it comes to fellowship with the Lord. Forgive me if that sounds judgmental, but even Gerald knows that you are alienated from God. He's come to me before and asked me why you never pray and why you never talk of God the way I do or the way JB did. He was so tiny when JB went away, but he remembers his father telling him about heaven and God. Proverbs 20:11 says, 'Even a child is known by his doings, whether his work be pure, and whether it be right.' It's obvious to those around you that things are not right." Beth saw a shadow of denial pass through August's eyes.

"I'd love for you to talk to me about what has hurt you and turned you from God. I'd love to be able to help you through your anger and frustration, but you won't let me. You turn away at every possible opportunity."

"Talking won't resolve anything," August stated firmly.

"And marriage will?"

"I love you, Beth!" August said as he pounded his fist against the table.

"And I love you, August," Beth whispered, ignoring the outburst. "But I can't marry you when your heart isn't right with God. It would always stand between us and eventually divide us. I can't serve two masters, and I won't give up God."

"The verse about two masters referred to money," August said stiffly, remembering Luke 16:13.

"The verse says, 'No servant can serve two masters: for either he will hate the one, and love the other; or else he will hold to the one, and despise the other. Ye cannot serve God and mammon.' I think it works in this situation as well," Beth said with a gentle tone.

"I can't hold fast to raising my sons as Christians who will respect the Word and fellowship with believers when their father denies the need. I can't love you and serve you properly as your wife, and hold onto my faith and serve God as well. Sooner or later, the two will clash, and the battleground will be our home. Would you really have the lives claimed be those of your adopted sons and wife?"

August stared in silence. Beth had forced him to face the one thing he'd refused to admit for so long. How could he explain to her that he'd faced such disappointment that he was no longer certain that he wanted God's will?

"Look," Beth continued, feeling suddenly strengthened, "God has a purpose in all of this, and I believe He has sent us to one another for a special reason. Maybe it's to help each of us deal with the past and the sorrows we've faced. Maybe not. But I know that this problem must be dealt with before we can marry. Do you understand?"

"I don't know," August said as he folded his arms against his chest. "I just don't know. It's all well and fine to use this as a reason to turn me away, but are you sure there isn't something more? You said you love me, was that true?"

"Yes," Beth said, nodding. "I love you very much."

"Then why not trust God to work everything out after we're married?"

"Because we're both old enough to know it doesn't work that way. August, I would love to marry you. Believe me, I don't like being alone, and I hate the fact that my boys have you only as a friend and not their father. I want us to be a family as much as you do, but I want us to be a family under the hand of God. If we married now, that wouldn't be the case, would it?"

August's dark eyes narrowed, and he clenched his jaw tightly. "If that's the way you want it, then I'll leave. I'm sorry I'm not good enough for you and your children."

August turned on his heel and stormed through the house. Beth followed after him, wishing she could say something that would stop him from leaving her in anger. "I love you, August," she whispered as he opened the screen door.

"But not enough," August replied. He slammed the door behind him and stalked down the drive.

Tears streamed down Beth's face as she watched the man she loved walk out of her life. "It's not enough without God, August," she whispered. "It would never be enough without Him."

Chapter 9

August faced each new day with bitterness and trepidation. The highway project kept his hands busy, but his mind continued to be haunted by images of the woman he'd left behind.

He was angry with Beth and with God, but mostly with himself. He knew he'd disappointed Gerald and Phillip by leaving without a word, especially after promising them such a grand day of fishing and storytelling. It grieved him that he was causing them pain. Why did life have to be so difficult?

From time to time, as news trickled in about the progress of the war, August felt his anger rekindled. He should have been one of the troops. If only God would have worked things out for him and heard his prayers. If only God cared.

Every day, August operated machinery, issued orders, and helped to assess progress. While he knew the job demanded his undivided attention, his mind incessantly wandered.

Log bridges were built to cross the multiple rivers and creeks, but the problem of boggy, wet ground made progress slow and uncertain. Riverbanks had to be reinforced to hold the bridges, and while gravel was readily available, the waterlogged land seemed to have an insatiable appetite. Load after load of rock was brought in to stabilize that which refused to be stable.

Danger lurked behind every tree, and each new and unexplored position placed the highway crew in jeopardy. Despite difficulty and hardship, the highway was steadily becoming reality. August wondered what he would do when the road work was completed.

Ralph Greening expected him to stay on and work for the Public Roads Administration. There were plans to make continued road improvements and to see to it that eventually the Alaskan/Canadian Military Highway would be more than a mud trail through the wilderness. But even for the promise of a secure job, August didn't know if he could live close to Beth and the boys and not be part of their lives.

August tried to put such thoughts from his mind as he joined his crew. Rains had slowed progress, and after a two-day dry spell, every man available was out on the road making up time. Testing the ground, August grimaced. It remained spongy from the deluge, and such conditions only added to the danger of the situation.

August climbed aboard a Caterpillar tractor and started his shift with great reluctance. His duties seemed meaningless, and his life once again held no purpose. But there were tree stumps to be removed and the road to be graded.

Paying little attention to the twenty-ton machine he maneuvered, August wasn't aware of how precariously close he had come to the edge of a sheer drop. His mind was too preoccupied to notice the ledge giving way, and by the time he recognized the danger, it was too late. In a mass of rubble and a cloud of diesel smoke, the machine slid down the embankment. All August could do was hold on.

It seemed an eternity of bouncing, pitching, and turning. Then the tractor came to rest on its side, pinning August beneath.

August felt the warmth of his own blood as it gushed from a cut above his left eye. He tried to assess the situation, but his mind was clouded and dull, and his eyes refused to stay open. He struggled to move his arms, but any movement was impossible.

I have to get out of this, August thought. He strained against the weight that pinned him firmly against the ground. He could feel cold, boggy dampness against his back, and he tried to remember if a lake or pond sat near where he'd been grading. His mind offered only hazy memories.

He heard voices overhead and knew his men would come to his aid. It was hard to figure out just where they were and how soon he could expect relief, but just hearing them gave him comfort.

"Why is this happening, God?" August wondered aloud. "Why must I suffer these torments and pains?" As it became a monumental effort just to breathe, August fell silent.

Minutes or maybe hours passed as August faded in and out of consciousness. He thought he heard people working overhead, but the roar in his head made it impossible to know for certain.

"August. August," a voice called out, and though he couldn't see the face, August answered.

"I'm here! I'm under here!"

"I know where you are. August, do you trust me to get you out?"

What a strange question, August thought. *Why would anyone ask me that?*

"I don't know who you are," August replied, "but if you can help to get me out of here, I'd be much obliged."

"August, do you believe in me?" the voice whispered.

August shook his head. "What are you talking about? Just get me out of this. I'll believe you, shake your hand, dance a jig, whatever you want. Just get me out from under this thing!"

August knew his words sounded harsh and ungrateful, but this man was beginning to bother him.

"August, you called upon me. Dost thou believe on the Son of God?"

A tingle ran down August's spine. Those words were Scripture. He remembered them very well. Jesus had asked that question of a blind man.

August's breath quickened. What was it that the man answered in the Bible? August thought for a moment before quoting John 9:36 in a hesitant voice. "Who is he, Lord, that I might believe on him?"

"Thou hast both seen him, and it is he that talketh with thee." The words paralleled Christ's reply in the Bible.

August felt a trembling that started in his toes and worked all the way up through his body. The love of a Savior whom he'd so long denied penetrated the darkness and cold that engulfed his body.

Suddenly all the bitterness melted away from August's heart. In an instant, the blindness of his anger lifted, and he could once again see. He remembered the closeness and comfort that came from being right with God.

"I've really made a mess of things, Lord. Forgive me," August cried out. "Please forgive me."

August wept tears of repentance as he thought of God's love. Even though he'd rejected that love, Jesus had reached through the wall of August's disappointment and denial to be at his side when August needed Him most. What a precious friend!

The presence of Christ at his side never subsided, even as the tractor was lifted from overhead. August struggled to open his eyes, but they felt heavy and weighted down.

"August, August, old buddy, wake up. Wake up!" one of the men called.

August opened his eyes to see the hazy image of several men. Above them the spruce trees parted to reveal a brilliant sky of cobalt blue. August tried to sit up, but firm hands held him down.

"Don't move, August. You're hurt pretty bad. We're going to get you some help. Just hang on."

August tried to remain conscious, but his mind flooded with blackness, and his body went limp.

"Maybe it's better this way," one worker said to another. "I wouldn't want to be awake when they moved me. Not with the way his body must be broken up inside." The men agreed as they waited for a stretcher.

Coming out of the darkness was much like surfacing after diving deep into a lake. Fighting against the urge to remain in the dark stillness, August awoke to strange voices and blinding pain. Feeling as though every part of his body was broken, August moaned in agony.

"He's awake, Doctor," a young woman's voice called.

A man peered down at August with a look of concern. "Mr. Eriksson, I'm Dr. Butler. Can you understand me?"

"Yes," August answered slowly. Even speaking seemed painful.

"Mr. Eriksson, you've sustained some injuries. We won't know the extent of those injuries until our examination is complete. You have a concussion and a deep laceration on your forehead. Other than that, it's hard to tell. We'll do what we can to make you comfortable."

"Where am I?" August asked, knowing that there hadn't been any hospitals in the area where he had been working.

"Anchorage. They flew you in yesterday."

"I've been unconscious that long?"

"I'm afraid so, but don't worry. It isn't at all unusual after sustaining a severe head injury. For now, I'd just like you to rest and let us do our job."

August gave a slight nod before drifting into a deep, peaceful sleep.

Three days later, August was propped up in bed, trying to absorb a full assessment of his condition.

"You are most fortunate, Mr. Eriksson," the doctor explained. "Had you landed on a hard surface, you'd most likely be dead. Instead, you landed in wet muskeg, which caused your body to sink beneath the weight of the tractor. When they were able to pull the machinery from you, they discovered that you were beneath the ground's surface. No one can explain why the tractor didn't sink right along with you, but perhaps the weight was better distributed. There's really no way of knowing," the doctor said as he glanced back and forth from August's face to the chart he held.

"Some might, in fact, call it a miracle. It took over four hours to free you, and you were unconscious the entire time. Fortunately, you didn't lose much blood," Dr. Butler added.

"But I remember being awake. I remember talking to. . ." August's voice fell silent.

"I can only go by what the pilot passed on to me from the road crew. However, it would fit with the nature of your injuries. Besides the concussion, you have a broken collarbone on the left side and some relatively minor lacerations elsewhere. We were fearful that you might have sustained several fractured lumbar vertebrae."

"Several what?" August questioned. Although his sister was a registered nurse, he had never taken the time to learn much more than the basics that kept him alive.

"We thought your back might be broken, but it appears that all is well. I'd say several weeks will right what's wrong, and you'll be able to return to your home. I strongly caution against any strenuous labor, however, for at least two or three months."

"That long?" August asked in a weary voice.

"I'm sorry, Mr. Eriksson," the doctor sympathized, "but as I've already stated, you're lucky to be alive."

"Not lucky," August said with a weak grin. "God saved me from death, and believe me, I'm grateful."

"Well then, I expect a good patient who's obedient to orders," Dr. Butler answered and turned to leave. "And I happen to agree with you, Mr. Eriksson. You were very blessed."

August nodded and relaxed as the doctor left. No sooner had he walked through the door than a gray-haired nurse entered the room.

"Good day, Mr. Eriksson," the pleasant-voiced woman said. "I'm Nurse Roberts. How are you feeling?"

"Well enough, I suppose."

"Good, good. I'll need to take your temperature and pulse now," the woman said as she automatically popped a thermometer in August's mouth and took his wrist.

The woman reminded August of his mother. She was firm, yet gentle in her touch, and her voice was like a spoken lullaby.

"I'll bet you'd enjoy some breakfast," she chattered after marking down his pulse rate. "Well, I have just the thing for you. Eggs, toast, juice, and maybe even some bacon. How about it?" she questioned, removing the thermometer from August's mouth.

"It sounds wonderful," August agreed.

"Then I'll fetch you a tray and be back in a jiffy," Nurse Roberts announced and hurried from the room.

August contemplated the tight bandaging that held his left arm firmly against his body.

He was grateful that it was his left collarbone rather than his right that bore the break. At least he could still use his right hand.

Nurse Roberts came into the room with a steaming tray of food. "Here we are. This ought to make you feel considerably better. You'll notice that I've brought you some coffee as well. Now, can I get you anything else?"

"I appreciate all that you've done. If it wouldn't be too much trouble, I'd be most grateful if you'd get me a Bible," August said, struggling to sit up. "I have some catching up to do."

"Here, let me help you," Nurse Roberts said as she put the tray down. She lifted August with ease and even managed to keep from causing him greater pain.

August looked into the soft brown eyes and sighed. He missed his mother.

"Thank you," August whispered.

"Not at all," the woman said, and brought the tray to his bed. "Now, you eat everything here, and I'll be happy to search out a Bible for you."

August reached out and placed his hand to cover the older woman's hand. "Would it offend you if I told you that you remind me of my mother?"

The woman broke into a big smile. "Certainly not. Is she nearby? Can I call her for you?"

"She's dead," August said thoughtfully. "No, she's gone, but she's in heaven. She loved God more than anything or anyone, and I know I'll see her again."

"That always makes it easier, doesn't it?" the woman observed. "Knowing that your loved ones are safe in the arms of Jesus and that you'll one day see them in heaven—it's all that gets me through each day when I think of those who have gone before me."

"You talk as one who knows," August replied softly.

"I do, son. I do. I lost my husband and children in the influenza epidemic. I decided to train and become a nurse after that. But even after all these years, it hurts to remember them and know that I must wait." The woman's voice was barely audible.

August squeezed her hand. "Someone is always left behind. I guess that's our job."

The woman smiled and patted August's hand. "Of course, you're right. Now, you eat, and I'll go find you a Bible."

It wasn't until the next day that August came to realize the doctor had given him a great deal of pain killer. As the medication wore off, deep, penetrating pain filled August's body. He struggled to forget it, forcing his mind away from the hospital and to the small rural village where Beth and the boys lived. He tried to imagine Beth at work and the boys at play.

He was grateful when Nurse Roberts brought him more pain medication. While August waited for the drugs to take effect, he leaned back against the pillows and prayed.

"Dear God, I need to be free from this pain. Such pain and misery takes my mind from the hope that I should have in You." August shifted uncomfortably. "I know I could just as easily be dead or dying—perhaps I really am—but Lord, I want to live. I want to see Beth and the boys, and I want to set things right with them.

"Father, I love Bethany Hogan, and I believe You sent me to her and her children to be a husband and father. I know I've doubted Your blessings, but I don't doubt them any longer. Deliver me, Lord. Deliver me and let me live. Amen."

Chapter 10

Beth discarded her mending and sat wringing her hands. She was miserable, her boys were heartbroken, and August was nowhere to be found. She blamed herself for driving him out. The image of August's angry face would forever burn in her memory.

She'd only said the things that needed to be said. She'd never meant to hurt August, but she couldn't be married to a man who was obviously fighting God.

The month had been miserable and rainy, leaving Gerald and Phillip bored and stuck inside. Mrs. Miller had graciously shown up to take the boys to her house, but Beth knew they were pining for August, and it was an impossible void to fill.

Then there was the constant worry of war. The Japanese still held strongholds in the Aleutians, and every day rumors fed fear and anxiety.

The army insisted there wasn't any immediate danger, yet there were practice drills from time to time, reminding everyone that the danger was close enough. Civil Defense officials spoke of blackout drills, insisting everyone have heavy curtains to place at their windows. Bethany wondered at this order, given that they were enjoying close to twenty hours of sunshine a day.

Rationing was tightened, and people were encouraged to do without and buy war bonds. Beth thought of the soldiers who labored long and hard to build the highway through Alaska. She thought them fortunate that no one was shooting at them while they worked. At least not yet.

People seemed more neighborly than ever, offering food, oil, and whatever help they could spare. In Alaska, life depended upon such generosity, but the war made their dependency upon one another more significant than ever.

The summer had been busier than Beth had expected, and it seemed there was never a moment to call her own. She had taken in laundry for highway workers, prepared baked goods for the army, and always had more requests for rooms at her roadhouse than she had rooms to offer. It kept her mind occupied for the most part, but not her heart.

Every day she passed by August's room, wanting to check whether his things were gone, and every day as she reached for the door handle, she stopped. She'd refused to rent August's room, hoping and praying that he'd return, but deep inside, Beth had lost any confidence in that possibility. Opening the door might prove once and for all that her fears were well founded.

Persistent knocking brought Beth hurrying to the front door, hoping that August had returned. The door opened to reveal Mrs. Miller, and Bethany couldn't hide a frown.

"I'm sorry, dear. Have I caught you at a bad time?" Mrs. Miller asked hesitantly.

Beth immediately felt bad for having given Mrs. Miller the wrong impression. "No, please forgive me. I'm just a bit preoccupied. Won't you come in?"

"Are you sure I'm not causing you a problem?" the older woman questioned as she followed Beth into the house.

"I'm sure. I must apologize for my demeanor these days," Beth said as she motioned Mrs. Miller to a chair. "Would you like some refreshments? I have lemonade and ginger snaps."

"No, I'm fine. I just wanted to visit with you. I know you haven't been yourself, and I wondered if I might help. I know how tedious widowhood can be."

Beth smiled and swept her blond hair back over her shoulder. "You are such a dear to me, Mrs. Miller. I seriously doubt I would have made it had it not been for Granny Gantry and now you."

"You mustn't let the past get you down."

"It isn't that," Beth said and bit her lower lip.

"Then what?" Mrs. Miller asked and reached across to pat Beth's hand. "I know I'm being a nosy old woman, but believe me, there are times when talking to someone who understands helps much more than keeping it bottled inside."

Beth smoothed imaginary lines in her olive green skirt. "It isn't the widowhood that grieves me, Mrs. Miller. The problem does relate to a man, however."

"What widow doesn't have man problems?" Mrs. Miller laughed softly. "What seems to be the trouble?"

"I've fallen in love," Beth said matter-of-factly. "But you mustn't tell anyone."

"Your secret is safe with me," Mrs. Miller insisted. "Now, why don't you tell me about it? Perhaps you'll feel better afterward."

Beth poured out all the details of August's appearance in her life and how her feelings had quickly developed into love. "I care far more than I ever thought possible. When JB died, I feared I could never love another, but God has graciously allowed me to love again."

"Then what's the problem?"

"I'm afraid I sent him packing," Beth said sadly.

"Why? What happened?" Mrs. Miller asked in surprise.

"August has something troubling him. Something that won't allow him to feel the closeness to God that I suspect he once felt. I tried to get him to talk about it, but he grew angry and stormed off."

"That was the day the boys helped me pick berries," Mrs. Miller stated.

"That's right," Beth agreed. "I felt so bad after convincing the boys that August would be here when they returned and then he wasn't. Gerald didn't even talk for two days, and when he finally opened up, all this hurt came pouring out. He felt betrayed, and I had to explain that I was responsible."

"But you weren't," Mrs. Miller said gently. "God is working in August's life. You were simply weeding a garden that God planted long ago. If God is striving to bring August back to the fold, you aren't responsible for anything more than living out God's goodness and standing on His Word. If that drove August away, then it is still part of God's plan."

Beth nodded. "Yes, I'm sure you're right. But—" She paused and lowered her face. "I love him, and I'm so afraid of losing him. What if he won't ever deal with his problems?"

"If it's meant to be, it will be," Mrs. Miller said firmly. "You must stand strong in your faith. God understands your grief and frustration. Trust Him."

Beth studied the older woman for a moment. Her gray hair had been pinned on top of her head without a single wisp escaping its bounds. It gave Mrs. Miller an extremely well-organized look.

The plump woman was wearing a cream-colored dress with pastel flowers splotching it from neck to knee. She carried an air of respectability and solitude, yet Beth was surprised that Mrs. Miller had never remarried.

"Mrs. Miller, may I ask you something personal?"

The widow nodded. "Certainly. I can probably guess what your question will be. But I have one condition upon which I will insist."

"And what is that?" Beth questioned.

"You must stop with the Mrs. Miller title and call me Hazel."

Beth smiled. "I would love to, Hazel."

"Much better. Now ask your question."

"I just wondered why you've never remarried. After all, you live in an area where women are scarce and the companionship of a wife is highly prized and sought after."

Hazel laughed. "That's true enough, and God knows there have been offers. Mostly men who needed a nursemaid or housekeeper, though. I guess the right man never came along."

"How do you bear the loneliness? I mean," Beth paused trying to think of a tactful way to speak her mind. "I have the boys as well as the roadhouse, and they keep me busy, but you're down there in town all alone."

The older woman sobered noticeably. "It does get hard, especially at night or in the winter. I've been widowed for over five years, and I don't think I'll ever get used to the winters. They're so cold, dark, and endless. The first year I would cry every time the sun set." Her eyes took on a distant look as she remembered those haunting days.

"You don't have to go on," Beth said sympathetically. "Unless, of course, you want to."

"That's all right," Hazel said and continued. "I know you understand. Those first months, I just wandered around trying to figure out what was what. I kept hearing my Zeke calling me, and when I'd realize it was just my imagination, my heart was heavier than ever. At night, I'd wake and reach out for him, but he was gone. When I'd come fully awake it hurt so much that I wished I'd never wake up again."

"Oh, Hazel," Beth murmured, "I'm so sorry."

"Sometimes I still find myself waiting for him to come home from working his trap lines, but of course he never does," Hazel concluded.

Beth nodded. "I know. I think it would have been harder on me, if JB hadn't already been gone for so long. When he left for duty in the air force, I probably felt his absence worse. When I knew he wasn't coming back, I comforted myself in God and my children, but I still couldn't bear living in the house we'd built together."

"I thought about leaving," the older woman agreed, "but I wanted to stay for the very reasons that you wanted to leave. I needed to feel Zeke close at hand. I needed to know his presence at least until the pain was less. The house was a strong reminder of our love. Every scratch or nick reminded me of something Zeke and I had gone through. I needed the comfort of memories."

"The boys are constant reminders for me," Beth said softly. "And though both bitter and sweet, they have been my lifeline. God was so merciful to give them to me. I don't know how I could have gotten through those first days without their love. They truly sustained me."

"Zeke and I wanted to have children," Hazel said honestly, "but God never blessed us with any. I guess that's why I take such pleasure in your boys. They are such joys to have around and so well behaved. They are a credit to you, Beth."

"Thank you for saying so, but teaching them manners has been the easy part. The hard part is playing both mother and father. I feel that my abilities always fall short of what they need, and now the only man they've truly known as father is gone. How can I possibly help them understand?"

"Trust God and wait, Beth. Trust God and wait," Hazel said firmly.

Beth nodded, but her mind was ever on her sons and their broken hearts.

That night, the silence hung heavy between Beth and her boys. Dinner was eaten with little interest, and when Beth suggested a game of dominoes, the boys only gave it a half-hearted effort. When the clock in the hall chimed nine, Beth ushered her sons to their bedroom.

"Momma, when will August come back?" Gerald questioned as he got ready for bed.

"I don't know, Gerry. He has to work on the road, and that takes him far from us. I don't know if he'll be able to come back any time soon."

"Is he mad at us?" Gerald asked in earnest.

Beth wanted to assure her son that August would never hold malice toward him or Phillip, but the words stuck in her throat. No doubt he was mad at her. He'd been so angry the night he'd left, and Beth was afraid he'd never want to see her again.

"I miss him," Phillip piped up from his bed.

"I know. We all miss August and want him to come back." Beth turned and made a pretense of picking up Gerald's discarded clothes to keep the boys from seeing the tears in her eyes.

"I'm going to ask God to send him back to us," Gerald said as he knelt to say his prayers. "I love him, and I still want him to be my daddy."

"I pray, too," Phillip said, scooting out from under his covers. "I want Daddy."

Beth opened the door and turned off the bedroom light. The boys' kneeling figures were illuminated by the shadowy light from the hallway.

She watched in silence as the boys prayed. Their little-boy voices lifted up pleas of love to their God, a God they trusted without doubt. Could Beth somehow do the same? Was it possible to regain the trust she'd once felt when life was more simple?

Seeing the boys safely tucked in, Beth made her way down the hall and to her desk. She'd long ago given August over to God, and there was nothing to be gained by taking him back.

Resting her head in her arms on the desk, Beth prayed for strength to endure the loneliness and for guidance for August. Wherever he was, God could reach him.

Chapter 11

Whenever Saturday came, Bethany awoke to a strange silence. Straining her ears for the sound of her children, she was more than a little surprised to realize they were quiet.

Enjoying the warmth of her bed, Beth reasoned that the children were simply extra tired. They had, after all, spent most of the previous evening helping Mrs. Miller pick berries again.

She was just fading back into dreams of August when something caught her ear. Bolting upright in bed, Beth waited and listened. Moaning sounds came from the boys' bedroom, and Beth knew instinctively that it was Gerald.

As Beth hastily threw on a robe and tore down the hall, a feeling of dread settled over her. By the time she reached the boys' room, her hands were trembling.

"Why am I so afraid?" she whispered to the air. "Surely he's only had a bad dream." She fought desperately to reassure herself. There was no reason for her uneasiness, yet a mother's heart told her something wasn't right.

She opened the door and found a bleary-eyed Phillip sitting beside his brother's sleeping form. All looked well, at least on the surface.

"Good morning, sweetie. How's Momma's boy?" Beth asked, fluffing her younger son's hair. Phillip scurried off the bed and into his mother's arms.

"Gerry's hot," Phillip said, planting a kiss on his mother's cheek.

"I'm sure he's fine. Let's go see," Beth whispered and shifted Phillip from one hip to the other. His legs draped down the side of her body, reminding Beth that he was quickly passing out of babyhood.

"Gerry," Beth said as she put Phillip on the floor beside the bed and took a seat by her sleeping son. She reached out and brushed back the sandy brown hair that had fallen across Gerald's forehead.

His skin was hot and dry, a sure sign of fever. "Gerry, wake up, honey." Beth shook her son gently.

"Mommy," Gerald moaned and opened fever-glazed eyes. "I hurt, Mommy. My head hurts real bad."

"You have a fever," Beth soothed, checking her son for any other symptoms. There weren't any spots to indicate measles or smallpox, and his body seemed free from any swelling or rashes.

"I'll get you an aspirin and a cool towel. You just rest, Gerry. Phillip and I will take care of you." Beth's calm voice masked the dread in her heart.

Beth carried Phillip from the room, speaking as she made her way to the kitchen. "We'll get Gerry some medicine and then he'll feel better." Phillip nodded as Beth hurried to get the aspirin.

Beth put Phillip down and rummaged through the cupboards until she found a small bottle of aspirins. Putting the medicine in her pocket, Beth then poured a glass of water.

"Me thirsty," Phillip declared as Beth picked up the glass.

"I'm sorry, sweetie. Here, have a drink and then we'll take a drink for your brother." Beth waited impatiently as Phillip satisfied his thirst. Then, after refilling the glass, she returned to Gerald's bed and gently lifted his head to swallow the tablet.

"Ouchy, ouchy, Mommy. It hurts," Gerald cried, recoiling from her touch.

Phillip had padded down the hall to find his mother bent over Gerald. "He sick, Momma?"

"Yes," Beth whispered. "Your brother is very sick."

"The light hurts my head, Mommy. Please turn off the light," Gerald cried softly.

Beth shook her head. Fever usually caused some pain, but never this much. Something was very wrong. She pulled the heavy curtains across the windows and turned back to face the situation.

"Phillip, I need you to stay here with Gerry while I go get the doctor. Can you do that for me?" she asked the tiny boy.

"I take care of Gerry," Phillip said as he planted himself firmly beside his brother.

"Good boy," Beth said. "Now, it's really important that you stay right here and that you don't get off the bed. Do you understand?"

"I be good, Mommy," Phillip said gravely. "I pray for brother."

"That would be good," Beth agreed. "I'm going to go change my clothes, and I'll check in before I go. I'll be right back."

Beth hurried around her bedroom, mindlessly choosing her gardening slacks and one of JB's old shirts. She quickly tied her blond hair back into a ponytail and made her way down the hall to the boys' room.

A light touch to Gerald's forehead confirmed her fears. The fever was rising. "Phillip, I have to go now. When I come back, I'll fix you a special, big-boy breakfast. Would you like that?"

"Can I have applesauce?" Phillip asked, requesting his favorite food.

"You be a good boy, and you can have whatever you like," Beth replied. "I'll be back in a jiffy."

She hurried down the hall, dreading the desertion of her children. She pulled on socks and boots to wade through the muddy roads of the rain-drenched community, and after one final peek at the boys, she rushed from the roadhouse and ran all the way into town.

Beth marveled at the transformation of her small town. The landscape literally became a sea of tents as the army continued to bring in men and supplies. She picked her way through the mud while soldiers whistled or waved in appreciation of a feminine form. The attention made Beth nervous, but she ignored it. Gerald's restless form filled her mind.

She breathed a sigh of relief upon finally reaching the doctor's office. Pushing open the door and mindless of the mud she tracked into the office, Beth made her way to where a nurse sat writing in a ledger.

"I need to see the doctor," Beth said breathlessly.

"What seems to be your ailment, Miss? . . ." the nurse fell silent waiting for Beth to fill in her name.

"Mrs. Beth Hogan," she offered impatiently, "and it's not for me, it's my son. He has a high fever."

"The doctor isn't here right now, but I can send him over as soon as he returns," the nurse replied.

Beth's brow furrowed as she bit her lower lip. "I suppose I'll have to wait then. Do you have any idea how long it might be?"

"Don't worry," the nurse answered sympathetically, "the doctor is setting an arm on the other side of town. He won't be much longer, and I'll send him right on to you. Now, why don't you tell me everything about your son's illness, and I'll pass the information to the doctor."

"He just woke up with a fever. I didn't bother to take his temperature, but I'm certain it's already very high, and it's climbing."

"Anything else?" the nurse questioned as she jotted the information down.

"He says his head hurts and his eyes are very sensitive to light," Beth replied and added in a near sob, "He's only five."

"Try not to worry, Mrs. Hogan. Tell me where I can send the doctor when he returns."

"I run the Gantry Roadhouse east of town. Just follow the road, and our place is a quarter mile past the crossroads," Beth directed in a trembling voice.

"All right, Mrs. Hogan. You go on back home and I'll do what I can. And Mrs. Hogan," the nurse paused, "please try not to worry. Give your son some aspirin and wash him with a cool cloth."

Beth nodded and made her way back toward home. She'd never run as much as she had this day, and by the time she reached the roadhouse, she was winded and every muscle in her legs ached.

Kicking off her muddy boots and slamming the door behind her, Beth raced to Gerald's bedside. Phillip sat faithfully beside his older brother, wiping the cloth over his forehead.

"What a good boy you are, Phillip," Beth said as she reached down and felt Gerald's brow. He felt as hot as ever, and Beth noticed that he didn't even stir at her touch.

"Come along, Phillip. I'll get you dressed and fix you applesauce pancakes."

"Yummy," Phillip said as he jumped down from the bed. "I took care of brother," he stated simply.

"Yes, you certainly did," Beth replied and helped Phillip off with his nightshirt. She replaced the gown with a shirt and pants and led him to the kitchen.

Beth hastily prepared breakfast between trips to the boys' bedroom. She alternated swabbing Gerald's fiery body and flipping pancakes. She had just placed a plate of pancakes and applesauce in front of Phillip when a knock sounded at the door.

"You stay here and eat. I'm certain that will be the doctor, and I'll have to talk to him about Gerry," Beth said as she left the room.

The doctor stood at the door, and Beth breathed a sigh of relief as she took his coat and showed him to Gerald's room.

"My name is Dr. Stevens," the man said as he began to examine Gerald. "My nurse tells me the boy's symptoms just started."

"Yes," Beth affirmed. "He was fine yesterday, although I do recall he seemed a little tired."

The doctor forced Gerald to sit, causing the boy to cry out in pain. Beth knelt by his side. "It's all right, Gerry. Momma's here."

"It hurts real bad, Mommy," Gerald managed between his cries.

"Son, can you bend your neck as if you were going to look down your nightshirt?" the doctor questioned.

Gerald made a valiant effort, but it only caused more pain. "No, no. It hurts," he whimpered. Tears formed in Beth's eyes as she watched her child suffer.

"It's all right, son. I'm a doctor, and I'm going to help you."

Gerald said nothing as the doctor eased him back on the bed. The boy reached out for his mother, and Beth immediately took hold of his hand. She waited in silence while the doctor finished his examination and took Gerald's temperature.

"You just rest now, son. I'm going into the hall with your mother so we can figure out how to make you feel better." The doctor finished putting his instruments into his black bag and motioned Beth to follow him.

Beth knew by the look on the doctor's face that the news would not be good. She felt her knees weaken as she pulled the bedroom door closed behind them.

"I'm afraid your son has all the signs of spinal meningitis," Dr. Stevens began. "I can't be certain without running a number of tests, including a complicated procedure called a spinal tap. I don't have the facilities in town to help your boy."

"What is spinal meningitis?" Beth asked anxiously.

"It's an infection that attacks the membrane surrounding the brain and spine. I'm afraid it's often fatal."

"What am I to do?" Beth questioned frantically. "He has to have help. I don't care what it costs or where we have to go."

"I know. I know," the doctor said as he put his arm around Beth. "What we have to do is get your son to a good hospital."

"But how and where?" Beth asked.

"My suggestion would be Fairbanks. I happen to know there's a supply plane headed there in two hours. I believe we should have your son on that plane."

"Then he'll be there," Beth said, regaining a bit of her composure. "I'll get him ready. Just tell me what to do."

"We'll need to keep him from getting chilled, so bring his blankets. I'll get my nurse to accompany you on the trip. She'll know what to do."

"What about Phillip?" Beth questioned. "He's my younger, and he shares a room with his brother." Fear reverberated in every word.

"He should be fine," the doctor replied, placing a hand on Beth's arm. "We don't quarantine for meningitis because there is no conclusive information about the risk of contagion."

Beth felt only minor relief at the doctor's words. "I'll need to get word to Mrs. Hazel Miller on Second Street. She'll need to come and stay with Phillip. I'm afraid I don't have a telephone. Could you send word to her when you get back into town?" Beth asked hopefully.

"I'd be happy to. I'll also get a couple of soldiers to drive you and your son to the airport. Just wait here until they arrive," the doctor instructed.

"I'll be ready."

An hour later, Beth waved a hesitant good-bye to Phillip and Mrs. Miller. The soldiers showed up as promised, and with them came the nurse who'd assisted Beth at the doctor's office. The woman literally took over and left Beth with nothing to do but look on in helpless frustration.

The drive to the airstrip was a short one, but to Beth, every minute smothered her in apprehension. The soldiers pulled up next to the transport plane and within moments had moved Gerald and the nurse to the stripped-out fuselage of a Lockheed Vega.

Beth's worried look caught the attention of the pilot. "Don't worry, ma'am. We'll have your boy to Fairbanks in less than two hours."

Beth offered the man a fleeting smile. "Thank you. I know you'll do your best." She allowed him to help her up into the plane, her mind filled with only one thought.

"Dear God," Beth breathed against the drone of the airplane's radial engine, "please help my son. Please heal my baby."

Chapter 12

August rotated his shoulder gingerly and waited for any indication of pain. When none came, he smiled. Finally, he was able to move with nearly the same mobility he'd had before the accident.

He offered a wave to the pilot who'd just landed him at the Northway airstrip, then went in search of the Public Roads office and his boss.

Several minutes later, August was sitting beside the cluttered desk that Ralph Greening continued to work from whenever in Northway.

"Catching up on paperwork is worse than dealing with the dirt, rain, and mosquitoes," Ralph griped. "I just got back from our old camp. You certainly gave us a scare," he added, offering August a cup of coffee. "This stuff's getting mighty hard to come by up here, so don't ever say no when somebody offers you a free cup," he teased.

August took the coffee and lifted the mug slightly. "To your health!"

Ralph laughed and joined him in the salute. "And to yours!"

The coffee tasted stale and was only lukewarm, but August didn't care. He was finally going to see Beth again, and he was anxious to complete his work with Ralph.

"Doc says I can go back to work, but nothing too strenuous," August said with a grin. "Whatever that means."

"It might mean that you're not to be dumping Caterpillars over the edge of muddy embankments again." At this both men laughed.

"Yeah, I suppose that's what he meant," August agreed and continued. "Anyhow, the way I see it, it's all up to you. You just tell me where to report, and I'll take care of getting there."

Ralph nodded, but then the thought of Bethany Hogan's hasty retreat from Northway came to mind. He'd only learned of her troubles that morning. His frown and knitted brows caused August to put his coffee mug down.

"What is it? What's wrong?" August asked.

"I went to see Mrs. Hogan today. You know, I wanted to tell her about your accident. I already felt bad that so much time had passed since you were flown to Anchorage, but I had no way of getting back here to tell her," Ralph said apologetically.

"I understand, Ralph, and I'm sure that Beth did," August offered.

"No, she wasn't there," Ralph said with a shake of his head. "Mrs. Hogan had one of her boys take sick. He was pretty bad, and they had to get him to a hospital. They flew out a couple days ago. I think they took him to Fairbanks."

August turned ashen. "Which boy?"

Ralph leaned back and closed his eyes. "I think it was the older one, but I can't be sure.

Can't picture him in my mind. You'd best go on down to the roadhouse and ask Mrs. Miller. She's been taking care of the place and the other boy."

August was already on his feet. "I'll do that. I guess it might be a spell longer before I'll be ready to work after all," August said as he made his way out.

"I kind of figured that," Ralph called after him.

August took off at a full run for the roadhouse. He came up the path panting and out of breath, with an aching in his shoulder that hadn't been there that morning. He pounded on the front door and waited impatiently for someone to open up.

"Why, Mr. Eriksson," Mrs. Miller stated in disbelief. "We thought you'd left for good."

"I was injured in an accident and flown to Anchorage. I just returned not more than a half-hour ago, and Mr. Greening tells me that Gerald is sick."

Mrs. Miller nodded, and her eyes turned misty. "Poor little boy," she said in a hushed tone. "The doctor doesn't expect him to make it."

"What?" August nearly yelled the word. "What in the world are you talking about? What's wrong with him?"

"Spinal meningitis," Mrs. Miller said ominously. "Beth flew with him to the hospital in Fairbanks, but the doctor said he might already be too far gone. With meningitis, there's just no way of knowing."

"What about Phillip?" August asked with dread.

"Oh, he's fine," Mrs. Miller answered with a smile. "We've been baking since before light. He's asleep right now, but I could wake him if you like."

August barely heard the words. He felt sick at the thought of Gerald dying and knew that it would be hard to see Phillip just then. He thought of Beth in Fairbanks, bearing alone the burden of her desperately ill child. "No, don't wake him. I've got to get to Beth," he muttered.

"I know it'd mean the world to her," Mrs. Miller said with a bit more composure. "She talked so often about you, wondering where you'd gone and if she'd ever see you again."

August nodded. "I've thought a great deal about her, too. Being in a sickbed does that for you—gives you plenty of time to think about the things you wished you'd done differently."

"I know she'll be needing you now," Hazel replied, touching August at the elbow. "She cares a great deal about you."

"I know," August said, turning to leave.

Hazel called out after him, "Please let us know how Gerald is."

"I'll do that. I only hope I'm not too late," August called over his shoulder as he bid the older woman a hasty good-bye. "Tell Phillip that Daddy was here and that I'll see him real soon."

"I will, Mr. Eriksson. I will," Mrs. Miller called out and waved. She whispered a silent prayer for the man as he rounded the bend and disappeared from view.

God was with August as he hurried back to the airstrip. He managed to secure passage on a plane going to Fairbanks, and after their scenic flight and bumpy landing, August went in search of the hospital.

The Fairbanks hospital wasn't a stately affair, but it was efficient. August hastened to find a nurse who could direct him and then made his way to the room where she said he'd find Gerald and Bethany.

At least he's still alive, August thought as he made his way down the corridor. Through the doorway of Gerald's room, August saw Beth.

She looked frighteningly small and helpless as she prayed at the bedside of her dying child. He could nearly hear her pleading words as she begged for the life of her son.

Hesitating on the threshold, August wondered how she'd react to his arrival. He glanced at Gerald's pale, nearly lifeless form and back again to the boy's mother. "Dear God," August breathed, "please hear her prayers."

August stepped forward. The noise caught Beth's attention. Her mouth dropped open at the sight of August.

"August," she breathed the word.

Beth looked gaunt and drawn, but August thought her beautiful. He opened his arms, praying that she'd come to him.

Without hesitation, Beth got to her feet, crossed the room, and wearily fell into August's arms. "Oh, August, I prayed you'd come. I prayed that God would find you and deliver you to me. Does that sound hopelessly selfish?" she questioned in a sob.

"He heard your prayers about that and then some," August stated. "I've come back to you, but only because I came back to God first."

Beth pulled back with tears streaming down her face. "Really? Oh, August, that's the best possible news. Now if only. . ."

August cupped Beth's quivering chin in his hand. "If only Gerald would get well," he answered for her.

"Yes," Beth replied. "August, he's so sick, and Dr. Matthews doesn't know whether he can get well or not."

"Is it meningitis as they feared?" August asked softly. He glanced over Beth's shoulders at Gerald.

"Yes," Beth answered and reached up to take hold of the hand that held her. "They sent for an experimental drug from the States, but it hasn't seemed to help."

"Well, we will have to pray together for him," August said tenderly.

Beth closed her eyes and nodded. "I've prayed alone enough for both of us, but I know there's strength in numbers. I'm afraid this time we need all the help we can get."

"Don't worry, Beth. You never have to be alone again. I've done a great deal of thinking and growing up as well. While I had nothing to do but lay in that hospital bed—"

"What?" Beth said pulling away from August. "You were in the hospital? But why? Are you all right?"

"Relax," August said, pulling Beth back against him. "I was in an accident a while back. It happened while I was grading the highway. The tractor fell over an embankment that had been weakened by rain. I'm fine now—just a little stiffness in my shoulder and a scar on my head."

Beth's eyes searched for the red welt. She reached up a hand and pushed back August's hair to reveal the scar. "Oh, August!" she exclaimed. "Does it hurt you still?"

"Not much. My collarbone was broken, and it still smarts a bit if I overdo, but really I'm fine. I just didn't want to send a letter to explain all that had happened. I wanted to wait until I could see you in person."

"I thought you hated me and had left for good," Beth blurted out honestly. "I felt so bad for sending you away." She glanced back at Gerald. "The boys were just heartbroken."

August nodded. "I knew they would be, and I hated myself for walking away. I knew I needed to listen, but I couldn't make myself turn around. What you said was exactly what I needed to hear. Of course, I couldn't see that until I was half-dead. Then, it was as if God had seen that simple methods wouldn't work with me, and He reached down with something I couldn't ignore."

"He usually does," Beth said with the slightest beginnings of a smile.

August acknowledged hers with a smile of his own. "God knew he was dealing with a particularly stubborn case. I'd run as far as I could, and when God couldn't pin me down any other way, I guess He used a tractor." August's words were lighthearted in spite of his ordeal.

"I confessed my sins, knowing that the only thing real in my life was my relationship with God. I remembered when my mother had put me on her knee and explained that each of us needed a Savior. Some people seek one in a lifestyle or a job, she said. Others try to force people into that role, but what we need is Jesus.

"I remember even now how amazed I was that Jesus had come to earth to save my soul. It only took remembering that simple wonderment to make me take a more realistic look at what I'd done to myself. You were a brave woman to stand your ground with me, Beth."

Moaning from the bed brought Beth and August to Gerald's side. "I'm not so brave," Beth murmured, looking fearfully into August's eyes. August placed his hand against the boy's fiery brow, while Beth took his hand.

"I'm here, Gerry. Momma's here," Beth whispered softly. Gerald calmed, opened his eyes, then closed them again. Beth began to cry softly. Exhausted by her vigil at Gerald's sickbed, she collapsed across the edge of the bed.

August came and lifted her to her feet. "Beth, come on. You have to rest."

"No! I must stay with him," she protested as August led her from the room. "He might wake up, and I don't want him to be afraid."

"We'll just be down the hall. I'll tell the nurse to watch over him. She'll let us know if he wakes up," August said firmly as he pulled Beth along.

Beth's protests only further weakened her. Finally, she gave up and allowed August to take her to the waiting room. August's strong arms offered her the strength that she'd prayed for. She breathed a prayer of thanks while August helped her to a chair.

"You wait right here, and I'll see if I can't get us a cup of coffee or something," August said.

Beth nodded and watched as he walked to the nurses' station. How grateful she was for his direction and strength. She had been so afraid of never seeing him again, and now, just when God knew she needed August the most, he was at her side.

The aching in her heart refused to abate, however. The doctor had told her there was no hope for her son. No hope whatsoever.

Beth knew better than to give up hope. While there was life, God could work. But it was hard to maintain hope in the face of such devastation. How could she explain to a doctor she'd only met that this child had to live, that without him a part of her heart would be forever broken? He was a man of medicine, and his cold, scientific attitude left Bethany empty.

Her eyes misted at the thought of Gerald's suffering. He was so little and defenseless. He didn't deserve this sickness. Beth felt weak to the point of being sick. How much more could either of them take?

God had heard her prayers, Beth reminded herself. After all, August was here, and he'd renewed his faith in God. God had surely sent August to help her through Gerald's illness. Leaning back against the chair, Beth closed her eyes and tried to pray. She was so tired, so weary of fighting alone.

Within moments, sleep washed over her. August returned to find Beth eased back against the chair sound asleep, but she still wore the worried concern he'd noted when he first saw her at Gerald's bed.

"Give her peace, Father," August prayed as he sat down beside her. "She's remained faithful and true, Lord. Please renew her strength."

Chapter 13

Throughout the long evening, August maintained his watchful guard over Bethany's sleeping form. He managed to find a blanket to cover her with and continued praying for both Beth and Gerry as she slept.

August watched the seemingly motionless hands on the clock. Nine, then ten o'clock dragged by, and still what sky he could see through the window showed streaks of light. The long summer night made it impossible to judge time.

Eleven, twelve, and finally one o'clock passed without word of Gerald's condition. August hesitated to ask for fear of waking Beth. She needed sleep more than anything else. He'd nearly decided to risk the disturbance when the nurse appeared with Gerald's doctor.

"I'm afraid I have bad news," Dr. Matthews said as he stood before August.

Beth stirred at the sound of voices and sat up. "What is it?" she questioned.

"Your son is failing rapidly. I suggest you and your husband come say your good-byes," the doctor replied. Neither Beth nor August sought to correct the mistaken reference to their relationship.

Beth began to cry, and August could only hold her close and stroke her head. He turned weary eyes to the doctor before asking, "Are you certain there is nothing else we can do?"

"I'm sorry," Dr. Matthews answered. "It is never easy to tell parents that their child won't make it. Gerald has fought hard to get this far, but he's too weak and the disease is taking too great a toll. He won't make it through the night."

"No, no," Beth sobbed. "He must live. He mustn't die!"

"Mrs. Hogan, please don't do this to yourself. It is of no help to your son. He's beyond our care now, and nothing can be gained by making yourself sick over his passing." The doctor's words seemed callous to Beth.

"You talk as though he were already dead," Beth replied as she pushed August away and got to her feet.

"For all intents and purposes, Mrs. Hogan," Dr. Matthews said without emotion, "he is. I can't do anything more for him. He's not responding to medicine, and his body is too spent to continue fighting. Let him go. You're a young, healthy woman, Mrs. Hogan. I'm certain you and your husband will have other children."

"I want other children, Doctor," Beth said with an undercurrent of anger to her voice. "But not to replace a dead child. I refuse to give up hope that God can deliver my baby from this illness. I have faith that He can work beyond your abilities."

The doctor shrugged his shoulders. "I cannot deny your tenacity, Mrs. Hogan. I only hope that your faith is not misplaced."

"It isn't," Beth stated firmly as she pushed past the doctor and his nurse. "If you can't give me any reason to hope, I know Who can."

August watched as Beth moved down the hall with renewed determination. He turned to the doctor and spoke. "I can understand a portion of your unemotional response to her, Dr. Matthews. You must see dying every day and find it as grotesque and unbearable as I do. However, I will take it as a personal insult should you feel the need to ever resort to crushing her hopes again."

"I assure you, sir," the doctor interjected, "that stripping that young mother of hope was never my intention. She has labored long and hard at the bedside of your child. She has demonstrated a strength beyond human capabilities. I admire all that she has done, but I also want her to understand that there comes a time when nothing more can be done. We have reached that point with your son."

August felt a tug at his heart with every reference to Gerald as his own child. "I cannot accept that the situation is without hope," he stated firmly. "I refuse to believe it."

"Most people do," the doctor agreed. "But people get sick, and people die. We doctors can only do so much. I have done everything in my power, and now I must stand aside and say it is out of my hands."

"You're absolutely right, Doctor. It is out of your hands, but not out of God's." August moved with determined strides to Gerald's room.

When he entered, Beth was stretched out over Gerald's tiny frame. He could hear her praying in a hushed whisper. She was a determined woman, August admitted. She had been determined for him to come back to God, just as she was intent on seeing her son healed of meningitis.

August thought back to those long moments spent beneath the tractor. His accident had opened his eyes to God's love and forgiveness, but it had also given him a glimpse into the power of prayer. Beth had been praying for him. His sister, Julie, and her husband, Sam, had both written letters of encouragement and mentioned their prayers for his well-being. Other people had prayed for August without him being aware of their concern.

That was it! August turned quickly from the room and went in search of a telephone. He would call Julie and ask her to pray for Gerald. He would ask her to gather as many people as possible and get all of them to pray. Then he would call and leave word for Mrs. Miller and the flock that attended church in Northway. There was power in prayer, of this he was certain, and August would leave nothing to chance where Gerald was concerned.

Locating a telephone, August quickly gave the operator all the needed information and waited impatiently while she connected him to his sister.

"Hello," a sleepy Julie sounded on the other end of the phone.

"Julie, it's August. I need you to pray about something!" August knew Julie would have received his letter explaining his return to God and the love he held for Beth and her sons.

"August!" Julie exclaimed. "What's wrong that would have you calling me at this hour?"

"It's Gerald. He's one of the little boys I wrote you about. He's the older boy, and he's terribly ill," August explained.

"What's wrong with him?" Julie asked in an authoritative voice. Her years as a nurse would require August to give her all the details.

"Spinal meningitis," August spoke the dreaded words.

"How long has he been sick? What have they done for him?"

"I guess he's been sick about three, maybe four days. I just got here myself and don't know what all they've done for him. I heard something about an experimental drug from the States, but the doctor says Gerald isn't responding and that there's no hope. He told us to say our good-byes."

"How awful," Julie whispered. "I'll be praying for you."

"That's why I called. I want you to pray for a miracle. Beth can't bear losing him, and neither can I. In my heart, he's already my son, and I want God to heal him so I can be a real father to him."

"A miracle is exactly what it will take," Julie said hesitantly. "I know God can do anything, but—"

"No but," August interrupted. "God can do anything. The doctor may have given up on Gerald, but Beth and I haven't. I want as many people praying and pleading for his life as I can get."

"Then you'll have Sam and me," Julie assured. "I'll even wake up our friends and get them to pray."

"Thanks, Jewels," he replied, using his sister's nickname. "I knew I could count on you. Now, if you don't mind, I'm going to make another call and get back to Beth and Gerald."

"I don't mind at all," Julie replied. "And August," she added, "welcome back to the family. I missed you and your encouraging faith. I knew God would work in a mighty way in your life, just as I know He will work in Gerald's. Good night, Brother."

"Good night, Jewels."

The warmth of his sister's love bolstered his courage, and August quickly made the call to Northway. Ralph Greening readily agreed to trek out into the night and rally the town to pray for Gerald.

Making his way back to Gerald's room, August found Beth sitting beside her son, holding his hand. Her eyes were closed, and August wondered if she'd fallen asleep or if she still prayed. He touched her lightly on the shoulder, and Beth opened her eyes.

"I was worried," she said. "Where were you?"

"I was rounding up support for our efforts," August said with a sheepish grin. "I've rallied the troops, so to speak."

"You've what?" Beth questioned, wondering at August's smile.

"I called my sister in Nome and Ralph Greening in Northway. They're in turn going to rally their friends and ask for prayer for Gerald. We'll have so many requests for healing going before God's throne, we won't be able to count them," August said with contagious excitement in his voice.

"How wonderful," Beth said and dropped Gerald's hand to take August's. "You truly amaze me, Mr. Eriksson. Not long ago you would have scoffed at God's power. Now you call upon it, knowing that even though the doctors have thrown up their hands, God can turn things around."

"I have you to thank for this," August said, pulling Beth into his arms. "You never lost faith that God could turn me around. I simply took that principle and put it into practice."

Beth allowed August to engulf her with his sturdy arms. Her blond hair fell across his arm, glittering like gold in the pale hospital light. She looked up into dark eyes that bathed her in love. Silently, she thanked God for answering her prayers for August's change of heart and then thanked God for hearing her prayers for Gerald. She felt hesitant at the latter, but it seemed important to trust God for those answers.

August felt his heart nearly burst with love for the woman he held. He longed to convey those feelings and ask Beth to marry him, but he knew the moment wasn't right. He didn't want her to say yes out of gratitude for his presence. Nor did he want her to refuse him because of the strain of Gerald's ordeal.

"I hate waiting," August murmured. Beth assumed his words were about Gerald's condition.

"I know. God has things under His watchful eye, but it doesn't always seem that way as we wait and wonder," Beth replied.

"Waiting all these years for someone or some purpose to come into my life has been difficult, too," August said cautiously.

"But now that you've waited, God has been faithful to send you people who care for you and love you," Beth whispered as she hugged herself close to August. "That little boy loves you nearly as much as I do. You mean the world to him, and I can't imagine God allowing Gerald to die without knowing that you're back here with him."

"All of this is a testing time," August stated firmly. "A time of trial such as Jesus said we'd experience in this world. But Jesus also said we could be of good cheer for He'd already overcome this world."

Beth nodded. "I believe that," she said, pulling away. "I believe that we will overcome this situation and that God will bless our boy." Beth thought fleetingly of JB and knew in her heart that he would approve of August as father to his son.

"Come on," August said and pulled Beth with him to Gerald's bedside. "Let's join our friends and pray for Gerald."

Chapter 14

It was close to three o'clock in the morning when Dr. Matthews reappeared to check Gerald's condition. The nurse ushered Beth and August into the hall while he conducted his examination. Within moments, the nurse brought them back. The doctor was writing notes on Gerald's chart.

Beth immediately went to Gerald's side, while August followed the doctor into the hall.

Dr. Matthews opened his mouth to speak, but August held up his hand. "There's nothing you can say. I know the odds are against that child. I know all of your medical expertise and skills have been tested and tried. Furthermore, I realize that even faithful servants of God lose loved ones in death. It's part of life."

August paused, pushing his hands deep into his jean pockets. His face took on a thoughtful look. "However, I also know the power of prayer."

Then with a smile of sudden peace on his face, August added, "Gerald's going to make it, and of that, I'm certain. He's going to get well because God will heal him."

Without waiting for a reply from the doctor, August turned back into the room, passing the nurse as she was leaving. August wanted to share his new feelings of peace with Beth. He entered the room and paused as Beth lovingly wiped her son's forehead.

"Gerry," August could hear her saying. "It's Momma, Gerry. I need you to get well. I'm asking God to make you well because He said I could ask for anything in Jesus' name and He would hear me. I'm doing that, Gerry. I'm asking in Jesus' name that your life be spared."

August could bear no more. "Beth, I know God will make Gerald well. I feel a calm and peace about it."

Beth stopped praying and looked up at August. "Honestly? You aren't just telling me that to give me hope?"

"I am telling you that to give you hope, but only because it's true. I feel such confidence that I want to sing it out. I even told the doctor that God would make Gerald well."

Beth crossed the room to where August stood. "I want to believe that, August. I know God is capable, but is He willing?"

"I believe He is," August replied. He looked into Beth's eyes and prayed she'd see the confidence in his own.

"Then I'm no longer worried," she said slowly. "If God has given you that certainty, then I shall praise Him for it and await my son's healing. I will believe!"

"That a girl!" August said, pulling Beth into his arms. "You're something special, Bethany Hogan."

Together they prayed and kept vigil at Gerald's bedside. Pulling chairs alongside the bed,

August and Beth sat together, holding each other's hands and Gerald's as well.

Shortly before dawn, August and Beth awoke. Gerry seemed to be in a deep, natural sleep. Beth reached out and touched the brow of her son.

"Oh, August!" she exclaimed. "He's not at all feverish. And look," she pointed to his chest. "He's not straining to breathe."

August stared at the rhythmic rise and fall of the tiny chest and nodded. "He's getting well, Beth. God is healing him even as we watch."

"Thank You, God," Beth said as tears ran down her cheeks. "Thank You for the life of my baby."

"Amen," August said in agreement.

Taking Beth with him to the window, August pulled back the heavy drapes to reveal a glorious sunrise bursting from the horizon. He reached out and wiped away Beth's tears. "Joy has truly come in the morning, just as the psalmist said. No more tears, Bethany. Now we will rejoice."

Beth nodded and threw her arms around August's neck. "I will spend the rest of my life rejoicing for the miracles of God," she whispered.

Just then another voice joined in. "Mommy!" Gerald called out. His voice sounded hoarse but strong.

Beth and August rushed to Gerry's side and found him not only awake, but also free of the glassy-eyed, feverish look. Staring in amazement, August and Beth could only smile.

"How do you feel, Son?" August asked as he bent over the boy.

"Daddy," Gerald said, forgetting himself. "You came back. I thought maybe you didn't like me anymore."

"That could never happen, Gerald," August replied. "I was very far away in a hospital, much like this one."

"A hospital?" Gerald questioned. "What's a hospital?"

"Oh, Gerry," Beth said as she sat down beside him. "A hospital is a place for sick people to get well. You've been very sick, but God has made you well."

"I had nice dreams," Gerald said, surprising them both. "I dreamed about lots of pretty flowers and a big river. Bigger than the one Phillip fell into."

Beth glanced in amazement at August and then back to her son's shining face. "I'll bet it was wonderful," she replied. "I'm so glad you're feeling better," she added, placing a kiss on his forehead.

"Me, too. I'm hungry, Mommy. Can I have some breakfast?" Gerald asked.

August laughed loudly. "Spoken like a true boy."

"Always hungry," Beth admitted. "We'll see if we can't manage to find something for you to fill that empty tummy of yours."

"I'll go right now and speak with the doctor," August said. But before August had made it to the door, Dr. Matthews entered the room and stared in shocked surprise at the sight of Gerald sitting up in bed.

"What's going on?" the doctor asked as he crossed the room.

"I told you God would make him well," August said with a hearty slap on the doctor's back.

"It's impossible," the doctor whispered in amazement. "That child should be dead by now." His words were spoken so softly that only August could hear them.

"Well, he isn't. In fact, he's very much alive and very hungry," August informed the man. Gerald agreed with an enthusiastic nod of his head.

"I simply don't believe it," Dr. Matthews said, walking over to Gerald's bed.

"Many people never do," Beth said firmly, refusing to take her eyes from her son's face. "And because of that, they never know the fullness of God's powerful love."

The doctor shook his head as he examined Gerald. He took a thermometer from his medical bag and put it into Gerald's mouth. While he waited for the results, the doctor felt for a pulse. His eyes registered surprise when he found a strong, steady beat.

Taking the thermometer from Gerald's mouth, Dr. Matthews again shook his head. "It's normal, and his pulse is strong and steady," he said, looking to Beth and August as if for an explanation.

"God has worked a miracle, Doctor," Beth said as she tousled Gerald's hair. "He has given me back my son."

The doctor nodded. "I suppose you're right." He had Gerald bend his head back and forth and from side to side. When he was satisfied that no symptom of the meningitis remained, he declared the boy could eat some breakfast.

Beth and August joined Dr. Matthews at the door of Gerald's room. "I'll need to run some more tests, but I must say, I am completely amazed," the doctor said humbly. "I have never seen God work a miracle such as this in the life of anyone, let alone one of my patients. Makes me feel rather useless."

"We want to thank you for all you did to help Gerald," Beth said as she extended her hand. "We know you did what you could, and we don't believe it useless for one moment. You simply operated under human limitations. We took it beyond that and expected divine results." Beth's words were gentle and supportive.

August nodded as his arm encircled Beth's waist. "If we could do everything ourselves, there'd be no need for God. Since we can't, we must turn to Him on a daily basis and pray for guidance, strength, and direction. I hope you feel inspired by this miracle."

"I certainly feel a wonderment about it," the doctor admitted. "It's like nothing I've ever seen, and it certainly bears consideration. Now, if you'll excuse me, I'll send a nurse in with a breakfast tray."

Beth smiled. "I know that'll make Gerry a very happy boy." The doctor nodded and turned down the hall, a baffled look covering his face.

"I guess that'll teach him to question a woman of faith," August said with a laugh as they turned back to Gerry.

"Where's my brother?" the boy asked eagerly. He was already trying out the bounce in the hospital mattress.

"He's back at the roadhouse with Mrs. Miller," Beth explained. "This hospital is in Fairbanks."

"That's far, far away from home," Gerald said, amusing both August and Beth. "How did I get here?"

"We took the airplane," Beth answered. "The soldiers helped us get here. Do you remember anything at all?"

"Nope," Gerald replied. "I just remember sleeping and sleeping. I'm glad you came back, August. You aren't going to leave again, are you?"

"No," August said, reassuring the child. "I don't plan on being far from you ever again."

"Good," Gerald said with a grin. "It made my mommy sad when you went away."

"Gerald!" Beth said with a finger to her lips. "You mustn't tell August about all that."

"Of course he must," August said with a grin to match Gerald's. He lowered his head to Gerald's and added, "I want to know everything that happened while I was away."

Beth shook her head at the grinning faces. "It isn't the past that matters," she chided with a smile. "It's the future that counts, and I intend that we should have a glorious one."

"I agree," August said, holding his hand out to Beth. "You can tell me all about it later," he added with a wink to Gerald.

"You are quite impossible, Mr. Eriksson," Beth said in mock exasperation.

"Not at all, Mrs. Hogan," August said as he lifted Beth's hand to his lips. "Just determined."

The touch of his lips on Beth's hand caused her to tremble. She could feel her pulse race and her breathing quicken. For the first time, nothing stood between her and August.

As if reading her thoughts, August smiled. He could feel her quiver at his touch. His eyes met hers, and in their reflection he saw all of his long-held dreams coming true.

"When's the food going to get here?" Gerald interrupted. "I want to eat, and then I want to go home."

August and Beth laughed and pulled Gerald into their arms. "I think that sounds wonderful," Beth agreed.

Chapter 15

Several bowls later, Gerald gobbled down oatmeal with raisins while Bethany told him about his days spent in the hospital. Meanwhile, August made arrangements for their trip home. He felt a lightheartedness he'd never known.

"Julie?" August spoke into the receiver of the phone. "It's August."

"August, how's the little boy?" Julie questioned through a static-filled line.

"He's fine. We got our miracle, Julie. Gerald rallied in a remarkable way," August replied.

"Praise God," Julie replied. "I knew He'd hear our prayers. How is Beth?"

"She's exhausted, but otherwise great. You would like her, Jewels. She has a strong faith just like you. She never doubted that God could make a difference," August said with pride.

"She sounds like the perfect woman for you," Julie remarked. The static played havoc with the line. "I'm sorry about the connection. I don't know if it has anything to do with it or not, but we're in the middle of a fierce storm. High winds and snow. You know the type."

"I do indeed. The temperatures dropped considerably here, but good weather is holding, which is another blessing. They're still trying to finish up the highway. I think they'll be done within a matter of a week or so," August replied.

"Will you be coming home after that?" Julie asked hopefully.

"I'd just begun thinking about that," August answered. "I want to come back, at least to get my things. I miss my dogs, and I want to teach the boys how to drive a sled."

"We'll look forward to seeing you," Julie said enthusiastically. "Sam has missed you a great deal," she added.

August thought of how much Sam would have enjoyed working on the highway. "I've missed him, too. Tell him hello and that I'll see you both soon. I'll talk to you again before I actually come back. Thanks again, Jewels."

"I'm glad we could be a part of your miracle," Julie replied. "It was good to hear your voice. Please take care of yourself."

"I will. I love you, Sis."

"I love you, too. Good-bye." Julie's voice was barely audible through the static.

After another quick call to Ralph Greening, August was free to return to Beth and Gerald.

"It's all set," August said as he entered the room. "As soon as the doctor gives his approval, we'll be on the first transport plane for Northway."

Gerald had finished his breakfast and waited eagerly for his mother's permission to get out of bed.

"Dr. Matthews said we could leave as soon as he has one of the other doctors take a look

464

at Gerald," Beth said with a smile.

August looked at her with appreciation. Now that his own bitterness toward God and Gerald's serious illness no longer filled his mind, August was beginning to recognize the perfection of the woman before him. She was everything he'd ever needed or wanted.

"Did you hear what I said?" Beth questioned.

"Huh? No, sorry. What did you say?" August asked as he crossed the room.

Beth laughed. "It wasn't important. I have you and Gerald, and soon we'll go home to Phillip. That's what matters."

Dr. Matthews came into the room unannounced just then. With him was an elderly man Beth didn't recognize.

"This is Dr. Barnes," Gerald's doctor announced. "I've asked him to evaluate our patient and give his opinion."

"How nice to meet you, Dr. Barnes," Beth said as she extended her hand. "So you've come to see our miracle boy."

"Yes, Mrs. Hogan," the man said, shaking her hand. "I must say, I was quite enthralled by the boy's recovery. I understand your son was only two days on the experimental medicine from the States."

"Yes, that's true," Beth said and added, "but I don't believe that's what cured him. After all, you folks had given him up for dead."

Dr. Barnes picked up Gerald's chart and studied it for a moment. Gerald finally broke the silence. "Are they going to let me go home, Momma?"

"I think so, Gerry, but you must be quiet and let the doctors do their job," Beth replied, giving her son a hug.

Dr. Barnes continued his examination of Gerald and finally turned back to Beth with a smile. "I see no reason to keep this child here any longer. Your son is completely healed to the best of my knowledge."

"Thank you," Beth replied. She threw a knowing smile at August, who had held back in silence while the men examined Gerald.

August stepped forward and put an arm around Beth. "How soon can we leave?" he asked.

"As soon as you're ready," Dr. Barnes replied. "I release the boy as of now."

Gerry let out an excited scream at the verdict, and August and Beth thanked the doctors once more for their help as the medical men turned to leave.

When the doctors had left, August turned to Beth. "Ready to go home, Mrs. Hogan?"

"Definitely," she replied, taking his offered hand.

August and Beth hugged Gerald close. August silently thanked God for the loving family He'd provided.

"You know," August began, "I think we should have a word of prayer and thank God for all He's done for us. Then I think we should get out of this hospital and head home to Phillip and Mrs. Miller."

"I agree," Beth said, lifting her eyes to August. In that moment she wanted nothing more than to spend the rest of her days loving this man and her children.

"Father, we come to You with thankful hearts," August began. "We praise You for the healing of Gerald's body and for the mercies You showed me in bringing me back to the truth."

Beth listened intently as August prayed, agreeing with his words and enjoying the blessings of God's love. Silently, she added her own requests.

I love him, Lord, she prayed. *I love him so very much, and if it is Your will, I pray You'll see us married quickly so that we can be a whole and complete family.*

August ended his prayer and Gerald joined in with a hearty "Amen." Beth lifted her face to reveal tears that she'd not realized she had cried.

"Why are you crying, Mommy?" Gerald asked with a worried look on his face. "Is something wrong?"

August turned, seeing the tears for the first time. "I think your mommy is happy, Gerald. Sometimes folks have a hard time expressing the wonder of how happy they are."

Beth dabbed her eyes with the corner of a handkerchief August offered her. "I am happy, Gerry. I'm so very glad that God has made you well and that He brought August back to us."

She turned to August, feeling confident for the first time that she could speak what was on her heart. "Please don't leave us again. We need you. I need you."

Beth's blue eyes pierced deep into August's heart. Years later he would remember the moment as one of the most precious in his life. She was so needy, yet so strong. Somehow, the two qualities balanced perfectly, creating one incredible woman.

"And I need you," August whispered, his dark eyes shining with love. "I'll always need you."

Gerald refused to be left out of the conversation. He was bored with the adult seriousness. "Can we go home?" he asked, breaking the spell of the moment. "I want to play in my tree house."

Beth laughed, and August lifted Gerald into his strong arms.

"Yes," August said enthusiastically. "Let's go home!"

Chapter 16

From Fairbanks to Northway, Gerald chattered about the plane and the view. August pointed out the highway below and explained to the boy about the work involved in building such a road.

Gerald listened in awe as August spoke of the powerful machinery that helped clear the way. "I'd like to do that, too," Gerald said in animated excitement. "I want to do work just like you."

"I thought you wanted to be a pilot," August replied, shifting Gerald so he could get a better view.

"That was what my old daddy did. Now I want to do work like my new daddy. You are going to be my new daddy, aren't you?" Gerald questioned sincerely.

"Would you like that?" August asked with a grin.

"I sure would," Gerald answered. "Phillip would, too. He told me so."

"Well then," August said with a glance at Beth, "we'll just have to see what the good Lord works out."

Beth felt a twinge of disappointment at August's words. She'd held her breath, waiting for his reply, and then she'd only heard a "wait and see" answer. Hiding her frustration, Beth was relieved that Gerald seemed satisfied with August's answer.

Folding her hands in her lap, Beth thought about the situation and glanced up to find August watching her. She offered the briefest smile, and when August winked and grinned back, Beth felt relieved. There was no way of knowing exactly what August had in mind, but Beth was certain he loved her and the boys. Wait and see wasn't an easy thing to accept, but it did offer the possibility of more, and Beth clung to that for reassurance.

The plane touched down shortly before dinnertime with Gerald already complaining that his stomach was growling. Stepping off the plane, August offered a hand to Beth.

"It's good to be home," Beth declared and breathed deeply of the crisp air. "I've missed it so much and Phillip, too."

August easily lifted Gerald into his arms and swung in step behind Beth. "I suggest we get your things, and I'll see about securing us a ride home. After all, this little boy is about to starve to death."

"I'll square getting the suitcase," Beth offered with a laugh. She watched as August hoisted Gerald over his head and onto his shoulders. What a great father he would be for her sons!

August waited until Beth was deep in conversation with the pilot before going off in search of a ride to the roadhouse. It was hard to believe that autumn had come in their absence. The fireweed was snowy with its cotton plumes floating through the air, and aspen shimmered with their hues of gold and orange.

In the distance, August could see that the Wrangell Mountains were already glistening with thick layers of snow. It wouldn't be long before snow would hug the ground in a white, insulating blanket. Thoughts of cold weather made August think of his dogs and sled travel. He'd have to find a way to bring them here from Nome and teach the boys to drive a team.

It wasn't hard to find a ride to Gantry Roadhouse; most everyone had heard of Gerald's illness and were anxious, even pleased, to lend a hand to the little boy.

The driver of the jeep turned out to be Private Ronnie Jacobs, one of the soldiers Beth had baked sweet potato pies for.

"It's mighty good to see that your boy is healthy and strong again," Ronnie said as he helped Beth into the seat.

"Thank you, Private," Beth returned. "Have they kept you well fed in my absence?"

The young man laughed. "Not on this army's food. I missed coming down to the roadhouse to buy the extras. I guess pretty soon we'll be out of here altogether. It'll sure be good to go back where it's warm. I miss Georgia."

"Who's she?" Gerald asked as August handed him to Beth.

Ronnie laughed. "That's not a girl. It's the state I live in."

"Is it as pretty as Alaska?" Gerald asked.

"I think so," the private responded, taking the driver's seat while August jumped in the back. "Now, if everybody's set, I'll get y'all home."

The drive to the roadhouse was over quickly. August had barely put a foot out of the jeep when Phillip came bursting out the doorway.

"Mommy! Daddy!" he called out. Running down the dirt pathway, he held out open arms for August's embrace. August tossed him high in the air. Phillip's giggles sounded like music to Beth and August's ears.

"Phillip, you must have grown six inches since I last saw you. Come give Mommy some love," Beth said, reaching out to take her son from August.

"I missed you, Mommy. I missed you whole bunches." Phillip's muffled voice fell in kisses against his mother's neck.

"Oh, and I missed you, pumpkin. I missed you so much," Beth replied. "And look here," she said as she put Phillip down. "Gerry's back, and he's all better."

"I helped take care of him, didn't I, Mommy?" Phillip questioned, catching sight of his brother. "Gerry!" he squealed as he rushed to hug his sibling. The boys were great friends and had missed each other terribly. Soon they were laughing and talking at once as they shared their adventures with each other.

Mrs. Miller came outside to join the reunion. "Gerald!" she called out and waved. As the foursome approached the older woman, Beth could see there were tears in Hazel Miller's eyes.

"Praise be to God!" she exclaimed, embracing Gerald.

"I was real sick," Gerald explained seriously.

"You sure were," the older woman agreed. "But God made you well, and I've made a celebration dinner to thank Him."

"Hazel, how nice!" Beth remarked. She was weary to the bone and anxious to drop into bed, but she wouldn't have spoiled Hazel's celebration for all the world.

"I could eat a moose," August declared with a grin.

"Well, I just might have some of that, too," Mrs. Miller said, laughing. "You'll just have to wash up and set yourself down to see."

The boys and August hurried in the direction of the washroom while Beth lingered a moment with Hazel.

"Hazel, I'm indebted to you for life," Beth said as she hugged her friend. "Without you I would have worried constantly about Phillip and the property."

"I'm happy to have helped. I finally felt useful, and I think it taught me something else," Hazel said, taking a step back.

"And what's that, Hazel?" Beth questioned.

"I've just been wasting myself and the talents the good Lord gave me. I've been hiding myself away, picking and choosing what I'll be a part of and what I won't. I hadn't realized how cloistered away I'd become."

"Don't be too hard on yourself, Hazel," Beth interjected. "You have done much to live for God. You teach Sunday school at the church and sing in the choir. Everyone who knows you or has had an opportunity to speak with you knows your heart."

"That may be, but I know I can do more and I intend to," Hazel replied. "But enough about me. What about you and Mr. Eriksson?"

"Oh, Hazel," Beth said, smiling broadly. "God has renewed August's heart. He's found his way back to the truth, and he loves me."

"How wonderful!" Hazel exclaimed. "God truly has answered our prayers. Has the man asked you to marry him?"

"Not in those words, but I am certain it's his intention. I can hardly wait until we're a family," Beth said happily.

"I believe you already are," Hazel stated and pulled open the door. "Now come along. My fine supper is getting cold, and those men of yours looked mighty hungry." Beth nodded with a smile and followed Hazel to the kitchen.

Dinner was as fine an affair as any Beth or August had ever known. Hazel had prepared so many specialties that Beth lost track of what she'd sampled.

Smoked reindeer sausages lay in long, steaming strips atop a bed of seasoned rice, while another pot held sliced moose in a tantalizing barbecue sauce.

Sourdough bread from a starter Mrs. Miller claimed was over seventy years old was quickly devoured with huge spoonfuls of homemade blueberry jelly.

Accompanying all this richness was an array of vegetables and fruit that bowed the table under its weight. On top of the stove sat strawberry-rhubarb pies and a fresh pot of coffee. There was decidedly more food than five people could eat, but no one seemed to mind.

"I know you'll want to put those boys to bed," Hazel said as she began to clear the table.

"Why don't you run on ahead and take care of them? I'll clean up this mess."

"I can't let you go on taking care of us," Beth said, stacking the boys' dishes together and reaching for August's.

"Now, I'll be gone in an hour or two and you'll have yourself and your family to take care of. Let me do this for you while you enjoy getting back to your routine," Hazel insisted.

"I think that's mighty fine of you, Mrs. Miller," August said. He got to his feet and patted his stuffed stomach. "I can't remember the last time I had anything quite that good. After they get done with rationing, you ought to open up a restaurant."

"I think that would be a grand idea, Hazel. Maybe that's the purpose you've been looking to fill," Beth remarked. "Better yet, maybe we could add it to the roadhouse. I know my boarders would be a lot happier if I offered meals with their rooms."

"And if you were careful with the things you served, you could probably get started before the war is over," August said, contemplating the possibilities. "We could build on to the kitchen, maybe over here." August walked to the south wall of the kitchen where the stove stood. "I don't think it would be all that difficult."

"I don't expect you to alter your roadhouse for me," Hazel replied evenly, but in her heart was born the first ray of excitement.

"It would be beneficial to both of us," Beth replied. "Besides, I don't expect to run a roadhouse all of my life. Maybe you could eventually buy me out."

Beth's revelation was news to August. He wondered what her plans were for the future.

"Well, you've certainly given an old woman a great deal to think about," Hazel murmured, moving the hot food back to the stove. "But right now, you have two boys who are nearly asleep as they stand," she said and motioned to where Gerald and Phillip were swaying on their feet.

"Come on, boys," August said, scooping a child into each arm. "I think it's time to tuck you in."

The boys needed little in the way of tucking in. They were both asleep almost before their heads hit the pillows. Beth stood for a moment at the door of their bedroom. She took a deep breath and sighed. The boys slept healthy and comfortable in their beds, and in the kitchen, August waited for her to join him. What more could she possibly want?

Gently, she pulled the door closed and went to August. "Seeing my children at rest has to be the most precious moment of the day. I never fail to be amazed at the comfort and joy it gives me," Beth said, taking August's hand in her own.

Thinking they would be helping to clean up the dishes, Beth registered surprise as August maneuvered her past Hazel with a wink and out the back door into the chilly night air.

They walked hand in hand for several yards, enjoying the solitude of the moment. Beth felt a peace she hadn't dared hope for after JB's death.

Pausing, she turned to face August. "I want to thank you for all you've done—especially coming to me in Fairbanks. I think I would have fallen apart if you hadn't been there."

August's dark eyes stared down at her for a long time before he spoke. He was eager to make Beth his wife, yet there seemed so much that had gone unsaid between them. "I needed to be there," he finally whispered, "as much as you needed me to be there."

Beth silently hoped that August would take this opportunity to propose to her. She felt light and airy, and her heart was fairly flying on wings of its own. Surely August felt the same.

Leading Beth to the long bench he had made for evenings such as this one, August searched for the right words to speak what was on his heart. "I brought you out here for a purpose," he began. "I needed to tell you something and explain."

Beth's brow furrowed. This didn't sound like the beginning of a marriage proposal. "What is it, August?"

"I'm going back to Nome," he replied.

Beth felt her chest tighten. Her mind whirled in a thousand directions as she wondered what August meant by his words. She gripped the arm of the bench and forced herself to be silent. Had she misunderstood his words in Fairbanks? Didn't he intend to marry her after all?

"I have an entire life back in Nome that you know nothing about," August explained. "I have a sister and a lifetime of mementos, not to mention a dogsled team to rival any in the territory."

August's words held such longing that Beth couldn't maintain her silence. "You're leaving us?" She dreaded hearing the answer.

"Only to get my things," August said with a grin. "You can't get rid of me that easily. I don't intend to be gone a moment longer than is necessary to pack my sled and mush my team back here." August noticed Beth's look of concern. "You didn't really think I'd leave you for good, did you?"

Beth shrugged her shoulders. "I didn't know what to think. I mean, I knew how I felt, and I thought I understood how you felt, but—"

"But then I told you I was going to Nome," August interrupted, "and you started to worry?"

"Nome is hundreds of miles away," Beth said, feeling little relief that August intended to return. "So much could happen to you on the way back. There's so much open, empty space between here and there. What if you have an accident or a storm comes up?"

"I've traveled those trails hundreds, even thousands of times. I know every inch of land between Nome and Nenana. Nothing is going to happen to me," August insisted.

"I wish you didn't have to go," Beth replied honestly. "I've said too many good-byes."

"Then we won't say good-bye," August stated firmly. "You could come with me. Mrs. Miller could watch over the roadhouse. We could fly to Nome and drive the dogs back together."

Beth shook her head. "I couldn't leave the boys that long. They need me to be a constant in their lives. They've said good-byes, too, remember? And their father never came home again. I couldn't put them through that, and taking them on the trail would be much too difficult, especially with Gerald just recovered from meningitis."

"I guess I wasn't thinking," August offered by way of apology.

"It's all right. I understand you have to go back, and you understand I have to stay. I guess the thing for me to do is give you over to God once again," Beth said, fighting tears that threatened to spill from her eyes.

"Who better to place me with?" August said, putting his arm around Beth's shoulders. He lifted her face to meet his and spoke with such tenderness that Beth thought her heart would burst. "I love you, Bethany Hogan. I've loved you for so long now, I don't remember a time when I didn't love you. And I love your children as if they were flesh of my flesh. I want to be a father to those boys, and I want to live my life in the warmth of your love."

Without waiting for her reply, August lowered his lips to kiss her long and deeply. He felt her tears fall against his cheek as she clung to him.

When he lifted his face, August was surprised to find Beth smiling. "Tears and smiles?" he questioned. Gently he brushed away a glistening drop from her face.

"I love you, August," she whispered in a voice more composed than August thought possible, given her reaction to his news. "I know your trip is necessary, but I wish you didn't have to leave me for so long."

"I'll be back before you know it, and when I return, I'll bring my mother's wedding ring and marry you. That is, if you'll have me," he added with a broad smile.

Beth reached out to push back his dark hair. The light from the moon illuminated his face as if it were day. "I'll marry you, August Eriksson. I'll be your wife, and bear your children, and all of my days I will love you as I have loved no other."

Chapter 17

August spent the final days of the highway project behind a desk. After eight months of tedious work and precarious conditions, the Alaskan/Canadian Highway was completed. Nicknamed "the Alcan" by those who worked it, the roadway was a miracle of cooperative countries and their people.

Destiny's road stretched over nearly fifteen hundred miles and constituted the efforts of more than eleven thousand individuals.

It wasn't much to look at, August decided as he flew from one isolated airstrip to the next, surveying the wonder from the air. Little more than a dingy brown ribbon, it wove its way through the countryside. Occasionally, strips of gray or blue indicated a lake or river, while either side of the narrow highway was lined with dark spruce forests and snow-filled permafrost meadows.

The army was pleased with the accomplishment. The road provided a way to transport oil and other goods to far north bases, should the shipping lanes become too dangerous. But an unanticipated benefit was what a morale booster the road had become. It proved to two nations and millions of their citizens that they could combine their energies on the home front to aid their loved ones serving in battles so far away. It made the people feel important, useful, and necessary for the war effort.

August smiled as the plane touched down in Northway. This was his final official duty for the project. After great consideration and prayer, August had decided against taking the permanent job offered by Ralph Greening.

Instead, August had shared with Beth his desire to raise sled dogs and help her with the roadhouse. She had enthusiastically agreed to having him around the house on a daily basis and had even begun to make a list of jobs August could be responsible for. August had laughed when he learned of the list.

"Good to know I'll be needed," he'd ruefully observed.

The weather had turned cold. Excitement gripped the town of Northway as it bustled with activities commemorating the new highway. But the dropping temperatures and significant snows signaled to August that it was time to go to Nome and retrieve his property. Once done with this, he would settle down to a new life with Beth and the boys.

August shook his head in amazement, remembering his first day in Northway when he was seeking a job on the highway. The road had given destiny to more than the countries through which it passed. God had used it to bring August his own destiny and a new life.

Snow blanketed the ground around the airstrip, leaving August to tramp out his own way to the crossroads. He didn't mind; it reminded him of days out on the trail hunting or checking trap lines. Remembering his father and the home he'd known as a boy, August was filled with longing to return to that life.

Nearing the roadhouse, August paused in order to take the sight in. Nestled among the tall spruce and leafless aspen and birch was the place he now called home. Black smoke rose from the chimney, contrasting against the gray, snow-heavy sky. The sight warmed August and prompted him to hasten his steps to the family he'd soon call his own.

Kicking off his snowy boots, August entered the roadhouse through the back door and pulled off his parka to hang it beside Beth's at the entrance to the kitchen. He was surprised to find Beth and the boys sitting at the table, smiling up at him as if they knew a secret.

"What?" August asked with a grin. "What are you up to?"

Phillip and Gerald giggled, while Beth lowered her eyes to keep from laughing out loud. August joined them cautiously at the table and looked on his chair for any sign of a pine cone or other such souvenir of the boys' mischievous behavior. Finding none, he sat opposite Beth, between the boys.

"Is somebody going to tell me what's going on here?" he asked, reaching for Phillip. "Or am I going to have to tickle it out of you?"

"Don't tell him, Phillip," Gerald squealed.

Phillip laughed in glee as August's fingers found his ribs. "You're going to be our daddy," Phillip laughingly gave up the secret.

"Mommy said you had to go to your old house and get your stuff, but that you were coming back to live here with us," Gerald added.

Beth looked at August with a shrug. "I couldn't help telling them," she replied. "And since you never said I couldn't, I gave in to my joy and let them be part of it."

August laughed as he reached out and pulled Gerald to his lap. Holding each boy on a knee, August gave them a squeeze. "And what do you boys think of that?" he asked.

"We like it!" Gerald exclaimed and Phillip echoed.

"Well, that's certainly a good thing for me," August proclaimed. "I guess I would have had a lot of trouble on my hands if you had said you didn't want me."

"I don't want you to go, Daddy," Phillip said with a pout.

"Me neither," Gerald agreed. Beth's expression confirmed that she felt the same way.

"Look, boys," August began, "I'm not going to be gone very long, and when I get back I'm going to be bringing my dog team. I'm going to teach you the old-fashioned way of getting around in the snow."

"We've never had a dog. How many dogs will you bring?" Gerald asked, suddenly interested.

"I'll probably bring twenty or so," August replied. "And twenty dogs are going to be a lot of work. I'll need extra help from you boys."

"Will we play with the doggies?" Phillip asked.

"Of course," August answered. "We'll give them lots of love and care every day. And we'll play with them and work with them. You'll see. It's going to be a great deal of fun."

"What about Momma?" Gerald questioned.

"Your momma is going to have fun with the dogs, too," August said with a wink at Beth.

"And it won't be long, boys," Beth added, "before you'll be ready to start learning to read and write."

"That's true," August agreed. "This roadhouse is going to need a lot of care, too. Your mother has already made long, long lists, so every day will hold plenty of things to keep us busy. And," August paused, looking purposefully into Beth's eyes, "I promise I'll never be away from here for any longer than I have to be, because I love you all so very much."

"We love you, too, Daddy," Gerald said, glancing at his mother. "Momma said we could call you that, if you didn't mind."

August choked up from the emotion surging through his heart. "I would love it if you would call me Daddy," he replied. "I want very much to be the best daddy in the world to both of you."

The boys hugged him tightly around the neck, while August and Beth exchanged a look of love that bound them forever to one another. *God is so good,* August thought. In His perfect way, God had saved the best in life for the last, and August could not imagine a sweeter future.

"Why don't you boys go play for a little while? I need to talk with August—your dad—for a moment."

"But he just got home," Gerald protested.

"Can't we stay?" Phillip moaned.

"Now, boys," August said, putting them from his knee. "You must always mind your mother and me. Sometimes your safety or lives might depend upon it. Right now, your mom simply wants to talk to me, but obeying her is always important. Do you understand?"

The boys sobered at August's serious tone. "Yes, Daddy."

With a smile, August broke the somber moment. "Good. Now, you run and play, and when I'm done talking to your mother, I'll come help you build something with your blocks."

The boys scampered off to their room, discussing at great length their plans for the toy building project.

"You have such a loving way with them," Beth remarked. "I'm amazed that you've never spent much time with children."

"There were never any around to spend time with. There was Julie, of course," he said, "but I was a child as well. I've always known, though, that I wanted to be a father. I've always wanted a house full of children and a home full of love."

"I feel like I've got so much to learn about you," Beth said wistfully. "You've never told me much about Nome or your sister. It's another part of you that I know nothing about."

August nodded. "Just remember, there's a great deal I don't know about you, either. But we have all the time in the world."

Beth frowned for a moment, remembering the war that engulfed the world. "It's a rather frightening time. The world is in such conflict. So many young men are dying to give us freedom and a future. It cuts my heart to imagine waving my sons off to war. I pray I never have to know that feeling."

"Yes," August said, remembering that he once wanted to be one of those marching away to war. "I've never looked at it quite that way. I was angry at God because He wouldn't let me be one of those going off to serve. I never thought of how it affected anyone but me. Now that two little boys I love could well face that responsibility, I feel the same way you do. I want to protect them and keep them far from the reaches of such a monster as war."

"Do you suppose the world will change so very much in the years to come? I mean after the fighting is over and the men have come home," Beth questioned.

"War always changes things," August said thoughtfully. "I remember reading about World War I. It seemed so far away and unimportant. Somebody else's war, I thought. Somebody else's land and people. But it wasn't that way, and neither is this. We're every bit as much a part of those who are fighting as they are of us. We give them a reason to fight, a reason to win. They need us, just as we need them."

"Is it selfish to want a good life with you and the boys, in the face of the adversity our soldiers are living with?" Beth inquired.

"I don't think so. I believe it's just as they would expect. Life goes on, and just as one war is over, another begins. Whether it's on a battlefield or in a hospital bed, it's a never-ending cycle, and God's hand is upon all," August replied.

"Then our destiny is in His hands, and nothing the world does or doesn't do will change that," Beth said with new certainty.

"That it is," August agreed and added, "A future with God's loving protection doesn't seem at all frightening."

Beth nodded and reached across the table for August's hand. His warm fingers wrapped around her own, and Beth knew there truly was nothing to fear. With God and a good man at her side, the challenges of the world seemed to shrink under a shroud of faith.

Destiny's road would be God's road, and though the way might hold pitfalls and obstacles, Beth and August would travel it together, always guided by the Creator of it all.

About the Authors

Mary Connealy

Mary Connealy writes romantic comedy with cowboys. She is a Christy Award finalist and a Carol Award winner. She is the author of the Lassoed in Texas Trilogy, the Montana Marriage Trilogy, and the Sophie's Daughters Series.

Mary lives on a Nebraska ranch with her husband, Ivan, and has four grown daughters: Joslyn (married to Matt), Wendy, Shelly (married to Aaron), and Katy. And she is the grandmother of two beautiful grandchildren.

Cathy Marie Hake

Cathy Marie Hake is a Southern California native. She met her two loves at church: Jesus and her husband, Christopher. An RN, she loved working in oncology as well as teaching Lamaze. Health issues forced her to retire, but God opened new possibilities with writing. Since their children have moved out and are married, Cathy and Chris dote on dogs they rescue from a local shelter. A sentimental pack rat, Cathy enjoys scrapbooking and collecting antiques. Since her first book in 2000, she's been on multiple bestseller and readers' favorite lists.

Tracie Peterson

Tracie Peterson, bestselling, award-winning author of over ninety fiction titles and three non-fiction books, lives and writes in Belgrade, Montana. As a Christian, wife, mother, writer, editor and speaker (in that order), Tracie finds her slate quite full.

Published in magazines and Sunday school take home papers, as well as a columnist for a Christian newspaper, Tracie now focuses her attention on novels. After signing her first contract with Barbour Publishing in 1992, her novel, A Place To Belong, appeared in 1993 and the rest is history. She has over twenty-six titles with Heartsong Presents' book club (many of which have been repackaged) and stories in six separate anthologies from Barbour. From Bethany House Publishing, Tracie has multiple historical three-book series as well as many stand-alone contemporary women's fiction stories and two non-fiction titles. Other titles include two historical series co-written with Judith Pella, one historical series co-written with James Scott Bell, and multiple historical series co-written with Judith Miller.

Kathleen Y'Barbo

Bestselling author Kathleen Y'Barbo is a multiple Carol Award and RITA nominee of forty-five novels with almost two million copies of her books in print in the US and abroad. A tenth-generation Texan and certified family law paralegal, she has been nominated for a Career Achievement Award as well a Reader's Choice Award and several Top Picks by *Romantic Times* magazine. A member of American Christian Fiction Writers, Romance Writers of America, and a former member of the Texas Bar Association Paralegal Division, she is currently a proud military wife and an expatriate Texan cheering on her beloved Texas Aggies from north of the Red River.